THE

Fishermen

C.P. HARRIS

Photographer: Rafagcatala, www.instagram.com/rafagcatala_13/?hl=en
Developmental Editing by Anette King, anette.king@gmail.com
Editing by Shauna Stevenson at Ink Machine Editing, inkmachineediting@gmail.com
Formatting: Allusion Publishing, www.allusionpublishing.com
Proofreading by Anette King, anette.king@gmail.com
Beta readers: Mihaela Zollinger, Vikki Elliott, vikkielliott@hotmail.com, Layla Nourreddine, and Irish T Hill.

AUTHOR'S NOTE

The Fishermen is book 2 in the Infidelity series. Themes include cheating (not between the MCs), possessive and jealous behavior, a twenty-year age gap, consensual non-consent, second chances, bi-awakening, hurt/comfort, and a scene involving exhibitionism. *The Fishermen* also deals with the off page death of a spouse. As always, I encourage readers to put their safety above their curiosity.

PART ONE

CHAPTER 1

Scanning a room for the man who'd piqued my curiosity wasn't easy while also balancing a tray of champagne filled flutes. Moving through the office space overlooking downtown Seattle, I did my best to smile as rich men in pricey suits measured their dicks. I tried to maintain a professional attitude, and do the job I'd been hired for, but what I really wanted to do was dump the contents of my tray over their three-figure haircuts and go hunt down the man I'd been low-key watching all night. The man everyone had either been watching or trying to get a piece of since he'd arrived.

Something cold hit my black dress shirt, soaking through the thin material and raising a hiss from me. "What a waste," a belligerent man said forlornly, holding an empty flute by its stem. The spilled bubbly quickly worked its way to my belt buckle. He grabbed another from my extended tray and stumbled away without so much as an apology.

I ground my teeth together and reminded myself that I needed the money from this gig to cover my half of the rent.

A tall, broad form moved past the reception area, exiting through the glass doors embossed with the Nexcom Global emblem, and suddenly all thoughts of toppled drinks and pretentious assholes were forgotten.

He bypassed the bank of elevators for the stairwell, and something told me he didn't decide he was in the mood to hike it down from the top floor of one of the tallest skyscrapers in the city. No, my gut instincts said he was going up.

Moving as fast as I could through the dense crowd of party-going pricks, I made it to the kitchen area sectioned off for the wait staff without another champagne shower or losing a toe under someone's expensive heel.

"Deb," I whispered urgently, hurrying over to where my best friend's sister sat texting on her phone. "I'm taking a break. I need you to cover for me." I rested my tray on the table, using the bar napkins stacked on it to pat my wet shirt.

"No way," she scoffed. "*My* break isn't even over yet."

"You owe me," I said, pointing to the name tag pinned to my shirt. Deb had gotten me the job last minute after someone else flaked on it. Even went as far as having the name tag filled out and waiting for me when I'd rushed off the service elevator with less than three seconds to spare.

I didn't understand why the catering company required us to wear them. In rooms like these, we were all called one of two names: hey and you. My favorite, though, was when they simply snapped their fingers to get our attention.

"Yeah, I kinda do owe you," she said, pretty proud of her handiwork. "But I'm on hors d'oeuvres duty tonight, not drinks."

"No one will notice," I said, jetting off before she could reply.

There were two groups of people in Seattle: The calendar people, who clung strongly to their belief that we had four seasons, and those who believed we only had two—wet and dry. After living here all my life and experiencing midnight summers in the park that damn near required a goose-down jacket, and times where we had up to twenty straight days of rain, I was part of the wet and dry crew. So I was smart enough to know I needed a jacket before heading to the roof, but not smart enough to ride down to my car to get one. The wind bit into me immediately.

"You're the young man who's been watching me all night."

Distracted by ensuring the empty bottle holding the door ajar was secure after I'd stepped onto the roof, I hadn't noticed Mr. Dark and Broody until I was hit with his curtness from somewhere to my left.

"Shit, you scared the crap out of me," I said, trying to catch my breath. I made a quick mental note: *Work on improving your stealth skills.*

This man intimidated people without even trying. I'd witnessed it downstairs, but even those who trembled in his presence wanted to be within his orbit. He was obviously someone important. He exuded too much power not to be, and that power was intoxicating. It had been what initially caught my attention.

Powerful and intimidating weren't the attributes that made him interesting to me, though. Beyond the authority and mystery lurked something familiar, something that kept my eyes glued to him all night. Because what could a man who seemingly had everything, have in common with someone who had nothing? I had to find out.

"Leelee Bear," he said, his eyes narrowing on my name tag. *I'm gonna kill Deb.*

I unclipped it, slipping it into my trouser pocket. "That was someone's idea of a cruel joke. I'm Leland."

He raised his narrowed stare to my face, his onyx eyes piercing and hot, providing warmth in the cold. *Fuck, he's intense.*

"This is usually the part where you offer me your name," I said, surprised my balls hadn't shriveled up under his scrutiny.

"You don't already know who I am?" he asked doubtfully, the chilly breeze ruffling the top of his jet-black hair. The patches of salt and pepper scruff riding his jawline shone white under the gleam of the moonlight.

I shrugged. "Why would I? I was told where to show up and when. Other than the check clearing, nothing else mattered."

His eyes hardened; a tough feat considering they were already as resistant as stone. I waited out whatever battle he faced internally, meeting the fire in those polished orbs, hoping my unflinching response conveyed honesty.

"Franky," he said, some of the tension around his jaw easing. "Franky," he repeated, as if trying the name on for size and realizing it not only fit, but that he liked it. It oddly felt like he'd given me more than a name. It felt like he'd given me a taste of his vulnerability without even realizing it. It didn't taste half bad.

"See," I said, "that wasn't so hard."

"No, it wasn't, Mr. Bear."

I scowled at the use of the fake last name Deb had made sure ended up on my name tag, and I could have sworn that earned me a tiny speck of a grin from him, but he'd shifted into the shadows of the roof again, so I couldn't be sure.

Franky gave his back to the brick wall supporting the door, so I did the same. We were a good distance from the lip of the roof, but that didn't hinder our view of the city. We were quiet for a while, content to take it all in.

"I'm afraid of heights," I admitted, breaking our stretch of silence. Franky craned his head my way, but I kept my gaze forward. "I was thrown from a fourth-floor window when I was eight. Spent months in the hospital, then a rehabilitation center. I've still got a nasty looking scar on the back of my leg. A souvenir, I guess."

"*Thrown?*" he asked.

"You heard right," I said, heart pounding. I could still remember the feeling of free falling, of reaching for my would-be murderer as I plunged to the pavement. Could still paint the look of freedom—of fucking jubilee on her face when she thought it'd be lights-out for me. I could still taste my tears as I laid on the curb, broken and still loving her.

"Who would do that to a child?" he demanded. I found his astonishment weirdly touching.

I turned to him then, hoping his expression of rage and disgust could erase *her* happy one from my memory. "My mother," I said.

We breathed into the wind together, our pace syncing and easing after a few minutes, like we somehow had calmed each other without words.

"Are you always this candid with strangers?" he whispered.

"Never," I whispered back, wondering if my tone had sounded as awed as his. Franky didn't apologize for something he didn't do, which was typically what people did after learning about someone's trauma. It was like a default setting in their brain or some shit.

Maybe his refusal to be sorry for me explained why I didn't regret telling him. I didn't wish I could take the words back and relock them in that place inside of me that I didn't allow anyone access to, even if I couldn't express why I'd told him in the first place.

"The trick is to look out, not down," he said. "That's what helps me."

Was he afraid of heights too? Were we just two idiots torturing ourselves for the hell of it? "So what are you doing up here, Franky?"

He sighed, staring straight ahead again. "I thought maybe I'd look down, for once. Maybe doing one brave thing will lead to me doing another."

"Like a domino effect."

"Precisely," he said. "And you?"

"Besides stalking some hot guy?" I joked. Franky glared at me in reprimand. "Sorry, I tend to flirt when nervous, or tired, or wired with energy, or angry, or simply breathing. Just ignore it—for the most part."

"For the *most* part?" he asked. "And what about the non-most parts?"

"As long as my frank and beans are covered, we're safe," I deadpanned, and naturally his gaze moved downward before flicking back up to my face. "What? Are they not covered? Are they just hanging out shooting the breeze? Please tell me they're covered," I said in mock horror, and this time his grin was unmistakable.

"I don't know why I'm up here. Maybe I came searching for a kindred spirit. Maybe I hoped I'd discover I was a daisy," I said under my breath.

"A daisy?" His brows puckered in confusion.

I shook my head. "It's nothing. Never mind."

A bright and equally stupid idea hit me. "Let's do this together," I said. "Let's look down together."

"No," he said resolutely, straightening and eyeing the partially open roof door. "This was a terrible idea, and I need to get back to the party." Except Franky didn't move. Getting back to the party seemed like the last thing he wanted to do.

"What's everyone celebrating anyway?" I asked, hoping my question reminded him why he'd walked out on the celebration in the first place, hoping it would get him to stay.

"Nexcom has just acquired a company on target to become one of their largest competitors."

"Sounds like a big deal," I said, and he grunted, still watching the door. I twisted to face him, resting a shoulder against the wall. "So you work here? For Nexcom?" There were more people than offices downstairs, and Deb had mentioned there being an employee list as well as a guest list. I'd assumed maybe he was a special guest with the way everyone whispered from their corners while pointing toward him, or how some swarmed him like he was their hive. But maybe they were the guests.

"Something like that," he said, evading the question, but at least he wasn't eye-fucking the door anymore.

"Come on," I said, holding my hand out to him and nudging my head toward the ledge. "What?" I asked in mock offense when he met my outstretched fingers with a raised brow.

"I don't need my hand held," he said sharply, anxiously spinning the wedding band I hadn't noticed before. I wondered how many people in his life knew he had a tell. Probably not many, if any. To the people downstairs he wasn't even a real person.

"I know," I said, because I doubted he would ever admit to needing help. I'd come looking for commonality and was finding it in spades. "But I do." Again, a truth I hadn't planned on spilling. Franky paused in the nervous rotating of his ring but said nothing.

"Things are less scary when holding hands," I said, wiggling my fingers. Franky shot me a skeptical look.

"All the iconic sad movies have hand holding scenes," I went on to explain. "Holding a dying loved one's hands as they transition. Holding a woman's hand as she gives birth to a twenty-pound baby," I exaggerated. "It's been proven by science."

"Science?" he asked without feeling.

"Science," I confirmed gravely.

Footsteps ascending the stairs on the other side of the door snagged our attention, and Franky backed up in time to miss the door hitting him in the face. The beer bottle holding it open rolled, bumping up against the toe of my shoe, and the man standing in the doorway reared away at seeing me there.

He took in my server's uniform and dismissed me. Franky appeared from behind the door, and even I shrank away from his murderous glare.

"Frank—"

"What can I do for you, Robert?" Franky asked curtly.

Robert's gaze pinged between me and Franky. "Is this server bothering you?" he asked with a hint of disdain.

"His name is Mr. Bear," Franky corrected, and I groaned inwardly. I'd have decked him if it hadn't amused me a little to see an imposing man with a bad attitude say *Mr. Bear* with a straight face. "And someone is bothering me at the moment, but it isn't him."

Robert either sucked at reading the room—in our case the roof—or he was used to Franky's hostility because he continued as if he hadn't heard him. "You're needed downstairs," he said, suffering Franky's staredown like a champ.

"I'll be right there," Franky gritted out. Robert offered a stiff nod before striding off. I caught the door and refixed the bottle.

"You're mean," I said, low enough to not travel through the cracked door and down the stairwell.

"Duly noted," Franky said. He exhaled at the gloomy night sky. "This place brings out the worst in me."

"What brings out the best in you?" I asked, earning myself a sardonic chuckle.

"When I find out, you'll be the first to know."

"So walk away from it," I said, like it was the simplest thing to do. "If it makes you miserable, then walk away."

"I can't."

"Why not?"

"People depend on me," he said, and I remembered the wedding band. He had a family to take care of.

"Well, maybe you can take some time off to figure out what makes you happy, then work toward figuring out how to support your family by doing whatever that is."

"Maybe," he said, but I got the impression he was humoring me. He felt trapped. I knew because caged men recognized other caged men, even if our prisons were of a different kind.

Franky entered the stairwell, gesturing for me to hold the door so I didn't get locked out when the bottle rolled again. I listened as he descended, thinking of something to do or say to prolong this moment, but there was nothing. Maybe a moment was all it was meant to be.

I peered toward the edge of the roof, remembering why we had been up there in the first place. A wave of sadness hit me as one thought filtered through my brain.

He left before getting a chance to be brave.

CHAPTER 2

Leland

The bed dipped behind me, and my roommate, Noon, was on me before the elbow I'd thrown connected with his ribcage. He chuckled, and I complained as he grabbed me up in a reverse bear-hug, planting kisses to the back of my head.

"Your reflexes are improving," he said, as I fought off his inappropriate affection like I did most mornings.

"Are you... Are you *naked*!?" I asked when something fleshy and hard tapped at my spine.

"It's morning wood," he said, and I felt his shrug. "Has nothing to do with you."

"Why are you like this?" I groaned, wiggling out of his hold.

"Because I love you, which means I love to torture you." He laughed, rolling away from me and deftly missing the headbutt aimed at his forehead.

"You keep this up and you're going to owe me a bed," I warned. The name Mr. Bear fit Noon more aptly than it did me, and my cheap Ikea bed frame couldn't handle one more of his annoying morning wake-up hugs.

"Maybe if you'd actually listen to your alarm when it screams bad '80s music at you, I wouldn't need to resort to extreme measures to get you up for work," he said, getting to his feet.

I slapped at my alarm clock until it quieted down, then flipped to my back, peeling one eye open to scowl at the grizzly bear staring down at me. "Who lets you fuck them with that?" I asked, his erection taking up most of my view. I often joked that it was the size of a small human and would need to start contributing to the rent.

"You did," he said with a snort, yanking the pillow from under my head and clobbering me with it.

"That was *one* time," I said, snatching the pillow off my face and sitting up just as he disappeared into the hall. "And it wasn't that big then!"

"Yeah it was," he shot back. "And you loved it."

I flopped down, scrubbing the sleep from my eyes. We'd fucked around with each other once in high school. Both curious and willing to be each other's guinea pigs. It was a disastrous mistake we never repeated. We were much better off as friends.

"Get your ass up before I eat your breakfast," he threatened from the kitchen.

I sniffed the air, fighting to get from under the tangle of sheets when the scent of bacon infiltrated my nostrils.

"What's the special occasion?" I asked, snagging a plate from the cabinet over the sink and loading it with the eggs and French toast sitting on the stove. Noon was still sans clothing, but at least the worst of his nudity was hidden under the cheap, Formica table.

I took the seat across from him, reaching for the bacon sitting in the center of the table.

"Has anyone ever told you how pretty your eyes are?" he asked, deflecting. "Seriously," he said in response to my deadpan expression. "They're like pools of caramel and gold. I think it's from all the sun exposure—which by the way you should avoid. All that UV radiation isn't good for you."

"Not gonna happen," I said. I loved being out in the sun. "And if you've resorted to flattery it must be serious, so spit it out."

He leaned his forearms into the table. "I'm moving in with Stacey."

It made perfect sense, and I couldn't say I hadn't seen it coming. Noon spent half his time at his girlfriend's place anyway, and we both knew why he wasted any time here at all. I couldn't afford the rent in this shithole on my own, and I wouldn't accept his help if he didn't live here at least part-time. I hated charity.

"I held off as long as I could, but I can't keep helping with bills in two different places."

"I get it," I said, even as I lost my appetite. My most recent job had only been seasonal. I could cover this month's rent—which was already a couple days late—with the extra money I'd earned from the server gig Deb had gotten me last night. I'd need to scramble to find something else, and fast, or I'd be screwed come July.

"I'll still pay my half of the rent this month—"

"Absolutely not," I said, shaking my head and pushing my plate away. "Unless you're staying here for at least half the month, keep your money. I'll manage."

"Actually, I've already paid the rent in full. Yeah," he said as I glowered at him, "figured you wouldn't accept it willingly."

"Then why did you say you'd pay your half? As if you hadn't paid the whole damn thing already?" I didn't bother hiding my annoyance.

"Because I was hoping you wouldn't be an ass about it, then I could take your half, add another half, and get the following month paid too."

"You know that would never happen," I said.

"Yeah, well, a man can hope. Will you let me—"

"Fuck no. One month is bad enough. I'll have something lined up by then. I'm thinking about getting my bartender's license," I said with as much enthusiasm as I could muster. Noon would make us both sick worrying about me.

He sighed, standing to snag a business card off the counter.

"What's this?" I asked when he dropped it in front of me.

"It's some ritzy art gallery downtown. Stacey knows one of the girls who works there. She got her to agree to take one of your paintings. It's on a consignment basis, though. It's the best the girl could do. Said the owner's a prick."

"No, thank you," I said, sliding the card away. "My work isn't good enough to hang in any gallery. Definitely not a ritzy one."

"Figured you'd say that too, which is why I took the liberty of handing over one of your pieces. They'll let you know if it sells. If it does, they may even commission more work from you."

"Noon," I grated out between my teeth. I knew exactly which gallery he was talking about. I'd walked past it several times, wondering if I'd ever be good enough to grace its walls. I wasn't, and they'd probably stuck my painting in a supply closet the moment Stacey left.

"It's not charity, Leland. If you won't believe in your talent, I will. It costs you nothing. Just let it hang there and see what happens. I'm leaving my best friend to fend for himself, and it's fucking killing me," he said, his eyes growing misty. "I had to do something to help you."

Noon's leaving me started way before today. We'd been growing apart for some time now because he had big life plans, and I kept my plans to a bare minimum. He was outgrowing me, and his moving felt like the final nail in the building of our friendship's coffin. It wasn't that he acted like he was too good for me, or that he'd never not be there if I needed him, but it felt almost cruel on my part to keep him at ground level with me just because I refused to grow with him.

But I knew he still loved me, and as threatening as he could appear, Noon was actually a big teddy bear, and I could never quite master being immune to his tears. I hauled my plate of food back in front of me. "Fine," I said, and Noon's huge paws were cupping my cheeks before I could get a proper eye roll in. He leaned over to plant a noisy kiss on my lips, causing me to drop eggs onto my lap.

"Thank you," he said, fake tears gone and walking away with an extra pep in his step and a smile in his voice.

I glared daggers at his back as I grumbled, "At least I won't have to put up with your saggy, naked ass anymore."

Noon tossed his head back laughing, flexing his muscular ass cheeks as he headed for the bathroom. "I love you too," he shouted back, his laughter resuming, the sound of it warming my heart until it vanished beneath the sound of running water.

◆◆◆

Two weeks of off-the-books grunt work at a construction site left me with enough cash to get the rent paid up for the rest of the summer, especially since Noon had covered June, leaving me with the money I'd scraped together for my half.

I never paid rent early. Shit, I could rarely swing paying it on time, but I didn't trust myself not to do something stupid like spend it on food or whatever else a human needed to survive, so I made my landlord's day by handing over the money order earlier that afternoon.

Back in the apartment, I propped myself against my headboard and recounted the measly pile of cash I had left, hoping I'd discover that I had, in fact, miscounted by at least a few hundred dollars in my favor the first ten times I'd counted.

"Nope," I said, blowing out a breath. It was just enough to pay for my bartending course. With any luck, I could complete the class in a few weeks and get work as a barback before September rolled around.

The tiny apartment felt empty without Noon. A different type of empty than the nights he didn't come home. This was permanent, and the emptiness in my heart reminded me that outside of him, I had no one. A reality I'd worked hard to maintain.

My gaze shifted to the rain pummeling my window. The gloominess of the day reminded me of Franky. Why had I shared so much with him?

"Are you always this candid with strangers?" he'd asked on that rooftop.

"Never," I'd said.

Yet I'd shared something with him so private and traumatizing that I often refused to allow myself to think about it. And now I racked my brain for a concrete answer to the question *why*. Had to be more than him handing over his name, no matter how big that felt at the time. I could've given him a number of less intimate secrets in exchange, but I'd given him the one that mattered most. The one that shaped me.

Franky wasn't lacking in the darkness and stoicism department. Dark and stoic men had always been my weakness, running a close second to men who didn't give a shit about me— because if they didn't care, I didn't need to worry about them wanting to stay. No one got to stay.

But what I'd felt toward him hadn't been attraction, not the physical kind, anyway. And even if it were, the wedding band on his finger would've put an immediate stop to that.

He was living a life he didn't want—to some degree—but seemed helpless in finding a way out of it. Or maybe he did see a way out but was too afraid to seize it. Too afraid to fail, or maybe, I was projecting my own shit onto him. What did it matter anyway? We were from two different worlds, and the chances were slim that those worlds would ever collide again.

My phone rang, bringing me back to the present, and I followed the sound to the kitchen table. It continued to ring as I stared at the unknown number populating the screen, contemplating if I should answer. Did I owe anyone money? The utilities were paid up to the end of the month, so it shouldn't be a bill collector. I tapped the speaker phone function, listening before tentatively saying, "Hello?"

"Hello, am I speaking with Mr. Meadows?" The voice was haughty but masculine.

"Depends," I answered, hesitant to confirm my identity. *Could* it be a creditor? "Who's this?"

"This is Neil Sanders. I'm calling about *A Winter Meadow*," he said.

Huh? I replied, then realized I'd said that in my head. "Come again," I said aloud.

"*A Winter Meadow*," he enunciated impatiently. "The painting hanging in my gallery, Mr. *Meadows*."

I haven't confirmed who I am yet, asshole, I wanted to say, but the words got jammed in my brain behind *A Winter Meadow* and *gallery*. I'd forgotten that Noon had confiscated one of my paintings for the gallery downtown. Mostly because I thought it was in a dark supply closet, or better yet, their alleyway dumpster. And I had no idea he'd given them *that* painting. Noon had named it *A Winter Meadow*. I simply called it the story of my sad fucking life.

"Mr. Meadows?"

"Ah, yeah, that's me."

"Your painting has sold. Normally, we would send payment by postal mail, but our client has requested to see more of your work." He sounded more shocked than me. "I promised we could have a few options for him to review by this evening." Now he sounded nervous, desperate even, as if he'd made a promise he wasn't sure he could keep.

I lowered onto one of the kitchen chairs. *Holy shit.*

"Mr. Meadows," Neil nearly growled this time, losing his snobby cool.

"Ah, yeah, still here. I can be there in an hour," I said, jumping to my feet and charging for my bedroom closet.

"Good," he said on a deep exhale. "See you in one hour. Bring your best." And then the line went dead.

Bring my best? They were all crap to me. They weren't aimless or pointless, because my art tended to depict whatever I was going through at the time, but that only meant something to me.

I dragged the wide chest from the closet, flipped open the lid, closed my eyes and grabbed whatever my hands touched first. My version of eeny-meeny-miny-moe. I didn't let myself think about the options I ended up with. I sandwiched them between foam boards, wrapped them in a sheet to protect them from the rain, then ran for the door.

♦ ♦ ♦

I waited at the front counter while Neil pranced toward a back office, bow-tie and glasses firmly in place.

He'd taken the two paintings off my hands as soon as I showed him my identification, explaining that I would be notified and expected to retrieve them promptly if his client wasn't interested. His attitude implied he believed the sale of *A Winter Meadow* was a stroke of luck, and that lightning would not strike twice for me.

Neil couldn't ruin my mood, though. Not after being told I'd be paid a thousand bucks for what took me no more than a couple of hours to create. He'd better hope his client didn't come barging in here for a full refund after coming to his senses, because like hell he'd be getting that money back. If it meant he'd then hold hostage the junk I just handed over, then so be it.

Neil returned with my check. "I bid you farewell, Mr. Meadows."

Who the fuck bids farewells in this century?

I took that to mean *get the fuck out of my gallery*, but once his back was turned, I got lost amongst the other art enthusiasts losing themselves in the world of interpretation. Figuring out what an artist attempted to say with their work was half the fun, making a piece mean something specific for you rounded out the whole of the experience.

I didn't know how much time had passed as I made my way back down from the third floor, but I could've spent all night there, especially after stopping in front of the empty wall space with the title tag that read *A Winter Meadow* by Leland Meadows. I could have curled up and slept right below the space, making it my home, making it my little slice of hope.

It'd been stuck in the back section near the restrooms, but I didn't care. All the better. It meant the person who now owned it deserved it because they took the time to find it. They'd ventured to this dark, dank area in search of something more, and they found me.

My steps were light and carefree as I made my way to the exit, tugging my umbrella from under my armpit in preparation of using it.

"I'll take them both," came a low, rumbling voice, halting my footsteps. It was full of command and take-charge energy, and if you paid close enough attention, you'd hear it was mostly bark with only a little bit of bite. I'd recognize that voice anywhere.

Neil stood in a lounge area off to the side, holding up my paintings for the inspection of a man in a maroon-colored suit.

The man's muscular body towered over Neil, the single recessed light above haloing him and glinting off the graying strands along his hairline the way the moon had a couple weeks ago on our roof. *Our roof?* Where had that thought come from?

"Are you sure?" Neil asked, and Franky glared at him as if he didn't appreciate being questioned on his decision. I winced, feeling sorry for anyone who had to weather that glower, even a prick like Neil.

Neil nodded repeatedly, backing away. "I'll get them wrapped and ready to go, Mr. Kincaid," he said wisely before scurrying off.

Franky's serious nature brought out an urge in me to tease him, to bend over backward for the pleasure of seeing one of his almost-smiles. But more important than that was the realization that *he'd* been the one to buy *A Winter Meadow* and the one buying my other pieces now. Was the universe on drugs?

"Franky?" I said, approaching him. He did a double take, a fleeting expression of shock dissipating to reveal his resting-in-difference face, and I felt it was my duty to ruffle his feathers a bit. "So you wear your armor to buy art, too, huh? What I wouldn't give to see you out of it." I grinned when the corner of his lip twitched.

"Hello, Leelee Bear," he said, and damn Deb and that stupid, childish name tag. My cheeks burned, because of course they did, and his eyes lit with victory. "What are you doing here?" he asked, thankfully not dragging out the shoe-on-the-other-foot routine. He didn't strike me as the playful or gloating type anyway.

"One of my paintings sold. Three now, from the looks of it." I nodded meaningfully toward the corridor Neil had flurried down.

"You're Leland Meadows," he said, and I had to admit it felt damn good that he hadn't said it as if it should've been impossible. I'd gotten enough of that from Neil, and from myself.

"The one and only," I said, feeling like a kid under his stare of appreciation.

Neil returned, steps slowing when he spotted me. "Mr. Meadows. You're still here," he said accusingly.

"Yeah, good thing too. Would've sucked to make a second trip down here in the rain. Although there isn't much I wouldn't do for two grand, weather be damned. Is it okay if I wait around for my payment?"

Neil blanched, and Franky's jaw turned to stone. I suppose it wasn't classy of me to discuss payment in front of a paying customer. No one ever blamed me for being classy, though.

"Two grand?" Franky asked Neil.

"Well, three if you count the first painting," I said, but doing so had made matters worse.

"W-well, there is the, ah, c-commission rate to account for," Neil stammered.

Franky's expression went from suspicious to angry, even though his tone remained even. "Are you telling me you have an eighty-percent commission rate?" Franky asked, and my gaze bounced between the two of them as I worked on the math. He'd paid five-grand for my work? For *each* painting?

"Ah—" Neil started before Franky saved him the trouble of coming up with a lie.

"Who exactly are you cheating here, Mr. Sanders? Me, or Mr. Meadows?"

I got the impression neither option was good.

"Is that how you run your business, Mr. Sanders? With a lack of integrity?" Franky asked, dialing the growl up a notch.

"No, Mr. Kincaid. I assure you it was a simple misunderstanding. I planned on rectifying it once I called him about the sale of the two additional pieces."

"I haven't purchased them *yet*," Franky said, and the background muzak fell away, the soft footsteps of the other patrons touring the gallery melted away, too, and the air itself seemed to have deserted me as the moment boiled down to what Neil would say next.

I couldn't blame Franky for wanting to abandon the deal, even though doing so would drastically affect me more than it would Neil. I'd been looking forward to eating something other than ramen and pineapple chunks for dinner.

"On behalf of the integrity of the gallery, and our long-standing relationship with you, I'll rectify this error by paying Mr. Meadows in full. My commission fee and all."

"*What?*" I asked, finally getting in on the fight. I could advance my rent for a full year with that.

"*Or open your art-bar,*" I imagined Noon saying. But I couldn't do that because this was a chance occurrence, with a zero probability of it ever happening again. I was no artist, not really.

"Excuse me while I get your payment in order," Neil said, ignoring my outburst.

"You didn't have to do that," I said to Franky once we were alone.

"You shouldn't let anyone get away with giving you less than you're worth," he said.

I lowered my eyes, not wanting him to see how much that meant to me, and collided with the empty spot on his finger where his wedding band had been. A sinking sensation gnawed at my gut, and I became consumed with needing to know if he was okay. "Franky—"

"Here you are, Mr. Meadows," Neil said, returning with my check. He didn't even look my way as he passed it off to me while addressing Franky. "Mr. Kincaid, your purchases have been left with your driver."

"Have a good day, Mr. Meadows," Franky said, shaking me free from my thoughts about his well-being. Neil was gone, and by the time I found my voice, Franky was halfway to the side entrance.

"Hey," I said, and he partially turned, waiting expectantly. "It's supposed to be sunny tomorrow. I hate wasting even a drop of sunlight."

There was a brief pause as Franky's gaze roamed my face and neck. "I can tell," he said. I clenched my umbrella with both hands to keep from touching my tanned cheeks.

"I'll be out attempting to be brave, if you happen to be looking for me."

"And why would I be looking for you, Mr. Meadows?"

"Is that what you're going to call me now that you know my full name?" I asked sedately.

"Maybe," he said, equally as sedate, which made me smile.

"Maybe you'll be looking for me because you'll need more art."

"So soon after today?" he asked.

"I have a feeling three Leland Meadows pieces won't be enough," I answered, folding my arms over my chest and nearly taking out an eye with my umbrella in the process.

"Oh really," he said, fully facing me now.

"Really," I confirmed with feigned gravity. His lips didn't flutter with amusement, but his eyes danced for a split second. I took it as a win.

"And what act of bravery will you be performing, *Leland*?"

The way he stressed my name made it sound important. Was it wrong that I wanted to ask him to make me feel important again? "The state fair kicks off down by the pier tomorrow," I said. "I'll be tackling the Ferris wheel."

He was silent for a few heartbeats, his expression blank. *Here's our second chance to be brave!* I wanted to shout, but I fell back on flirtation instead.

"I mean, don't let my charm and good looks persuade you. You need to want to do this for you."

"Your charm and good looks?" he asked, and I pointed at him when he grinned, my own smile nearly breaking my face. *Gotcha.*

"Goodbye, Leland."

“Goodbye,” I said to his retreating back, but I privately hoped this was somehow the first of many hellos.

CHAPTER 3

Franklin

"**M**r. Kincaid?" my assistant called, poking her head into my office as I glanced up from the paperwork on my desk. "Sorry, I tried your phone, but it's on do not disturb."

"That's usually what I do when not wanting to be disturbed, Patricia." I instantly regretted taking my bad mood out on her. "I apologize. It's been a trying morning. Did you need something?"

She smiled sympathetically. "Robert's here insisting he speak with you."

"Send him in," I said, shuffling the papers together and sticking them in their folder. Patricia nodded, stepping back so Robert—Nexcom's leading attorney, and my late father's friend—could storm into my office. I pushed to my feet, preparing to meet his anger with a reality check.

"Tell me you aren't serious," he said, by way of greeting. "Tell me I heard you wrong in there." He jutted a thumb over his shoulder to where the conference room resided beyond my door. "And why did I have to find out about this in a meeting with everyone else?"

"I'm very serious, and this is exactly why you found out the way you did," I said, tone hard. Robert watched me create Nexcom with my bare hands, guided me— not so willingly—through the merging and liquidation of my father's business after his untimely passing, then he came to work for me. He was the closest thing to family I had left, and he tended to stick his nose into areas of the business that didn't pertain to his role within it. Our shared history often left me having to remind him who was in charge.

"You can't just take a summer off, Franklin. You don't get to do that. Not without advanced notice and proper planning. With much of our cash flow tied up in the new acquisition, Nexcom is vulnerable right now." Robert stopped on the other side of my desk. "We hit our lowest profit margins this past quarter, and we're preparing to negotiate our second-biggest deal yet. Until those contracts are signed and the new partnerships made, you need to be as visible as possible. You can't expect the company to stand if it's missing one of its legs—"

"Then let it fall," I cut in chillingly, not even sure I didn't mean it. "I'll be available for anything urgent, but short of our headquarters crumbling to the ground—"

"The building is shaking as we speak—"

"I expect you and Chris to handle things," I continued over him.

"But—""Are you telling me that my lead attorney and CFO are incapable of tackling things while I'm away, Robert?" I asked, leaning my palms on the desk. The move drew his gaze to my left hand and the absence of my wedding ring.

"What's going on, Franklin?" he asked, temper cooling.

"I'm fine," I said, sliding my hands into my trouser pockets.

"How's Selene?" he asked next, the wrinkles at the corners of his gray eyes deepening further.

"The boys aren't coming home this summer. Use this time to figure out what you want, Franklin, because we can't live like this anymore."

"I will, if you promise to do the same, because this goes both ways, Selene."

Shaking my last conversation with my wife from my head, I took in the opulence of my office, the business awards lining the display case along the wall. I peered down at the suit I wore and thought about the hundred others like it lining my closet. I glared at my leather-bound planner resting on the end of my desk, packed to the brim with meeting reminders and business dinner engagements.

I resented them all, resented everything they represented, and most of all, I resented that even in my temporary reprieve from a life I wasn't sure I wanted to live anymore, I couldn't escape them completely.

"You know how to reach me, *if* necessary," I said, scooping up my cell phone and ignoring his last question. The well-being of my wife wasn't his business, and I didn't know how to answer it even if it was.

"Franklin," he said as I reached the office door. I stopped with my hand on the handle. "I know the lines between us can often be blurred, and I know sometimes you look at me and see your father. You see his failings as a parent, and how much he and I are alike. But I do care about you, and I hope you know you can talk to me."

Robert's intentions were good, but he was of the same mind-set as my father. It was what made them the best of friends. He wouldn't understand what ate at me, and at the end of the day, we weren't friends. At least not by choice. We'd inherited one another, and I was sick and tired of not having a choice.

"In some ways you're like him too," he whispered.

"He and I are *nothing* alike," I said, pushing through the door because I couldn't spend another minute in that office being suffocated by the weight of antiquated expectations, and because I knew if I'd turned to him, I would've been greeted with his pity and the realization that he was right.

◆ ◆ ◆

Samuel waited near the curb for me, holding the back door of the SUV open. Wanting to put miles, instead of mere feet, between myself and Nexcom, I didn't waste another second clearing the lobby's revolving doors and sliding in.

We rode out of the city in silence until he pulled into the driveway of the waterfront property I'd recently purchased. I stepped out, inhaling the scent of the Pacific Ocean, loving the way the light breeze ruffled my hair.

"Samuel," I called as he shut the rear door and prepared to climb into the driver's seat.

"Yes, Mr. Kincaid?" Samuel had been my father's driver; another person passed down to me—albeit a more welcome in-heritance gift.

"Take the summer off. With pay," I added when his sage eyes widened in alarm.

"Are you sure?" he asked, his salt and pepper brows lowering.

"Yes, I'm sure. Enjoy your grandchildren this summer. Take your wife on that Italian vacation she's been not-so-subtly pestering you about. I'll be fine." Another invisible manacle fell from my wrists. How many more could I break free of? I wanted to rely on myself this summer. I wanted to drive, to walk, to ride the damn bus, and imagine my father turning over in his grave because of it.

Samuel scanned the two-story coastal home surrounded by evergreens on both sides, then swept his gaze along the tree-lined road we'd turned off of, probably noting how isolated I'd be out there. How alone I'd be. His forehead creased with further concern when he observed my ringless finger.

"I'll be fine," I stressed again when his expression shifted to one of indecision. "I swear it."

"Only if you promise to call me if you need me or if you need *anything*," he demanded.

I squeezed his shoulder, and he rested a weathered palm on top of mine. "I promise."

With a stiff nod, he got into the SUV, reversing out and pulling off with a wave.

I sighed and turned to the back of the house, which faced the winding road, leaving the front of the home to overlook the ocean and mountain view.

Entering from one of the side doors, I moved beyond the mudroom, through the open kitchen and into the living room, unlatching and sliding back the glass wall to let in the sea breeze and early morning sunlight.

I tore my blazer off, tossing it onto the white sofa, the only piece of furniture I had in the house. My tie went next, and I kicked out of my dress shoes like they were on fire.

Slowly circling in place, wondering what I should do next, my gaze bumped up against the painting perched on top of the mantel. *A Winter Meadow.*

It called to me, like it had that day in the gallery, and I went to it now, just as helpless as I had been then.

I'd gone there in search of something to spruce up the place. I didn't have anything specific in mind, but I figured I'd know what I wanted once I saw it. I almost walked out empty handed after spending an hour unimpressed by the unimaginative pieces hanging on the gallery walls.

But then I'd discovered a small, poorly lit alcove on my way to the restroom where *A Winter Meadow* hung crookedly, with a price tag that couldn't have been more insulting in comparison to what everything else in there was going for.

At the foot of the fireplace, I reached up to adjust the painting's positioning.

Withering wildflowers hung their heads in the vast, shadowy meadow. Fearsome storm clouds colored the grass beneath their stems gray. A spattering of trees was painted in the distance, their bare limbs cradling a light dusting of snow and their trunks curved as if folding under unseen pressure.

The portrait would have been depressing if not for the bright, yellow daisy drifting on the wind toward a sliver of sunlight visible through a tiny break in the bleak clouds.

What made the daisy so different? Why had it survived when everything else around it hadn't?

The other two paintings of Leland's that I'd purchased were beautiful too, but not quite as thought-provoking as this one, and I suddenly needed to know what drove him to create this. I wanted him to translate it for me, to explain its symbolism and how it related to him personally.

"Maybe I hoped I'd discover I was a daisy," he'd said that night on the roof. I touched the corner of the framed canvas, now even more intrigued by him.

I suppose I should've been stunned to find out he was the man behind this magnificent work of art. I'd been more shocked about the coincidence of it being him more than anything, though, because I'd come to learn from our peculiar, shared experience a couple of weeks ago, that Leland was full of surprises—and that I shouldn't be surprised by any of them.

"Maybe you can take some time off to figure out what makes you happy, then work toward figuring out how to support your family by doing whatever that is," he'd said, and I'd descended the roof thinking him idealistic and naive. Men like me didn't get to walk away, and I was too terrified to even dream of what walking away would look like if I could. Because as much as I believed that I hated my status, my privilege, and my grasp on power, there was also a large part of me that felt I'd be no one without it, and that I'd lose everyone if I let it all go.

But then, learning I was on the verge of losing everything and everyone anyway, left me with a sense of now-or-never.

"We haven't been happy for a very long time, because you haven't been happy for a very long time, Franklin. If ever."

I screwed my eyes shut on the flashback, not wanting to recollect what she'd confessed after. Instead, I focused on what Leland's last words to me were.

"The state fair kicks off tomorrow. I'll be tackling the Ferris wheel."

It wasn't even noon yet. I hadn't given his invite much consideration yesterday, but now, after the morning meeting I'd had, and after ruminating over his art, I found that I wouldn't mind seeing him again, if only to pick his brain about *A Winter Meadow*.

I didn't know what time he'd arrive there, but he said he loved the sun, and it was at its peak around noon. It wasn't much to go by, but I had very little to lose.

Upstairs, I stripped out of what remained of my suit and legged into a pair of dark jeans before tugging a navy Henley over my head. The transformation from my usual attire made me think of something else Leland had said.

"So you wear your armor to buy art, too, huh? What I wouldn't give to see you out of it."

The comment had been purposely salacious, meant to fluster me, but it had got me thinking instead. If I wanted to experience something different, I'd have to start with shedding my armor.

I smoothed my hands down the cotton shirt, the change of clothes feeling refreshing, and I wondered how long I'd get to enjoy this before having to leave Franky behind and return to being Franklin Kincaid.

Deciding not to dwell on that, I shoved my wallet into my back pocket and made for the garage.

Exactly one hour later, I pulled into the graveled parking lot near the pier. Leland's main objective was the Ferris wheel, but it didn't hurt to keep an eye out for him on my way to that side of the boardwalk, so I took off at a leisurely stroll in that direction while keeping an eye out for him elsewhere.

I'd never consumed food from a truck, or hot dogs boiled in the compartment of a metal cart, but the scents overwhelming the air made my stomach grumble, reminding me I hadn't yet eaten.

I narrowly avoided slamming into a running toddler holding an ice cream cone, her mother not far behind, and I winced when a man with a bullhorn in a dart throwing stall shouted for willing participants to "come on over."

It was a lot to take in, and I almost backtracked to the parking lot, but then straight ahead, a man as tall as me, with sun-kissed cropped hair and fists jammed into his hoodie pockets, caught my attention.

Leland stared up at the Ferris wheel in abject horror, his face drained of color. His jeans hugged his defined legs, proving he wasn't as slender as he'd appeared the last two times I'd seen him. His work slacks, and then the cargo pants he'd worn at the gallery, were a lot looser on his seemingly slim frame.

I skirted around the carnival ride, careful to keep out of sight until I stood behind him. "It won't bite," I said.

Startled, his shoulders bunched, then relaxed as they vibrated from a silent laugh. "What a shame," he responded in a seductive tone.

"Are you always this amorous?" I asked, as he turned to me. Begrudgingly, I did enjoy his devilry, although I'd never admit to it.

"Always," he said shamelessly, and I smiled, unable to help myself. Leland was light and fun, that much was evident, and I desperately needed some fun and levity in my life. Loosening up would just take some getting used to after having it drilled into my head since I was a child that showing enjoyment was equivalent to showing weakness. *"Fear garners respect,"* my father would say. Through his guidance I'd become a dismal boy.

"Couldn't stay away from me, huh?" Leland said.

"Don't make me regret my decision."

"Always so testy. You look good without the armor," he said, nodding with approval.

"Thanks."

He nudged his head in the direction of the spinning wheel. "Are we ready to do this?"

"We?" I asked incredulously. "No, *we* are not ready to do anything." I couldn't even look up at it. I expected him to try and convince me, maybe even offer up a loaded retort. Instead I got his serious side, which aged him beautifully.

"Okay," he said. "I understand." His shoulders rose and fell with his deep breath. "Wait for me?"

"Yes," I said. "I'll wait right here for you."

Leland whirled to face the Ferris wheel, only pausing for a heartbeat before moving with determination toward the short line of people waiting for their turn to look death in the eye. Guilt poked at my chest. Hadn't he been there for me a few weeks ago in spite of his own fear? Hadn't he been willing to look over the edge with me?

"I was thrown out of a fourth-floor window when I was eight," he'd admitted when he didn't have to.

"Wait," I called out against my better judgment. Leland reached back without looking, wiggling his fingers. "You're such a child," I said as I caught up and took his hand, because *"things are less scary when holding hands."*

◆ ◆ ◆

"I looked you up," Leland said. We'd survived the Ferris wheel, and while that had been more than enough adventure for me for one day, it had the opposite effect on him. If it moved fast and launched itself skyward, Leland tackled it while I stood back and watched with a mixture of admiration and nausea. "You're a pretty big deal. Why'd you tell me your name was Franky?"

"The woman who helped raise me used to call me Franky when no one was looking. My father hated the name, which of course caused me to favor it," I said, as we ambled toward the pier. Leland grinned, shaking his head at me. "What?" I asked.

"This might sound weird, because I hardly know you, but it's so *you* to refer to a nanny as 'the woman who helped raise me.'"

"Nanny feels too—"

"Privileged?"

"More like insulting to the person who shaped the most important part of me." The part I desperately sought to recover now.

"Oh," he said, all traces of humor replaced with something mirroring respect. "I mean, nanny *is* fewer words, though. I would've guessed that would appeal to you."

"Normally it would, but Gloria deserves more than that, so I suffer through the pain of using more words than necessary for her," I said with a feigned, agonized sigh.

"That also seems so like you," Leland said, offering me a piece of cotton candy. I turned the soft, blue confection over in my hand before taking a small bite, then another, marveling at the way it quickly dissolved against my tongue. "You've never had cotton candy?" Leland said, aghast.

"No," I said, stealing a bigger piece.

"How old are you?" he asked.

"Forty-five," I answered, and he didn't even bat an eyelash. "And you?"

"Twenty-five." A young couple vacated a bench up ahead that overlooked the water. Leland veered in that direction.

"So, do you have kids?" he asked.

"I thought you looked me up," I said, settling down next to him.

"Yeah, but there was a lot of information to sift through, and I'd rather paint than read. Plus, I figured it'd be cool to hear it from you." He kicked his feet up on the pier railing, balling up the empty cotton candy bag and sticking it in his pocket.

"What if we never saw each other again?" I asked.

"I bookmarked the webpage in case of such an emergency," he said, then pointed a finger at my lips. "That's three smiles now."

"The second one doesn't count. There's no such thing as *hearing* a smile."

"You're a sore-loser cheater," he accused, and this time I skipped past the smile and settled into laughter. It was low and swift, but Leland's breath caught and held anyway.

"Fine. Three smiles. I won't make the fourth one easy for you."

"At least you admitted there will be a fourth."

"Only because you're ridiculous, and apparently ridiculousness is hard to fight against when exhausted."

"Tired already, grumpy old man? The sun hasn't even set yet."

"I'm not grumpy or old," I grumbled, probably proving him right on the grumpy part.

We soaked in the cool air in companionable silence, neither of us in a hurry to break it as our gazes chased the seagulls flying low over the still waters. I wasn't sure what it was about Leland, but I found him increasingly easy to talk to. Perhaps because he didn't know me, which made it possible for me to be whoever I wanted to be around him. It was much easier to change in front of someone who didn't know who you were before. Or in my case, who I'd been pretending to be. He didn't look at me and wonder where the old me went and when he'd be back. I was Franky, and we were both getting to know me.

"I have two sons. Cole and Jasper. Jasper's my stepson, but that's a technicality I often forget. They're away at college."

"You're married to Jasper's mother," he said.

"We're separated at the moment, but yes, we're still married." I rubbed the spot where my wedding band used to be, feeling the loss deep in my soul and the ache deep in my bones. Would I find my way back to her? An even scarier question was did I want to.

My chest constricted around the guilt I carried there. I was failing my family, and I didn't do it lightly, but I'd reached the brink of how much more I could tolerate failing myself.

Leland and I observed the water again, as somewhere behind us the roller coaster blasted down its wooden tracks, and the subsequent screams played background music to our thoughts.

"I'm losing my best friend," he said out of nowhere, closing his big brown eyes and tipping his head back, his face bathing in the late afternoon sunlight. "I know saying that sounds random, but it's not. His name is Noon, and we grew up in the same shitty neighborhood. He's a freaking giant of a man who can cry at the drop of a hat. *Literally*," he stressed. "You drop a hat and he's crying."

I smiled at his description of him, and Leland's smile-radar must have pinged because his head snapped my way just in time to witness it. He didn't call me out on it, though. Didn't proclaim himself the winner. He simply returned the gesture before sweeping his gaze over the harbor again.

"He's also inappropriately affectionate, and I *always* pretend to hate it. Anyway, he's in love with his girlfriend," he said drolly.

"Blasphemy," I said, appalled on his behalf.

"I know, right?" He cut a glance at me and grinned. There was deep affection under the surface of flippancy. Hurt too, but it was clear he cared for Noon, and something like jealousy rolled through me. *What I wouldn't give to have a friendship like that.* And on the heels of that thought I remembered that I *did* have a friendship like that once.

With Theo.

"We've lived together since we were old enough to work whatever crappy job we could get our hands on to hustle up rent money. He moved in with her the day after your office party, and I have a feeling that was only the first of many moves that will take him farther away from me."

"That can't be easy," I said, feeling his sadness like a thick layer of fog around us.

"He's the only friend I have. I kind of make it a point to keep it that way." He twisted to look at me then, his typical childish glee replaced with something soft like vulnerability. It made me curious about the sarcastic, flirtatious side of himself he so readily offered up. Was that merely to disguise the pain hidden underneath?

"I get the feeling you have even fewer friends than I do, Franky. Why else would you be here, with me, when you're... when you're *you*," he said. "I have absolutely nothing to offer you, but if you're in need of a friend, I may have an opening."

"As someone who makes it a point to avoid friendships, why would you offer me one?" I asked, not only confused by his touching gesture, but by the warmth it infused inside of me. I doubted we could be friends. I had too much baggage, too much going on in my chaotic life, in my chaotic head. Not to mention I was old enough to be his father.

But he'd been the first person I met, so to speak, on this new journey of mine. And without Gloria and Theo, Leland was the only one who knew Franky, to some extent. I secretly wished I didn't have to let that go, even though it was barely anything to hold on to to begin with.

I thought Leland would answer my question with sarcasm or any other defense mechanism he kept in his arsenal. Nothing too heavy or too revealing. Instead, he kept his veil off, giving me something real, something I instantly connected to.

"Because you somehow feel different. A possible exception to my rule. And because I'm lonely," he admitted softly, opening something in me and leaving me speechless.

CHAPTER 4

Easing off the gas, I strained to see the ocean beyond the densely packed trees blocking my view. I patted Betty on her dashboard, silently thanking the old Beetle for surviving the trip outside the city.

Last night on the pier, Franky asked if he could commission me to create a piece for him, and I'd easily agreed. He'd overpaid for the portraits he purchased from the gallery, and I'd seen this as an opportunity to right that wrong, because little did he know, I wouldn't be charging him a red cent. I had no clue at the time that my blank canvas would be his living room wall.

I pulled into the driveway, stopping in front of the first of three garages and whistling up at the house appreciatively. Cutting the engine, I slouched in my seat, reaching back to grip my headrest as I closed my eyes and breathed in the scent of ocean air drifting through my lowered window.

Serenity hummed through me, filtering out the unnecessary noise of life until all I could hear were the birds eagerly chirping from within the tall canopy of evergreens surrounding me. I'd need to make the most of this before getting back to the blaring car horns and thumping music I was subjected to at my apartment.

Fast approaching footfalls interrupted my moment of bliss, and through the rearview mirror I spotted Franky jogging up the drive. He stopped at the front passenger window.

"Have you been waiting long?" he asked, sweat traveling from his hairline and disappearing into the scruff overtaking his strong jaw. "I thought I'd be back from my morning run before you arrived."

One could learn a lot by looking into Franky's eyes. They were nuanced, and most times they did the talking for him. I wanted to become an expert at deciphering the meaning behind every shift. Like what it meant when they seemed to spark with life, or when they were dull, or round, or narrowed. They were shining like burnished brass now, full of excitement. Was he happy to see me? Did I want him to be?

"It's fine. I just got here, and I'm early anyway." I kept my gaze trained above his neck and off the broad expanse of chest area exposed below.

"Come in," he said, using the running shirt tossed over his shoulder to wipe down his forehead. "I'll make us breakfast before we get started."

"You can cook?" I asked, quickly getting out of the car.

"I guess we're about to find out." He sounded uncertain as he moved toward the side of the house.

"Great, so I'll either be your guinea pig, or your victim."

"Or both," Franky said, laughing, the sound a deep rumble and more effervescent than his brief laugh on the pier last night. He was different today. More relaxed and less contemplative, and as much as I didn't want to assume the credit for that, it was hard not to, because I was different too, and it definitely had something to do with him.

"Wow," I said, as we rounded the front of the house. Puget Sound was an inlet of the Pacific Ocean, and Franky's home had an amazing, unobstructed view of it. I'd passed other homes on my way up, but they were nothing more than specks in the distance from here.

The patio felt more like an extension of the interior with the way the glass wall opened up from end to end. At the far side, a set of stairs built into the home's rocky foundation led to a small dock and an anchored boat.

"It's peaceful here," he said.

Pine ceiling fans hung from the exposed beams inside, and the white walls and matching washed-wood floors gave the home a nautical look. It was beautiful, and aside from a sofa and my painting, it was also unfurnished. "Did you just move in?"

"Yeah," he said, bypassing the living room for the open kitchen. There wasn't a single stool around the marble island, and the breakfast nook was just a square, empty space.

"When's the rest of your furniture coming?" I asked, peering at the two Adirondack chairs surrounding the firepit on the patio. There was easily enough unused space out there for a twenty-seat outdoor dining set.

"I didn't order any more furniture," he said, plucking a carton of eggs from the fridge.

"Do you at least have a bed?"

"I have a comfortable mattress," he said absently, eyeing the eggs like they required a code to crack.

"Tell me you have a bowl for the eggs." I chuckled, circling to his side of the island and opening cabinets until I struck gold.

"I've got cooking utensils, bathroom supplies, light bulbs, and even a canister of air freshener. I just don't have much furniture." He pressed his back into the counter behind him, crossing his legs at the ankle as I cracked six eggs into the porcelain bowl.

"Why not? Are you a minimalist or something?"

"No," he said, unsure. I didn't know him well, but I knew that tone was unlike him. I glanced over, waiting for him to give me more. "I'm going to make it all."

"You're going to do what?" I accepted the whisk he pulled from a drawer near his hip, mixing the eggs as he continued.

"You remember Gloria?"

"Your nan—" I caught myself. "The woman who helped raise you?"

"Yeah. Her husband was a carpenter. He did most of the work on my family's estate. I'd sneak off and help him whenever my father wasn't around. And there were rare occasions when my father would allow me to spend the night with Gloria and her boys, and we'd get to build things in their garage all night." He smiled, but his pupils were dim. *Dim means sadness.* I made a mental note of it.

"Anyway," he said, grabbing the salt and pepper from the cabinet above him. "Thought I'd see if I still had it in me."

"Do you keep in touch with Gloria and her family?" I secretly hoped he had someone to call for help, because I had a feeling this project of his might end with a missing finger or three.

"No. My father abruptly let them go one day. He claimed it was because I'd outgrown my need for Gloria."

"But you knew better?" I asked.

"I usually hid the satisfaction I got from working with my hands really well. Maybe he saw me smiling one too many times after being with Gloria and her family. Who knows. But my father had plans for my future, and he eventually saw them as a distraction to those plans."

"What did your mother have to say about that?"

"I lost my mother at a young age, but she never had much interest in me. She was a socialite through and through. I used to pretend things would've ended up differently had she still been alive. Pretending eased the pain for a while. She'd hand-picked Gloria herself, though. I suppose I owe her for that."

I wanted to apologize, but I hated receiving apologies from those not at fault. They never felt genuine. How could they be when the issuer had nothing to be sorry for? And since Franky hadn't done that to me on the roof that night, I wouldn't do it to him now.

"Do you ever think about looking them up?" I asked.

"I'd planned to keep in touch with her eldest son, but they ended up moving and changing their numbers. I'm sure my father had something to do with that. He and I were from two different worlds, anyway." He shrugged. "It wouldn't have worked. Not at that time."

"We're from two different worlds," I pointed out, having thought the same thing not too long ago.

"That doesn't matter to me. It never did. The loss of my friendship with Theo was out of my control. We were young, and neither of us had the power then to change the outcome." Franky unhooked a frying pan from the pot rack hanging above the island and placed it on the stove.

Theo. He'd said the name like it pained him too. I thought about my friendship with Noon, and how it was slipping away from me. I understood Franky's pain completely.

"Looks like you'll make it out of here alive, after all," he said, handing me a pack of sausages from the fridge.

"Yeah," I replied wryly. "Funny how this all worked out."

"I'll make it up to you with lunch," he promised, but if he couldn't get eggs right, what would be in store for us with lunch?

"Give me a few minutes to shower. Then we can eat before going over the mural."

"Sounds good," I said, turning the burner on under the pan as he exited the kitchen.

With breakfast cooked, and nowhere to sit and wait for Franky, I wandered into the living room, tilting my head curiously at the wall surrounding the fireplace. I peered out over the ocean before returning my gaze to the wall, instinctively knowing that Franky wanted me to paint a mural of the ocean, and that he wanted it done here.

The surface was smooth under my fingertips, and a rush of excitement coursed through me at the prospect of creating something so grand—which was strange considering I didn't believe I had the talent to pull off something this big. I'd need a ladder to get it done. The only painting I'd ever done on a ladder was when I'd slapped primer over the brown water stain on my kitchen ceiling.

Painting had started as an outlet for my anger. A school counselor had suggested it, and I kept at it because it worked, not because I thought I had what it took to be the next Picasso. But if Franky believed he could furnish this whole house with items he created with his bare hands, then maybe I could believe I had what it took to do this.

Noon had an enviable understanding of who he was and where he was going in life. Always had. So I found it hard to trust his praise because he couldn't comprehend what it meant to be conflicted. To be afraid of anything.

It was easier with Franky because he seemed as lost as me. And sometimes, it was nice to have a little company as you found your way.

"I've been staring at that a lot since I bought it," Franky said, coming to stand beside me. I'd been so caught up in my thoughts, I hadn't realized I'd inched over to the mantel where my painting rested. "I'm curious about what you were trying to convey."

I pursed my lips, working out how to simplify the explanation of something so personally complex. "Did you know the daisy is one of the strongest flowers? They spread like wildfire and are hard to keep at bay."

"No," he said, eyes expanding below hiked brows.

"I kind of went down a daisy rabbit hole once. My elderly neighbor had once given me a single daisy as thanks for helping her upstairs with her groceries. She told me to change the water every few days and to enjoy it for the week or two that it would last. I used an empty beer bottle as a vase, and she ended up lasting a whole month."

"*She?*" he asked.

"Yeah, she gave off feminine energy. I named her too."

"Let me guess," he said. "Daisy?"

I smiled, and he shook his head with amusement. "The highlight of my day was racing home from my shitty temp job to see if she'd beat the odds again. She did every time. Well, until the last time. Still, Daisy was resilient. She wasn't supposed to last that long outside of her environment, but she thrived despite the odds stacked against her."

I paused, digging deeper, to that place inside me often left ignored and untouched, then got back to the meaning behind the painting. "This daisy has hope," I said, pointing at the vibrant, floating wildflower. "It's taking a chance on the unknown, while the rest of the meadow opts for the familiar, even if it will possibly kill them. They go through the winter cycle. They go dormant. A consequence of fear." My explanation sounded childish and stupid to my own ears, and I braced for Franky's laughter and judgment.

"And which one are you?" he asked, turning his body toward me. "The daisy, or the winter meadow?"

"Definitely the meadow," I whispered with raw honesty, splitting my chest cavity open for Franky to have a peek inside. I never tried for anything more than what I had, because there was safety in the predictability of my mundane life. I'd rather die in the meadow not knowing that something better waited for me, than to reach for the stars only to come crashing down. No one else could hurt me in my meadow. I'd made it that way. I'd made it so nothing good lived there because everything good would eventually leave.

Franky and I were so close that I could feel the heat pouring from his gaze, and my heart crashed against my sternum like rough waves. Did he think I was weak? Had my answer reflected my age?

All my internal angst melted away when he smiled at me softly. "Me too," he whispered back. "But maybe one day we can both be daisies."

Warm and delicate, I added to my mental vault of his eyes. *Warm and delicate means he understands me.*

◆ ◆ ◆

I worked until the sunlight faded and the night sky turned the ocean black. Until darkness cloaked the trees and the mountains beyond with its shadow. And then I chewed nervously at my thumbnail as I looked from the outline I'd completed on the wall, to the photos I'd snapped earlier of the view outside.

Franky's litany of curses from out on the patio cut into my overthinking. He'd dropped his hammer again. It stopped being funny hours ago, though, and now I just felt bad for him. At least he hadn't made any life-threatening mistakes while working the table saw.

His phone rang, and he fumbled through the copious pieces of scrap wood and tools scattered around to find it.

"Cole?" he asked, as if he was the last person he expected his kid to call.

I zipped into the hoodie I never left home without as a gust of ocean breeze blew inside. The air smelled of impending rain. I began straightening up my work area, preparing to call it a night and do the long drive back to the city. Within minutes I had everything situated, and I'd been about to send a goodnight text to Franky when his call ended.

He fell onto the edge of the unlit fire pit, his shoulders slumped like the world had fallen onto them. Before I could ask if everything was okay, he shot to his feet, grumbling about needing at least one thing to go right tonight. Franky hammered in the final nail on the table he'd been working on all day, then flipped it right side up onto all four legs, only to have it tilt to one side.

As if he couldn't trust his eyes, Franky rested his phone in the center of the table, and it slid to the left before nose diving to the ground. He lowered onto one of the Adirondack chairs this time, cradling his head with his palms.

Not wanting to leave him alone with his misery, I went to the fridge and grabbed the six-pack I'd brought in earlier when I'd gone to the car for my paint supplies.

I placed the beer in the empty seat next to Franky's, then picked through the scrap wood littered about until I found a piece that would fit perfectly under the defective leg of the table.

"Voila," I said, after setting the case of beer on the now leveled table. Franky didn't find me funny at all.

Sawdust caked his t-shirt and jeans, and his hair had been matted down by sweat. He looked exhausted, but I had a feeling it had more to do with his phone conversation than the slip 'n slide table.

The string lights running overhead provided enough lighting to hang out on the patio, but I needed heat if I planned to keep his bad mood company out there. I worked out how to get the fire pit going and then fell onto the seat next to him.

Using my keys, I popped the cap off a cold bottle of Stella before gesturing for him to take it. Franky stared at it, debating whether or not to accept. He ended up reaching for it with a resigned sigh and a nod of thanks. I opened my own and took a healthy swig.

If talking was what Franky wanted to do, he'd have to make the first move. I was content to simply be there. To be whatever he needed from me at that moment.

"How'd you know this was my favorite?" he eventually asked, picking at the bottle's label.

"That night on the roof you used an empty bottle to prop the door open." I shrugged. "It could've been roof litter, especially since we were only serving the good stuff that night, but I took a gamble that it wasn't."

He grunted, his sour mood still lingering. "I keep the small fridge in my office stocked with it."

Stella was my favorite as well, and it felt damn good—in a way it shouldn't have—to know we had that in common too.

"Maybe I'm not cut out for this," he said defeatedly, glaring at his botch job.

"It's not so bad," I said.

"It's unusable," he countered with a huff, wrapping his full lips around the mouth of the bottle before angling his head back.

"It's eclectic," I challenged, then winced when the leg gave out completely, breaking and taking the others down with it. Luckily it had tilted my way, and with cat-like reflexes, I swooped up the beer pack by its cardboard handle before it hit the ground. I whipped my head toward Franky, holding my breath, the beers clutched to my chest.

He cracked first, doubling over, shoulders shaking, and I sat unsure if he was laughing or crying.

"Are you... Are you laughing? Please tell me you're laughing." Because I needed to be certain before releasing the howl of laughter caged in my throat. And because his laugh from earlier didn't hold a candle to this. *This* laugh was a building roll of thunder chocked full of perfect white teeth. *This* laugh invaded his whole body.

"Yes," he managed to get out, body trembling, tears peppering the corners of his weary eyes.

"Oh." I swallowed down my stalled amusement in favor of watching and enjoying the sound of his. I placed the remaining beers on the wide arm of the chair as he settled.

"It was either laugh or punch something," he said, using the heel of his dusty palm to wipe his eyes. "Shit," he hissed, blinking rapidly.

"Here, let me," I said, using the end of my sleeve to wipe the dust away. "Better?"

"Yeah," he said, blinking a few more times to be sure.

"It's your first time trying in decades, maybe more. Give yourself a break and some credit. Watch a few videos online or sign up for a class," I suggested.

His eyes brightened like a light bulb had flicked on in his brain. "Be right back." He drained the rest of his beer, taking the empty bottle with him as he maneuvered around the fallen table to enter the house, returning minutes later carrying a large box.

"What's that?" I asked, standing to haul the broken table out of the way so he could rest the box on the ground in front of his seat.

"An old box of junk I had stored. I came across it while searching for something else and brought it with me. I haven't looked inside since... God, since Gloria left." He tore the lid open, rummaging through its contents in search of something.

"What are you looking for?" I leaned forward to snoop inside.

"I took notes whenever I got the chance to help Paul," he said distractedly. "And even when I wasn't helping him, I'd ask tons of questions and jot down his answers. Sometimes he'd even hold on to the book and add to it for me. It's gotta be in here somewhere."

I'd been about to ask if Paul was Gloria's husband when Franky snatched a tattered notebook out of the box in triumph.

He flipped through the stiff, creaking pages, complaining about the faded ink.

"I think this can still be useful." He brought the book so close it practically touched his lashes as he tried to make out the aged penmanship. My curiosity detoured to the photo he hadn't noticed floating from between the book's pages to land gracefully near my foot. I scooted to the edge of my seat to pick it up, gaze flying over the image.

Franky was easy to spot. He lacked the pounds of muscle he had now, and his facial hair hadn't grown in yet, but he had that mad-at-the-world expression I'd come to know him for.

He sat on a freshly mowed lawn that seemed to roll on for miles behind him, his arms wrapped around his bent legs as he stared broodingly into the camera. A boy who looked no older than ten kneeled beside him holding an action figure, and a man and woman stood behind them, their arms linked, heads touching. *Maybe Gloria and Paul?*

What really caught my eye was the blonde boy standing off to the side like he'd opted out of being in the picture. Whoever snapped the photo had done a bad job of keeping him outside of the shot, though.

He seemed closer to Franky's age. Both in their mid-teens, if I had to guess.

I couldn't take my eyes off him, and as Franky shuffled through the pages of his notebook, clueless to the piece of his past I currently dissected, I racked my brain to understand why I couldn't turn away.

Eventually, I worked out what had captivated me about the seemingly innocent photo. It was the way he stared down at Franky when he thought no one was looking, unaware he'd be a part of the moment being captured. *Longing.* The pained look on his face was longing.

"Franky," I said. He stopped what he was doing when he saw the picture I held up. "Is this Theo?"

He took the photo from me, scanning it as if he'd never seen it before, or like he'd forgotten about its existence. "Yes," he said, sitting back slowly. I watched his eyes, watched the way they grew distant beneath his lashes, the way they seemed to shrink—or wither like the wildflowers in my meadow.

Regret.

"Why was he looking at you like that?"

"Like what?" he asked quietly, his finger tracing Theo.

"Like he misses you, when you're only a few feet away."

The corners of his mouth tipped downward, and his brows met in the middle. "This was taken after my father broke the news to us. By the time I'd gotten the film developed, they were gone. I told myself he was upset. That he was hurt that we couldn't be friends anymore."

"You *told* yourself?" I asked, focusing on that part of his explanation, because what we told ourselves wasn't often the truth, and we knew it.

"We were young," he said. "What else could it have been?"

That's what I wanted to know. I didn't push, because I couldn't afford to be wrong, but if my suspicions about Theo were correct, could it also mean the longing went both ways?

I decided to let him in on something about myself I never hid, but that I hadn't outright told him yet. Maybe I could be a source of inspiration. Maybe there was nothing to inspire. Still, it felt like the time and the perfect opening.

"Would it surprise you, or bother you, to find out that I'm bi-sexual?" I asked, as we both gazed thoughtfully into the fire.

If Franky thought my questions were random, or if he felt the change in my energy, he didn't acknowledge it. "No, it wouldn't bother me. Would it surprise me?" he mused. "Well, you do have a tendency of being provocative, but flirtatious remarks meant to provoke a reaction wouldn't be cause to assume anything. So while I wouldn't be surprised, I'd never jump to conclusions about something as important as that."

As far as stances went, that was a damn good one, and it made me proud to know him. It made me want to know him better. "That was your son on the phone earlier, wasn't it?"

"My oldest. Cole."

"Do they know you're here?" I asked meaningfully, opening two more beers and passing one over to him.

"No, they have no idea that Selene and I have separated."

Selene. A name made it more real. Made her an actual person.

"Why not?" I asked, swiveling my head his way. "They're adults now, you don't need to hide things from them."

"They're always your kids, Leland. And that primal instinct to protect them from emotional and physical pain never goes away. Especially when you'd be the one inflicting it," he explained, but on that, I couldn't relate. All my parents had ever done was hurt me, and so each word he uttered sounded foreign to my ears. My heart was another matter. My heart understood he was in agony, and it ached for him.

"I never fail to harm them anyway," he added more to himself, staring off at something the eye couldn't see. "Especially Cole."

"Are you leaving your wife, Franky?"

"I don't know," he said honestly, twisting the beer bottle by its neck as the butt of it perched on his knee.

"You still love her," I said.

"Yes," he whispered like the sharing of a secret.

"You're still *in* love with her," I then ventured.

"I... I don't know. If I am, it's buried beneath the mess I've made of my life."

"Then why not roll up your sleeves and dig through the rubble?" I asked.

He sucked in a deep breath, tipping his head to the sky as he considered his next words. "Sometimes it's easier to start from scratch than to fix what's broken. And sometimes it's harder to be yourself, or to find yourself, with someone who has only ever known you as someone else," he said. "I don't expect you to understand—"

"She wants the version of the man she married. She sees you as a stranger who kidnapped her husband, and she wants him back," I said.

He rolled his head in my direction, relief written all over him. "Yes," he breathed. "I feel unfulfilled, and although I love her, and we've lived an amazing life, something's missing. I fear it always has been, but it becomes harder to hide once your kids leave home, because then it's just the two of you, no distractions, no more need to pretend. There's no longer anyone other than yourselves to pretend for. To fight for.

"It starts with the little things like not showing up for something important because you've shown up a hundred times before, so this time is no big deal. And then there are the promises you forget to keep because something else was your number one priority that day. The canceled date nights, the conversations you fake being present for... Then one day they're no longer spilling their secrets to you, no longer sharing their ambitions with you. You think you're grateful for the reprieve, until you find out someone else has filled the emotional void you left behind."

"She cheated on you?" I asked.

"She claims she stopped it before it got physical."

"And you believe her?"

"Yes. He was someone she could talk to because I had stopped listening. We tried therapy, but it didn't work. It didn't *fix* me."

"Maybe because you're not broken, Franky."

He nodded indulgently at the sentiment. "She doesn't blame me for her mistakes, but it doesn't mean that I am blameless. I owe it to her to figure myself out, and the only time in my life that I've ever felt whole was when I was with Theo and his family. When I wasn't Franklin Kincaid, heir to the Kincaid legacy. I was just a simple boy, doing honest work with honest people, and it felt good to be treated as such. So I'm trying to get back to that place, if only for a little while."

"What about your company?"

"I took some time off, although something tells me my time away will be a lot shorter than I'd hoped for," he said.

Our night on the roof came back to clobber me over my head. I'd suggested he take some time off to figure out what he'd wanted to do. I hadn't known I was encouraging him to walk away from his life and marriage. "Is this partly my fault?" I asked, opening my arms to encompass the house behind us and the ocean ahead of us.

"Of course not." He forced a smile for reassurance. "My life was unraveling long before we met. If anything, your words were confirmation to my unspoken thoughts. I should be thanking you, really. Maybe finding myself will help me find my way back to Selene. Maybe I won't have to live with hurting our children after all. Perhaps it'll make me a better father, if it isn't already too late for that."

Someone so capable, so honest, so wise, and with more years of life experiences than me had no business looking at me as if I'd somehow saved him, as if I held all the answers. And I had no business wanting to hunt every answer down to every asked question—even the unasked ones lingering behind his eyes—and lay them right at his feet.

You know better than this, Leland.

"I should go," I said. Franky was two decades older than me, had adult kids, and his marital status was set to complicated.

This had run-as-fast-as-you-can written all over it, and if I were smart, I'd tell him I couldn't finish the mural and cut my losses.

A heavy palm landed on my arm, stopping my escape, its warmth burning past the heavy fabric of my sweater to scorch my bare skin. "It's late, and it's a long drive back to the city," Franky said. "Why don't you stay."

"It's not that late," I said, hoping I didn't sound as winded as I felt.

"Okay, so maybe I don't want to be alone," he confessed, and why did his confessions have to affect me the way they did? I would've made a terrible priest, because no way could I have ever handed Franky's problems over to God. As it stood, I wanted to be the one to absolve them all.

"There's a mattress and clean sheets in the guest bedroom. Please, stay," he begged, and begging had never sounded so good.

"Okay," I whispered, even while knowing that *this* would be the moment I lived to regret.

The moment I stayed.

<h1 style="text-align:center">CHAPTER 5</h1>

Franklin

"So where'd your love of art come from?" Leland asked with his feet kicked up on the Jeep's dash, his face pointed toward the beam of sunlight streaming in from his window. His car wouldn't start that morning, so I insisted on covering the cost to have it towed and driving him to his apartment for a change of clothes. It was my fault anyway. If he hadn't pushed its limits by driving so far outside the city, it'd probably still be functioning well enough to get him around.

"Selene, actually. She's a big supporter of the arts. One leg of her charity is devoted to funding art programs in schools throughout the inner city and shining a spotlight on up-and-coming talent who may normally be overlooked."

"Okay. How many times have you been in love?" he fired off next.

"No more questions until you agree to let me pay you for the mural," I said. Leland had been rather inquisitive today. By my count, we were on question number fifty. I'd spoken more in the short time we'd known each other than I had all my life.

Keeping my eyes on the road, I felt around the center console for my sunglasses before slipping them on.

"Like I told you before," he said, making a sound of displeasure when the sun dipped behind a cluster of trees. "You over-

57

paid for the other paintings. I'm not taking any more of your money."

"And like I told *you*, I'd underpaid for them. Seattle is an expensive city. That money won't get you far." We'd spent the better part of the morning, in between his Spanish Inquisition, arguing over it.

"It's already gone," he said with a shrug. "Paid my rent for a full year."

"You advanced your landlord? That wasn't a good investment," I said, trying my best not to come off as a chastising father.

"I know," he said, and I waited for something more, but Leland kept his eyes closed and his face upturned in his reclined seat. I let it go. It wasn't my job to lecture him about his life choices, especially when mine weren't any better.

"Twice," I said. "I've been in love twice." I felt his gaze fan over me, and I risked looking at him before refocusing ahead. "Cole's mother, Annabeth, was my first love. We met in college. Got married soon after, and she wanted to start a family right away."

"And you didn't?" he asked.

"I wanted to get Nexcom off the ground. I wanted to show my father I could make something of my own, something that could surpass the success of Kincaid Industries. I gave her what she wanted and ended up paying for it. She died during childbirth."

"That couldn't have been easy," he said.

"I threw myself into my work for years instead of dealing with it, and it was hard to not see Cole as a reminder. I loved him, but I can admit to avoiding him too. He'd had his own version of Gloria after his mother died." I'd spent years wanting to be better than my father. He was a tyrant, thought he knew what was best for me, and cared more about work and upholding a certain image than he ever cared about me. But in the process of trying to be better than him, I ended up proving that in many ways, we were one and the same. I'd failed my son, and he still bore the scars to prove it.

"And then I met Selene—"

"And you saw your opportunity to give Cole a mother. Someone to take care of him in a way you weren't capable of," Leland said.

I couldn't deny that Selene was an excellent mother. I couldn't say that the way her eyes lit up when she spoke about her son the day we met didn't factor into how quickly I eventually fell for her. Who knew how Cole's life would've turned out if Selene and Jasper hadn't walked into it when they had, but it wasn't the only reason I'd married her, even if it was the driving force behind my decision to. "I loved Selene," I said. "I *love* her."

Leland gestured for me to turn right at the approaching stop sign and then instructed me to turn left at the fourth light up ahead.

"Why the sudden curiosity with my love life? Wouldn't you rather know why I'm afraid of heights?" I slowed at the next red light, able to now drag my stare to him for more than a split second.

"Oh, I'm sure it has something to do with a lack of control," he said, guessing correctly and writing that topic off as completed.

"I don't know. You're so..." He struggled for the right word.

"Cold, distant, unfeeling..." I supplied, having heard those attributes used to describe me before.

"No," he said, considering me. "And if anyone says that, then they haven't been paying close enough attention. Maybe in most instances you're a man of few words, and the words you do say can be sharp, but your eyes say a lot."

He cocked his head, as if searching through his mental vocabulary for something to sum me up. "You're formidable," he decided. "I can see how that can be daunting and intense for someone who doesn't get you. It makes me wonder what it's like to be loved by you. If you're different when in love." He turned back to the sun just as the light turned green.

"I am different when in love," I said, thinking long and hard. "Softer, maybe. But I don't know if that's by choice or out of fear." That last part had been meant for me, as it wasn't something I could even begin to explain, nor had the thought ever crossed my mind until then. Through the astonishment of my reveal, a fire I'd known was there but had never tapped into before began raging inside of my core. It only ever simmered below the surface, as I tended to hold that piece of myself back when in love, even while making love. I was too afraid that whatever it was would consume me if I gave into it. Too afraid it would make me even more unlovable.

"What about you?" I asked, circumventing a follow-up question from him. "Ever been in love?" I drove two city blocks and Leland still hadn't answered. I had no intention of prompting him to. Just because discussions of love weren't a trigger for me, at least not when talking to him, didn't mean they weren't triggering for Leland. The person who should've loved him most did try to end his life, after all.

"My mother had an addictive personality," he eventually said. "If she found something she liked: cake, candy, a particular brand of diet pills... You name it, she'd *gorge* herself on it until she became physically ill." He dropped his feet to the Jeep's floorboard, then raised his seatback, putting an end to his relaxation. "Our neighbor had won a thousand bucks once on a scratch-off. Seemed like big money to me at the time. I would daydream about being old enough to buy a scratch-off. I had big plans for the money I would no doubt win. On my eighteenth birthday I won five dollars on my first try. I ended up blowing that month's rent in one hour. I just kept playing and playing and playing." He hitched his elbow on his door, rubbing a finger over his top lip. "Noon had to come haul me out of that gas station convenience store by my collar."

I got to the fourth light and made the left, and he pointed for me to pull into a vacant parking spot in front of a rundown night club that hadn't yet opened for the day. I turned off the engine but didn't make a move to get out.

"The one thing she couldn't get enough of was love. She fell into it easily. Obsessed over it, lost jobs over it; the highs were so high, and the lows were fucking scary, Franky." His eyes were so wide they trembled from the strain. I removed my sunglasses, needing to experience the full scope of what this recollection was doing to him.

"She'd dance with me in the rain after finding a new guy, completely euphoric. And she didn't hesitate to throw me from a fourth-floor window when he decided he'd had enough of her smart-mouthed kid."

A loud crack echoed around us, and I looked down to see my glasses snapped in two, a piece in each fist.

"And that's only the half of it. Wanna know what my worst fear is, Franky? Ending up like my mother. So, no, I've never been in love. I've actively avoided it."

I felt compelled to say something, but I'd never been good at saying the right thing in the face of someone else's pain. And when it came to my own pain, I'd shut down, go inward, and often stay there for way longer than what was acceptable for the people around me. But the deeper I allowed myself to sink, the harder it was to dig myself out of whatever hole I'd plunged into. I'd been told it made me come off as frigid, indifferent. I didn't want to be either of those things right then.

Leland had already moved on to staring out of his window in thought by the time I reached over to uncurl the fist he had planted on his thigh. He turned back to me, brows drawn together in question. I squeezed my hand around his and said, "'Everything's better when holding hands.'"

"I believe it's: 'Things are less scary when holding hands,'" he corrected.

"Same thing, smartass," I said, snagging a chuckle from him.

♦ ♦ ♦

"Quit acting like you've never seen a crummy apartment building before," Leland muttered as he flipped through his set of keys. I'd already walked the length of the third-floor landing, examining the discolored paint on the patchy walls, peeling it back like a child, and then moving along to see what other trouble I could get into. "You've at least seen them in movies. Bad plumbing, the heat and hot water doesn't work half the time, and there's even the occasional mouse."

I got the impression he wasn't speaking in general, and that he was preparing me for what to expect once we got inside. He only had three keys on the ring, so we should've gained entry to his apartment already, yet he was flipping through them for the fourth time.

"Did you want me to wait in the car because you thought I would negatively judge your home?" I asked. He'd wasted five minutes trying to convince me that he didn't need an escort upstairs.

"Maybe," he said. "This isn't exactly 'estate' standards."

"This is the first time I've been over to a friend's place. Well, the first time in around three decades. I'm excited," I said.

He gave me an odd look. "You've never been to someone else's home?"

"Sure. Family, business acquaintances, my investment broker..." I stopped there, but the list of people I'd had to sit at a dinner table with over the years and pretend my interest in being there went beyond quid pro quo was endless. "This is different. I actually *want* to be here."

Leland finally inserted the correct key into the lock's cylinder, appearing less anxious. "You first," he said after pushing the door open, then bolted it again once we'd both made it into his narrow hallway.

"It's really a one-bedroom," he said, brushing past me to lead the way, "but the previous tenants put up a door, turning the living room into a second bedroom."

We reached a fork in the short hall in no time. "Kitchen," Leland said, pointing right. I eagerly stepped inside. The space couldn't hold more than two people. Leland wore that odd look again.

"Um, and this is the bathroom," he said, pointing to the door that stood ajar to his left. "Can't get it to stay closed to save my life, but it's not like my roommate had been modest to begin with."

"Noon," I said, remembering his best friend's name.

"Yeah."

I exited the kitchen to push the bathroom door open. A pedestal sink and mirror greeted me, the toilet and shower adjacent to it. Unlike the kitchen, only one person could fit in the bathroom at a time, unless one of them was in the shower. "What else?" I asked.

"You're really getting a kick out of this, aren't you?"

"Weren't you excited to see my home?" I asked.

"Have you seen your home? This isn't much in comparison."

"I don't need much," I said. "I've lived a life of excess, and when I stop to think of my happiest moments, they aren't the ones involving fancy cars, homes that could house a small country, and making million-dollar deals. Trust me, you could have all that and still feel empty."

He nodded, regarding me with understanding, but in true Leland fashion, he said, "Still, it must be nice to wake up to that view every day."

I laughed, unconsciously reaching out to brush a strand of hair off his forehead. The lump at Leland's throat bobbed, and I let my hand fall to my side. "Sorry," I said, "if that crossed a boundary."

"It's fine," he replied, his small smile putting me at ease.

He showed me to the makeshift bedroom that had belonged to Noon. A mattress was all that remained. Leland's room contained a queen bed, a night stand, a closet, and a worn dresser that caught my interest. I trailed a hand over the ornate carvings in the wood. "It was my grandmother's. Or at least that's what Uncle No One said. He can't always be trusted to tell the truth, though."

"Uncle No One?" I asked.

"Yeah, he's sort of a nomad. Disappears for years on end only to show up having reinvented himself. No one knows where he is, and no one knows who he'll be when he shows back up. Hence, the moniker Uncle No One. It's been a year since he last popped up, throwing pebbles at my window. He was doing private investigative work then. Without a license, I'm sure."

I ogled the dresser one last time before moving on. "Where do you paint?"

"Right here," he said, motioning to the small square of space we stood in. The only floor space free of furniture. "I set up the easel, sit at the foot of the bed, and paint."

A commotion started in the apartment above us. We peered at the ceiling as cursing rang out.

"Ignore it," he said. "They'll fight for about an hour, then fuck for a few more. They're getting started pretty early today, though. They're usually night owls."

"Doesn't the noise keep you up?" I asked.

"No more than the loud music and drunken alleyway blow jobs from the hole-in-the-wall nightclub next door."

Leland was resilient, I'd decided right then, and a newfound respect colored the lens I viewed him through. I wanted to know everything about him. All that he'd faced, survived, and even the things he hadn't, because some things we never quite make it through. We merely learned how to walk through life while still living in our own hell. I didn't think either of us noticed that our gazes were latched on to the other's until something heavy hit the ceiling, snapping our connection in two. My stomach did a somersault, and there was suddenly not enough air in the tiny room for the both of us.

"I'm gonna grab a quick shower." We switched spots so he could get a few items out of a drawer, then we shuffled, switching positions again so he could get to his closet. We went to great lengths not to come into direct contact with each other. Something was off; there was now an awkwardness that hadn't been there five minutes ago.

"How long do you think they'll have my car?" he asked, picking through a stack of folded shirts on the closet shelf. The mechanic shop offered pick-up and drop-off service, but we wouldn't know how long it would take to fix the vehicle until they diagnosed the problem. Leland had agreed to stay at my place in the meantime so he could continue his work on the mural.

"Bring enough clothes to last a few days. I have a laundry room in case it ends up being longer," I said. *I hoped.*

He laid clothing on the bed, telling me to make myself at home as he left for the bathroom.

I exhaled a long string of air when the water came on, scrubbing my hands over my face. I felt jittery, like I was crawling out of my skin, and I worked my brain to sort out why.

I grabbed a bottle of water from the fridge, in need of something to wet my parched throat. When that didn't help the thirst, or the feeling of being suffocated, I decided fresh air was what I needed.

I'd been about to tap on the bathroom door and shout to Leland that I'd be waiting outside, but the door creaked part way open on its own. I thought perhaps he was on his way out, but the shower still ran, then I remembered he'd said he couldn't get it to stay closed.

Leland's wet back taunted me through the mirror, the muscles of it flexing with his movements. I held my breath, taking a step closer, seeing a little bit more of him.

He let out a moan, and something in me screamed to walk away, but instead I pressed forward.

He lowered his head, slapping one hand to the tiled wall to hold himself up as the other hand tugged wildly on his cock. I couldn't see it, but I knew.

My gaze roamed over the curve of his ass, even though it shouldn't have, even as guilt, confusion, shame, and *heat* percolated in my core.

Leland quickened his pace, and I backed away, disappointed in myself, and at a loss for what was happening inside of me.

He threw his head back, his body going rigid as he uttered something hoarsely, and I'd barely made it to the apartment's front door without choking on the knot settling in my throat.

By the time Leland jogged down the building's front steps, I'd worked out three different speeches for why we couldn't continue this friendship. Yet I allowed him to climb into the passenger seat and toss his duffle bag in the back. He smelled fresh, too clean for the dirty images now replaying in my mind.

All my speeches went out the window when he looked at me innocently, the sun striking his honey-brown eyes and turning them golden from that angle. "Ready?" he asked. I was positive he meant whether or not I was ready to leave, but my brain supplied other options.

Ready for more? Ready to confess why you really asked me to stay last night? Ready to admit why you'd asked the mechanics to take their time with my car?

I had a feeling every word he uttered moving forward would have at least ten different translations to my over-analyzing brain.

I stifled a shudder as those pools of churning honey held me hypnotized. I should've said no, that I wasn't ready for any of it, especially as a familiar feeling warned me that I'd been here, in this exact predicament, before.

"Well?" Leland asked, his mouth kicking up into a slight grin. "Are you ready?"

"Yes," I breathed, my answer just as ambiguous as his question.

CHAPTER 6

Leland

"**U**nbelievable," Franky hissed from the patio, and I froze with my paintbrush suspended in mid-air. It was hard to make out his form amidst the piles of debris and tools, but movement drew my eyes to where he crouched on the other side of the table saw.

"Was that a *good* unbelievable, or a bad one?" I asked, because he'd been in a bad mood ever since leaving my apartment a few days ago, and while I'd done my best to not take it personally by chalking it up to his numerous failed attempts at building something stable, it was kind of hard not to feel like my presence had been the thing ticking him off.

It wasn't in what he said, but the opposite. As the master of quiet, his silence tended to be chillingly loud in its intensity, a red flag to my instincts, warning me to give him space.

Last night, I'd watched him stare into the still, black water beyond the dock from my bedroom window for over an hour before finding the courage to brave whatever had him so far inside his own head. After creeping up behind him and asking if he wanted me to leave, he'd turned on me, the action slow, making it apparent that he'd known I was there, even though it had taken me minutes to finally speak.

His eyes, the color of a starless night sky, had bored into me, and I'd backed up a step as something resembling pain swirled through their dark depths. *"No,"* he'd said, the low illumination of the dock lights throwing shadows along his tensed frame. *"The last thing I want is for you to leave."*

Then why had it felt like leaving was what he'd *needed* from me?

"The good kind," he said from the patio, bringing me back to the here and now. I descended the ladder, discarding my brush into a mason jar on my way outside.

"A coffee table," I guessed, squatting next to him and running a palm over the top of it.

"Careful," he warned, gripping my wrist with more strength than was needed. "I haven't sanded it yet." Franky let one knee hit the ground, his other knee bumping into mine as he examined my hand for splinters. His touch lacked the delicate finesse of someone concerned, but his face twisted with concentration as he inspected my skin. I assumed he didn't realize his own brawn, or that he didn't believe he had to be gentle with me.

His warm breath hit my palm, and I instinctively curled my fingers as a metaphorical fist clamped around my heart.

"I'm fine," I said, or maybe panted, as he released me and got to his feet. Shit was getting weird really fast between us, and I quickly did the math on the last time I'd had sex. Was that the problem? Was the seclusion getting to my libido, which seemed to kick into gear whenever Franky looked at me the way he did now, like he again didn't want me to leave, but needed me to go?

"It's a little too high," he said, sliding his hands into his back pockets, but not before I noticed them flex as if fighting against taking a hold of something. "My measurements of the legs were off, but at least it's level. Doesn't look like much now, but it'll come to life after it's sanded and varnished."

"You did it," I said, my smile growing until it ached, the weirdness from a second ago forgotten as it hit me that we wouldn't be adding another piece to the furniture graveyard that one of the garages had been turned into. He'd done it. "You fucking did it."

Franky dragged a thumb and forefinger down the corners of his mouth as he nodded cooly. "Yeah."

"For fuck's sake, Franky," I said, a touch exasperated but mostly amused. "Drop the cool-kid act and be flipping happy. You did it!" I attempted to lift him into the air, but he was all muscle and didn't budge. "Someone needs to hit the gym," I muttered, rubbing my lower back.

"Are you alright?" he asked, steadying me by my shoulders. "You can't pick me up, Leland."

"No shit. I got carried away in my excitement. What the hell are your bones made out of anyway? Bricks? I'll be fine," I said when his concern lingered tightly around the corners of his mouth. "You did it, Franky," I said again, getting us back to the victory at hand. We stared down at the table in a moment of silence.

An earthquake erupted around Franky's lips until they parted and gave way to sound. He laughed without restraint, and I watched, reacquainting myself with this side of him after drowning in his tension for days.

I grinned like a loon as he shoved his hands through his thick hair, the gravity of what he'd accomplished finally hitting him.

"I did it," he said.

"Fuck yeah," I agreed, as the light in his eyes reignited. "You did it. You made something we can actually use."

"I've gotta make the island stools next, or maybe a dresser, or end tables for the living room," he said absently, ideas tripping over themselves in his head.

"Not so fast, Mr. Carpenter." I held up a hand. "First off, it's going to rain." And as if waiting for a proper introduction, steel-colored clouds swarmed the sky. "And secondly, we need to celebrate."

"I could always work in the garage." He rubbed at his cheek, transferring the grime on his hand to the smooth, freshly shaved surface. "I'm only kidding," he said when I scowled. "What do you suggest we do?"

"There's a cool jazz bar not too far from my place. Josephine's. Nothing fancy, but they have great beer on tap, a couple pool tables in the back, and if you bump your hip into the jukebox the right way, it's free." It was also where I went when needing a quick, no-strings fuck in one of the single occupancy bathrooms. After having Franky's indelicate hands on me, I needed the rough handling of a man tonight. I wouldn't be picky, though. Something soft with great tits would do as well.

Franky scanned the twilight sky with mistrust. According to the weather forecast, we'd be getting a bad storm tonight.

"Or we could keep it local if you want. I just need a change of scenery. We both do," I said pointedly.

"No, Josephine's is fine," he said. "We'll be near your place if it gets too bad to drive back here, and besides, I feel terrible about how I've been acting."

"Oh, and you think taking me to my favorite bar will make up for it?" I asked.

"I'm hoping it will," he said, giving me sad puppy dog eyes without even trying to. Yeah, I needed to get laid, and fast.

We loaded his tools into the garage before separating to get ready.

My eye color came courtesy of my dead-beat dad, but I got my straight hair from my mother. It required styling when in between haircuts, or else it would stick out at odd angles until long enough to properly flop over my ears and forehead. Tonight, I gave myself a slicked-back do, finishing the look with faded tight jeans and a t-shirt purposely one size too small.

Franky waited at the bottom of the landing dressed similarly, except his outfit didn't scream bargain shop the way mine did.

It didn't bother me, though. Not after he'd treated my apartment tour like the world's most hidden treasure. We were too alike to dwell on the superficial areas where we were different, because we were different in ways that didn't matter to either of us. "Great minds think alike," I said, in reference to our matching ensemble, and he agreed.

"Ready?" he said, then winced. "I mean, to go to the bar."

"What else would you have meant?" I asked with humor in my tone. I cleared the bottom step, which put me directly in front of him. Franky may have had me beat in the muscle department, but we were the same impressive height.

"Nothing, just didn't want to confuse you," he said, being weird again.

"My car or yours?" I asked. The mechanic had dropped Betty off earlier, finishing up with her sooner than anticipated.

"Mine," Franky growled, the possessiveness emanating from that one word felt out of place. Had he misheard my question? He seemed angry, which in turn raised my internal temperature. Now I not only wanted to be fucked, but I wanted the fucking fueled by rage. *What the hell is wrong with me?*

"Your car?" I asked, just to be sure we were on the same page before the heat in my core traveled southward.

"Yes, my car," he confirmed with a stiff smile.

"You okay?" I asked.

"Of course. With the weather being as bad as it is, it's probably best we take my car. That's all."

"Makes sense. Betty isn't known for her reliability," I said, as he moved past me and toward the door leading to the garages.

♦ ♦ ♦

We parked right outside Josephine's doors, but neither of us had thought to bring an umbrella, and the storm was now in full swing. We hurried inside and over to the two unoccupied bar stools closest to the entrance, grabbing handfuls of napkins to dry off with.

Josephine's had a good crowd for it being mid-week. I did a quick once-over for intimately familiar faces and came up short. I avoided repeats, but tonight I would've made an exception. Desperate times and all.

"So *questionably* raised by your Uncle No One after your mother ran off, and completely on your own—well, with Noon— by the time you were fifteen?" Franky asked, picking up the conversation we were having on the car ride into the city.

"Pretty much," I said, ordering two Stellas. "My uncle isn't built for a domesticated life, but he stuck around long enough to see me out of the hospital and turned over to him. Then he'd come and go—mostly go—with strict instructions to not answer the phone or open the door for anyone." I slipped the bartender my bank card before Franky could get his wallet out. "Keep the tab open," I told him, ignoring Franky's glower. While intimidation tactics may have worked for him in business, he didn't scare me. I hid my smirk around the mouth of my pint glass.

"Noon and his mom lived next door to my uncle's place. She hated my uncle, likely because he wouldn't give her the time of day, but she made sure I had a hot meal every night. And she'd let me sleep over whenever he was gone for too long. She had a nasty drinking problem, though, so it didn't take much to convince Noon to strike out with me. His sister Deb lived with her father."

Franky sipped at his drink thoughtfully, probably thinking my life was one long, bad movie. I trailed his gaze toward the stage behind us where an older man sporting a fedora and dark shades worked on piecing his saxophone together.

"That's Stan," I said. "He comes in a few nights a week to serenade the crowd for tips."

Stan sprinkled a few singles inside his open sax case to get the ball rolling.

"This place has character," Franky said, staring at the pool tables in the back.

"Ever played before?" I asked.

"I'm probably not any good," he said.

I finished my drink, licking the beer froth from my top lip. "Let's go," I ordered. Stan belted out something jazzy, the sultry sounds of a tune I didn't recognize following us to the rear of the bar. A few guys conversing near the available pool table moved off to the side with their drinks, allowing Franky and me access.

"Do you know what this is?" I held out one of the cue sticks I'd plucked from the mount on the wall.

"I said I'm probably not any good, doesn't mean I don't know what all the parts are."

"So you know what all the parts are, you just don't know what to do with them." I winked, and his stare turned scolding. "Come on, you left yourself wide open for that joke." I shoved a stick at him, leaning mine against the table so I could rack the balls. "I'll take it easy on you in the first round. It's every man for himself once you get the hang of it. Or at least once you get the rules down."

"Should we play for something?" he asked, attempting to chalk the wrong end of his stick.

I took pity on him, finishing up with the balls and then turning his cue stick right side up. "Maybe let me give you a lesson first, then you can decide if you're in the mood to lose the contents of your wallet to me."

Franky's eyes danced with delight, taking a good chunk of my breath away. He then smiled that big, once-in-a-blue-moon smile, robbing me of what little oxygen I had left. "Playing for money isn't fun."

"Because you have plenty of it," I said.

"Will you even accept my money if you win?" he asked, brow cocked. How fucking well he knew me already.

"Probably not. I'm sure I still owe you fourteen grand for those paintings you bought as it is," I muttered.

A server I'd never seen waiting tables at Josephine's before laid a tumbler of brown liquor on the edge of the pool table before winking at me and biting her lower lip. It was a toss-up between what would spill first, her ample cleavage sitting atop her low-cut shirt or her messy, brown bun being held up by a single pen.

She strode away, hips dramatically swaying as she went, and I turned in the direction of the heat burning a hole in my cheek. Franky watched me with an unreadable expression, the smile I loved now gone.

"Uh," I started stupidly, rubbing at the back of my neck. "I think she brought me someone else's drink."

"It's yours," he said, his voice unreadable too. "I ordered it before following you over here."

"Where's yours?" I asked.

"I'm the designated driver." His lopsided grin returned, and the sick feeling of guilt after having been caught ogling her melted away, leaving behind confusion as to why I'd felt guilty in the first place.

"Oh, I see."

"See what?" he said innocently.

"You're banking on winning because I'll be too drunk to keep my shit together."

"Are you accusing me of playing dirty?" he asked.

"Yes, that's exactly what I'm doing." I wet my tongue with the scotch, humming in appreciation. "How about we play for truths?" I blurted out.

"Truths," Franky said flatly, as if waiting for the punchline.

"Yeah," I said breezily. I wouldn't be the one losing anyway. "Winner gets to ask three questions, nothing we'd readily admit to each other. It has to be something big, and the loser has to answer them truthfully."

"Okay," he said without pausing to think it over. That should've been the first sign that things weren't as they seemed.

Feeling sorry for him, I declared the first game a practice round. Franky couldn't get the hang of holding the pool stick, so I ended up coming in behind him more than once to guide him through the move of striking a ball.

The scent of sandalwood infiltrated my system every time I got close enough to inhale it from the back of his neck. I was wound tight, and thank goodness Franky was too preoccupied with learning the game to notice.

Between the drinks that kept coming, and the hot server—who introduced herself as Sam—delivering them, I was off my A-game. Sam moved in closer with each drop off, brazenly brushing my arm with her breasts and tucking my cash tips between them. Franky watched intently each time, and my face sizzled at knowing he could see my body's reaction to her.

By the end of the night, I owed Franky three truths, and he owed me none.

"That's considered cheating," I said and frowned as Franky hung up our cue sticks. He not only knew how to play, he excelled at it. He'd pulled the oldest con known to man, and I'd fallen for it. "You said you didn't know how to play."

"I said I'm probably not any good. It's been too many years to count since I shot pool. Who knew it was like riding a bike," he said with a shrug.

"You bamboozled me and you know it," I said sourly, but he simply chuckled. My palms grew damp as I asked, "So, what do you want to know?"

"I think I'll save my questions for a later date," he said tauntingly, setting my teeth on edge. I hadn't expected to be the one on the literal losing end of the stick, and I wanted to get his questions over with before he had the luxury of time to come up with even better ones.

"Fine," I said, the rush of booze lighting up my veins. "But just know the trust is gone now."

Behind Franky, Sam moseyed toward the corridor leading to the restrooms, smiling coyly at me before disappearing down the hall. "I'll close out the tab so we can leave," he said.

"*You'll* close it?" I asked, perplexed.

"Yeah, I had them move everything over to my card when you went to the bathroom," he said. *Of course he did.*

"Ah, I'll meet you up front. Scotch runs right through me," I said as airily as possible.

He took on that vacant stare again, the one I now hated because it said nothing while giving everything away. Something was bothering him. "Take your time," he said. "I'll wait in the car." He craned his head over his shoulder knowingly to where the restrooms lay beyond, then strolled off.

My stomach churned at seeing him go, and the alcohol did zilch to numb the guilt I still couldn't explain. Figuring, again, that it had everything to do with needing sex, I made it to the restroom and did what I always did with no emotions involved. Only this time, I didn't feel the rush of anticipation as I slid the condom down my length. This time I didn't appreciate the warmth of a soft mouth wrapping around my dick, and this time, after I spun her and held her steady by the hips, I wished it were me being slammed into from behind.

My orgasm fell flat and fizzled through me disappointingly, leaving me unsatisfied and hungry for more. Hungry for something new, for someone different. And for the first time ever, I felt dirty afterward.

I told myself fucking Sam was for the best, and I continued to try and convince myself of it the whole silent, tense ride back to Franky's place. I repeated the mantra as I showered, attempting to scrub the last five minutes at Josephine's away.

It was for the best.

It was for the best.

It was for the best.

I kept at it as the rain pounded onto the skylight above the guest bed, and even when it stopped an hour later. Even when Franky's footfalls then passed my door, dragging me to the window where I knew I'd find him thinking at the ocean from the dock.

It was for the best.

It was for the best.

It was for the best.

Then why did it feel like a betrayal?

CHAPTER 7

Franklin

The wind had picked up markedly after the rain stopped, and so I made my way down to the dock to ensure the boat was securely moored. It helped that I couldn't sleep and needed something to do other than envisioning what took place in the bar restroom between Leland and Sam tonight.

Those thoughts shouldn't have been occupying my mind. I shouldn't have cared. So why did I?

Tightening the dock lines around the deck cleat, I reflected back on our night at Josephine's.

"How about we play for truths?" Leland had suggested.

I had every intention of letting him win. I was too jaded, or maybe too old to take pleasure in beating him. With Leland I wanted to have fun, not win, and besides, I owed it to him after how I'd been behaving.

But *truths?* I couldn't turn that down. Not that I believed he had many, or that he wouldn't share them if asked, but I wasn't sure I had the stomach to ask him the things I *really* wanted to know otherwise. Not without the game—and the rules he'd come up with—to hide behind.

I wasn't afraid, but I *was* confused, and to be honest, it was easy to forget how new we were to each other, and that there were things I didn't have the right yet to know. Either way, the prize was too good to pass up.

I'd taken the coward's way out after winning, choosing to save my questions, instead of asking if I'd been imagining things when I'd heard him hoarsely moan my name as he got himself off in the shower that day in his apartment. My gut wasn't ready for that conversation.

I thought about asking him to leave, but then remembered how feral I became when he asked if we were taking my car or his tonight. I couldn't risk him not having a reason to return home with me if we'd driven Betty. If I'd taken a moment to think reasonably, I would've concluded that he had to come back, or else I would've been stranded. No, him leaving wasn't the answer.

The cool air nipped at my arms as I searched the ocean for answers. Answers to questions like why our conversations went well beyond the line that should've been drawn with us. Leland was here to do a job, not listen to my confessions. And yes, he'd extended his friendship to me, but it didn't explain why talking to him had felt easy from the start, and why our silences felt even easier. Was that normal? Did that just happen? Did two people meet and click that instantaneously?

It happened with you and Selene, I reminded myself. We'd met and married quickly, but I hadn't been this conflicted about it then, so why now? Maybe because there were other reasons at play, then, because marrying Selene had been just as much about wanting her for Cole as it had been about wanting her for me. Maybe because the reasons why I shouldn't feel the way I do now hadn't applied to my situation with Selene. I was available when I met her, and I was unavailable now.

I rubbed at my forehead until it hurt, purposely redirecting my thoughts to the pain there so that I wouldn't have to face the answer to my question.

"You still love her," he'd said to me one night. I cursed the voice in my head for taking me back there.

"Yes," I hissed to myself, dropping my head into my hands. It was the same answer I'd given Leland that night, but I needed to hear myself say it again.

I loved Selene. But did I love my life with her? Was it enough? Why couldn't it be enough?

I was successful, I wanted for nothing materialistically, I had a loving, beautiful wife who had breathed fresh air into my life and my home at a time when I was still sinking from the loss of Cole's mother and my inability—or refusal—to be there for my child. A child Selene loved as if he were her own, right from the start. Why couldn't I be grateful for the life I had instead of wishing for something...*else.*

You're being selfish, I internally scolded myself. Plenty of people felt unfulfilled, had imperfect marriages, and hated their jobs. They didn't destroy everything and everyone around them just for a taste of something new. A taste of something they couldn't even name, something they weren't sure they would even want once they had it.

The grass isn't always greener on the other side, Franklin, I reminded myself.

And my kids... I'd promised Jasper I would protect him and his mother, that I wouldn't hurt either of them the way his father had hurt them. And Cole and I already had an unaddressed, awkward relationship because of all the past mistakes I'd made. The things I didn't get right. I'd been distant the first half of his life. I put the growth of Nexcom first and turned a blind-eye to the guilt he harbored behind his mother dying so that he could live.

Things had only gotten marginally better between us these last twelve years thanks to Selene, but truth be told, I'd never stopped making mistakes with Cole. Jasper either. I still didn't believe I was a good parent, and I didn't have the courage to ask if they held anything against me, because if the answer was yes, it would need to be dealt with, and I wouldn't know where to start.

Selene symbolized the one good thing I ever did for Cole. Was I really contemplating destroying that?

I stopped those thoughts before they had time to stretch their arms and get comfortable. It was the fear talking, and I'd already decided to use this predetermined amount of time to sort out what I wanted. To decide if what I wanted included saving my marriage. To decide if the happiness of one man was worth the destruction of countless others.

"You have a right to change your mind about who you want to be in this world, Franky. To decide you've had enough of living a lie." Leland had said those words to me on our ride to Josephine's. Maybe if I repeated them enough I'd start to actually believe them.

My bones were suddenly too heavy for me to hold up, so I shuffled to the house, my bed calling my name.

In the living room, the box of old junk my notebook had been in peeked out from the corner of the sofa, and I padded over to it, catching my yawn in my hand.

Nostalgia trumping my exhaustion, I settled onto the couch, placing the box on the coffee table. I hadn't gotten the chance to inspect everything buried inside of it. I'd been too preoccupied with digging up my old notes.

Reaching in, I withdrew my high school yearbook, flipping to the dog-eared page and huffing a tired laugh at the state of my hair back then. I remembered the photographer telling me to brush it back from my eyes, but it was my protective barrier. I was hiding, even back then.

I waded through the mementos that no longer made sense to me until my fingers brushed up against the photo with Gloria and her family. The one that included an unsuspecting Theo.

I hadn't seen the picture since I was a teen, and now I found myself musing over it twice in a matter of weeks.

Theo hated taking pictures and had opted out of this one. I couldn't recall who took the photo, maybe a groundsman, but Theo ended up making an appearance in it anyway.

Memories of my friendship with him were pretty crisp when I let myself think about it. I'd been less fond of his brother, Clark. He was too young, and while he wanted to play with toys, Theo and I had wanted to build things.

My father blamed my disinterest in the family business on Gloria and her family, but it couldn't have been further from the truth. I came alive when with the Palmeros. Much like the way I came awake with Leland.

Leland...

I brought the photo closer, so close I could hear my breath beat across it. How had I not noticed this before?

The light hair, the straight nose, the hard strike of his brows, the fine delicateness of his cheekbones that almost made him pretty... Leland resembled Theo.

I gazed down at Theo, processing why Leland had felt familiar to me from the second we met. Their personalities couldn't have been further apart, though. Leland had a wry, wicked sense of humor, and while he didn't have a Rolodex full of friends, I would still classify him as extroverted. Theo was shy, preferred books over music, frowns over smiles, and liked to go unnoticed, hence his aversion to cameras. But they shared the ability to make me feel comfortable, safe, and understood.

Relief coursed through me. That had to be it. Leland called to the surface feelings I hadn't felt since I was fifteen, and I hadn't recognized them for what they were. I'd been contorting myself into a pretzel trying to work out the acute reactions I'd been having toward him, not understanding where they were coming from and why they were coming on so fast. I'd been unknowingly living in a constant state of déjà vu, and it had been making me crazy, moodier than usual over the last few days.

He reminded me of Theo. That explained it.

Dropping the picture to the table, I stumbled to my feet, finally ready to get some sleep. I felt lighter than I had in days, regretful too. I hadn't been the best person to be around.

I stopped in front of Leland's door, pressing my ear to it when I thought I heard movement. I owed him an apology, but it would have to wait until morning.

Back in my room, I got undressed, checking the weather app before setting the phone on the nightstand and settling onto my stomach, arms tucked under my pillow.

Tomorrow's forecast: sunny with clear skies. Leland's favorite. I hated the heat, but I drifted off making plans, knowing tomorrow things would be different.

♦♦♦

Leland entered the kitchen the next morning to me waving a dish towel under the blaring smoke detector. Breakfast was supposed to be a nice surprise, not a fire drill.

He sauntered in, eyes still heavy with sleep, wearing only a pair of boxer briefs. I waited for the inappropriate feelings to pour in, holding my breath for it, but there was nothing but fondness and sincere remorse for having woken him up that way.

"I thought we agreed you wouldn't cook anymore," he said, stretching his arms over his head.

"What's wrong with my cooking? And when did we agree to that?"

His eyes widened, the last of his sleep gone. "Er, I guess I dreamt that," he said while I rushed to turn off the smoking oven. I slid the pan of burnt biscuits onto the stove before slamming the oven door shut and coughing into the crease of my elbow.

The alarm abruptly stopped ringing, and I turned to see Leland hopping off the island with the smoke detector in his hand.

"What?" he asked, looking down at himself. I'd been staring too long at him.

"Nothing, it's just…you're lean, but not as lean as I initially thought you were." Aside from the partial back view I'd gotten of him while he'd come with my name on his lips in the shower, I hadn't seen him with barely any clothes on before. I'd been too distracted by my own presumed interest, and resulting paranoia, to take in much at the time.

I'd noticed his physique last night through his body-hugging jeans and t-shirt, but this was different. Now every sinewy muscle down to his ankles was on display. I checked in with myself and still felt nothing inappropriate going on.

He inspected his slim but defined arms. "Yeah, well, my body type is something else I can blame my mother for." He leaned a hip against the counter, picking through the bacon for the one piece I miraculously hadn't torched. *Maybe I* shouldn't *be cooking.*

"Do you have any pictures of her?" I got the plates and silverware set up on the island as we talked.

"No, but there're photos of her online from her modeling days."

"Your mother was a *model*?" I'd assumed she was a sociopathic, love-obsessed attempted murderer from the heartbreaking tidbits he'd shared. However, if he looked like her, then a model made sense.

"Yeah, before I came along and 'ruined everything,'" he said around air quotes.

I glanced over at my phone, biting the inside of my cheek.

"Go ahead," he said, taking a wooden spoon from the utensil jar on the way to the stove to dish up a helping of dry scrambled eggs. "Her name's Willow Meadows."

I gave in to my curiosity as he loaded our plates with over-cooked waffles. "Wow," I said, looking between Leland and the magazine spread I'd pulled up. She was young, maybe eighteen, and aside from his eye color, Leland was the spitting image of her. "She's beautiful." Her pin-straight blond hair fell to her lower back, her moss-green eyes bright and innocent, her limbs long and dainty.

"Where is she now?" I asked delicately. I hoped she was rotting in a prison cell somewhere.

"Your guess is as good as mine," he answered, now sitting on the island, our food the only thing separating us. "It was touch and go for a while. I was banged up pretty badly. She was long gone by the time I came out of the coma. The official story was that I fell. I didn't refute it."

"Jesus, Leland," I breathed. He'd propped a heel up on the island, leaning back into his palms. I'd opened my mouth to chastise him about having his feet where we ate, but the gnarled skin reaching toward his shin from the back of his calf stopped me.

I moved in close, standing between his legs to trace my fingers over the old wound.

"It doesn't hurt anymore," he whispered. "You don't have to treat it like it does."

"Of course it does," I said. I wasn't talking about the physical pain in his leg. Neither of us were. Without having to say it, we were discussing the ache in his heart, and that wound would hurt forever.

"You don't have to pretend to be unaffected by what she did to you. Not with me," I said, my fingers idly exploring the webbed scar tissue. The way Leland spoke about his mother suggested the things she'd done were only her problem, not his.

I didn't care what any therapist said. The sins of our parents became our problems too, because we were left to find a way to deal with them, to get past them. My children included.

"Maybe I just like when you don't handle me with kid gloves," he said.

That wasn't it, or maybe that wasn't *only* it, but I dug my fingers into him anyway. His cheeks reddened and his cock shifted in his underwear.

I spun away, busying myself with cleaning up, although I hadn't even eaten yet.

"I, ah... I'm gonna go put some clothes on now that I don't need to run for my life. No more cooking. Ever," he called back unsteadily as he bolted from the kitchen.

He returned wearing sweats and a shirt, and we ate the salvageable parts of our breakfast.

"I could have the mural finished in a few weeks," he said. I covered my disappointment by adding our plates to the load in the dishwasher.

"Take your time," I said nonchalantly. "If you think you need to rush on my behalf, you don't."

"It's not you. I've got plans I need to get back to," he said. He'd moved to the edge of the living room, his eyes closed as he soaked up the sun shining in from the patio.

"Sorry," I said, meaning it. "I didn't stop to think about what I may be keeping you from."

"You're not keeping me from anything," he said serenely, the sun transporting him to his happy place. "I just have something I need to do in a few weeks. I could always fit both into my schedule if I have to." He moved farther onto the patio-turned-construction zone, and I joined him.

"How about we take the day off?" I asked, running my thumb over the keys in my pocket.

"To do what?" he asked in a sun-drunk state. I bit back a laugh, jangling the keys to get his attention. Leland cracked an eye open.

"I haven't taken the boat for a spin yet. It'll be even sunnier on the water."

"Hell, yeah," he said, letting out a whoop and reaching for the keys. "Who needs work anyway?"

"I'll grab the beer and sandwiches I made us," I said, and his mouth opened in alarm.

"Look, I may not be the best cook—"

"'Not the best' implies you can still cook, and well...you can't," he said, as if breaking the news to me gently.

"It's just bread and turkey. You can't mess up bread and turkey," I said.

"I'll be the judge of that," he said, missing out on my eye roll as he bounded for the stairs leading to the dock.

◆ ◆ ◆

I hung back near the sun lounger on the stern, giving Leland time to soak in everything the mini yacht had to offer. Experiencing it through his eyes brought me a level of pleasure I hadn't felt since I was a kid, way before I knew to expect this type of opulence from my life.

His hands scaled over the upholstery and siding of the boat as he moved beyond the wet-bar and deeper into the cockpit. More than once his gaze returned to the sunbed I stood beside.

"There's a sunbathing area on the foredeck as well," I told him, then chuckled when he dashed to the front of the boat. I unclipped my sunglasses from the collar of my shirt, slipping them on in preparation for the blast of sunlight awaiting me, then met him up front.

"I'm not gonna lie," he said, already sprawled out on his back with his own shades on. "I was kind of hoping you'd one day invite me on board."

"Why didn't you ask?" I held on to the railing as the boat swayed mildly.

"I don't know," he said. "It's not easy for me to ask for things."

"Why not?" I crouched along his supine body, giving in to the urge to remove his shades. I wanted to hear his explanation, as well as see it play out in his eyes.

He squinted up at me, the yellow of the sun deepening the honey hue of his irises. "Because what if I ask and the answer is no?"

"What if?" I asked, always burning to understand him, to get more of the deeper parts of him. "What if the answer is no? What then?"

"Then I would *know* I couldn't ask you for anything instead of assuming I couldn't. I'd know I couldn't rely on anyone but myself, instead of hoping that wasn't the truth."

As always, we were talking about more than this moment, more than this boat, and more than *us*. "Ask me for something," I whispered. Leland laughed but quickly quieted when I didn't join in. I hid his shades behind my back when he reached for them, my probing stare never leaving his. "Ask me for something that you've been wanting to ask me for but haven't."

His chest rose and fell rapidly as the seconds ticked by. I didn't know what I was doing, what I hoped to accomplish, but like I always had after Leland opened a wound for me, I operated on instinct. "Let me drive your boat," he settled on.

"No," I said, and he turned away from me. "Only because you have no interest in driving it. You'd rather spend your time up here. I'm using one of the questions I won, Leland, and according to your rules, you have to give me honesty. What do you really want to ask me right now?"

"I don't like this game," he bit out. While I'd seen brief glimpses of Leland's sadness, for the most part he hid behind humor and sexual provocation. Until now, I'd never seen him upset.

I considered him a while longer, determining it wasn't anger rippling off him. Leland was scared.

"You made the rules, now play by them," I said, refusing to let him off the hook.

A mischievous glint lit his eyes, rivaling the gleam of the sun, and I knew he'd resort to making light of whatever he planned on saying. He pillowed the back of his head with his hands. "Let me spend the rest of the summer here with you. After the mural is complete."

That took me by surprise. "I thought you had something to do once you finished."

"It's just a bartending course. My homebase could be here," he said, a little less sure. His breezy, I-couldn't-care-one-way-or-the-other facade crumbling under the suspense. "Maybe just a couple days out of the week. It's...sunnier here."

I didn't think highlighting how adorable that was would go over well, so I didn't. "No," I said, watching unfettered vulnerability crush him. He didn't have the strength needed to hide it. "I want you here every day. If you can do whatever it is you need to and make it back here—back home—then please, stay."

"O-okay," he said, that sweet blush of his washing over his tanned skin.

"Wasn't the possibility of getting what you wanted worth the risk of rejection?" I asked, returning his glasses to him. *Wasn't I worth the risk?*

Leland stilled with his shades halfway on, his eyes searing into me over the rim of them. I hadn't realized I'd said that last part out loud, but the way his mouth and stare softened said it mattered to him that I had.

"Yeah," he said without clarifying which question he'd answered. Both, I hoped. "Can we get this show on the road now?"

"From fear of rejection to demanding," I tsked. "Do you want a below deck tour first?"

"Nah. The view is much better from here," he said significantly. He was once again hidden from me behind his tinted lenses, but his face was angled up at me. My breath quickened as I tried to work out the intention of his comment, but then his brows wiggled above his frames, and I huffed out a laugh.

"Your flirting is going to get you in trouble one of these days," I said as I made my way to the rear of the boat, Leland's laughter chasing me.

I unwound the dock lines from the cleat, going over a few things in my head as I got the boat ready for departure. Had Leland wanted me to invite him to stay when he'd mentioned needing to leave once the mural was complete? Moving forward, I would be mindful of instances when he could be hinting for more instead of outright asking me for it.

I set off, steering us aimlessly and suffering from the helm as Leland first removed his shirt, then his pants in an attempt to achieve an even-bodied tan. At one point he took a nap on his stomach with his boxer briefs pulled below the meaty part of his ass cheeks. The elastic waistband pushed the round globes higher, making them appear plumper than they already were. He couldn't have known what type of view I'd have from here.

When I couldn't take it anymore, when I could no longer pretend that my budding attraction for him was some misplaced sentiment from a childhood friendship, I dropped anchor and left Leland sleeping while I took off to berate myself below deck.

Entering the small bedroom, I fell back on the bed, squeezing my eyes shut. Visions of long, sun-bronzed limbs assaulted me, and a blush so vibrant it reminded me of fresh cut watermelon on a summer day made my pulse thrum furiously.

Some force beyond me possessed my body, and before I knew it I had a spit-slicked fist wrapped around my cock, tugging and strangling it with a mix of lust and anger. I just needed to get this urgent need out of my system before facing him again. I didn't want it to feel good, but it did, which made me angrier, which in turn made me harder. I'd never been a violent man, but someone needed to pay for how good it felt to touch myself to thoughts of him, and since it couldn't be Leland—could *never* be Leland—it had to be me.

My biceps flexed, and my hips jutted off the bed as I pumped my cock, needing to orgasm to prove that once done, I could then put this madness behind me.

Within seconds I'd come all over my hand to thoughts of Leland. I panted at the ceiling where Leland slept peacefully above, eyes still closed because I couldn't look down and face what I'd done.

Feeling around, I untucked one end of the sheet, speedily wiping my hands and groin area off before lifting my hips to right my pants again. My breathing evened out, and I began to drift off when a deep, sleep-filled voice startled me into a sitting position.

"Everything okay?" Leland asked from outside the bedroom door. How long had he been standing there? I began internally panicking, but he just stood there rubbing the sleep from his eyes.

"Yeah," I croaked through my dry throat. "Just needed a break from the sun."

"Oh." He smiled cutely as he held out his sun-painted arms. "I think I may have gone overboard."

"You look good," I said, clearing my throat.

"I do, don't I?" he said roguishly, raising his arms to grip the molding above the door. The action made his chest expand and his muscles lengthen. "Ready for those *killer* sandwiches you made?"

"Very funny," I said, standing and hoping all signs of what I'd done were gone. "I'll have you know I won the national sandwich making contest four years in a row in high school."

"Please tell me such a thing did not exist, and that if it did you weren't uncool enough to participate." He looked downright horrified.

"It didn't. But if it was a thing, I would have won."

Above deck, Leland and I polished off our sandwiches and a six-pack of beer while getting to know each other better.

"My favorite time of day is right before sunrise," I said, after he'd shared that his favorite time of day was when the sun was at its highest, something I'd already figured out on my own. "Every morning I go down to the dock in my running gear, then head out before the day gets too hot."

"I know," Leland said. The beer had loosened him up, made him careless about how long he stared at me. Or maybe I was the one too loose, the one letting my imagination run wild.

"How?" I asked.

"I wake up early every morning to watch you drink tea on the dock as the sun breaks past the horizon," he said. "I love how the sun looks when it rises around you, when it makes room for you."

What did that mean? I waited for him to laugh or for his teasing grin to make an appearance, but neither happened. I stared down at my three empty bottles on the table separating us, wondering if maybe I'd had too much to drink and was now starting to see things in his eyes that didn't exist.

"Where did the time go?" I said, checking the time on my phone. We'd been talking for over five hours. "We should go. It's getting late."

"Yeah," Leland agreed, exhaling and averting his gaze. We docked and went our separate ways for the night. The break was needed, even if my heart said it wasn't welcomed.

The following morning, a mug of hot tea waited for me on the counter. It had a splash of milk and a hint of lemon in it, exactly how I preferred it. I watched the sunrise, resisting the urge to peer back at Leland's window to see if I'd find him there. I didn't need to anyway. I could feel him.

From that day on, I looked forward to Leland's tea, and his company, even though it was from afar, even though I never gazed back to confirm it.

Then one morning there were two steaming mugs of tea, and a very bright-eyed Leland waiting for me. I accepted one of the mugs he held and led the way to the dock. We sipped in silence, eyes trained on the rising sun. He reached out a hand to me just as the first rays broke free.

"Scared?" I asked.

"Of the moment ending," he said, trying unsuccessfully not to grin.

"You're such a child," I said, grinning in return. "An unoriginal one." Unoriginal but effective. I wrapped my hand around his. He went back to bed after, and I set off for my morning run.

That went on for another week, and then one day, Leland waited in the kitchen with our tea and his own running gear on. We watched the sun rise, then ran five miles together. I'd had to cut my mileage in half to accommodate his poor endurance, but it was worth it. I'd learned a lot more about him during those runs, like how shamelessly he could beg when sweaty and exhausted. I'd learned that I loved to hear him beg, and I loved seeing him sweaty and exhausted.

The weeks rolled by, and the word "strangers" could no longer be used to describe us. Maybe not even the word "friends." We were terrifyingly something more, at least to me we were. I couldn't speak for Leland because his penchant for flirting made it difficult to know if the line was becoming blurred on his side too.

Guilt scorched my stomach like acid, and I thought about my marriage less and less during those weeks, which worsened the guilt.

I was in trouble, and my mood began to darken because of it.

CHAPTER 8
Leland

"Franky," I called from the living room, but he kept sawing away out on the patio. I bit down on the wooden tip of my paintbrush to free my hands, wiping them off on my paint-splattered jeans before fishing my phone from my pocket to pause the music coming through the Bluetooth speaker. "Franky," I tried again, pulling the brush free, but got nowhere. I needed his opinion on the shade of green used for the trees in the mural.

Franky wasn't childish, so I knew he wasn't outright ignoring me. He'd been in a funk for two days now, and when stuck inside his head, the outside world had no chance of getting in. He'd have to crawl out of his cave to meet me.

It took effort not to plummet into a black hole right along with him, because Franky was an all-consuming force. When he was happy, life couldn't get any better than that moment for me, but when he was sullen, it felt like hanging on to the edge of something for dear life as a tornado ripped through. The highs and lows were equally dizzying and intoxicating.

I'd let him have his mood while I kept busy with the mural, but forty-eight hours was more than enough time to wallow in whatever had been bothering him, and I needed a second set of eyes.

I kicked my way through a small mountain of rubble and got between him and the sunlight he needed to see by. He jerked upward from where he knelt over what looked to be the beginnings of an end table, removing his protective goggles with splintered and calloused hands. Hands that had been soft and well-cared for when we'd first met.

"Hey," he said out of breath, falling to his haunches as I hovered over him. Sweat glistened between the gray hairs at his temples, and also traveled down the pronounced veins along his chiseled forearms.

"Hey," I parroted back, forgetting why I was standing there to begin with.

"Did you need something?" he prompted, expression fierce. And fuck the second pair of eyes I needed on the mural; it now became my mission to remove the stick lodged deep inside his ass.

"Yeah," I said. "I'd like to paint you."

"Okay," he said confused. "Maybe later, after I've showered and changed—"

"No," I said, interrupting him. "That's not what I meant. Although, I would love to do that now that you mention it..."

"Leland, what are you rambling on about?" he asked, wiping the moisture from his forehead with the hem of his shirt. The move revealed his rock-hard abs and the salt and pepper hair trailing south below his navel.

Gripping my paintbrush like a pen or pencil, I made a squiggly motion inches from his face.

"Don't," he said gruffly, the word hitting hard like a mallet, which only further encouraged me.

"I'm sure that tone has gotten you far in business, but you don't scare me, Franklin Kincaid. You barely even impress me." I flourished a hand over the four *impressive* counter stools lined up and ready to be carried into the kitchen. He stared blankly at me.

"Are you *that* intent on being grouchy?" I asked, because if so, then maybe he *was* a child after all.

Franky sized me up and then I was on my back, a stack of boards toppling over as Franky straddled me, fighting to get my paintbrush from me.

Our laughter weakened us, making it impossible for either of us to maintain control over the brush. I fought to keep it cradled to my chest, and green paint smeared over the front of us both now.

"Let it go," I demanded between peals of laughter.

"Not a chance," he said, his thighs tightening at my hips.

Franky had the advantage of size and brute strength, but I had a few dirty tricks up my sleeve. I sacrificed one of my hands holding the brush's handle to palm his cock through his dusty jeans. He reared back in shock, falling off of me and onto his ass with a grunt.

I scrambled to get on top of him, quickly drawing a green stripe across his nose and proclaiming myself the winner. We laughed through our inability to breathe, our chests heaving under the sweltering heat of the sun.

Our laughter faded, and I waited above him, the shape and shade of his eyes telling me he had something to say. "Jasper and Cole would like you," he said.

Now wasn't the time to make fun of him for being insanely random, so I rolled with it. "Introducing me to the family now?"

"Maybe." His heavy palms rested on my thighs. "Why not?"

"I mean, I guess. But wouldn't you need to tell them how we met? *Why* we met?" Jasper and Cole didn't know their happy family wasn't so happy after all. Franky turned away, teasing his bottom lip with his teeth.

"Is that what's been bothering you? Are you thinking about telling them?"

"Jasper and Cole have been on my mind, but no, I'm not telling them anything. At least not now."

"Have you been thinking about Selene too?" I wouldn't blame him. I'd been thinking about her. I'd given in to my curiosity and searched images of her online. She was beautiful, and for some reason that had made my heart hurt. I wondered how she was using their time apart. Her actions, while wrong, had been partly a result of what he'd stopped giving her, and partly a result of her own personal crisis—I assumed. I wondered if the balance of pain was evenly scaled because of it, or if he carried most of the load.

"Yes and no," he said. I badly wanted to follow it up with why and why not, so I didn't. A want that strong couldn't be good.

"She's their patron saint," he said, looking at me again.

"So you think they'll take her side?"

"Choosing her over me would be the easiest choice either of them would ever have to make. They'll hate me for hurting her, then I'll lose them. I'm not so sure I ever had them to begin with."

Franky and I had done a lot of talking over the last couple weeks. We'd take the boat out on sunny days and speak for hours on the ocean. We'd sit by the firepit on cool nights, tossing back beers—or something stronger if the topic required complete oblivion to get through it. Franky's central theme was guilt. He traveled through life bogged down by an abundance of it, and it all traced back to his parents' neglect of him, then the loss of Gloria and her family. It may have originated there, but it had continued into how he saw himself as a husband and parent.

"It's not too late to fix things with them. With your kids," I clarified, refusing to examine why I felt a clarification was needed. Why I felt the need to leave Selene out of it.

"Maybe," he said noncommittally.

"What else has been bothering you?" I brushed back the clump of hair sticking to his damp forehead. I had a need to comfort him, and I would've apologized for the intimate touch if he hadn't closed his eyes to it, inhaling and exhaling in relief.

Franky blinked up at me sluggishly, his eyes hot and fierce, paralyzing me. He shook his head, ridding it of whatever thoughts had been boiling up inside him. I felt powerless to do anything but wait for his next words, or his next move.

"What *isn't* bothering me," he said bitterly, his eyes now devoid of anything good. I'd been holding myself up on my knees, but the sudden change in his demeanor jarred me, dropping me onto his lap where his hard cock waited.

Franky's fingers dug into my legs, and the air exiting my lungs reversed direction.

I expected for one of us to freak out any second now, but the freak out never came. We were both too stunned to do anything but remain suspended in time. My dick responded to his, and without a direct order from my brain, my hips thrust forward, picking the worst time to go rogue.

"No," Franky gritted out angrily, eyes flaring with panic as his fingers did damage to the tops of my thighs.

We staggered to our feet, straightening our clothes and clearing the lumps from our throats. *Would shit be extra weird now? Would he ask me to leave? What the fuck was* that, *Leland?*

"That one tilts, and it's driving me crazy," Franky said, flicking a hand at the stools, his voice pinched. "And that one's too short, and the middle one is too tall."

So we were pretending nothing happened. I could do that. I could *try* to do that. I prayed a silent prayer that when I opened my mouth to respond, I could manage more than a fucking sweet moan. "But the fourth one is perfect." I inwardly patted myself on the back for sounding unfazed. "I know this because I tested it out this morning. Now all you've gotta do is make three more just like it. You've mastered it."

He didn't respond, the mask of pretense slipping as he paced a circle with his hands bracketing his hips. I didn't want to leave. I didn't want another person tossing me out the window because they'd decided I'd become "too much."

I was determined to show him that we could forget what happened and move on, determined to get an enthusiastic reply from him about his damn stools.

The paint on his nose had dried, but the end of my brush remained caked with paint. I pointed it at him threateningly. "Repeat after me," I instructed. "I did it."

"Leland—"

"Uh-uh," I said, and he watched the bristles for sudden movements. "Say: I did it. Say: I didn't know what the hell I was doing when I first started, but I didn't give up and I'm the fucking man," I said in one rush of words.

"I will not—"

"Say it!" I shouted, flaunting my weapon at him. "Say: I'm the fucking man, and I can overcome any fear and do anything I put my damn mind to."

"Please don't make me—okay, okay!" he said, holding his hands up in surrender as I swooped in. "I'm the man—"

"The *fucking* man," I corrected.

"Must you swear so much?" he asked with a sigh. I flew my brush in closer. "I'm the fucking man, and I can overcome any fear, and do anything I put my damned mind to." The corners of his eyes crinkled, and he brandished a grateful smile. Saying it had made him happy. I quickly added two green polka dots above the stripe on his nose, smiling when he frowned at me.

"See," I whispered. "You're a daisy after all."

His grin was boyish and bashful as he whispered back, "So are you, Leelee Bear."

CHAPTER 9

Franklin

Dumping my wet umbrella and shoes by the door, I walked briskly toward the stairs, not wanting to waste any more time in getting some medication into Leland's system. I halted with a foot on the first step, seeing a tightly coiled bundle on the couch.

Backtracking, I placed the bag containing chicken soup and cold meds on the coffee table so I could unbutton my suit jacket.

"Company still standing?" Leland asked, blanket to his neck.

"Sorry I had to leave you." I sat beside him, angling my body toward him so I could lean in and feel his forehead. "I'd been putting off going in for a couple weeks now. This meeting was unavoidable."

"We need you back, Franklin," Robert had implored. *"We lost the deal."*

"It's fine," Leland said, reeling me back from my wayward thoughts. "I told you it's just some stupid bug. I was tired of lying in bed all day, and I wanted to sit in front of the fire." He nudged his chin over my shoulder to the finished mural. "Isn't it fucking beautiful?"

The fire crackling in the hearth morphed it into something majestic. "Finally you see what I see. You're talented, Leland," I said. He'd never called any of his masterpieces beautiful before. Leland grinned his charming, lopsided grin.

He'd finished the mural a couple days ago, and I'd successfully built four functional counter stools. I'd let him convince me to dive fully clothed into the ocean in celebration—during a rainstorm, on the coolest summer day yet. As the one who'd raised two kids who loved to play in the rain no matter the sickly consequences, I should've known better. But Leland tended to make me feel like a kid again, or maybe even for the first time.

A cool draft caressed the collar of my shirt as the sound of rain meeting the ocean escalated.

"It's hot," Leland explained when my lips thinned. I'd left the doors and windows closed so he wouldn't get any worse.

"But you're swaddled like a baby," I said, rubbing the furry blanket between my fingers.

"That's because it's also cold," he said, shivering.

"It's the fever." I shook two tablets into my palm and handed him the half empty bottle of water sitting on the coffee table. "I'll heat up your soup."

Thankfully, it hadn't gone cold, and within minutes I'd returned, balancing the hot soup and crackers on a tray. I instructed Leland to sit up before settling it onto his lap and encouraging him to eat when all he wanted to do was sleep. I kept a watchful eye as he finished his soup and hydrated with water, and I continued to monitor his temperature until it broke. All the things I'd missed out on doing when Cole was a little boy. His nanny had taken care of the brunt of it.

"Thank you," Leland said, folding his feet under him. "You're good at this."

"At what?" I asked.

"Taking care of people."

"I'm not," I objected. "Not really." I stood, ready to run from his searching gaze.

Leland latched on to my wrist as I passed him, urging me to sit back down. "What makes you bad? Tell me, Franky. What do you think makes you so terrible?"

I sighed wearily, needing to know the answer myself. "I never held Cole when he was sick. Jasper either."

"But you would sit by their bedside while they slept. You would sneak into their rooms at night to make sure their fever broke," he said, repeating the details from a conversation we'd had days ago on our walk. It had started out as a morning run, but we'd been talking too much to maintain our fast pace.

"I didn't make it to the parent teacher meetings or show up to their equestrian lessons."

"But you were there for every competition, and you left an important business meeting to be there for Jasper on bring-your-dad-to-school day. He said you saved the day. You told me he said that." Leland's warm hand cupped my chin, bringing my head up and my gaze to his. The flames made his light eyes nearly transparent, and if I looked hard enough, I could see right through them and into his soul. I didn't want to look hard enough, though, because then I wouldn't want to look away.

"So you weren't the most nurturing parent, and you weren't there for everything. You were building a company. Something to pass on to them. You were there when it mattered, and I'd bet my life they know that. Your brand of love isn't perfect, but it's still love, Franky."

"You make it sound so noble, but the truth is far harsher than that. Any good I've ever done by them, Cole in particular, had been inspired by the good being done by someone else."

"Selene?" he asked.

"It started with Annabeth," I said, referencing Cole's mother. "Had she lived, she would've been his primary caretaker. It was why I'd agreed to the pregnancy. I wasn't just building a company, I was building something that would surpass what my father, and what his father, and *his* father before him had created. My life's objective was to prove I could be better than him. I was heartbroken when Cole's mother died, but secretly I was more resentful than anything. Sometimes I forgot what shade of blue his eyes were. That's how many days would pass by before I went in search of him." My pulse thudded in my throat, and I thought I might choke on my shame.

"I fed myself the same lie you just offered me. That I was building something great, something he could one day have and be proud of. And when we did spend time together, Nexcom was all I would talk about, in the hopes that he would understand why he couldn't have more of my time. In later years he became eager to discuss the day-to-day operations of the business, even working summers for me. But now I wonder if it was because he truly cared for the job, or because he thought that was the only way to connect with me. And that in itself is its own form of expectation, of pressure."

Leland listened intently, his thumb absently brushing my chin.

"Yes, Selene ensured I was there for the big stuff, and yes, she made me want to do better, but at my core, I'm not better, Leland. I'm just like my father, and I don't know how not to be," I admitted.

"Even with Selene's influence, I wasn't an active participant in our life. I'd only ever been an observer. Standing back and watching them thrive, happy that I'd finally gotten something right when it came to Cole." I ended my purge on a ragged breath, feeling drained but not fixed in any way.

"I don't believe you," he whispered. "You paint yourself to be a monster, but from what I know of Selene, she wouldn't have fallen in love with a monster. There must be some good in you. I *know* there's good in you. You just can't seem to see it."

"I appreciate the sentiment, Leland. But you haven't had the privilege of seeing me fall apart. I hope you never have to see what I'm truly capable of." I dove into a black hole when Cole's mother died. A hole I hadn't had to slink back into in some time. One I never wanted to live in again.

"What aren't you telling me?" he asked drowsily.

"You should be resting, not trying to solve puzzles—" My words died on my lips when he swooped in to plant a warm kiss on my forehead.

Leland snuggled back into the sofa cushions as if what he'd done was no big deal. He must have been sicker than we initially thought. "Better?" he asked around a yawn.

"Not even close," I breathed.

"Speaking about influence, I think I've been under Noon's for too long. He thinks a forehead kiss can cure anything."

"So hand holding and forehead kisses," I said with a lightness I didn't feel.

"Hey, you like holding my hand." Leland scooted lower and turned onto his side, resting his head on the sofa's arm. He looked young and innocent, and I had to remind myself that he was only twenty-five, and I had to warn myself not to hurt him too.

"Sleep," I said, standing.

Leland hummed. "It's still early. I'll take a quick nap while you change." He was snoring before I hit the top of the landing.

I took my time, knowing once I returned, Leland would wake up and pretend to be well enough to converse all night like we'd been doing lately. I showered, dressed in sweats and a tank, then perched at the end of my bed pondering what my next life choice would be, and who it would ruin.

It was well into the evening when I crept downstairs, the light of the fire guiding my way through the dark. As predicted, Leland stirred the moment I entered the room. He had a skill for feeling my approach, as if he were that in tune with me. To be fair, I could feel him advancing from a mile away too.

"How do you feel?" I asked, circling the couch and retaking my seat.

"Like a million bucks," he said, the heavy bass of his voice deeper upon awakening.

"Liar," I said, helping him untangle himself from the blanket so he could swing his feet to the floor. "Hungry?"

"No," he said. His lips were red and puffy from either sleep or fever, and his hair needed to be brushed. He'd slipped out of his shirt at some point because it now lay damp with sweat on the floor, and he still seemed exhausted.

"Go back to sleep, Leland."

"But—"

"I'm not going anywhere. I'll sit right here until you wake up again. I'll sit here all night if I have to."

He flushed, looking adorable as he did so.

"I enjoy your company too," I said. "You have nothing to be embarrassed about. Now sleep. That's an order."

"I kind of like it when you order me around."

"I guess in sickness and in health applies to flirting too," I said, and he chuckled as he hunkered down at the other end of the couch, stretching his long legs over mine.

"Now you're trapped. I'll know if you move."

"I'm sure you'd know either way." I kicked my feet up on the coffee table, preparing to shut my eyes for a beat as well, and between the light pattering of the rain, and the soothing sound of wood splintering in the fireplace, it didn't take long for me to go under.

The howling of the wind jarred me from sleep sometime later. Rain pummeled the glass, as if begging to be let in, and the fire had burned down to pulsing embers, leaving the room stuck in limbo between light and dark.

I breathed deeply, stretching my neck from side to side before noticing Leland's head on my thighs. He slept on his back with one foot on the floor and a hand jammed down the front of his cotton joggers. It scared me how much I wanted to be his hand.

Beads of sweat decorated his upper lip, and his bare stomach rose and lowered with his even breaths. I hadn't known he was a wild sleeper, or perhaps the restlessness was a side effect of being sick.

I needed to move, to get the blood flowing in my numb limbs again, but I didn't want to wake him. I also needed to check the time, because he probably needed another dose of medicine if the heat working its way through my sweats was any indication.

A bad idea brought a tremor to my hands, and I fisted them, pressing them into the sofa cushions.

"...a forehead kiss can cure anything," he'd said earlier, and maybe there was something to it, because I did feel better after, if only marginally.

This is just to see how hot he is, I told myself, hearing it for the lie it was but proceeding without caution anyway.

My lips touched his fevered skin, and I swallowed down the pain I'd been lugging around for so long, feeling both a sense of freedom and the cold sensation of chains tightening around me.

That's enough! I shouted at myself when one second turned into two, then three, then eight. But it wasn't enough. Not when I'd been in a drought for so long.

Leland shifted in his sleep, and I recoiled guiltily as he mumbled incoherently before curling into a fetal position. I sent a sigh of relief and remorse into the room, then stiffened when his arm circled my waist, coming to rest in the arch at the small of my back.

I peered down my chest at him, watching in horror as he blinked awake.

He licked his lips, turning away from my crotch area to gaze up at me, his eyes glassy and distant, as if he were still half asleep. "Franky?" he asked, voice raspy. The arm around me unwound, his hand traveling to feel around my face.

"I'm here," I said. "Your fever's back."

He groaned, closing his eyes briefly before lifting them to half-mast. "Franky?"

I helped him into a sitting position, his hand sailing over my jaw, nose, and mouth, trying to make out my identity in the near darkness. My breaths were quick against his palm, his long fingers scorched the skin at my nose. I inhaled him like a drug, my cock hardening, getting high off of it. "Give your eyes a second to adjust," I said, my tone desperate.

"*Franky*." It wasn't a question this time, and his delirium had been replaced with what sounded close to want.

What happened next happened too fast, a blur of movement, and I didn't know who initiated it. I didn't know who was to blame.

I hefted him up from under his arms, and he straddled me, tugging my head back by my hair before crashing his lips into mine. All thoughts, all feelings of uncertainty and guilt, were gone under the touch of his mouth, and under the weight of his hard body against mine.

Our movements were frantic as we swallowed each other's moans, as the kiss turned sloppy and ear-splittingly loud. We were two dogs finally allowed off our leashes, and being caged had made us savage.

I slithered my hands into the back of his pants, kneading his hot ass cheeks as he ground himself on my heavy erection.

Hot. The word stabbed through the building lust, batting at my brain for entry. *Hot.*

I snatched my hands away as if I wasn't more than willing to be incinerated by Leland's fire. His waistband smacked against his lower back as a feeling of abandoning home washed over me.

He was sick, and likely unaware of what we were doing, and while a locked door had suddenly been thrown open in my heart and mind, I didn't want him unknowingly taking part in something so wrong, even if to me it felt like the first right thing I'd done in years.

"Leland, wait," I said, urging him away. He strained toward me with swollen, pursed lips, his eyes closed. He was tempting and hot—in more ways than one—and I almost faltered, almost hauled him back in to give him what we both wanted. What *I* wanted.

I held him by the hips and scooted to the edge of the sofa so I could stand. Leland took advantage of those few seconds by wrapping his arms tightly around my neck and blindly kissing my face.

"*Leland,*" I groaned, unstrapping his arms before dumping him on his back and pinning them across his chest. "Wait."

"Why?" he asked, "Haven't we waited long enough?" His words were slurred, a mixture of drowsiness and confusion, but my heart catapulted up my throat regardless.

I left him there, returning with a glass of water and two cold and fever pills, demanding he swallow them both down. I slid the empty glass onto the coffee table as I lowered shakily to the edge of the couch. My elbows dug into my knees as I cupped my hands over my tingling mouth. "You don't know what you're saying, Leland, and I'm a mess. I've got fires burning in every corner of my life, and the last thing I need to do is start another one." Life was bigger than what I wanted, and until two minutes ago, I hadn't been sure what that was. And now...

Leland's soft snores cut into my speech. How much of it had he heard before losing consciousness? I sat there long enough for the glowing embers to die out on a whisper, then I spread the blanket over Leland before making my way upstairs.

I stopped at his open bedroom door, glancing behind me to make sure the coast was clear before quietly entering.

I'd given in and ordered bedroom furniture after realizing building a whole house's worth on my own would take more time than I'd anticipated, especially with my re-learning curve.

I ran a shaky hand over the untidy bed, imagining him tossing and turning, kicking himself free of the sheets in his sleep. I also imagined occupying the space next to him and being held in his strong arms the way he'd held on to me downstairs.

A wild sort of panic rocketed through me, and I took a seat on the soft mattress before I did something silly like fall over or run back to the living room and demand he hold me and never let go this time.

Feeling unmoored, I hugged one of his pillows to my chest for something to anchor me, bowing my head and unintentionally taking his scent into my body. My cock thickened again, and I groaned in agony, the feathered filling eating up the sound. *What the hell am I doing?*

It took all my might to rip the pillow away from me and not reach into my pants and strangle my erection between my fist.

"Damn it," I bit out, feeling my temper rise. Why now? Why him? Why *me*?

You know why, Franklin.

I slammed the door on that voice while also slamming the pillow back onto the bed. Two sheets of pastel paper floated onto the floor. It was the type of paper Leland sketched on in between painting the mural. I thought back on what he'd said to me when I first discovered his hidden talent.

"I'm not all that good at sketching, but it relaxes me when I get too in my head about how crappy a painting is turning out. Sketching reminds me that there's something I'm better at, so then I go back to my painting with renewed confidence. It's a trick of the brain, really," he'd said.

At the end of every night, I'd find sheets of charcoal drawings scattered throughout the house. They were amazing, like everything else he'd done, and I secretly kept a few of them.

I picked up the sheet closest to me, turning it over and leaning closer to the bedside table to get a better look under the lamp light. The rough sketch depicted a man from behind. A *nude* man from behind.

He stood on a balcony, palms pressing into its railing, his head lowered, the ocean—expanding in the dark distance—spot lit by the moon.

I pursued the muscular planes of his back with a trembling finger, chasing the hard line of his spine down to the beauty mark atop his right butt cheek.

The second rendering was more explicit. Two men in bed, their faces hidden, leaving me to identify them using other means. The one from the first sketch hovered between the other one's spread thighs. I knew it was the same man because of the matching beauty mark. And I knew the man below him was Leland because of the scar marring the leg he had wrapped around...*my* lower back.

Storming from Leland's bedroom, I charged into mine, throwing my balcony doors wide and stepping into the warm rain. I held up the first drawing, now bunched in my fist, staring between it and what I could see spread out in front of me.

The same ocean. The same moon.

I turned my back on the view, rain water sluicing down my body as my gaze landed on my open bedroom door. *He'd been watching me.*

Balling up the wet paper, I pressed into the railing, adopting the same pose in the sketch. Leland wasn't fevered and delirious when he drew this, not like he had been when we kissed tonight. And suddenly the mishap on the patio when we'd gotten aroused as he straddled me could no longer be ignored or summed up to our adrenaline pumping and my need for sex. This thing bubbling inside me wasn't one-sided.

I struggled to pinpoint the moment it had started for me. Had I known that I wanted him the instant he'd stepped on to that roof, refreshingly oblivious to who I was? Or had it begun when I took his hand before marching onto the Ferris wheel with him? Or perhaps when I watched him get off in his shower?

And when had it started for him? As his gaze stalked me all night at the office party? Had it begun with the very first flirtatious comment he'd directed at me?

Some missing part of me slid into place, making me whole while also tearing down the world around me.

A rash sort of recklessness came over me, and I warred with wanting to barge downstairs and take what I wanted—now that I knew Leland wanted me back—and packing up his things and returning him safely to his apartment before the sun rose to shine its light on my indiscretions.

He didn't deserve me making a mess of his life, which was precisely what would happen if I laid another hand on him.

I sank to my haunches, still holding on to the balcony railing for support as the rain picked up in force, attempting to pound some sense into me. I thought of my wife.

"Use this time to figure out what you want, Franklin, because we can't live like this anymore."

An insidious voice crooned romantically in my ear, whispering that Selene's words had granted me permission to cross every vile line I had in mind.

Bile cruised up my esophagus as I made a tough decision. I had to get as far away from Leland as possible before I gave in and pursued the thing that had haunted me ever since *then*. Ever since Theo. That voice had given me a terrible excuse to do it now, and I wasn't above using it.

CHAPTER 10

Leland

For once, the morning sun was the last thing I wanted to see after waking up on the sofa with a stiff neck. My mouth was dry, and the rest of my body felt clammy, but all that was forgotten by the sight of Franky dressed and sitting at the kitchen island. Not sitting, more like *waiting*.

"How are you feeling?" he asked with zero emotion.

"Better, I think. Hard to tell when every part of me needs a shower and sustenance." I stretched, getting to my feet.

"I'd like to make sure you're okay. My physician was able to fit you in this morning. After that, I think it's best if you went back to your place. Now that the mural is complete."

I'd been about to tell him I didn't need to see a doctor, that I was fine, that I could stay, even though he was being weird. I'd already accepted that "weird" came with the territory when being Franky's friend. I'd rather deal with his mercurial moods than not deal with him at all.

I couldn't tell him that, though. Not when my packed duffle bag sat at the bottom of the stairs, sending a new round of sickness through me. *What the fuck?*

Flashes of last night assaulted me then, and my stomach rolled with anxious energy. I'd attacked him on the sofa unprovoked, then basically admitted to wanting to do it all along.

"Franky," I breathed, unsure of what to say next to make things right. He averted his gaze, something like embarrassment had lingered there, confusing me. I should've been the one embarrassed. I *was* embarrassed.

I swung back to my packed bag. *Fuck.* He'd had to go into the guest bedroom to pack up my stuff. He'd found my sketches.

"I can explain," I said, surprised I could even form words through the marching band wreaking havoc on my frontal lobe.

"Not now. Get cleaned up and changed. We need to get going."

"I don't need a fucking doctor, Franky." *I need to make this right.*

"It's not up for debate, Leland. It's my fault you're sick. I need to know you're okay before—" He stopped abruptly, but I finished it for him.

"Before you wash your hands of me?" Why did people find it so easy to get rid of me? To walk away? My father, my mother, my uncle, and even Noon.

"No," he said, adamantly, as if he knew where my thoughts had gone. "You've done *nothing* wrong."

"Then why?" I understood that I'd fucked up. He was married, with grown children. *We* couldn't happen. Shouldn't happen. But I'd felt his hard cock under me as we tussled for my paintbrush that day on the patio. I'd smelled the musky scent of his cum in the cabin of his boat that one afternoon, and while I couldn't prove it had anything to do with me, my gut told me that him jerking off had *everything* to do with me.

"You have the bartending course I've been keeping you from, and I'll be going back into the office earlier than expected." He lifted his chin, displaying his authority and making it perfectly clear the decision had been made and wasn't up for discussion.

I wasn't dealing with the Franky I knew. He'd slipped back into his armor. Before me sat Franklin Kincaid.

"So that's it? You're locking this place up and returning to the colossal estate you love so much? Returning to the *job* you fucking love so much? Going back to your wife?" Sarcasm and anger oozed from me. And something else entirely. Something I had no right to feel. Something I didn't want to name.

"We're going to be late," he said, standing, the legs of his stool scraping against the kitchen floor.

"I said I don't need a damn doctor," I snapped, charging for my bag. "I'll shower at my place, and I can drive myself there."

"You come with me under your own steam, or I carry you there," he threatened. Any smidgen of warmth that had been lurking below his increasingly frosty exterior had disappeared. He'd do it. He'd drag me there kicking and screaming if he had to.

"You're not paying the bill," I spat, matching his coldness. I grabbed up my bag and made my way to the bathroom.

♦ ♦ ♦

Franky paced the small room we'd been confined to in the ER, his expression severe. I'd ended up refusing to see his fancy doctor after asking the billing coordinator for the cost of the visit. Franky's options were to make a scene trying to keep me there or take me to the hospital emergency room three blocks over where my bullshit state insurance would be happily accepted.

"I told you I was fine. You can leave now. I'll find a way back to your place to pick up my car." I'd been diagnosed with the common cold, which had been more fever and exhaustion than anything. Now we were waiting for the discharge papers.

"I'll wait," he said, stuffing his hands in his pockets.

My temper cooled as I noticed how tired he seemed. Had he gotten any sleep last night? "Franky—" The door swung open then, slamming the brakes on our conversation.

Noon stormed in, and I let out a string of muttered curses. Stacey worked in the ER. I hadn't seen her, so I'd been optimistic that I'd be in and out of here without Noon knowing.

Without a word, he tilted my head up by my chin, examining me as if he'd heard my face was broken.

"Stop overreacting," I mumbled around his grip, swatting his fussy hands away. "And isn't your girlfriend letting you know I was here against hospital policy or something?"

Noon hadn't spotted Franky over in the corner yet, but how he hadn't felt the sudden dip in the room's temperature was beyond me. I didn't need to see Franky's eyes to know he wasn't pleased. I just didn't know if it was the interruption of what I'd been about to say that had pissed him off or Noon specifically.

"Screw policy," Noon said. "She thought I was here to see you, though. I was actually surprising her with lunch."

"Is there anything she can do to speed up the discharge process? I'm ready to get home." *And forget this day, and every other day since meeting Franklin Kincaid, ever happened.*

"You're sick," he said. "I'm off for the next few days. You can stay with us until you're back on your feet."

"It's a fucking cold, Noon. A pitiful one at that. I have yet to even blow my nose."

"It's still early," he said. "Sometimes it takes a few days for all the symptoms to kick in."

Franky stepped forward then, startling Noon. "He'll be coming home with me."

After getting over his shock, and Franky's audacity, Noon turned his questioning stare on me. "Who the hell is this?"

"I'm Franklin Kincaid," Franky answered tersely, obviously not appreciating being dismissed by Noon.

Noon's chest puffed out as he faced Franky head-on. I jumped in before things could get out of hand. "Noon, this is Franky. A-ah friend. Franky, this is Noon."

"An, a-ah friend?" Noon asked, invisible quotation marks coating his words as he stared Franky down. "Must be something different than a regular friend, because I'm the only one of those you've got."

Franky glowered at him, and I narrowed my gaze at the back of my best friend's head.

"Stop being an ass, Noon."

"No, I'm just a protective friend defending you from some stranger who thinks you're leaving here with him."

"If you were such a great friend, instead of a neglectful one," Franky said, tone dripping with contempt, "you'd have known he's been living with me for weeks."

The testosterone levels rose, pushing at the ceiling, and although Noon had a few inches and more than a few pounds of muscle on Franky—which said a lot—Franky didn't fumble under the weight of Noon's formidability. If anything, he seemed ready to prove that size didn't matter.

"I've actually been trying to reach you for weeks now," Noon said, turning his guilt-ridden eyes on me. "You haven't returned my texts or voicemail messages. I even stopped by the apartment this morning."

"*Weeks?*" Franky asked. "Did you scour the city from top to bottom for him? Did you report him missing? Was an APB put out for him?" Franky asked, challenging Noon's sudden concern. His tone went darker with each rhetorical question. "I'm terrified for him if you're all he's got. I haven't known him for a fraction of the time you have, but I'd rain hell down on this city if even a day went by without hearing from him."

I couldn't deny that Franky had a point, even if I wasn't clear on what drove it. I'd actually been the one trying to reach Noon, and not the other way around, but my texts and voicemail messages had gone unanswered. I'd checked in with Stacey, so I knew he was alive and well. *"We've just been busy,"* she'd said.

He'd only just gotten back to me yesterday, but with being sick, I hadn't gotten the chance to return his missed call.

"Franky," I said. "Can you give us a few minutes?"

He nodded, reining in whatever it was he'd unleashed. "I'll see about your discharge papers."

Left alone with my best friend, I inched over so he could sit next to me. He snorted, pulling up a chair instead. No way could he have fit on the narrow gurney with me. The gesture was meant to be an olive branch.

"Why'd you lie?" I asked.

"I couldn't give that asshole the pleasure of knowing he was right," he said, gazing back at the door Franky exited through. "I'm sorry. I've been a shitty friend. I've just been—"

"Busy," I cut in with. "I get it. You've always had big dreams, and I've always wanted to play it safe. We were bound to outgrow each other." I smiled weakly. I'd tried to follow his lead after high school, even enrolling into community college alongside him. Didn't last long. I would've eventually flunked out, if I hadn't been kicked out first for fraternizing with the faculty.

"That isn't what's happening, Leland."

"Isn't it? I overheard you and Stacey talking a few nights before you moved out. I know about the big job offer she got in New York. She decided to accept it, didn't she? And you've decided you're going with her, right?"

Noon took my hand, looking ridiculous squeezed into the tiny hospital chair at my bedside. It groaned under his bulk. "That's what I was calling to tell you. We've been getting things in order for the move. I would've told you sooner, but time got away from me."

"You're a bad liar," I said.

"Alright, maybe I feel guilty about leaving, knowing you don't have anyone else, but..."

"But you've gotta go," I said, when he couldn't.

"Yeah, I've gotta go." He squeezed my hand tighter.

Noon glanced over at the closed door again, as if only just remembering about Franky. His eyes came back to mine with a million questions lingering behind them. I couldn't hold his stare.

"Am I wrong about you not having anyone else? Who is he?" he asked, and I blew a raspberry, dropping my head back on the pillow. I told him as little as I could but enough to satisfy his curiosity, ending things with Franky hiring me to paint a mural. I left out the part about him being one of the wealthiest business-men alive. Those details meant nothing to me, so I opted out of mentioning it.

"You're into him," he accused afterward.

"No, I'm not."

"I've never seen you into anyone before."

"Because I'm not," I said.

"Is he single?" he asked, ignoring my denial.

"It's...complicated," I said, giving up the act. I was tired of acting anyway, and this was Noon, he knew me better than any-one. *Almost* anyone.

"Please don't tell me he's married," Noon begged.

"They're *separated,*" I stressed.

"Since when?" he asked, unconvinced.

"The start of summer."

"Leland..." he warned.

"But things weren't good between them prior to that," I said defensively. "Doesn't matter anyway. I finished the mural, and we don't plan on seeing each other ever again." God, it hurted to say it. Noon watched me doubtfully. "What?" I snapped.

He jabbed a finger at the door. "That didn't look or sound like a man who plans on never seeing you again, Leland. I believe his exact words were 'He'll be coming home with me.'"

"He just feels guilty," I said. *Always guilty.* "I'll grab my car from his place once we leave here, and be back home before the sun goes down."

"Your non-existent dating life has made you stupid," Noon said with a snort. "That man isn't guilty, he's territorial. He saw my hands on you, and he nearly blew a blood vessel. He's a married man, and he hardly knows you. He shouldn't be that intense about you." He'd lowered his voice to a concerned whisper. I didn't point out that Franky knew me in ways he didn't.

Was Noon onto something? I'd already convinced myself on the car ride from Franky's house that anything I believed meant something more than it did had been a figment of my imagination.

A good defense attorney could call a medical professional to the witness stand to explain away the boner Franky popped out on the patio. It didn't need to mean anything simply because I wanted it to. I'd sometimes get hard while thinking about food whenever the wind blew the right way.

And him getting himself off on the boat didn't have to mean anything either. He'd likely gone from having regular sex to having to do without overnight. I'd jacked off for much less.

But the kiss... He'd kissed me back. *Hard.* There was no explaining that away, was there?

I'd been about to ask Noon what else he'd picked up from Franky's actions, but the man in question reappeared, entering without knocking like he owned the place.

Franky's stare darkened at the sight of Noon holding my hand. I slid my palm free, locking my spine against the shiver racing up it. "Someone will be by with your discharge papers shortly," he said tightly.

Noon rose from his chair, a mischievous glint to his eyes that only I could see. "Don't—" My warning hiss was sliced in half by his lips smashing onto mine. He gave me a loud, smacking kiss, smiling against my mouth as he held my head, then backed away before I could draw blood.

"Do you make a habit of touching him against his will?" Franky asked, deceptively cool as a cucumber.

"Oh, trust me," Noon whispered near Franky's ear as he moved toward the door, "he's willing." He'd all but told Franky we'd fucked, and then I went and confirmed it by blushing with mortification. The idiot even had the nerve to wink at me. *I'm gonna kill him.*

Franky's nostrils flared as he nailed me to the bed with his black, sinister stare.

Noon reached the door, stopping with a hand on the handle. "Leland," he said, all traces of humor swapped for misgivings. Made it hard to be upset with him. "Don't forget about the scratch-offs."

If I wasn't already struggling to contain my embarrassment, my face would've reheated, tipping Franky off to what Noon's comment implied. Franky knew about the scratch-off story, but luckily he was still boiling over Noon's previous innuendo to notice his latest insinuation.

Noon vanished, leaving me alone to weather the storm he'd caused. Maybe that was his point. If I hadn't seen what was right in front of me before, Noon had made sure nothing blinded me from it now.

"We need to talk," I said, done with denial and with fighting my feelings.

"I know," he replied, haggardly. "I know."

CHAPTER 11

Leland

The silence stretched to full capacity during the ride back to Franky's place. We'd made an unspoken agreement to keep our words to ourselves until we could share them uninterrupted and without distractions. Neither of us wanted to pour our hearts out as we sped along the highway.

Franky didn't waste any time getting comfortable for the approaching confrontation, yanking off his blazer and tie as soon as we walked through the door. It was like he'd thought putting it on in the first place could take him back to how things were before he'd decided to try his own happiness on for size, but it didn't work. Of course it didn't.

Ambling into the living room behind him, I idled near the sofa while he opened up the living room wall and breathed in the ocean air before lowering his chin to his chest.

"What was that back there?" I asked, taking the lead. "Between you and Noon."

"I was jealous," he said, stunning me. Not because I hadn't been teetering toward that conclusion, but because I'd expected it to take a round of shock therapy to get him to admit it. No, not admit it, because for the most part, Franky was an honest man. I'd expected it to take more prodding for him to *realize* it.

"I hated that he had the privilege of touching you in a way that I..." He faded off, leaving me to imagine how his sentence would have ended if he'd had the courage to complete it. *In a way that I don't.*

"And then he wanted to take you from me. To care for you when I'd planned to basically dump you at the curb." He grunted, then said under his breath, "No one takes anyone else from me."

Anyone else? I thought curiously. I didn't know where to go next, didn't know if I should be apologizing or rejoicing. The atmosphere felt heavy and wrong, yet liberating and right. We weren't pretending anymore. His answer had given us the freedom to be truthful, no matter how ugly the truth would be.

"Last night while in bed," he began, as I stood there clutching the sofa back, wading through my mangled emotions. "I stared at the empty space next to me, wishing someone was there. That someone wasn't my wife." His pain was audible, screaming over his whispered words, and I wanted to rip myself from my spot and comfort him as he lifted his head to the churning storm clouds outside.

"I climaxed to the memory of a lean body, of someone who shouldn't even be in my life, let alone my fantasies. That person wasn't my wife, Leland. I experienced an orgasm so intense it felt like I'd exited my body, and it wasn't Selene's name I called to get me there."

"What are you saying?" I asked, locking my knees when they promised to buckle.

"I'm dying here, Leland," he said gruffly. "Don't finish me off by making me spell it out for you."

But I needed him to spell it out, to write it out, to fucking *bleed* it out. This was too big to leave anything up for interpretation. Neither of us could be left guessing. Maybe he needed me to put myself on the line too. The way he had just done.

"I didn't know it at the time, but I've wanted you since the day I laid eyes on you. That day on the roof, your fears called out to mine. You made me want to be brave before you'd ever said one word to me. That's how much you affect me, Franky."

Franky took the two steps needed to place him on the patio. I followed, more like chased him. I didn't want him moving farther away from our current reality. Farther away from me.

"You scare me," I admitted, closing in on him with purpose. "But I want to face you anyway, because you make me want to face everything that terrifies me. You're married, and I... I've tried to care. I mean, I've tried to *still* care. But no matter how hard I try, your marriage doesn't stop me from wishing I was in that empty space you spoke about, and it doesn't stop me from blowing my load every fucking chance I get from just thinking about your sinful voice, or your dark moods, or the way you surprise even yourself when you laugh." I sunk my fingers into his silky hair, feeling sympathy for the terror written across his face, but I pressed on anyway.

"You're more than complicated. You're a stick of fucking dynamite, Franky. Capable of blowing me to pieces, but I want you anyway."

"I-I'm married," he said, which came out as more of a reminder to himself.

"I don't care," I said, out of breath. "Not anymore. And maybe that makes me a bad person, but I want you too much to fucking care, Franky. You taught me to ask for what I want, even if the answer is no. I'm asking if I can have you, even if it's only for a little while."

"We can't," he said resolutely, spinning away from me, leaving my hands empty and my heart bruised. My first reaction was to retreat from his rejection, a turtle backing into its shell. It was a cold reminder of why I didn't depend on anyone. I'd bled for him and was wounded deeply for my troubles. Then I remembered something he'd once told me.

"Wasn't the possibility of getting what you wanted worth the risk of rejection?"

"Why can't we?" I asked, allowing him the space he'd put between us. "You're technically separated, and you said this summer was for figuring your shit out. How do you plan on doing that if you don't actually figure your shit out?"

"I'm not sure an affair, which is exactly what this would be, constitutes as figuring *anything* out. If anything, it complicates things further, Leland."

"She cheated first," I said quickly, before I lost my nerve. "Emotional cheating still qualifies as cheating."

The sky rumbled, the ocean grew agitated, and birds abandoned their branches. Everything, including us, waited on a precipice, waited for what would happen next.

"I won't use that as an excuse," he said. "I refuse to. And besides, it isn't even a good one."

I disagreed, but because I wasn't sure if my disagreement came from my core beliefs or because I wanted him, I didn't challenge his point.

"What do you want, Franky?" This was no longer about us, about taking what we wanted. I cared about him, and I needed to know—needed *him* to know—what he wanted for not just this moment in time, but for his life. And maybe hearing it from him would help me decide what I wanted from my own life too. As it stood, I couldn't see beyond wanting him.

"A new job?" I asked when he remained mute. "Not to have a job? Friends? Do you want to move to Alaska? How do you see the rest of your life playing out? At what point do you start living for yourself? Not for your revenge against the two people who brought you into this world or in penance for being an imperfect father and husband." I walked around him, chasing his gaze. "Let yourself have this. Let yourself have me."

"What do you want from me, Leland?" he asked breathlessly.

"The truth," I said with a helpless shrug.

Franky took a deep breath, lacing his hands behind his neck before releasing one and palming the side of my throat with it. I closed my eyes, gripping his forearm and enjoying his touch in a way I'd never let myself do before.

"The truth is, I don't have the answers to any of those questions, Leelee Bear." He'd called me that plenty of times in jest. This time he said it with a type of despair that left me unable to think. He said it like maybe it could be the one good, normal thing in all of this. "Truth is, the only time I'm not lost, the only time I have a clue about anything, is when I'm with you." He squeezed my neck, making it difficult to breathe. Or maybe his confession had been what cut off my air supply.

"So you do know what you want," I said.

"Yes," he answered, as if that ugly truth had been torn out of him.

"Then fucking take it," I dared before I could stop myself. If he'd been hoping I would talk some sense into him, he was wrong.

"Just because it's the truth doesn't mean we should act on it, because an even bigger truth is that this won't end well. I can't make you any promises. I will likely regret what comes next, and I'll likely hurt you beyond repair."

"I. Want. You. Anyway." I turned each word into a punch for maximum impact. *Don't forget the scratch-offs.* Noon's reminder worked its way into my resolution, but I was in a gambling mood, ready to risk it all, and I was done with pretending otherwise. "Take what you want, Franky, and I promise I won't ask for more."

"I'm married," he said, a warning, not a reminder this time.

"I promise," I said again.

"Leland—"

"I *promise*, Franky."

Thunder cracked overhead, stealing his attention, and I glared at the roaring sky, ready to curse the fucking gods judging us from beyond it.

"It's not that simple," he insisted.

"It *is* that simple. But you want to act like it's not. You want to first turn yourself inside out for an eternity before you finally lay more than a hand on me, because in your mind it shouldn't be such an easy thing to do." My statement reminded him of the hold he had on me, and I slapped my palm to the back of his hand when his grip loosened on my neck, afraid I'd lose my mind—lose him—if he let go of me.

"You own a company you hate running, you have grown children you tiptoe around, and a wife who doesn't really know you or understand your restlessness. What decent human being would risk all that for a chance to feel good, right? Not without first making himself sufficiently sick with wanting." I wasn't trying to pressure him. Wasn't trying to be a bad influence either. I was merely telling him what he wanted to hear, what he *needed* to hear. We were working through every objection out loud before falling into our selfishness.

I would've stood there all night daring fate to strike us down, would've risked being burned to cinders by one errant spark of lightning if it meant I'd end up in his bed. It should've shamed me to admit that, even if it was only to myself, but I had a metaphorical stack of scratch-offs in front me now, and there was no turning back.

"You don't know what you're asking for," he said, shouting to be heard over the rain that had given no warning before pouring down on us. I let him drag me inside as he complained about me already being sick.

"Maybe I don't," I conceded. "But I know *you*. Your foul moods are equivalent to a fucking earthquake, and all I can do when you're experiencing one is hold on to something and grit my teeth until they pass. You're a category-5 shit-storm on a good day, Franky, but on a bad day? God, on a bad day, I wanna be the thing you take it all out on. When you feel good, I feel like I can take on the world or ignore it for one more second to be with you.

"I know you like a bottle of Stella right before dinner because it helps you unwind, making it easier to walk away from whatever you're hacking away at on the patio. I know you love your family, and that you wish you could be different for them. More nurturing, more present, and less regretful... But before you can be different for them, you need to be different for yourself."

"Leland," he said, cradling my face between his strong hands. "I didn't know my being withdrawn affected you so much."

"I love your darkness, Franky. And I would take being in the eye of your storm over being on the edge of it any day. You've been struggling with this, haven't you? I know that now."

"Leland," he pleaded, eyes erratic, unable to choose a spot on my face to crash land on. He tapped his wet forehead against mine, then pulled away, looking over my rain-splattered clothing with a frown.

"I'm fine," I said, holding back a sneeze. I let him pull my t-shirt off anyway. He dried my hair with it, effectively forcing us into an interlude.

"Who else knows you, Franky?" I asked, getting the conversation back on track. "Not who knows Franklin Kincaid, but who knows *you*." I rubbed a hand over his heart, feeling it pitter-patter faster than a hummingbird's wings.

"No one," he said, shuddering from my touch. He glanced over to the photo on the coffee table. It had been there for a while now, but neither of us had mentioned it. "At least not anymore."

I rewound my mental recorder, playing back something he'd said a little while ago.

"No one takes anyone else from me."

Suddenly, I was both curious and jealous, and the hand on his chest curled into a tight fist. Theo would have to wait until later, though, because right now it was about Franky and me.

"Please," I begged, my lips approaching his. Franky cupped my cheeks, his arms shaking with the emotional strength it took to hold me back. *"Please."*

"I'm not good for you." His voice broke.

"I've been warned," I whispered before he closed the gap. Our lips collided with an intensity that literally knocked me off my feet.

Franky steadied me with an arm banded around my waist, crushing me to him, our hard cocks thumping against each other. The kiss was feverish and messy, and several times we had to break apart to suck in air before diving back in again.

He tugged my hair like it had somehow offended him, and I squirmed my hands between us to rip open his dress shirt, sending the buttons flying everywhere. He stopped me before I could undo his belt buckle.

"I haven't changed my mind," he said, accurately reading my panicked expression.

"If you're worried I'll get you sick, it's a little too late for that."

He shook his head, his hands dropping to my shoulders. "It's not that."

"Then what?" I asked.

"Maybe we should take it slow."

My first reaction was to be disappointed, maybe even scared that we'd both have a change of heart if we let this moment slip away. But I'd never taken anything slow, and he'd never done this before, and I surprisingly wanted to savor that. For once I didn't want to rush in so that I could just as quickly rush out.

"Okay," I agreed, kissing him again and peeling my lips away with tremendous effort. "Slow. But promise me that when we fuck, it'll be anything but slow."

"The antithesis of it," he swore, but I didn't miss the hard swallow he gave.

"You're going to be a natural, Franky," I swore in return before handing myself over to the kiss again.

We kissed until the rain stopped, until the moon replaced the blood-orange sun, and until the skin of our lips was raw to the touch and swollen.

We kissed our way to Franky's bed, where he released his full weight on top of me, uncaring about my inability to breathe as he explored the inside of my mouth with his greedy tongue.

Franky prodded, and swept, and licked every crevice, and I patiently let him, even as my balls tightened painfully inside my jeans.

He still wore his now buttonless shirt, providing easy access to his muscled chest and back, and my hands took advantage, roaming and squeezing and imagining how they would bunch and release as he fucked into me.

"Top or bottom?" I asked during one of our rare breaks where we used the time apart to stare into each other's eyes, expressions both excited and afraid. I knew better than to assume, even though my ass already knew what it wanted. It clenched around the emptiness as I waited in suspense for Franky's answer. It was possible he didn't know, and that would've been okay too.

"Top," he said with a confidence at odds with his experience. "I have this need to be inside of you, Leland. I've always had that need."

"*Fuck*, you're making me wet, Franky." I dug my heels into his lower back as my cockhead grew damp inside my boxers. Franky moaned from the assault against his dick and resumed our kiss, becoming consumed again.

"What about you?" he asked, chest heaving as he dragged in all the air around us, leaving me without.

"Bottom, Franky," I breathed. "Fucking bottom."

His eyes darkened as he held himself above me to take in the clothes covering my body with scorn. Franky's scorching stare returned to mine, and I knew we were doing this. Fuck taking things slow, and inexperience be damned, we were doing this.

"There's so much of you," he said, already playing with my pebbled nipple through my thin shirt as our hips instinctively undulated against each other. "I don't know what to do with you..."

"Are you calling me chunky, Franky?" I teased in a raspy voice, arching up, pressing my pec to his teasing fingers.

"No, I just don't know if what I've done in the past would work now." He avoided directly mentioning his wife, but I wasn't a fool. My lip curled with jealousy, which should've been the first sign that letting Franky touch me was a mistake, that going any further would be an even bigger one. "Everything in me wants to tear you apart, Leland. And I'm sorry," he said, with a hard thrust between my spread legs, "but I don't think I can hold back. Not after holding back for so long." The haunted gleam in his eyes said his refrain went further back than the day we met, and a thrill rocked my whole body because I'd be his first, I'd be on the receiving end of everything pent up inside of him.

I gripped two handfuls of his hair, tugging until it hurt, until the pain sent his eyes rolling heavenward, until he understood what freedom really felt like, until those eyes became ravenous for it. "You couldn't fuck this up if you tried, Franky. Do whatever you want to me. Be as rough and as selfish as you need to be." I swallowed, lowering my tone as I voiced the thought I probably should have left inside my head. "Use my body in all the ways you felt like you couldn't use hers." I tugged his hair harder to distract him from the guilt leaking into his expression, and he moaned, lust hardening every angle of him until even his pitch-black eyes had turned to stone. The bed rocked, beating against the wall as his cock attempted to cut through our layers of clothing to get at me.

"What if I hurt you, Leland?" His question held a double meaning, but I addressed the more pressing one, the one that would get his cock inside of me.

"My body can handle you, Franky. You don't need to use caution with me. Never with me," I whispered meaningfully.

That was all the permission he needed before ripping our clothes off in under sixty seconds.

"Christ," he moaned, his gaze eating up the expanse of my naked body, the sight of my dripping dick. Franky scooped up the pearly bead dangling over the rim of my cockhead, eyeing it as if it were one of the seven wonders of the world.

He brought his finger to his nose for a sniff, seemingly swaying to one side from the scent's potency before sucking his digit clean. The bedframe shook with his full-body tremor.

"Tell me you have lube," I said, rolling my balls in one hand and teasingly stroking my cock with the other. "Tell me you needed it for all the nights you wanted me but had to make do with your hand instead."

"Yes," Franky breathed, reaching into the bedside drawer for the lube, then swore. "*Please* tell me you have condoms."

"Fuck," I hissed. "I'm all out."

Franky swiped the tip of his tongue over his lips, closing his eyes as if tasting the remnants of my pre-cum there, and I knew this night couldn't end like this.

"You can trust me, Franky," I said, giving him all he needed to know with my intense stare.

"I do," he said, giving me the same potent stare in return. "And you can trust me."

"I do," I said. "God, I fucking do."

"Show me what to do to you," he demanded.

I drizzled lube over our cocks before stroking his shaft. He shivered from his kneeled position. "Shit, Franky, you're big."

"So are you," he said, thrusting into my hand.

"There's big, and then there's *this*," I said, squeezing him, my fingers almost meeting around his girth. "This is... *Fuck*, your cock's gonna do a number on me, baby." My hole clenched around nothing, and I needed that problem rectified sooner rather than later.

"Come closer." I encouraged him forward by his dick until he hovered over me, forearms braced on either side of me. Holding on to our twin erections required both of my hands, and Franky caught on quickly, pumping his hips, gliding the underside of his slick dick along the pulsing vein of mine.

I rocked with him, matching his excitement, unable to do anything but hold on to us as he grew bolder and less cautious above me.

"That's right, Franky," I crooned. I wanted to save the best for last. To show him the type of pleasure he never imagined he could achieve with nothing more than foreplay, then I would give him my ass and send him skyrocketing into addiction.

He kissed me savagely, encasing my throat in one large palm, tightening his hold unconsciously as he bucked in and out of my excruciating grip. He'd leave bruises, for sure, and would possibly kill me in the process, but I didn't care, because what we were doing felt that good. What we were doing was worth dying for.

I let loose a strangled whimper when my lack of oxygen became too unbearable to hide. Franky released me, and I expected a string of apologies to follow, but he was too far gone in his lust-haze to spend a second on regret.

He sank his teeth into my shoulder, nearly breaking the skin, replacing one near-death pleasure with another. Our dicks slipped from my grasp as I cried out, but Franky kept bucking like a bull, his dick sawing a path through my pubic hair in search of my erection.

He dragged his teeth higher, and I lifted my chin, giving him room to tear my fucking throat out if he so pleased.

Franky's fingers scraped across my scalp as the digits bunched in my hair, and he sucked at my neck so hard I felt it in my asshole as if there was a direct line there. I needed to be fucked. I needed Franky's obscene cock inside me, pulverizing me.

He moved on to my earlobe, then my jawline, meanwhile he'd sealed off the space where my hands had held us together, now rutting against my cock with such accuracy that my assistance was no longer needed.

Franky attacked every area on my body that he could manage to bite or bruise without sacrificing what we had going on down below.

"I'm sorry," he panted, popping his mouth off my nipple. "But I *need* to hurt you."

I got it. I understood from the feral glaze in his eyes, from the barbaric way he moved above me... Franky was now a changed man. His world would never look the same once we left this bed. Lies that he'd convinced himself were true would no longer be the easy pills to swallow. He'd just discovered his latest addiction, and he wanted to make me pay for it.

"Don't ever fucking apologize while you're fucking me, Franky." My nipples burned to the third-degree, my throat was on fire, and I'd likely be bald by the time he was done with me. "Destroy me, Franky." I turned my head the other way, presenting the other side of my neck in offering, and he didn't waste a second before sealing his mouth over the unblemished skin.

We were drenched in each other's sweat, the sheet simultaneously popped off all four corners of the mattress, and the nightstand wobbled. I shuddered at imagining what would happen when he eventually shoved inside of me.

Franky's hair glistened, the dark strands swinging like a pendulum as he raced like a fucking horse toward his orgasm. We were both so damn close to drowning each other in cum.

He dug his forehead into mine. "I'm close," he gritted out before stealing another tongue-battling kiss.

"Not yet. Not until your cock is inside of me, Franky. I *need* your cum inside of me," I panted, feeling my own climax tap at my lower spine. "Just the tip. For round one, just give me the tip, then jerk off while it's inside of me." I wanted to be tempted and teased. I wanted my hole ungrateful and hungry for more. And I wanted him crazed, his hold on reality gone. I wanted him violent and needing more than what the tip could offer us both.

"What do I need to do?" he asked, moaning as he fought back his orgasm.

"Sit up," I said.

Franky backed into a kneeling position, his face contorted with genuine torture as he gripped his drooling cock at the base. He needed to come. We both did.

"Lube your fingers," I said swiftly, hauling my knees to my ears as I continued to work my shaft.

Franky fumbled the bottle twice before popping the cap and making a mess in the process. "Slip one finger in, *slowly*, at first," I said, leisurely whipping my dick. "Fuck!" My head fell back and pressed into the pillow when one finger breached me. I hadn't had anal sex in a while. Franky would be a terrifyingly tight fit.

"That's it," I said, peering down my chest again, needing to see every centimeter of his thick fingers vanish inside my hole. "Another, then crook them."

Franky did as told, adding another finger, sliding them in to the very last knuckle. "You're so damn hot," he said, showing his teeth, and now fucking his fist too.

Now four digits deep into me, my ass sucked on his hand while the pace of our jack-off session exceeded the speed necessary to keep our loads in their sacs.

Working on instinct, Franky crooked his fingers, tapping my gland until I fucking detonated. Keening, I called out his name, spurting cum until I'd left a fucking stream of it all over the front of my body.

"Leland," Franky said between gritted teeth, still finger-pounding my nub, still painfully jacking his cock.

"Now," I said, wringing every drop of cum from my dick. "Stick it in now, Franky."

Franky fell over me again, leading just his cockhead into my snug entrance like we'd agreed. I hissed through the burn, my orgasm lengthening.

He pumped himself in short, punishing strokes, his crown swelling just beyond my hole before a river of warmth went barreling through me.

"Christ...*fuck*," he spit out.

"That's right," I said, fully spent, head rolling to one side. "Don't pull out until you're done, Franky."

The hand holding his weight up slipped, taking him down, the air whooshing out of me as he fell onto my sticky chest, his cock breaching me more than halfway now. I cried out from the invasion.

Franky plunged all the way inside, shooting me higher up the bed until my head banged against the headboard. His mouth and throat moved as if he were gagging on his words. "So-sorry," he said, even as he unapologetically kept plowing and fucking me full of his spunk.

I'd never felt so full, so overwhelmed, so fucking complete as I did with his dick fully sheathed in me. My hole spasmed, puckered like a set of lips, opening to accommodate every sinfully thick inch of him.

Franky secured the headboard with one hand, using it as leverage as he continued to roll into me, in complete denial that the sex was over. "More," he said as his climax ebbed. "I need... more."

"There's plenty where that came from," I said, completely and utterly annihilated.

Franky sat up, slipping wetly from me, gaze chained to my jizz-smeared chest, then lowering to his cock and balls, both stained with his own release. Next he stalked the helping of cum leaking from my ass to soak through the sheet.

I lowered my legs, my feet hitting the bed.

"Can I?" Franky asked, his tongue darting across his lips.

"I'd be mad if you didn't," I said, bearing down until a gush of cum erupted from my used hole.

Franky sucked me clean, slurping and moaning, mouth sealed over my asshole. His need to ingest cum was a physical thing, so intense that he hadn't even stopped to consider whose cum he so eagerly gulped down.

Stretched out on his stomach and writhing, Franky ate from me indiscriminately, lapping and praising me as his palms split my cheeks apart. I gripped the backs of my thighs to make the deep dive easier on his tongue.

I circled my hips, watching him go to work on me. "I don't think you got it all, Franky," I said, taunting him to do something about it. He sent a middle finger straight into me, withdrawing and sucking the white off the thick digit before sending it back in for more.

Once satisfied that he'd digested it all, he crawled up my body, his tongue flattened to my skin, licking up the mess I'd made. He even got the drop under my chin, then retraced his steps, devoting all his attention to my nut sac and dick.

"Fuck, wait," I hissed, my cock sensitive to the touch.

"No," he growled, batting my hands off his hair. He buried his face in my groin, chuffing and smelling and kissing my short pubic hairs.

Franky's knees spread wider on the mattress, and I savored the sight of his ass tensing and releasing as he fucked the memory foam. In no time, my cock hardened again.

"Let me ride you, Franky. Let me show you how good I can make you feel."

He rose to his hands and knees with interest in his eyes. His balls hung between his legs, his cock filling, aiming at my center like a loaded weapon. The burly crown stretched until it shone like a gem, the long, heavyset shaft veiny and darker than the rest of his body. Franky licked the creamy corners of his mouth.

"Say yes, Franky. Say you'll let me fuck your cock," I said with feigned bashfullness, undulating as he watched.

"Jesus, Leland." Franky slid to his haunches, lifting and squeezing his pectorals as if he needed to be milked there too.

I clambered to my knees, suctioning my mouth over the perky nipple he fed to me, suckling enthusiastically as he roughly kneaded his other pec.

"Damn it, that feels good," he whimpered, his cock thumping loudly against his lower abs as he humped the air. Franky held me by the back of the head, mouth slack, eyebrows shooting into the air in disbelief.

"I think you've found yourself a fetish, Franky," I said when I was through. "I wonder how many more we'll discover." Our knees touched, our chests heaved, and our cocks stood tall as we took a split second to soak in the moment. Franky hadn't let go of his pec yet, and my saliva glistened from the pert nipple.

"I think so," he said with wonder, quickly wrapping a hand around his base and quivering. I mopped up the clear fluid at his tip with my tongue.

His fingers grazed along his neck as he fixated on the hand-prints lining mine. I couldn't see them, but the sweet sting of my skin told me they were there. More pre-cum spit from his slit at the sight of them. "I've left marks on you," he said.

I didn't answer. I was too busy fucking myself open on a hand drenched in lube. "Are you going to let me ride you, Franky? Are you going to let me ruin you?"

"Yes," he said in a trance-like state as he absently fondled his balls.

I slapped his hand out of the way and squatted over his lap, then swallowed his dick with my hole. "Has it ever felt like this, Franky. Has someone ever wanted you this much?"

"No," he breathed.

"This is my cock now," I said, even though time would prove that to be a lie. For now it was the ultimate truth. "I'm the only one who fucks this dick from now on, do you hear me?" My thighs ached as I fucked him with exuberance. "We get to say and do what we want when we're like this, Franky. We can be whoever we want, live out all our fantasies when we're together like this."

Franky dug his fingers into my hip, getting high off the game, deciding to join in. "Your ass belongs to me, Leland," he growled, the tip of his nose touching mine. "And so does your cock and your mouth. Your whole damn body is mine." Franky's palm whistled through the air, crashing against my ass and tug-ging a yelp from me. "Say it," he snarled.

"No," I said on a whimper, only to have him spank me hard-er next time. "Fuck!"

"Say it!" he shouted, fine droplets of saliva pelting my chin. I said nothing, fucking him with a stone-cold expression, causing him to get carried away.

"I can do this all night," he said, hand cracking against the now raw flesh of my ass. I could no longer move. I sat on his dick, taking my punishment, sweat blinding me. "Say it," he hissed.

"My-my body is yours, Franky."

Franky took control then, force-fucking me on and off his erection. "I fuck this snug ass from here on out. No one else. And your cock gets no action unless it's in my mouth or my hands."

"Fuck," I said shakily, the slapping sounds of my ass meeting his lap getting me off just as much as his threats. "You're good at this, Franky."

"This isn't a game," he said, ripping me off his cock and dumping me onto my back. I bounced on the mattress and then he was on me and in me again, manhandling my wrists above my head. "You fuck anyone else, or allow anyone to fuck you, and you'll have to answer to me, Leland."

I rolled us, planting my fists into the pillows next to his head, expertly riding his dick, purposely ruining him for anyone else. Our sweat mingled, the sound of our sex boisterous and slippery as his fingers slotted into the handprints at my hips. We were going to break the fucking bed.

"Who do you answer to, Franky?" I asked, anger taking over as my thrusts became more determined, more point driven. "Who else has handled your cock this good? Who else have you been able to fuck so thoroughly and with all your goddamn might, Franky?" I leaned over his mouth, licking across the seam. "You can't break me, Franky." *At least not my body.*

The fucking turned animalistic, more so than it had already been, as if my final words were a challenge to him, and I braced myself against the headboard as he planted his feet flat on the bed and tore into me. All I could do was stay on my knees, hold on for dear life, and accept him as his cock charged in and out of me, slipping and catching on my rim.

Franky heaved up and wrapped his teeth around a nipple. I tossed my head back and cursed, my dick thrumming as it leaked against my belly. He stilled, biting and sucking my flesh as he unloaded inside me again, trembling and groaning around my beard-burned skin.

"Touch me, Franky," I managed to get out. I was coming before his fist had fully enclosed around me.

A few minutes of heavy breathing passed before I was on my back again with a wild-eyed Franky hungrily taking in my cum-splattered abs. "Hold on," I said, as his head lowered. "Answer my question."

"After," he said, consumed by yet another found addiction.

"Now," I ordered, holding him by the hair and fighting against his resistance, fighting harder when he stretched his tongue toward my navel.

Franky blinked, his cum-lust clearing, and my heart skipped a beat as I waited for him to say something. "For as long as this lasts, be it one night, one week, or several months... You'll be the only one I have sex with, Leland."

I chuckled inwardly at his use of the word *sex*. "So it's only called *fucking* when you're high on dick, huh?"

He swatted my outer thigh, hard enough to make me flinch, hard enough to make me swallow. He tongued me spotless, moaning during the process, then ordered, "Get on your hands and knees, Leelee Bear."

He wanted me positioned like a dog, adjusting my limbs until I painted the picture he had in his mind. "This is how you should be," he whispered, trailing a finger down my arched spine. "You're beautiful like this." He ate his cum from my hole again, complaining about there not being enough.

Franky didn't give my ass a break all night. When his cock couldn't keep up with the rest of him, and his tongue had had enough, he fingered me, watching me intently as he learned what angle and what pace pleased me the most.

He became a student on the subject of my desires. At times his exploration felt clinical, but that's what made it hot. I was his test subject, and I'd teach him all he wanted to know and then some.

We showered as the sun rose and then I filled the empty space in his bed. *I'm here now,* I wanted to say, *for however long this lasts.* My body was too fucked out, and my brain too tired to articulate anything.

Franky hesitated for a brief second before hauling me into his chest, stroking my hair as our breaths evened.

"I don't like Noon," he whispered.

"Why, because he's not afraid of you?" I asked, yawning. Noon didn't intimidate easily, if at all. That had to be an unwelcome change for Franky.

"No," he said, "I can respect him for that."

"Then why?" I knew the answer, but I needed him to say it, and not for clarity's sake. I needed to know he was jealous. I needed to know I wasn't the only one who was imperfect in that way.

"Because he's had you," he said, exhaustion weighing down his words.

"It was a long time ago, and it didn't mean anything."

"Say it again," he said, the hand stroking my hair now twisting tightly in it.

"It didn't mean anything," I said, giving him what he needed, nestling into him further when his fingers relaxed and scratched at my scalp. I thought that was the end of it, the end of our night, until whispered words pulled me from the tugging hands of sleep.

"I know you prefer one great friend over many, because it lessens your chances of people hurting you. Of them leaving you. I know you also prefer one friend over none, because being completely alone reminds you of how lonely you are. I know deep down you believe in your artistic capabilities, but you do things like spend all your money prepaying your rent, because it gives you an excuse to not pursue your secret ambitions. I know you have one-night stands because you're afraid of what falling in love will do to you. I should be petrified of hurting you, of being the one to prove you right, but I'm selfish, and I want you, Leland. Even if it's just for a little while."

I could hardly hear him past the pounding of his heart and the fevered screaming of mine. I tried to lift my head off his chest, but he held me there.

"And I know that what your mother did to you still haunts you. And not just because I can hear you cry out in your sleep for her sometimes. I know it because your beautiful soul, and your beautiful golden eyes, tell me every time the wall around them opens up for me. And I know you never open either of those things for anyone. Maybe not even for Noon. I'm not even sure you know they're open for me."

We were quiet for a while, listening to the birds raise their voices outside.

"What are we doing, Leland?" Franky asked.

"I don't know," I admitted.

I knew what I thought we were doing, but I had a bad feeling that what I thought and what was fact were two totally different and complicated things.

What I did know, right then, was that Noon was wrong. *Franky does know me.*

CHAPTER 12

Franklin

"**I** feel like shit on wheels," Leland complained, blowing his nose. "Sorry for getting you sick." His cold symptoms had fully developed. It started with a sneeze for me that morning and a hacking cough from him.

"It's not your fault," I said, pushing up in bed to recline against the headboard with him. "I knew you were sick when I kissed you."

"Do you regret it?" he asked.

I thought his question over for as long as it took, not wanting to lie or give an answer that didn't encompass the whole truth. "No, I don't regret it. No matter how much I should."

I plucked a Kleenex from the box on the nightstand just in time to catch my sneeze with it.

"Tell me about Theo," Leland said. "That picture hasn't left the coffee table in weeks. And I see you staring at it sometimes. He was more than a friend, wasn't he?"

"No, he wasn't. At least I'm not sure. I cared for him a lot, and at some point I did suspect that something had shifted between us, but I was young, figured I didn't know myself or know what I was feeling. My father sent his family away before we could figure anything out, and I'd never experienced those same feelings again." I shrugged.

"How did it start? When did things change between you two?"

I waited out Leland's coughing fit, using the time to think back on all the little things, the little signs I'd had from Theo. The ones I thought maybe I'd imagined. "I'd catch him watching me, and he'd blush before turning away. We used to race to our favorite pond on the property, holding hands. Nothing unusual for us. Then one day the way he held my hand changed. His hold on me became...protective, I suppose. Maybe proprietary is a better word.

"Gloria used to make these delicious hoagies for us to take to the pond. And homemade iced-tea. Theo and I would fight over the biggest piece, because she could never quite manage to cut it evenly. We grew older and closer, and one day Theo gave up the bigger half graciously, and continued to do so. And then one day, seeing him became an event. Something I had to shower and pick out the right outfit for." I shook my head at the memory. "He made my stomach flutter, but we were both still too young and too scared to examine why. And then he was gone, and so were the flutters."

"And you've never felt those flutters again?" Leland asked.

"Not for a long time," I admitted, staring into those gorgeous brown eyes of his as tiny waves rippled through my core. "Not until you."

Leland and I spent the next several days curled up together in bed, or recuperating on the sofa, and on one warm night, the boat. We picked over soup, drank a profuse amount of hot tea, and even attempted to kiss, but it either ended with Leland coughing until his ribs ached or me pulling away to sneeze. We were magnetic, and even through sickness, we craved one another.

We settled for holding each other through our fever-induced chills and taking turns hand feeding each other. I'd never felt so cared for before. Maybe because I could never afford to be sick, or maybe I'd simply never given anyone else the opportunity to, had never given myself permission to be vulnerable enough. Another thing to feel guilty for. I'd set everyone up for failure when it came to me."

I'd learned a lot during those days with Leland. I learned I could be a baby when sick so long as I didn't have the pressure of always needing to be the strong one. I learned I could be nurturing, and weak, and childlike when I could trust that the person I was with didn't need me to be a pillar for them.

My kids needed me to be strong, my wife needed me to be strong, and Nexcom did too. Leland just needed me to be me.

Leland and I shared a different kind of intimacy that week. One I was afraid to lose after only recently discovering how much I needed it. Being with him felt like thriving. It felt like progress after feeling stagnant for far too long.

My heart beat differently with him. It beat like I imagined it was supposed to. Wild with excitement, then steady as it filled with peace. I never wanted it to end.

But how many people was I willing to hurt to hold on to my peace? That was the part I struggled with.

◆ ◆ ◆

"Leelee Bear!" I called, rounding the patio from the side of the house. I yelled it again, amused as he cursed the day I was born.

"Is that how you treat the person who went through the trouble of making sure dinner was ready when you got home?" he said when I crossed through the open wall and into the kitchen. I didn't spare a glance for the food. I enveloped him in a hug, kissing him passionately, showing him how much I missed him.

"Someone's in a good mood," he said.

"Yeah, I can finally breathe through both nostrils and my appetite's back."

"*And* because you haven't been away from me for more than five minutes in a long time, so you missed me. Admit it," he said, circling his arms around my back. We'd separated to run our individual errands. Leland needed more art supplies and to hand in paperwork for the bartending course he'd registered for, and I needed to put out another fire over at Nexcom.

Normally, the latter would have affected my mood negatively for the duration of the day, but seeing Betty haphazardly parked in the driveway, and knowing her owner waited inside for me, had inverted my frown.

"Should I be admitting that?" I asked. I'd told Leland I couldn't make him any promises. I'd said I was no good for him and would likely hurt the both of us. He'd in turn said that he knew what he was getting himself into. He was the guy who didn't commit, who didn't allow himself to fall. I'd been counting on his boundaries to help me create my own, but here we were, two teen lovebirds, chirping and flying into each other at all hours of the day. It felt good, and somehow that felt bad. Like skydiving without a parachute.

"Sure," he said, without a care in the world. "If we're going to do this, let's not be miserable while doing it or hold back in the process."

"I'm not so sure that's a good idea, Leland." I fondled the shell of his ear.

He nodded, his lips forming a hard line. "You're right. Sorry. I'm as new to this as you are. It's just, you're my friend, too, you know?"

"Yeah, I know." It made it hard to draw straight lines. Made it hard to know which of those squiggly lines shouldn't be crossed, because even if we weren't lovers now, I still would've missed my friend. "I don't want to lose our friendship by trying to keep our distance as lovers. If that makes sense."

"Makes just as much sense as all that sexy caveman shit you were spewing when I rode the fuck out of your cock," he said, and I groaned, covering his mouth with my palm. He pulled at my fingers, trying to free himself so he could embarrass me further. It seemed to be a new hobby of his.

Leland pinched my nose and smacked his other hand over my mouth, leaving me with no backup option for air supply. His eyes glowed with delight and anticipation of me waving the white flag first. I let him go, gasping for air once he released me as well.

His cheeks were rosy with joy, his shirt askew. *My* shirt askew. He'd taken to helping himself to my clothes now that he'd moved into my bedroom. They swam on his smaller frame, often drooping off one creamy, pale shoulder, calling my mouth to his exposed skin. I suspected that was why he wore them. I didn't complain.

"Laugh it up," I said, "because you'll regret every word when I get you back under me."

"And when will that be?" he asked huskily, flushing for a completely different reason now.

"Soon. Now. Immediately," I said, bringing his fingers back to my nose. Leland snatched his hand away, hiding it behind his back.

"Give me your hand back," I said.

"No," he replied, squirming as I fought for his hand and won. I uncurled his tight fist, inhaling noisily from the heel of his palm all the way to his finger tips, closing my eyes after getting a hit of the dark aroma. "I thought that's what I smelled."

His cock lengthened inside his shorts, but that didn't mean anything. At twenty-five, Leland became aroused whenever the wind blew, which happened a lot when living close to the ocean. Keeping up had never been an issue for me in the past, but Leland would definitely be a challenge to my stamina.

"What were you doing before I walked in here?" I crowded him into the island.

"Nothing," he answered, stuffing his hands in his pockets.

"It doesn't *smell* like nothing."

"Like I said, I cooked. There's a burger and fries waiting on the stove." He motioned his head over my shoulder.

"I'm not hungry for that." I flicked my tongue over his bottom lip, and he gave a hum of approval.

"You never know until you try it," he said. "I made a dipping sauce for the fries. It's thick and salty. Just the way you like it."

For the first time since arriving home, I took my eyes off him. The burger and fries were already plated, a clear portion cup containing a creamy, white sauce sat next to it.

"You should try it," Leland insisted, but I was already on my way over there.

I brought the portion cup to my nose, nearly drowning my nostrils in the heady cum in my impatience. "Jesus," I croaked, my salivary glands activating. I buried my tongue inside Leland's cum, the sounds coming from me inhuman. I scooped up a mouthful and tilted my head back, feeling it slide like honey down my throat to pool in my belly.

Leland clicked his tongue. "If I were a different man, I'd say you had a problem."

I was too deep into my new addiction to offer a retort, so I dipped a couple fries into the cum cup instead before shoving them all into my mouth. "Why does it taste so good?" I asked.

Leland shrugged. "Could be all the pineapple I eat. Should I be worried you'll swap woodworking for cum eating as your new, favorite pastime?"

"That would be a valid concern," I said. "I'll be sure to keep the fridge stocked with pineapple." I wanted to pin him down and suck my next meal from him. My cock throbbed painfully behind the confines of my clothing.

I fingered what was left in the cup, making sure I didn't miss a drop. I wasn't satisfied. It wasn't enough. "I need a little more,"

I said greedily, and Leland nodded, reading the question in my eyes. "Now?"

He nodded again, tugging the waistband of his shorts over his erection.

"You're already so close," I said, caging him in, our heads touching as we gazed at the fluid beading at his slit.

"Yeah," he agreed, tucking the shirt hem between his chin and chest as he spread his pre-cum over his pretty, pink crown.

"Faster," I ordered, nails scraping along the island's edge.

"Fuck, you're impatient," Leland gritted as he worked the top half of his shaft. "Put a finger in me, Franky. The biggest one you got." He yanked his shorts lower with his free hand, then spread his legs as far as he could with them now hovering around his knees. "I need something in my ass."

Leland was the one doing all the work, but my heart pumped frantically.

"Spit on it," he said, when I licked a stripe up my middle finger. "Make it dirty, Franky."

"Damn it, Leland," I swore, shutting my eyes briefly. I was dangerously close to unloading unassisted in my pants.

"Do it now," he panted. I felt every bit the fumbling virgin, following Leland's more experienced lead. "Don't go slow. Do it like you're taking what's yours. I wanna feel it burn, Franky."

My knuckles pressed against the warm skin of his inner thighs. I had my finger lodged deep inside him before he'd said my name. On fire now, and with a sense of entitlement, a sense of ownership over him, I wrapped a hand around his throat, forcing my way into his mouth and eating his cries. "Like that?" I asked, working his prostate and taking his mouth again. The way his ass sucked on my finger as he jerked himself off harder and faster was all the yes I needed.

His Adam's apple bobbed below my palm, and feeling bold, I freed his neck to squeeze a thumb and forefinger between his jaw, forcing his mouth open and spitting straight into the back of it. Leland came on a shout, and I gobbled that up too.

His cum dribbled down his chest to the nest of short curls at his groin. I fell to my knees, ferreting through his pubic hair for what fell there, then sweeping the flat of my tongue from his navel to his chest. There were a few cum smears on his fingers, and I got that too before unzipping my pants and hauling my cock out.

The rush of hot cum exploded up my shaft, and I came all over the island's white cabinets. Leland's spread legs played goalie post.

"Sharing is caring, Franky," Leland said as I tilted toward the streaks of cum with an open mouth.

I offered him a finger full, then selfishly ate the rest. "You greedy fucker," he said, pushing me to my back before falling on top of me. He kissed me with the intention of stealing the morsel I hadn't swallowed off my tongue yet. I held him tight, transferring what was left to him.

"You really do have a problem," he said, stroking my hair, staring into my eyes with an expression that should have scared me, an expression that probably would after this moment passed.

"Yeah, I do," I agreed, not sure we were talking about the same problem, because I was looking at mine.

CHAPTER 13

Outside of Noon slipping into bed with me when in the mood to piss me off, I'd spent my entire adult life actively avoiding sharing a bed with anyone, then Franky came along and made it so I couldn't sleep without him.

That should've terrified me—and most nights it did, but tonight when I woke up to his cold, empty side of the bed, I wanted nothing more than to have him returned to me, wanted nothing more than the feel of his broad back nestled into my chest, because big, bad, Franky had a thing for being the little spoon.

He'd said it was a new phenomenon he couldn't quite grasp. I said it was because he'd always had to be the one to protect, but here, safe with me, he now got to be the one protected. He kissed me breathless for that.

A cool breeze pebbled my skin beneath the thin sheet covering me. I rolled to my side, turning on the lamp to confirm the balcony doors were open. I knew where I'd find Franky.

I kicked out of the sheets, first snatching my t-shirt from the floor, but it'd been shredded beyond repair by Franky's urgent hands. I tried my underwear next, but he'd slammed me against the wall and tore a football sized hole into the back of those so he could get his cock inside of me.

Franky hadn't kept his hands, or his dick, off or out of me ever since we were both well enough for him to do so. In the last forty-eight hours we'd done everything from hand jobs to blow jobs to finger fucking to fighting over cum.

He'd been more than familiar with the concept of sixty-nine-ing. It was obvious he'd had hands-on experience with it. I had to remind myself that being new to having sex with a man didn't mean Franky wasn't exceedingly proficient in the act of sex itself. He'd mastered the art of fucking, something that came with practice, a skill he'd had long before ever touching me.

Thinking about what that meant angered me in a way it shouldn't have, in a way I'd promised myself it wouldn't. But a fed ego kept the anger under control, and my ego fed off of knowing that although he'd without a doubt pleased others with his mastery, no one had ever truly pleased him. No one but me.

This will end, Leland. I'd begun mentally preparing myself for the end of this part of our relationship by repeating those words daily, and I did so now as I rounded the bed and exited the bedroom naked.

This will end, Leland.

The living room wall was partially open. We'd closed it before going to bed. Well, before Franky had rushed me up the stairs only to tear into me right outside the bedroom door.

"We were so close," I'd said, face smashed against the drywall as he spit-shined his cock and launched it into me.

"I couldn't wait any longer," he'd said, his harsh breaths jabbing at my ear. He'd spun me around after, peeled my damaged underwear off and pitched one of my calves over his shoulder so he could fish his tongue inside my sticky hole.

He'd licked my cum from the inside of my underwear next, then ordered me onto the bed as he relaxed onto his knees, manipulating his cock, pleading for it to cooperate. *"I need you one more time."*

"Can't keep up, old man?" I'd taunted. That had done the trick.

Blinking out of those delicious memories, I folded my arms against the chill as I approached Franky near the dock.

He wore his black silk robe, the sash and lower half billowing behind him like a cape.

I hugged him from behind, and he exhaled deeply, melting into my touch. I took that to mean whatever was wrong with him, I'd made it better. I shot a warning down the line to my heart. *This will end, Leland.*

Franky pivoted to face me, jaw hardening in disapproval from my lack of clothing. "Do you want to get sick again?" he asked. "It's freezing out here."

"So keep me warm, then," I said sweetly, kissing the patch of salt and pepper stubble on his cheek. I looped my arms around his t-shirt clad back, and he wrapped the two ends of his robe around me.

"What's wrong, Franky? Why's your sexy ass out here instead of arched into my crotch as we sleep?" I groped his buns of steel.

"Jasper called. I didn't want to wake you."

"I'm not the lightest sleeper in the world. I'm pretty sure stepping into the hall would've been sufficient enough."

"And then I came out here to think."

"You and your ocean," I said. Franky brought all his problems to the water. "It's almost midnight, is everything okay?"

He grunted, kissing the wrinkles between my brows as his arms tightened around me. "He didn't expect me to be asleep. I'm usually finishing up with work around this time." Franky sounded torn up about that.

"Is that what's got you so restless now?" I gently eased his bottom lip from the clutches of his teeth. "Are you feeling guilty about how much you worked?"

"There's that, but... Forget it." He shook his head. "It's probably nothing, and I shouldn't be talking to you about—" Franky quieted abruptly.

"Talking to me about what?" I asked. "Or about *who*?" I tried when he didn't respond to my first question. "Is something wrong with Selene?"

Franky glanced over to the ocean again as if searching for solace. I wanted to be the one to give him that.

"Hey," I said. "You're talking to your friend now, not the man you've fucked twelve ways to Sunday all over this house. What's wrong?"

"He said he spoke to his mother earlier, but only for a short while because she was exhausted."

"Okay..." I said slowly, running his words back in case it was a riddle that my midnight-brain was too dense to solve.

"Selene is never exhausted, Leland. She thrives on the day-to-day, wants to make every minute count, and often needs to be bribed to sleep. If she was tired she would never readily admit to it."

I swallowed hard, not expecting his undisguised reverence of her to hit me like a battering ram to the gut. *He loves her.* Of course he did. He'd never claimed otherwise, and just because he now enjoyed cock, didn't mean he suddenly hated—

"And more importantly," he said, putting a plug in my line of thinking. "She's never too tired for them. She'd pin her eyelids to her forehead if it meant staying awake for them. Even if it was just to sit and watch them sleep. *Always.*"

"She sounds like an amazing mother," I said. *An amazing wife too,* I thought resentfully.

"She is," he said, clueless to the not-so-nice emotions swimming through me. "It's got me concerned, but I don't know if I have a right to be." Franky looked at me, looked *into* me like I was his crystal ball. Like I was his...*friend.*

I put my confusing feelings for Selene aside, reminding myself that *this* part of Franky's and my relationship, the part that made it okay for our cocks to align the way they were now, would likely end.

I'd promised him—but mostly myself—that I could handle this affair for however long it lasted, that I wouldn't push him for more or try to influence his decision about his marriage. They had history, they had kids, they had reputations to uphold, they had love. Him being the happiest he's ever been when with me didn't mean ending his marriage was a done deal.

I ignored the pesky voice that said my promise had been made before he touched me. That said I couldn't have known his touch would feel like my missing piece.

Whether he left Selene or not had to be up to him, and him leaving didn't mean he'd choose me. Did I even want to be chosen?

"Call her," I said. "If not tonight, then in the morning. You have every right to be worried about her."

He hugged me closer, pressing the side of his face into mine and whispering his thanks. He'd needed to hear that, needed to hear that he could still care for her, still love her. *And maybe even still want her.* My blunt nails dug into his back, causing him to eye me curiously. I dropped my gaze.

"Come, let me get you out of the cold." He removed his robe and held it out for me to slip into it.

"Only if you promise to ditch all those clothes when we get inside," I said, disguising my distress with flirtation. Nothing convinced Franky that I was okay quite like when I flirted with him.

"Promise," he said. I now had a love-hate relationship with that word.

Franky led me inside by the hand before fisting and tugging his shirt over his head and removing his pajama bottoms. He wore nothing underneath, and it was a damn good thing because his cock was stiff enough to have busted a hole through the tight, fancy boxer briefs he typically wore.

He reclined along the length of the sofa, one foot flat on the floor and the other settling over the arm on the opposite side.

This created a sliver of space between his thighs, which he gestured to. "Come lie with me."

"This couch wasn't made for the both of us," I said, even as I let the robe drift off my shoulders to pool at my feet.

I dimmed the lights to something romantic and insinuating, then stopped at the arm of the sofa where his foot perched.

"I'm actually counting on that," he said, holding an arm out for me. "Makes for a tighter squeeze."

I ignored his outstretched hand until it fell. He grinned seductively, tucking both arms behind his head, more than okay with me taking my time to drink him in. "Why do you have to be so fucking sexy?" I asked, disgusted by how much I wanted him at all times. It was tragic, really, because with every hour, with every fucking minute that passed, my craving for this man grew without limits.

"You sound torn up about it," he said, chuckling. The rich, harmful-to-my-heart chuckle that made me think of more nights like this and an infinity of morning afters.

This will end, Leland.

I swirled a finger around the pad of one of his perfect toes, and his humor faded, replaced with a flash of warning in his eyes as he inched his foot away from my exploring hands. Franky was ticklish. I'd discovered that little nugget after a morning of breakfast in bed where I ate my French toast off his abs. There'd been a lot of clean up required. Syrup had gotten *everywhere*.

He'd gone red with the effort of not squirming away from my tongue as it swept over every part of him.

"I'm just glad I get to enjoy it before it's gone, old man," I teased.

"I'll have you know my father had a six-pack until the very end."

"Mmmm," I hummed. "So sexiness is in the genes."

"Stamina too," he said, canting his hips, his ridiculously well-proportioned cock hard as steel. I enjoyed playful Franky. To be honest, I enjoyed every shade of Franky I could get; the darker the better, though.

His body was a work of art, and the graying at his temples and beard only amplified his hotness. Made him distinguished. And he fucked like a zoo animal, like a beast trying to break out of its cage. Sometimes it felt like his goal was to snap me in two and leave me for dead on the side of the road—or bed.

My mouth watered as he laid there watching me watch him, his dick spasming as it stretched further. The tip of my hard cock grew wet. *Always wet for Franky.*

"I don't want to fuck you, Leland," Franky said with a barely-there grip on his aggression. "At least not yet. But you're making it hard."

"Yeah, *really* hard," I said, wondering if tonight would be the night I managed to suck down more than half his dick without gagging on it—although gagging until I cried was half the fun.

"Get over here," he said, silently laughing, his shoulders not the only thing shaking as a result.

"I give up my view if I lie down, though," I complained, entranced by his strong, thick thighs and the light dusting of hair along his calf muscles.

"Ask yourself," he said, readying his argument. "Do you want to watch the game from the sidelines or on the field?"

I was between his legs in a nanosecond, snuggling into him and moaning as our cocks rubbed together.

"You're so easy," he said.

"Hey, no slut shaming," I said, balancing my chin on his chest.

We were okay with letting our lust cool, although it never went cold. I idly sifted through the thin spattering of hair over his pecs, sucking his nipples at his request as he drew shapes along my back. For now we were content to let things unfold naturally moment to moment.

"Tell me more about your art-bar," Franky said. He'd asked me the dreaded *where do you see yourself in five years* question yesterday, and because I was no closer to an answer now than I'd been when my school counselor had asked me the same thing at fifteen, I gave him the first thing I could think of, which was the art-bar, even though it would never happen.

I hadn't turned the question on him, because I didn't want to hear about all the great things he'd have going on in five years that didn't include me.

This will end, Leland.

I should've known I'd only bought myself a reprieve, because Franky was determined to see the best in me, to see what great things awaited me, and he was good at tempting me to see and believe it too. He'd never let the mention of an impossible dream of mine skate by without making a concentrated effort to support it, and I did the same for him.

I'd put a listing on one of those marketplace sites for a few of his furniture pieces that were sitting in the garage. I'd done it behind his back, not wanting to discourage him if none of it sold.

"*It sold!*" I'd yelled a couple days ago, stampeding onto the patio and scaring Franky to death.

"*Damn, it,*" he'd cursed, dropping the hinge he'd been screwing onto a wardrobe.

"*It sold,*" I'd said again, calmer this time, shoving my phone, which displayed the listing, at his face.

"*It sold?*" he'd said, taking the device from me. "*Is that the chest from the garage?*"

"*Yup. It sold in less than twenty-four hours.*"

"*It sold,*" he'd said again, this time in a whisper.

"Earth to Leland," he said, snapping his fingers in front of my face, forcing me to leave my memories behind. "The art-bar," he prompted.

"Only if you tell me more about your storefront idea," I said.

"Deal," he said, pinching my cheek when I frowned up at him. Should've known he'd be willing to do anything to get me talking. "I'd love to open a small shop where I would sell custom pieces, where no two would be the same. I don't want to go into the business of mass production. I want to make items people will cherish for years to come and hand down to their children because they know something like it could never be bought again. I don't want a factory full of machines and people bringing my ideas to life, watering them down and cheapening the quality. I want to build it all myself," he said. "I want my work to have integrity."

"What's stopping you?" I asked. "Do it."

"Yeah, I could see the headlines now," he said, his hands smoothing over my shoulders. "Franklin Kincaid walks away from Nexcom to sell chairs."

"You could start the company up under a different name. A pseudonym," I suggested.

"I may not be recognizable by the average person walking along the street, but Franklin Kincaid venturing into a new sector of the business world would not go unnoticed, no matter what name I used. Someone like me doesn't get to just vanish. The vultures would hunt me down, and the press would make me their next meal. Everyone would know."

"Would that be so bad?"

He smoothed his knuckles along my cheek, one side of his frown ticking up into a weighted grin. "Maybe not, Leelee Bear."

The nickname didn't even upset me anymore. Not when he stared at me like that while saying it. I'd rather use my energy in holding on to the feelings his indulgent gaze stirred in me. *Because this will...* Oh, fuck it. I couldn't finish the habitual mantra. Not now, not when all I wanted to do was capture this moment to memory, to charcoal-pencil-and-paper it.

"Where are you going?" Franky asked as I rushed for the stairs. "We still need to discuss the art-bar!"

"That can wait until later. Don't move a muscle!" I jogged into the guest bedroom—which I'd converted into my art supply room—and grabbed my easel, a pad of sketch paper, a pack of charcoal pencils, and lube before charging back downstairs.

"I thought I told you not to move," I said, scolding him. He sat upright now, hair mussed, cock lazing over his thigh. "Actually, I like that position better."

"What in the world are you doing?" he asked, confused but highly amused as I moved the coffee table over and set up my work station.

"I'm going to sketch you. Now stay still."

"An after-midnight sketch," he said in bewilderment. "One thing you're not is predictable, Mr. Bear."

And there goes that look again, the one that made my heart dance and my brain shake its head at my stupidity. "Just don't move."

I refused to turn the lights all the way up and kill the vibe, so I'd mostly need to go on instinct not sight. I didn't care, I just needed to get him down on paper right this second.

I got lost in my task, and only came up for air when Franky's complaint reached my ears.

"What are you doing over there?" he asked, shifting restlessly.

"I'm sketching you," I said faintly, my hand flying over the paper.

"You haven't looked my way in the last thirty minutes. If you're sketching me by memory, at least let me move my arm. It's falling asleep."

"Don't be a baby," I said. "And your hands are resting on your thighs, how can they be numb?"

"Maybe they're not numb, but they are lonely." His admission had the quality of a shrug. Like his words were no big deal, merely a statement of fact.

How could he possibly see himself as distant and cold? Or *only* distant and cold, because I definitely understood firsthand that he could be both of those things without apology. But he was *this* too. He was giving, supportive, humble, and he saw the best in me. Being with Franky was equivalent to floating on air, and I'd become addicted to the high.

Could it be that I brought this out of him? I shut the door on those assumptions. They would lead me nowhere.

"Done," I said, dropping my pencil on the easel's ledge and dusting my hands off. I did initially need Franky to sit still to get the job done, but my direction for the sketch had changed without my permission. Seemed my heart had a mind of its own.

My body warmed with shyness at knowing in a few seconds he'd see what I'd created.

"Well," Franky said. "Are you going to show me?"

"Depends."

"On what?"

"On if you want me to show you, or *show* you," I said.

"Aren't they one in the same?" he asked.

"No," I said, stalling, running my clammy hands up and down my bare thighs. It was always like this when showing my work, and I was sure every artist could relate. But this was different. This was *more*.

"It's late, sweetheart. I don't have the brainpower to translate that," he said.

Why am I being annoying about this? He'd seen my work before, and he was more than fluent in all my filthy ways. This was just both of those things combined. Art and filth.

With the pad of paper in hand, I moved to stand between his knees, holding it out to him. I had to gesture twice for him to take it before he snapped his gaze away from my rising cock.

There was a reason I hadn't needed to look at Franky as I sketched. The only thing visible on him in the drawing were his sturdy legs and the large, calloused hands he used to spread my ass cheeks as I rode him on the sofa.

I'd sketched myself from behind, the hard lines of my spine and traps prominent, feet flat on the cushions along his hips. I'd drawn one hand securely fastened to the back of the couch, the other behind me, braced on his right kneecap.

Franky's cum spilled from me, drenching his scrotum and inner thighs, and with my head blissfully thrown back on my neck as I lowered onto his colossal cock, it was clear that I was in heaven.

Franky set the sketch aside. It tumbled off the sofa and onto the floor as he scooted lower, his legs falling open to make room for his balls and erection, his feet spreading wider in preparation of gaining the leverage needed to fuck me as hard as the picture had implied.

"I showed you," I said, vocal cords overtaken by horniness.

"Now *show* me," he ordered, finally understanding the two weren't one and the same.

I lubed our cocks up for longer than needed, stretching out the torture, then gave him a view of my ass as I turned and bent over to open myself up. I quivered when he informed me with authority that his face had second dibs on my hole. His cock would breach me first.

Facing him again I settled onto him, and he gathered my ass cheeks in his hands, his first couple fingers resting along my exposed cleft, as we recreated the sketch.

I rose up and down, pushing through the balls of my feet, curling my toes into the cushions, as my cock clobbered my stomach repeatedly.

"Look at us, Franky," I whispered, short of breath and already sweaty.

Franky's gaze fell to where his cock disappeared inside my hole, only to reappear, and then disappear again like a fucking magic trick.

He began to fuck me harder then, his dick giving my ass a delicious beating, as if the visual of our connection had angered him. Maybe it reminded him that he'd made me no promises, and that this would all be temporary. Or maybe those reasons were projections of my own thoughts. Regardless of where his anger stemmed from, I took it. I'd always take his rage. I'd always welcome more.

"Hear the beautiful music we make when we fuck?" I asked crudely. I would make him remember this. I would engrain this sound into every fiber of his being. Any time he heard the slapping of water, the slippery, squelching sound of slickness, the hard smacking of sweaty skin colliding with sweaty skin, of wetness personified, he would think of me. I would be his ocean, and he would fucking yearn for me.

I fucked him ruthlessly, accepted every hard upward thrust with a wicked smile, which lit a match to his rage. I dug my nails into his knee as I fought to stay seated on this wild ride.

"You c-can't hurt me, Franky. I-I told you I can t-take you," I stammered, finding it hard to fuck, breathe, and talk at the same time. "Told you I can handle your big cock."

"Jesus, Leland. Your mouth." He hit my sweet spot, and I let out a symphony of moans.

"You like it when I talk shit, don't you? Like it even better when I let you ruin me, right, Franky?"

"Yes," he hissed. "I want to hurt you for making me feel this way."

"Hurt me, Franky. And next round, rip me off your cock when I'm so close to the edge that the loss of your dick makes me cry. And then stuff my mouth with it. Pump my throat with so much cum that I gag on it. And don't stop pumping, not even when I fight to get away."

"I'm coming," he gritted out. I slapped both hands to the sofa back, circling my hips and pounding onto his lap. I'd have bruises by sun up.

"Make sure it's enough to drown your balls, Franky," I panted. "Just like in the sketch."

"Ughhh!" he shouted, neck snapping back as he violently bridged into me one last time, nearly cleaving me in half, holding me down on the weapon he called a cock as his cum shot into me.

My own dick jerked without direction, painting us white. "Fuck, Franky," I breathed as my cum flew between us.

Our cocks twitched and eventually sputtered to a stop as I continued to grind on him. I ran my hand through the puddle of cum on my stomach, feeding it to Franky and sitting patiently as he held my wrist so he could suck every finger clean, even getting around my cuticles.

"What are we doing here, Leland?" he asked through a shredded voice, sinking a possessive hand into the wet hair at my nape. The rough touch felt like a stacked claim, like ownership. Like an answer to his question. Those feelings were too dangerous to have.

"I was hoping you knew," I said.

Franky's eyes went from confused to angry again, and a hand cracked against my ass cheek hard enough to send me forward, screaming out from the jarring pain. Only his hold on my hair kept me steady, and I struggled to read the sudden change in him. Struggled to comprehend what had brought about uncompromising and unfeeling Franky. It was his version of a wall, I told myself, because I knew him that much.

"You know what I want," he said in a monotone voice.

I popped off his cock, hissing from the vast emptiness left behind, then crawled onto the coffee table, assuming the position. I almost lost my balance when Franky knelt behind me and yanked me onto his face, eating my ass like it wasn't connected to my body. Like he didn't need to be careful or caring at all.

Even in this he could do no wrong, because while I enjoyed it when he touched me like I was more precious than all the stars in the sky, I *loved* when he treated my body like a soul didn't exist within it. Like my heart wasn't included.

I stared at my sublime reflection in the glass wall, mouth parted to release shallow breaths, eyes brimming with moisture as my cock thickened, filling to the brim with blood.

Franky and I were driving nowhere fast, and at some point, we were going to crash and burn. It scared the shit out of me, but not enough for me to smash on the brakes. Not enough to make me stop.

Once done, Franky hauled me up and off the table by my throat, the scent of sweet musk sighing over my lips as he spoke dangerously close to me. "Why do I need you again after just having you?"

"The feeling is mutual," I whimpered, trembling through my need for him. Franky screwed his eyes shut, his frustration tickled my skin, the ache in his heart reached for the ache in mine. When he opened his eyes again they were blank. He'd won the battle in the fight for distance. *Lucky him.*

"You're going to tell me no," he said, voice chilling. "And I'm going to take you anyway. Do you hear me?"

"Fuck. Yes. Loud and clear."

"Do you want me?" he asked, testing me.

"No."

"Do you want my cock, right now, Leland?"

I peered down at his intimidating dick covered in drying cum. "No," I said adamantly, backing away only to be ensnared by him again.

"Too bad."

Franky fucked me across the cold, hard floor like we were nothing more than strangers, and I'd lost count of how many times he'd interrupted my sleep to demand I hand over my body.

Each time he fucked me, the foreboding sense that things were coming to an end grew like weeds in the pit of my stomach, expanding until every corner of me had been touched and poisoned by it. Yet I didn't want him to stop, and after each time, I prayed there would be another. Another chance for me to say no, another chance for him to use my body anyway. And as the sensation grew, so did my hunger for him, until my mind and my body were at an impasse, both wanting different things and refusing to bend. My body would win, though, because that was where my heart resided, and my body would always follow my heart.

He didn't say a word to me, only took and expected me to accept it. I'd died and gone to sexual nirvana.

As the next thirty nights passed, we grew closer in a way we didn't know how to prevent. It mostly went unacknowledged, by either of us, and I often wondered if Franky had his own mantra, similar to mine, that he chanted daily inside his head.

We were locked away from the rest of civilization here on the ocean, and without any outside interruption—aside from the stress of what waited for us out in the world—it was easy to pretend we'd never have to actually face it. Too easy. And the more we fucked, which turned out to be always, the more blinded I became to the line separating our friendship from our friends-with-benefits-ship.

Franklin Kincaid was highly flawed, uncivilized, possessive, and entitled when it came to me and my body, but he was also good, and I'd go down fighting anyone who believed differently.

I wasn't the only one forgetting about the promises he didn't make and the regrets he assured me he'd have. Forgetting wouldn't make the inevitable go away, though. Forgetting would only make us kick ourselves harder when the end finally hit us in the face, because we'd tell ourselves we should've known better, we'd ask ourselves: *how could I have been so stupid?*

We'd make love during the day, or something similar to it, something not as soft, because we weren't the tender types. Not when chasing orgasms and inner demons.

At night, though... At night our fucking became a history lesson in decadent violence as it became clear with the setting of the sun that we'd used up another day. Time moved way too fast for us.

It was never too much, but sometimes my body didn't agree. And that was okay, because even when he couldn't outright fuck me, there were always other things he came up with to do to me.

I'd let sleep drag me by the ankle into its black cave only after Franky was done having his way with me. It would end with him breathing "enough" into the room, and then placing us on our sides and guiding my mouth to one of his taut nipples. The sucking soothed us both, lulled us both to sleep.

And every night, without fail, one recurring thought chased me into the void: *This will end, Leland.* And following behind that came a new realization: *But not before he breaks you.*

CHAPTER 14

Leland

Selene Kincaid mingled with the attendees all vying for her attention. I maintained a healthy distance, huddling in a corner of the art museum, stalking her every move.

I'd become increasingly curious about her over the last four weeks, and so after overhearing the follow-up conversation between Franky and Jasper, where Franky assured him that his mother's exhaustion was simply a result of long hours spent preparing for the annual Save the Arts charity event she spearheaded, I did the one thing I shouldn't have. I submitted a piece for the auction portion of the event, and it got accepted. It was either come as a participating artist or sell a kidney to pay the cost of admission.

Maybe it was all the nights Franky and I had spent on his boat cuddling under the moon as we exchanged childhood traumas. Maybe it was the way he trusted me with his tortured soul, trusted that I could endure it. It could've even been the way he clamped his arms around me when I whispered that summer was almost over as I rode him in front of a roaring fire. Maybe it was simply the Willow Meadows in me, but I had to get a glimpse of the person who probably thought they knew Franky better than me.

The harder I fell for him, the more I needed to convince myself that she wasn't right for him. I needed to uncover her flaws to justify my role in our affair, to justify not wanting it to end.

I spent my spare time plugging her name into every search engine under the sun, getting familiar with her philanthropic work, reading every journalistic write-up ever done on her, and obsessively scanning her images. I'd blamed filters, Botox, and corneal pigmentation for her unnatural beauty. I mean, eyes that vibrant shade of green didn't actually exist, right?

I'd wanted to hurl my phone at the wall every time. My jealousy would turn to anger, and sometimes I'd operate under the steam of both emotions, and then I'd fuck Franky because I needed to remind him of what she couldn't give him. I needed to remind myself of how much he wanted me, of how good I made him feel, and that I was the better choice because I was built tough and could take him on at his worst.

Technically, her body was equipped with all the orifices a cock could ever need, giving her yet another advantage over me. But I'd seen and experienced the lawless side of Franky, and there was no way that at one-hundred and thirty-pounds soaking wet, and five-feet seven-inches in considerable heels, could she handle Franklin Kincaid unchecked.

At least that was what I told myself as my thighs ached from riding his dick repeatedly, as my body burned in all the places he'd attacked with his hands and teeth, and as he rage-fucked my throat raw. I told myself that whenever I bullied my way onto his lap, ignoring his bad temper and sinking onto his mountainous shaft as he swore to me that *"Now isn't a good time, Leland."* It didn't matter whether or not he was in the right headspace; his cock never lied, and it always wanted me. And I told myself that now as my nails bit into my palms after getting my first in-person look at her. *She can't handle him.*

I'd missed the registration deadline for the bartending course that started last month. Nothing could've torn me from Franky, and he'd been too distracted with me to remember anything about it until it was too late. He'd made sure I signed up for September's class, though, even sending me off this morning with a good-luck-on-your-first-day fuck.

I'd pushed Betty to her limits, racing to my apartment to change into the one decent suit I owned and still make it to the museum on time.

I smoothed my expression and plucked a flute of champagne from a passing server's tray, then slunk deeper into my corner to watch her smile and make small talk with everyone she came in contact with, shaking hands and offering her thanks to them for attending.

It didn't matter if it was a man in a designer suit, one of the museum curators, or a young, disadvantaged artist whose piece had been selected to hang on the walls for the day. Selene greeted them all with the same warmth, the same respect, and never once appeared as if she'd rather be doing anything but speaking with them.

"Excuse me," I said, apologizing to an older woman after stepping into the crowd and startling her. I circled the roped off floor designated for the event, sticking close to the perimeter of the room as I trailed Selene from afar, the classical music playing overhead too atmospheric to drown out the sound of my speeding heart.

I faked being absorbed by the nearby painting of an apple tree when she stopped in front of the painting I'd submitted as if compelled to, placing a hand over her sternum as she moved in closer to it.

The online images of her didn't do her beauty justice. She was petite, but her weight filled in her lush curves, which the lacy, body-hugging emerald dress she wore did nothing to disguise.

Her ashen hair sat high in an intricate bun fastened with a rose-gold clip, stray strands fell and curled past her nape to brush against the pale skin of her upper back. I felt inferior to her already, and I hadn't even heard her speak yet.

I hadn't planned on making actual contact with her. I only needed to get close enough to point out her faults, to prove the internet and Franky wrong about her, both things I'd convinced myself I could do from across the room.

But there was something magnetic about her, so without thinking I allowed myself to be pulled into her orbit. I put my game face on and slithered over to the vacant spot on her left.

Selene studied my painting, wringing her hands now, not even noticing she had company. I wondered what she thought about it, wondered what about it had her so preoccupied.

It was just an abstract painting of a white dove caring for an abandoned baby blue jay. Nothing special. Nothing a toddler with some finger paint couldn't manage.

"I know what you're thinking," I whispered. Selene peered up at me, and I noticed that she *did* look tired around the eyes, but it didn't steal anything away from her beauty. If anything, it added something delicate to her regalness. It softened her confidence to something more approachable.

"Do you, now?" she asked, not missing a beat, her voice wrapping me up in a warm hug.

"You were wondering how something like this made it through those doors, and now you're asking yourself what a young, hot stud like me is doing in a place like this."

Selene's girlish laugh was all sunlight and wind chimes, and I was disappointed when it came to an end on an extended sigh. "Well, you're certainly entertaining," she said. Her smile didn't reach her eyes, but it didn't feel personal, she seemed to have a lot on her mind. Of course she did. Her kids were hundreds of miles away, and her husband had decided he wasn't sure he wanted to hold on to their life together. *Of course* she was tired, and unbeknownst to her, I was adding to her exhaustion.

"I was actually thinking about how much this reminded me of my son, Cole."

"Does he look like a bird?" I joked, filled with a need to make her laugh again, if only to erase some of my guilt.

"Good heavens, no," she said. "My children are gorgeous—and I'm not just saying that because I'm their mother either." She pointed at me in reprimand as if knowing those would be my next words. I held my hands up in mock innocence.

"Cole's technically my stepson," she said, focusing thoughtfully on the painting again, "which is why this piece connects with me the way it does. He's my baby-blue."

The dove hadn't given birth to the blue jay, but due to a number of possible circumstances, she'd decided to care for him like he was her own.

Her vulnerability took me by surprise, and I wondered if she only seemed unguarded to me because I had the advantage of knowing so much about her. Selene brought her fatigued gaze back over to me, and even managed a soothing smile. Suddenly, my plans to poke holes in the theory that she was a saint felt like an impossible task, and a mission I no longer wanted.

I began thinking of polite ways to end our conversation before she could say or do something else absolutely perfect to make me question my recent life choices.

"What's your name?" she asked.

"Noon Waters," I said, not wanting to lie to her. Well, it was a lie, but it matched the lie I told to get in here, and it matched the name on the silver plaque below my painting. And for a reason I couldn't explain, I wanted her to know it was me who had made her feel good for even a second.

Her eyes broadened along with her smile. "It's you," she said, and I shifted uncomfortably under the respect in her tone. "I can't tell you how tempted I am to remove this from the auction block and keep it for myself."

"You may still get a shot at it. I doubt anyone will bid. It took me less than a few hours to make it. Nothing crafted without effort and angst can be worth much, right?"

Selene stared at me, stared *through* me, seeing past my blasé ramblings. "You're talented, Mr. Waters. But I think you already know that, or at least you're beginning to suspect you are," she whispered conspiratorially. "I think you like to be reminded of your talent because every reminder fills your cup and takes you one step closer to never needing anyone's validation again, and to believing you deserve what you *truly* want from life."

"Philanthropist *and* mind reader," I said. "Impressive."

"No. I'm just a mother. And a fellow cup holder," she said with a wink.

She was right. If I could convince myself that I wasn't any good, then I had an excuse for not doing something with my gift. It became harder and harder to keep up the charade every day. Especially with someone as validating as Franky in my life.

"What you're doing here is amazing," I said, adding some validation to her cup, returning the favor. "Not enough people in your position care about getting art programs funded for the underserved."

She didn't say anything to that, but her blush and the awakening of her tired eyes was thank you enough. Her assistant, I assumed, interrupted us, letting Selene know in a hushed tone that she was urgently needed. Selene nodded to me before allowing herself to be whisked away.

My painting did end up selling, and under the rules of entry, a portion of the sale went to me. I donated my half to the cause, leaving a note on the check for Selene.

Dear, Selene... Use this to fill more cups.

♦ ♦ ♦

I drove back to my place to think and change out of my suit, and ended up falling asleep with a killer migraine. I woke up in the dark, disoriented, and to the sound of pounding on my apartment door.

I felt around the bed for my phone, cursing at the insane number of missed calls from Franky.

"Coming!" I shouted over the knocking. I flipped on the hall light, shielding my eyes as they adjusted to the brightness.

"Are you alright?" Franky asked before the door had fully opened. Rain water dripped from the ends of his hair, leaving dark circles on the shoulders of his white shirt. "I've been calling you."

"Yeah, didn't you get my text?" I asked, still waiting for my brain fog to clear.

Franky moved into the apartment while I locked the door. "You said you weren't feeling well and were going to take a nap."

I leaned against the wall opposite him in the hall. "I had a headache. I just woke up." It wasn't a big deal. I didn't get why he was so panicky.

"Leland," Franky said. "That was *ten* hours ago. It's after one in the morning. I thought I'd find you passed out on the floor or something."

"*What?*" Seeing his missed calls had distracted me from my purpose of searching for my phone in the first place. I'd wanted to know the time. Franky wasn't pleased, and his fear for me came off as annoyance. "Sorry, I um... It was a brutal headache."

"Did you take anything for it? How are you feeling now?" Less than two feet separated us in the narrow hall, and Franky cut that distance in half, stepping into me and sinking his hands into my hair. He meticulously examined my expression for signs that I wasn't okay.

"I'm good," I said, but my assurance didn't loosen the tightness of his lips. I wanted to talk to him. I wanted to tell him we couldn't do this anymore. It had been the plan I'd formulated before diving into a ten-hour coma. But when Franky touched me, the way he touched me now, every plan I ever had for myself changed.

"Franky," I breathed as he kissed along my forehead and cheekbones. I flattened my palms against his chest with the intention of pushing him away but balled his shirt between my fists instead.

"I was so worried," he said, kissing my closed eyelids, then kissing lower, and lower.

You need to make a choice, I wanted to say, but his mouth brought mine to silence.

This isn't right. It never has been, I wanted to say next, but his tongue got in the way.

I know we said no promises, and I know I swore to myself that I wouldn't fall in love with you, but we both know things have changed. That everything *is changing.* I said none of that, though.

I wanted to shout for him to stop kissing me like he'd rather die than to tear his lips away from me. To stop touching me like he wanted to rip my skin away to get to the important parts of me. To stop making me believe that I'm something more than what I am when he gazed at me.

But saying any of that would've required the ability to breathe, and right then, my every breath belonged to him.

"Franky," I said quickly as he yanked at the drawstring of my sweats, loosening the baggy waistband so his hand could dive in. He pretended not to hear me, recapturing my mouth, forcing my head and spine flat against the wall at my back as he tried to kiss me right through the plaster.

I unclenched my fists and shoved at his chest, sending him to his side of the hall, but he launched himself at me with a snarl, shredding my t-shirt between his hands.

Franky slammed the front of his body along mine, hands tightening in my hair until my scalp sizzled, the fabric of his jeans rough on my exposed cock. I pulled at the back of his shirt, tugging until the thin cotton ripped, then swallowed huge gulps of air when he ceased the attack on my lips to tackle my neck.

This was bigger than him being worried about me. Bigger than me feeling empathy for his wife. This was Franky knowing exactly what I'd been about to say and making sure I remained voiceless because of it. This was him understanding that my headache started from a pain in my heart. This was terror and agony on both sides, denial and selfish need.

Franky let me go long enough to get rid of the scraps of shirt clinging to him, and I took the reprieve to dart for the bedroom. He grabbed my arm, swinging me around until we'd switched places. The impact on my back punched the air from my lungs.

He pinned me to the wall by my neck, his lips pulling away from his teeth in warning as he wrangled his jeans open one-handed. His cock spilled lewdly from the opening, fully inflating as my sweats pooled at my ankles.

"Stop fighting me," he said, catching my hand before it connected with his cheek. He forced his hips into mine, smashing our bare cocks together.

"Shit," I moaned from the impact of his heat and then we were both fighting to get each other's pants out of the way.

We were frenzied but focused, determined to get what we were after. The only noise came from our joint panting and the slap of my palms against the wall when Franky roughly spun me away from him and pulled my hips back.

"Fuck, fuck, fuck," I heaved at the wall, my lips brushing up against paint. I couldn't think, I could barely see; all I could do was feel, and it all felt like too much.

In a flurry of movement, Franky spit into his palm and kicked my legs wide before catapulting right through me, sending me to my toes on a shout of pain mixed with undeniable pleasure.

He fucked me like the clock was winding down, like the world was coming to an end and he'd be damned if it did so without him claiming me thoroughly one last time.

I welcomed it, loved it even. Because for once I had someone in my life who was torn up by the possibility of losing me, and I relished in the way it felt to see him fight to hold on to me, even if he only fought in the physical sense.

Franky's thrusts were too swift to keep count, the power he put behind the fucking comparable to being hit by a freight train. He interlaced our hands above my head as he cursed God and praised my cock-taking abilities less than an inch away from my ear. "Fucking you feels like freedom, Leland." Franky got to be all he could be with me, and I got to reap the benefits of his liberation.

"I need to come, Franky," I said brokenly as my bones rattled beneath my skin. He wasted no time in reaching a hand around to take care of me.

I came, roaring his name, streaks of cum sprinting down the wall.

Franky's rhythm increased, shaking me like a ragdoll as he chased down his own release. Too soon he stiffened, his orgasm kicking through me as his heart quaked against my back. I pinched my eyelids shut, recording to memory the sensation of his cum filling me as I internally begged the moisture cresting behind my eyes to return to wherever the fuck it came from.

He rubbed his forehead against the back of my skull, still coming, still holding me to the tips of my toes.

"No," Franky breathed, pressing his hips in tighter when his softening cock began to slide from my hole. A traitorous tear rolled down my cheek.

He kissed my sweaty neck, then licked his way down my spine, kneading my ass hard enough to bruise as his tongue lashed around in my opening.

Cleanup tended to take longer than the time it took to make the mess, because Franky left nothing on the table. He was arrogantly dirty, his hunger never satisfied, and had a bottomless pit of an appetite.

I gave myself over to it, fucking his face as my tears and sweat created a salty stream down the front of my body.

Once finished with me, Franky used his tongue as a sponge to collect my cum off the wall, then stood and snaked his arms around me, kissing along my jaw from behind.

"Franky?" My voice quaked.

"Yeah," he said into my skin.

I thought about everyone involved, everyone who'd be affected by our affair if it got out. I thought about Selene and how tired she seemed, how unfair this was to her, and how not being able to hate her meant I had to hate myself more.

I should sacrifice myself and end this now, because one broken heart was better than many. I knew that. I understood it. But maybe they wouldn't work out anyway, because Franky had been on the hunt for something more long before I'd entered the picture. Bottom line, he was unhappy with his life before he'd met me. Still, it didn't mean I needed to take part in the breaking of a family.

I thought about all of this as he suffocated me with his arms, waiting with a held breath for me to answer him.

I thought about all of that and more. I thought about the type of man I wanted to be, and how much fuller my cup was today than it had been yesterday, and how Selene had done more mothering of me in those few minutes of conversation than my own mother ever had.

Was I better than this? Did I *want* to be better than this? I did. I *did* want that.

But I wanted Franky even more.

"Leave her," I whispered.

CHAPTER 15

Franklin

The leather chair squeaked under my weight but Leland didn't stir. I alternated between staring into the night-shadowed ocean through the open balcony doors and gazing at Leland as he slept peacefully in my bed.

Staring at him for too long caused my mind to jumble, and a glance into the water's vastness provided a reset; it brought clarity to a complicated situation.

"We'll talk later. Let me get you home." Those were the words I'd said to him after taking him with an edge sharpened by fear, and after he'd asked me to leave my wife for him. They were the last words spoken by either of us for the remainder of the night—or rather early morning.

I tilted my head back, downing half of my beer in an effort to forget how he'd dejectedly stared out of the passenger side window as we rode through the desolate streets to get here. Then— without any suggestive commentary or sneaky tactics meant to tempt me into taking him again—he allowed me to bathe and towel us off before tucking him into bed.

I'd been up ever since, and with the sunrise not too far off, I figured I might as well stay up to watch it.

I'd been too aggressive with him, which wasn't unusual, and neither was my reasoning for behaving that way. But I had to stop taking my issues out on him, out on his body, no matter how much he swore it was precisely what he wanted. It wasn't the aggression that bothered me, but the motive behind it.

Saying I panicked when I couldn't get a hold of him earlier would've been minimalizing the emotion. After fearing that maybe he was alone and unconscious, I then feared that he'd simply had his fill of me. That he'd had a sudden attack of conscience and no longer wanted to be a participant in the wrong we were doing.

As much as he would've had the right to walk away from this, and as much as he *should* have walked away from this, I wasn't ready to let him go. So I'd demonstrated that in the only way it seemed I could these days, by unleashing my cock on him. On the maturity scale, it ranked decently low.

Rolling my head on my neck, I released a silent sigh as the tension eased a little, watching as the beer bottle's condensation spilled across my bare knee, cooling my warm skin.

Rustling came from the bed, and I snapped my eyes open to find Leland sitting up, the sheet pooling in his lap as he reached over to click on the lamp. He blinked slowly, eyes hooded with exhaustion, even with all the hours in total he'd spent sleeping.

He was young and cute with his hair tousled and lips sleep-swollen. Seeing him like this, one would never know how... *accommodating* that adorable pink mouth of his could be. A perfect match to his adorable pink hole.

Leland wiped the sleep from his eyes before taking in the room, as if trying to remember how he'd gotten here. He wet his lips, his breathing quickening as his gaze flashed up and down my naked body.

I finished my beer before setting the empty bottle on the floor near the others. "Now we talk," I said before lust got the best of either of us.

"Okay," he said, even as his slightly curved cock tented the sheet. I discreetly pressed a palm along my own burgeoning erection, ordering it to stand down.

"I thought you were done with me," I said, jumping right into the heart of things. "When I couldn't get a hold of you..." I shook my head, unable to finish.

"How did that make you feel, Franky?"

"Relieved, mostly, at first. I thought it left me with only one option. Taking the coward's way out." *Going back to my life.* "But after that thought came an intense ache. I wasn't ready to let you go."

"Yet," he said, a muscle in his jaw feathering. "You weren't ready to let me go *yet.*"

He wanted a promise I still couldn't give him, a renegotiation of our terms. He wanted me to break apart my family for him, but he didn't understand that while he had everything to gain in me doing so, I had everything to lose.

"Where do you see yourself in five years, Leland?"

"Not this again," he said, annoyed.

"Answer me."

"I already did."

"Yes, the art-bar, which I still know nothing about. I need a broader answer to the question."

"You know I hate that question—"

"Answer it anyway," I insisted.

"What does that have to do with any of this? With right now?"

"I can't afford to only account for right now," I said.

"You're acting like you were happy. Like life was a fucking dream before I came along and made things complicated. You were searching, Franky. Searching for—" He clamped his mouth shut before saying *me,* but it was there between us anyway.

"You were searching for...something. You were unhappy when we met on that roof. You left your home to move in here. You took a sabbatical from your job. Hell, from your fucking life!" His voice rose an octave. "But now you're looking at me as if somehow your misery is my fault."

"It's not your fault, Leland. But if you want me to make a permanent decision that will inflict maximum damage to those I care about, you better damn well know that you'll want me long after the excitement and newness of this has ended," I said with equal passion. "Because good sex—life-altering sex even—can only take a relationship so far."

"I don't know, Franky," he said unconvinced. "It kind of sounds like you're blaming me."

"I'm not," I swore. "I'm not blaming you for the condition of my life, but do you understand why leaving Selene, why risking a further divide between myself and my kids isn't something I can take lightly?"

"Are you saying that if at some point down the road we don't work out you would regret walking away from your marriage? Because your decision to leave shouldn't just be dependent on me. You aren't happy with her. Not anymore."

That was only partially true. It was myself that I'd been most discontent with. The type of ostentatious life I'd been living, the type of unfulfilling work I'd been doing, the type of father I'd been...

And yes, I'd been missing the kind of human connection I'd found with Leland, but to say I would have ultimately walked away from it all would've been a lie. Outside of taking some time away, I hadn't known what I planned on doing. Not in the long run.

"I know it feels like we've known each other forever, but in terms of actual time it hasn't been that long. Not nearly long enough to base a rash decision on."

"So, what, you need more time to fuck me in private and keep Selene in limbo before you can be sure that I'm worth the risk? Is a year long enough? Two?" he asked. "I don't get it. You were planning on walking away from her before I got here. Weren't you?" Leland asked, his eyes rounding with childish hope. I wanted to race over and take him into my arms.

"Probably not," I said gently. "I would've liked to believe I would have, but ultimately, I don't think I would've found the courage to. Because I don't think I would have discovered what it was I needed to make me whole if I hadn't discovered you. And I doubt I'll ever find another you, Leland." I loved building things with my bare hands, but doing so alone in that house for the summer wouldn't have been enough of a catalyst to make me uproot my life. It wouldn't have been the thing that left me feeling full. "There's no one else like you, Leland."

"Not even Theo?" he whispered.

"Not even Theo," I whispered back.

His mouth and jaw softened, as if he'd finally understood where I was coming from. This wasn't as simple as me finding someone else if he and I didn't work out. There *was* no one else. The feelings I had for him were solely based on, and reserved for, him. What I'd been missing was him.

I'd said I would enjoy this for as long as I could. Until the end of summer, which was barreling down on us swiftly. But now we were dreaming up the possibility of more, and it terrified me.

I loved Selene, and I could walk away from Leland now and go back to my old life and find some measure of peace because I'd know that other than him there was nothing else out there in the world for me. But I couldn't break their hearts for anything less than forever with him.

"So tell me, please, Leland. Where do you see yourself in five years?"

Leland regarded me as if I were the biggest idiot he'd ever come across before whispering, "Somewhere still wanting you."

My breath hitched, and I rose to my feet, kicking the bottles over and sending them rolling in opposing directions. "Are you sure?" I asked from the foot of the bed, a death-grip on one of the spiked posts.

"Positive," he said, scooting backward and watching me warily. I didn't need a mirror to know my gaze had darkened, and I didn't need to look down to know my cock was ready to pound into something.

"I'm not an easy man to deal with," I warned him, planting a knee on the bed.

"Tell me something I don't know," he said.

"I'm not an easy man to love."

"Loving you will be worth the fight it will take to do so, Franky."

We tussled for control of the sheet, and I easily tore it away from his white-knuckled grip before catching him by the ankle and dragging him to the end of the bed. Leland's legs went around me, and I lifted him into my arms, holding him up by the soft globes of his ass.

"I'm stubborn, and selfish, and can get in my own way, and I sometimes show that I care by doing things that prove the opposite." I nibbled at his lips as he scraped his nails along my scalp.

"How many times do I have to say that I'm not afraid of you? When will you finally believe me, Franky?"

"Maybe after you've loved me through my worst, Leelee Bear."

"Bring it on."

"I'm going to make love to you this time," I said, as something like a purr climbed the walls of his throat.

"Just promise me I'll still feel you tomorrow," he said, inhaling my kisses.

Grabbing the lube off my nightstand, I got us ready, then lifted him by his ass cheeks before sinking him onto my shaft. "Slow down," I whispered into his mouth when he began bouncing on my cock. He stopped, letting me take the reins, and I moved him up and down effortlessly as I walked us onto the balcony, shifting my hungry kisses to soft pecks across his nose and mouth.

"Franky," he said on a groan when I settled his ass onto the railing and dipped him back a fraction to thrust in and out painfully slow. Not once did he flinch from the vulnerable position I'd placed him in. I held him steadfastly, both arms slung across his back as he interlaced his hands behind my neck, trusting me not to let him fall.

I'd had every intention of watching the sun rise over his shoulders, but all I could do was watch the heavy emotion building behind his bright irises.

I strung the love making out for as long as I could, eventually carrying him to bed before finishing inside of him and then massaging my cum into his skin after drinking every drop of his.

Afterward, Leland hugged me from behind, inhaling and breathing into my sweaty nape.

"This will take some time," I said, yawning and closing my eyes. Me leaving Selene wouldn't be an overnight thing. It would need to be done right. I needed him to know that.

"Just don't change your mind, Franky." His arms eventually grew slack, his breathing evening.

Falling asleep should've been the easiest thing for me to do by then. I'd officially been up for twenty-four hours, and I'd fucked well beyond my limits for the day when running on no sleep, little food, and inadequate hydration. But Leland's plea was a strong wind blowing the fog of slumber away.

I held on to his arms tighter, focusing on his soft snores pelting my neck, and ignored my phone, which now vibrated with an incoming text.

Sleep eventually took mercy on me, but I woke up feeling unrested and wondering how long I'd been out for. I reached for my phone to check the time, seeing the text message waiting for me. It was time stamped three hours ago, and the name on the locked screen read: **Selene.**

I swiped up, fingers folding tightly around the device as the five-word message sank deep into my bones, sending a chill through me.

Selene: *The boys are coming home.*

CHAPTER 16

Franklin

I was on my third cup of hot tea by the time Leland trudged downstairs. I couldn't shake the cold dread clinging to my bones.

"You're going to crash at some point today," he said from the hall beyond the kitchen.

I entered from the patio, sliding my mug onto the kitchen counter, waiting as he advanced on me. His sweats hung low, revealing the trimmed hairs between the deep V at his hips, and his cock tapped against the gray fabric with every step. "Good afternoon," I said, placing a chaste kiss along his smooth jaw.

He smiled boyishly, then grabbed a bottle of water from the fridge.

"And you're going to be climbing the walls all night," I said. "Between the hours you spent asleep at your apartment last night and then again once we got home, there's no way you'll be finding rest tonight."

"I'm sure you can manage to put me to bed," he said, his brows dancing as he stepped into my space again.

"Is sex all you think about?" I asked.

"No, it's not," he said seriously. "But I love having sex with you. And to be honest, I guess I feel like I have something to prove."

"And what's that?" I asked.

"That I'm a great lover. A *better* lover than most. That I can keep you satisfied. I don't want you wanting for anything—or anyone—else," he said.

"You don't have anything to prove," I assured him.

"That's easy for you to say. You're not the one trying to steal a married man. You get to just sit back and reap the benefits of my insecurities," he said.

"Leland... That's not—"

"I don't have money or a fancy education. I can't give you more children, and I have zero prospects, but I can take your cock like a champ, Franky. So let me," he ended with a plea.

He'd rendered me mute. Leland and I were relatively truthful with each other, but this went beyond that, brutally so. Even after our talk last night, he still doubted me, doubted my commitment to him, and it also seemed he doubted his ability to hold on to me by means outside of sex. It made what I had to tell him all the more difficult.

"You're my listening ear, Leland. You're the friend I never knew I needed. You stroke my passion, yes, but we are about more than just sex."

"I know," he said, exhaling and combing a hand through his hair. "Between yesterday, then last night, and the early hours of the morning... It was a lot. I think I'm still coming down."

"What happened yesterday? Did something go wrong in class?" In all the mayhem, I hadn't even gotten to ask him how his first day went.

"It was fine," he said, a little too quickly.

"You'll have to tell me all about it later. Right now, I need to tell you something."

"Sounds like I'm not going to like it," he said, cocking a hip against the counter. The move jostled his already loose waistband, sending it lower, revealing a sliver of tanned skin at the root of his shaft.

I meant what I'd said to him a few minutes ago. Our relationship wasn't based solely on sex, but Leland was a sexual creature. Every move he made suggested something, every look he gave dripped with desire, and almost every word uttered had a double meaning that could be tied back to fucking, or being fucked, or something equally as charged and orgasmic. He was vivacious in the bedroom, or on the floor, or forced up against a wall. His sexual energy knew no bounds.

"Let's have a seat in the living room." I chose the sofa. Leland chose to stand in a corner on the opposite side of the room, probably not trusting himself to be near me until he knew what was going on.

"What is it, Franky?"

"Selene texted me this morning. The boys are visiting in a few days—"

"The *men* you mean, right?" he said, cutting my sentence off at the knees.

"*Cole* and *Jasper* will be visiting," I tried again. "It's suppose to be a surprise—"

"For your birthday," he said before I could, his impatience and agitation now a third entity in the room. This would be a fight.

"Yes," I confirmed. "But given our current situation, she thought it would be best to make me aware of it now."

"So what's the plan?" he asked, folding his arms. "Will you ask Selene for a divorce before they get here? At least by then you two can present a united front when breaking it to them."

"You know that's not what's going to happen," I said with as much sensitivity and care as I could, but my own agitation began to rise to the occasion. He was being unreasonable, and his tone suggested he didn't give a damn.

"Why not? She'll use this time to try and get you back. She'll realize she still wants you."

"You can't expect me to blindside her with this news and then expect me to crush my children all in a matter of *days*. Do you even care about what this will do to them?"

"Of course I care. I don't want them to hate me, Franky," he whispered, and it struck me that I had more than one battle ahead of me. Not only would I have to walk away from my marriage, and destroy my kids and beg for their forgiveness in the process, but I'd then need to introduce them to the man I set their world on fire for, and hope that we could all...get along.

"You'll change your mind," Leland continued, shaking his head manically, inspiring my own mania. This new realization made things more complicated, and I was losing my grip on the situation. "Regardless of what was said last night, if you go home and pretend everything is perfect, you'll change your mind. You'll reminisce about the good times over dinner. You'll miss the parts of your life that weren't so bad. You'll wonder if you can make things work with her, wonder if you owe it to your sons to give your marriage one last chance. You'll forget about me, Franky. I know you will."

"No, I won't. None of that is true. But I need more time," I said, suddenly more conflicted than I'd ever been, and by the look of his wild gaze, my feelings had translated through my words.

I could almost hear his heart tearing in two, and it felt like someone had taken a sledgehammer to my chest. I couldn't think past the ache.

"They'll be gone in a few days, and I'll be back here with you. We'll make a plan then," I said, trying to appease him, wanting to remove the look of pain from his eyes, also needing to buy myself some time to consider how we would all work as a blended family. "I'm not unsure about you, Leland. You have my word on that."

"Will you fuck her?"

"What?" I asked.

"Will you *fuck* her, Franky?!" His voice thundered through the lower level of the house, and I breathed, summoning every ounce of patience I could dredge up instead of showing him whose anger was boss. "I mean, you're fucking me bareback, so I think I have a right to know."

"No. I don't plan on having sex with her. Jesus, Leland." I jumped to my feet.

"So no sex, then. Let's see…" He gripped his chin in thought. "What about kissing? Holding hands? Sleeping in the same bed? How exactly does this whole playing house thing work, Franklin?" he bit out like I was obtuse. His questions stunned me. I hadn't thought that far ahead.

"You still love her. How could you not? She's perf—" He stopped himself, leaving me curious.

"She's what?" I asked, lowering my voice.

"Nothing," he said, dragging his hands down his face. "Just don't do this."

I exhaled, sitting again and motioning to the spot next to me, trying to get a handle on the conversion. "Have a seat, please," I said.

"Tell me you aren't going to do this first," he said, a defiant fire igniting behind his golden brown eyes. I said nothing. He wouldn't have liked my answer anyway.

"On second thought," he said, "maybe you should do this. We've been cooped up here all summer. I could use a breather, some fresh air. Maybe I'll meet up with Noon. It's been a while since we hung out. Maybe I'll even hit up Josephine's," he said threateningly. He couldn't get his way, so the next best thing was to play on my possessiveness.

I prowled over to him, taking his face between my hands, the heel of my palms pressing against the stubborn jut of his chin. Jealousy flared from some place deep within me, cramping my gut and raising the volume on the sudden silence overtaking the room. "Don't do something you'll regret. I'm warning you, Leland."

"Don't threaten me with a good time, Franky," he said, not even blinking under the strength of my fierce stare. If anything, the threat of facing my anger seemed to embolden him further. "Don't worry, I'll wear a rubber—"

I shut his mouth for him, holding it closed as he tried to wriggle from my hands. "I'm a powerful man, Leland. I hold more influence than you can ever imagine. Don't make me ruin someone's life all because you're in the mood to test me," I whispered maliciously, the air pumping through his nostrils hot against my face as I drew in closer to him. "Don't play games you can't win."

Leland had experience with my mercurialness, and his body had long ago adapted to receiving me in anger. But up until then, he'd only known me as Franky.

Franklin Kincaid would call in all favors owed to dismantle the life of anyone who laid a hand on Leland. Franklin Kincaid would buy out Josephine's just to have the pleasure of setting it afire and watching it burn.

"What is it you want? Hmm?" I asked, one palm moving to clamp around his nape, the other freeing his mouth to choke his words off at his throat. "What do you win by sending me into a jealous rage? Is your goal for me to fuck you? Spank you until I break skin? Do you need me to make it so you can't sit, let alone ride a cock or fuck a pussy while I'm gone?" I snapped crudely, beyond thinking before I spoke. "What I'm about to say next is unfair of me. I know this." I increased the pressure on his windpipe before continuing. "I don't want anyone else's hands on you, and I'm afraid of what I might be capable of to ensure that doesn't happen." I'd backed us deep into his corner, my shoes bumping up against his bare feet. His cheeks were rosy, his eyes screaming bloody murder, but I didn't care. "Don't push me, Leland. You end things between us before you push me that far."

If there was one thing Leland excelled at, it was antagonizing me—for good or bad—and never backing down. I took a firmer hold around his throat, and he glared at me defiantly, welcoming the suffocation, as if he didn't need to breathe, as if my jealousy would sustain him.

A small part of my brain still operating on reason understood that I needed to let him go, even though I knew without question I wouldn't like his reply. I was right, and I regretted freeing him instantly.

"I'll do whoever the fuck I want, unless you give me a reason not to," he said angrily. "You don't own me. Now back the fuck off."

I didn't back off. I crowded him into the wall, afraid that while I was off pretending my life hadn't changed, he'd be out falling into the arms of someone who deserved him. That fear prevented me from seeing straight.

"Franky," Leland said, shoving at my chest.

"Take it back," I said, unmovable. "You take it back right now."

"Say you won't leave me here to go be with her, and I'll tell you anything you want to hear."

I bared my teeth at him but couldn't get my mouth to spill the words he wanted to hear.

"That's what I thought." Leland ducked to slip under my outstretched arms caging him to the wall, but I was faster. Slamming him back in place, I took his mouth in a savage kiss, leaving him with no choice but to take it or risk losing the chunk of hair I held him by.

"Take it back," I snarled.

"No," he breathed, uselessly pushing at me.

"I've never had to deal with you according to your age, Leland. Don't make me start now."

"Says the grown man fucking someone other than his wife."

Checkmate. I released him, stumbling back from the blow of his spiteful words.

"I-I'm sorry, Franky," Leland said, reaching for me. "I didn't mean—"

I held a hand up, stopping him. "I think we need a breather. Some time apart," I said.

"Won't we already be getting that when you leave?" he replied.

"I'm going to work on the patio—"

"It's about to rain—"

"Then in the garage!" I shouted. "We need space. We'll talk later." And because he still hadn't taken his threats back, and because I was five seconds away from taking him over my knee, I turned and vanished into the garage before he could issue another reply.

CHAPTER 17

Leland

Hunkered down inside the guest room, I spent the rest of the day taking my frustrations out on a blank canvas. I'd considered going to my place, but the very idea of leaving him, after learning he'd soon be leaving me, hurt like a stab to the chest.

For once I welcomed the afternoon storm clouds and then the early evening rain as I purged my emotions via paintbrush.

I could've lied to myself and said that the version of Franky I'd left downstairs wasn't real, that it didn't exist outside of our heated argument, but I didn't want to. Because whoever that man was—Franky, Franklin, or someone else entirely—having him promise to make the life of anyone who touched me a living hell, felt good. Too good to question or regret, and I hadn't been an angel either.

I'd pushed him because I needed him scared, just as scared as me, because maybe if his terror reflected my own, he wouldn't leave me to go be with *her*.

Shoving him over the edge meant I didn't have to fall head-first alone, and it confirmed, more than words ever could, how much he wanted me. Yeah, it was an unhealthy way of thinking, but I owned it. I didn't give a shit.

More than anything, I'd wanted him to know how it felt to feel like I was slipping from his grasp, because I damn sure felt like he was slipping through mine.

Stepping off my milkcrate, which doubled as a step stool and paint supply holder, I shuffled to the bedroom door to take in the full scope of my painting, squinting up at the seven-foot canvas. It was chaotic, dark, and the biggest piece I'd ever created.

I added a few finishing touches to the bottom, then dumped the brush next to the others in the jar of murky water and began kneading the headache building behind my forehead.

"Fuck." I pulled my hands away, remembering they were covered in black and blue paint, which now meant my face was too.

The storm kicked up outside my open window. Rainwater screamed as it made impact with the earth and ocean, and the growl of thunder competed with the growling of my stomach. In my stubborn determination to avoid Franky, to not be the one to seek him out first, I hadn't eaten all day.

My forearms were also covered in paint, and the stench bubbling up from my armpits nearly knocked me to my ass. Food would need to wait until after I'd showered.

After thirty minutes of standing under the hot spray, hunger pangs cut into me, and I began to sway on my feet. I held myself open a little while longer, letting the water wash over and soothe the place Franky had claimed so completely last night. Despite what I'd said in the heat of the moment, Franky did own me, and he always would.

I finished up, snagging a towel off the floating shelf and haphazardly drying off as I trudged into the bedroom. My nerves elbowed their way in, forcefully overtaking hunger's space as I quickly dressed and then descended the stairs.

Banging came from the side door leading to the garages, which was where Franky worked whenever bad weather ran him from the patio. I spread my palms over the door, needing but refusing to cross over the threshold and go to him. If we only had a few more days together, we should be making the most of it, not spending time on separate ends of the house, but I wanted to be the one pursued. I wanted him to feed into my insecurities by showing me what I already knew. I wanted him to show me that he cared.

We'd dealt with each other's crankiness before but never had we been so *angry* with each other. Never had we done and said things with the sole purpose of inflicting pain.

I'd started it, the hurling of hurtful words part. All he'd done was tell me the truth about his plans at the first opportunity he could, even if that truth stung.

The hammering in the garage stopped, and the hammering in my chest picked up. I'd bet ten scratch-offs that if I opened the door, I'd find him shirtless and grimy, staring my way with that look he often got when waiting for me to turn a corner and enter a room. A mix of raptorial hunger and hard affection. Like he missed me and wanted me badly enough to not take his time or be nice about it.

My world freeze-framed as I pictured Franky cocking an ear in my direction, sensing me.

Footsteps pounded beyond the slab of wood, closing the distance to the door. Not wanting to be caught lurking there when it swung open, I hurried on light feet to the kitchen.

Franky wrenched the door wide like it weighed a ton, probably hoping to catch me in the act of missing him.

I lined the cold cuts and condiments I'd taken out of the fridge along the island, pretending I didn't see him watching me from the end of the short hallway that separated the garage from the kitchen.

The heavy thud of his work boots hitting the hardwood floor vibrated up my bare feet, past my thighs and beyond. Franky's mammoth shadow crossed the kitchen entryway before he did, and I kept my head down, slapping turkey and cheese onto two pieces of bread and then working on slicing the tomatoes.

He relaxed into the trim of the archway, his hands going into his front pockets. I stole a glance at him, regretting it when the longing seeping from his eyes made me want to open my body to him, welcoming him home.

I took a few bites of my sandwich, not tasting anything, but it gave me something to do other than wait mutely for him to make a move.

He moved behind me to the fridge. The door opened and shut, followed by the sound of a cap being popped and a thick throat working to get a bottle of Stella down. I took a third bite, my appetite now gone—at least for the sandwich—but I forced it down anyway.

A second pop, chased by a continuous gulp before the bottle slammed down onto the counter.

Franky breezed in behind me, smelling like a hard day's work and beer. "You missed a spot," he said, wiping behind my ear and then showing me his paint-coated thumb.

"Thanks," I said, the ends of the bread crumbling in my clenched hands.

"I'm sorry," he said, holding on to the island at either side of my hips and rolling his nose through my hair. "I don't want to fight with you." He backed up enough to let me turn around, then connected his forehead to mine. We stayed like that for a while.

"If you need to sleep in the same room with her, you don't sleep in her bed." I couldn't bring myself to say *their* bed. "If you need someone to talk to, you call me. *I'm* who you go to for comfort, Franky." I continued with my list of demands, asking for what I wanted even if the answer would be no. "If you need something to let your frustrations out on, if you need someone to fuck, you come find me in the middle of the night. I'm your secret keeper, your shoulder to lean on, your ocean when there isn't one, and my ass is your goddamn punching bag. Do you hear me?" I asked, thumping a fist against his chest.

"Yes," he said, kissing me. "Yes."

"I need you," I said, needing to feel possessed by him after our fight. "Fuck, Franky, I need you."

Franky picked me up, my legs latching around him as he carried me through the kitchen and into the pouring rain. We kissed like mad men as he carefully maneuvered the stairs leading to the dock with me in his arms.

We were soaked by the time we reached the boat's cabin, bumping our heads on the low ceiling as we peeled out of our clothes while trying to remain glued to each other.

I rode him as he perched at the edge of the big bed, my palm flattened to the ceiling in the confined space. We didn't talk, just fucked and stared into each other's eyes, living in the moment.

Franky flipped me onto my back, and the boat began to rock. Could have been the heavy wind, the heavy rain, or the heavy impact of his thrusts shoving me to the top of the bed.

My stomach dipped, and I couldn't say if I was seasick or love-sick, but I didn't care.

We eventually switched positions again, causing him to lose the suction he had on my neck. He sat up, chewing into my shoulder as I whipped my ass up and down his cock.

"No one will want to touch you when I'm through with you," he said, clamping his mouth over my nipple next.

"Fuck," I hissed, the vein along my bouncing shaft throbbing. "Two can play that game, Franky." I raked my nails down his back, drawing blood.

"Ugh!" he bit out, throwing his head back before pinning me to the mattress again. He shook his hair from his face, sweat raining down on me as he grunted, hauling my lower body onto his lap and hitting my sweet spot with deep jabs of his cock.

"Not my face," he said. "Anywhere but my face."

I clawed into his chest next. Lines of crimson formed, running parallel down to his midsection.

We took turns damaging one another as the heat rose in the windowless room and the scent of sex hovered on the verge of suffocating us.

By the time we were through, the sheets were ruined and we were hard pressed to find an area on our bodies not stained red. The cabin itself would need to be hosed down.

"I'd like to use my second truth," Franky whispered after we'd limped back to the house, showered, and collapsed into his bed. He'd already used one of the truths he'd won after hustling me in a game of pool. I'd forgotten I still owed him two more. He could ask me anything, and I'd have to answer honestly. My heart lurched up my throat as I waited.

Franky shifted me off his chest so he could see me clearly, wincing as doing so agitated his bruises. "When you promised you wouldn't ask me for more, did you already know you would?" He was asking about the day we left the emergency room. The day he said he couldn't make me any promises. The day I'd promised I would never ask him to. Yet here we were...

"Yes," I said truthfully. "Did you go into this knowing I'd break my promise?"

"Yes," he whispered. "I knew, but I wanted you anyway. It was the worst of the many selfish acts I've committed since meeting you. One of many selfish acts I'd committed *against* you. I'm scared it won't be my last, Leland. You deserve better than me."

"Just come back to me, Franky," I said, wiping the tears from the corners of his eyes. "Just come back to me."

CHAPTER 18

It'd officially been twenty-four hours since Franky went home to his family, and to say I wasn't handling it well was a fucking understatement. Especially since he hadn't called, texted, or sent a freaking carrier pigeon with a message letting me know he was okay. Letting me know *we* were okay.

Did they hug for the sake of their kids? Did they hold hands at the dinner table while laughing at some random Christmas memory? Did she ask him for help getting the zipper down on her dress before bed? The oldest fucking trick in the book. And did he fall for it? *Willingly?*

My phone vibrated on my thigh, and I nearly sent my whole body up in flames, fumbling my lit Marlboro to answer it. It was only Noon. "I'm out front," I said. "Just walk around the side of the house." I hung up and went back to staring into the fire pit.

He'd called earlier saying he wanted to see me before leaving for New York. I'd invited him over instead of risking Franky showing up and me not being here. There was also a petty part of me that wanted to upset Franky by having Noon in his home, even if he ended up never knowing about it.

"Cigarettes," Noon said, stepping onto the patio. "Must be serious."

I had quit the habit five years ago after having been lectured to death by him. "You could say that." I took a drag.

"Smoking and self-loathing," he mused, picking up on my tone. "A dangerous mix." Noon leaned in to kiss the top of my head, then rearranged the chair next to me so it faced me, then took a seat. "So this is where you've been spending your time," he said, checking out the interior of the house, then surfing his gaze over the ocean. "Nice view."

"Yeah," I agreed absently, checking my phone again.

"You look terrible, Leland. What's going on?" Leave it to Noon to poke the elephant. I was in rough shape. I didn't have the energy needed to lie, plus I needed an outside perspective, even if his point of view would be too honest for me to digest without a fight.

I dragged in another lungful of nicotine. "He's going to leave his wife for me—and before you accuse me of breaking up their marriage," I rushed in to add defensively, "she cheated on him first, and they both agreed they could use some time apart to figure shit out. He wasn't happy in the first place, but I make him happy now."

"Okay," Noon said, cool as a fucking cucumber. "Go on."

"We agreed we would give us a shot. He wants to be with me," I emphasized.

"Uh-huh," Noon said.

I snuffed out the cigarette on the small dish I'd been using as an ashtray. "His sons are in town from college. They don't know their parents' marriage is on the rocks, and Franky doesn't plan on telling them. At least not yet. But he will soon."

"Because he's going to leave her for you," Noon said helpfully.

"That's what I said," I snapped, then breathed deeply. "Sorry. Anyway, he went back home." I swallowed down the bile rising at the use of the word *home*. "It's just for a few days. Then he'll be back, and we'll come up with a plan to break the news to everyone."

Noon kept quiet, and I gestured annoyingly at him to say something.

"Oh, I can speak now?"

"Yes, you asshole," I gritted out. Noon smiled a sad smile, like he didn't take pleasure in what he was about to say to me.

"You two are living in a vacuum right now. Have you ever considered what being attached to Franklin Kincaid will mean? Yeah, I know who he is," he said when I gaped at him. "He bumped into Stacey that day at the hospital. Demanded a rush be put on your discharge papers. He dropped his name. I'm pretty sure he gave his attorney's name as well."

"That last part's a lie," I said. Franky would have given his name—if asked. But he wasn't some pretentious asshole waving his power around and threatening hospital staff with lawsuits if he didn't get his way.

"Point is," Noon went on. "You'll be the man who broke up a powerful family. His wife is revered. They'll dig into your past, they'll say you're with him for his money—"

"I'm not," I said indignantly.

"The truth won't matter, Leland. Not to the vultures. They'll say he's going through a midlife crisis, that he's old enough to be your father. They'll say you're young enough to have played in the sandbox with his kids..."

"That last one's a stretch," I huffed. Cole and I were a few years apart in age, and Jasper was even younger than Cole.

"His kids will be embarrassed by it all. They'll be pissed, and they likely won't accept you. It'll affect his business, the thing he's worked half his life to build—"

"He doesn't care about Nexcom. He wants to make furniture," I said weakly, and for the first time it sounded stupid to my own ears.

"Furniture. I see," Noon said. "So you'll be the guy who made him turn his back on his family's legacy to what, build coffee tables? How long before he resents you? They'll label you as his downfall. And once you two step back into the real world, who will you become in the face of the force that is Franklin Kincaid, one of the wealthiest men in the world? Leland the bartender?" It wasn't said with cruel intentions, but I flinched away from it anyway.

"Look," he said, taking pity on me. "I'm not saying he doesn't want to leave her. I can list a million reasons why you're the better option without even knowing her, but reality will kick in, and he'll see that he has too much to lose. He'll see this fantasy you've both been living for what it is, and he won't choose you. They rarely ever do."

"Franky and I are different," I said, my voice pitched low.

"The exception to the rule?" he asked. "I sure hope so, Leland. For your sake, I really do."

"You've always had your shit together, Noon. Even when we were busting our asses to make rent, hopping from one dead-end job to another. You knew our way of life was only temporary for you. I don't understand how it feels to be sure of myself, and you don't get how it feels to be unsure of anything. Franky and I are different because we are the same." It was that simple, and I'd never felt more certain of something than I did that singular fact. While Noon was shooting forward, Franky and I were scrambling to get our feet under us.

Movement over my shoulder pulled my attention away, and I was on my feet and short of breath in one second flat. "Franky." I sighed, gripping the back of my seat for support.

From the shadows of the living room, Franky approached the patio wearing an all-black suit, his dress shoes clicking ominously against the floor.

Noon stood as well, nodding at Franky's hard stare. "Franklin," Noon said, addressing Franky by his given name.

"Good to see you again, Noon," Franky replied, accepting Noon's extended hand. He managed to sound like he meant it.

"Just thought I'd stop by and keep Leland company. Can't feel good being left alone in this big house," Noon said, being irritatingly antagonizing.

"How nice of you," Franky said, stepping into my side and kissing me passionately. He settled a possessive hand on my lower back. "But I'm here now."

"I'll walk you out, Noon," I said, before the pissing contest flooded the place.

We took the shortcut through the house, and I caught him by the arm when we got to his truck. "Hey, sorry we didn't get to catch up. When are you leaving?"

"In a couple days," he said. "I wanted to see you sooner—"

"I'm sure you've been busy with packing and stuff," I said, giving him an out. To be fair, I'd been so caught up in Franky that I hadn't noticed Noon's absence.

"Yeah, I have been," he said, giving me a grateful smile. He dropped his voice to a near whisper. "If he wants you, he'll find a way to choose you no matter what. Remember that. Okay?"

Words failed me, so I nodded.

"I'll be calling you next week," he said, climbing into the cab of his truck and starting up the engine. "Pick up the phone, or I'll fly back and tell your boyfriend how you *really* like it." He wiggled his eyebrows at me and peeled off before I could slug him through the open window. I watched his taillights fade around the bend before heading back inside.

"New habit?" Franky asked, holding up my Marlboro pack.

"Old one. I just had a couple."

He turned the pack upside down to demonstrate that it was empty. "Looks like you eviscerated it." He kissed me again when I got within range. "Tastes like it too."

"How much time do we have?" I asked, sliding his jacket off his shoulders, letting it fall to the ground.

"A few hours. Maybe more."

"Are we really going to spend a moment of it discussing nicotine?"

"I'd rather not," he said, brushing my hair back. "You look tired."

"I'm worried more than anything," I admitted.

"Come, let me take care of you."

Franky ran a hot bath while I patiently waited. "Arms up," he said, removing my shirt. He angled my head up and over to get a good look at the saucer-sized hickey above my collarbone, and then checked the one on my bicep. That one looked closer to a bite than a bruise.

He pinched the waistband of my jeans and underwear, tugging them low on my hip. The fingerprints there were subtle, not like the matching set on my wrists.

He slipped his hand around to my back, feeling for the teeth indentation below my shoulders, smoothing his fingers over it apologetically and shutting his eyes. We'd torn into each other pretty badly the night before he left.

"I allowed my emotions to get the better of me," he said, kneeling in front of me and kissing my belly. "I'm sorry."

"You shouldn't be," I whispered above him, running my fingers through his hair.

"No?" he asked, pained.

"Not for the reasons you're sorry for. Marks don't mean you've hurt me, Franky. I've always bruised easily. I love it when your lips are on me, when your teeth sink into me, and when your hands are too firm," I said. "Rough sex is my favorite. Rough sex with you is my favorite. And I more than returned the favor."

"That you did," he said, smiling against my ribcage.

"Take off your clothes," I said.

"You want to see your handiwork?"

"All of it."

Franky dipped a finger into the water to check the temperature, then turned the valve off before getting rid of his clothes. He was a thing of fucking beauty surrounded by candlelight. His dark edges sharper, the hard planes of his body menacing.

I grazed my fingers over the vicious claw marks already scabbing over on his chest, then lower to the ones on his burly thighs. "They're sexy," I said, his cock swaying slightly as it thickened.

"Oh no you don't," he said, peeling my fingers off his cock. "This is about you."

"But it's your birthday," I complained, gawking at the network of veins below his succulent tip.

"Which means we get to do whatever I want." On his knees again, he unbuttoned my jeans and peeled them down, stopping as my tight, lace briefs came into view. "What's this?" he asked, hauling my pants farther down.

"A birthday gift," I said as he skimmed his nose up and down the front pouch holding my dick hostage.

"I love lace," he said, now mouthing my caged bulge. I'd learned that tidbit of information from an interview Selene had done where she'd jokingly mentioned that her penchant for wearing the delicate fabric was due to her husband's appreciation for it. She'd sported a fitted lace jumpsuit on the cover of the independent magazine.

Franky tore the front of the underwear away, his tongue out and waiting to catch my chubbing cock as it fell free from the gaping hole.

"Fuck, Franky," I groaned, unable to breathe past the hot steam stifling the air.

Franky released my cock with a pop, falling to his heels, one hand on the tub's ledge, the other strong-arming the base of his erection. "Get in," he ordered, barely holding on to his sanity.

I legged out of my jeans and the shredded underwear, then submerged myself into the hot water with a hiss when my bruises protested. The pain faded away within minutes. "You're going to have to take care of that first if you expect me to relax while being bathed." I gestured between my legs to where my cock saluted below the water as Franky reached for the bath sponge and soap.

"Maybe I want you to suffer," he said, even while reaching below the surface to take care of me. I got comfortable, bending my legs until my knees rose above the water and then letting them fall to the sides of the tub.

"How long are you going to keep me in suspense?" I asked, undulating as he worked me at a leisurely pace. "How was the reunion?"

"I was happy to see the boys," he said. "Although, how I felt on the inside about their return didn't translate well on the outside. I mostly stood back as they fawned over their mother."

"You're too hard on yourself. You think they don't know you? They love you anyway." Knowing Franky, he greeted them with a handshake-hug and said something like "welcome home" with a stony expression. "I mean, they did fly in for it."

"Yeah," he said with a hint of a loving smile for his sons. He didn't apply enough pressure to bring me over, just enough to mellow me, to make me feel drugged as we spoke.

"And Selene?" I whispered.

He didn't waste time pretending that I was asking about her well-being. "She was respectful of where we still are with things. I haven't changed my mind. I'll find the right time to tell her."

"Did you get to open my birthday gift?" I asked, fingers digging into the edges of the porcelain tub as Franky tightened his fist.

"I excused myself to the kitchen with my slice of birthday cake and added the extra frosting you provided me with."

"A-all of it on o-one piece of c-cake?" I stuttered, body blistering with beads of sweat as my orgasm took shape. I'd managed to jerk off a couple times, filling a portion cup with my cum before he'd left.

"All of it," he stressed, water splashing as he jerked me off.

The back of my head cracked against the tub as I came on a silent scream, tremors overtaking my body.

Franky stalked the streaks of cum floating along the water's surface, his gaze entranced.

"Eat it," I breathed.

"This night isn't supposed to be for me," he said roughly.

"I like knowing that I can give you something she can't."

"It's not a competition," he said.

"Feels like it."

He ripped his attention away from my drifting seed. "I can't breathe when I'm not with you, Leland. My heart doesn't beat the same. It took being without you for a day to realize I've taken being here with you for granted. I couldn't wait until the house was quiet, until everyone had fallen asleep, so that I could race back to you. No one can compete with you. *No* one."

Franky took one last regretful look at my bathwater as I digested his heartfelt speech, trying not to let my conversation with Noon worm its way in.

He's choosing me. I recited those three words in my head, making them my new mantra, as Franky washed my body and my hair. I recited them as he toweled me off before taking me to bed, and even as we fell asleep, our bodies connected at every point.

No sooner had we drifted off, Franky startled awake, checking the time.

"I have to go," he said, slipping his arm from under my head.

"Wait," I said groggily, pushing him onto the mattress and sitting astride him.

"I can't, Leland. I've already stayed too long."

"I'll be quick," I promised, kissing and licking his lips as I readied us. I fucked him with long, slow strokes, only punching my hips down when close to his base, wanting to make sure my ass wasn't spared an inch of him. We came together, eating each other's moans, and although he was impatient to leave, he couldn't resist staying a little while longer when I pressed my open mouth to his nipple. I hollowed out my cheeks, sucking on the pert bead and then showing love to the other one.

"That's enough," he said as I reached between us to palm his semi-hard erection. "I have to go."

I sat up abruptly, stuffing my hole with his cock before he was fully erect.

"Leland," he said sharply, but with half of him already inside, and me working my hips to get him hard enough to allow for me to swallow the rest, the battle had already been won in my favor.

"Don't," he said weakly, trying to pluck me off of him. I dug my knees into his sides, bouncing on and off his dick with purpose as I gripped the headboard.

Franky remained still, irritation burning through his eyes as he stubbornly fought against his natural instinct to cooperate with the fucking, as he fought to not give me what I wanted.

"Mmmm," he eventually groaned against his will. That and the twitch of his cheek were the only signs that he was flesh and bone and not made out of pure stone.

It was unfair of me to put him in this position. If he was caught sneaking back into the house, he'd have to come up with an explanation for where he'd been. *Should be easy enough to manage,* I thought as I continued to fuck him through his anger.

"Stop," he breathed, his order less convincing than the last one, especially after his body began to move punishingly beneath me.

I leaned over him, riding the fuck out of his dick as I whispered threateningly, "Not until you come. Not until I milk you dry. Not until you're mine."

The first two demands were easily fulfilled, and I collapsed on top of Franky afterward, falling asleep before the cum had cooled. I vaguely remembered him planting a kiss on my forehead and complaining about there being no time for cleanup before it was lights-out for me completely.

The next time I woke up I was alone, reaching for my phone to read the incoming text that had woken me up in the first place. Fear clamped around my heart and throat as I stared at the screen, realizing I'd forgotten to account for something. I'd forgotten to account for the day I met *her*.

I read the text one more time and then eventually a fourth, knowing I would need to do something about this, knowing it could potentially ruin everything.

Selene: *How about a hot lunch and a filled cup?*

CHAPTER 19

Franklin

I was in the mood to break something, and since Leland wouldn't be home from his bartending course for at least another hour, I'd have to find something else to take my frustrations out on.

Pulling into the driveway, I tapped the remote attached to the visor, opening all three garage doors simultaneously. One I used as a work area, the center garage stored my functional pieces that Leland had convinced me to sell, and the third served as a graveyard for my failed attempts.

I'd spent the last three days wearing my wedding band, and showing up to Nexcom—to Robert's delight—as if the past few months hadn't happened. I'd even had to bring Samuel out of summer retirement for a few days to chauffeur me around. Luckily he wasn't still in Italy.

The boys were now on their way back to Massachusetts, and removing the ring felt like the first truthful thing I'd done in days.

I dropped it in the cup holder before exiting the Jeep and rolling up my sleeves as I entered the graveyard. I skipped over the heavy tool options lining the cabinets along the back wall, choosing the metal bat leaning in the corner instead. A saw or drill wouldn't help with the type of aggression I needed to work out. I needed to beat on something.

By the time Leland arrived, grinding Betty to a screeching halt, I no longer needed that evening workout session I had planned. God only knew where my shirt had disappeared to, probably under all the rubble hiding the floor, and even my eyeballs felt drenched with sweat.

"What's got you Hulking out?" he asked, kicking a slab of wood out of his way to get to me. He'd left his car running and the door open, and the worry lines creasing his forehead betrayed the easy attitude his question implied.

"Don't worry, your ass isn't in trouble—pun intended," I said, figuring he probably thought my mood would transfer over to him. It was quite the opposite. Seeing him had made everything better.

"That's a shame. My ass likes your brand of trouble." His concern retreated, although there was still something anxious about his expression.

"I've missed you," I said around a sigh, because maybe he needed some reassurance, and because it was true. I let go of the bat as Leland admired the corded muscles along my forearm. They tended to be more pronounced after heavy exertion.

"I wasn't expecting *that*," he said, "but I'll take it. So, what did I miss?" He waved hand at all the destruction.

"Well," I said, dropping a kiss to his lips. "I was told that I needed to 'get my head out of the clouds' as I prepared to leave Nexcom's headquarters earlier. I was informed that I don't get to lead a normal life because too many people depend on me, and the success of my company, to feed their families. My future grandchildren are depending on me. My great-grandchildren are depending on me..." I made a so-on and so-on motion with my hand. "You get the idea."

Leland snorted. "Robert?"

I wasn't sure I'd nailed my imitation of Robert, as hyperbole wasn't my style, but Leland guessed it after having only met the man once. "His last-resort was to guilt me with Cole."

"How so?" Leland asked. We'd moved beyond the construction zone I'd created and now stood near his car.

"Cole came into the office with me one day. Sat behind my desk, spun around in my chair. He wants this," I said, squinting against the sunlight. "Robert said the least I could do was preserve it for him."

"Cole's interested in running the company?"

"Looks like it. This wasn't the first sign either. I used to think his interest in Nexcom might've come from pressure on my part throughout the years. I'd always told myself it was the one area where my father and I differed, but I could see now that while my brand of pressure may have been more subtle, it was nonetheless pressure. Nexcom was the only thing we shared, really. I'd thought maybe that connection had translated to him as pressure to be my successor. But his interest seems genuine."

"So you're going back full-time?" Leland asked.

"It's not like I planned on faking my death and skipping town. I just thought I could play a lesser role. Bring someone on as acting CEO perhaps." I shrugged. "But the market is volatile right now. The economy isn't doing well, and the tech industry is feeling it. Nexcom has seen some losses. I need to be visible. I need to do this for Cole."

"So then you go back," he said. "But you fight to still find time for *you*."

"Yeah," I said, lips thinning. Summer was coming to an end, and the real world waited at autumn's front door. The days were whizzing by too fast, as Leland once eloquently put it. "But not right now. Not today. Today I want to get reacquainted with you."

"What do you want to do?" Leland asked, already bouncing on his feet.

"I want to take you to dinner."

"Like dinner outside this house, dinner?" he asked.

"Yes." I chuckled. "Didn't you forbid me from ever touching the stove again?"

"Yeah, but is it okay for us to be out together?"

Aside from that night at Josephine's, we'd never gone farther than the ocean together. And we were just friends then, and on the wrong side of town, chances were slim we'd run into anyone who knew me or knew of me. It was sort of an unspoken agreement to be discreet after we'd altered the dynamics of our relationship. It'd be impossible for us to keep our hands off each other while in public, and anyone with the slightest bit of intelligence would pick up on the fact that we were more than friends. Going out hadn't been worth the hassle or the risk. Besides, we'd had everything we needed right here, with each other. But I missed him, and I wanted to do something different tonight.

"I'll rent something out if I have to," I said, rubbing my nose against his. "But first, let's go for a swim." I had him in a fireman's hold and jogging around the side of the house before he could warn me not to do something stupid like jump into the ocean. I at least placed him on his feet at the dock to strip him first as his laughter rustled the tree tops.

We played beneath the water like children, splashing and chasing one another, laughing until it hurt. We didn't make it to dinner that night, choosing to stay home where we didn't need to hold back our affection, where we could make love undisturbed and without restraint.

We spent the next three days patching up our bubble, locking the outside world out, and taking each other in.

With Leland's help, I painted my first portrait, and with my guidance he made a questionable stool to replace his milk crate. And I *almost* got him to cough up more details on his mysterious art-bar. Leland was determined to make me work for it.

Every night I got to rip him out of something lacy. One night in particular, Leland wore a lace catsuit that came with a built in opening at the front and back. I did my best to keep that one intact but was unable to do more than let my erection fall through my open zipper before taking him on the patio.

We shared baths, we shared our bodies, and we made plans. I couldn't wait to get our life started.

That all changed on day four.

CHAPTER 20

Leland

The shrill ringing of Franky's cell phone woke us up with a start. The digital clock read two in the morning.

"Hello?" Franky said into the phone, voice alert considering the time. Then again, a call at this hour could only mean an emergency. Franky sucked in a sharp breath. "I'm on my way." Throwing the sheet off, he hurried into the closet. I did the same.

"What's wrong?" I asked as Franky tore clothes off their hangers. "Are Cole and Jasper—"

"Selene's been rushed to the hospital. I have to go."

"I'll go with you," I said, already moving to the other side of the closet where I kept my things.

"You can't," he said, stopping me. I'd never seen him so afraid, so anxious, and I didn't want to cost him more precious seconds by debating all the ways I could've been there for him without being in the way, and without being seen. I would've stood in the pouring rain outside the hospital doors if I had to.

"Okay," I said. "I'll be here if you need me." I wanted to ask for details. Details he probably didn't have given the short duration of the call. Instead, I fell back as he put his shirt on inside out, then followed him to his car.

"I'll call or text as soon as I can," he said, kissing me with trembling lips. He was pulling off before I could kiss him back.

I sent up a silent prayer that whatever had happened, Selene would be okay.

Going back to sleep was out of the question, so I alternated between pacing a hole in the living room floor and chewing my nails down as I blankly watched the sun rise through the closed living room wall.

I debated calling the hospital, but I knew I wouldn't get any answers over the phone. I just wanted her to be okay. For everyone's sake, including my own, she needed to be okay.

Day transitioned into night again, and I still hadn't heard from Franky. I didn't want to call him in case Cole and Jasper were around, or potentially other family members. I didn't want to add to his stress, but my own stress levels had reached dangerous heights.

I gave in at the eighteen-hour mark and phoned the hospital. All they would tell me was that only family was being allowed in at this time, but at least that meant she was alive.

She'd been tired, I remembered Franky telling me once, and I'd seen it with my own eyes. *Could that be related to this?*

My phone vibrated, skidding across the coffee table, and I lurched forward from the sofa to grab it.

Franky: *She's awake and stable. I'll be here for a couple more hours, until she falls asleep, then I'll stop by.*

Leland: *Take all the time you need. I'll be here.*

I hit send on my reply, my exhaustion crippling me now that I knew she'd be okay. He'd said he would stop by, meaning he wouldn't be staying, but I'd expected that. Knowing I'd get to lay eyes on him, hug him, breathe him in and give him some strength to deal with whatever lay ahead, was enough.

I managed to eat something for the first time that day, then showered before crumbling wet and naked onto our bed.

The clap of thunder jerked me from sleep four hours later, way beyond the time Franky said he'd be here. Lightning lit up the room, revealing Franky's foreboding shape as he watched me from a dark corner in the room. "Shit, Franky," I hissed, scurrying to the headboard. How long had he been standing there?

"Put some clothes on and meet me downstairs," he said as he started for the bedroom door. The smell of scotch lingered moments after his footsteps had receded down the hall.

Entering the kitchen, I tightened the string on my sweats, stopping at the uncapped bottle of brown liquor on the kitchen island. It was full last night. A little more than half now remained.

Another clap of thunder rang out, followed by two bolts of lightning that illuminated Franky's stern profile as he peered through the glass wall and toward the ocean.

"Hey," I said softly, padding over to him. Franky sidestepped my touch, glaring at me with harsh accusations in his eyes. Had something changed since our text exchange? "Is Selene—"

"She's fine. For now," he amended. "That could change as early as tomorrow or as late as next year, or the year after." His voice echoed with hysteria, and he worked to calm himself down. "She has dilated cardiomyopathy. It's a heart condition. There are things that can be done in the short term, but she'll need a new heart to survive it. And maybe not even then."

"Franky," I whispered, reaching up to touch his face. Franky laced his hands around my wrists before forcing my hands to my sides. He backed away until he'd reached the fireplace, as if he didn't trust himself to be near me. I stood there as rain crashed against the wall, heart throbbing.

"Why were you nervous when you came home the other day?"

"The other day?" I asked, confused. There seemed to be multiple things going on here at once, and I was the only one left out of the loop on any of it. I thought over his question, as he didn't seem to be in the mood to repeat himself or offer any assistance in jogging my memory. I hadn't left the house in days, not since... *Fuck.* Not since the day he'd taken a bat to the furniture in one of the garages. Two days after I'd woken up to a text from Selene. My gaze fell away from him.

"Not ready to share yet?" he asked, his anger tugging at its leash. "Fine, I'll go first."

I counted each of the three deep breaths he took before he spoke again.

"Selene called her assistant. She wasn't feeling well and needed her help in getting to the hospital. She didn't want to risk driving but didn't think it was serious enough to warrant an ambulance." The drop in his voice, signaling rage, felt directed at himself. Either he was upset she hadn't thought she could call him, or he felt guilty that she'd had to face this alone. Probably both.

"She collapsed during their brief conversation. Tricia acted quickly. Calling for help as she sped over to the estate. The paramedics had to administer CPR." He paused there, shoving his hands in his front pockets to hide the way they trembled. My fingertips scratched against the glass at my back in search of something to hold on to, since it was clear that something wouldn't be him.

"I spent the next several hours, as she lay in a hospital bed unconscious, searching for answers. Raging at every nurse and doctor who couldn't give me a straight one, and firing Selene's assistant for keeping her secrets from me." His nostrils flared savagely as he fought for control over himself, and I fought to stay on my feet.

"I didn't know whether or not to call my sons, because I didn't know what news I'd be delivering to them, and instinctively I knew that had she wanted them to know something was wrong with her, they would have already known. So I waited, and it was the hardest decision I ever had to make. Every hour she remained asleep, and those machines hooked up to her continued to beep, I thought I may lose my mind. Her cardiologist finally showed up, shedding light on the situation."

I wanted to comfort him, to say fuck it, fuck his anger, fuck what he was leading up to, fuck my fear of the outcome. I wanted to run to him and hold him, and beg him to forgive me. "Franky, please—"

"She eventually opened her eyes, and the first thing she said to me was under no circumstances should I tell the boys about any of this. We went over her diagnosis with her doctors and came up with a treatment plan, but there was a somber note in the room as we all understood what she'd need in the long term. With nothing left to do but sit and worry, Selene decided she'd distract me with frivolous conversation, and the more I encouraged her to rest and not worry about me, the more she worried, and the more she talked."

I couldn't stop my tears from brewing as his pain pricked at me from across the room. His beautiful eyes pivoted from hurt, to sorrow, to guilt, to helplessness. But mostly there was anger, and he needed somewhere to put it. He always did. I braced myself for the inevitable impact of it.

"I was going to tell you," I said in a small voice.

"How convenient," he sneered, and I closed my eyes, turning my head away from him. "Imagine my surprise when she told me about a young, charismatic artist she met at her last charity event, and how much she'd love to have his work headline her next For the Arts fundraiser."

I swallowed past my dry throat and took a step toward him.

"No!" he shouted, sending me back into the glass. "Don't come near me."

"Let me explain," I begged.

"I didn't even have the strength to feign interest in what the hell she was going on about. I was too consumed with the shock of nearly losing her, too consumed with the fear of possibly losing her still. But then she whispered his name. *Noon Waters.* And that got my attention."

"Franky—"

"How odd, I thought, that there were two people out there with the same, uncommon name. First and last. So I asked her for a description. She smiled and said jokingly from her hospital bed, 'Sunshine on legs,' and I knew she was talking about *you.*"

Selene may have said it as a joke, as a means to distract him, but Franky said it like it was a weakness he wished he no longer had, and the first fissure cracked down the center of my heart, because he would use this to end us.

"She's still waiting for you to get back to her," he gritted out.

I'd never responded to her text, hadn't given much thought to how my meeting her under false pretenses would come back to bite me until I'd received her message. We'd one day meet. One day, Franky would need to introduce me to her, because she would be a part of his life in some way forever, and she'd know. She'd remember me.

I'd somehow thought he'd already known when I showed up to find him demolishing shit in the garage. But he didn't know, and we then spent the next several days refamiliarizing ourselves with each other, being obscenely obsessed with one another, and I willfully forgot.

"Don't use this as an excuse to walk away," I pleaded, each word a struggle to utter past the lump swelling at the back of my throat.

"An *excuse?*" he asked, appalled. "You lied to me! That was the day..." He stopped to add a few things up in his head. "The charity event happened on the first day of your course. Did you even attend?"

"You're scared—"

"Answer me!" he roared, face turning red. The patio chair scraped across the floor as the howling wind picked up, the sound only audible because of the sudden break in the continuous cracks of thunder. It was like Franky's outburst had made even the storm hold its breath.

"No," I admitted, panic churning in my stomach. "I didn't plan on approaching her. My feelings for you were changing, and I got curious. I knew I didn't want our affair to end yet, but I didn't know we would end up together. I didn't know that I would ask you to leave her for me. I didn't think it through, but what I did isn't some impeachable offense, Franky. It was a mistake. We can get past this," I said, my legs taking me to him.

Franky held a hand out to stop me, his feet carrying him away until the coffee table and sofa separated us. He was running from me, and my heart couldn't take it. My lungs were forgetting how to function without him already.

"What the fuck is happening here?" I asked, staring into his red-rimmed eyes. His hair looked as if it'd been run over, like he'd been cruelly tugging at it, and his scruff had sprouted into a small beard since I last saw him. The stress had aged him too. He seemed frail, and I didn't miss the way he pressed his palms into the sofa back for support. Had he gotten a wink of sleep?

"I bet you're thrilled about this, aren't you?" he asked. "Things would be so much easier for you if she were gone." He couldn't have hurt me more if he'd punched me with a brass-knuckled fist.

"Don't pretend you don't know me enough to know I'd never wish for that."

"But I don't know you, Leland," he said, his voice trembling as he retreated a step in response to my one step advancement.

He's running from me. And then another realization infiltrated my mind. *He's pushing me away.*

"Don't do this." A rogue tear dripped onto my cheek. Franky dropped his gaze to it, shuddering through an expelled breath, and backed into the hall until his spine met the wooden balusters. "You came here to hurt me. Why, Franky?"

The light from the upstairs hall trickled down the staircase, spotlighting his wet eyes, and whereas he'd been operating on pure rage and pain before, he now looked lost. "I need you to hate me," he whispered.

"Don't you know that I love you too much to ever hate you?" I'd never said the words out loud before. Maybe a part of me was always afraid I'd scare him off, like maybe our foundation wasn't strong enough to handle a bombshell like love. But I'd said it with every look, every kiss, and every single touch. And it had been reciprocated. I'd felt it whenever I was beneath his capable hands, whenever pinned by his body and unforgiving cock. I felt it with every tortuous and possessive claim he'd made on me, and even through his most unpleasant moods. I couldn't hate him if I tried.

I took advantage of the momentary distraction my admission bought me. I scaled the coffee table, leaped onto the sofa, then jumped off the back of it. I had his face in the palms of my hands before he could move a muscle in the opposite direction.

Franky sagged in on himself, like my hands on him were both the last thing he needed and the only thing that could save him. He couldn't pretend anymore, not when we were like this. "You can't love me," he said.

"Why not?" I asked, kissing his tears away.

"Because... I can't leave her now." The words were ripped from deep inside him, and they cut open some place deep inside of me.

"You mean now, like right now, right? Because I wouldn't expect you to. Fuck, she almost *died,* Franky. I don't expect you to storm her hospital room with divorce papers. Is that what this is about? We'll make it work. You said there's a treatment plan in place. We'll wait until she's stronger. Until she can handle the news. M-maybe w-we'll tell the boys first?" I rambled on.

My panic rose at the look of guilt and pity in his eyes, and I used all my strength to keep his head still as he moved it slowly in the gesture of no in my hands. "Yes," I breathed. "Yes. I can wait for you. We can even take care of her together. *Please.*"

He stood taller, holding my face in his hands in return, my naivety reflected in his sorrowful eyes.

"Don't say it. If you aren't going to say the right thing, then don't say anything," I ordered, yanking at the collar of his shirt. Franky didn't say anything, which said it all. Two excruciating heartbeats turned into ten, and I couldn't stand it anymore. "Say something!" I yelled, shaking him.

"What do you want me to say, Leland?" He brushed a thumb under my damp eyes.

"I want you to say we'll find a way to make it work. I want you to say it'll be hard, and it will take longer than we thought, but nothing will tear us apart. Because if you want me, Franky…" I stopped to swallow down a sob. "If you want me, you'll find a way to choose me, no matter what." I skimmed my fingers along his brows, his lips, and his chin. Wanting to kiss him, to remind him of how good we were together. Of how worth the fight we were. The upstairs light flickered as another round of furious thunder and lightning battled for dominance over the booming of our hearts, and volts of electricity sizzled across the points of our skin that touched. "We can be a secret. For however long it takes. Just…*please*, choose me."

"Can't you see how selfish of me that would be, Leland?"

"No," I said determinedly. "Because all I can see is how terrified you are. Choosing me doesn't mean you don't love her, or that you can't be there for her. It just means you love me enough to fight for me. No matter what it takes."

"Noon was right. Everything he said to you on the patio that night was true. We were in way over our heads to begin with." He'd heard our conversation that night, I realized, and he'd said nothing until now. "The odds weren't in our favor from the start."

"Fuck the odds," I said, refusing to let him run through excuse after excuse as to why we couldn't be. "I'd face down anything to be with you. Now *please* do the same for me."

His fingers curled tightly in my hair, and I slapped my hands on top of his, as if I could siphon some of his pain into me, proving that I could carry some of the burden if he'd only let me.

"You could never be my priority. Your needs would come last to hers, if I could even tend to your needs at all. You would get the scraps of my time. I'll make promises I won't be able to keep. You'll live in a constant state of waiting for me. She's *dying*," he said, agonized. "They won't say it, but she is. And my heart is broken because of it. Every time I see you, I'll be looking for something to ease the pain, something to dump my pain on, something I can rage against. You would be getting the worst parts of me every time, because I'll need to give her my best. It will slowly eat away at you, and you'll eventually hate me."

"You don't scare me. Your darkness doesn't scare me, Franky. How many times do I have to prove that I can handle you?"

"You shouldn't have to," he said angrily, trying to shake some sense into me. "You shouldn't have to handle me. You deserve better than that."

"I don't want better! I want *you*. I'll take your fucking scraps without complaint if it means one day I get to have more. If it means that sometime in this lifetime I'll get to have the good parts of you again." I smashed my mouth against his. If he wouldn't listen to my heartfelt words, I'd show him in the only other way I knew how—with my body.

"Stop it," he snarled, wrestling me away from him. He turned for the side door, and I grabbed him by the back of his shirt.

"Fight!" I yelled. "Fight for us!"

Franky swung around and hauled me into his chest with a painful grasp on my wrists. "Can't you see I'm doing the right thing here?! Can't you see how much this is killing me?!" The volume of his voice reached a fevered pitch, and in the midst of me trying to break free of his hold, my fist connected with his upper lip, slitting it wide open. Whatever sliver of restraint he'd managed to cling to, immediately evaporated.

I didn't back away as he wiped his lip, staring at his bloody digits as his breathing accelerated. And I didn't flinch when his blank gaze flicked to mine.

"Do your fucking worst," I said resolutely.

Franky crashed into me, sending us barreling over the sofa back and onto the floor, wedged in by the coffee table. My shoulder collided with the sharp, wooden edge of it, and Franky shoved it out of our way. It screeched across the floorboards, knocking into an end table and pitching the porcelain lamp to the ground. Chunks of its shattered pieces skidded over to us as Franky forced his way between my thighs.

I could've made things easy for him, but he needed this. *We* needed this.

His rage grew as we tussled, pouring from his eye sockets like twin beams of light, and I'd knowingly stepped in the way of it.

Franky kissed me like he hated me, tasting of tears, blood, and scotch, and I struggled to get free of the attack as all three flavors watered my tongue.

He broke the kiss, his palm clamping around my throat as his gaze flitted around the living room in search of something. I bucked against him, but he just sank his hips deeper into me, lightly humping my erection.

"Get off of me," I croaked, trying to peel his fingers off me. I followed his stare to the bottle of lube lying amongst the lamp's wreckage. It must have fallen off the end table as well.

A war waged within his vibrating body. He needed to get the lube, but he didn't want to risk me getting free. "Stay put," he warned, but I flipped onto my front and scurried on all fours toward the stairs as soon as he'd hefted himself off of me.

I'd gotten half way up before he'd caught up to me, grabbing one leg of my sweats and tugging. My chest met the hard tread, and I held tight to the one above me as he attempted to drag me back down.

I kicked out, breaking free of his hold, and managed to crawl up a couple more steps before his hands were on me again. Franky dragged my pants down by the waistband, and I crawled right out of them, continuing up the landing as he tumbled backward, meeting the bottom step with a groan and a curse.

The air whooshed out of me as he grappled me from behind, using his strength to his advantage, sending me front first to the floor and then straddling me.

"Yield," he gritted out, subduing me with an arm to the back of my neck as the sound of his zipper lowering rang out.

"That isn't what you want, Franky," I said, clenching my ass shut against the cool lube hitting it, forcing him to peel one cheek aside before fitting his crown inside of me. He wanted a fight, someone to rain pain down on, and I wanted to show him that that someone would always, willingly, be me.

I dug my fingers and toes into the floorboards, gaining an inch of forward momentum, causing his cockhead to slip from my opening.

"Damn it," he spat as he repositioned his legs so they were between mine, then used his knees to push mine higher, situating me in a frogged position before fully seating his cock in my vulnerable hole.

"Fuck," I moaned, smacking a palm against the wooden floor as he took off, thrusting faster than the lightning still jetting wildly across the sky.

Franky didn't fuck me with caution, didn't once stop to care about his size, about my limits, about whether or not I had any. He used and abused my hole, throwing his weight into me and driving us down the hallway without restraint.

The fucking wasn't romantic. It was archaic, barbaric, graceless, and inconsiderate. All we were missing was the club needed to hit me over the head with and the cave for him to drag me into.

He was giving me a taste, an example, using this as a teachable moment for what he'd have to offer me moving forward. What he didn't understand was that I'd take it, because I loved him enough to, because *something* was a fuck ton better than nothing. "Let me have it, Franky. Give me your pain, your anger, your fight... I can take it."

Franky pulled my head off the floor by my hair, my lower back arching enough to keep my cock from scraping against the hard surface as he delivered brutal thrust after thrust, deeper and deeper, propelling us down the long hall.

Franky was a carnivore who wouldn't be satisfied until my bones were bare, until I paid for him falling in love with me to begin with.

"I love you, Franky," I said, biting my lip to still the quivering. His groan sounded wounded, and I wondered if the wetness hitting my ear was sweat, blood, or more of the moisture I'd seen behind his eyes downstairs.

This felt like goodbye, like him saying this was all he could give me, and like me falling apart, never to be whole again.

Franky reared back, taking me with him and slinging his arms across my chest, crushing me against him as he shoved his dick in and out of me.

"Let me see you," I said, edging toward orgasm. "I need to see you."

He reluctantly let go of me, and I popped off his cock, turned to him, then lowered back onto his dick.

Franky tried to hide his face in my neck as we began to move again, but I fought to hold his gaze to me. "Touch me," I cried, the jagged pieces of my heart stabbing at my breastbone. Franky blinked, the last of his unshed tears falling before he wrapped his fingers around my cock.

"I'll be here," I said, riding him hard. "I'll be here waiting for you. You need a few days to think. I know that, but I'll be here when you're ready." I slammed down on his cock one last time, my vision blurring as thick strings of cum spurted into the air like confetti, bathing his knuckles and lower abdomen white.

Franky spasmed as he came, dropping his forehead to mine as he filled my hole to the point of overflowing.

The cold claws of reality crept in, and he spread me out on the floor so he could heave to his feet and zip himself back into his pants. He hadn't even cleaned me first, which I'd come to need after we fucked because it reminded me that he cared. The reverent ritual had also become a sort of apology in my eyes, one I didn't know I needed until now.

"Franky," I said, and had to say it again to gain sound. He looked away in shame.

I knew better than to get mixed up with Franklin Kincaid, but I hadn't cared about the risks because every fiber of my being wanted him. I should've cared, because I could feel every snap, every break of something vital happening inside of me as he stumbled along the wall toward the stairs, moving farther and farther away from me. "I'll never be the same, Franky," I promised, giving in to the pain and devastation contorting my body. "Please don't fucking break me."

"I'm sorry," he whispered. And then he was gone.

I waited for him for nineteen whole days, with nothing to nourish me but fleeting hope. I waited, and he never came.

He never chose me.

CHAPTER 21

Leland

Two Months Later

Neil Sanders was the last guy I wanted to see again, but since we had history, my chances of getting him to buy another piece from me would be greater than if I'd gone to a gallery where I'd be an unknown. I needed cash, and he could smell it on me, and the disdainful curl to his top lip said he wouldn't make this easy.

"Five hundred," he said.

"One thousand," I countered, holding on to the edge of the large canvas with a death grip. It was my last connection to Franky. I could've brought any other painting here, but I'd chosen this one for that specific reason, and now I thought I might be sick if I let go of it.

"Six hundred," he said with finality, taking pleasure in having the upper hand.

I only needed money for gas, food, and a few other essentials until I could get work. The bartending school had taken pity on me, crediting me for the course I hadn't completed, and waving the registration fee for December's class. So I didn't need funds for that.

There'd been an influx of cash into my account a few weeks after Franky walked out on me, way more money than the mural was worth. Knowing Franky, the extra was to compensate for his

239

guilt. I'd had every dime returned to fucking sender immediately. Money couldn't fix what he'd broken.

"Sold," I said dejectedly, my tone matching my overall appearance.

"Great. I'll get the paperwork drawn up," Neil said, scurrying off and leaving me to mourn in peace.

I'd created this painting the day Franky and I fought after he'd told me Cole and Jasper were coming into town for a few days. It had been a form of release then, but I'd quickly decided I wanted it to be a gift. I'd worked tirelessly to perfect it, barring Franky from the guest room where I kept it hidden from him. He'd never get to see it now. Never get to see himself through my eyes.

Neil cleared this throat, startling me. "Change of heart?" he asked, and I released my tight grip on it, stepping several feet away.

"No," I said, the word cutting into the rough edges of my heart.

I signed the contract and collected my check, rushing out into the misty afternoon air before the ink had fully dried. I wasn't any closer to knowing how to live without Franky than I had been the night he left me naked and hurting on the hall floor pleading for him to take mercy on me. Pleading for him to not break me.

I'd left voicemail messages that went unreturned, sent text messages that went unanswered, and during my lowest point, I waited for him one morning outside of Nexcom's headquarters, but he hadn't shown up.

I'd spent weeks occupying the home we shared for the summer, weeks of fucking weeping in front of the fireplace, praying he'd come back to me, praying that he was okay. I'd become a desperate man, and when I looked in the mirror, it was my mother who stared back at me tauntingly.

Sometimes I would sleep on the ocean, curled into a fetal position in the boat's cabin, remembering the nights he'd make love to me with a vengeance in the tiny space. The nights he'd explode inside of me, then place his mouth over my hole before hollowing his cheeks and extracting what he'd just poured into me. Franky was selfish in that way too. Always demanding I return what he gave to me.

I used booze to mask and numb the pain I'd suffered from the loss of his warmth, the loss of his belief in me, and the loss of his uncompromising force when wanting and needing me. It literally hurt to breathe during that time, but as the days passed by in a blur, it hurt a little less to hate him. The hate became the thing that would sustain me.

He'd changed his number around week four, and so I began writing him letters. Some were angry, requiring a whole note pad to complete. Some letters were short and sweet, containing a simple *I love you, Franky.*

Then there were the tear-soaked letters that included some of our best memories, like when I'd hold him against my chest as he slept, snoring softly into my neck, dampening the skin there.

Or that time I'd thrown my legs over the arms of the chair on the patio, stuffing my cum into my hole after jerking off less than two feet away from him. He'd refused to fuck me, saying my body needed a break after the night he'd had with it, so I'd taken my time, getting myself off as the most wicked things spilled from my mouth in an effort to tempt him into taking me.

"Enough," he'd said defeatedly, but I continued sawing my fingers in and out of my hole as he watched helplessly. Franky was no match for my games, especially not when cum was involved.

I'd agreed to stop, dropping my feet to the floor, but the damage had already been done. Franky strong-armed his way between my legs, licking and swirling his tongue around the nail-beds and cuticles of my cum-drenched fingers before tackling the web of skin between the digits.

I then spread myself out on the patio table, lifting my legs and pulling my cheeks apart as he fought with his desires. *"Well, are you going to kneel there and pretend you don't want the rest of this clogging up your throat?"* I'd asked. I bore down as he rimmed me through his annoyance, he even got the dried stains on the underside of my shaft before standing and wrangling me to my knees.

"Why do I get the feeling you like seeing me this way," he'd said, speaking past a tired tongue, his scruff and nostrils shiny and wet.

"What way?" I'd asked, as he angrily undid his pants, his cock springing into the air.

"On the brink. Like..." He'd faded off, in search of the right words.

"Like you'd do anything to have me?" I'd said. *"Like the only way for you to cope with wanting me is by taking it all out on me? Your anger, your lust, your guilt... Your sadness too?"*

"Yes," he'd said, seemingly shocked at how in tune I was with him. I could feel the rage in him boiling because of it, boiling because he was about to prove me right, and there was nothing he could do about it.

"You're a tortured soul, Franky, but I can handle it. When no one else can, I can handle you," I'd promised him.

"Your hole may not be ready for me," he said, words garbled like he'd been eating rocks, not cum. *"But your mouth seems to be functioning just fine."* He'd fucked my throat then, coming shortly after on a rabid snarl.

I reminded him of all that in my letter, even spilling my cum onto one of them, hoping my scent would win me his change of heart. I never mailed them, though. I'd tossed them all into the fire.

There was one letter I'd actually sealed and stamped, intending on forwarding it to him, but I ended up shredding it with hands and teeth before dumping the bits into the trash. That was the day I'd left our sacred place for good.

I'd gone back to my apartment, where in between religiously jerking off to dreams or nightmares of Franky, I found time to have a mini breakdown after receiving a text from Noon. Things were going well in New York.

With Noon gone, and now Franky, I was the one thing I feared more than anything. I was alone. I'd been thrown out of a window again.

The mist grew to an impatient drizzle, shaking me from my thoughts. I moved to the side, allowing a couple to hurry out of the rain and into the gallery as I breathed through my heart palpitations, as I went over what I needed to do next.

I needed to seal myself off, make myself immune to this type of pain, immune to the feelings of others. There was only one way to do that. I had to find it in me to not care about anything.

Three hours later, I found myself at a seedy gay bar across town, strategically drinking the hard stuff in hopes that it would take half the money needed to get wasted to the point of unconsciousness than it would have had I been guzzling beer.

"Can I buy you a drink?" a guy asked nervously, taking up the empty stool next to mine.

I paused with my drink to my lips, side-eying the tan line where his wedding band should be. "They're all the same," I slurred, huffing a laugh before downing my drink. "You can buy the next two." I rolled my eyes at his eager expression. "Well, what are you waiting for?"

His green eyes sought out the bartender, flagging him down from the other end of the bar. "He'll have another—"

"No. This is the cheap shit." I slid my empty tumbler away from me. "I'll take a round of the best you've got," I said directly to the bartender. "And make it a double." Seconds later I had another drink in my hand and was already asking for more.

"So, what's your name?" he asked, inexperience written all over him. His sandy brown hair had been combed to precision, and his plaid shirt had been buttoned up to his neck. A little too preppy for me. Too nice, and too...*smiley*. The only time Franky showed that much teeth was when they were tearing into my skin. This guy was nothing like what I preferred, which made him perfect for me.

He sipped his beer, looking around as if his spouse might charge in at any minute, and I mentally stabbed the voice telling me this wasn't right, that this was how I ended up here in the first place.

Things would be different from here on out, because I'd promised myself I wouldn't give a fuck anymore. What this guy had going on outside of the hot fuck I intended to get wasn't my problem.

"How about we skip the small talk and get down to why we're both here tonight," I said.

"Ah, okay," he said, seemingly waiting for me to be the one to do something. I'd have to get used to being treated like what happened next was up to me.

"Have you never picked up a random dude for a one night-stand before?"

"No," he admitted, sighing and shaking his leg under the bar top. "I don't normally do stuff like this, but life right now—"

"Rule number one," I said, interrupting his sad song. I couldn't care less why he was here. I wasn't the moral police. "Keep your problems to yourself. It's better that way, and I don't give a fuck about anyone's problems anymore." I winced through the burn of my shot going down and then promptly ordered another. "Add that one to his tab too," I informed the bartender before returning my attention to preppy-boy.

"Rule number two: no names. And rule number three: no repeats. You got a condom?" I asked.

"Yes."

I nodded to the bartender, then chugged my last shot. "Good. Let's go." I staggered toward the restroom, feeling drunk enough to not feel anything, drunk enough to ignore the warning signs of an impending mistake. I wanted Franky gone. I wanted his scent off my skin, wanted his imprint removed from my heart and mind, and I wanted every space in and on my body that had been reserved for his cock only to now be open for walk-ins. I wanted someone— many someones—to fuck him out of my system.

I wanted that guilty, shameful feeling that came with giving away something that belonged to someone else. I wanted there to be no going back for me, just like there had been no looking back for him. I wanted that flimsy string holding what remained of me together to break. I wanted to be the old me—someone who never got too attached—and a mix of someone new, someone stripped of all compassion. I wanted to be walled in where nothing or no one could ever hurt me again.

The bathroom had seen better days, and from the drying streaks on the stall door, we weren't the first to use it for unintended purposes.

"Don't take your time with me," I whispered, fingers trembling against my belt buckle. "Pretend I'm not even human."

"Okay," he said easily, all traces of the shy guy at the bar gone now that he was seconds away from having what he'd come here for. The sound of the condom wrapper being torn open hit my ear, and true to his word, he worried only about getting himself off.

He fucked me as I gripped the top of the rattling stall door, focusing on the place inside me that still clung to hope, focusing for the sole purpose of obliterating it.

He pawed at my hips, but his hold lacked the proprietorship that Franky's contained. His dick rocketed in and out of me at a fast clip, but it lacked the punishing edge that drove each and every one of Franky's devastating thrusts. Our bodies clapped together, but absent was the thunderous crack that filled the air and nearly deafened me whenever Franky crashed into me.

And preppy-boy was a man of many words, prattling on about how good I felt, how hard he was going to come, and how he planned on ruining me with this one, sad fuck.

Franky was a man of few words, a man who could ruin me with one look, a man who could make me come with the promise of a single touch, a man who could make hate sex feel like the greatest expression of love ever known.

I grew dizzy as a vortex of emotion gained momentum in my core, aiming for that final thing tethering me to the man I'd been with Franky. The internal snap came with the shedding of tears, cleansing me of love as the first of many strangers to come finished inside of me.

Next came numbness. I couldn't even feel myself silently crying anymore. Couldn't feel the organ I assumed was still beating within my chest. Couldn't even feel myself orgasm as he reached around to jack me off, adding more white streaks to the collection on the door.

It was over. I was done. I would never be hurt by anyone ever again. It was all wrong, but it was everything I needed.

PART TWO

CHAPTER 22

Franklin

Two Years Later

Josephine's had gone through a renovation since the first and last time I'd walked through its doors with Leland. They now served dinner and had added dimly lit alcoves with high-backed booth seating, providing an area for patrons to have a more intimate and private experience.

I was there because I could no longer sit in the home where my wife had died mere days ago. I couldn't stomach the way I'd emotionally shut my children out, leaving their grief to fend for itself as I hid away like a coward. I needed to be someplace where I could disappear, where I wouldn't matter. Someplace that felt closer to the version of me I hadn't seen for some time.

Those were the numerous reasons I'd given myself for being at Josephine's. I hoped to God they weren't actually excuses.

"Ready to order?" my waitress asked, interrupting my self-flagellation.

I quickly perused the menu. "I'll just have a Stella."

"Sorry, but this area is reserved for diners," she said.

"Add an order of fries, then." The mention of fries, coupled with the nostalgia of this place and everything that came after it, made my chest hurt in a way it hadn't in two years, compounding the pain that had already made a home there. I gripped the small bundle of bar napkins on the table, feeling the tissue tear beneath my hands, beneath my agony.

Left alone, I slipped Selene's last journal entry from my inside pocket, unfolding the sheet of paper and smoothing out the edges. It went into detail about Cole and Jasper's intimate relationship, something I knew nothing about, another complication I didn't need, one I didn't know how to address.

It didn't help that if my suspicions were correct, it meant this secret played a role in Selene collapsing and taking her final breath inside Jasper's bedroom. A vivid imagination wasn't required to paint a picture of what she'd likely walked in on. I'd seen it written all over Cole's and Jasper's faces when I pulled up to the house that night to find her being loaded into a waiting ambulance. I hadn't understood their identical expressions of culpability until later finding her journal.

The entry ended with her needing to make things right with Jasper after making him promise he'd end things. A promise she'd extracted on my behalf, because she didn't want the news to break my heart. If only I'd been just as mindful with her heart throughout our last years.

I couldn't help but also believe she was afraid the revelation would cause me to cast Jasper aside. With her gone, we were the only family he had left, and she probably assumed a transgression this big would've rocked an already fragile foundation.

A part of me blamed them both for what happened to their mother. The irrational part of me that didn't want to carry the burden of blame alone. It was easier to make it through the day if I could direct some of the rage swimming inside me onto someone else, a nasty habit of mine, which of course made my guilt that much worse.

I'd been about to start on my second beer, my fries going cold and untouched, when a familiar sensation prickled at my spine, stiffening it.

"How many times I gotta tell you, you don't shit where you eat, Leland," a stern voice said in a paternal tone. The mention of

Leland's name sent my world spinning. I hadn't dared to speak it since I'd abandoned him to his heartbreak. I hadn't even deserved to dream of it.

There was a pause, in which I wrapped my head around the fact that he was here and that I was so close to being discovered by him. Thankfully, my seat back reached beyond the top of my head, hiding me from the face on the other side of the booth, although I felt the heat of his gaze burning through the wood.

"And how many times do I have to tell you it's called taking a cock, Johnny. Not shitting," Leland eventually said. I flinched from his brashness, from his crude delivery, and maybe even from the act he'd confessed to itself. I badly wanted to stand, to peer over the top of the seat to see if his sweet face had hardened the way his tone had implied. Words delivered like that couldn't have come from anything with a trace of softness inside of it.

"And besides, I'm not on the clock yet," he said to Johnny, letting me know he worked there.

"You are now," Johnny said. "Get behind the bar, Leland." Johnny may have been at his wits' end, but there was fondness under the exasperation too. "And cover up that hickey, will ya? One of these days I'm going to make good on my promise and fire you," he grumbled.

He'd been fucked and branded by someone other than me, and I shouldn't have given a damn. Not now, not with everything I had going on in my life, not ever again. I shouldn't have been there, yet, I had to see him now that I was. I prepared myself for what I might see before peeking my head out of the booth.

Leland was busy wiping down the bar. He wore a fitted thermal with the sleeves tugged up to his elbows, and he hadn't done anything to hide the bruise from the view of customers as Johnny had requested. He'd need a turtleneck to hide something of that size anyway. Instead, he wore it proudly, a scarlet letter he paraded around without shame.

Leland didn't exude the impishness I'd come to know him for during our time together. His eyes weren't as soft around the edges, and the boyish smile that had always teased below the surface of his lips no longer existed. He'd hardened.

He was still handsome, more so now, if that were possible. But he no longer reminded me of sunshine. Leland was a cyclone of pain. I'd tarnished him.

Maybe this was what I'd come here for. To hopefully see him and be reminded that nothing good ever came from me getting too close to anyone. First Theo, then Annabeth, then Cole, then Jasper and Selene. And now Leland. I was better off in my mental isolation, trapped inside myself where I couldn't hurt anyone but myself. Where the hurt I'd already inflicted paled in comparison to what I could do if I made myself available to those who needed me most.

I stuck around long enough to witness him hit on every paying customer who sat at his bar. I didn't bother waiting for the bill. Instead I dropped enough cash on the table to cover my tab and gratuity, then gnashed my teeth as his flirtatious laughter followed me into the cool night air. A laugh that held a dark edge that hadn't been there before.

◆ ◆ ◆

Selene smiled at me from the picture frame atop the armoire as I tore at my tie, adjusting it for the tenth time.

"How am I supposed to get through this day?" I asked, closing my eyes on her. We had an hour to be at the church. An hour before well-meaning people joined us in saying our goodbyes. An hour before the plethora of apologies began rolling in. An hour before we were forced to smile and offer gratitude for their sympathy, when all I wanted to do was lock myself away and forget that one of the most important people in my life was now gone.

An urgent knock sounded on the bedroom door before Cole barged in, breathing raggedly.

"Cole?" I said, spinning away from the mirror. We'd all been sitting in our separate corners, licking our wounds these last couple weeks since her death. I knew what guilt looked like, knew the awkward energy it exuded, knew the gazes it made one unable to hold. Cole and Jasper felt guilty, and their guilt caused them to avoid me, and mine caused me to let them, so I was surprised to see him here now. "What's wrong—"

"Jasper's leaving. He won't even stay for the funeral. You have to do something. Talk to him. *Please.*"

"Did he say why he's leaving?"

"Just... Just that he needs time away." He folded his arms defensively. Lying had never come easy to Cole. He was a man who spoke plainly, but he lied to me now, or at the very least only gave me a half-truth.

The right move would've been to assuage his distress. I should've told him that I would do whatever it took to keep what remained of our family intact. That would've been the fatherly thing to do. I couldn't form the words he needed to hear, though, because I was in no condition to keep anything together. And a part of me approved of his and Jasper's separation. A big part of me. Most of me.

"Everyone copes in their own way," I said, unable to hold his stare. "If he wants to leave, there's nothing we can do about it."

He blanched, stumbling back as if I'd struck him with an open fist. "But he's your son," he whispered, cutting out what remained of my heart.

"I know," I said. What I knew and what I felt resided on two different planes. "But forcing him to stay may not be what's best for him."

Cole battled with indecision, likely knowing that if he wanted more from me, he'd need to offer me more. He wouldn't, though, because then we'd have to deal with why we'd lost Selene just hours before being notified that she'd made it to the top of the donor list. We'd have to deal with the fact that he and Jasper had grown from stepbrothers to lovers practically under my nose.

There was a sense of betrayal that came with that knowledge, but it also further highlighted my inadequacies as a parent. How had I not known? How had I not seen it before, when *all* I could do was see it now. There was no escaping the way they looked at each other.

"So...so you're just going to let him go?"

God, his watery blue eyes bore into me the way mine had beseeched my father after learning I'd lost Gloria and Theo. I swung around, giving his pain my back, but its reflection gaped at me through the mirror anyway. "Some time apart could be good," I said. My father had said something similar to me. "I'm sure he'll return."

"I can't lose him too," he said. "She would want you to fight for him."

"So now you're the expert on what my wife would want?" I snapped, pivoting to him again. He was right, of course, which was what set me off.

Cole's cheeks were now hollow, and his suit hung loose on his frame. Peering down at how my own suit swam on me told me I wasn't faring so well either.

"No, I'm not. Had I been..." His anguish cut him off. "I'm sorry."

"You have nothing to be sorry for," I said.

"But I do." He chuckled self-deprecatingly, blinking up at the ceiling.

I squeezed my eyes shut. *Don't say it. Don't make me face this now. Not now, and maybe not ever.*

"You loved her, and now she's gone. And I get to be sorry about that." Cole chewed his lip while I swam in the ocean cresting behind his blue eyes. Physically we were so close, yet we were millions of miles apart.

Too many secrets and lies separated us, and not just his. I'd offered them my fair share, even if most were by omission. I'd partaken in withholding Selene's diagnosis from them until we no longer could, and even now neither of them knew about our marital crisis. We'd fed them a fantasy, and I continued to feed those fantasies with my silence in Selene's absence.

I knew what haunted Jasper and Cole, what kept them awake at night, and I could have made it all better with a few well-placed words of comfort, instead I began withdrawing from them even more because I was angry. So damned angry.

"Why can't I ever do right by you?" I'd had no intention of giving voice to that thought, but nothing seemed to be functioning properly. Not my heart, nor my brain. Both organs were filled with so much of everything that this one thing had found its way out.

"What?" he asked.

"Nothing," I said, getting back to my tie.

"What is it you think we needed from you that you didn't give?" he asked, deciding not to let it go.

"Everything," I breathed, feeling the world crumble around me with that admission. It'd been the most honest thing I'd ever said to him. The most vulnerable I'd ever been with the people who should have, but never did, get all of me. Why was it so hard? Why was it *still* so hard?

We were all so broken, I realized right then, but I couldn't be the one to fix us. I wasn't strong enough, or brave enough, to do that. Not since *him*. I was capable of very little without him.

An incoming text shattered whatever spell we were under. "Samuel is waiting outside for us," I said, flinging aside my uncooperative necktie.

"I'll meet you in the car," he said, and I nodded. Cole stopped on the threshold of the bedroom, glancing back at me, then into the hall again, seemingly torn between saying more and letting it go.

"You're there when it matters most," he said.

"No, I'm not," I replied, self-disappointment using my insides to sharpen its talons. Because it mattered now, and I couldn't get past my own deficiencies, my own discomfort, and my own guilt to do anything about it.

I wanted to punch something, preferably myself, but I tucked the need into its tiny compartment, right next to everything else I wasn't ready to face.

We made it through the funeral services and sped home at Cole's insistence. He was out of the SUV before Samuel had pulled to a full stop outside the estate doors. I took my time going inside, in no rush to see him dash from room to room in search of something that wasn't there.

All signs of Jasper were gone.

Jasper didn't wait around to say goodbye, and I hadn't hunted him down before leaving for the funeral to tell him that I loved him. That no matter what, I loved him with all of me, even if I'd never been the best at showing it.

Selene's worst fears had come true. Her son had no one, and I threw myself into my work, determined to make my life as miserable as it could be as penance for my shortcomings.

"You're a tortured soul, Franky," Leland had once said. Now I wondered if I'd ever had a soul to begin with.

CHAPTER 23

Leland

"**Y**ou're late," Johnny griped as I hurried behind the bar. Betty wouldn't start this morning, so I'd had to take two buses over to Josephine's to start my evening shift. I used to live within walking distance, but my apartment had become another reminder of Franky, so I moved once my lease was up.

Josephine's was packed for a Tuesday, and Johnny didn't seem pleased to have to work drink orders. He could be cantankerous, but he had a soft spot for me. Probably because I was the only one who allowed him to work them like a war horse without complaint. He was too cheap to hire more staff, and I needed the added distraction, so it worked out well for the both of us.

"Take it easy on me, Johnny. I've been working doubles for weeks. I got four hours of sleep last night, and my car broke down this morning."

"According to my calculations, you had more than enough time to get a full eight hours of sleep, which means you decided to do something *else* with that time," he said, his graying brows raised. "Hopefully that at least means my customers are safe from you for the next twenty-four hours." Johnny hobbled away, and I hustled to get the bottleneck of orders filled.

I slept around—safely. It was the only way I could make it through the day. The only sleeping aid that worked, and the only time I felt in control of my emotions because I didn't have any while fucking. I was completely numb, and it was difficult to hold on to that illusion when not.

But contrary to Johnny's penchant for overexaggerating, I only fucked customers who were passing through, and only when I was desperate. I left the regulars alone. That was a hassle I didn't need.

I'd been counting bills and inserting them into their correct slot in the cash register when someone tapped the bar top behind me. "What can I get you?" I asked, focusing on my task.

"Gin. Neat."

"Coming right up," I called over my shoulder, slamming the drawer closed. I reached for the bottle of Sapphire on the top shelf and poured two-fingers into a tumbler. "Here you—" The glass slipped from my hand, crashing and splintering at my feet as the rest of my words lodged themselves in my throat, refusing to budge.

A carbon copy of Franky perched on the stool in front of me, only he was over two decades younger, and his eyes were blue instead of a blazing onyx. *Cole.*

He peered behind him, as if my hard glare couldn't possibly be directed at him. "Are you okay?"

"What are you doing here?" I demanded.

"*Excuse* me?" He looked out of place on this side of town, and now that my initial shock had worn off, I noticed the dark circles under his eyes and how unnaturally pronounced his cheek bones were.

"Your expensive suit tells me that you could literally go anywhere in this city to grab a drink, so why are you here of all places?"

Molly, the barback, came over with a broom and dustpan, cleaning up the glass shards as the other customers waited impatiently for me to pull it together. I thanked her, then asked if she could take a few orders from my side of the bar as I dealt with Cole. I stepped aside so she could drop a bar towel onto the puddle of gin.

"Do all drink requests come with an interrogation? And is your employer aware that you profile and discriminate against paying customers?" he asked, hackles rising, ready to lay waste to me for insinuating he couldn't be wherever the hell he wanted to. And he didn't have to raise his voice to do it either. I'd heard him clearly over the music and buzz of conversation around us.

I searched the bar for Franky as Cole waited for my comeback. What the fuck was happening?

"Are you alone?"

"Are you high?" he countered.

"H-how did you find this place? You're not from around here."

"And the insults keep coming," he said acerbically. "Will telling you get me a drink?"

"Yes," I said, my body going cold.

"If you must know, I didn't want to attract attention to myself tonight. I found one of your bar napkins in my father's SUV and took it as a sign. Now can I get that drink? And make it a double."

So Franky *had* been here that night. I hadn't seen him, but I'd felt him. There was an electrical charge that zinged through whatever room he occupied. A raising of neck hairs and a quiet, but unmistakable, call of everyone's attention that he wasn't even aware he possessed. Or maybe he knew but saw acknowledging it as being beneath him.

I'd searched high and low for the source of it after finishing up with a quick fuck in the restroom, but I'd come up empty. Except... Except the booth in the far-right corner in the back. The only place I hadn't looked because Johnny had cornered me.

"If you were looking for a place to go unnoticed," I started, getting back to my current panic attack, "you should've left the Rolex at home." My fear made me cruel, or maybe I had the years of not giving a fuck to thank for that.

"Thanks for the tip," he snipped. His shoulders slumped as he massaged his forehead. Whatever zap of energy he'd gained from my inappropriateness was now gone, replaced by a sadness tangible enough to mold with my hands. "I'll have that gin now. And keep them coming."

If Franky had been here, did that mean... No, it couldn't mean *that*. Could it?

"This might sound strange," I started cautiously, "but did something happen to you? Or to someone important to you?"

"Christ, does therapy come as a side, too, in this place?"

"No, it doesn't," I said, backing away, the raw grief in his eyes giving me my answer. "Your drink's coming right up." Selene's son sat in front of me, devastated by the loss of her, and I had to bite into my cheek to make myself not care. *It isn't your problem, Leland.*

I made his drink and then begged Molly to switch ends of the bar with me as an extra precaution, because I refused to fucking give a damn.

I worked the rest of the night on autopilot, doing my best not to notice him move through the stages of inebriation. It was kind of hard not to once his cheek met the bar top, though.

"Good night," Molly said sympathetically, flipping over the open sign on her way out. It was my shit luck that I had to close up, and so I was stuck, alone in Josephine's, with a shit-faced Cole.

I rinsed the last martini glass in the bar sink, then ambled over to where he now slouched over his empty glass.

"Do you have a driver waiting outside?"

"My mother, and my best friend. He was the love of my life," he slurred.

"Come again?"

"Earlier," he said, struggling to raise his head to me. "You asked me if something happened to someone important to me. My mother died, and the only man I'll ever love left me because of it."

The second half of his confession didn't make any sense. Probably the gin talking. It didn't matter. It wasn't my problem. "Maybe there's someone you can call—"

"We killed her, and my father doesn't even know it."

Don't do it. Don't fucking care, Leland.

"He loved her," he went on belligerently, "and we took her away from him—"

"So why don't you go home and tell him all of this? I'm sure you two can work it out, be there for each other." Even now I couldn't take hearing about how much Franky loved her. I'd need a hard fucking and a bottle of Jameson to knock me unconscious tonight.

He huffed, tossing back the imaginary contents of his glass, scowling at its emptiness before shoving it aside. "Are you always this blunt and abrasive?"

"Yep."

"Maybe that's what I need. I have no one else, and those that are paid to care..." He trailed off pensively. "They'll just tell me what I want to hear. I could never tell them the truth anyway."

I barely caught that last part.

"Look, I'm sure you didn't kill her. Either way, I'm not the person you should be tell—"

"Isn't that part of your job description? To listen to me?" He swayed before catching himself. "I fell in love with my stepbrother, and that secret killed our mother," he confessed in a hushed voice.

"What?" I gasped. That couldn't be right. "Does your father know?"

"No. He could never. We've broken his heart enough. He lov—"

"Yeah, I know. He loved her." I sighed. "Look, I'll get you an Uber home." I strode to the opposite side of the bar where I had my cell phone charging, glancing back in time to see Cole steady himself again. He'd almost fallen off his stool this time. In his state, he was liable to be mugged and dumped at the curb rather than driven all the way home.

I pinched the bridge of my nose, the events of the day weighing on me. I could ride in the Uber with him, then have it take me home, but the chance of running into Franky was too great, even at this late hour.

I cursed this fucking night, my life, and the whole Kincaid clan. I'd worked non-stop for two years to be done with all things Franky. Turned myself inside out until I wasn't even recognizable to myself. I'd built so many walls around me that not even sunlight could get in, only to find myself faced with our shared past again.

"I have no one else."

Cole's saddened voice echoed through my head again. He didn't have me either. We were strangers, even if we sort of weren't, and if he knew the truth about me and his father, the truth that would surely blow the lid off the false image he had about his family, he wouldn't want anything to do with me.

But Selene had been kind to me once. She'd mothered me, filled my cup when all the while I'd been sleeping with her husband. I owed it to her to make sure her son made it through the night unharmed. I could do that, but that would be it.

"Up you go," I said, after cutting the lights off and setting the alarm.

Outside, I nearly buckled under Cole's dead weight as I lowered him into our waiting Uber, and again thirty minutes later when having to help him out of it.

My elevator picked the perfect night to be on the fritz, and by the time I got Cole up the four flights and into my apartment, I was in need of a lung transplant.

I let him fall face down onto my bed while I wheezed obnoxiously, folding over and gripping my knees.

Massaging my lower back, I considered what to do next. My studio apartment consisted of one large room with an attached kitchenette. I'd have to knock down a few walls to expand my bathroom if Cole needed to use it.

Cole's phone rang from an inside pocket, and I backed away, instincts telling me it was Franky. I could almost feel him in the room now.

The backs of my knees met my futon, and I collapsed onto it as the ringing stopped and then picked up again. He was probably worried. Well, too fucking bad. I'd done my good deed for the night. I wasn't looking for extra credit.

Next came a ping, probably a text or voicemail notification. I ignored it, kept ignoring it, and also ignored the following six times it rang.

My anxiety heightened during the following fifteen or so minutes of silence, because then thoughts of Franky tracking Cole's location and showing up here needled my brain.

"Fuck." I lunged toward the bed as the phone blared again, patting down Cole's pockets with my clammy hands. I retook my seat at the edge of the futon, the call going to voicemail again as I stared at the word "Dad" until the tiny seed of terror blocking my throat sprouted into a golf ball.

I answered it on the first ring the next time, bringing it to my ear and scanning Cole for any signs that he may be lucid.

"Cole?" Franky's cutting voice demanded through the line. His angry and worried voice still sounded the same, and I envisioned him scowling and pacing with the phone pressed to his ear.

His voice was sex and booze and scratch-offs. All things I'd had an obsession with at some point in my life. The former two still plagued me. I closed my eyes, sitting back and accepting that all the hard work I'd done to cut myself off from any feelings for him had been in vain. Franklin Kincaid still got to me. I didn't have to let him know that, though.

"No. It's me." I waited for his breathing to escalate, waited for him to say my name, waited for anything that would indicate that hearing my voice did *something* to him. *Anything.* Good or bad. I got nothing, which shouldn't have hurt me as much as it did because nothing was what I'd already had.

"He showed up at Josephine's," I said, saving him the trouble of working out why I had Cole's phone. The rest came out in a tumble. "He got pretty hammered, so I brought him back to my place to sleep it off. He said he found a bar napkin in your car. That's how he ended up there." At least this time he offered me a sigh. I searched my memories for what a sigh slipping from Franky's lips meant and came up with a number of possibilities. One being his sigh of apology after unceremoniously doing whatever the fuck he wanted with my body—I immediately derailed that train of thought.

"You were there," I said angrily into the silence. "This is your fault." Had he stayed away instead of pointlessly seeking me out, my world wouldn't be turning itself upside down right now.

"I didn't know you worked there," he whispered.

"It doesn't matter," I hissed, looking over at Cole again and lowering my tone. "You left me broken on the floor dripping your cum." I took pleasure in the audible wince that pulled from him. It was vulgarity at its finest, said with a heartlessness I wished I could also feel.

"You had no right to show up in any space you knew meant something to me." I exhaled a shaky breath. "And now what am I supposed to do? What am I supposed to do with him?"

"He needs someone," he said. "Please, take care of him."

"I'm no good for anyone—" The line went dead, and I caught myself before hurling the phone across the room, remembering that it belonged to Cole.

My chest heaved as Cole snored. I'd let him sleep it off, then put him out before the sun came up.

I strode over to the fridge, cracking open the bottle of Jameson I kept on top of it and taking a healthy swig. I let the Irish whiskey flow freely down my throat, hoping it would somehow burn my heart to ashes on the way down.

I wouldn't get any sleep tonight, and more than ever I needed a hot body on top of me. I'd have even settled for being inside something soft and warm, although my mood called for something hard and unforgiving intent on making an example out of me.

Punching the pillow I'd snagged from the bed into submission, I spread out on the futon fully clothed.

"I'm not an easy man to love."

Franky's words from a time that felt both ancient and recent unfurled in my mind.

I craned my head around to stare at Cole. Knowing what he could expect from his father had me for once feeling sorry for someone other than myself. Franky shutting down, icing his son out wasn't my problem, though. Who Cole had or didn't have to help him through this rough time *wasn't* my problem.

Don't do it, Leland. Don't. Fucking. Care…

CHAPTER 24

Leland

In dire need of washing the scent of sex and alcohol off of me, I bypassed the small cluster of people waiting for the janky elevator and opted for the stairs instead. My ascent slowed to a full stop after spotting Cole sitting on the top step of my landing.

He'd shown up to Josephine's four nights in a row now. Even had a favorite seat in the back where he ordered gin by the bottle, then spent the night drowning his troubles away.

I mostly ignored him, except when I couldn't, which was all the damn time.

"Stalking me now?" I asked, too tired to pack the question with venom. I'd worked two shifts and managed to squeeze in a threesome. I was dead on my feet. Exactly what I needed to be to get some shut-eye tonight.

"I came to return your shirt, and to apologize for being sick all over your bathroom floor the other morning." He got to his feet, holding out the laundered t-shirt I'd lent him. It'd been too small for him, but I hadn't the heart or the time to tell him he'd have looked less indecent shirtless.

"That's nice of you," I said, taking the last few steps, "but you've seen me more than once since that morning. You could've returned this to me any one of those times. At my job. So why are you really here?"

"You know who I am." It wasn't a question, but I debated answering in the negative anyway.

"Yes." I took the shirt and stepped around him, flipping through my keyring as he followed me down the hall.

"What did I say to you that first night at the bar?"

"Nothing I'm interested in repeating, if that's what you're worried about."

One of my neighbors walked off the elevator, greeting us before disappearing inside her apartment.

Alone again, Cole returned to the reason for his visit. "No one can—"

"Your secret's safe with me, Cole," I said with a tight smile, eager to get this over with. I inserted my key into the lock, halting at his hushed thank you. It said more than it should have, meant more than him being appreciative of my discretion. It said he thought I was a good guy. It said that he could use one of those in his life right now.

I faced him, wholly unprepared to be hit with the hemorrhaging of his pain. Franky would've never given just anyone the pleasure of seeing him come apart. My armor suffered a crack, because as much as I wanted to put fifty feet of security between myself and Cole, I couldn't help feeling sympathetic.

At twenty-four, Cole was still young, we both were. But I understood his pain. I knew what his heartache felt like. I knew the texture of it, the stench it gave off, and I knew how impossible it was to navigate its constant fluctuations, the unpredictable agony of it all.

We'd both been abandoned by a Kincaid. In his case there were three; Selene, Jasper, and his father.

Losing my hold on Noon had been part of the reason I'd been drawn to Franky, so I could relate to Cole's need to latch on to something as he fell from his cliff. It just couldn't be me.

With his good looks and wealth, Cole could've had a whole mob of friends if he wanted to. What the hell made me so damn appealing?

"You must think I'm pathetic," he said.

"You lost your mother and stepbrother, who you also happen to be in love with, all in the same week. No, Cole. I don't think you're pathetic. I think you're justified. But we don't know each other, yet you stare at me like you want something from me." *Like I even have anything to give.*

He fidgeted with his misbuttoned shirt, and he was in bad need of a shave. "I have nothing," he whispered.

"Yeah," I whispered back. "Welcome to the club."

◆ ◆ ◆

I showed up to work Monday after taking a rare but much-needed day off. I'd been pushing my body to its limit—in more ways than one. I'd just clocked in and been about to take my first order when my gaze smacked up against the back of Cole's head. He sat at his preferred table again, fighting to hold his head up. I gripped the edge of the bar as my blood ran hot.

"Molly," I called out as she settled her purse over her shoulder. Her shift ended when I showed up to relieve her. "Cover me for a couple hours. I'll pay you double."

◆ ◆ ◆

There were houses, and then there were estates, and Franky's home fell under the second category.

The wrought iron gates parted for me and Betty to enter, and I rocketed down the cedar-lined driveway, vaguely catching a glimpse of a pond and what looked to be horse stables in the distance.

After what felt like miles, a palatial home surrounded by rose bushes appeared out of thin air. Franky waited at the front door for me, hands deep in his pockets.

The house was beautiful but overstated. It wasn't Franky's style. There was no ocean here. Where did he go to think?

I was too jittery to still be upset about Cole. Too overcome with an emotion I thought I'd fucked and drank out of my system.

Circling the fountain, I came to a stop, cutting the engine and getting out before I lost my nerve too. "Are you normally the welcoming committee?"

"When the person at my door is you? Yes," he said, eyes sunken but as keen and appraising as ever. "Come in."

The contemporary living room had a woman's touch and lacked any of Franky's creations. I wondered if that would change with time or if he'd continue to live in a shrine to Selene, much like he'd admitted to doing when Annabeth died.

Franky stopped at the open french doors overlooking the side garden, which offered an immaculate view of the setting sun. I took advantage of having his back to me, noting how every posterior muscle that had once expanded outward, now appeared concave. He was grieving, and I needed to check some of my righteousness at the door before proceeding.

"It's good to see you," he said hesitantly, so unlike himself. "Hard but good." He turned to me, and those rich, obsidian eyes that had been unreadable on his doorstep now screamed at me, sending me back a step.

They brushed over me as if they were hungry for the sight of me. They begged for me to understand *everything*, and although bone dry, they cried out for something I couldn't give. For something I knew to my marrow he wouldn't have accepted anyway. He was alone, and if he'd given in to his nature of making a home for his guilt, that meant he wanted it that way.

I laid an extra mental layer of bricks, building another wall in front of the three already stacked there. I couldn't let him break me again. I couldn't let him see that I was broken already.

"Cole keeps showing up at Josephine's," I said. Franky nodded as if he'd suspected this.

"The two people he depended on the most are gone," he said. "He needs time—"

"He needs more than time," I snapped, then softened my tone to something more sympathetic to his pain. "He needs his father."

"I can't be there for him," he said.

"You're all he has left," I stressed, stepping around the loveseat and moving closer to where he stood with his back straight.

"I can't," he said, adopting a glacial façade as if that would make me back down.

"Why not?" I asked, but he was unwilling to answer. "Why not, Franky?"

"You wouldn't understand."

"He's your son. You have to—"

"I can't."

"Yes, you can."

"Leland—"

"You have to—"

"I can't!" he yelled, his overgrown hair flopping onto his forehead. "I am *incapable*." The confession had been torn from him, and he sagged against the door at his back as if he'd used up whatever reserve of strength he'd been holding on to, or pretending he had in the first place, to admit it.

Had I been anyone else, he would've fought to the death to remain stoic and on his feet. I hated how good it felt to know he could still be weak in front of me, despised how much I wanted to shoulder his weight, how much I wanted to take him into my arms and relieve his excruciating pain.

"It can't be me," he whispered.

I tilted my head, narrowing my gaze. "Do... Do you *know*?" I asked.

"Yes," he said.

"About Jasper, and about Selene?" I specified, needing to be sure we were talking about the same thing.

"Yes, and yes," he said. "I can't be what he needs me to be. And he needs you more than I do," he said meaningfully, and I had to feel around internally to make sure my guards were still up. They were, and he'd seen beyond them anyway.

As if a trap door hiding my dirty secret had opened up in my mind, it suddenly occurred to me that I didn't want to commit to a friendship—or a commiserationship—with Cole, because if Franky was going to come for me, I didn't want the added complication of befriending his son in our way. I understood Franky would need time. I wasn't completely heartless or insensitive to his situation. But even now, I wanted him to choose me.

What I'd been doing these last couple years, who I'd had to turn myself into... It wasn't to toughen me up, to make me immune to the pain, immune to *him*. I'd simply done what was necessary to get by, to survive in hopes that one day he would come for me.

"You're just like your father," I said, lashing out, embarrassed that he'd seen through me. "I used to tell you that wasn't true, but it is. This is what you do, right? You can't connect with your kids because of your own issues, so you find someone who can give them what you lack."

"That isn't true," he said.

"Oh no? So you're not *gifting* me to him now? Like you gifted him Selene?" I was sorry the minute I'd said it. It needed to be said, but it didn't mean I wasn't sorry it hurt him. Regardless of how I felt, he was hurting enough, his pain was real.

Franky flinched as if the verbal strike had physically touched him.

"Isn't that what your father did with Gloria?" I asked softly. "Allowed Gloria and her family to raise you so that he wouldn't have to be bothered with facing you, only removing them when it got in the way of his life plans for you? And then what? He avoided you until the day he died."

"It isn't the same," he said, but I could see he was considering it.

"Except it is the same, Franky. At the very least it's eerily, fucking similar." I couldn't be his therapist. Not when some would say I needed one of my own. He'd need to come to his own conclusions in his own time. If ever. "Believe what you want to believe," I said, resigned. "I've gotta get out of here."

"You need him too," he said quickly as I marched from the living room.

"What I need is you!" I swung around and roared, trembling from head to toe. Every vein in my body pulsed, my head throbbed, and the sound of the final piece of my heart fracturing filled my ears.

"I know," he said sadly. A hand twitched at his side, and my sick, traitorous heart hoped it was because he was fighting the need to reach for me. "But I can't be what you need either."

I pivoted on my feet and kept moving, my shoes squeaking on the marble floor. I would not let him see me break down.

"Just one," he whispered, his voice trailing me into the foyer. "Just one, Leelee Bear."

Franky's parting words bounced around Betty's interior as I punched at the steering wheel. They forced me to go back in time, forced me to remember how much he knew me.

"I know you prefer one great friend over many, because it lessens your chances of people hurting you. Of leaving you. I

know you also prefer one friend over none, because being completely alone reminds you of how lonely you are."

I started the car and peeled off, ignoring the figure at the front door getting smaller in my rear view.

♦ ♦ ♦

Monday nights were the slowest at Josephine's, so with the place relatively empty, Cole stuck out like a sore thumb. Not that he wouldn't have anyway. He had money written all over him, and he had the same I-own-the-place vibe that his father gave off. Even in his current drunken state.

I paid Molly like I promised and then sent her on her way.

Cole had made his way to the bar during the time I was gone. I lined up four shot glasses, filling his two with that fuck-awful gin he loved, and mine with whiskey—the good stuff. Johnny could be pissed about it later. He'd probably dock me for it too.

Cole didn't need prompting. He chugged the shots and gestured for a refill.

"You really want to know why I keep coming back here?" he asked, his words heavy and slow. "I'm here because maybe this is where he likes to be. My father," he added on, as if I didn't already know. "Maybe he'll come find me here."

"He won't," I said, bursting his bubble of hope.

"You're mean."

"Then get out," I deadpanned, to which he chuckled.

"I think I'll stay, because maybe deep down, you're not as mean as you pretend to be. Maybe, you're not mean at all."

"That's a whole lot of fucking maybes," I said, nodding to the only other customer in the place as he made his exit.

Cole sighed, a waft of gin-infused breath knocking me in the face. "I don't blame him for not coming. My father," he said again. "There isn't much I do blame him for. Well, not since he brought Selene and Jasper into my life."

"Maybe you should tell him that," I suggested, already on my fourth shot.

"Look who's got a case of the maybes now," he said, lilting to one side. "Oh! You can smile!" he exclaimed a little too loudly for how close we were.

"Don't get used to it," I said, finding it harder to wear my angry mask when all I wanted to do was wallow in my self-pity.

"Is jazz the only thing that jukebox plays?"

"What do you want to hear?" I dug inside the tip jar for some coins.

"Claude Debussy," he said. Franky did mention once that Cole was a classically-trained pianist.

"You're on the wrong side of town," I said, the coins pelting the bottom of the jar as I tossed them back in.

I moved us on to water next, because I wouldn't be accompanying him to the hospital for alcohol poisoning. We drank in silence, both lost in our own thoughts and problems that, unknowingly to him, ran parallel to one another. Some probably met in a head-on collision.

"Have you ever been crushed by the one person you would've done anything for or given anything to?" Cole asked, leaning his forearms into the bar top.

"Yes," I answered.

"How did you handle it?"

"I let it change me," I said.

"Did it help? Did it make it hurt any less?"

"I thought it did, but fooling yourself has an expiration date." The bell above the door chimed, and I left Cole to think that over while I mixed two vodka tonics for the ladies who had entered.

"Do you plan on coming back?" I asked, returning and refilling his water.

"Would that be weird?"

"No weirder than it already has been." I pushed the business card Johnny had wasted on me toward him.

"Dr. Mulligan?" He read with a furrowed brow. "A therapist? Where did you get this from?"

"I keep a stack under the bar for crybabies like you." We chuckled, and I had to admit, it felt good. "Don't be like me, Cole. Get yourself some help."

Cole came in every day after that, eventually drinking less, and in due time our conversations moved past the irreparable condition of his life.

Things unfolded naturally between us, and soon, our interactions went beyond Josephine's doors. Later on, our topics of discussion didn't include much mention of his father at all.

The guilt I carried for the secrets I had to keep never went away, but I over-compensated by being more of a friend to him than I'd ever allow him to be to me. I told myself the scales were evenly balanced that way, no matter how much my inability to accept anything from him annoyed him.

Slowly, parts of my old self returned. And because Cole avoided Franky as much as possible due to his own guilt behind Selene's passing, it made it easy for me to avoid him too.

There were occasions where Cole would try to drag me to some fancy Nexcom function, now that he'd begun working for the company, but those were simple enough to get out of.

I indulged his obsession with attending boring medical conferences, and he supported my need to be in the sun, although he complained the whole time we had to do something outdoorsy.

I still fucked a lot, way more than what was psychologically healthy. But a man had to do what he had to do to sleep, because no matter how much progress I made, there were some things about me that couldn't be fixed. Some things that could only be fixed by Franky.

Cole's friendship ended up being the life raft I needed. Franky had gotten it wrong. I didn't need just one friend. I specifically needed Cole.

CHAPTER 25

Franklin

Four Years Later

Three raps sounded at my home office door, and I locked away the dog-eared photo of Leland I'd been staring at all morning before calling for whoever waited to come in.

Cole entered, his long-legged gait eating up the carpet as he strode for the seat across from my desk. The sunlight streaming through the windows glinted off his cufflinks.

He poured himself into the seat, resting an ankle over his knee. "Thought I'd stop by to make sure you weren't having second thoughts," he said, getting straight to the reason for his visit.

"It's a little too late for that now," I said. "The staff is already getting things in order for the celebration tonight, and the florists will be arriving any minute." I'd be announcing the changing-of-the-guard tonight. As of tomorrow morning, Nexcom would officially belong to Cole.

He'd worked hard for it, and I could no longer pretend to stomach my role in the company. A role I hadn't played well in the last year or so. Behind the scenes, Cole had been responsible for Nexcom's boost of success with his passion and fresh ideas. At this stage, I was nothing more than a figurehead.

"Until the papers are signed, it's never too late. And sometimes, not even then. You taught me that," he said. Cole was a far cry from the man who'd lost everything less than a handful of years ago. He reminded me of myself, but due to Selene and Jasper's influence, he was softer in areas that my losing Gloria and her family had hardened in me.

"No second thoughts," I promised, and he nodded once, the corners of his mouth relaxing now that he knew this conversation wouldn't end in a war.

Cole cleared his throat. "Full disclosure. I intend to move our headquarters to New York. It'll be my first order of business—in tandem with the acquisition of several competing tech companies."

I gripped the pen I held tightly as I digested the bombshell he just unloaded on me. "That's not what's best for my company. Not now. I won't sanction the move."

"Nexcom will no longer be your company," he reminded me gently, and I eased into my seatback, loosening my grip on the pen.

"Is this so you can be closer to Jasper?" I asked and then thought: *Or farther away from me?*

We never discussed Jasper. There wasn't much we did discuss outside of business, but Jasper had most definitely been the elephant in any room Cole and I were in together, along with all the other secrets we held on to.

"It's a good business move," he said. "But I'd be lying if I said Jasper had nothing to do with it. I miss him, and maybe enough time has passed where we can at least be friendly with each other."

I'd kept tabs on Jasper throughout the years, and I assumed Cole had done so as well. If that were the case, he was well aware that Jasper had recently gotten married. If that news had hurt Cole, he hadn't shown it. Not to me anyway.

"I didn't have to tell you this now, but I didn't want you to feel tricked or blindsided by the news once the final documents were signed."

I steepled my fingers in front of me as I riffled through my incoming thoughts and concerns, deciding to address the one that held superiority over the others. "And what about Leland? You two have become inseparable."

"How do you know that?" he asked, his brows pursed.

As far as Cole knew, Leland and I had only met once when he'd accompanied Cole to an office party Robert had organized in honor of Cole's first big promotion. Cole had briefly introduced us, but seemed more than happy to leave things at that. He'd protectively remained at his friend's side, likely aware of his discomfort, probably assuming it stemmed from Leland feeling out of place. Leland and I knew the truth, though. It had to have taken a lot for him to agree to attend, knowing I'd be there, and he'd actively avoided direct eye contact with me the entire night.

"You're never home." I motioned around us as if my home was his. "And you two are friends. I just assumed that when you aren't working, you're with him."

"I haven't lived here since..." His words receded, but yet they were somehow still there between us. My home hadn't been his since Selene died and Jasper left. And although I lived there—if it could be called living—it hadn't been mine since then either.

"This hasn't been my home for a long time," he said instead.

"You're right. I'm making assumptions about a relationship I know nothing about." I began drumming my fingers anxiously on my desk.

"Are you okay?" he asked, angling his head at me.

"I'm fine," I said, hoping he hadn't gotten too distracted and forgotten about my question. I needed to know about Leland.

"There's nothing for Leland here. I'm hoping I can convince him to leave," he said.

"Do you think he'll go?" I did my best to sound disinterested. Going so far as to sign a document that didn't require my signature.

"Possibly." He shrugged as if that possibility wasn't important to me. "He's got an old friend there and nothing tying him here. I'm hoping the idea of reconnecting with Noon will sell him on the idea of moving."

Hearing Noon's name set my jealousy afire, but I kept an even expression.

"You should rethink this. Our shares may already be headed for a slide once tonight's announcement goes public. Then you want to add something as big as a cross-country move? This could frighten investors, who, by the way, are already leery of you taking the reins."

"Which is exactly why it's the best plan. I need to separate what this company used to be from what it will be. I need to separate it from *you*. I'm decisive, shrewd, and everyone needs to know I'm not afraid to take charge and take chances. I think you know this."

It made sense when phrased that way, but of all my vital organs, my heart held the least sensibility. It was one thing to not have the best relationship with my son, and to not have a relationship at all with Leland. It was an entirely different story to lose all traces of them.

"What about the hundreds of employees this will affect?" I asked.

"I've considered everything," he said. "Trust me to know what I'm doing."

I'd ambled over to the window to put some distance between myself and Cole's expectant stare. It reflected back at me through the pane anyway. I nodded, and the strain around his eyes smoothed away.

"Will Leland be coming tonight?" I couldn't help but to ask, even if it ran the risk of Cole's suspicion.

"Took some arm pulling, but yes. Although I'll be lucky if I can get him to stay long enough for cake." Done with talks of his best friend, he moved on. "What are your retirement plans?"

"I try not to think that far into the future."

"Well, that future will be here come morning."

I hummed in answer. I had no clue what my next steps would be.

"You could always come along," he said with care. "We could talk to Jasper together. Try and reclaim what family we have left."

I wondered if he was being polite or genuine. Likely the latter, since unlike me, he'd been doing the work needed to find some measure of healing. If his secrets weren't also Jasper's, I was sure Cole would have confessed them to me by now, but he'd never do that without Jasper's explicit permission.

"Maybe," I said, unwilling to commit.

"Yeah, maybe," Cole parroted back, as if he'd expected as much.

◆ ◆ ◆

Leland did show up later that night, issuing me an awkward greeting before vanishing to the outskirts of the backyard. He seemed content to remain there watching the other guests mingle and dance under the chandeliered tent.

Every so often Cole would tear himself away from someone important to the future of Nexcom to check on him, while I lurked, pretending not to notice every move he didn't make. Lurking had become a vice where Leland was concerned.

At one point their exchange turned heated, and Cole gestured for Leland to follow him along the path to the south gardens. I sat my drink down and excused myself from a discussion I had no interest in, trailing Cole and Leland from behind the tall row of hedges.

The band continued to play, but the music thinned the farther away they walked, and I strained to hear their conversation over the chirping of crickets and katydids. My own footsteps crunching the grass reverberated in my ears, and I gave up on getting closer for fear of being caught.

"I'm not accepting any handouts," Leland said.

"You're the most stubborn person I know. Actually, my father might have you beat. It wouldn't be a handout. I'd be paying you," Cole said.

"Do I look like I could be anyone's executive assistant?"

"And you think you look like a *bartender*? Have you seen your cheekbones?"

"This ends now if you plan on making fun of my devastatingly handsome looks," Leland said, sounding more like the man I'd known before I went and destroyed everything good inside of him.

I was envious of Cole. Jealous that he got to be the one to breathe life back into Leland, that he was the one to experience and laugh at his outlandishness.

Cole took his time with his amusement, laughing until it seemed to hurt, and although I felt unrightfully possessive of Leland's humor, it felt good to hear my son happy.

"You're chewing on your bottom lip, that means you're thinking about it," Cole said.

I knew all too well how Leland teased his lip with his teeth. I'd had to rescue it from his sharp incisors many times. Blood would collect right under the soft flesh if he'd been at it long enough, turning the blush pink beds crimson. I'd sometimes save it from him only to break the skin myself to get a little taste of what pooled beneath it.

"You'll never build enough capital for your bar if you stay here. You're living hand-to-mouth, Leland," he said softly. "And since you won't let me invest the seed money, at least allow me to do this. I wouldn't be paying you any more than the position is already offering. If you won't do it for me, then do it for yourself. For once, do something for yourself. For your future."

I ground the heel of my palm into the ache at the center of my chest as Cole continued with his persuasion. It hurt to know Leland had shared his dream with someone else when he'd held it so close to the vest with me. I'd thought I would one day earn the details of his art-bar. From the size, to the color scheme, to the pieces he'd choose to display on its walls. Pestering him about it had become a game of mine. I used to live for the excitement of wondering if *this* would be the time he actually answered my questions. If *this* would be the time he felt safe enough to. But I hadn't earned hearing about it from his own beautiful lips. I hadn't fought hard enough to earn anything.

"I don't know, Cole," Leland said, but there was no fight left in his tone. Cole would win this. "This is my home."

"Is it?" Cole challenged. "What's keeping you here? I'm the only friend you have in this city."

Leland's silence terrified me, and as if scenting blood in the water, Cole charged forward.

"Come to New York and you'll get to reconnect with Noon. Besides, you've already gone through every man in Seattle who would have you—and don't even get me started on the women. It's time to diversify your dickfolio," he said.

"Well, why the hell didn't you lead with *that*?" Leland quipped, pulling a guffaw from Cole. I, on the other hand, didn't find it funny at all. I ground down on my back teeth, went in search of Robert as Leland continued on with his amorous tirade.

"Franklin!" Robert called from the chocolate fountain as I weaved through the crowd to get to him. "Where's Cole? We should probably do the toast."

"Follow me," I said cavalierly, entering the back of the house and moving purposely down corridors until I'd reached my office.

"What's going on?" Robert asked from close behind me.

"Close the door behind you," I instructed before pacing pensively.

"Talk to me, Franklin. Where's Cole? Did something happen—"

"It's too soon," I said. "Cole taking over. It's too soon."

"With all due respect, Franklin, he's got more of a stomach for this than you. Don't let your cold feet get in the way of your better judgment. His ideas are fresh and honorable. Don't underestimate him. Not *now*," he said, flicking a hand toward the celebration happening outside.

"I'm not, but did you know he's planning on uprooting our headquarters to New York?" I hissed, feeling my tether to Leland pulling tight as a bow. The panic was all encompassing and resounding throughout my body.

"*New York*? He'll lose half the staff if he does that," he said in a whisper, drawing in closer.

"He says he's got a plan in place to prevent that, but maybe he's in over his head."

Robert dragged a tired hand down his mouth, pushing his suit jacket aside to brace his other hand on his hip. "He's going to hate you for this,"

"I know," I said wearily. "But it's only temporary. I just need more time." The last part was said under my breath.

"More time for what, exactly?" Robert asked, his sharp ears never missing a thing.

"More time to let go," I admitted, Robert and I no longer speaking about the same thing. "Just a little more time. He'll understand."

"He'll understand what?" Cole asked from the doorway. Apparently, Robert had left the door ajar.

"I'll leave you two to talk," Robert said, head down as he exited.

Cole drew in closer, looking back at the door Robert had dashed through, then back to me questioningly.

"Let's sit," I said, motioning for the lounge area.

"No," he said. "I think I'll stand for this."

CHAPTER 26

Leland

"He *what*?" I exploded up from the garden bench. I'd been hiding out here while Cole had gone to investigate when the announcement would be made, no doubt picking up on my itch to be anywhere but here but wanting me to at least stay for the most important part.

"He rescinded the deal. He's no longer turning Nexcom over to me." Other than the pulsing muscle in his cheek, Cole exuded restraint. "He swears it's only temporary. The projections and the actuals didn't align the way he'd hoped this quarter. He said we'll revisit things at the end of the next quarter."

"What the fuck does that even mean?" I asked, losing my cool enough for the both of us. Cole had been working so hard for this. His dream of improving the artificial heart had been the main thing driving him these last few years, and he needed the power of Nexcom behind him to do it.

"It means he's full of shit and I should've seen this coming."

"But you said he was okay with things. You said as early as this morning he seemed okay with things."

"He did. I don't know what changed." Cole exhaled, taking up the seat I'd vacated. "It doesn't matter. I'll build my own damn company, and it'll rival his."

How achingly familiar that sounded. It was what Franklin

had done to his own father. Were the Kincaid's doomed to perpetually repeat history?

"It'll take too long to grow it to where you need it to be," I said, hoping to steer him away from those thoughts. "Maybe it is just for a few more months. You've waited this long, right?"

He didn't answer, and I didn't blame him. There was a whole fucking ball happening behind us in honor of Cole taking up the mantle. This had to be equally disappointing and embarrassing for him. Franky was a lot of things, but this seemed too cruel even for him, and he hated running Nexcom. *So why would he...* A terrifying thought came to me. "Did you tell him about New York?" I asked and then hesitantly added, "Did you tell him that I may go with you?"

"Yeah," he said, eyes shrinking to tiny slits. "You think he did this because of the move?" He didn't even stop to think that this could be because of me. Of course he wouldn't, because he trusted me and had no clue how many lies were wedged between us.

"No," I said, failing to hide the danger in my tone. Cole was too preoccupied with his frustration to notice. "Where is he?"

"I don't know. Somewhere inside, I'm guessing. Or maybe he went to walk the grounds. He said something about needing to think."

I immediately knew where I'd find him. "Will you be alright if I leave for a couple hours? I promise I'll come back."

"You don't have to," he said, standing again. "I know this isn't your crowd. I'm going to get out of here, myself. I'll walk with you to valet."

Less than an hour later I pulled into the driveway of the waterfront home I'd shared with Franky for a summer. Seemed like forever ago and yesterday at the same damn time. Nostalgia triggered the nausea flipping around in my gut, but overriding it was the near-debilitating anger singing through my veins.

I entered through the unlocked side door, my careful footsteps carrying me to the living room. Ambient light drifted in from the open patio wall, providing enough illumination to see what was in front of me.

The cool night breeze ruffled the edges of the dust covers draped over the furniture, and a hint of stale air lingered inside the home. I wondered how long it had gone unused.

Perking my ears, I listened for movement upstairs but nothing came, or at least nothing loud enough to be heard over the warning bells going off in my head. I'd been about to leave—about to run, actually—thinking I'd gotten it all wrong, hoping I had. Hoping my worst dream and favorite fucking nightmare wasn't somewhere in that ghost town of a house where no one else knew to find me.

My escape came to a screeching stop when my gaze bumped up against the painting leaning in a corner.

Something misfired in my brain, because where it had never taken effort to walk before, I now had to inwardly shout orders at myself to move.

I squatted in front of the forty-by-forty canvas, scanning the kaleidoscope of amber and green filling the sunflower field. It was one of my first paintings ever, and I'd sold it during the lowest point in my life.

My breath quickened, and I swiveled in my stooped position, taking in everything around me covered by white sheets. I began tearing them all away, revealing painting after painting, all done by me and sold over the course of the last four years to the art gallery downtown.

Only one remained hidden now. It loomed at the foot of the mantel, taller and wider than the others. The humming in my head intensified the closer I got to it, and I tore the sheet away before I lost the nerve to.

The unveiled painting depicted Franky as storm clouds. The fingers of smoke wrapped around my ankles and wrists, tugging them wide, reaching and sliding through my partially exposed cleft to smother my cock. My back arched off the bed of dark clouds in ecstasy as the gray tendrils snaked around my neck in the sunless sky.

The painting was provocative, for sure, but I'd kept my face in shadow, which made it more of a discussion piece, something left up to interpretation, rather than something pornographic.

I trailed a finger over the rough canvas. First over the bolt of lightning arcing across the sky and then the more menacing clouds charging my way—signaling an even deeper and darker degree of brutality approaching. It illustrated our relationship better than any photograph ever could.

I'd titled this one *His Storm,* because Franky was the storm, and I was at the center of it. And because I'd naively believed that the storm had belonged to me.

I could still remember the heartbreaking day I'd handed it over to Neil for a measly six-hundred bucks. Bit by bit I'd had to sell off every piece I owned just to make ends meet.

"This is how you see me," Franky said from somewhere behind me. I'd felt him enter the room, same as I always did, but I was paralyzed to do anything about it.

"This is who you are," I whispered. "You're a storm that intoxicates and then destroys everything in your path. Why is this here? Why are any of them here?"

"I issued strict instructions to the gallery after purchasing my very first Leland Meadows piece. They were to contact me immediately if anything else of yours came through their doors."

I spun around, anger escalating to unfiltered rage. Franky waited for it less than a dozen feet away, dressed in all black, his matching eyes devouring me. "I don't get you. I used to think I understood you better than you understood yourself, but I was wrong."

"Yes, you were, because you can't know a man who doesn't know himself."

"Bullshit," I called. "You knew who you were, and for a split second you were brave enough to be that person. You used to be a man who said what he felt and felt what he meant. You were warmth through your coldness, and light through even your darkest moments. You used to be a man who wanted to be better, even if you didn't know how to be. And now you fucking relish in the worse parts of you. In the *scared* parts of you. You've let the little boy in you run rampant. You've spoiled him. You've let him indulge in his own pity for so long that you no longer know what it means to *try*," I ended, shaking my fists at him, pleading for *something*.

Per usual, I didn't know how to be near this man and not be honest with him. I hadn't cracked the code on locking my shit up tight and faking indifference. No matter how many years passed, no matter how many beds I hopped, no matter how many times I told myself I was over it, one second of staring into his eyes as he stripped me bare with his gaze, and my lies went tumbling down.

And my honesty didn't only extend to pointing out his flaws, because reading Franky his rights was akin to holding a mirror up to my own imperfections. My own weaknesses. Many things that I accused him of could be said about myself. We were both little more than monsters in our own way.

"Whatever good there was in me is gone now," was all he said. It was like beating my head against a brick wall and not expecting to bleed.

"Give it to him," I said, skipping straight to my reason for being alone in a room with him. Comparing who this man was now with who he used to be would only lead me to trouble. Would only aid in making me remember the good. He already had the advantage by me being there surrounded by the walls he'd once thrown me up against, standing on the floors he'd eaten me out on, breathing in the ocean he'd take me sailing on before drowning me in his sweat and cum.

And the look in his eyes, and the way his posture dipped forward, said he would take any opportunity he saw to personally remind me of it all.

"Now's not the right time," he replied coolly.

A harsh and humorless laugh bubbled up in me, and I scrubbed my hands over my face. "You don't even want it, Franky. I'm sure if it weren't for Cole wanting it you would've sold it off to the highest bidder a long time ago. So why did you dangle everything he's been working toward in front of him, only to snatch it away tonight?"

"That's not—"

"Why!?" My voice echoed through the hollow shrine of the past we stood in, putting an end to the lie he'd been about to deliver with ease. "You wanted me to be there for him. You thought I needed someone to be there for me. Well, you got what you wanted, and now I want you to tell me why you fucked over the only person left in my life who means something to me," I seethed.

He took a step toward me under the guise of shifting on his feet. My heart pressed against my spine in search of a way out, in search of a place to hide. I had to remind myself not to be afraid of him, remind myself that fear shouldn't feel this good.

"What's the matter, Franky? Cat got your tongue?"

"You wouldn't understand," he said. He'd said those words to me before, but this time I understood quite fucking well.

"I'll do you one better," I challenged. "Fuck understanding. I *know* why you did it, because it's the same reason I've been so resistant to Cole's pleas for me to go with him. You found out I'd be leaving, and you panicked, because even though we're not together, and even though we never will be, there's something about us being intertwined in the sick, passive way that we are that keeps that insidious spark of hope alive. It burns away at our core until we can taste the acidic burn of it at the backs of our throats, and the thought of snuffing out that flame completely feels deadly. It feels like dying."

Franky released a trembling breath as my words hit the bullseye.

"You think I don't know that you sometimes watch me?" I asked. "That on occasion, you lurk outside my window, just behind the wide bark of the elm tree in the park, and you watch me."

"You..." he started but couldn't finish.

"Yes, I know, because no matter how much time evaporates, I can't stop fucking *feeling* you. And I know some part of you hoped I knew, because maybe that would mean I haven't let go of you either, right?"

Franky didn't answer, but the roll of the knot at the center of his throat said enough.

"I bet Friday and Saturday nights are the hardest for you to bear. Isn't that right, Franky?" Those were the nights reserved for relapses. The nights when after a full business week of celibacy, I failed at being better. I'd binge, making up for lost time, catching up on the sleep I'd lost while thinking I could change. My front door was a revolving one, and it didn't turn away anyone who wanted to enter it. Franky never hung around for the show, but *knowing* had to have eaten him alive.

"No," he said, shocking me. "Sunday nights are always the hardest. That's when you close your curtains to me, but it's the *why* of it that breaks my heart, Leland."

It took a herculean effort not to show my surprise or vulnerability. Sundays were reserved for my shame. They were my reset days. The day of the week when Cole's influence led me to believe I could do better, that I could try again. Sunday was also the day I attempted to paint, but my hands shook so badly I could never manage to pick up the brush. I'd shut him out because I refused to let Franky know that without him I couldn't find it in me to be a daisy. But he knew anyway, and it fucking hurt like hell.

"What do you want from me?" he asked.

"Me? Nothing." That wouldn't have been the truth a few hours ago, but now it had to be. What he'd selfishly done tonight changed everything, and I needed to find a way to walk out that door and mean it when I said I was done with him. I needed it to not just be true on the surface where it was easy to believe when miles away from him. I needed it to be true beneath the lies I told myself and beneath the pain I soothed with sex and booze. "Cole is another story. You're going to step down graciously, exactly as planned—"

"I can't."

"Yes, you can."

"I won't." He said it like he meant it too.

"Franky, so help me God—"

"You're not the only one I stand to lose!" The sudden panic and rage seeping into his voice jarred me, and it took a dozen heartbeats to formulate a reply.

"Then fight for him. Why won't you fight for him?" I threw my hands up, letting them fall and slap at my sides.

Franky peered out over the ocean, and I *hated* that I knew he needed a moment to collect himself. I hated that I allowed him that moment, because I knew I wouldn't get anywhere otherwise. I didn't want to know him anymore. I didn't want to love him anymore.

"Do you know what happens when you try to be something you're not?" he asked. "It doesn't stick. I can turn on the television, or search the internet, or open a book to learn what it means to be a great father, but it wouldn't matter because no matter how good my intentions are, I can't be anyone other than *my* father. Any moments in the past where I'd gotten it right were driven by guilt, not desire. Or by the person in my life thinking I could be a better man, and me wanting that to be true. Left to my own devices, I can't get it right."

"Cole doesn't see it that way. He doesn't think you're perfect, but he doesn't think you're a lost cause either. Why don't you get that?"

"Because he can't see into my heart and mind. Only I can, so only I know that any measure of good he sees in me is a lie."

"That isn't how he sees it," I repeated.

"Probably because my neglect made it easier for him to get away with having an intimate relationship with his stepbrother. Have you ever thought of that?"

"I... No." *I hadn't.*

"Of course you didn't. And did you ever stop to think that maybe the reason he doesn't see me as all that bad is because his judgment is clouded by the guilt of killing their mother!" He sucked in a sharp breath, eyes wild. He hadn't meant to say that.

"You don't believe that," I whispered, again hating how vehemently I knew that.

"I've had to," he said. "It's the only way I can get up in the morning. The only way I can survive this."

"But you're not surviving, Franky. Have you ever thought about just asking them? About having an honest conversation and asking your kids how they truly feel about you?"

"No," he said, shaking his head.

"Why not?"

Franky stared at me with disappointment laced with terror, like the answer to my question should've been obvious. "Because what if they tell me the truth?" And to him there was only one version of the truth. *His.* The reality of Cole and Jasper hating him was much scarier than the thought of it.

"I'm amazed at how well you juggle being both utterly selfish and self-sacrificing," I said. "You think if you're unhappy, then that means you're paying for everything you've ever done wrong, but really, you're just compounding your sins. Your suffering isn't a gift, Franky. What you're doing isn't okay just because you're not happy while doing it."

Once again I found myself reflecting on our conversations from the past, on some of the obscure things he'd said, most of them making sense now.

"You're definitely a tortured soul, Franky, but you aren't that bad," I'd said after he apologized for waking me up with rough sex, penalizing me for some unwanted emotion he woke up feeling.

"You haven't had to suffer through one of my dark hours," he'd replied grimly.

I'd waved it off, thinking it was just Franky being broody as always, thinking I had seen how dark it could get with him. This was different. Tonight was more. It went deeper than wanting to live a simple life, deeper than wanting to be a more present father, deeper than realizing he was in love with me.

Franky's problem with his kids was only a small slice of what haunted him. Beneath his bed resided the ghosts of Gloria, Theo, Paul, his mother, his father, and Selene. They completed the fucking torture cake he loved to lick the icing off of.

I couldn't help him, though, and he wouldn't let me even if I could. Finally, the voice in my head screamed for me to exercise some self-preservation, and I swallowed, my next words spoken through a voice filled with resignation. "Give him the company."

"Will you stay if I do? Will you convince him to stay?"

"No," I said. "We're both getting as far away from you as possible."

"Then I won't do it," he said, brazenly moving toward me.

"Stop." I raised a palm, warning him not to say another word or to take another step closer. He listened, but his stance spoke volumes. His halt was nothing more than a pause of what he believed was the inevitable.

"Don't leave, Leland."

"Why not? So we can spend the next however many years pining in silence? So we can stay stagnant, dwelling on what can't be? I waited for you. God, I'm *still* waiting for you." I shook my head, a sudden wave of grief threatening to do me in. "You once asked me where I saw myself in five years. Do you remember that?" I asked.

Franky dropped his stare to his shoes, but not before nodding once.

"My answer is sadly still the same." I closed my eyes, going back to that night.

"Where do you see yourself in five years, Leland?" he'd asked.

"Somewhere still wanting you," I'd answered.

I opened my eyes, the memory of that night floating away from me. "After tonight, my answer won't be the same. It can't be. I can't do this anymore."

"Leaving you was the right decision," he said, "no matter how much it hurt me to do it." Franky stalked forward, his strides conveying that he had nothing to lose. "How I left you is another matter—"

"Stop it, damnit—"

"I'll never forgive myself for it," he pressed on, his words a jumbled snarl. This wasn't a profession of love or regret, it was an accusation, it was Franky exercising his fury the only way he knew how, it was him arrogantly thinking that after all of this time, he could punish me for how he felt, for his inability to control it.

"Not another fucking step, Franky," I warned with rising apprehension. He was so close I could count the gray hairs scaling his jawline.

"I've never stopped wanting you," he sneered. "Why can't I stop wanting you?"

"Don't you lay a fucking hand on me." My hiss clashed with his scream as my back met the wall. His hands, ready to lacerate anything in their way, froze near the buttons of my shirt. "This isn't our summer of love, Franky. Those days are over. You touching me now without my explicit consent will not be the turn on it once used to be. I won't be *yielding* to you this time."

I couldn't imagine what him fucking me right then would've been like. From the look of crippling desperation on his face it would've taken a stretcher to wheel me out of there afterward or a search party to find my scattered remains after he was done tearing me apart.

"I won't be the thing you release your self-hate on. Not anymore. I've already endured you rage-fucking me and then leaving me in a heap to recover alone. Once was more than enough. And more importantly," I said, driving him back with my intensity, "you don't want me. Not if it means hurting Cole in the process, even though no one hurts him quite like you do. And isn't that some tragic, fucking irony."

His eyes widened at my venomous outburst, but he kept his hands to himself and kept backing away long after I'd stopped moving.

"Give him the company or I'll tell him *everything*," I threatened before walking away from him for the last time.

CHAPTER 27

Franklin

Months of living out my retirement off the grid had caught up with me. I'd moved to the insignificant town of Lockwood, South Carolina, where Bertha successfully delivering her calf was considered front page news, and where Nexcom and Franklin Kincaid didn't exist. Being far removed from everyone and everything came with its perks, but also a substantial emotional cost. I was lonely. Even more lonely than I'd already been before.

I was tired, too, and felt every bit my age as I hauled my weary body beyond the lake cabin walls to the quaint coffee shop less than a quarter mile down the road. The bell chimes hanging above the door tolled as I entered.

"Well, if it isn't the town's favorite Debbie Downer."

I peered over my shoulder, then back to the elderly man wiping his hands on his apron behind the counter.

"Yeah, I'm talking to you," he confirmed. "You're not usually in here this early. We're barely open for the day."

I couldn't sleep and had started my trek here before the sun had fully risen.

"I know what you want," he said as I'd been about to order my usual. "You're the only person I know who orders tea in a coffee shop."

"It's on the menu," I said.

"Because we're nice people, but no one actually orders it. Take your favorite seat with the view of the lake, and I'll bring it right over."

Did I have a favorite seat? And if so, how did he know? I could only vaguely recall ever seeing him here before. Definitely not enough for him to know what my usual or favorite anything was. Without thinking, I headed for the booth I always sat in—answering my own question—but then thought better of proving him right and took a different seat instead. I scowled as he laughed while working on my order.

"Lexie will be pissed that she missed you," he said, dropping off a steaming mug of coffee and standing there expectantly with his arms crossed. "Go on. Try something new."

"Lexie?" I asked, since it seemed keeping my head down and flying below the radar wasn't in the cards for me today. I wasn't much of a coffee drinker, but I sniffed the contents of my mug, appreciating the toasty scent of hazelnut.

"She's the young lady who always manages to draw the tall straw in the fight to serve your table."

"Excuse me?"

"Yeah, they all want to serve the town hermit." His chuckle made his facial wrinkles more pronounced. I chose not to join in on the fun, especially when it was at my expense. He sobered and cocked his head at me. "Son, you moved to a friendly town, but you aren't all that friendly, now are you?"

"Then why are they all fighting to serve me?" I asked, stirring sugar into the coffee I hadn't asked for.

"Ha! Aside from your looks? I'm guessing it's because you tip well. Lexie was able to clear her light bill with the hefty tip you left her a couple days ago. Maybe today I'll earn enough for that fancy car I've been wanting."

"Don't count on it," I said, taking my first delicious sip and stubbornly withholding a groan.

"Yeah, well, it doesn't hurt to dream. I suppose when you're deficient in one area, you try to make up for it in other ways. But think of how much money you'd save if you just smiled instead of leaving your whole bank account on the table." His laughter followed him as he limped back behind the counter.

I wanted to tell him it did hurt to dream, but that would have required me to speak, something I tried to do little of.

"I suppose when you're deficient in one area, you try to make up for it in other ways."

I mulled over that and the other flashbacks it conjured up.

"You can't connect with them because of your own issues, so you find someone who can give them what you lack."

"That isn't true."

"Oh no? So you're not gifting me to him? Like you gifted him Selene?"

The next sip wasn't taken carefully, and so it scorched the inside of my mouth. At least it took my mind off of the more severe pain overtaking me. That was until another memory of Leland telling me what I didn't want to hear infiltrated my mind.

"You think that if you're unhappy, then that means you're paying for everything you've ever done wrong. Your suffering isn't a gift, Franky."

Leland's voice continued to berate me and then my father's voice took a turn.

"Franklin, I'd like you to meet Gloria. She'll be taking care of you from now on."

I needed a distraction from the noise in my head, and since this seat didn't offer a view of the lake, that left me with only one other option. "What's your name?" I asked. The old man and I were the only ones there, so even though my gaze hadn't moved from my coffee, he knew I had to be talking to him.

"Joe," he said. "Same as it was when I introduced myself to you on your first day here. Same as it says on my name tag. If the one syllable is too hard for you to retain, you can always look up at the name on the sign outside. Or the logo on the mugs and napkins." It was obvious he found me amusing, and through my grouchiness I found it in me to be slightly embarrassed.

"I thought Joe stood for coffee," I said.

"Are you being funny?" Joe leaned into the counter. "I can't tell past the frown you're wearing."

"If I buy you a car, will you leave me alone?" I asked.

"Hey, you're the one who asked for my name."

I grinned tiredly. "That I did."

"Your place is the one tucked between the cluster of red maples." It was a statement, not a question.

"Is there anything you don't know?"

"Someone as good looking as you showing up in a small town draws attention. But small town or not, I suspect the only place you can truly hide that face of yours is on the moon. At least that's what Lexie says." He vibrated with laughter, rocking and holding his stomach as if his intestines would fall out otherwise.

I rolled my eyes, then stared down at the tea he traveled back to my table with. It was too light to be my usual order.

"It's my specialty. Just made it up on the fly, actually, but don't ask me to tell you what's in it." He mimed zipping his lips shut. I took a sip and couldn't resist the full body shudder from absolute delight if I wanted to. "I said don't ask," he warned, pointing a scolding finger at me. It was missing its tip.

"Old war wound," he said after catching me staring at the partially amputated digit. "That and the bad hip—and don't you dare apologize for it."

"I wasn't planning to," I said. "Yes, it's my place." Other than the coffee shop being so close, the home was secluded, which I preferred. Neighbors tended to want to talk.

"Right on the lake," Joe said. "Much better view of it than what you get from that seat over there," he said, motioning toward the back. "Your *favorite* seat. Have you done any fishing yet?"

"No."

He hummed thoughtfully. "Smallmouth bass are my favorite. Absolutely scrumptious. But they're shy. Takes time and patience to catch 'em, but you'd be surprised at how much quality thinking you can get done while you wait, and you look like a man who could use some high-quality thinking."

A middle-aged woman shouldered through the door, arms overflowing with files, her glasses askew. She grumbled a hello before falling into a booth closest to the door.

"Who's that?" I asked, since Joe seemed to know everything.

"That's Beatrice, the town shrink. Be right with you, B!" he said before getting back to me. "Uh, what was I saying?"

"High-quality thinking," I prompted. "I didn't realize there was low-quality thinking."

"Oh yes," he assured me. "There's low-quality, bad-quality, and good-quality too. You won't find what you came here for if you don't get some good-quality thinking in. Maybe high-quality talking too," he said, dipping his head toward Beatrice pointedly before ambling off to take her order.

I stayed at the coffee shop longer than I normally did, ordering another round of Joe's specialty. An hour later I had a paper bag filled with Joe's homemade crumb cake, driving directions to Henry's Sporting Goods store, and strict instructions on which fishing instruments to buy.

"Guess I'll put anything I catch on ice and bring it to you," I said.

"Nah, you enjoy it. The wife has me on a strict diet of fruits and vegetables for the foreseeable future."

"I don't eat fish," I admitted. Something else that reminded me of Leland. Something else we had in common.

"Well, then, that means keeping the fish won't serve you," Joe said, patting me on the shoulder. "Catch and release. And maybe the fish won't be the only thing you let go of, because holding on to things that don't serve you is just bad for the soul."

◆ ◆ ◆

By day five I'd concluded that Joe was a quack who knew nothing about fishing or thinking. I hadn't caught anything, and the only thoughts that ran through my mind involved flying back to Seattle and chaining Leland up in my wine cellar to stop him from leaving.

He and Cole were heavy into their plans to move Nexcom when I left. Stock prices were up, and Cole had been labeled "the king of business." I had to go. I couldn't take it anymore.

Not that I wasn't happy for my son, because with all my faults and warped ways of demonstrating it, his happiness was important to me. But with every financial news update, and with every congratulatory praise aimed at him, he grew more confident in his decision to leave.

"To hell with this," I muttered. I'd been about to call it a day when my fishing rod jerked in my loose grasp, nearly causing me to tip overboard. Carefully getting to my feet, I reeled in my line.

I quickly set the flailing fish into the pail of water near my foot, holding it on its back and covering the head and eyes—the way Joe had instructed—before removing the barbless hook.

I crouched over the aluminum pail, winded and feeling accomplished. The fish swam, adjusting to its new environment, or maybe trying to find a way out of it. It didn't huddle in a corner, licking its wounds and giving up. Not like I did.

Digging my phone from my pocket, I did a search for smallmouth bass. The scales on my fish were so silver they almost appeared white in the light of the sun, nothing like the blotchy fish on my screen.

"This has to be for something," I said to the fish. "My being here has to be for something." I gazed at the water surrounding me and then to the cabin in the distance. I couldn't stay here forever, but I couldn't go back the same.

"Catch and release. And maybe the fish won't be the only thing you let go of, because holding on to things that don't serve you is just bad for the soul."

I contemplated Joe's parting words from last week and got an idea. I needed to make the inconvenience I'd caused the fish worth something. Maybe if I could let go of something, *give* something to the fish, he could carry it away for me.

There was so much to weed through in my mind. So many lies and negative thoughts rushing forward to act as tribute, and yet so many clung to my brain's synapses as if I wouldn't be able to survive without them.

I reached in and randomly plucked one. This was a practice session, after all, and with any luck they'd all get a chance to swim.

"Cole and Jasper can't possibly love me," I whispered. Everything in me fought against letting that one go. *Start smaller,* my internal voice said. *Keep that one,* it said next, *that one is true.*

Grabbing both ends of the pail, I upturned it over the side of the boat before I lost the nerve. Within seconds the fish was gone, taking my lie with it. Joe didn't tell me how terrifying letting go would be. He forgot to mention that my thought would reach back for me, begging to be saved, and that I would want to latch on and pull it back into the safe confines of my mind where it would find comfort.

I felt naked without that one untruth, and the others rallied together, getting creative, trying to fill the void left behind.

Maybe they do love you, but that doesn't mean they like you.

Right behind that thought came one so vile and believable that it sent me to my knees.

Or maybe they love you out of guilt, because they believe they had a hand in the death of their mother, the death of your wife, the wife you failed, the wife they think you would never hurt. The wife who was your only saving grace with them.

Out of breath, I hurried to grab my fishing pole. I needed another fish. I needed to let more of this poison go before it absorbed the tiny speck of space I'd freed up.

Your father hired someone else to love you because he couldn't. Because you were unlovable.

That one got to me the most, and my hands shook with the force it took to maintain my hold on my rod. My father had only barely tolerated me when my mother was alive, and she'd allowed his neglect of me, had even participated in it. My purpose was to serve the legacy. My worth came from my name, which is why for so long—even now—I battled with giving up what came with the name Kincaid in exchange for what I truly wanted out of life. And if I wasn't lovable for *me*, for Franky, then I had no right loving anyone else or allowing anyone else to love me in return.

Gloria and her family leaving without looking back was proof of that. Finding, and then losing, the one person who'd ever made me feel that I could be the man I wanted to be was also proof of it. *Leland.*

I loved Selene, but I loved Leland more. I'd wanted Selene, but *never* with the bone-aching ferocity I experienced when wanting Leland. I was distraught by the loss of my wife, but what damaged me most was still wanting him even while grieving for her. All of that had been more proof of how unlovable I was, and how little I deserved love.

The sun dipped, and my mind grew tired from all the mental gymnastics required to keep the naysaying voices under my control, instead of being under theirs. And just when I'd been about to call it a night, when leaning against the floodgates became too much, my line tugged again.

I fished for days, for weeks. *Months.* I fished until I ran out of my own lies and began taking requests from Joe or using my time on the water for simple reflection.

During one of those reflective moments, I realized that for so long I lived with the delusion that my unresolved problems were manageable, but in actuality the compartments I'd kept them in just hadn't been full yet. By the time Selene died they were bursting at the seams, then spilling over the edges until I was standing knee-deep in the mess I'd made.

In some ways, I felt entitled to my pain. It was mine. I owned it. It was my excuse to barely exist, and without my baggage, who was I? Without it, I had nothing.

As the months passed, I understood that trauma was a cancer of a different kind. It ate away at everything good, and it blocked any attempts made at refueling my life with additional good. I'd been more than willing to let it eat me alive before, but now I wanted to starve it. More importantly, I wanted to take my time in doing so. This wasn't a race, because races could be lost, and I didn't want to have to run this one ever again.

While my lake was helpful, I needed to use every tool at my disposal to heal, to do it right, because I wanted my new way of thinking to stick. I'd one day return to the real world to face the consequences of my actions head-on, and I needed to be mentally strong enough for the job.

Eventually, the summer heat made it harder to sit out on the lake all day, and so I began spending more time at Joe's, and gazing at it thoughtfully through the window near my favorite seat. I could've done that from the cabin, but doing it from Joe's came with an ulterior motive. I got to study Beatrice.

"Are you sure she's even licensed?" I asked Joe, who took to sitting across from me and droning on incessantly whenever business was slow.

He twisted around to eye the eclectic therapist, who I learned paid him rent for the isolated corner she occupied and saw patients there twice a week. She picked the two slowest mornings, and to be fair, everyone left her table seeming lighter and looking happier than when they'd come. It was odd, but no more than she was.

"She's the best," Joe said proudly. Beatrice also happened to be his niece. "Hey, have I steered you wrong yet?" he said at my look of apprehension.

"No, you haven't," I admitted reluctantly. His green eyes danced as he left me alone so he could greet an incoming customer. I sighed, the long and suffering kind, before heading over to Beatrice who read last Sunday's newspaper over the rim of her colorful glasses. I could've seen anyone, could've afforded the best, but I was discovering that the best didn't always come from the places you'd expect them to.

"Do you have room in your schedule for a new patient?" I asked. Beatrice folded her paper neatly before tucking it into the corner and offering me a quirky smile that somehow eased some of my hesitancy.

That first session I said nothing, and she didn't push me for more. By the third I'd given her something she already had: my name. But the sixth appointment I'd given her the one thing I wanted. *Leland.*

I gave her little pieces of my past every time after, and some days the vulnerability of it all became near unbearable to sit through. On those days it felt like I'd walked out of Joe's without a stitch of clothing on, like the whole world could see every ugly part of me.

Still, as the season rolled by, I found myself eager to get to our weekly, unconventional sessions, and once the early morning air cooled with the return of fall, I combined thoughtful fishing with my talks with Beatrice.

I couldn't stay locked away there forever, though. I had to get back home and make things right. I had to fight for what remained of my family.

"Leaving already?" Joe asked as I entered the coffee shop.

"How did you know?"

"You've got a sorry look on your face. More sorry than usual. And because it's been a long time coming," he said.

"I need to catch my son before he permanently leaves for New York, and the tea is abysmal here," I joked half-heartedly.

Joe fidgeted with the espresso machine as he spoke. "Well, good riddance. No more of you drinking up all my specialty and hogging up Beatrice's time. I sure won't miss your grumpiness at all. Not one bit. And maybe now Sarah can stop drooling over your tight behind whenever you stop by the house." Sarah was his wife, and she said she only drooled to make him jealous.

My shoulders shook, although my laughter didn't feel joyous. I'd miss him too. "Does that mean you and Sarah won't house sit for me while I'm gone?" I dangled the cabin keys in front of me. "I mean, there'll be nothing but reminders of me there. I'm sure it'll be hard—"

"Give me those," Joe said, snatching the keys from me and smiling at my dumbfounded expression. Who knew he could move so fast. "My platoon didn't call me Speedy for nothing," he said. "Don't let the limp and crow's-feet fool ya."

"I wouldn't dare," I said.

"You come back soon, you hear? I don't want Sarah getting spoiled living in all that house. It'll only make dragging her home harder."

I had no intentions of returning, at least not for more than a quick visit, and by tomorrow, Joe and Sarah would get the deed with their name on it by certified mail. Their home wasn't equipped for Sarah's wheelchair, and between that and Joe's bad hip, they hadn't seen the upstairs of their home in years. They'd had to turn their tiny den into their bedroom. I'd started on the accommodations for her months ago, knowing I would be leaving my home to them.

"Enjoy it," I said, and he nodded, clearing the emotion from his throat before squeezing my shoulder.

"Get out of here before you change your mind. I've already got plans for that patio of yours."

"Already?" I asked. "You haven't had the keys for a full two minutes."

"Speedy doesn't just apply to the way I move. I think fast, too, you know."

In many ways Joe had been like a father to me during my time in Lockwood, even keeping me company on the lake some days. All my valuable lessons started with him, and mostly by example, by the way he lived his life.

If I had to choose the most valuable of them all, though, it would be that reaching in and grabbing hold of the pain wasn't the problem, hanging on to it once you did was what killed you slowly.

Catch and release.

CHAPTER 28

Franklin

Even before Selene's passing, the estate had become a symbol of pain for me. From the years that Cole and I drifted through its halls in a fog of grief as he grew into a young man under the primary care of others, to the eventual neglect of my marriage, then my race to save my wife, to learning that saving her was out of my hands.

In the most recent years I'd welcomed that pain. I relished in the guilt and the reminders that came with not leaving this place. With not starting over.

This home was now a stranger to me, and I dropped my bags in the foyer, knowing that if I went any farther I'd run the risk of me reverting back to who I was before Lockwood. The bad voices were already tapping at my ear.

I sent a text off to Cole.

Franklin: *I just got back, are you available for dinner?*

His response came immediately.

Cole: *We left for New York ahead of schedule. I got an invite to Jasper's surprise birthday celebration, and I couldn't pass it up. I forgot to mention it to you. Things have been hectic.*

Franklin: *I take it Jasper doesn't know you're coming?*

Three dots appeared and vanished several times before he settled on a reply.

Cole: *No.*

Another text came behind that one.

Cole: *I hope your time away helped. Sorry I missed you.*

Franklin: *I hope so too, and no need to apologize.*

I didn't know what else to say, so I left it at that. He was gone, and I had no business being hurt or upset about it, but I was anyway, and it was on me to deal with it.

Outside of business-related matters, Cole and I hadn't spoken as often as we probably should have while I was gone, so I was excited to get back to him, to maybe spend a few days together before he left, to perhaps see Leland too.

I'd had it all planned out in my head. We'd grab a bite to eat, I'd apologize, we'd have a good cry, and my son and I would promise to work on our relationship. I had to remind myself that fixing things wouldn't happen on my timeline. If Cole and Jasper decided to let me in, and if by some miracle Leland decided to let me in too, it would need to be on their terms and when they were ready.

My phone vibrated with another text.

Cole: *You can always join us.*

Franklin: *I think one Kincaid showing up to a party he doesn't even know about is more than enough. But thank you.*

I smiled distantly, hitting send and choosing to feel grateful for the invite instead of over-thinking whether or not it was genuine. Negative thinking would get me nowhere.

Jasper was a married man now, and the stepbrother he'd once had an intimate relationship with was on his way to re-insert himself into his life. Adding myself to that flame right now would only burn the whole damn house down. I'd give them a little time—but not too much.

Invigorated with hope, I scooped my bags up and left the house I no longer recognized for the one I'd spent some of my happiest days in.

Arriving at the waterfront house, I stuffed the speeding ticket I received on my mad dash here into the glovebox before entering the home. *Our* home.

I went through every room, tearing away the dust covers and opening windows and balcony doors, breathing life into the place again. I ogled Leland's mural before moving on to *A Winter Meadow,* still perched atop the mantel, still capable of bringing me to my knees with its beauty and the remorse it stirred in me.

"Maybe one day we can both be daisies."

I'd told him that once and then I'd turned around and made the feat impossible.

"Catch and release," I reminded myself.

Sliding open the glass wall, I stepped onto the patio, inhaling the scent of ocean water just beyond and squinting at the setting sun. Soon the moon would be high, bringing with it memories of the countless times I'd made love to Leland right under its light.

Will he ever forgive me? I asked myself. He had every right not to, and for so long I reveled in the idea that he never would.

My last stop was the garages where my other love awaited me. I swiped a hand over the chest of drawers I never finished, wiping the dust from my fingers onto the leg of my pants as I moved over to the table saw.

What's he doing right now? Without permission, my mind had reserved every other second for thoughts of Leland. I gave up on fighting it long ago.

It occurred to me then, that today was Sunday, and I was hit with something I'd confessed to Leland the last night we were here together.

"Sunday nights are always the hardest. That's when you close your curtains to me, but it's the why of it that breaks my heart, Leland."

With a burst of energy and inspiration, I began hauling everything onto the patio.

Maybe it wasn't too late for us, and even if it was, maybe I could give Leland back some of what he'd lost because of me.

I changed into something more comfortable, slid my goggles down, and began working on my most important project yet. By my rough calculations it would take me a little more than a month to finish if I worked around the clock.

Just in time to make it to New York for Christmas.

CHAPTER 29

Babysitting my beer on my cold-as-fuck fire escape, I listened for the click of my apartment door letting me know that the two strangers I'd let in my bed tonight had dressed and left me to beat myself up without an audience.

Every day was a struggle. Living in a new city, doing a job I hated but was surprisingly good at, and still fucking every chance I got for less than a moment's peace.

It didn't help that my window now faced a brick wall belonging to an apartment building more dilapidated than my own, instead of a park and a peeping Tom I loved to hate.

"Leland!"

Cole. Always showing up when I needed him, but because of the lies I had to keep, the ones that would follow me to my grave, I could never lean on him. He could never *know*.

I dropped my chin to my chest, taking repeated deep breaths and letting the mask of the man my best friend knew slide over my face. This version of me was all I could give him.

"I'm here," I said, entering my kitchen through the window and then slamming it shut on the frosty night air.

"You move fast," he said, looking back at the front door, then over to me. Like any professional addict, my first order of business was to get the lay of the land, to know where to go for my supply, except my drug of choice was distraction in the form of sex.

"So you think I'm a slut," I said, shit-eating grin in place. If Cole sensed a problem with me he'd pounce and then I'd have to spend the night deflecting or outright refusing to tell him what was wrong with me. "What else is new?"

"I don't think you're a slut. I think you're in pain, but you won't tell me why." His gaze became probing, the atmosphere suddenly heavy. I turned the topic to him, lightening things up with a joke that teetered too close to the truth.

"Ready to wreck a marriage?" I asked, sucking down my beer.

"I respect Jasper's vows." The lie rolled smoothly off his tongue as if rehearsed a thousand times in preparation for the showdown he'd be facing at his stepbrother's surprise birthday party tonight. "I'm just hoping for a place in his life."

Cole would never not want his stepbrother, and not a day went by since he learned Jasper had tied the knot that Cole didn't drift off during a conversation, or a business call, or a meeting, with thoughts of him. If he had a chance to slip into Jasper's bed and his heart, Cole would snatch it up without a second thought for Jasper's husband. I knew the feeling.

I wanted him to be happy. For him, I wanted to believe that true love could win no matter what. I tried never to let my own cynicism get in the way, so I let him have his slice of denial without any interruptions from me.

"Okay," I said. "Are you nervous about tonight?"

"It's been six years since I've last seen him. I'm eager, not nervous."

Cole resembled his father to an uncomfortable degree, and sometimes, especially in moments where his confidence and strength rivaled that of a god, it was almost too much to bear. I averted my gaze to the folder he tapped against his suited leg.

"What's that?" I gestured with my bottle to the folder. Cole handed it over. Confused, I set my drink on the kitchen counter and accepted it. A sticky note with a hand-drawn smiley face clung to the first page of the paperwork inside.

"It's perfect," Cole said when I gaped up at him. I'd re-written the damn mission statement at least twenty-times on account of him. He'd wanted to help in some way with the process of me opening up my own bar, and since I refused to accept money from him that I hadn't earned, I figured allowing him to look over my mission statement was harmless enough. That was until he picked it apart—repeatedly.

"You think so?" I asked absently, looking over a few harmless notes he'd left in the margins. Hard to believe I'd gone from daydreaming about owning a bar with a gallery space reserved for art—the creating and selling of it—to now considering a possible chain of them. Well, minus the art part. My dream had been downgraded to just a bar, and lucky for me, Cole didn't have a clue.

"Yeah," he said, voice dripping with pride.

"You could have emailed this to me, you know," I said, holding it up.

He shrugged. "I needed a reason to check in on you." Cole worried about me. Worried about the neighborhood I lived in, worried about how much sex I had, worried about how I was adjusting to the move. I hated his worry because I didn't deserve it, and so I refused to feed into it.

"I'm fine. I had a little night-cap, and now I'm ready for bed." We both understood the beer bottle on the counter wasn't the night-cap I referred to. "Go," I said, motioning for him to leave.

"Okay, fine, I'm going, but call me if you need anything."

I pushed him out the door without promising him anything. Cole would be the last person I called if I needed something. I had to save all my unused favors for if—or when—the day ever came that I needed his forgiveness.

♦ ♦ ♦

Weaving my way through the teeming bar, I kept my eyes peeled for Noon. I'd been back and forth to New York many times in preparation for the move, but each visit had been short, every minute accounted for, crammed with meetings and a list of things to do. A month of being here permanently and things were finally starting to normalize. Reconnecting with Noon hadn't been possible until now.

He wasn't hard to spot. Even seated, his head rose above the fray. My heart danced wildly as I approached his table. *Fuck,* I missed him.

Noon pushed to his feet, his laughter infectious, and I let mine break free as I prepared to be crushed to him.

"Get over here, you idiot," he said, grabbing me up into one of his rib-breaking hugs.

We placed our order and jumped right into conversation, as if only days had passed and not years. Noon wasn't the type to leave room for awkwardness. His guards were always down, and with overbearing affection, he broke through any wall that stood in his way.

"So," he said, gesturing around the bar he'd suggested we meet up at. "Will it work?"

I'd mentioned my plans to him during our brief phone conversation, and he'd mentioned that he knew someone wanting to sell their building and the bar attached to it.

The bar's location was my main concern. Regardless of my looks, I wasn't a glitzy, cosmopolitan-drinking kind of guy. I wanted my business to reflect who I was at my core. I wanted to open my doors to the construction-working father of two who had just enough money after payday to grab a few beers on tap with the crew. I wanted struggling artists. Locals. And *maybe* the occasional bar fight to keep things interesting.

The East Village provided all of that, and I couldn't have asked for a better neighborhood than Alphabet City.

"It's perfect," I said over the music. Worn and rustic, which aligned with the look I was going for. It would require minimal work, from what little I could see through the dim lighting. Maybe a fresh coat of paint in a few places and a complete renovation of the bar area itself.

"That door over there leads to a huge open space the size of this room. Maybe bigger. You could knock this wall down and open the place up some more. Do your art exhibits and sip-n-paints back there."

"Yeah," I said, "eventually." I'd need to first figure out how to paint again. I fisted my hands under the table to keep the tremors under control. They tended to take over on Sundays. "For now it'll just be a bar."

Our waitress delivered our drinks, giving us both a minute to collect ourselves after the initial euphoria of seeing each other again. We sipped and nodded to the music as I scoped out the place a bit more.

"Most of the people who frequent here are residents of the area. Steve's on a first name basis with damn near everyone." Steve was the guy selling the place.

"Exactly what I'm looking for," I said. Loyal customers who felt like family. They would be the ones to keep the place in business.

"What made you decide to finally do it?" Noon asked, then looked around as if envisioning the place being mine.

"Age and maturity, I guess."

"That simple, huh?"

"Yeah," I said.

Noon leaned forward, moving his tumbler out of the way of his forearms. "Leland, this is me you're talking to. Outside of making enough to keep the lights on, the man I knew had no plans for the future. You've changed, and while age and maturity is a damn good answer, I want the truth."

Noon had never been one for small talk, bullshit, or beating around the bush. And it had been so long since I didn't have to pretend I was okay, that not doing so now took a momentary retraining of my brain.

"Honestly? Sheer exhaustion. I was so fucking tired of thinking I was outrunning something when actually I was merely running in place. My life and my emotions had become one big fucking Groundhog Day. Living a lie isn't easy, yet I continue to fucking live it," I said, giving no context for my statement and surely confusing the fuck out of him. "Truth is, I'm scared I don't know what I'm doing here, but I have to do *something*. And I'm almost positive I'll fail. What do I know about operating a business? So you see, I haven't changed at all." Felt good to say it, felt good to drop the playboy persona for one goddamn second and actually let someone in.

Noon considered me for a beat. "Let's tackle the second half of your rant first. What if you had a crystal ball that showed you the future, and it showed that you would absolutely, unequivocally fail at this. Would you try anyway?"

Leave it to Noon to simplify shit and carve out all the extra stuff clouding my vision. "Yeah, I would." Because my only other alternative was to continue to age into a bitter old man, and I couldn't go on being pissed at Franky for not being better if I couldn't manage to be better myself. Plus, I had a feeling Cole wouldn't have let me get away with my previous retirement plan of being a sex-addicted drunk.

"So see, you have changed. The old Leland would've tucked-tail and taken the first job offering a barely livable wage."

"Gee, thanks," I said dryly. Noon raised his glass, and I clinked mine to his.

Two drinks later and a shared basket of fries, and Noon decided to touch on the one topic I could've done without. The man responsible for the first portion of my mini, emotional purge.

"Whatever happened with Franklin?"

"Let's see," I started. "He left me for his wife—who later died," I added delicately. "I turned into someone you wouldn't have recognized, then later became best friends with his son Cole, who took over the company, hired me as his executive assistant, and moved me here to New York. And in some ways I'm still not the person you once knew."

Noon slowly lowered his glass.

"Oh! I forgot to mention the kicker. Cole has no idea I once had an affair with his father, or that said fucked-up father and saintly stepmother's marriage wasn't the picture of perfection."

"Oh," Noon said, for once at a loss for words.

"Oh indeed."

Noon considered his drink, twisting the glass between his hands, before swallowing it down with a grimace. "So, let me guess. You haven't been in a serious relationship since. I'd take it a step further and say you don't do casual relationships either."

"Maybe we should revisit the part where you said I changed, because obviously I haven't if you still know that much about me."

"You don't like to be hurt."

"Does anyone?" I challenged.

"No, but hurt looks different on you. You refused to stare out of a window after what your mother did to you."

"Could you blame me?"

"Not the first few years, no. But how long would you have held on to that phobia had I not started that trash can fire in my bedroom, then woke you up by screaming fire, and insisting the only way out was through the window? And you've never gotten over your fear of heights."

Franky had actually helped me with the latter fear, but I kept that to myself. "I still can't believe you did that. You could've burned the whole damn house down."

"Point is, you nurture your pain like it's something you gave birth to, and you already had a no-love policy before falling for Franklin. Afraid you'd end up like your mother."

I *had* ended up like my mother. Obsessed and unable to see life without Franky in it. "No, I don't do serious or casual relationships," I said. "And the world's a better place because of it. Now, can we please move on to lighter topics, like maybe why your shirt's two sizes too small for you?"

We laughed and reminisced until Stacey called him home.

"Is it past your curfew?" I asked as he ended his call with his wife.

"She can't sleep without me," Noon said. Good to know I wasn't the only one who suffered from insomnia when the man I loved wasn't in the bed next to me.

"I'll pay the bill," I said.

"No way. You've got a building to pay for," Noon said, fetching his wallet and flagging down our server. "Which side of town are you heading to? We can share a cab."

"Nah, I'm not ready to go home yet."

Noon checked the time and then eyed me questioningly.

"I, ah, need to stop and grab something to help me sleep," I said, and something in my expression must have tipped him off, because his confusion was then replaced by something so soft it made me turn away.

It was late, and I could've saved myself some time by taking the redhead at the bar up on the offer in his eyes, but if these people were regulars, and if by some miracle I could secure a loan large enough to take over this place, I had no intention of shitting where I ate. *Johnny would be proud.*

Noon and I slipped our coats on and hugged goodbye outside.

"Do you think you have room in your arsenal for *two* friends?" he asked, backing toward the curb where his cab idled.

"Yeah, I think I can manage two," I said.

"See," he said, his eyes twinkling under the street light. "You have changed."

"Not in the ways that matter," I mumbled to myself. I waited for his taxi to pull off before making my way to the nightclub I'd passed on my way there.

Stumbling into my apartment a couple of hours later, I had just enough strength to peel out of my clothes before tumbling face-first onto my bed. The scent of sex and cigarettes surrounded me. It ended up being one of the best night's sleep I'd had in a while.

The next few weeks were a blur of getting things in order for the purchase of the bar, working for Cole, and trying my best to be there for him as he navigated his ever-changing intentions for his relationship with Jasper.

I'd found my rhythm. I knew how much sex I needed per week to get the bare minimum hours of sleep every night. I knew how hard I had to work at being a good friend to keep my guilt under control. And I'd even come to terms with the fact that I may never hold a paintbrush ever again. Things were going great, and then *he* showed up. And then everything changed.

PART THREE

CHAPTER 30

Leland

Seven Months Later

Not only did I have my Christmas holiday ruined when Franky decided to show up in town, but I also had my whole life thrown off its axis when he decided to stay. Indefinitely.

After the new year, I spent months focusing on the purchase of the building that housed the bar, then the renovations of it because there was more to be done than I'd initially thought.

As soon as the loan had been secured, and I was sure that I could stay afloat for a few months unemployed, I handed Cole my resignation. I needed to direct all my attention into getting the place up and running, or so I'd told him.

Cole understood from the beginning that my working for him would be temporary. A means to get me to my dreams, so there were no hard feelings on that front. He did, however, have a problem with how little access to me he got afterward. Avoidance had become my main objective, and so I'd kept myself too busy for everyone.

It wasn't as hard as one would think, because Cole had eventually won Jasper, and with Jasper's now ex-husband out of the picture, he and Cole had begun making up for lost time.

A few months of needing to stay afloat turned into six, because nobody told me that contractors sometimes lied, and that nothing would work according to plan.

I refused to tell Cole, because he would've offered me another job or outright transferred me the cash, so I'd been living off my credit cards instead, which was why I should've been at my bar waiting for the electrician to show up to fix a wiring issue that threatened to delay my grand opening, and not across town riding the elevator up to Cole's penthouse.

He'd made it clear in his message that if I didn't come to him for this meeting, then *they'd* come to me, and I couldn't have Franky in my space, tainting it with our tumultuous past.

The elevator doors parted silently, revealing Cole's expansive marble foyer. I ran a nervous hand through my hair, preparing myself for the lecture I'd for sure receive from him, while also preparing to be cut open by the sight of his father.

Cole's booming voice came from the living room, where I assumed he was speaking with his *other* best man. Per his text, he wanted to meet in person to go over details for the big day. He and Jasper were getting married.

"There he is," Cole drawled, glaring at me from the sofa. I bit back my snarky reply because I deserved his bad attitude. What I didn't deserve was to be hit with the overwhelming emotions that came from seeing the man sitting in the armchair across from him. I'd never get over him. I'd accepted that. Didn't mean I had to like it or put myself in situations where those feelings crippled me.

Franky gracefully unfolded from his seat, which, for me, happened in slow motion as my brain took its time recording every moving part of him. "Hello, Leland." The deep rumble of his voice sent my toes curling in my shoes. He was still the type of man who preferred *hello* over *hi*.

Such a fucking gentleman.

His dark eyes widened and his lips twitched.

Fuck. I'd muttered that out loud. Cole, seemingly too upset with me to have heard, dug into me before my embarrassment could set it.

"Where the hell have you been? I didn't realize the end of our working relationship meant the end of our friendship, too, Leland."

"Have you always been this dramatic?" I asked, hitting back. His annoyance melted away, a slice of hurt taking its place. "I'm sorry. Of course we're still friends. I've just been busy getting the bar ready for tonight's grand opening."

"I've been offering to help. Jasper and I both have. You don't have to do this alone," Cole reminded me.

"But I want to," I said abruptly, my anxiety elevating the longer Franky and I were in such close proximity to each other.

"Doesn't explain why I haven't seen or heard from you since my birthday party nearly a month ago." His pale blue eyes implored me to help him understand, to tell him what he did wrong. It was on the tip of my tongue to tell him the truth—or at least part of it. That I couldn't be around his father because when he watched me as if walking away from me all those years ago had been the biggest mistake of his life, it threatened to re-open old wounds I'd fought hard to keep barely scabbed over.

I chanced a glance over at Franky, and he didn't even have the decency to turn away, to pretend he wasn't staring at me in a way that said he was ready to lay the truth at Cole's feet right then and there if it meant he could have me.

Caught up in the darkness of his gaze, I hadn't heard Cole call out to me until it was too late. Until he'd gotten to his feet as well, his narrowed stare shooting between me and my kryptonite.

"Is *he* the problem?" he asked, pointing to Franky. They were a lot more similar now. A result of the quality time spent rebuilding their relationship. Franky had a refinement that Cole missed out on, though. Probably because Jasper had shown up at the right time in Cole's life, softening some of his hard edges. Franky would always seem out of place in certain environments, even though he was humble at heart. Cole tended to blend in better, expensive clothes and all.

"Is that why you've been missing in action?" Cole went on to ask. "Do you think he's taking your place? Or is it that he makes you nervous?"

"No," I said at the same time his father told him to not be ridiculous.

Franky's eyes remained glued to me, and Cole's stare thinned further, bouncing between his father's rapt attention of me and the blush I could feel warming my cheeks.

Franky used to have the best poker face in town, but he seemed incapable of closing himself off now, and whereas he didn't seem to care, I was terrified it would get us caught.

I cut between them, skirting around the coffee table to take a seat on the couch next to where Cole stood. "I'll be around more often," I promised. "Now, can we discuss the ball and chain Jasper's about to lasso around your ankle? I've gotta be out of here soon if I plan on opening tonight."

An hour later, I had my list of wedding responsibilities, and Cole walked me to the elevator while Franky stayed behind. "Hey, this friendship works both ways," he whispered. "Let me be there for you."

Not for the first time, I wanted to tell him what haunted me, but what haunted me would break us apart. It would also screw up whatever progress he and Jasper had made with Franky. "I know, and I will. I could actually use help with the bar tonight," I said, extending an olive branch.

"Sure," he said, shrugging, as if a recently minted billionaire taking drink orders and working for tips was no big deal. "And if you need more help, I'm sure my father can—"

"No," I said in unison with Franky as he crossed into the foyer.

"I have a few furniture pieces I need to finish up at home," he said. He must have been in the middle of that before coming here. His tight, worn jeans and even tighter white t-shirt were both smeared with varnish and paint. One wrong move and his whole ensemble would've ripped away from his hard body, and it pissed me off that I wanted to see that happen.

"He's doing physical labor now," Cole said, snorting his disbelief. Franky affectionately rolled his sexy midnight eyes at him. How many nights under the stars had my own eyes rolled to the back of my head as he took his time with me? I had to get the fuck out of there. "Says he's finally living his truth," Cole continued, oblivious to my momentary lapse into ancient history. There was confusion in his tone but obvious approval too. After all they'd been through, Cole was happy for his father.

I turned my back to them, pounding at the elevator call button and rushing on before the doors had fully opened.

Cole shot his arm out, preventing them from closing me in.

"You two might as well ride down together," he said.

Fuck it to hell, I groaned inwardly.

"I'll catch it when it comes back," Franky said. Was he determined to get a rise out of Cole's brows?

"Get on," I said meaningfully, willing to do anything to avoid Cole's probing.

Franky considered me a moment, then clapped Cole on the back before slipping in next to me.

We rode a few floors down in silence, his scent choking me, his size practically forcing me into the side wall of the cabin. The phrase "better with age" was invented for him. He was too potent, too distinguished, too fucking handsome for his own damned good, and when he swiveled his head my way as if he'd read my thoughts, the last of my resolve snapped like a twig.

"You've got to stop looking at me like that."

"Like what?" he asked in that new infuriatingly innocent, yet challenging way of his. He was daring me without even knowing it.

I didn't know where the hell he'd dumped his baggage since that night I left him standing in the living room of our summer home with an ultimatum, but he needed to go back and collect it because new-Franky did not work well with the current-Leland. Current-Leland was braced for a fight, but this new and improved version of him left me with nothing to fight against.

"Like you want to fucking eat me alive," I gritted out.

"Leland," he said, like a plea for me to give him an opportunity to explain, an opportunity that I'd been denying him since he'd touched down in my new city.

"Don't," I hissed into the confined space. "Too much time has passed. You don't get to be different. You don't get to go off on some spiritual journey, or whatever the fuck you did, and then expect me to suddenly fall into your arms because you've now changed. I have the right to not want you. I *don't* want you, Franky." The lie tasted bitter on my tongue. "Respect that."

"I've been trying to make amends," he said softly, the ongoing plea in his tone getting to me. "But you've rejected all my calls and ignored my text messages." He'd been wise enough not to show up to my place uninvited, though. Proving he'd learned the meaning of boundaries since I'd last had the privilege of experiencing him.

"I apologize for the strain my presence has caused on your friendship with Cole. I never wanted that," he said.

"I know you didn't," I whispered, staring straight ahead at our twin expressions of sadness reflected in the mirrored doors. "But it happened anyway, and now Cole is going to figure out the truth if you can't control your emotions."

"Would that be so bad?" he asked.

"For fuck's sake, Franky," I said exasperated. "*Now* you're ready to risk it all? Do you know how long I waited to hear those words? It's too late. I'm different now too, and not in a good way. And you're his father. He'll forgive you. I won't be so lucky." I was too jaded, too hardened in too many ways to even entertain him. He didn't get to lay waste to me, to forfeit so much of our time, then have a sudden awakening and expect me to jump on board.

There was a time I could have possibly forgiven him for what did and didn't happen between us before Selene had died. Time offered clarity on how impossible our situation was, even if that time had done nothing to repair the trauma endured. But everything *after*? All the years I'd spent waiting on him while continuing to destroy myself in the process, giving myself away as if my body meant nothing to me, creating new addictions that never quite trumped my addiction to him... All the yesterdays I spent wanting him to offer me what he dangled so temptingly now... *That* I wasn't sure I could ever forgive him for, and I honestly never expected to be put in a position where I'd have to.

Not to mention what he'd done to his own son. I'd felt every hurt he'd inflicted on Cole, and all I could do was stand by and silently relate to him.

No, it didn't matter what my fucked-up heart wanted. I didn't know how to trust Franky, or how to let go of *everything*. And I didn't think he deserved the effort it would've taken for me to try.

The elevator chimed as we reached the ground floor, and with a pounding heart and an ache at its center, I gunned for the lobby's revolving doors before Franky could convince me to change my mind.

◆ ◆ ◆

Other than handing out fliers in the area to establish myself as the new owner, I hadn't done much advertising for the grand opening. I'd rather gain popularity organically, and I hoped to hang on to the regulars. They'd need to get used to a new bar name, a semi-new look, and a new sheriff in town, but that feeling of being home when they walked through those doors wouldn't change.

Cole showed up—dressed in a three-piece suit. I shook my head good naturedly before running down the basics of mixing drinks, even providing him with a little cheat sheet in case he got stuck while I was off checking on food orders or mingling with customers.

The menu was simple: fries, sliders, wings—basically, the shit I liked to snack on while boozing.

"What's with the bar name?" Cole asked as I took one last pride-filled look around before I unlocked the front door.

"It means something to me," I said vaguely.

"Maybe one day you'll deem me worthy enough to share," Cole replied tightly before stalking off. I'd have to deal with the state of our friendship sooner rather than later.

I propped the door open with a rubber stopper, letting the warm summer breeze in, before selecting an upbeat song on the jukebox. Then I waited for the magic to happen.

"Jesus, Leland," Cole said hours later over the cacophony of conversations. "I think we're in danger of exceeding maximum occupancy." He smiled from ear to ear.

"I know, isn't that great?" I popped a cap on a bottle of beer and then slid it into a waiting customer's hand.

Drinks flowed, music played, pool balls were pocketed, and by the end of the night we'd run out of wings.

Cole pushed through the kitchen's swing door, lifting the flip-up countertop to sidle up next to me behind the bar. "Dishes are clean, trash has been taken out, and I told the guys they could leave. Anything else you need help with before I go?"

"Nah, I'm good," I said, finishing up with the liquor inventory. "It's almost midnight. Go home to your jealous fiancé." Jasper and I were cool. He'd long gotten over the times I'd purposely made it seem that Cole and I were more than what we were. But they were both possessive and twisted as fuck. Didn't take much to get their hackles up where the other was concerned.

"What's behind the locked door?" Cole asked as he shrugged into his blazer. I followed his gaze to the bolted door near the jukebox.

"Just extra stock space," I said.

"You've already got enough space for that. How big is it back there? Maybe you can expand the bar. From the looks of it, you could use the extra square footage."

"Not that big," I lied.

"Okay," he said, noticing the lone person finishing their drink at a table in the back. "Need me to close out his tab? Rush him along?"

"You could barely rinse a glass without fumbling it, and now you wanna take a stab at the register? No, thanks, rich boy. I got it from here."

"Fuck you." He chuckled.

"Thanks for your help," I said seriously. "I know I don't accept it often—"

"Try never," he cut in wryly.

"Hey, I let you give me a job, didn't I?"

"That's different. We both got something out of that."

"Well, I let you help me tonight, and I'm trying to thank you, but you're ruining it."

"Yeah, yeah," he said, rounding the bar and heading for the front door. "You're welcome," he called back.

"Love you!" I shouted as the door closed behind him.

Owning the building meant I got to make the apartment above the bar mine, so I cashed the final patron out, locked the place up, and was home in no time. I'd thought about hitting up a club and dragging someone back to my bed, but for once I was determined to get to sleep on my own. It happened rather quickly once I gave myself permission to imagine oceans and daisies and nights in front of a fire. When I gave myself permission to mourn the fact that the person I most wanted to share my success with that night, hadn't been there.

CHAPTER 31

Franklin

He'd named his bar The Daisy. I stood back on the curb, choking on my admiration of him as I reread the two words scrawled across the black awning in white block letters. It was simple, like its owner, yet said so much.

Inside, business was slow, but it was early. With no sign of Leland, Cole, or Jasper, I took the opportunity to explore the place. My exploration ended at a locked door in the back. This was supposed to be an art-bar, but so far all I'd seen was...bar.

"What are you doing here, Franky?"

I pivoted toward the voice that kept me up at night. Leland waited for an answer just outside the kitchen, hints of it revealed by the swinging door still flapping back and forth. *God.* He was even more gorgeous now than when I'd last seen him a week ago at Cole's place. Golden brown eyes, framed by thick lashes, glistening under the sun rays bursting in through the windows.

"I'm meeting Cole and Jasper here to go over wedding details with you. They're probably stuck in traffic, or they would've been here by now." I scrunched my brows together, peering outside. Cole's text had said to be there by noon, and I'd purposely arrived late to ensure I didn't arrive first. I went as far as walking there from home instead of riding the train, which added an extra forty-minutes to my commute.

Of course I *wanted* to be the first one here. I'd have given anything for a moment alone with Leland, for a chance to simply talk to him, or listen to him rage at me, or suffer through his ignoring me. But what he needed from me overrode what I wanted from him, even if what he needed wasn't me.

Leland pulled his phone from his back pocket at the same time I opened my text conversation with Cole.

"Oh," I said, feeling foolish.

"Yeah, you're a day early," he confirmed.

"Right," I said. *What now, Franklin?* "Mind if I stay for a drink?"

"You've got your pick of high-end bars on the upper east side. Why slum it down here at my crummy bar?"

"You know where I live?"

"Cole may have mentioned it." The long column of his neck reddened. A tell that he wasn't being completely honest. Had he looked me up? My heart raced at the thought, and I silently warned it not to get ahead of itself.

"What can I say? I like obscurity." I shrugged, sinking my hands into the front pockets of my jeans. "And this place is far from crummy. It's..." I scanned the rustic bar again with its understated style. "It's you."

"You? Obscure?" Leland snorted, ignoring my last comment—and its implication that I knew him. I took his heading around the bar as a good sign, though. "The thing is, you stick out like a sore thumb, Franky." He turned to pass through the raised counter flap, putting the bar top between us.

"Thank you, I think?" I said, straddling one of the stools and setting my baseball cap next to me. I combed my fingers through my flattened hair.

He chuckled at my confusion. The sound was light, carefree, and at odds with the heaviness that normally surrounded us. "That was definitely not a compliment," he said.

The corners of my mouth tipped up. I missed the way he used to give me a hard time. My smile seemed to trigger his anger, because his lips thinned and he whirled away from me to grab a beer glass.

"Stella?" he asked, already tugging the lever on the tap before I could confirm.

"You know me well," I said, my mouth working before my brain.

"Do I?" he asked, setting my drink on top of a bar napkin. "Because one word comes to mind when I think of you, Franky. Whiplash."

I walked right into that one. "Leland—"

"Don't tell me that I know you. It's insulting." The door opened, and a young couple strolled in holding hands. I'd forgotten where we were. Hadn't even noticed when the man sitting at the other end of the bar when I'd arrived had left.

Leland hustled down to pick up the cash he'd left behind, then made small talk with the newcomers before making their drinks. The woman asked him a question I couldn't hear, and Leland smiled, pointing past me to the jukebox in the back. With nothing left to do, he hesitantly returned to me.

"I thought you wanted to open an art-bar," I said, steering the conversation to what I hoped was lighter territory. Granted, I'd never gotten much from him personally about the art-bar, but the name had given some indication to what he'd wanted this place to encompass, and with not one bit of art in sight, I knew this wasn't it.

"That was another time, Franky. A lot has changed since then." His words were loaded, and I sighed. Seemed there was no getting anywhere with him. Any direction I took, whether it was being upfront about my feelings, apologizing to no end, beating around the bush, giving him his space...none of it mattered or got me anywhere.

Maybe humor was the way in. Leland had always enjoyed a good laugh, especially at my expense. "If you're not too busy, I've got a bare wall that could use—"

"You're kidding me, right? Wild horses couldn't drag me through your front doors, Franky."

"What about regular horses?" I'd thought my bright idea had backfired, but eventually he returned my grin, tugging his bar towel off his shoulder.

"What is this, Franky? What are you doing here?" He wasn't asking that in the literal sense, because we'd already established why I'd shown up there. He was speaking more in the grand scheme of things.

"I'm trying to earn your forgiveness. Please let me."

"Is that all you want?" he challenged.

"It's more than what I deserve," I said, because the truth would've set us back five minutes, and I couldn't afford to lose any progress.

His top teeth toyed with his bottom lip. "I don't know how to do this with you, Franky, but I need to try for Cole. I just... I don't know *how*. I don't think I can."

"What can I do to fix things?" I asked, hearing the desperation in my tone.

"*Fix* things?" he exclaimed, turning heads at the end of the bar. I'd said the wrong thing, but to be fair, anything could've been the wrong thing. That was how built-up anger and resentment worked.

Leland took a deep breath before continuing with a lowered tone. "You think you can show up and wave a magic wand to make *years* of pain go away? You think you can show up as a brand-new man, ready to cleanse his sins, and I'm supposed to do what? Go along with it? Break my friend's heart? Take you back? Do you know what I've done to myself since that summer?" He stared down at his body in horror.

"I…" I didn't know what to say. Anything I said would be wrong. "Would you have preferred it if I hadn't come to New York?"

He screwed his eyes shut, as if he didn't want to admit what he would say next. "Cole and Jasper needed you. *They* need you. I'm happy they have you. I just don't know where that leaves me, because seeing you only hurts, and I can't pretend where you're concerned. Cole will eventually know enough to ask the right questions—and don't you dare say we should tell him the truth, because that is not something you get to decide on your own."

He was right. If it were up to me, Cole and Jasper would know everything, but the truth wasn't mine alone to tell. It was why Cole had never told me the truth about Selene's death or his intimate relationship with Jasper. He hadn't had the okay from Jasper to do so.

"Okay," I said. "Maybe for now we can coordinate. Work as a team to lessen the instances when all four of us need to be together."

"How?" he asked skeptically. "There's the wedding, and your son is hellbent on us being one big, happy family."

It was true. I'd received more invites for Saturday barbeques and Sunday family dinners than I could count. I'd had to talk Cole out of starting up a group text. "We'll figure it out." It was the least I could do for him.

Leland was flagged down for a refill, and I pushed up from my stool to catch his arm as he made to walk away. "But let me make myself clear," I said. "The moment you tell me you're ready, we tell him. I won't hesitate, Leland. I won't make the mistake of not choosing you again."

He backed away slowly, his eyes watching me distrustfully. He spun toward his customers, and I fell to my seat, downing my now-warm beer in one continuous gulp.

The woman giggled above the music, and her boyfriend tossed an arm over her shoulder, smiling sappily down at her as Leland poured their drinks. He handed them off, then disappeared into the back.

The front door creaked open, and a few more people staggered in, taking seats at various high-top tables. One guy, there by himself, sat a few stools down from me. Average height, deep-set blue eyes, good looking enough. He drummed his fingers on the bar and craned his head around in search of something or someone.

Leland returned, his gloomy expression evaporating at the sight of the young man. "Alex," he said, with a familiarity that made my stomach knot. "Back already?"

"What can I say? You make the best Old Fashioned in town." Alex ended his not-so-subtle flirtation with a wink. He couldn't have been older than twenty, and looked more like the frozen margarita type, I thought pettily.

"Nah," Leland said, turning to reach the bourbon off the top shelf while *Alex* checked out his tight backside. "That would be my mixologist, Marrissa. She works the night shifts. You should stop by in the evening sometime."

"Do you work the night shifts too?" Alex asked a little too eagerly.

"Yeah, I do," Leland said. "I'll be here all day every day until we work out the kinks." He joked with Alex for a few minutes before finally sauntering back over to me.

"Things are starting to pick up," he said, a clear hint for me to leave. "Your drink is on the house."

I nodded, standing to fetch my wallet from my back pocket to pay for my drink anyway as he exited the bar area to take orders from the other customers chatting patiently at their tables.

I pushed my hair back and slipped my hat back on, heading for the door.

Stopping at Alex's shoulder, I looked behind me to confirm Leland was out of earshot. "Alex, right?"

He startled, swiveling his stool until he faced me. I took pleasure in the neck ache he'd have come morning for having to strain to gaze up at me. "Ah, yeah. Do I know you?"

"I'm a friend of Leland's," I said, which cleared his leeriness away. "You live around here?"

"Oh, no. I'm a student at Cooper Union. Finishing my undergrad this summer. It's not too far from here. I came in for the grand opening with a friend. Been here four times since," he said sheepishly. "Drinks are good. Food too."

"I do hope that's the only thing you're coming in here for, because *he* isn't on the menu." I traveled my stare to Leland, who made polite conversation with the folks at a nearby table, and Alex followed. I stepped in closer, forcing his back into the bar. "Cooper Union, right?" I didn't wait for him to answer. "Education is important, and I'm in search of new philanthropic opportunities. Maybe I'll swing by there some time." I crowded him in further, adding a hint of threat to my whisper. "Perhaps I'll run into you when I do."

"Th-that would be great," he said in a shrill tone. "Enjoy your drink, Alex," I said before exiting. Some things about me may have changed, but some would always remain the same. Leland was mine.

CHAPTER 32

Leland

Ambient music played below the din of hushed conversation in the restaurant. The hostess led me to the corner table where Cole already waited, scowling down at his phone.

"Your father would have stood for me," I said dryly, hesitating before taking the seat across from him. I'd considered taking the one next to him—the one reserved for Jasper, if only so I wouldn't have to sit next to Franky and be subjected to feeling his heat. But then I'd be stuck facing him, stuck watching him, and stuck with him watching me. I didn't know which fate was worse.

Cole chuckled, setting his phone on the table. "Is *that* what it'll take to get you to come around? Standing for you? Wish I would've known sooner. Maybe I'll even throw in a curtsy next time."

I laughed in return, a sharp pain poking me in the heart. I missed him. Missed *this*. Our easy banter. "I'm here now, aren't I?" I asked. "Even though fancy places make me itch." I tugged at the collar of my button up. My back was to the front of the French restaurant, and I glanced toward the entrance. "Where is everyone?"

"They'll be here soon. We're early," Cole said.

"I see." He'd given me an earlier arrival time so we could speak alone.

"Jasper tells me I'm overbearing where you're concerned. Too needy—"

"Are you sure that's not his jealousy talking?" I asked with a grin.

"Is it?" he asked, the tealight candle at the center of the table throwing shadows across his big baby blues. "I think I have been coming on too strong lately, but we were thick as thieves back in Seattle. You were there for me when no one else was, not even my father." He pressed his forearms into the table. "You've always been a private person. I get that. I don't like it, but I get it. But something's changed. Ever since Jasper and I got back together…" He trailed off, as if not wanting to think his relationship had caused a rift in our friendship. "I just don't want you to think I don't have room in my life for you both."

"I know that, Cole. I love that you finally got your happily ever after. And I love Jasper. Trust me, what's going on with me has nothing to do with you." The lie was out before I could comprehend the dishonesty in my words. What I was dealing with had everything to do with him, just not in the way he thought.

"If I come around more often will you promise to stop pretending you're into all of this wedding planning crap?" I said, lightening the mood.

"Is it obvious that I'm using it as an excuse to connect with you?"

"As obvious as the boner that springs in your pants whenever Jasper enters a room." We laughed, raising eyebrows, and damn it felt good. I had to find a way to make this work, even if that meant finding a way to coexist with Franky.

Our server came by with a bread basket and a carafe of water, upturning our glasses and filling them before nodding and striding off.

"So what time will the two of them be getting here?" I discreetly checked my watch. I had less than an hour before Noon's rescue text would come in. It would've been nice to at least get through an appetizer before ditching my entrée.

"Jasper's finishing up with a client, but his office is a short walk from here. My father's date ended twenty minutes ago, so he should be here soon—"

"*Date?*" I asked, voice loud and cracking unintentionally on the word. My jealousy made me forget where I was and who I was speaking with. "I mean, isn't he too old to be dating?" I said calmly, as if I didn't care much but wanted to make conversation.

"I'm fifty-three and virile," Franky's steel voice corrected me from behind, causing me to sputter the sip of water I'd just taken. I went rigid as he slid onto the chair next to me.

"I could have done without hearing that," Cole complained while I shook out my folded cloth napkin to dry my mouth and the front of my shirt.

"And it wasn't a date," Franklin said to his son, then to me he said, "It was a business meeting."

Cole scoffed. "Does he know that?"

He. I didn't have the good sense needed to maintain the pretense of not giving a fuck. "Who's *he*?" I asked Franky. He wore navy slacks with a matching collared shirt, and he smelled like heaven and sin. Yeah, sitting next to him was not the brightest of ideas, especially when it meant I couldn't hide my reaction to him from Cole.

"My neighbor owns a chain of furniture stores throughout the city. I met with him and his partner to discuss possibly working on a line for them."

We were brought menus, and Cole perused his, informing us he'd be ordering for Jasper to get the ball rolling on dinner.

"Partner?" I asked, hoping that meant what I thought it did.

"*Business* partner," Franklin clarified, and my stomach filled with lead.

"So he's available, then?" My mouth refused to shut up.

"Very," Cole said. "And you should see the way he looks at my father."

Our server returned to pour water for Franky, and I unclenched my jaw and turned to Cole. Thankfully, he was still busy scanning the food options.

"You should put him out of his misery," he said absently to his father. "Tell him you're straight."

"But I'm not," Franky said, pausing to take an audible gulp of water. "Straight. I'm not straight."

There was a brief pause in which Cole dropped the menu too close to the candle, nearly setting it on fire as he stared at his father open-mouthed. "Oh," he said.

"Is there a problem with that?" Franky asked in his usual self-assured way, but I didn't miss how his hand trembled as he lowered his glass. Admitting this to Cole wasn't a simple thing for him.

"No," Cole said, slightly offended. "Of course not. I just... This is the first I'm hearing of this." He also appeared hurt, I realized. He was probably wondering when this revelation occurred, and depending on when, how it fit into Franky's marriage to Selene.

"We'll talk later," Franky said to him.

Cole's phone vibrated, breaking up the awkwardness. "It's Jasper. Excuse me," he said, before leaving the table.

"Are you trying to make me jealous?" I snapped, our bodies twisting until we faced each other. I should've been asking for details on what their talk would entail, but Franky wouldn't tell Cole about us without the go-ahead from me, so instead I focused my attention on the neighbor I didn't know but secretly wanted to murder anyway.

"No. Jealousy isn't the road I want to take to your forgiveness, Leland," he said sincerely, which made me feel even more embarrassed and idiotic, because I'd been provoked when it wasn't even his intention to provoke me. I'd shown him exactly how much I still cared.

A surge of grief overflowed in me, because I knew right then that I would have to give up Cole. I couldn't coexist in his world with his father. If this little exchange proved anything, it was that Franky would one day move on, and that there would be a line of eligible people waiting for that to happen, and I'd have to watch someone get the best parts of him. The parts I still dreamed about having.

Since landing in New York, Franky had been watchful, patient, and tentative when addressing me, even if most of those communications came through ignored text and voicemail messages. He'd treated me like a man who was sorry would, and like he didn't want to make my life any harder than it needed to be. And maybe I'd taken that for granted. Enjoyed it, even. How long would he wait for me, though? I swallowed around the realization that I wanted him to, that I saw his pining as some sort of punishment he needed to endure. What would happen, though, when he decided he no longer deserved my punishment?

"Your furniture will be in someone else's store?" I asked. "It'll be mass-produced." That was the opposite of what he'd once dreamed of. He'd wanted a quaint store that doubled as his workshop. He'd wanted to make and sell one-of-a-kind pieces and be home in time for dinner. A simple life, he'd called it.

"I think this is better for me. I'd have more time to create if I didn't also have to run the operation on my own."

"No," I whispered. "That's not why you're doing it." But before I could further call him on his bullshit, I remembered that I'd also tailored my dreams to make room for my fears. The Daisy was just a bar with no art involved. I guess we were both doomed to live and die in the winter meadow.

My face prickled from where his gaze currently touched it. My heart pounded a staccato rhythm for the beauty of him. We'd gotten so close that our tongues could reach out and touch if they wanted to, so close I could feel the breeze fanning from his long lashes, so close that one twitch of either of our hands and they'd be entwined from where they rested on the table.

"*Please,* Leland."

The sight and sound of Franky begging would never cease to make me feel both honored and unworthy. A man like him shouldn't have to beg, yet he did so for me.

"What if you lose them? What if choosing me ends up being the worst decision you ever make, Franky? What if we tell them the truth and we fall apart? Who we are now might not work well together. I don't even know you anymore. I don't even know me," I whispered shakily.

"I—" He was interrupted by Cole and Jasper swooning over each other as they strode hand in hand to our table.

"I-I have to go," I said.

"No," Franky said quickly. "Let me. If you need to be away from me right now, let me be the one to leave. Cole misses you."

Cole and Jasper were on us before I could reply, and Franky plastered on a smile as he stood to hug his stepson.

We ordered our food and drinks, and while the three of them chatted, I plucked a chunk of bread from the basket, tearing and eating tiny pieces at a time for something to do.

It was a whole hour later when Noon's tardy text pinged through my phone. "I, ah, gotta go," I said, standing and waving my phone in the air. "I've got a...thing."

"Can't your booty call wait another hour?" Jasper said, ribbing me playfully as he leaned into Cole.

"A gentleman never keeps a lady waiting," I said. "Or a man, for that matter." A sour taste filled my mouth when Franky's silverware clattered to his plate. He wiped the corners of his mouth with his napkin but didn't look at me.

"What's your week look like, Cole?" I asked, hoping if I made an effort to get a guys' night on the calendar that he'd let me slip out now without a fight.

"I'm free Wednesday evening," he said.

"Okay. Wednesdays are slow. I should be able to get away from the bar early. Pencil me in."

We said our goodbyes, and I didn't release my held breath until I'd escaped into the muggy night air. I stopped at the corner of the busy intersection, spinning around to face the direction I'd come from, fighting against the urge to go back and collect the other piece of my soul.

I backed up a step, and then two, and then a few more. Car horns blared and pedestrians screamed for me to look out, but I didn't take my eyes off the restaurant that still held the other half of my heart. Not until headlights blinded me, not until the sound of tires screeching deafened me. Not until a delivery van barreled down on me. Not until it was too late.

CHAPTER 33

Seeing Noon's hands on Leland didn't inspire thoughts of violence the way it used to, but that didn't mean I was okay with it.

"Should you be touching him?" I asked, returning to Leland's hospital room with a hot cup of tea. "You might be unknowingly causing him pain." I counted the seconds it took Noon to remove his lips from Leland's forehead. If anyone's forehead kisses were going to make Leland feel better, it would be mine.

"As opposed to *knowingly* causing him pain?" he asked, his pointed jab perfectly aimed at my heart.

"What the hell is that supposed to mean?" Cole asked in defense of me from where he stood at the foot of Leland's bed. We were all on edge thanks to the argument he and Leland had been having before I'd decided to take a break from it to grab some tea.

"Enough," Leland said. "I think I'd know if he was causing me pain."

The vehicle he'd been struck by, mercifully, wasn't going fast enough to cause any real damage. He'd suffered a few minor scrapes and bruises, and a fractured arm and leg. Nothing that a few weeks or so recuperating couldn't fix. They'd kept him a couple nights for observation—something he was well enough to complain about during every waking hour.

"As I was saying," Cole began.

"No," Leland said. "My answer is still no."

"You heard the doctor," Cole said. "Your dominant arm has a fracture, and you've suffered a complex break in your left leg. Between the splint and cast, you'll need round the clock assistance for at least the next four weeks. His words, not mine." Cole jabbed a finger toward the door, to where Leland's doctor was making his rounds somewhere on the other side of it.

"I don't need you to take care of me," Leland said, sending my son into a tailspin.

"You're so damn stubborn," Cole exclaimed, but Leland's obstinance was unshakable.

"You can stay with us," Noon said.

"No," I said sharply, and everyone's head snapped to me. I breathed through my irrational jealousy before giving a rational answer. "Noon's got a new job and a wife. He doesn't have the bandwidth to help you in the way you'll need. And Cole has a company to run and a wedding to plan."

"This is more important—" Cole tried, but I made a downward motion with my hand to calm him.

"I know, but pausing your life to take care of him isn't necessary. Not when I'm retired and wouldn't need to sacrifice anything to do it. He can stay with me until he's back on his feet."

"You shouldn't have to—"

"I want to," I assured Cole. "If he's important to you, that makes him important to me." I hated that I had to pretend I was doing my son a favor. I would take care of Leland because I wanted to. Because I loved him.

"I'll hire a nurse," Leland said, setting Cole's rage on edge. Frustration and worry guided Cole, and I was sure Leland understood that.

"Brilliant idea," Cole said dryly, "and I'll pay for it, because we both know you can't afford to right now."

"No," Leland barked, cursing when his splinted arm hindered his movements.

"Are you alright?" I asked Leland while resting a hand on Cole's shoulder, silently asking him to take it easy.

"I'm fine," he said, dropping his head to his pillow. "I won't take your money, Cole."

"Then you're stuck with one of us," Cole seethed, pressing his palms into the footboard and leaning in, all while subtly looking Leland over to make sure he was okay.

"Fine," Leland bit out, eyes flicking over all of us. "I'll stay with Franky—" He stopped short. He'd never called me by that name in front of anyone. No one else knew of its importance. "I mean Franklin. I'll stay with Franklin *until* I'm able to manage on my own."

"Until a medical professional says you can manage on your own," Cole warned.

Noon whistled low and slow. "I wouldn't want to be on his bad side," he murmured, watching the stare down happening between Leland and Cole. Cole didn't back down until Leland agreed. And then we spent the next few hours convincing him that between Cole, Noon, Jasper, and the other staffers, The Daisy wouldn't fall into ruin while he spent the next few weeks recovering.

That evening he was discharged, and I was helping him out of my truck in front of my townhome. The wheelchair seemed excessive, but he couldn't hop around on one leg all day, and with only one good arm, he couldn't operate crutches.

"I'm not getting on that," Leland said, glaring at the wheelchair lift hooked to the side of the porch stairs. I'd fully expected him to be difficult about this.

"I can always carry you up," I said, gripping the handles of his chair as he debated his options.

"Are you sure that thing is even secure?"

I chuckled, wheeling him onto the ramp and securing him in before ascending the steps slowly to keep pace with him.

"You've got to be shitting me," he said when we entered the foyer to an identical lift attached to the staircase straight ahead.

"My offer from outside still stands," I said, to which he craned his head around to scowl up at me.

"Why do I even need to go up there? And when did you even have time to do all of this?" he grumbled as I rolled him onto the second lift, careful not to hurt his injured leg.

"That's where the bedrooms and showers are, and Stacey called in a few favors," I said. "You can take the primary bedroom. Its size can accommodate the chair, and the bathroom shower is bigger too. Cole dropped your clothes and toiletries off earlier. Everything you need is here."

"Where will you sleep?" he asked as we entered my bedroom.

"In the room across the hall."

Using the chair's joystick, Leland spun toward the bathroom. He didn't compensate enough for his extended leg and ended up nailing the chest of drawers with it. "Damn it!"

"Let me help—"

"No," he gritted out. "I need to be able to do something for myself." It took him five minutes of working up a good sweat, but he finally got the chair through the bathroom door.

"You thought of everything." He scanned the wall-to-wall shower and the medical-grade bench inside of it. "You'll need to help me with more than just making a sandwich," he said with trepidation. "Fuck. I didn't think this through."

"I won't make this uncomfortable for you," I said, trying to reassure him.

"You'll have to see me naked, Franky. You'll have to strip me naked, and likely help me shower and do...other things," he said, chest rising and falling rapidly. "How will that not be uncomfortable?" He had a point.

"I'll do as little or as much as you need me to, and we'll come up with ways that you can help yourself. Your arm splint should be off in a few weeks, a month at the most. You'll gain more mobility and independence," I said, but he couldn't see beyond that bench.

"What do you want to do first?" I asked, blocking his view of the shower. "I can make you that sandwich you were just talking about. Won't require fire to make it."

Leland huffed at my bad cooking joke, then blushed down at the tiled floor. "I need to wash the hospital scent off of me."

"Okay," I said decisively. If I wanted him to be at ease with what came next, I had to pretend that showering him was no big deal. I'd need to keep things clinical. "Give me one second."

I returned wearing swim trunks and a tank, then helped him up and against the wall so I could remove his clothes. I didn't linger in any spots, and I made sure my fingers didn't graze any areas considered private.

"Not yet," he said, breathing rapidly and clutching the waistband of his boxer briefs with his good hand.

"I'll set you down, then get the scissors. You can shower with them on, and I'll cut them away once you're ready." I lowered him onto the bench, slipped on the waterproof cast protectors, then got the showerheads going while I rushed for the scissors.

By the time I'd returned, Leland had already gone through the bench's caddy for the sponge and soap, and had begun lathering up his chest.

I waited at the threshold of the bathroom, allowing him any amount of independence he could achieve. His chest area was all he could manage, especially since he didn't have the use of his dominant arm. I pushed off the doorjamb and hurried in when he nearly tipped over. "I've got you," I said, holding the sponge under the spray of water until it was sufficiently wet, then scrubbing him down as gently as possible without also making him feel fragile.

I soaped up his back, his good arm and good leg, counting every healing scar and bruise he'd sustained from the accident. Bruises and scars I hadn't created physically, but emotionally, I was responsible for them all, and I planned on atoning for every last one of them.

"Tilt your head back a little," I said, turning on the handheld showerhead and removing it from its mount on the stone wall. I held it over his hair, rinsing the suds away.

I was soaked from head to toe. Maneuvering around the bench had put me directly under the fall of water, and if we stayed in there any longer, we'd both turn into prunes. I'd stalled as long as I could.

With the scissors in hand, I crouched and began cutting the boxer briefs upward from the leg.

Leland's stomach went taut, and the volume of his anxious panting rose above the sound of both running showerheads. "Fuck. Wait," he said, but it was too late. I'd already cut high enough for his erection to pop free. He quickly released the punishing grip he had on the side of the bench to desperately tug the wet flap of cotton over his cock.

I bit into my tongue, needing the physical pain to consume me before my arousal could. I stood, unintentionally lining up the junction between my hips with his gaze, and thankfully I hadn't been erect.

"I've got it from here," he said, closing his eyes. He was already flushed from the steam, but the color had deepened. He was embarrassed.

"I won't go far," I told him.

"I said I've got it."

I backed away, grabbing a towel from one of the shelves and drying off as best I could before leaving him alone. I waited out of sight but close enough so I could be there if he needed me. Water dripped down my legs to pool on the floor at my feet, and I wrapped the towel tighter around me.

First came a breathless whimper and then shortly after, a bottle crashed to the shower floor, likely the bodywash, followed by a string of curses. I charged in to find Leland sliding down the bench, his one-handed hold on the side not helping him, especially not once the bench began to teeter to the side.

"Jesus," I hissed, dropping the towel and rushing in to help him. I righted his seat and lifted him up by the armpits. A speck of blood had seeped through the shallow cut above his brow. I dabbed it away. "Are you okay?" I asked, looking him over and noticing what could have been a drop of cum in his pubic hairs. My eyes then went to the droplets working their way like sludge toward the drain.

"I don't like you seeing me like this," he panted. He seemed more ashamed than embarrassed, and I noted the way his shoulders hunched forward. "I must be a real turn on, huh?" He laughed darkly.

I switched the water temperature from hot to cold, to relieve some of the oppressive heat stifling us, while turning his words over in my head. Had my body's reaction—or non-reaction—been the cause of his humiliation? I'd thought I was doing the right thing, but maybe now, more than ever, Leland needed to know he was still desirable. He needed to know he was seen as whole, full of vitality, and not a man made up of broken flesh and bone. Leland needed to know he was still capable of capturing my attention, even if he had no plans of doing anything with it once he had it.

"I'd had to nearly cut my tongue in half to keep my lust under control," I said, and even now the taste of copper swam between my teeth.

"Oh yeah?" he asked with feigned indifference, examining the waterproof covering protecting his splint.

"It took extreme pain to not react to you, Leland. I promised not to make you uncomfortable, but I imagine that while you're living here, my nights will end with me bringing myself to climax with the taste of your name on my lips. And even the nights that you aren't here."

Nothing about Leland's situation was sexy to me. Not his pain nor the bruises I hadn't inflicted with my own tongue, hands, and teeth. I could have lost him. Stepping outside of that restaurant for air and seeing the activity of people and first responders at the corner was like seeing my own life flash before my eyes. My priority now was seeing him back on his feet and, hopefully, earning his forgiveness. That didn't mean I wasn't still attracted to him; it just meant my attraction wasn't my main focus. But what he needed now was the red-hot part of me that saw him and instantly wanted to tear him apart and swallow his cries, so I gave it to him. I'd give him any and everything.

"God, Leland. If I could slam you against that wall and take you right now, I would. I would fuck you for all the years I hadn't been able to. For all the years I loved you and wasted that love on my pain. I would fuck you until you couldn't see straight."

He looked at me then, his expression probing, as if he thought maybe it was my pity for him talking. I unloosened the string of my trunks, then kicked out of them while keeping my eyes trained on him. "This is for you, Leland," I whispered, holding on to my erection. "This is *because* of you."

Leland licked his lips. "It's still so big," he said in fascination, then his eyes widened as if he hadn't meant that for my ears.

"Why wouldn't it be?" I asked around a huff of amusement.

"I heard it shrinks with old age." He shrugged, and the mood felt lighter already.

"You're going to pay for all these old-man jokes," I warned, shaking a finger at him. A devilish smirk played around his lips, one I hadn't seen in years. "Let's get out of here," I said, leaving my erection to be dealt with later.

"What's that?" he asked, lifting one end of my now transparent tank when I bent to help him up.

"It's a daisy," I said as his fingers brushed along the tattoo taking over my flank, making me shiver. "You have one too." An identical wildflower graced his upper back; its petals reached up and around the mound of his right shoulder. I'd noticed it while undressing him but hadn't wanted to say or do anything to make bath time more awkward than it needed to be.

"What's your story?" he asked.

"One lonely night stroll home from Cole's place," I said, "I came across a tattoo shop with flowers in the window. Seemed serendipitous. Do I even want to know your story?" I asked.

"Probably not."

"Tell me anyway," I whispered. I'd suffer through whatever it was, so long as he was telling me things.

"I got it after one of many lonely fuck sessions," he said, and I tried but failed at hiding my flinch. I'd never adjust to hearing him speak about having sex with someone other than me. "I just...needed something to hold on to that night. Something to help remind me that I could be more."

"You are more," I said. "You're everything, Leland."

Leland closed his eyes, and I didn't comment on the look of contentment overtaking his face. I was sure it would have only angered him if I pointed out that I'd made him feel better.

Once dried and dressed, we moved to the kitchen, where we waited for the sandwich and soup order I'd placed to be delivered. I'd been kidding when I said I'd make it myself.

Leland managed to feed himself the sandwich with his left hand but nearly gave himself third degree burns with the soup.

"What were you doing in the middle of on-coming traffic, Leland?" I asked, blowing a spoonful of soup before bringing it to his parted lips.

"Resisting the urge to run back to you," he admitted, as if the earlier shower ordeal, and the accident itself, left him too tired to lie or pretend.

"I hope this taught you to never resist. Open up," I cooed, spoon already reloaded with noodles and broth. Leland frowned but did as told.

"You're enjoying this, aren't you?" he asked.

"Immensely."

He chewed slowly, swallowing before speaking again. "You have the painting I made for you hanging in your bedroom," he said, accepting another helping of soup.

"*His Storm*," I said, voicing the title of it.

"What did Cole and Jasper say about it?"

"They haven't been in the bedroom since I hung it there."

"They'll eventually see it. What will you say when they ask why my watermark is on it?"

"I'll tell them the truth."

"Which is?" He shook his head, refusing to eat more until I answered.

"That the man I love created it for me. That it depicts the passion we once shared. The darkness of that passion."

Leland shoved the spoon away, not even wincing when the broth fell on his pant leg. "You can't tell them *that*."

"Why not?"

"Because we're not together, Franky. And I never said we would be. You'll ruin everything for nothing."

I set the carton of soup aside and gripped the armrests of his chair when he tried to drive away. "Listen to me, Leland. Stop looking at this in terms of what you and I will be to each other, and start thinking about what you need to be free of the secrets and lies holding you prisoner. It's a burden, and it's killing you. It's killing me too."

Leland tried to stand, then yelled in frustration at his inability to easily move. I let the armrests go, allowing him to back up a few feet, giving him the breathing room he needed. He nibbled at his lip in thought, scanning the countertops and cabinets. "You say you love me," he whispered. "But I don't even know you anymore." He'd said as much in the restaurant.

"Brown is still my favorite color. Specifically the shade of brown that shines like burnished honey in the sunlight. Like now," I said as the afternoon sun shone through the kitchen window to light up his honey-gold eyes.

"I no longer prefer to work by the water. It distracts me, slows me down because I'm constantly drawn to it, and the view causes me to get lost in my thoughts. I prefer to get my work done first and then reward myself by taking a stroll along the river."

"With a bottle of Stella?" he asked hopefully, as if he needed something about me to be as it used to be.

"Yes, because some things will never change," I said. "I made a friend. He's sometimes more of the father I never had than a friend, but I care about him, and his sage advice helped me a lot. His name is Joe."

"Just Joe?" Leland asked.

"Yeah, like coffee," I said. "I'm still capable of being jealous of anyone who thinks they have a claim on you, and I still find it hard to be a decent father to Cole and Jasper, but I'm trying to be better at everything."

"Would it be easier between the three of you if you could tell them the truth?" he asked quietly.

"Yes, but I would never do that unless you were ready to."

Leland gnawed on his bottom lip again before asking if I'd gotten any better at cooking.

"I can successfully boil an egg and build a meatless salad," I said, to which we both laughed.

We ended up taking our conversation to the sofa, where I spent hours sharing my new self with him and confirming which areas of me would forever be unchanged.

For the most part, the conversation went well and felt good. But there were moments when something innocuous would set him off. When a joke didn't land the way it should have, and instead triggered his anger toward me.

I took his hostility in stride, because at least it meant he was talking to me, at least it meant he was unleashing everything he'd kept bottled up for so long. And every time I became afraid that he'd wheel himself out my front door and never look back, I'd tell myself this was progress, that I was one step closer to having the other half of my heart back, and he was one step closer to accepting the other half of his.

I told myself that, one day, our half hearts would meet in the middle. One day, our hearts would join and be whole.

CHAPTER 34

Leland

"So your knees are shot," I said, tilting my head back so I could soak up the sun.

"I said I quit running. I never said my knees were shot," Franky said distractedly from the shady side of the backyard.

"Same thing," I said.

He stopped hammering. "My knees are fine. I'd just rather reserve what I have left of them for...other activities," he settled on.

I snapped my head up. "*Other* activities? Have there been *other* activities, Franky?"

"Leland, I didn't mean to upset you—"

"Then fucking answer me," I insisted, but he watched me like I was a wild animal instead. "Actually, don't answer that." I wheeled for the open patio doors leading into the house, but Franky got in my path. It was either roll over him or stop, so I kept going.

"Damn it, Leland." He grabbed the arms of my chair while avoiding my casted leg. His face was now inches from mine, and we were breathing as if we'd run miles or fucked for days.

"Get out of my way," I said.

"No. Not this time. You've been running from me all week. We're okay one second, laughing even, and then you give me the finger, or a derisive curled lip, or nothing at all before you bolt on me. I understand why, and I can handle it, but just this once, don't run. Talk to me instead."

He was right. This whole week had been dedicated to taking one step forward and two steps back, and we were likely to continue experiencing setbacks. I didn't know how to let go of the past for more than a few minutes at a time. Any and everything triggered me.

Discussions about a film he watched during our time apart would upset me because had he not been so selfish for so long, we could've watched it for the first time together. Mentions of travel made a veil of red fall over my vision because we could have seen those parts of the world together. And his recollections of nights gazing into a fire made me wonder who he'd been flame gazing with.

Asking was out of the question, because knowing he'd found sanctuary inside anyone but me would've sent us all the way back to ground zero. But not knowing did that anyway. More importantly, I was jealous and resentful that he'd grown, that he was able to do so without me, and that in the areas where I needed to be changed the most, I was still the same. I wouldn't be able to appreciate that he was in a better place until I was in a better place too.

"I know what upset you, and I can even come up with the reason why, but I want to hear it from you," he said.

Why did he have to be so close to me? I could see the grime caked into the sweat along his neck. The debris from his hard day at work trapped between the strands of his hair. I could smell the scent that made him the perfect man for me. The scent of exertion and need.

"I was your first," I started. "It shouldn't mean that much to me, but it does. It did. And you were so fucked-up for so long that I assumed I'd be your last too. I thought it would be impossible for you to feel your way through the dark to someone else, especially when I was right there in the dark with you. *Waiting* for you. Why didn't you just say the right things to make us better? Why didn't you come to me?"

"I was depressed, Leland. I thought I was doing the right thing by everyone. I had it wrong, and I'm so sorry." He knelt in front of me now, the sun cascading across his remorse.

"Did it mean something to you? Did *they* mean something to you? Did you...enjoy it?"

"*Never*. And I always regretted it afterward."

"Do you promise?" I asked, needing him to swear it. Needing to know that no one had satisfied him, because *no one* else had satisfied me. Not since him.

"I swear it."

I inclined my chin, absorbing the love in his stare. "Did you get down on your knees for them? Is that the real reason they're shot?" I asked, the corner of my mouth curving upward.

Franky laughed, tossing his head back and letting his amusement pour out of him in relief. My heart shifted. It felt like waking up to a nice stretch after a good night's sleep. It felt like something had been repaired. "I kneel for no one but you, Leland. No one."

The resulting silence said too much, so I changed the subject. "Won't Lucas be here soon?" I asked. Lucas was his neighbor with the crush who Cole spoke about. He actually lived around the block. His backyard faced Franky's, though. He'd popped his head over the planked fence separating their yards yesterday to double check that they were still on for their meeting about the furniture line today. Franky had introduced me as his eldest son's friend who he was helping out after an unfortunate accident. Lucas had seemed relieved that I was nothing more than a temporary inconvenience for Franky. I'd bristled at Franky's description, though, not appreciating being drilled down to an inconsequential friend of the damn family.

"If you want me to claim you, Leland, just say the word," Franky had said.

I'd wanted to say the word. I'd wanted to say the word in every damn language and dialect known to man, even the ones that had long gone extinct. But I'd chosen the language of silence instead.

"Yeah," Franky said, putting a pin in my thoughts of yesterday. "I should get cleaned up."

"He wants to have sex with you, you know."

"I know," Franky said, rubbing the back of his neck. "But he's professional. He'd never say or do anything to hurt this deal."

"Just making sure you can see what's right in front of you. That you haven't gone senile in your old age."

"Believe me," he said, "I see *exactly* what's in front of me. Everything else, including Lucas, is merely background noise." With that he was gone, dashing into the house and up the steps to shower and change.

I let Lucas in like a good boy, even managing a nod of hello before escorting him to the backyard to wait for Franky. He busied himself on his laptop while I returned to my patch of sunshine and contemplated him.

"How much can you see from your place?" I asked, staring up at his windows. From the top level he'd easily be able to see into Franky's backyard, and he'd most definitely have a perfect view into his curtainless bedroom. The bedroom Franky helped to dress and undress me in daily.

Lucas stopped punching the keys to gaze over at me. He was closer to Franky's age than I was. A decade younger than Franky at most. The gap wasn't substantial enough to be considered scandalous, though. He had that going for him.

"I can see enough," he said. The pity in his tone prickled. He probably viewed me as the poor disabled guy who needed his best friend's daddy to take care of him. Probably thought of me as a burden to Franky. Yet I was the one getting naked for Franky every night. The one being stripped naked *by* Franky every night. The one being waited on hand and foot by him, bathed by him. Adored by him. *You hold the power, Leland.*

"You want him," I said.

Lucas shifted uncomfortably, staring into the house, checking if the coast was clear. "It doesn't matter," he said, not wasting either of our time with denial. "We're going into business together."

"That's a stretch. You're working on one line together. What are you hoping for after?"

They weren't compatible. They had the same disposition, gave off the same pheromones of aggression. Franky liked an imbalance of power in the bedroom. He wanted to conquer. Wolves didn't want to eat other wolves, they wanted to feast on lambs.

"Should we be having this conversation?" he asked.

"Why not?"

He cocked his head as if trying to figure me out. Likely wondering if I played a bigger role in Franky's life than the half-truth he'd been fed. He was curious, that much was clear in the way he'd watched me a moment ago when he thought I wasn't paying attention. He may have been professional enough to not mix business with pleasure, but business would be over soon, and I knew a hungry vulture when I saw one.

"What's the deal with you two?" he asked.

"Like he said, I'm his son's friend." I had to be careful not to let my ego get in the way of good sense. At the moment I was just Cole's best friend, and I knew he'd already come into contact with Cole and Jasper and likely would again. I couldn't afford to screw everything up because I wanted to prove to Lucas, and to myself, that he could never get Franky. Didn't mean I couldn't bluff my fucking ass off, though.

"So," I nudged. "What are you hoping for in the future?"

"A date might be nice, for starters."

"Yeah, a date is a nice appetizer, for sure. But what about the entrée?"

Lucas cleared his throat. "He should be down any minute now, and I've gotta get this presentation set up," he said, going back to his laptop.

"You strike me as a top," I said, not giving a fuck about his excuse for being here. "And two tops don't make a bottom."

He closed his laptop, a thin smile on his thin lips. I didn't give a damn about his annoyance. "Look, I don't know if you're bored or—"

"Or," I said. "If bored is my only other option, then what I am definitely falls under the category of *or*."

I mentally ran down a list of what could've slipped from his mouth after the word *or*.

Or if you want him...

Or if he's yours...

Or if you don't want to see him with anyone else...

I could've gone on for days. *Yeah, definitely an or. A fucking capital OR.*

"Maybe he's open to trying something new," Lucas said, a fire lighting behind his gray eyes. He made pushing all his buttons too easy. "Maybe he just needs to find the right person."

"And you're the right person?"

"Maybe."

"You can't teach an old dog new tricks, Lucas. Franklin Kincaid is not riding anyone's cock. That's one hole of his that a dick won't see any action in," I said breezily, examining my nails.

"Maybe I'll be the one to compromise."

"And what do you know about taking a cock? About breathing through the stretch, grinding your teeth against the burn, all while bearing down and telling yourself you were built to take all of him."

"*Him?*" he asked, as if he'd caught me.

"Generally speaking." I fluttered my one good hand.

"Sex isn't all about penetration," he said. "You're still young. I wouldn't expect you to understand that."

At this stage in the game it wasn't even about Franky anymore. At least not for Lucas. Now it was about riling me up in return, taking some of his power back. I laughed dryly. "Oh, he'll definitely want to penetrate you. Over and over and over again. And I hope you like pain with your pleasure, because whether or not it's his hand crushing your windpipe as he uses your hole as a cum dumpster, or his teeth at your jugular, or his nails scraping along your beard-burned skin, you won't walk away from the fucking looking the same way you did when you marched into it."

"And how do you know all of this, 'son's best friend'?" he parroted with a hint of mockery.

"As the son's best friend, I've seen and heard all sorts of things throughout the years," I said nonchalantly.

"I bet you have," he said.

"Sorry I took so long," Franky said to Lucas, but his long gait ate up the distance to me. "Is Cole still coming to pick you up?" he asked.

"No, I texted him not to after you headed upstairs to shower."

"I thought you wanted to lay eyes on The Daisy?"

"I'm much more interested in the business of furniture tonight," I said as Lucas assessed our exchange.

"Alright," Franky said. "Hungry? Thirsty?"

"I'm good for now, but maybe after your meeting you can feed me before bathing me."

Franky gazed down on me in displeasure. All week I hadn't let him do either of those things without a fuss, and now I was offering him my obedience. "Be nice," he murmured for my ears only.

"Too late," I whispered back. "I'll be right inside where I can hear *everything*," I said for Lucas to hear, rolling away from them with an unhidden smirk.

I ended up feeding myself, to Franky's disapproval, but there was no getting around my needing help in the shower.

"Did I ruin your deal with Lucas?" I asked as he soaped up my feet.

"Are you the reason something urgent suddenly came up?" he asked.

"Maybe," I said.

He hummed as if he'd suspected as much. "I'm sure it's fine. I don't need the contract, though, Leland. I'll be able to put food on the table regardless. It was just something to do, I suppose."

"You know, for someone whose knees are shredded, you sure have spent a lot of time on them this week," I said.

"Keep it up," he threatened. "I'm keeping score, you know." He pushed to his feet, rinsing the washcloth clean before adding more body wash to it and handing it out for me to take.

Franky now only washed the areas I couldn't get to, respecting my boundaries as much as possible. He'd ditched the ridiculous swimming trunks around day four, and my bath time had become *our* bath time. He'd stand under the showerhead and clean himself off, back turned to me as I took care of my more exciting parts.

He gestured for me to take the washcloth again, and my breaths became too thick to release. I struggled to articulate my thoughts, eventually managing to string three words together. "You do it," I said, my cock rising below the hand towel spread over it.

Without making a big deal out of my request, Franky got down to one knee again, peeling away the hand towel. My cock sprung up from its nest of curls, and Franky held it by the crown while he soaped up the shaft. My stomach flexed involuntarily, and I couldn't hold back my hiss of pleasure.

"Are you okay?" Franky asked, the shower water beating at his back.

"Yes, just... Don't...stop," I gritted out.

"Can you scoot to the edge?" he asked. I managed with his help, and once my balls were no longer confined by the bench, he turned his attention there.

"What do you want, Leland? There's no room here for guessing games." He wanted to know if I was looking to be cleaned or looking for more.

"More," I said, hips undulating. I wanted to grab hold of his hand and wrap it around my dick, but one hand was trapped in a damn splint, and the other couldn't give up the hold it had on the bench.

Franky took his time fisting my cock and the obscene sounds of soap squirting around and through his fingers made my balls tighten.

"Don't play with it, Franky," I whispered. "I need to come." Now that his hands were on me I realized that everyone that had touched me during our time apart were poor excuses for the real thing. No one played my body the way Franky did. No one had ever controlled my body's responses like he had. And he reminded me of that with only a teasing grip that would drive me insane before it drove me to orgasm.

"You need *me* to make you come," he said, fingers gliding along the raised veins of my arched cock. We both knew I could have gotten myself off, but I'd asked him to do it. *Needed* him to do it. We weren't at the point where I could admit that out loud, though.

"Jack me like you mean it, or..." My words were gobbled up by an extended moan.

"Or what?" Franky asked, easing up on the pressure again. His cock was hard and intimidating, but it was like he didn't even notice because his predatory gaze stayed hyper fixated on me.

"More," I demanded in frustration as he swiped a thumb over my wet tip. "Harder. F-faster, Franky."

"You forgot to say please," he whispered, enjoying my misery.

"Please, damn it," I whimpered. "*Please.*"

It was like my begging flipped a switch in his head, reminding him that this should be simple, that he shouldn't be enjoying it, that it didn't mean anything. Franky immediately began pumping my dick at a fast clip from root to tip. My body seized up instantly, and within seconds I came on a shout, my vision blackening around the edges as my orgasm didn't seem to want to let go of me.

I would've slithered to the shower floor if Franky hadn't held me up, and I crash-landed back on earth to catch his hot stare on the soapy cum sliding down his hand and my inner thighs.

"Franky," I said raggedly. He snapped out of his haze and hurried to wash his hand off before carefully rinsing me down with the handheld showerhead.

His own cock was ready to burst, the plum-colored head shiny and wet. Franky ignored it, getting us out of the shower and dressed for bed. We were silent throughout the routine, and he refused to even sneak a glance at me.

Fuck. I'd been selfish. I wasn't ready for more, yet I'd asked him to negotiate the line drawn to give me exactly that anyway.

"Text or call me if you need me," he said, when all I'd had to do before was whisper his name and he'd come running from across the hall. Kind of hard to do that now since he'd closed the bedroom door behind him, and seconds later I heard the guest bedroom door close too.

I woke up hours later to the feeling of Franky being gone. I couldn't get back to sleep, not even after I felt him return home in the wee hours of the morning. I spent the next couple weeks waking up all hours of the night to that void but hadn't found the courage to question him about it. Too afraid to learn why. Too afraid to learn he had somewhere—or someone—else to go to for release when he couldn't release on me. Too afraid I'd want to do something about it.

CHAPTER 35

Leland

"**T**hat's enough," Franky said, as I tugged once more on the resistance band. "You heard the doctor. Light stretching—"

"Twice a day," I finished for him, using my good forearm to wipe the sweat from my brow. "I know."

"Are you in that much of a rush to get out of here?" he asked, setting his dumbbells onto the rack. I'd finally gotten the splint off. The leg cast would take longer, and unfortunately that meant I still needed some assistance since my arm wasn't strong enough to work crutches.

"I have to get back to The Daisy, and don't think I haven't noticed you all doing everything in your power to keep me out of there." Cole or Noon would either pop over or call daily with updates on the bar, but I'd only gotten to go there a handful of times.

"We just want you to put your recovery first, and to trust that the people who care about you have everything under control," he said, moving around his home gym, putting everything back in its place.

"It's still a baby, and I'm the owner. I need to be there."

"You check the balance sheets every night. You know it's doing well. Better than well," he said, and I grunted in response.

"You hate that it's doing well without you, don't you?" he asked, settling onto the workout bench adjacent to me.

"Yes," I said, staring straight ahead. His question implied more than he intended it to, and so had my answer. "It means I'm not crucial to its survival. It means I'm not special at all. The Daisy doesn't need me, but I damn sure need it." I looked at him then, and sure enough, he saw me.

"That isn't true, and you know it."

I faced forward again. The blank wall held more appeal than the honesty in his eyes. I was in a rare mood, somewhere between apathy and feeling so much that it hurt to breathe.

"You've been pensive this past week. More so than usual. What else is on your mind, Leland?"

Where the hell he constantly disappeared to late at night was on my mind. Also on my mind was why he returned every morning, right before sun up, bone tired and in need of an urgent shower. But after the hand job fiasco the last time we'd showered together, I swore to myself I wouldn't do anything to lead him on ever again, and giving him the impression that I cared about where he might be, and who he might be with, most definitely fell under the leading-on category. It said *I want you.* It said *I give a fuck.* And I did want him, and I absolutely gave a fuck.

I had to be certain that what I wanted was what I could let myself have, though. There was still the big matter of trust. There was still Cole and Jasper to contend with, and although we'd made some strides toward forgiveness over the weeks, there was still that last bit of resentment I couldn't quite kick.

"Just thinking about all the bad choices I've made throughout the years," I said, which was true. There were multiple things occupying my mind. He could have that one. "All the relationships I may have sabotaged."

"Why'd you do it?" he asked, the scent of his sweat prickling my nose and making my mouth water.

"I want to say I don't know, but that'd be a lie." I hadn't purposely sought out unavailable people, but I didn't exactly have my hookups fill out a questionnaire on their relationship status either. Don't-ask-don't-tell was my motto, and in the instances where it was blatantly obvious, instances when they didn't even have the decency to remove their wedding rings or make up some excuse to get their boyfriend out the club doors before fucking me in the bathroom... Well, I'd told myself if it wasn't me, it would have been someone else.

"The truth is, I saw it as proof that I was wanted. That I was worthy, and special, and so goddamned irresistible that everyone would want to risk it all to have me. For a moment, someone wanted me more than they wanted their next breath. In my mind it made you wrong for not wanting me. It made everyone who ever mattered wrong for not wanting me. And some part of me also relished in causing harm, because I felt harmed." I exhaled deeper than I ever had, feeling a small vacancy open up in my soul for having admitted that out loud, for essentially getting rid of it.

"I'm sorry," Franky whispered.

It wasn't an empty gesture, because Franky didn't do those, but I understood something just then, and so I said, "You don't need to be sorry anymore, Franky. What I did was on me. It's about time I own my shit. Let me have this."

"Okay," he said.

We were at the tail end of August, which meant summer was winding down, and the sweat on my body, mingled with the cool breeze flowing in from the open window, made me shiver. "I'm gonna head up and take a hot shower," I said.

Franky didn't ask if I needed help. I'd been showering alone since the night my cock exploded all over his fist. It had taken me twice the time at first, but now with the splint removed, bathing myself moved from impossible to a minor annoyance.

"I'll do the same," he said, standing. "I was thinking about walking along the pier. Maybe grabbing some dinner while I'm down there. Feel like joining me?"

"Sure," I said, then leaned forward to whisper, "right after we swing by the bar."

♦ ♦ ♦

From the moment we arrived at The Daisy, I'd done nothing but get in the way. It wasn't wheelchair friendly I realized, and made a mental note to do something about that. I'd hopped around on my one good leg until it cramped, almost taking me to the floor if it weren't for Cole catching me. I took the hint and allowed Franky to get us the hell out of there.

We hung out by the pier where I watched Franky get lost in his thoughts, still one of my favorite pastimes. Then we grabbed tacos and Stellas from a food truck before spending the next two hours eating and chatting at one of the seaport's outdoor eating spaces overlooking the water.

"You're kidding me?" Franky said, setting his beer down on the bistro table we sat at.

"Nope. Noon literally swept him off his feet." We laughed as I went over the first time Noon and Cole met. Cole and I had been hanging out at my apartment when Noon stopped by. Cole opened the door for him, and instead of exchanging pleasantries, Noon picked him up and spun him around before landing a kiss to his cheek and thanking him for dragging my sorry ass to New York.

"I would've loved to see my son's face," Franky said.

"I tried to get them to recreate it, but Cole was too stunned to cooperate."

Franky still had a smile on his lips as he brought his beer bottle to them. "I never got to thank you for being there for Cole," he said.

"You act like I had a choice in the matter," I said, lashing out. The atmosphere instantly shifted, moving from light to heavy. I pinched the bridge of my nose. "I'm sorry... I—"

"Are you tired?" Franky asked.

"Ah..." *Was I tired?* I'd just fucked up a perfectly great moment, and in the middle of my apology he wanted to know if I was tired? "No, I'm not, but Franky—"

"Don't apologize for going through your process, Leland. You once told me that you could handle me at my worst. Let me return the favor."

I nodded. "Okay."

"Now, come on. I want to take you somewhere."

"And leave your precious water?" I asked.

Franky came behind me to grip the handles of my chair, leaning in to whisper as he moved us farther away from the sun setting over the river. "There's more water to be found," he said, making me equally curious and excited for our next stop.

◆ ◆ ◆

"Coney Island?" I said, as I hopped out of the passenger seat and into my waiting chair. The seaside amusement park overlooked the Atlantic Ocean and was nestled within a residential area in the southern part of Brooklyn. There were roller coasters, bumper cars, carnival lights, and games. And the scents that assailed me from the many greasy food stalls made me forget we'd already eaten not too long ago.

"I can't count how many times I've been here since they opened for the season," Franky said as I followed him deeper into the park. "It's the best at night. When the boardwalk is lit up and the beach is empty of everything except the sound of crashing waves."

"Do you still come here? At night?" I added. Maybe this was where he'd been disappearing to. Maybe I'd been stressing myself out for nothing.

"No," he said. "Not since before the accident."

"Right," I mumbled under my breath. I felt the switch in my mood coming on, but this was the first time in forever that I'd been so excited about something, and I didn't want to ruin it with another outburst, so when Franky stopped to buy a spool of cotton candy and then offered me a piece, I stuffed my jealousy into a mental drawer to be dealt with later.

"What brings you all the way out here when you've got a perfectly toxic river closer to home?" I asked, which bought me a laugh from him.

"I think you know," he said, stopping to gaze down at me.

I did know. It was the same reason I was beyond happy to be there with him now. "The Seattle state fair," I said.

"This place reminds me of the day we became friends," he said. "I come here and life suddenly feels simple. Easy. Like it was between us that day." Franky shut his eyes, a shy smile tugging at his mouth, as if the images of that memorable day were floating around on the inside of his eyelids. Things were so simple then. We hardly knew each other, yet we'd faced a fear together, and that had somehow bonded us in a way.

The amusement park wasn't overly crowded, but kids and teens whizzed by us as they raced to the next exhilarating ride and experience.

"So what do you do when you come here?" I asked, ripping off another chunk of his cotton candy, trying not to care that his lips were now adorably blue. "Besides thinking on the beach."

"I get on that," he said, pointing to the Ferris wheel straight ahead.

"The Ferris wheel?" I asked, my blood pumping faster at the idea. I hadn't been on one since our day at the fair, and even though I wouldn't say I was terrified of heights anymore, I still had a healthy respect for higher altitudes.

"Keeps me focused on my goal," he said. "Keeps me focused on *you*."

"We almost shit our pants up there," I said, my voice a bit breathy from his intensity.

"Care to do it again?" he asked, studying the wheel and then staring daringly down at me. He held his hand out to me when I stayed quiet with indecision, because things were less scary when holding hands, even if that *thing* was revisiting the era when my feelings for him began to unknowingly take shape.

"Shitting my pants has never sounded so good," I said, closing my hand around his.

The ride operator was nice enough to keep an eye on my chair while we took a spin on the wheel. Franky and I sat across from each other as we climbed higher, the wind blowing our hair as we gripped the sides of the cart and smiled through our anxiety.

"It never gets easier," Franky said. "But it's always worth it in the end."

I yelped when the cart swayed, and Franky had the nerve to laugh at me.

"Shall we pretend?" he asked, and I cocked a confused brow at him. "I still remember every word."

I got it then. He wanted to recreate our first ride on the Ferris wheel. "I remember too," I confessed.

Franky shut his eyes, and I wasted a few seconds to admire how handsome he was. To admire the additional gray hairs along his jaw and the strands of white mixed into his thick, jet-black hair.

"It doesn't count if you don't open both eyes," I said, and Franky cracked one eye open, just like before.

"Both eyes," I said. Franky opened them both, even managing the same look of exasperation he had that day, before raising his gaze to the night clouds.

"Now look down," I said, in the tone used to convince babies to take their first step.

"If I have to look down, then so do you," he said, and I swallowed on cue.

"We do it together," I replied. "We're in this together."

"You don't even know me," he whispered. "And I don't know you."

"Makes sense," I said with a shrug. "Because *I* don't even know me. Not really. And I'm betting that you don't even know you."

Franky paused. The exact same pause he'd given me then, except this time his eyes said that he knew me. They said that I knew him too. "You're stalling," he said.

"No, you're stalling," I shot back.

"The ride's almost over, Mr. Bear." And it was. We'd already gone around several times. It was now or never, but I couldn't get my mouth to form my next line. I wasn't the same flirtatious guy looking to get a rise out of the grumpy older man. I'd since been hurt by that older man, and I was scared that he would know that this time the words actually meant something to me, that this time they would be the truth.

"The ride's almost over, Mr. Bear," Franky said again, nudging me to keep it going.

I licked my lips. "What if I don't want it to end?" I asked. Franky's smile gleamed with hope but he managed to stay on script. Managed to keep us from veering off memory lane.

He daggered me with the same unimpressed look that shouted he was over my antics, when I was only getting warmed up. "Enough talking. Should we see what we're made of?"

"Hell yeah," I said. "Let's do it." With a synchronized deep breath, we squeezed hands and looked down.

◆ ◆ ◆

Franky and I played games and ate funnel cake on the boardwalk until the amusement park closed and we were forced to leave. We talked the whole drive back to the city, and our conversation didn't end when we got home. It didn't end when he said good-night from our bedroom doors, yet didn't move. It still hadn't ended when I dragged myself over to the bed and relaxed against the headboard before patting the spot next to me. It didn't end until my head drowsily hit his shoulder, until I vaguely registered that I still wore my outside clothes, until he kissed the top of my head, running his fingers through my hair, lulling me to sleep.

CHAPTER 36

Leland

I woke up hours later alone and more upset than I'd been all the previous nights Franky had vanished. Not only had he left the house, but he'd left my side to do it, and that somehow felt much worse. Worse because at some point during the night, we'd gotten tangled up together, which meant that whatever he was getting out there, was powerful enough to tempt him away from my fucking arms.

I'd searched the place from top to bottom, knowing I wouldn't find him, and then I waited in the dark shadows of the living room for him to come home.

Franky didn't creep in until the hazy orange hue signaling dawn coated the sky, and by then my anger and my jealousy had skyrocketed from something hot and boiling, to an icy-cold whisper.

"Where do you go when you leave me here alone at night?" I asked, tone deceptively calm.

Franky swung around with a hand to his chest. "Jesus, Leland," he said breathlessly. "You scared the crap out of me. What are you doing up so early?"

Slower, and with more force this time, I repeated, "Where do you go when you leave me here alone at night?"

"I didn't realize you noticed I was gone," he said, his breath evening out.

"Is it a shock that I still can't sleep without you?" I asked, disgusted with myself. I'd gotten the best sleep I'd had in years there with him—prior to his nightly disappearing act. "Do you really think the best way to win me over is to sneak out for quickies at odd hours of the fucking night?" The living room brightened in degrees as the sun rose higher and higher. With more light to see by, I could make out how disheveled he looked. "Must have been a great fuck," I spat acerbically.

"That's not what this is," he said, moving closer to the sofa.

"So, what, you expect me to believe you've been slinking off to the East River to get some thinking done?"

"It's not that either," he said, lowering onto an armchair, nothing but an ottoman separating us.

"I'm leaving here today. I'm leaving *now*," I amended, "And you're not going to fucking fight me on it."

"Leland—"

"Or talk me out of it, so save your breath." I pushed up and hopped over to the stairs.

"Alright," he said, catching me off guard. I hadn't expected him to give in so easily. I leaned against the banister, out of breath from my journey there. "I'll let you go without a fight, but only if you let me take you somewhere first."

"Fuck you," I spat. I'd allowed him to take me somewhere last night, and that nostalgic ride on the Ferris wheel had robbed me of my guards and my good fucking sense. I wouldn't be going anywhere with him again.

Franklin prowled over, an expression I hadn't seen since our summer on the ocean falling over his face. "You come with me now, or you stay here. Those are your only options, Leland."

Thirty minutes later our Uber driver came to a stop in front of The Daisy. "What the hell are we doing here?" I asked. Franky didn't answer. He got the wheelchair from the trunk and dropped the brake as I hobbled over and fell into it.

Next, he unlocked the bar door and held it open, motioning for me to go in and then following behind me.

"Why are we here, Franky?" I tried again, but he simply strode for the door at the back of the bar, flipping through the spare set of keys I distinctly remember giving to Noon out of necessity after the accident. My original set had a daisy keychain on it. Those were with Cole.

"Come on," he said, waiting until I rolled in to switch the lights on.

The expansive room had been painted white. It had been a dull gray the last time I'd entered it. Art hung on the tall walls. *My* art hung on the tall walls. Every piece that Franky had gotten his hands on.

Strategically placed track lighting haloed them and their title plaques. The art work itself had been encased in what appeared to be handcrafted wood frames. I sucked in a sharp breath, raising a trembling hand to trace the hand-carved daisies that had been carefully etched into them before being varnished in bronze.

Wooden folding chairs were situated in a semi-circle in the center of the room, the birchwood seat backs and legs all bore the same deep grooves of daisies as the frames did. The easels in front of them were a thing of beauty, too, their holders containing pine and cedar stemmed paintbrushes bearing daisies of their own. More of them, too many to count, lined the glass supply cabinet in the corner. Round brushes, flat brushes, fan brushes... All intricately lined with the wildflower.

How long had it taken him to do this?

I made my way onto the small stage where I would instruct classes from, settling onto the swivel stool with Franky's assistance.

My easel was majestic. Larger and grander than the others, so it could be seen by my future crowd of pupils, and to set me apart from everyone else. My brush bristles were made from Ko-linsky Sable, which had to have cost him a small fortune.

It was everything I'd wanted. Everything I'd hoped for but knew I would never have, down to every last detail, every last petal. But I'd never told him. I'd always been too chicken-shit to speak this into existence, and I knew if I told Franky, he wouldn't have rested until it happened, and so I'd made a game out of him finding out, knowing he never would because I'd never be brave enough to tell him. So how...

"How did you—" The sound of something crinkling shut me up. Franky pulled a weathered, taped together sheet of paper from his pocket, unfolding the square carefully before reading its contents out loud.

Thank God I was seated, because I knew exactly what he held, could remember the day I wrote it, the day I cried over it and then ripped it into a million tiny pieces before tossing it in the trash and leaving our summer home alone and broken-hearted. It was the only letter that hadn't met its death by cremation.

He'd found it and put it together again, the same way he'd been putting me together ever since the accident.

"'Dear, Franky,'" he started. "'Fine, you win. I'll tell you about my imaginary plans for my imaginary art-bar.'" Franky looked up from the letter when I laughed. I wrote that letter many moons ago, but if I closed my eyes, I could still see which paragraph had held my tears and which corner of the page had felt the grip of my desperation.

He went on to describe the white walls and spotlights, and how the most important thing was that there was enough space to not only hang my art but everyone else's, because no matter who walked through that door, we'd all be in this together.

I laughed again when he got to the part about the chairs.

"'None of that fancy high-back shit,'" he read. "'I want to keep it simple. Mostly, I want something easily storable so that the space can be multi-functional. I want them to feel like they're home.'" Franky paused to gaze up at me, a shy question written on his face.

"Mission accomplished," I answered around a rush of emotion. The backs of my eyes stung with it.

He nodded and pressed on. "'I want to work with schools and disenfranchised kids. I want to host charity events there, and I want the community to feel as if they're a part of it all. And I want daisies, Franky. Daisies everywhere so I'll never forget to be brave ever again.'"

Franky cleared his throat. I wasn't the only one overcome by the moment, by how symbolic it was, by how long it took us to get here.

"'And lastly,'" he continued. "'I need a sign. A literal and figurative sign. Something that'll hang on the wall of my art-bar and at the back of my mind at all times. What should it say, Franky? I've got a few ideas, but I haven't settled on one yet. I'll give you a few options I've had bouncing around in my head, and I want you to choose. You get to choose because this dream will be as much yours as it is mine. I want you to help me craft it with your bare hands. I want you to help me make my dreams come true. Will you do that for me, Franky? I know you will, so you get to choose. Surprise me.'"

He looked at me through damp eyes before reading the letter's closing, as if he'd read it so many times it was now etched onto his brain. "'Love, Leelee Bear.'"

"Fuck, I was young," I said, downplaying the written thoughts of my twenty-five-year-old self because this moment was too much to shoulder. Too big to experience. And because somewhere in that art studio was a sign made up of words he'd chosen, and I was afraid seeing it would obliterate the final wall protecting my heart from him. Afraid to learn that wall had been obliterated a long time ago.

"You were beautiful," he said. "You still are."

I blew out a shaky breath as the sight of him grew blurry. I wanted desperately to blink away my tears, but my eyes were too full of them for that now. One blink and they would stream down my cheeks.

"Turn around, Leland," he said hoarsely.

"I can't," I said.

"Be brave, Leelee Bear."

So I did. I stood and carefully twisted to the wall behind my stool, lifting my chin to read the elegant letters carved into the sign hanging high above. "Maybe one day we can both be daisies," I said, tears tumbling down. It was my favorite of the three options I'd given him in the letter, because not only was it something he'd said to me before, it was my way of begging him to choose me. My way of reminding him that we had plans to be great together.

It still spoke to us, but now it would also speak directly to every person who'd step foot into this room. It said *you and I are in this together. No matter who else is in this space, it's just you and me.* It said *I'm just as scared as you, but together we could all be daisies.*

Franky cupped my cheeks, wiping away the wetness there.

"When did you have time to do all of this?" I asked.

"I worked around the clock on it before coming to New York. I'd intended it to be a Christmas gift but quickly realized you wouldn't have been receptive to it. So I waited, which gave me time to add more pieces."

"Thank you," I said with every part of me.

"You're more than welcome, Leland."

I gripped his wrists, rubbing circles along the undersides as we stared into each other. "I haven't painted in years. I might not know how to anymore."

"So you'll practice. Every day and every night, with me by your side, you'll remember how," he said.

"Okay," I said, then his expression turned conflicted. "What is it?"

"I want to call in my last truth."

"Your what?" I asked.

"I once beat you in a game of pool, and my prize was three truths. I got to ask three questions, and you'd have to tell me the truth. I still have one left."

I licked my lips nervously. No matter what he asked, I'd have to give him unfiltered honestly. "How long have you been waiting to say that?"

"*Years*," he said, voice trembling under the weight of that one word and the wasted time it conveyed.

"I'm pretty sure we've passed the expiration date on that," I said, and he chuckled. "Ask me anyway." I steadied myself for whatever would come next.

"Where do you see yourself in five years, Leland?"

I groaned. "Not this question again."

"Answer me, *please*," he said seriously, his eyes roaming my face anxiously. I placed a palm over his chest, feeling his frantic heartbeat under my fingertips.

"Why stop there?" I asked. "Why not half a century?"

"How about several millennia?" he whispered.

"I think I like the sound of infinity more," I whispered back.

"Where do you see yourself in this lifetime, and every lifetime after, Leelee Bear?"

I swooped in impossibly close, holding his face and his gaze the way he held mine, and I gave him the same answer I'd given him all those years ago. I gave him the truth.

"Somewhere still wanting you, Franky."

CHAPTER 37

In the time it had taken me to grab my phone from upstairs, and our beer refills from the fridge, Leland had ambled from the patio armchairs we'd been enjoying our nightly conversation from, to the easel he'd set up over on his favorite side of the backyard. It was the area least protected by tree foliage, so it received the best sunlight during the day. It was also the section of yard space I'd chosen for the garden, for that same reason.

I rested our Stellas on the short table in front of our chairs before coming up behind him to drop a kiss along the column of his neck. "You're cold," I said, running my hands up and down the gooseflesh along his arms. As if to punctuate the sudden dip in temperature, a faint breeze snuffed out the flames of several of the lanterns surrounding us.

"Which means you're not," he said, craning his head toward me.

"I admit this weather agrees with me, but we can take your easel and our drinks inside."

He turned back to his current project. "I get more done out here."

It'd been a couple weeks since he picked up a paintbrush, and my walls would be eternally grateful for the work he'd blessed them with in that time. He'd had a few false starts, and more than a few confidence-shaking moments, but Leland had always been a natural, painting was in his blood, and it came back to him relatively easily. Now he couldn't stop. I couldn't even get him down to The Daisy, when before I'd had to get creative with my distractions to keep him from attempting to work shifts at the flourishing bar.

"Will you at least allow me to keep you warm?" I asked, already heading for the fold-up chair I kept perched against the fence for those spur-of-the-moment requests that I sit so he could paint me.

"No way," he said as I opened it behind him, preparing to sit and wrap him up in my arms. "I get nothing done when you touch me."

"A jacket, then?" I'd been overly needy and protective of him since the art studio reveal. I took offense whenever the night air ruffled his hair, or when the afternoon sun threatened to burn him alive.

He didn't seem to mind. It went unsaid that we were making up for lost time. Things were still tenuous between us, which played a part in how I'd been behaving. The past hadn't miraculously disappeared as if it never existed. There were still occasions when he stared at me like he was unsure or like he was certain but scared.

Cole and Jasper learning the truth continued to sit wedged between us too, but Leland wanted me, and he could admit to it now, admit that he wanted to try. It was more than enough. More than I deserved.

Cole and Jasper had been by for dinner last night, and pretending there was nothing but friendship going on between us, when there was plenty more going on, had been easier than when we'd had to pretend to be one step above strangers.

"No need," Leland said, interrupting my musings. "I'm done for the night."

"And what's this?" I asked, lowering into my chair anyway and resting my chin on his shoulder. Leland didn't do abstract much, but he was equally as good at it.

"I don't know yet," he said, angling his head at the canvas. "I let my hand lead instead of my head. I'll come up with a name for it eventually."

I ran my nose up and down the crease behind his ear, breathing him in. "Have I been touching you too much?" I whispered in a love-induced haze, getting high off the scent of him.

"Too much?" He chuckled, the sound reverberating along his skin. "Franky, all I dream about is getting this boot off my leg so I can fuck the shit out of your cock. No, it's never too much." He'd gotten the cast removed earlier that day. The boot was a hindrance, but he'd gained his independence back. I wouldn't touch him in *that* way, though, until he was fully healed.

"Always so tasteful," I quipped, brushing my lips against his cool skin.

"Hey, decorum has always been your department, and it's such a fucking turn-on when you lose all traces of it." He tilted his head to give me better access. "Fuck, Franky. Look at what you're doing to me," he breathed. My eyes moved to his lap where his cock had tented the soft fabric of his sweats, and where a pin-sized wet spot had graduated to the size of a dime right before my eyes. "Always making me wet, Franky."

I backed off, and he whimpered. "There are a few ways I can take care of that for you, but you can't tempt me into hurting you. I won't fuck you until you can take it."

He twisted around. "The doctor said the boot can be removed in a week," he said.

"He said one to two weeks, Leland."

"Can we fucking think positively?" he asked, pent-up lust agitating him.

"One week. But then you've got to rehab the leg. You haven't used it in a while."

"Oh, for fuck's sake. How long, then?"

My laughter rumbled up from my chest. "By my estimate, and according to the way I want to handle you, at least five weeks."

"What if I work out with you daily to strengthen my leg? What if I don't complain while doing it?"

"Then maybe four weeks."

"That's it? Just one week shaved off?" he asked petulantly.

"You have to ease your way into an intensive workout, Leland."

"Fine. But I'm sending you a calendar invite for four weeks from today. If I'm not ready by then, I'll saw the fucking leg off and ride your cock with a bloody stump."

"I wouldn't expect anything less," I said, grinning and shaking my head at him. We'd made up for all the lost kisses throughout the years, and my hands had become intimately reacquainted with his body, but I wouldn't cross that final boundary until I was sure I could do so without restraint, because I had a strong feeling I would lose all of it once inside of him.

"Franky," he began, still staring back at me. "I don't want anything between us when the time comes. I'm always safe. You can still trust me."

"I know," I said, brushing the backs of my fingers down his cheeks. "And I hope you know that you can still trust me."

"In this I do," he said. Neither of us addressed the clarification of his trust in me. I knew I still had work to do.

Leland yawned, his lust forgotten for now.

"You're tired," I said.

"I'm fine. It's still early, and I'm not ready for the night to end." He sought out the patio where our beers were waiting for us. "How about I shower all of this paint off of me and change into something warmer, and you get the fire table going?"

I agreed, removing the protective lid from the concrete table as he entered the house. The doorbell rang minutes later, and I wondered who it could be as I made my way inside the house.

"Lucas?" I questioned in greeting.

"From the look on your face, I'm guessing you forgot about our meeting," he said, and I flipped through my mental calendar in search of an evening meeting I may have scheduled with him.

"Come in," I said, coming up blank but not wanting to leave him on the doorstep while I figured it out. With my sole focus being Leland, it was highly likely that I'd dropped the ball on this. It was late, but not late enough, and with him being my neighbor, our meetings tended to be less formal and fluid.

He took Leland's unoccupied seat, pushing his beer bottle aside to lay out a folder.

"Lucas," I said delicately, as he'd been about to withdraw his schematics. I'd never been the type to tiptoe around a deal, and I wouldn't start now, so I got straight to the point. "I've decided to go into business for myself. I apologize for wasting your time, but it's something I've been thinking about for a while, and I've finally decided to act on it."

Lucas gazed at the unopened beer bottles, as if only now noticing them, and then glanced over his shoulder into the house. He sighed, falling back in his seat. Lucas was handsome in a rugged sort of way. He came from a good family and had inherited the business after his father passed away some years ago. He would never speak to my soul the way Leland did, though, and in the bedroom, he wouldn't be as malleable beneath my hands as Leland was. Lucas and I may have been similar on a surface level, but Leland and I were the same on a cellular level.

"Does this have anything to do with the jealous ward you've been charged with taking care of?" A playful, albeit disappointed, smile tugged at the corner of his mouth.

"He's not as young as he looks," I said, but I was sure he knew that. "And what do you mean by jealous?"

"Didn't he tell you? He all but told me that your cock was a wrecking ball, and that my ass wasn't built to withstand it. Can't remember if that was before or after he insinuated that sex with you was an experience akin to violence," he said, and my brows leapt up my forehead. "Good violence, I assumed. I got the impression that brutality was his foreplay. And yours," he added.

"Well, I can't say that I'm sorry for his behavior..." I started, wondering what I *could* say instead.

"No," Lucas said, with a knowing grin. "You look too pleased to be sorry."

Lucas assured me all was forgiven, and I asked for his discretion. He wasn't friends with Cole and Jasper, but my sons were friendly with him whenever they stopped by while Lucas and I were speaking across our yards, and Cole had sat through a few of our meetings at the house before. It would've been easy for Lucas to slip up and say something that Leland and I weren't ready to share.

Leland returned bundled up and sporting a scowl.

"Sorry, did I take your seat?" Lucas asked, but he made no move to relinquish it. In fact, he crossed an ankle over one knee and settled in further. At this point, he was toying with Leland good naturedly, but since Leland hadn't heard our conversation, he still viewed Lucas as a threat and clearly didn't take kindly to him infringing on his territory.

Lucas didn't know Leland the way I did, though. Leland would always win at games like these.

With a saccharine smile that didn't reach his hostile gaze, Leland planted his ass in my lap, bracing his hands on my spread thighs and explicitly undulating onto my cock. "No," he said. "This is my big, fat seat right here."

I groaned, subduing his hips and peering around him to see Lucas coughing into his fist to hide his laugh. "Leland," I said tightly. "I just finished telling Lucas that I'll have to back out of our deal."

"You did?" He wheeled around to look at me. That took some pressure off my cock as he was now mostly seated on my thigh. "Does that mean...?" He ended his question there, perhaps needing me to say the words.

"It means a quaint shop, custom pieces, local customers, and coming home to you at the end of my work day." Something about what I'd said scared him. I could see it in his eyes, but he kissed me long and hard before I could sort it out. We kissed like our lives were on the line, like if we stopped, we'd both die. I'd forgotten all about Lucas, and when we looked up, he was already gone.

"You're giving me that look, Franky," he said, scratching at my stubble.

"What look?" I asked, falling deeper in love with every curve of his face.

"The *I want you to suck my tits* look."

I never knew I was capable of laughing as much as I did when with him. He was my sickness and my remedy. "Maybe I do," I said, capturing his bottom lip between my teeth.

"Well, then whip 'em out, baby." He sat straighter, giving me room to slip out of my t-shirt, and then I helped him down to one knee while he shot his booted leg out to the side.

"Are you comfortable like this? We can go upstairs—"

"I'm fine. Don't baby me when we're like this," he said.

I cradled the back of his head, bringing his mouth to my right pec, to my most sensitive nipple. "God, Leland," I breathed, tugging one-handed at the button of my jeans.

He nibbled and sucked as we both struggled to get our erections clear of our pants. I couldn't reach his cock from this angle, so we settled for jerking ourselves off.

He popped off of my nipple to spit on my cock and then lick a stripe up the palm he used to work his own before plastering his mouth to my chest again. The faster he pumped his shaft, the harder he sucked on my tight bud, and the closer I got to erupting all over us both.

Once close to orgasming, I yanked him to my mouth by his hair, forcing my tongue between his lips as our arms shook with the speed used to bring us over the edge. Within seconds we were coming and swallowing each other's groans and then fighting about how I selfishly ate all of the spilled cum.

"I'm making up for lost time," I said, licking my fingers clean.

"Four weeks," he said, typing something into his phone. My own phone pinged with a calendar invite.

"Four weeks," I agreed, hitting accept.

◆ ◆ ◆

The next morning Leland was already dressed by the time I got out of the shower. "Where are you going?" I asked, tightening the towel around my hips.

"I told you. I'm going to be at The Daisy full-time now." He patted his pockets down and scanned the bedroom we now shared. I plucked his phone off the dresser and walked it over to him.

"I know, but it's barely sunup, and I get the impression you wanted to be gone before I got out of the bathroom." I held his chin, my gaze imploring him to talk to me.

"What gave it away?" he asked dryly.

"The disheveled hair, but mostly the t-shirt you're wearing backward. What's going on?"

Leland pulled me in by the hips and rolled his forehead along mine. "I don't know. Sometimes things are fine and I'm hopeful. Then out of nowhere this nauseating feeling of terror comes over me. I can mostly talk myself down from it, but sometimes I just need space to breathe."

"Are you having second thoughts about us?" I asked. We'd agreed to try again, and I'd conceded to doing so without telling Cole and Jasper the truth—for now. Leland had said it was because he wanted a moment where the two of us could reconnect and be happy before throwing the four of our lives into turmoil with our confession. I understood where his hesitancy truly came from. He thought he'd lose me again once the truth was revealed. In this he still didn't trust me.

"No second thoughts," he said. "How about you?"

"I've never been more sure about anything," I swore, but it did nothing to erase the tension in his body. My words wouldn't do, and I vowed right then to stop using them. I'd have to prove myself to him through actions.

He moved to playing with the short hairs at my nape, closing his eyes, and therefore completely taken off guard by my kiss. I wordlessly conveyed what I would no longer verbally say, hoping to lessen his doubts, begging for him to take reassurance from it, for him to believe that I needed him more than I needed my next breath. I poured everything into the kiss, and his eyes burned brighter once we separated.

"Are you still coming tonight?" he asked.

"I wouldn't miss it for the world."

Leland had revamped the bar's website to now include the art portion of it. He'd be hosting his first sip-n-paint. I happily volunteered to handle the art studio's food and drink orders while his head bartender and other staffers took care of the front.

"Okay. Cole will be making an appearance," he said, a reminder that we couldn't touch, ogle, or say anything too inappropriate to each other.

"I'll be on my best behavior," I promised.

He left, and I watched the clock all day, counting down the hours, minutes, and seconds until I saw him again, even giving in and making my way to The Daisy a whole hour earlier than planned.

Leland worried that the noise from the bar would interrupt the art session happening in the back, but the volume didn't travel too terribly, and what did, seemed to elevate the experience—rather than diminish it—by creating an easy-going atmosphere for the first-time artists.

I did the job I was hired for, only screwing up one order, and I made sure to treat Leland as if he were my son's best friend, and not the best thing that ever happened to me.

When it was safe to, I found a corner and gave in to my urge to drop the facade and watch with pride as Leland shined brightly. And he didn't only instruct from his raised platform. He came into the crowd, providing individual attention and offering tips and tricks. He'd picked something simple tonight. A single daisy floating in a cloudless blue sky.

I caught up with him once Cole left a couple of hours before closing. "You did great tonight," I said, taking up a stool at the bar. Leland practically preened as he refilled the napkin dispenser.

"It was amazing," he said. "And I heard back from the art school a few blocks over. They're willing to partner with me in some way. We just need to hash out what that would look like."

"You're unstoppable," I said, both of us forgetting the no staring rule. A customer tapped the bar top to get Leland's attention. "Go ahead. I'll wait here and then help you close up once the night is over."

"You don't have to. I might as well start sleeping in my own place again. Traveling downstairs versus across town will be less of a hassle now that I'll be here every day. And we can't exactly explain away my staying with you now that I can get around on my own." His tone may have given the impression that he meant everything he'd just said, but his big brown eyes pleaded for me to stay. They begged me to demand he come home to me. I wouldn't, though, because that wasn't the key to passing this test, and there would be a series of other tests tomorrow, and the tomorrow after that, so I committed to acing them all, starting with this one. Leland wanted a more meaningful gesture. He wanted me to work for him. To work for *us*.

"Okay," I said. "Call me tomorrow?"

"Yeah, of course," he said, offering me a tight smile.

I couldn't kiss him goodnight, so I settled for nodding before slipping through the door. I crossed the street, finding a lamppost to lean up against before pulling up the Uber app on my phone.

A little under two hours later, Leland and the remaining staff exited the bar and bid each other goodnight as he locked up before turning to the steel door leading up to his apartment. He stared at it as if he didn't recognize it, as if he hated that he'd have to walk through it. I typed out a quick text and hit send.

Franklin: *Look across the street.*

At this hour, the streets were deathly silent, so I heard the ping sound off in his pocket. He dug around for his phone, his head whipping toward me as soon as he read the message. I sent him another one.

Franklin: *Come home with me.*

Leland read it, biting his bottom lip.

Franklin: *We've got three minutes before the Uber driver leaves us.*

He peered toward the black SUV idling two buildings down. Truth was, he'd been there a while now. I'd paid him handsomely to wait as long as it would take. Leland tapped away at his phone, and mine vibrated in my hand.

Leland: *You mean three minutes before you both leave me, don't you?*

Franklin: *I'm not going anywhere without you, Leland. Never again. You either come with me or I stay here with you.*

He didn't make a move, and I eventually headed for the Uber. I told the driver he could go after tipping him extra, and I turned back in time to see Leland slipping through his apartment building door. "Leland!" I called, and he whirled around, surprise splashed over his face as he took in the retreating taillights of the Uber.

"I thought you decided to go," he said.

In terms of actually fighting for him, this could be considered a minor scuffle. It didn't do much to prove my intentions in the long run, but he needed it, so I didn't question it. Anything he needed I would willingly give.

"Nothing could make me go, Leland. *Nothing.*"

He brushed a thumb over my lips, and I bit down on it gently. "I can't believe you waited out here all of this time for me."

"You're worth the wait. Now, do I get to see your place?" I asked, backing him into the hallway, mindful of his booted leg.

"Yes," he said.

"Do I get to spend the night too?" I asked, shutting us into the hall.

"Yes," he said as breathlessly as the first time.

I leaned in to whisper my next question directly into his ear. "Did I pass the test?"

"A-fucking-plus," he whispered back.

CHAPTER 38

Leland

Every test, every game of mine that Franky played and won equated to a tiny shot of dopamine. He never took the opportunity to remind me that we were adults, to remind me that asking him to get out of bed to grab me a glass of water simply to prove he loved me should've been reserved for teens and their lovesick angst.

Franky was unwavering in the weeks leading up to *the* night. And I didn't know why I needed him to do half those things. Or maybe I did. I'd gone without the source of his love for so long, and I already knew what having it snatched away again would do to me, and so I needed constant reminding that it was still there, that today his love was as sharp as it had been yesterday, and the day before. Hell, an hour before. And maybe if he didn't tire of me, maybe if he could give me what I needed no matter how immature and silly those things were, then maybe he could give me the big, mature, not-so-silly thing when the time came.

It all made sense in my head. Said out loud was another matter, but give anyone a dash of fear, a spark of hope, and recollections of a failed love affair in the past, and they might do the same.

I hadn't lied when I said I'd be somewhere still loving him in the next lifetime. I hadn't lied the first time I'd said it either.

I would *always* want him, and I now knew that no matter how much I prepared myself for him, no matter how much hindsight I now had, and no matter how much more my own life had to offer me, Franky still had the power to break me because there was no protecting oneself from the type of love we shared. You went all in, guards down, hearts exposed for the taking.

No task fulfilled, or metaphorical scrimmages won, or grand gestures made by Franky would prepare either of us for the ultimate test to our relationship. I had to believe we would survive anything, and that would require my complete and utter blind trust in him, and I was ten steps closer to surrendering my sight than I had been weeks ago. But whatever happened later, I wouldn't regret tonight.

The calendar alarm went off, the piercing sound setting off the tripwire connected to my nerves. I silenced it on my way to the full-length mirror. The black catsuit I wore didn't have an opening at the ass like the one I'd worn for Franky years ago had, but it just meant he'd have to tear it open to get to me.

My cock and balls hung through the front beautifully, though, and the diamond cutout at the chest area showed off my muscular cleavage. I'd never been more grateful for the grueling workout sessions with Franky. I flexed my pectorals, pinched my pink nipples through the lace fabric and watched as my dick stiffened and curved upward in response. With nothing left to do, I went in search of Franky.

We'd stayed apart for most of the day to build anticipation, then a couple of hours ago I received a text from him with strict instructions to remain upstairs until it was time, and that he'd left a bowl of pineapple slices for me outside the bedroom door.

I used those hours to prepare my body, my heart, and my mind for tonight.

My heart rate leveled up with every spare bedroom and bathroom that came up empty. I'd even checked the walk-in closets. I knew he wasn't upstairs. I would've felt him there, but I needed more time before I completely handed myself over to him.

With a deathgrip on the banister, I took my time descending the stairs, noting how eerily dark and quiet the first floor was. Half way down, cool air hit my bare toes, telling me the patio doors were open. Maybe he was waiting in the backyard.

My breath faltered when I rounded the bottom step. Aside from an unobstructed path leading to the back of the house, every available surface and square inch of floor space had been swallowed up by daisies and glass-encased pillar candles.

I moved slowly down the aisle lit by candlelight, passing the open kitchen that now resembled a flower shop. The candles wrapped around the living room, caging me into a circle of love. It felt ritualistic, and I was more than ready to offer my body up as the sacrifice.

I stopped behind the sofa, needing something to hold on to while I absorbed everything Franky had done to make this night special. Directly ahead of me, the patio doors stood open, and candles flowed well beyond it to where flower pots stuffed with daisies overwhelmed the backyard. He'd created our very own greenhouse. That was what it felt like. From the coffee table, to the mantel, to the kitchen island and counters... There were daisies *everywhere*.

No, not a greenhouse, I realized. Franky had created a meadow. One where everything thrived. One filled to the brim with courage.

"There you are, Mr. Meadows," Franky crooned seductively from somewhere behind me. I spun around, hand to my heart. I'd forgotten all about him.

"Franky," I breathed, but then lost all train of thought at seeing him naked and leaning with arms crossed against the front door. He'd been watching me.

He pushed off the door, his confident stride languidly eating up the path toward me as the candle flames worked their magic along his chiseled body and obsidian eyes. "Lace," he said, or more like hissed. "I love lace."

"I know," I said, the words shivering.

"I love lace on you," he clarified. I knew that too. And *fuck*, his cock was already hard and weeping, his crown tapping the top of his navel as he stalked closer.

"This is beautiful," I said as he took his time getting to me. "No music?" I needed something to drown out the frantic drumming of my heart.

"No. All I want to hear are your rough pants and your hoarse shouts for more...or less."

"More. Always more, Franky. Even when I beg you for less."

Franky hummed his pleasure at hearing that.

"But where are you going to fuck me?" I asked. There wasn't an available patch of space large enough for him to lose his control on.

"Right where you stand, for starters," he said, and I eyed the back of the sofa I now gripped from behind.

"Oh," I said, swallowing.

"Are you nervous?" he asked, reaching me and securing my neck between his hands.

"Not nervous. I just need you everywhere, right now, and I can't decide which of those places needs you the most." My mouth watered for him, my fingers tingled with the need to touch him, my cock throbbed for his hand, and my hole clenched for something of his to hold on to. His dick, his hand, his tongue... It didn't care, so long as something belonging to him was inside of it.

"Don't worry, you'll have been touched by all of me before the night is over." And as if to punctuate his point, he drew in closer, so close our bare cocks bumped heads.

"Are you going to be nice about it?" I asked, slightly pulsing up and down so our dicks rubbed.

"No, Leland," he said regretfully, his thumb stroking the pounding vein at my neck. "I'm afraid not."

Contrary to his apologetic words, he kissed me softly then, as if to say this was all the gentleness he could offer me until this unspoken, ceremonial reclaiming was over with.

Franky broke the kiss, then slid a hand through the chest opening of the catsuit, squeezing my plump pectorals as I leaned into the rough handling, feeding him more of my flesh.

I played with the clear fluid at the tip of his cock while he tugged at my nipple. His own hickey-bearing nipples beaded and begged for my lips. I plunged my sticky finger into my mouth, groaning when the salty flavor hit the back of my tongue.

Franky reached between the daisies on the sideboard behind him for a bottle of lube, squirting it messily over his cock before forcing my hand on him.

His patience didn't last long, and within seconds my back was to his chest and I was shoved over the couch, one knee positioned on the back of it as Franky kicked my standing leg wide.

I panted hard, disoriented, and pushed up onto my hands as Franky fisted my ass cheeks through the lace, spreading and lifting and closing them repeatedly while he swore this wouldn't be quick.

I blew my hair from my face and looked straight ahead, stiffening when I thought I saw movement through the cracks in the fence. I narrowed my eyes. It was a good distance away, but there was something... There it went again, a flash of white where there had been darkness, a t-shirt maybe, as if he'd moved over a plank to get a better view. *Lucas.*

Lace ripping away from my lower body jerked me back into the moment with Franky. I dug my hands between the cushions to white-knuckle the front of the sofa frame.

I relaxed my elbows, lowering my chest to give Lucas an unhindered view of Franky spanking my opening with his slicked, meaty cock. Lube splashed onto my skin with every heavy beat he delivered, and my hole shook under the weight of it.

"You're going to pay for giving this away," he said, voice thick and gravely.

"Make me pay, Franky," I said on a loud moan.

"No one else but me gets in here ever again."

"No one," I swore, gaze fixed on our voyeur while Franky remained clueless about him. "Can you give me everything I need, Franky?" I asked, antagonizing him.

"Watch me," he said threateningly, fingers poised at my entrance.

"Don't waste time on easing me open. I took care of that already. Just send your cock all the way in—" My words snapped away on a shout of surprise as Franky buried himself to the hilt, holding my waist to keep me from careening headfirst into the daisies lining the floor in front of the sofa. *Fuck*, he was huge.

He held me so firmly, I thought my bones might shift under his hands, and he took off at a pace so blindingly fast it felt like the world had begun spinning around us. "Did any of them fuck you like this, Leland?" he asked. "Did any of them make you feel like you were splintering apart?"

I tried to form words but the overwhelming pleasure got in the way.

"Answer me!"

"No!" I screamed.

"Your hole is mine to take, to use, to abuse, whenever the fuck I so please," he snarled, and my teeth clamped so hard together I thought for sure they'd shatter.

"My hole, my body, my *everything*," I managed to get out, "is all yours." Already I needed to come, and with the friction of the sofa pillows and the lace covering my stomach, I thought I just might.

"Think you can handle this?" I asked, way above a whisper, my gaze laser focused on the backyard fence.

"I know I can," Franky said, unaware that my question wasn't directed at him.

Now that I'd been sufficiently opened, my hole intimately reacquainted with its puppet master, I began to rock against him as best I could.

Franky pulled out abruptly, landing an open-handed blow to my ass. I cried out from the sudden emptiness and sting of pain.

"Don't fucking move, Leland. Your only job is to take this." He hauled me up by the front of my throat before loading my ass with his dick once more.

"Fuck," I croaked, my fingers digging at his pulsating hand as I fought for air.

"You don't need to breathe," he hissed in my ear, his sweat soaking through my skin. "All you need is me, and all you need to focus on is the fucking I'm giving you."

My hitched knee dug into the sofa back, and Franky moaned as he fucked in and out of me unrepentantly. His fingers at my throat didn't relent until his teeth had sunk into my shoulder, swapping one suffocating pleasure-pain for another.

The daisies in front of us went toppling down as the sofa screeched forward along the floor, and all I could do was hope the candles didn't tip over to join in on the fire already burning me up from the inside out.

"Wait," I begged convincingly, now taking his teeth and his cock and the fingers attempting to bury themselves inside my hip bone. "Franky, stop," I shouted loud enough to be heard beyond a backyard and through a planked fence.

Franky popped his mouth off the scorching bruise he'd cemented into my skin. "It's too late for that, Leland," he said, still fucking me, not even making an effort to slow down, not even trying to see if he were capable of following my direct order.

I smiled triumphantly as Lucas backed away, as Franky's breath punched at my ear, and as pearls of sweat decorated my upper lip. Lucas's back door slammed shut, but Franky was too consumed with the tight grip my hole had on his dick to notice. Now that we were alone, I dropped my chin, pointlessly voicing how I really felt.

"Don't stop," I said around a strangled moan as he artfully located my bundle of nerves. "Don't you fucking dare."

I didn't tell him I was coming before I came. I didn't want him to stop me. I didn't want him to warn me of what would happen if I did. I reached behind me and tangled my hands in his hair as my cum shot into the air.

"Dammit it. Squeeze yourself at the base," Franky ordered, plunging deeper and deeper. It was too late, my orgasm was in mid eruption, and there was no clogging up this fountain now.

Franky turned me toward him urgently, lifting me and launching back into me as I circled his hips with my legs. My cock rocked with aftershocks as he marched us down the aisle of candles to the front door.

"Easy, Franky," I panted, his swift movements working my overstimulated body.

He slammed my back against the door, clamped a hand over my complaining mouth, and growled, "*My* hole, remember?" and then he did the opposite of easy; he fucked me hard, his feet sliding on the floor as he shoved into me until he came.

"Tell me... Oh *God*." He moaned. "Tell me you feel it, Leland. Tell me you feel my cum marking you, branding you as mine."

With his hand still covering my mouth, all I could do was nod wildly as my nails dug into his shoulder blades.

"Good," he breathed, circling his hips and standing on his toes, as if he wanted to climb inside of me. "Good."

He let my feet hit the ground, then overpowered me to the floor. With the top of my head pressed to the door, and my knees folded to my temples, I could do nothing as he tongue-fucked his cum from my hole and into his hungry mouth. He moaned and slurped and shouted orders for me to shut up and stay still when I squirmed beneath the onslaught of his ravenous tongue.

"Let's go to bed," he said with one final lick up my cleft. It was clear he didn't mean to get a good night's sleep.

"I-I can't," I said from my puddle of sweat and bones on the floor.

"You don't get a say in this," he said, his body heaving above me, lips swollen and scented with cum. "Not tonight." His muscular thighs put tree trunks to shame, and the thin layer of softness covering his abs only made him appear stronger, wilder, like something birthed in the wilderness. He scooped me up, tossing me over his shoulder before making his way upstairs.

It was a while before he was hard again, but he took that time to blow me to my second and third climax for the night, and to brand my body with his mark.

By the time he instructed me to hold on to the headboard as he entered me from behind, I couldn't even say what day it was.

"There's still some in there," he said, amazed, exiting and reentering my hole, the sound of slickness sending electric currents racing along my body. "I thought I got it all." And then his mouth was at the apex of my thighs again as he sucked deep breaths in through his mouth, retrieving what he'd accidentally left behind downstairs.

All night he situated me how he wanted me. He spread his weight over me without a care for how I would get enough oxygen to live through this. He molded my orgasms into what he wanted them to be. Tempered, earth shattering, or somewhere in between. He'd once promised me I would pay for the old man jokes, and he'd kept his word. Except in the past he'd treated my body as something that never belonged to me through a lens of anger and pain, and this time he'd done it all with reverence and love. *Always* love.

Cum handprints left a trail on the wall above the headboard, and tatters of black lace hung from the bed posts. Speckles of dried blood from our combined wounds covered the sheets, and my ass was raw from beard burn, and now the glorious spanking he was giving me.

"My hole!" he shouted with every grueling blow.

"Your hole," I agreed laboriously, body taxed but still backing onto his massive cock and into his cruel palm.

"I love you," he said, landing strike after strike. "*God*, I love you, Leland."

"Then don't stop making me pay," I said gutturally, loving his unmerciful torture.

The festivities didn't end when the sun broke through the clouds. And not after he'd fucked his full length to the back of my throat, making me gag and cry. Not even after he'd then wiped my tears while demanding I ride him hard until we came. It ended when we were both too spent to see straight, and when the inside of my ass and his belly were too full to consume another drop of his seed.

I lost the battle to sleep in our final sexual position, straddling his hips, my chest on top of his from where I'd fallen forward after fucking his cock like I'd been trying to escape something, like only the speed and force of his dick could save me.

I woke up groggy, in need of at least ten more hours of sleep, and still sprawled over Franky on the half of the mattress still on the bed frame.

Franky snored softly beneath me, and for the life of me I couldn't understand why I was awake. I turned to the bedroom doorway and suddenly knew what had woken me up. The two figures, with matching expressions of betrayal, looming there.

"What. The. Fuck," Cole whispered.

CHAPTER 39

Leland and I showered and dressed separately—at his insistence—before meeting Cole and Jasper downstairs. The candles had burned out, but the place still resembled a botanical garden. Nothing like the crime scene upstairs.

Cole stopped his pacing of the foyer to scrutinize his friend, gaze narrowing on the bruises surrounding his neck. Leland drew his collar up self-consciously.

Jasper stood protectively next to his fiancé, his anger reserved and calculating compared to Cole's. From the look on Cole's face, his anger was a thing that couldn't think or reason. His mind would likely be too clouded by it to see past the obvious.

Of the two, Jasper's quiet rage was the one to be frightened of. It saw far more than Cole's did.

"Did you take advantage of him while he was in your care?" Cole's question for me sounded more like an accusation. "Did you?" he snapped, a strand of hair slipping out of place.

"He wouldn't—" Leland interjected, but paused when I rested a hand on his forearm, a silent request that he let me handle this. Cole didn't miss the gesture, and some of his anger gave way to confusion.

"I would never take advantage of him, Cole."

"Well, then maybe he's the one taking advantage of you," he said, then turned his attention to Leland. "So you're fucking my father now? Is the whole of Manhattan not enough for you? Do you not have *any* boundaries or self-control?"

Leland flinched from the insults hurled at him, and I had to remember that Cole was my son when everything in me screamed to physically defend Leland's honor.

I looked at Leland, and written across his face was everything he believed he was about to lose and have a hand in destroying. I'd never seen him so terrified before. Not even when I'd walked out on him all those years ago.

"How long has this been going on?" Jasper asked, leveling a shrewd stare at me.

"Isn't it obvious," Cole said. "They barely knew each other. It had to have started after the accident."

"No," Jasper said. "This feels...older. It's always been this way between you two."

"Maybe we should all have a seat and talk this out more rationally," I tried.

"Have a seat where?" Cole asked, motioning around us. "You've turned this place into a fucking conservatory."

"Alright, well, give us a couple of hours and we'll come to you." My heartbeat threatened to strangle me, and I couldn't bring myself to meet Jasper's burning gaze. He'd see it all if I did. He'd see the truth, and I didn't want to have to deliver, or confirm, it like this.

Cole continued with his litany of questions as if he hadn't heard me. Thankfully, it seemed he was too upset to have heard Jasper either. While Leland attempted to calm him, I swallowed and chanced a glance at Jasper. He watched me like I was a puzzle piece he was trying to make fit, and I saw the terrifying moment it did.

"This goes further back than the accident, doesn't it?" Jasper asked, and that snagged Cole's interest.

"We don't have to do this now," I said, unable to do anything to staunch the guilt in my tone. "Let's go to our separate corners, cool off, and meet again with clearer heads. You'll be more receptive then."

But Jasper was a dog who now had his bone, and he had no plans on relinquishing it. "It's been right in front of us," he said. "The way you two stare at each other when you think no one's looking. The tension has been there since Franklin showed up for Christmas," he said to Cole, then angled his head at Leland. "And then you pulled away... Did this start while you were both in Seattle? After you and Cole met?"

I inched closer to Leland until our shoulders tapped. Cole tracked the movement.

"No," Leland answered cautiously. "Not...then."

"Not then," Cole whispered, seemingly digging through his memory bank for something that would timestamp my relationship with Leland.

"That bar napkin I found in your car the day of Selene's funeral," he said, pointing a finger at me. "That's what led me to Josephine's..." He faded off in thought, then approached us looking downright murderous and sneered, "How long have you two known each other?"

♦ ♦ ♦

"Eight years?" Jasper repeated, and what little color he had, drained from his face. His green eyes were wide and desperate.

"What about Selene?" Cole asked, lacing his hand with Jasper's, forming a united front.

"We were separated when Leland and I—"

"Separated!?" Cole shouted. "Wh-what the fuck is going on here? Has our whole life been a goddamn lie?"

"Cole, let me explain," I said, but he'd already pivoted for the front door. "Jasper, please—" I tried, but he tugged his arm away from me, shaking his head in disbelief before following Cole.

"Let's talk about this," I said to both of their backs while Leland watched with hunched shoulders.

"Not now," Cole said. "I can't stand the sight of either of you right now." And with that, they were gone, the door slamming in their wake.

"This will all work out," I said to Leland. "But know that no matter what, I *will* choose you. Do you hear me?" I asked when he remained despondent.

"Don't worry about me," he said. "If you can fix the relationship with your kids, then do it." And exactly as Cole and Jasper had just done, he turned and walked away.

Another test, I thought. One I would pass with flying colors, because Leland was worth everything I potentially stood to lose, and I wouldn't sacrifice our happiness ever again.

◆ ◆ ◆

Neither Cole or Jasper would take our calls, and we'd been removed from the approved visitors' list at their residence. Didn't take a genius to deduce that we wouldn't be welcomed at their places of employment either.

I'd told Leland we'd give them a few days to cool off, but then a few days turned into a week, and by week two, Leland had gone from trying unsuccessfully to end things between us, to being virtually catatonic. I'd had to convince him not to cancel the intimate art auction he already had planned at The Daisy for the following week.

With my help it went well, and he'd donated half the proceeds to the art department of a local middle school, and as previously planned, the balance went to Selene's charity, which

Jasper now spearheaded. The final straw came when Jasper returned the check to Leland in pieces.

"Where are you going?" Leland asked with underlying panic. Didn't matter how I answered, his tension wouldn't ease until I returned. It'd been the same anytime I left his sight.

"I'm going to see Cole. I don't care if I have to fight through a line of hotel security, I'm not leaving until I see him."

"Okay," he said resigned, settling back into the sofa, the spot he'd been watching the sun from all day. I slid my jacket on and left, knowing nothing I said would make him feel better. Only my son could do that.

After a near scuffle in the hotel lobby, and several threats of having the police called on me, Cole relented and allowed me up to the penthouse. I charged off the elevator, aiming straight for the living room, where I knew I'd find him brooding over his piano.

I slowed at seeing him, my temper simmering as the face that looked so much like mine stared back at me haggardly. "Cole," I said with a sigh. He shoved to his feet and moved to the sofa. I took the seat across from him.

"Are you alone?" I asked.

"Yes. Jasper went into the office today."

"How're the wedding plans?" I asked as both an icebreaker and a stall tactic. They'd put them on hold after Leland's accident and had only begun talking about it again the week Leland and I were literally caught with our pants down. Cole remained stubbornly silent.

"I've missed you both," I said. "And Leland's been beside himself. None of this is his fault. It's been my fault since the day I met him."

"Since the day you met him," he said bitterly. "And what day was that, exactly? The day you abandoned your sick wife?"

"I didn't know she was sick at the time. We'd separated months before I found out."

Cole laughed without humor. "You think calling it a separation doesn't make you an adulterer? Were there legal documents signed to give credence to this *separation*?" he asked.

The question was hypocritical of him, seeing that Daniel and Jasper were not only married but still sleeping in the same bed with each other when he and Cole's affair began. But this was Selene we were talking about. This was their mother, and I understood that this was different for them.

"No," I said. Selene and I hadn't gone through the proper legal channels to make our separation official, and while implied that I needed to do whatever was needed to be sure of the direction I wanted our marriage to go in, my freedom to have sex with others hadn't been explicitly stated by either of us. And even if I'd been able to wave a legal document at Cole, signed and stamped by attorneys and court officials, a separation didn't mean a severing of our vows. We'd have technically still been married. And in their hearts, in all our hearts, that meant I'd had an affair. "But I don't want you or your brother believing I would have walked out on her knowing she was ill."

Cole leaned forward at that. "Is that the reason you went back to her? Because you found out she was sick?"

"That wasn't the only reason," I said honestly.

"Did you love her?"

"Yes, of course, I did. I *still* love her, Cole."

"But you love Leland more," he said, shocked, as if in all of this he hadn't once stopped to consider that Leland and I were in love. That we were more than maybe past fuck buddies revisiting old times. "What about everything you told Jasper when you showed up here?"

I'd given Jasper what he deserved. Liberation from his grief. And after everything I hadn't done right after his mother's death, I owed him that, by any means necessary.

"You helped him get over his guilt and grief by sharing your own pain surrounding her death. Had everything you said to him been a lie?"

"It wasn't a lie," I stressed, "but the whole truth was much more complicated than what I had a right to disclose at the time. You, of all people, should understand that."

The wrinkles lining his forehead cleared, and I exhaled, seeing it as a sign that he was now listening with the intent to understand, instead of to blame.

"I have a million more questions now than I did before you arrived, but even if I were willing to sit through your answers, Jasper won't. His forgiveness won't come easy."

Cole loved Selene deeply, but Jasper's bond with his mother went deeper than Cole's ever could. Jasper and Selene were all each other had for a good while before we were married. They'd been through tough times together. She was his mother *and* his best friend. And not only did I make him a promise to always do right by her, I'd also been instrumental in Jasper forgiving himself for the part he believed he played in her death. His sense of betrayal wasn't necessarily bigger than Cole's but definitely different. And while Cole tended to stand up and fight when things went wrong, Jasper had a nasty habit of running away.

"He'll follow your lead," I said. "If you can get past this, then perhaps so can he."

"So you want me to beg on your behalf?" he scoffed.

"No, but can you at least get us in the same room?"

"I'm still not sure either of you deserve forgiveness. I may be able to understand why you hadn't told us sooner, but I can't promise to ever understand how you two got started in the first place. And do you plan to keep this *thing* going between you two?" He couldn't even bring himself to call it what it was.

"I love you, Cole, but you and Jasper aren't children anymore." Something I wished I had learned a long time ago. "I no longer have to lie to protect you, no longer have to pretend my marriage was something it wasn't in order to maintain your sense of stability or to ensure that you like me. And I don't have to surrender my happiness to please you. Not anymore." I was sure I'd answered at least half of his unasked questions with that proclamation alone. Cole sat back, his hard features softening.

"Is that what you thought you needed to do?"

"Yes," I said truthfully. "Will it destroy a part of me to lose you and Jasper? Yes, it will. Will I miss you every second and never stop fighting to have you both back in my life? Absolutely. Will I give up the only person who has known every ugly part of me and loved me anyway? No, I won't. If you make me choose, Cole, my choice will be Leland." When it became evident by the following silence that our conversation was over, I nodded and stood to leave.

"Dad," Cole called as I reached the archway of the living room. I kept my back to him, letting that three-letter word wash over me, perhaps for the last time. It hurt to even consider never hearing it ever again. "You're choosing him, and I understand why, because I'll forever choose Jasper above all things. I owe you for him, and having him made everything that happened be-fore him worth it. And if it's any consolation, we were too in love to be concerned with what you weren't giving us. What you gave was more than enough, because we got everything else we need-ed from each other. I'll talk to him for you. I'll see what I can do."

"I love you," I said raggedly, letting myself believe his words, letting them sink in and work their magic on my heart.

"I love you too," he said back.

◆ ◆ ◆

Leland waited on the staircase for me, his duffle bag packed and on his lap. He took the last few steps down and met me in the foyer, speaking before I had a chance to. "I've given it a lot of thought," he said. "Your relationship with Cole and Jasper trumps your relationship with me. I get that. And I won't hold the choice you obviously had to make against you—"

I placed a finger over his lips. "Shut up, Leland." I took his duffle bag and marched up the stairs and into the closet where I began unpacking it for him.

"Franky, what are you doing?"

"Top or bottom drawer?" I asked, holding up his t-shirts. "We never did sort those details out. If we choose according to our bedroom preferences, that would mean you get the bottom." My joke only seemed to baffle him more.

"I'm not staying here. I'm breaking up with you because I won't survive you breaking up with me again."

I let the shirts fall from my hands and grabbed his face between my palms. "I chose you, Leland. I will always choose you, no matter what."

"You'll resent me," he whispered, bottom lip quivering.

"Never," I vowed. "You are the best thing that has ever happened to me. Nothing is worth anything without you."

"Are you sure?" he asked, his hands and eyes restless on my chest and face.

"I'm positive." I kissed the corners of his trembling lips before giving in to my need to taste him. I explored his mouth with my tongue, taking my time while taking his breath and giving him mine. I reluctantly pulled away, returning his shy smile with a brazen smile of my own. "Did I pass the final test?"

He chuckled, eyes closing as if in prayer before reopening on a silent Amen. "Yes," he said. "You passed them all."

"Now, while you are my greatest reward, I still think I deserve a prize for passing. What have I earned?"

"Whatever you want. Just name it."

"Trust," I said easily. "I want you to finally trust me, Leelee Bear."

"I will. From now until forever, I will," he promised.

CHAPTER 40

Leland

The weatherman predicted rain all week, but what we got was a monsoon. It affected business, but I kept The Daisy open because it gave me something to do other than mourn my friendship with Cole. It had been two weeks since Franky had stormed his place. Jasper still hadn't warmed up to the idea of forgiving him, but he and Cole had been able to reconcile since then. I, on the other hand, still hadn't heard a peep from my friend.

I got lost in the rain spilling down outside as Franky began bussing the table of a departing party of three. He'd been here helping me as much as possible. Help I didn't need, but I understood that he was concerned for me, so I let him hover.

"Watching the door won't make him appear," Franky said from across the room as he loaded the plates and cutlery into the bus bin.

"I know," I said, shaking my head as if that small action might shake off the funk I'd been in. I turned to the liquor shelves behind the bar and began the menial task of making sure all labels faced forward. I dragged out the process and was able to distract myself for ten whole minutes.

I'd just made up my mind to close up for the day when the brass bells above the door chimed. I finished with the last bottle and spun around. "Welcome to... *Cole,*" I said with an exhale. He dumped his umbrella in the metal pail at the door, brushed the droplets of rain from his suit, then wordlessly took up a seat at the bar.

I got to work on his usual. Two fingers of gin and an order of fries with extra mayo. He hadn't asked for it, but I hoped he'd feel obligated to stay and finish it. I'd have done anything to keep him in that seat.

"Your fries will be out in a minute." I brandished a nervous smile, but he just squeezed his tumbler between his hands and watched me thoughtfully. In the background, Franky stood still as a statue, probably wondering if this would be a reconciliation or a fight. Cole hadn't given him a hint on where things stood between us. When Franky had pried, Cole simply said he would find me when he was ready to.

It was one thing for him to find out his father was more imperfect than he'd already known, but another to learn that his best friend had been a complete stranger. I'd helped him through the most challenging time of his life, and he hadn't even known that I'd played a vital role in the ugliest, hidden part of it. I'd betrayed him, and it had to have cut deep.

"Did you really get that scar on your leg from falling off of a dirt bike?" Cole asked. I couldn't read him, and I didn't know if honesty was the fastest way to get through to his heart or if it was the quickest way to send him running for the door. I wrung the bar towel between my hands.

"No," I said, choosing honesty. "My mother threw me from an apartment window when I was eight."

Cole averted his gaze, as if he didn't want me to see the pain there, as if he hadn't counted on my breaking through his icy exterior so soon.

"Why did you think you had to hide that from me?"

"It wasn't you, Cole. There are things about me I don't share with anyone, not even myself," I said. I'd shared it with

Franky, and Noon had known, too, but it was one of the things I'd put back in its box after Franky broke my heart. Telling Cole would've meant acknowledging the trauma all over again, and I'd had more than enough trauma to deal with at the time. But I'd more than willingly open that sealed box now if it meant earning his trust again.

"Who are you?" he asked achingly, and I had to grip the edge of the bar to keep from crumbling around the truth of it. "I feel like I could spend years sifting through all the lies and never crack the surface of who you really are."

"I'm sorry," I said, which of course would never be enough. He'd thought I was someone he could trust, and now he was likely going over everything I'd ever said to him, questioning fact from fiction. It had to be hard knowing you were the only one keeping it real the whole time, because even when I was forced to give him a deeper piece of me, that piece had always been watered down. "Not everything was a lie—"

"But it wasn't the whole truth," he said.

"No. It wasn't. It couldn't be."

"And you were so good at keeping the heat off yourself, at giving me just enough, or barely enough, before turning things back to me, before being there for me. Our friendship has always been built around what you could do for me, Leland. Can't you see how unfair that is?"

"I've always known it was unfair, Cole." My inability to let him be there for me in any shape or form constantly got in the way of our friendship.

"It was mostly my guilt and the secrets I had to keep that held me back," I said. "How could I let you help me through a bad day, when that bad day was caused by memories of your father? How could I tell you my heart was in a constant state of pain, when that pain had been caused by Franklin Kincaid?" I didn't gaze over Cole's head to see if my words had hurt Franky, but I knew he'd want me to tell the truth, no matter how brutal. "I couldn't tell you," I said. "So I'd lie or change the subject. That doesn't mean our time spent laughing wasn't real, or that I don't value or need you in my life. It just meant I had to give you more than what I could accept from you. And that meant giving you less of me. I needed you to know when the time came that I was in this for you, not for what you could do for me or for access to your father. I was in this friendship for you, Cole"

"One thing I've been certain of all these years, though," Cole started, "is that you'd been hurt by love. That's what drew me to you, but you'd never confirm nor deny. My father was the one who hurt you," he said.

"Yes." I didn't care that it wasn't a question, it was the truth, and that was all Cole would get from me from here on out.

"And I'm guessing he *didn't* renovate the back for you at a discounted rate?" Cole looked toward the art studio.

"No, that was another lie," I admitted. "He did it for free. He did it out of love."

"Love," he whispered, as if he still couldn't wrap his head around it. "What's your mother's name?"

"Willow," I said, even though it wasn't easy to. I hadn't spoken it in years. I'd kept her in a dungeon located in the recesses of my mind where she'd been easy to ignore because all my mental focus went toward getting over Franky. Something else I'd failed at.

"Willow Meadows," he whispered. "Pretty name."

My throat shrunk in on itself at the mention of her full name. I could hear the gate of her dungeon creak open, and could feel the binding keeping that box shut loosen at the corners.

"The name doesn't match the woman," I said blithely.

"No more of that," he said sharply, drawing me up a peg. "No more pretending you're okay, or that you don't care about what you've been through. No more."

I hadn't realized I'd done that, and right on the heels of swearing that I'd be honest with him too. Old habits were hard to break. "It stops now," I confirmed.

Cole sipped his drink, letting the burn run its course before firing off another question. Felt like we were speed dating, except I was the only one on the receiving end of the get-to-know-you phase. There wasn't a stone left unturned with Cole. He'd given me all of him from the start, and what he hadn't handed over to me, he'd left unguarded for me to draw my own conclusions.

"What's your favorite color?" he settled on.

"Colors on the first date?" I joked. I'd never lied to Cole about anything as pointless as favorite colors or favorite foods or movies... The question was more symbolic than anything. We were starting from scratch. Building from the ground up.

I glanced beyond Cole to Franky, who smiled encouragingly at me with admiration and love bursting from his pupils. "Black," I said, and Franky grinned knowingly, his ebony eyes pleased with my answer.

"What are you most afraid of?" Cole asked.

I relaxed against the bar, getting into the rhythm of our exchange, enjoying it even. "It used to be heights and windows. Now my worst fear is losing your friendship, Cole. Or if I've already lost it, never getting it back."

He let that sink in a bit, taking his time to mull things over. "I get to know you now," he said, lighting the wick of hope, voice bogged down with emotion.

"Yes," I said eagerly.

"No more evasion, no more lies," he warned, and I promised it all ended here.

"I have so much to tell you," I said, pushing through the glee squeezing my heart.

"Can't wait to hear it all," he said, before adding sarcastically over his shoulder, "You can breathe now, Dad." He'd known his father was there the whole time.

Franky dropped the bin to the table and hustled over, ruffling Cole's hair and leaning over the bar to meet me for a kiss.

"That's gonna take some getting used to," Cole said, nose wrinkled. We laughed, hugged, kissed, and fought over Cole's fries. We talked with a freedom we never had before. We talked with no barriers and no secrets between any of us. It felt healing, like a breath of fresh air, but there was one thing still missing, one person we all needed to make this family complete.

"Jasper and I decided to have a small ceremony at the house," Cole said. He and Jasper had a beautiful, sprawling home outside of the city, where they spent weekends and any other spare time they got. "We never wanted anything big anyway."

No, that had all been for me. A way for him to pull me back in after I'd pushed him away.

"And I'm paying for your tux," he said, brow raised, daring me to turn down his kindness. Tuxes weren't cheap, and The Daisy was doing well, but I was still on a tight budget.

"Fine," I said, and he scarfed down a fry, smiling victoriously. "But I don't like charity. That much about me is accurate."

"But you feel bad for all that you've done, and so you're going to let me help you with this, and with whatever else you may need help with, for all the times you wouldn't let me help you in the past. Isn't that right?" he asked, and I scowled at his laughing father.

"Within reason," I gritted out.

"Great, because I'd like to invest in The Daisy. We've got other locations to open up, after all."

I groaned, tossing a limp fry at his smug face.

"Am I still invited to the wedding?" Franky asked.

"Of course you are," Cole said. "Jasper will come around. Give him a little more time."

"I'll give him as long as it takes," Franky said.

I closed the bar up and took Franky to my place. It was my turn to be strong for him, so I pulled back the curtains in my bedroom, undressed us, and held him under the blankets as we watched the rain come down.

"You heard, Cole," I said, after an hour went by and Franky hadn't said a word. "Jasper will come around. And we've got Cole on our side now. Jasper will listen to him."

"I hope you're right," Franky said, and I tightened my arms around him.

"Hey, I've got an idea," I said, shooting up, laying on the enthusiasm extra thick.

Franky rolled to his back, staring at me like I'd sprouted two heads. "Is this idea an attempt to get my mind off Jasper?"

"Yes, but that doesn't mean it isn't a good idea."

He pushed up to lean against the headboard. "Okay, what's the idea?"

"Getting your business up and running won't be an overnight thing, but what if we can do something that's more immediate? Get the buzz going before business even begins?" I'd climbed to my knees in my intensity, hoping my genuine excitement would be contagious.

"I'm listening," Franky said, in the even tone of a party pooper.

"There's an event space a couple blocks up. A storefront. Street level. Why don't we rent it out and do a furniture pop-up shop."

"A pop-up shop," he said slowly, brows pinched.

"Yes. You've got all that inventory in your basement, and I'm sure you have everything you made in Seattle in storage somewhere. More than enough custom pieces to draw a crowd for a few days and still have plenty left to get things rolling when you officially open Kincaid Wood."

"Kincaid Wood?" he said, cracking his first smile.

I shrugged. "It was the first thing that popped into my head. Didn't help that your wood is actually on display right now," I added, and Franky's gaze dropped to where the blanket stopped below his hips. He barked out a hearty laugh then, and my heart unclenched.

Franky sobered and reached for me. I let him pull me onto his chest. "Thank you," he said, kissing my nose.

"For what?"

"For being ridiculous just to see me smile."

"Okay, it did start out as a way to brighten your mood, but it is a good idea. What's stopping us? Give me one reason why we shouldn't do it? We could even invite Cole and Jasper." Bringing up Jasper again was a gamble, but I decided to bank on Franky being positive about him showing up, versus him sliding back into a funk at the mere mention of his name.

He thought about it for a while, sifting a hand through my hair as I waited. "Kincaid Wood," he repeated again. "It does have a nice ring to it."

"Is that a yes?" I asked, tickling his ribcage.

"Not if you keep that up," he admonished, tensing under my moving fingers.

"Yes!" I said, jumping up and dashing for the living room.

"Do we have to get started on it now?" he complained as I returned with my laptop.

"The sooner we start, the sooner you reunite with Jasper. He knows how important this dream of yours is. He'll show up for you, Franky." I settled down next to him in the bed, waiting for his response.

"Okay. Let's do it," he said.

"Perfect." I began typing furiously, creating a list of things to do. "We could pay for social media ads, create a website, and get Cole to make a few calls. Kincaid Wood will be huge—"

Franky slammed my laptop closed and silenced my eager rambling with a kiss. "How about we just spread the word locally?"

I'd been about to argue, but he dropped another kiss to my mouth, then whispered a reminder. "A simple life, Leelee Bear."

I smiled against his warm lips. "A simple life," I repeated.

A week later we had the event space rented, the furniture transported, and the doors opened on the first Kincaid Wood pop-up shop.

We'd kept promotion to the bare minimum. We asked neighboring businesses to hang the flyers in their windows, and we handed out flyers with drinks at The Daisy.

The locals came out in droves, and by day four we even had some out-of-towners. Word-of-mouth was spreading fast, and Franky's wish for a simple life might not end up being so simple after all. Furniture was figuratively flying off the shelf, and his list of requested commissions was as long as my arm.

"This is unbelievable," Noon said, as two strapping men hauled a cherry wood chest of drawers into a U-Haul out front.

"I know," I said, watching Franky talk prices and care instructions with customers.

"He isn't so bad, you know," Noon said.

"Is that how you really feel, or are you just high off the fifty-percent discount you got on that dining set?" I asked. Noon clapped me on the back as he chuckled.

"Nah, he's good to you. Good *for* you. He found a way to choose you no matter what, and as your friend, that's all I could ask for." Noon had visited me at Franky's house several times while I'd been recovering there, and since he knew about our past, Franky never felt the need to shield his feelings for me around him, even before I began returning those feelings. Noon also clandestinely shared his copy of the bar keys with Franky so that he could work on surprising me with the art studio. He'd witnessed Franky atone for his mistakes, so if he said he thought Franky was good for me, I knew he meant it.

The front door opened again, and again Franky snapped his

head in that direction, his chest caving in when it wasn't Jasper's face that greeted him. He went back to helping customers.

"Jasper still isn't talking to him?" Noon asked.

"No. And today's the last day. I thought for sure he'd show up." Didn't help that Cole's return flight from a last-minute business trip was delayed, causing him to not be here. He was bummed he couldn't make the grand opening, but he assured us he'd be here today. One son's support would've been better than none.

"There's still time," he said.

"Yeah, you're right," I responded, but my tone lacked optimism.

"Alright, I gotta go." Noon dragged me into his chest for a hug. "Call you tomorrow." He waved to Franky on his way to the door.

Evening rolled around, and the last customer said their goodbyes. The only thing left was a coffee table and a few chairs. I handed Franky a Stella, and we took a seat, drinking in silence.

I didn't know what to say, especially when I knew nothing would make him feel better. Only one person could do that. I'd been about to lock up for the night when a familiar face walked nervously through the door. Franky hopped to his feet, and so did I.

"Jasper," he whispered.

"Franklin," he said, his long, blond hair wavy and wild. He looked just like Selene.

"I'll leave you two alone—"

"Stay," Jasper said to me. "You're a part of all of this, so stay. Please." He gestured for us to sit, then came over, removing his satchel and taking up the empty seat across from us.

Franky and I set our beers aside, then I held his shaky hand for support. He gave me a grateful squeeze.

Jasper dug a stack of photos from his bag, then began quietly laying them out one by one along the coffee table. I glanced at Franky for clarity, and he shrugged, confirming his own confusion.

The first photo was of a kid wearing a tattered shirt and shoes with barely any rubber left around the soles.

"This is me one year before you came into our lives," Jasper said, his finger on the picture. A row of homes was in the background, some abandoned and some just run-down. None of them looked up to code to live in, though. "This was where we lived at one point," he said.

The next photo was of Selene. She was scarily thinner than what was classified as petite, but she held a birthday cake and wore a smile that didn't reach her eyes. "My father was supposed to pick me up from school on my birthday. He promised me ice cream cake. He never showed up. My mother spent every dime she had on this cake to make up for it, even though that meant we wouldn't have food for the next week or so. Not until she got paid again."

Franky squeezed my hand tighter, but otherwise he kept quiet, letting Jasper have the floor.

"And this photo," Jasper said, "was taken at a shelter we'd had to stay at for a while when Mom couldn't afford the rent increase." Jasper slept curled up on a cot in a tiny room. A thin jacket had been thrown over him in place of a blanket. "It was cold, and there were more displaced families than resources," he said. "Mom gave me her jacket while she went without."

The next photo showed Jasper and Selene having a picnic in a rose garden. She'd gained some weight, and Jasper's eyes were no longer a dull green. They were both smiling into the camera, so unlike their expressions in the other photos. "This was a month after moving in with you," Jasper said, his breathing going shallow.

"And this," Jasper said, moving on to a photo of Franky sitting at his bedside while he slept. "This was you sneaking into my room to sit with me while I slept. I'd been sick."

"Do you remember this day?" he asked Franky, pointing to a photo of him sitting astride a horse and dressed head to toe in equestrian gear.

"Th-that's the day you won your first medal." Franky picked up the photo, bringing it in close. "I was there that day. I was there for that," he said, as if he'd forgotten all about it.

"Yeah, you were," Jasper said hoarsely.

"You'd wanted me to come to your practice lesson the day before, but I couldn't make it," Franky said.

"Funny," Jasper said. "When I think back on winning my first race, *this* is the day I think about. The day you were there."

Franky nodded, blinking back tears. He picked up the next photo and chuckled. "Christmas morning. You'd snuck down to open your gifts while we were asleep, but this year your mother didn't label them, thinking it would stop you. Instead, you opened all the gifts under the tree. She was so upset. She'd worked hard wrapping all these herself. She'd wanted me to help, but I had business to take care of at Nexcom," he said, sounding a little dejected about it.

"Wanna know what I remember?" Jasper asked.

"Yes," Franky said like it was a plea.

"You'd had extra gifts hidden around the house—granted you hadn't wrapped them or shopped for them yourself, but you were prepared for my Christmas mischief, and your gifts came in handy. Everyone had something to open on Christmas morning."

"You were a Christmas menace," Franky said playfully.

"And once again, you saved the day."

Jasper pointed to the next photo, no longer explaining, because by now we understood the meaning behind all of this. There were photos of Franky at Cole's piano recitals, photos of him at their graduations, and even pictures of him and Selene during happier times. Seeing a shot of them hugging would've sent me into a jealous spiral in the past, but not anymore. I would welcome fond memories of her, welcome getting to know her through their eyes, welcome comforting Franky during bouts of sadness because she was gone. That was what families did for each other.

Franky applied pressure to my hand once more, his silent way of letting me know he was okay, before letting go. He scooped up photo after photo, adding commentary for some, while simply smiling down at others.

"What do you see when you look at these photos?" Jasper asked Franky. "Do you see the bigger picture they make?"

Franky dried his eyes with the hem of his shirt, then looked at them all again. "There was a time when all I'd see were the ones that were missing. A time when I would think for every single photo here, there were at least ten others that would show the truth. Show the times I hadn't shown up for you all, the times you weren't my priority, the efforts I hadn't made."

"But now?" I said, chiming in. "What do you see now, Franky?"

"Now I see that I wasn't perfect, but I wasn't all bad either." He caught his sob in his hand.

"That's what we all see, Franky," I said, scooting my chair closer to him and gripping his nape. "That's what we all are. Imperfectly perfect." I wanted to kiss him, to hug him, to whisper all the words to make his tears recede, but this was their moment, and so I fell into the background again.

"I understand you in a way that Cole doesn't," Jasper said, sniffling through his own emotions before running down the list of things that made him and Franky similar. "I was married—unhappily so. I married Daniel for reasons other than love. I had an extramarital affair and then for a short time I gave up the man I loved for my marriage." Jasper looked to me then, to the man Franky had given up for his own marriage. "Cole swears it doesn't make me a bad person, though."

"It doesn't," Franky said vehemently, his unconditional love on full display.

"Thanks," Jasper whispered thickly, as if he'd needed that validation from Franky. "I looked at all these pictures and realized that you aren't a bad person either. You *saved* us. You gave me and my mother a life we wouldn't have had without you. You gave me Cole. Things happen. I know that. And as much as I loved her, I needed to accept that things—good and bad—were allowed to happen to her too. To the both of you."

Franky completely broke then, giving sound to his pain and his happiness. They both did, and seeing them stand and meet to cry into each other's arms made me break too.

Franky needed this. No matter how evolved he'd become throughout the years, there had been a cap on that evolution, a ceiling he couldn't break through because of our secrets and lies. He was free now. We all were. And we'd grow even stronger because of it.

"I made it!" Cole said, bursting through the doors out of breath. "I made it." He scanned over all the wet faces in the room, including mine, and took in Jasper and his father hugging. "You came," he said to Jasper, rushing over to join in on the hug.

Jasper and I exchanged a look over Franky's trembling shoulder. I gave him a nod of thanks, and he gave me one in return before reaching out for me. I was out of my chair so fast it toppled back in my wake.

We eventually separated, laughing at how much of a mess we were. Eyes red, shirts drenched in tears. But we were laughing because we were happy too.

"Sorry I missed it, Dad," Cole said, peering around the bare space. "Looks like it was a hit, though."

"I'm sorry too," Jasper said. "Sorry it took me so long to come around."

Franky felt around his pockets for his phone, instructing us all to gather in close for a selfie. "It's okay," he said, "because when I think back on this time, *this* is the moment that I'm going to remember." He held up his phone, held up the photo of his family. "This is the moment that will matter."

EPILOGUE

Leland

Ｔhe nightmares involving my mother returned with a vengeance after Cole's round of twenty-one questions at the bar, and they had only gotten increasingly more frequent ever since Franky and Jasper made amends a few weeks ago. It was as if my brain was bored now that I had zero distractions, and it wanted to remind me that not everything in my life was perfect, and wouldn't be until I'd dealt with *this*.

I'd wake up nightly to shrill screams, then quickly realize the feral sounds were coming from me. Franky would towel me down, clearing the sweat away from the night-terrors attempting to drown me.

The dreams were always the same. Me free falling-toward the pavement, but before I hit the ground I'd be back at the windowsill again, being *pushed* again. It was a never-ending cycle of terror, and I'd reverted to not being able to get too close to a window that wasn't on ground level. I wasn't new to the nightmare, but it'd been a while.

The exhaustion was killing me. The dreams would hit within minutes of me falling asleep and then I'd be too terrified to go back to bed. Even Franky's eyes were bloodshot and heavy, because he never let me suffer awake alone.

Last night Franky asked if I'd be willing to talk to someone. Someone other than him. I told him I'd talk to a damn wall if it meant making this go away.

By sunrise we each held a one-way ticket in our hand and were rushing to catch our flight.

Lockwood, South Carolina in the fall felt more like the final weeks of spring leading up to summer elsewhere. No wonder Franky had instructed me to pack light. He wouldn't tell me much, just that this was where he'd learned how to be happy. The place that contained a few of the most important people in his life.

I rolled the window down, letting the breeze have fun with my hair as we took the scenic route from the airport. It was peaceful here. Green and lush, and quiet and homey.

We pulled onto a rocky backroad that opened up to the most beautiful lake I'd ever seen. "Makes sense why you loved it here," I said to Franky, stepping out of the car, only now noticing the one-story cabin. As grand as the home was, the water was the real showstopper.

We reached the screen door and Franky knocked. The front door had been left open, so we could see inside. No one approached from within. "Are you sure they're home?" I asked. Before he could respond, an elderly man with a cane appeared. Joe, I presumed. His confusion shifted to a pleasantly surprised smile.

"Well, look at this," he said, then shouted to someone we couldn't see. "Sarah! Look who's here." He managed two steps in our direction before a wheelchair came barreling past him, nearly knocking him over if it weren't for the nearby wall.

Franky opened the screen door, stepping inside just as Sarah—Joe's wife, according to what Franky had told me—came to a stop and threw her arms up at Franky, demanding a hug.

"How long you plan on being here?" Joe griped as he caught up to us in the entryway. He rubbed the hip he'd knocked into the wall when Sarah had zipped by him.

Franky chuckled, ending his hug with Sarah. "Don't worry, not long enough to ruin your marriage."

"She loves me more than you, you know?" he muttered, as if we all couldn't hear.

"Oh," Franky said, playing along, "I hear she can't even stand me."

We all laughed, Sarah included, who then granted Joe the kiss he'd bent down for and then took over the massaging of his hip. I'd never seen Franky this easy, this playful, this...*him*. Whatever magic this place possessed, I wanted it to work some on me.

"Oh! You brought a friend," Joe said, his eyes crinkling at the corners. I stepped from behind Franky and said hello, bending to accept an embrace from Sarah.

"Why didn't you tell me you were coming?" Joe asked, tone reprimanding. "And how *dare* you give me this beautiful house that I can no longer live without. It's too late to take it back, you know?" He'd said all of this in a rush, each question flowing right into the next, the last one ended with a finger pointed at Franky. It was clear these two cared for each other, and that Joe was happy to see him.

"I don't want the house back," Franky said, but Joe and Sarah's adoring expressions said that he didn't have to. They would have given it back or welcomed him to live there with them, without question.

"So," Joe said to Franky, getting back to the topic of me. "Is this the young man you worked so hard on that lake for?"

"Yes," Franky answered, simply kissing the spot above my brow where it creased in confusion.

"That's nice," Joe said, his grin bouncing between the both of us. "Well, stay as long as you like. We've got plenty of room here."

"That won't be necessary," Franky said. "We'll stay in the guest house, if that's okay with you? Better view of the lake."

"In other words, he's a screamer," Joe said, then complained when Sarah backhanded his thigh in disapproval. I hid my smirk behind my hand, and Franky ushered me out, letting Joe and Sarah know we'd be around for dinner.

"Oh, where can I find Beatrice these days?" Franky called back.

"She's in the office today. Give her a call. She'd love to hear from you," Joe said.

We collected our bags from the trunk and trekked to the guest house where we made ourselves at home for the next few weeks.

We spent our mornings watching the sun rise and taking long walks before stopping into Joe's Coffee Shop for his specialty tea. It was called The Sourpuss. Named after Franky, and item number one on the menu.

In the afternoons we planted daisies around the property and took the boat out on the lake. Evenings were reserved for dinners with Joe and Sarah or sessions with Beatrice, and our nights were dedicated to making love.

I hadn't even scratched the surface yet with Beatrice, and some nights the dreams returned with an intensity that made me feel like they were mocking me and the progress I'd thought I made. Still, I didn't want to leave. I didn't understand how Franky ever had. Everything felt right in the world here. It felt like we were in our *own* little world here.

"I'm not ready to leave," I whispered as Franky moved between my legs. He'd been taking me gently lately, per my request. Thrusting in and out of me at an agonizingly slow pace as I touched and memorized the sharp planes of his body. I was in my soft season, he'd said to me once. The season where I made love to remember, instead of fucking to forget.

"Then we won't," he said, kissing me with one forearm pressed into the mattress near my head while his other hand swept delicately along my collarbone. I crossed my ankles at his lower back, enjoying the feel of his cock diving in and out of me at a speed that said we had hours, days, *years* until this needed to end.

"What about the bar?" I asked, panting into his mouth as he kissed me again and again.

"It's running like a well-oiled machine," he said, pausing to groan my name. "You hired a manager, and you've got a great team of employees working there. And you know Cole isn't going to let anything go wrong while we're gone."

I flipped him to his back, the move creating a breeze that blew out the flame of one of the candles surrounding the platform bed. Franky was gorgeous beneath me, with the light of the moon hitting him through the open balcony doors. "One more week," I said, my orgasm stretching its arms as Franky's hand hugged my erection. One week wouldn't be enough. The little boy in me had been repressed for too long, had suffered one too many atrocities, and with all the good the town of Lockwood had brought to my life, my nightmares, when they came, still threatened to break me.

"Two weeks," he countered, jacking me off as I played with his nipples.

"Three," I breathed, deciding we only lived once, and that I wanted to do it here, with him inside of me and the lake bearing witness to it.

"One...month," he countered, then groaned, stilling and filling me with his spunk.

"Yes," I hissed, letting my head fall back as I rocked my hips back and forth until I came.

Franky removed all traces of cum from our bodies, rubbing his belly and licking his lips once done. We lay facing each other on our sides, petting and massaging exposed skin.

"I think I want to find my mother," I whispered, as if saying it too loud would somehow conjure her up.

"Did Beatrice suggest that?"

"Not in so many words, but it's time. I need to resolve this part of my life. I need to know why. I need to know what made her that way. Maybe then the nightmares will stop." For once I was beginning to question what her past must have been like for her to have turned out the way she had. We were all a sum of our experiences and trauma, and I wondered about the horrors she must have faced for her to do what she did to me. "I might not find her."

"We will," Franky promised.

"She might not even be alive."

"Then we'll deal with that too," he said, refusing to let me wallow in pessimism.

The rising sun stole our attention away from each other, and we watched it climb over the water, as if it were the first time it had ever accomplished something so impressive.

I sighed, dragging my nails through his chest hairs. "Did coming here even make sense if we can't stay long enough for me to make headway with Beatrice? I know we can't stay a month. Or three weeks. Or even two," I said, convinced it had been the racing orgasms talking.

"We can do whatever we want. Whatever you need, Leland."

"What about Cole and Jasper?" I asked, resting my chin on his chest when he shifted to his back. "Don't you miss them?" They'd gotten married soon after Jasper and Franky made amends, and they'd only recently gotten back from their honeymoon before we left, so we hadn't gotten to spend a lot of time with them.

"Yes, but you're my priority now. Choosing you means I go where you go. It means what makes you happy brings me unmeasurable joy. You come first, Leelee Bear."

"Will I never outrun that damn name?" I asked, smiling up at him.

"You know," Franky said, stroking my hair as his gaze grew distant. "Now that I think about it, as boys, Jasper used to refer to Cole as Coley-bear."

"Great," I said, pressing my mouth to his skin. "So I'm part of the cub-club now."

Franky laughed briefly, then turned earnest. "Seriously," he said. "We can stay."

"What if it takes years to resolve all the childhood shit I've kept bottled up? There's the dead-beat dad shit to unpack too. What if I talk to Beatrice until I'm blue in the face, and still a few nights of peaceful sleep here and there is all I'll ever get?" I knew I was being negative and impatient, but I didn't want to resort to narcotics to get a decent eight hours of sleep, and I knew that was where I was headed. "What if nothing works, Franky?"

Franky looked out onto the water again, as if my answer waited there. "Then we'll try something else."

"Like what?" I asked.

"We'll fish," Franky said simply and shrugged.

My laugh rumbled through his chest where my lips were still pressed against him. "So we'll be fishermen? *That's* what will cure me?"

"Yeah, why not?" he said, smiling at me. "It'll be the cure for all the bad things life will throw at us, because there will be plenty. Nothing is ever perfect, Leland. But we can choose how we deal with it."

"And we're going to choose fishing?" I asked to be sure. "When life tosses us a curveball, we're going to go fishing."

"Yes," he said.

"What will we do with them? We don't even like fish," I pointed out, even while the thought sent my heart crashing against its cage with a joy so potent it left me breathless. So long as I was with him I would do and try anything, because he made me believe anything was possible.

He hauled me higher up so he could look deeply into my eyes, the place where he would forever find all the love I held for him. "It's okay," he said, one corner of his mouth lifting. "I'll teach you how to catch and release."

The End

Bonus Scene

For a SWOONY bonus scene, other works by CP,
social media links, and to subscribe to C.P.'s Patrons
for EXCLUSIVE content, visit: www.cpharrisauthor.com

Pinterest Board
The Fishermen - Pinterest Board

https://www.pinterest.com/authorcpharris/
the-fishermen-infidelity-2/

OTHER WORKS BY C.P.

Visit here for all books by C.P. Harris
www.cpharrisauthor.com/books

FIND C.P. HERE

Website

http://www.cpharrisauthor.com

Newsletter

https://cpharrisauthor.com/#newsletter-signup

C.P.'s Patrons & Stalkers Reader Group

https://www.cpharrisauthor.com/subscriber-access

Amazon

https://www.amazon.com/stores/C.P.-Harris/
author/B088P988MF

BookBub

https://www.bookbub.com/authors/c-p-harris

Goodreads

https://www.goodreads.com/author/show/20305771.C_P_Harris

Instagram

https://www.instagram.com/authorcharris_?igsh=MWtjN-
G01aDdiajcyOA==&utm_source=qr

ACKNOWLEDGEMENTS

Thank you to everyone who cheered me on during the writing process, and to all the amazing editors and beta readers I worked with. And thank you to the readers who have been with me since the beginning, and the ones who have found me along the way.

A special mention to Mihaela. I literally don't know what I would have done without you.

The
McDougalls
of
Second Chance Bay

Annie Seaton

Her Outback Playboy - Jenni's story
Her Outback Protector - Don's story
Her Outback Haven - Dane's story
Her Outback Paradise – Matt's story

Book 1

Her Outback Playboy

Jenni's story

Annie Seaton

Dedication

This book is dedicated to the wonderful readers we meet on the road as I research my books!

Chapter One

Jake Jones stood on the bridge of his sleek white motor cruiser as it approached the mouth of the Norman River. He closed his eyes, lifted his face to the salt-laden air, and took a deep breath. The fresh, clean smell of the coast and the sharp tang of the mangroves soothed him. Ten years away from home had been way too long.

The smell of this landscape; there was nothing like it.

No matter where Jake had been in his time away, he'd never smelled sweet, untouched salt air like the Gulf of Carpentaria. He stood, unmoving, absorbing the familiar sounds and smells for a few minutes before he opened his eyes again. Ahead, the short, stubby mangroves covered the edge of the water like a dark green curtain as the sun sank low in the winter sky. The waters of the Gulf glinted silver as the light faded in the gathering dusk. There was no movement apart from the water birds pecking around the tree roots, sending sea creatures scurrying for shelter. In the distance, shards of sunlight glinted off the rod of a lone fisherman on the point. This was not a pretty coastline like the surf beaches of the east coast of Australia, nor did it have the rugged grandeur of the Mediterranean, but it was quiet and serene.

And it was home.

Monaco had been pretty, and the boats at Monte Carlo had been luxurious, but the smell of diesel and petrol had always hung around the huge marina. It had been noisy and busy no matter what the hour and the hum of traffic around the harbour was constant. Last winter it had been the smell of snow covering Mont Agel above the harbour that had filled Jake with homesickness until he'd decided it was time to go home.

Almost. He wasn't going to return to the town that he had left beneath a cloud of shame until he could return triumphantly. He'd had to put some final business plans in place, and when everything was settled, he made his move to come home. He was coming back to Second Chance Bay on his terms; it had taken a long time to get himself to the position when he was confident enough to come back to the Bay. He had a lot to prove to the community he'd left behind as a young man almost ten years ago.

'Do you want me to berth at the docks over town?' Gus, his deckhand, gestured with his head to the dock ahead. They'd picked up *Moonshine*, one of his new motor cruisers in Darwin, and it had taken a couple of days for the paperwork to be organised before they'd headed east along the coast to Second Chance Bay. Jake had booked a helicopter to fly Gus back to Darwin tomorrow to pick up the second charter boat he'd bought. Gus would bring the rest of the crew with him on the way back. The first charter was already booked and filled with the maximum number of clients on each vessel.

Jake had ticked all the boxes and had organised every last facet of his business before he'd come home. He wasn't leaving himself open to any criticism.

He was successful, and he wanted the town to see that.

With a shake of his head, he answered Gus. 'No. Keep going. We'll refuel in town tomorrow. I'm keen to get berthed. I have a visit to make.'

'Rightio, captain.' Gus saluted with a wide grin.

'Piss off, Gus. You can cut the captain stuff.' He knew Gus was teasing him, but he wasn't in the mood. Even though he was trying hard to look calm on the outside, coming home to the town that had done him so much damage made his gut churn.

Jake stared at the hotel on the point at Karumba as they approached the entrance to the river. Second Chance Bay was a small village across the river from Karumba, a town famous for its sunsets and not much else apart from the prawn industry.

Unless you counted its fame for being the place where Jake had lost his dreams along with the respect of the people who were important to him, but that was something he didn't talk about. But when the time to travel back approached, the memories of the past had filled his waking hours and his dreams.

'You really grew up here?' Gus looked at him, his face a study in disbelief.

Jake nodded. 'Sure did. What's the problem with that?'

Gus shrugged. 'Doesn't seem to be much around here. Always had the impression you were a city boy. You know, learned to sail in Daddy's yacht on the north shore of Sydney.'

'Mate, you're a long way off. This is where I was born, and this is where I learned my way around the water. Mightn't look much, but there's plenty to do if you love the sea.' Jake picked up a rope and wrapped it around his hand, ready to moor when they reached the Bay. 'You've gone soft being on the *Cote d'Azur*.'

'Hey captain, I did my time out of Darwin when I was a young bloke just like you. I know the tropics. I just can't see why you'd leave what you had in Europe to come home to this.' He lifted his hand from the helm and spread his arms wide.

'*Home* is the key word, Gus.' Jake crossed to the side of the deck and watched as they motored slowly past the small town of Karumba. A low timber bridge on a narrow neck of the river provided access to the few houses across at Second Chance Bay, but most residents of the settlement found it quicker to go across the river by boat, leaving their cars near the boat ramp at Karumba.

The boat's wash ruffled the water, and the sound of the small waves breaking on the shore behind them was louder than the quiet inboard motors.

Jake stared as they passed the large fish co-op on the riverbank just past the zinc pipeline.

'It was time to come home,' he said softly.

Home on his terms.

Jake swallowed, unsure of how he felt. **McDOUGALS FISH CO-OP** was still emblazoned on the rusty roof of the big shed. He knew at least one of the McDougal boys had stayed in town and taken over from old Bill McDougal. He'd kept in touch with a couple of local friends in the early years—those who stayed loyal to him—and they'd let him know that Bill had died a few years back. Considering the way Jake had left town, he hadn't been tempted to express his sympathy for the passing of a man who'd called him a liar and a thief.

Besides, anything he'd sent—cards or flowers—would have ended up in the bin with the fish scraps if he knew the McDougal family. They were loyal and stuck together. Okay, he was sorry old man McDougal had died, but he'd been a right bastard to Jake, and he'd caused him a lot of grief in the year before he'd fled town when he was only nineteen.

Straight after high school. Straight after—

Nope, he wasn't going there.

With a shrug, Jake turned away from the view of the co-op and looked across to the other side of the river. Two jabirus picked their way along the muddy bank in the mangroves looking for food, occasionally wading into the water in their search for crabs and fish. He stared at them until the cruiser passed the docks on the portside, lost in his thoughts.

'What's the go with all the big ships?' Gus pointed to a large vessel at one of the docks, his words pulling Jake from his memories.

'Karumba is the main port up here on the Gulf,' Jake replied. 'Mining, fishing and live cattle exports are its lifeblood. Not to mention the tourism. You'll be surprised how busy it gets here in the river.'

'And you're about to make it busier with the new charter business. Showing off the crabs and crocs and a bit of fishing on the side.'

Jake shook his head with a grin. 'And a little bit more upmarket than what they're used to, mate. I did learn a bit over in the Med. I'm planning some big trips up the coast. The best fishing in the world around here.'

'Sounds good to me. But you'll need the crew that I'm picking up to make it work.'

'Don't worry. I picked well. It was worth taking the week for the interviews.'

Gus nodded and stared ahead as the river curved in a wide arc.

'Okay, take her across to the other side when we get past the next bend in the river.' Jake headed across to the wheelhouse. 'The Bay starts a couple of hundred metres past the bend. The entrance is narrow but deep enough to get this baby into the jetty. There's a deep-water dock just near my house.' Jake rubbed his hand over his chin and hid a smile.

The house. The Jones' family mansion.

'Right, captain.' White teeth flashed again in Gus's tanned, leathery face. The older man had become a good friend to Jake over the past few years and had jumped at the chance of a job as the master on one of Jake's new boats back in northern Australia.

It seemed a long time since Jake's first night in Monte Carlo, when as a raw nineteen-year-old, he'd found a bar where he could afford to buy a drink—not that there were many affordable bars for a backpacker looking for a job and somewhere cheap to stay. When he'd heard the Aussie drawl at the other end of the bar, Jake had finished his beer, made his way up to the group, and watched Gus holding court.

Once he'd listened to the conversations and established that the men were all deckies like he was, he'd made himself known, and within twenty-four hours Jake had his first job on a boat out of

Monte Carlo marina. Having his Master four qualification, and his marine engine driver's ticket had made him very employable, and he'd worked hard in the marina and on the boats out of Monaco for five years before he'd bought his first boat. Jake had soon found if you were prepared to work hard, and not drink your money in the local watering holes, there was good—and fast— money to be made.

'Okay, swing her hard to port. You're almost there.'

As Gus steered the cruiser to the decrepit wooden jetty, he stared at the house ahead.

'You're kidding me, right?' Gus's eyes were wide, and Jake grinned.

The derelict house was no worse than it had been when he'd grown up here. The only difference was his mother had passed away not long after Jake had left town.

Jake had never known who his father was, and the experience of seeing Bill McDougal in action with his sons had left him with no desire to ever find out. He'd been quite happy the way things were.

Maybe if he was honest, it could have been the lack of a father figure in his life that had led him to make the wrong choices when he'd lived in Second Chance Bay. "Punching above his weight" had been the term used by Bill McDougal.

It was ironic that he'd discovered who his father was when Mum's solicitor had written to him three years after her death; his life had changed dramatically from that moment.

Jake shook his head. If he was going to spend his time back in town regretting the past and getting maudlin, he might as well turn around and head back to Europe now.

He jumped up onto the side of the boat and turned to Gus with a big grin. 'No, Gus, this is home. This is where I grew up.'

Still with sagging windows, the rusting roof, the broken gutters, and the faded paint, the house was a mess, as much a mess as it had always been—yep, he was home. It looked no worse than it had when he'd left. Maybe the jungle of weeds was a bit longer and the fence between the house and the dock had fallen over, but it was the place he wanted to be. The place he was going to make his home again.

'Welcome home, Jake,' he said softly under his breath.

Chapter Two

After *Moonshine* was tied securely to the end of the dock, and he and Gus had checked out the house, Jake lowered one of the rubber tenders from the back of the cruiser and headed across the river.

Gus had scratched his head as they walked through the house. Cobwebs formed intricate patterns, catching the last sunlight of the day. In a couple of rooms, the vines had grown through the windows and creatures had deposited their waste on the old wooden floorboards.

'You really grew up there?'

'I did.'

A frown this time. 'And you wanted to come back here? In fact, from memory, it's all you talked about over in Monaco.'

'Yep. This is home.'

Gus shook his head and his grey curls fell over his forehead. 'Mate, I know childhood memories colour our perception of things, but are you really goddamned serious about living here?'

'I'll live on one of the boats between charters until I do the old place up. This is going to be my home. Nothing that a good builder can't fix.'

'I don't just mean the house. I mean in this town.'

'Yep.' Jake's voice was clipped.

'So you're serious about basing your charter business here?'

'I am.' Jake didn't see the need to explain himself to anyone. 'You want to come on board, you're welcome. If you want to go—' He shrugged and waited for Gus's reply.

The older man stared at him intently for a long moment. 'I committed to you, Jake, and I'm in. I just wonder about the financial viability of setting up here.' Gus turned and looked at the house and Jake's gaze followed the older man's eyes. He let himself see it as someone else would.

Someone who was looking at the house without the memories that he held; the memories that had helped him through the ten years away from home.

The timber slatted boards had weathered to a dull grey, and the rusted roof was missing a couple of sheets of iron. Vines had grown over the front porch and the whole picture reminded him of an old house he'd seen on the bayou in Florida when he'd visited there on a boat-buying trip a couple of years ago. Long grass almost reached the top of the old fence that separated the house yard from the river, and he swallowed when his throat closed as he stared at the two timber posts holding the wire of the old-fashioned clothesline.

He could still see Mum there, an apron with a pocket for the pegs wrapped around her slim figure as she hung out the washing. Her black curls flying in the breeze and a perpetual smile on her face.

Jake closed his eyes as nostalgia sat heavily in his chest. This was the place he'd grown up and had had a happy childhood.

Just him and Mum.

He hadn't been able to afford to come home for her funeral. Her sister from Sydney had come up and taken care of the details and Mum had been buried in the cemetery on the other side of the river. The Jones—he had taken his mother's name— had been original settlers in Second Chance Bay in the early 1900s. He had to hold the happy memories and make a life here on them.

Jake turned to Gus and kept his voice upbeat. 'The financial prospects of a charter business aren't your worry, but rest assured you'll get paid, no matter what.'

'I'm not worried about that. I'm worried about the long-term prospects for you. You really think you can make a go of it here?'

'Not your worry.' Jake had turned to the tender at the back of the cruiser. 'Get yourself settled. Grab a couple of beers from the fridge. I'm going across the river to get us a feed of the best prawns you'll ever taste. I won't be long.'

The dock at the back of the fish cop-op was one he was very familiar with. He'd lost count of the number of times he'd tied various boats up to it over the years. From the first rowboat, he'd had when he'd been a young boy to the small inboard launch that he and the McDougal boys had fished in right through high school, to the afternoons when he'd served in the shop after school so Helen McDougal could go home and cook dinner for her family.

It was the place where he and Jenni had sat and shared their dreams.

He wondered which, if any, of the brothers was in the fish co-op today and more to the point what sort of reception he'd receive, if it was still held by the McDougals. Jake looped the rope of the tender around the post and pulled himself up the bank. The car park was empty and for a moment he paused, wondering if the co-op was still trading. The prawns weren't his reason for coming across river; he needed to see if any of the McDougal family were actually still in town, because if there was one thing his future—his success— was going to ride on, it would be their reception to his reappearance. He was sorry that old man McDougal wasn't here to see him come back to town. He was pretty sure the boys would have stayed here; he couldn't see them leaving the Bay.

Jenni was a different matter; she'd be long gone. Shame she wouldn't see that he'd made it.

A successful businessman who'd made something of his life.

The brothers—he couldn't bring himself to think about Jenni's dismissal of him—had believed their father.

Always the bad boy of Second Chance Bay, Jake had left town in a hurry.

***

Jenni McDougal stood by the window at the back of the fish co-op and dragged in a breath of fresh, clean—non-fishy—air. Her three brothers owed her big time for this; she'd only been home one day and already she'd been seconded into the fish shop, despite their promise that if she came home for her winter holiday, she'd not have to work there. Donny and Dane were out on the two boats on a week-long charter, and Matt had driven down to Normanton for a meeting with the bank.

Pah. She should have known better than to believe a word they said. After being the baby sister of three boys for the past twenty-eight years, she knew what her brothers were like. She might love them all dearly, but she'd forgotten that they'd do anything to get their own way. Eight years in the city, completing her degree and working as a casual teacher had taught her to trust again. In the classroom, the five-year-olds she taught kept their word and taught her to look at the world with fresh eyes. Trust and faith in others had come back slowly, but Jenni was still wary.

But not enough apparently. Home one day, and Jenni had fallen for the spiel of her eldest brother; hook, line, and sinker Matt had reeled her in.

'Come on, Jen. It's only for a couple of hours.' Matt had been at his most persuasive, as she'd looked up at him and folded her arms.

'No.'

'It'll save Mum having to work there before she goes off to cook at the pub.'

Jenni had wavered a tiny bit and then shaken her head. 'Hire someone. What would you have done if I hadn't been at home?'

'There's no one to hire. All the young blokes have headed off to the mines. We have enough trouble getting deckies on the charter boats now, let alone work in the shop'

'I'll do the charters anytime, but you know how much I hate working in the co-op.'

'What's the difference, sis? You don't mind handling fish on the boats. There's no difference.'

'Oh, give me a break, Matt. You can tell *you* never go out on the charters.' Jenni stood at the back door of the co-op and looked across the river to Second Chance Bay where their house was. 'There's fresh air out there, and there's nothing like the thrill of landing a big one. It's a bit different to being in and out of a fishy-smelling cool room all day, lugging ice, and serving cantankerous customers. And seeing those poor dead fish.' She shivered. 'All those fishy eyes staring at me from the display cabinet.'

'Cantankerous? I don't have cantankerous customers.' Matt shook his head.

'Well, they must all save it up for when I work there.'

Jenni had worked in the co-op when she'd been at high school and had hated every minute of it. Her father had finally given in and hired Jake Jones, much to Jenni's delight. A couple of weeks later she'd been caught out; Dad was supposed to be on a charter, but the boat had come in early. When he'd walked into the shop and spotted her sitting on the bench swinging her legs as she talked to Jake, Dad's eyes had narrowed.

'You can come back and work at the shop seeing you find it so interesting all of a sudden. There's no point in me paying that boy if you're going to be hanging around.'

Jenni had flinched and shrunk back when Dad's eyes had narrowed on Jake.

'It's okay, Dad. I was just getting something for Mum.' She'd nodded and scurried away, leaving Jake to wear Dad's temper.

Jake Jones.

The boy she'd had a crush on right through high school; the boy who'd eventually shown her you couldn't trust anyone. She pushed away the memories; her plan had been to stay in town and study externally and get a job here in the local high school, but life had put paid to that. A couple of years after she'd finished school and had saved enough to leave home, Jenni headed to Brisbane and studied for her teaching degree, and worked at night in a variety of jobs.

Anything was better than staying home and working in the family fish co-op as her father had expected her to.

'Jenni?'

She jumped and stared at her brother as he looked at her, his head tipped to the side and a pleading look in his eyes. 'Please?'

'Oh, all right then. But if you're not back by lunchtime, I'm closing up early.' She jutted her chin out and glared at him, and was rewarded by a kiss on the top of her head as Matt headed back to the small office at the side of the co-op.

'Love ya, sis. It's good to have you home.'

And now here she was here again in the shop, almost as soon as she'd come back home.

But this time, she was here to stay.

All she had to do was tell her family she wasn't going back to the city.

Of course, Matt hadn't been back by lunchtime. Jenni had handled smelly fish, doled out kilo after kilo of frozen prawns to a constant influx of grey nomies, kept a cheery smile on her face, assured them that yes, the fish were caught locally, as well as recommending tours for those interested in going on a charter. The famous McDougal tour out to the sand island at low tide every afternoon or night—depending on the tide—was the main thing that kept their business in the black. In the winter anyway, when the grey nomies were in town. They took the groups out to the sandbar to watch the sunset, fed them marinated fish and prawns, champagne and beer, and gave each guest a glass or stubby holder imprinted with the McDougal Croc Tour logo.

She'd been so cranky with Matt, that for a brief second, she'd even thought about closing up the shop at two.

When she'd rung the house at three o'clock to see if her brother was back, Mum had laughed.

'Matt won't be home till later tonight.'

'Why? What happened? Did he get a flat on that dreadful road?' The road from Karumba to Normanton was notorious for flat tyres as vehicles headed into the ditch on the side of the narrow red dirt road as they tried to avoid the big road trains.

'No, Jen. He's got a girlfriend in town. Getting some salt, I'd say.' Mum's giggle came across the phone line. 'She's a sweetheart. The new librarian at the Shire library. I think our Matt's in love.'

'Salt? What on earth are you talking about, Mum?'

'Then again . . .' Mum sounded thoughtful.

Jenni could see Mum standing in the kitchen, tapping a finger on her lips.

'Then again what?'

'It could be lust.'

'Please, Mum.' Jenni rolled her eyes.

Was she seriously having this conversation with her mother?

As she stood in the cool room with stinking prawns surrounding her and with a horrid pair of yellow Wellington boots on her feet, Jenni put her hand over her eyes and then quickly dropped it to her side.

Ergh. Her fingers smelled like fish guts.

'Mum, you're not losing the plot are you?'

'God, no. I'm too young for that. Although thirty years with your father—God rest his soul—was probably enough to send me troppo.'

'So what were you talking about?' Jenni leaned forward and frowned as a huge flash motor cruiser motored up the middle of the channel, a tall guy with dark brown hair standing near the edge of the deck. For a minute, it was like a blast from the past and she blinked before she spoke.

Kill the memories.

'Salt?' she said.

'Don't worry about it, sweetheart. If you don't know what salt is, I'm not the one to tell you. Ask your brothers.' There was that giggle again. 'I'm off to work now. I'll cook dinner for you before I go.'

'Thanks, Mum. See you later.' It was good to hear Mum sounding so happy, but Jenni's voice was distracted as she placed the old-fashioned phone receiver back up on the wall.

All morning Matt had bemoaned the lack of money to put into the business. The co-op building needed repairs, and the cost of fuel was going up every time they set off on charters that were getting harder to fill each trip as customers looked for five-star luxury accommodation and meals on the week-long charters.

The fishing charters had been one of Dad's ideas that had worked.

Probably the only one.

Summer was a different matter; at least she'd come home in the winter and the town was alive with visitors and business was brisk.

Finally, there was a lull in the shop. There were no customers at the counter and the car park was empty so Jenni took the opportunity to step out the back to the small patch of lawn between the building and the river. Leaning back on the sun-warmed wall she inhaled deeply; the fresh cool air was pleasant after the cold air of the shop. Tipping her head back she looked upriver and smiled. It was so good to be home. Since she'd left, she'd only been home once—for Dad's funeral. Her guilt at fleeing soon after school hadn't eased at all.

Not that her family had known why she'd left, although she'd always suspected that Mum had known there was more to her leaving than a burning desire to go to university.

I should have gone into acting, she thought with a grim smile.

As she stood there watching the gulls swoop over the water, the bell on the shop door tinkled. Tucking her hair back behind her ears, and picking up the heavy plastic apron she'd slipped off, she pushed open the door.

'Good afternoon, what can I—' Jenni's mouth dropped open and her world tilted. For a moment she could only stare. The apron slipped unheeded from her fingers and she took one hesitant step forward as her heart set up a tattoo of beats to rival an AC DC song. It was the man she'd seen in the motor cruiser a few minutes ago. The man she'd thought looked like Jake Jones.

It *was* Jake Jones.

Chapter Three

'J-J-Jake?

Swallowing. Jenni stopped and gripped the edge of the counter as she fought to regain her equilibrium. The cocky good looks, the same cute dimple on his chin, and the gold-flecked hazel eyes that picked up the sunshine when he was outside. The tumbling curls had gone, replaced by a sharp short haircut, but the semi-unshaven look was still there; a narrow short beard followed his jawline.

Jake Jones was still as gorgeous as ever. Jenni's heart beat harder; she put a shaking hand to her hair and then dropped it abruptly. Her knees were trembling and she fought for calm.

'That's me.' He took his eyes from her for a moment to look at the fish nestled on the ice in the glass display cabinet next to the cash register, and Jenni took a deep breath to steady herself. Bending down, she picked up the apron, slipped it over her head, and then wiped her sweaty hands on the back of her jeans.

When she looked up again, that golden gaze locked on hers so quickly, that a tremor ran down her spine.

'Back for a visit?' she finally managed to splutter. 'I'm surprised to see *you* in town, Jake.'

'Me? Why would you be surprised?' He moved closer to the counter and she took a step back. Surely he wouldn't have the hide to touch her? 'I thought you'd be long gone,' he said.

'Well, I'm not as you can see.'

'I can. And a very nice picture it is too.' He grinned and she looked down at the bright yellow plastic apron. 'It'll be good to have a talk and catch up, Jenni.'

A simple request, but one she wasn't having a bar of.

'I don't think we've got anything to talk about, Jake.' She lifted her chin and kept her voice even as she stared back at him.

'I think we do, Jen.'

'Don't call me that.' The retort slammed out before she could pull it back, but he ignored it.

'I was sorry to hear about your father,' he said, those hazel eyes boring into hers.

Those words fired her up even more. 'Were you? There's no need to be polite for the sake of it. I think you of all people have a damn hide setting foot in the shop.' She folded her arms to stop them from shaking. 'In fact, I think you have a hide setting foot back in town.'

'Well, sweetheart, it's a free world, so they say.'

The lazy twang of his voice sent a familiar shiver down Jenni's spine. She swallowed but Jake kept talking before she could speak.

'I am surprised to see *you* still in town. What are you doing wasting your life serving fish? What happened to your dreams?' His gaze was intense.

'Wasting my life? I'm quite happy with the life choices, *I* made, thank you.' There was no need for him to know what those choices were and that she was only here under sufferance this afternoon.

He had barely changed; his face was still boyish, but there were laughter lines around his eyes that hadn't been there before. Jake shrugged, and Jenni couldn't help raking her gaze down his lean body. His shoulders were broad and the white polo shirt with the navy blue insignia moulded a muscled chest. He put his hands on the counter and she stared at his forearms; they were tanned, sprinkled lightly with fair hair, and whipcord strong. He was too close to the counter to see his jeans, but her memory sufficed there. She swallowed again as she remembered the strong muscular thighs of his youth.

Heaven help her.

The boy she had known so well had grown into a man since she'd last seen him—almost ten years ago. The night he'd come tapping on her bedroom window, begging her to talk to him, but the events of that afternoon had been imprinted on her heart, and she'd slammed the window shut in his face.

The memory of him walking dejectedly away across the paddock to his rowboat had stayed with her for a long time.

But the memory of Jake's betrayal was one she'd never forgotten.

##

Jake cursed himself for coming to the co-op the minute he'd hit Second Chance Bay.

Bloody fool. You couldn't stay away, could you? he castigated himself silently. Although the last person he'd expected to see in the shop was Jenni. He hadn't even expected to see her in town.

He'd suspected the brothers were still around because the charters that their family had run for years were still going. He'd Googled them and also found the Facebook page for the Gulf fishing charters that had run here since he was a kid.

Of course, he'd Googled; it was good business sense. You had to know the opposition when you were setting up a business. And depending on which of the brothers was running the business, he had a proposition to put to them.

He might be a fool, but old habits die hard.

It was old man McDougal he'd had the problem with, but he was gone now.

Knowing that had let Jake begin to plan to come home.

The reception he was going to receive from the town and the McDougal family was going to be interesting, but he was a big boy now and he knew he wouldn't take the shit that had been doled out to him back then.

The silence between them was broken only by the hum of the freezers at the side of the shop, and the constant vibration of the cool room door behind the counter. Jake walked across to the large glass-fronted fridge at the side of the store where the fresh prawns

25

had been kept when he had worked here in his late teens. He looked around, raising his eyebrows, surprised at the state of the equipment. The fridge was rusted along the bottom and the glass door was scratched, and it was hard to see what seafood was behind the glass door. The shop looked uncared for—and old. Even the smell of the seafood was stale; the fresh clean smell of salt was overlaid by the smell of old fish.

He turned back to the counter. 'Do you have any fresh king prawns?'

Jenni's eyes widened. She had been expecting to continue their conversation.

'Um, yes. There's some in the cool room. How many do you want?' Her voice was as chilly as the ice in the front cabinet.

'A couple of kilos.' He gestured to the cool room. 'Are they fresh?'

'Of course, they are.' She turned with a flourish and opened the door of the cool room. Jake couldn't help admiring the cute bottom in the snug-fitting jeans as she disappeared into the depths. He waited until she came out and placed two plastic bags of prawns on the newspaper on the counter.

'Will that be all?' Jenni folded her arms as she waited for his reply. Her light brown hair was still tipped by fine blonde streaks where the sun had lightened it. Her complexion was pale but flawless—he smiled to himself as he remembered her insistence on always wearing a hat the minute she'd stepped outside. Her green eyes were wide as she stared at him waiting for him to answer.

'I guess it will be for today.'

Jenni's movements were deft as she quickly wrapped the plastic bags in newspaper, and put them into another white plastic bag. 'That will be forty dollars please.'

Her voice was impersonal as though he was a stranger.

Jake pulled out his Amex business card and passed it over but she shook her head and pointed to a sign next to the cash register.

Cash only. No EFTPOS.

Digging into his wallet, he pulled out a fifty-dollar note. Jenni's eyes were downcast and she didn't meet his gaze as she took the money and rang up the sale.

'Thank you,' he said as she handed him the change. Her fingers brushed against his and she pulled her hand back as though she'd burned her fingers.

He stood there for a moment and she finally lifted her eyes to his.

'I was sorry to hear of your mother's passing, Jake.'

'Thanks.' He nodded as he took the bags from the counter. 'I guess I'll be seeing you around. Are the boys still here?'

'They are.' As she replied her eyes dropped to the Moonshine Charter insignia on his polo shirt and her cheek coloured as her lips tightened. 'Moonshine?' she said. 'You're working for the new charter company?'

He couldn't help himself as he turned for the door.

'No, Jen. I *am* Moonshine. It's my company.'

Chapter Four

Jenni was quiet as she pushed open the front door of the house she had grown up in at Second Chance Bay. As she'd crossed the river, she leaned forward and stared upriver to where the sleek white cruiser was moored at the dilapidated jetty of the Jones' house. Her mood was black; Matt hadn't shown up and after she'd cleared the till, put the cash in the white bank bag and secured it in her backpack. Jenni had pulled down the blind on the front door of the shop. The mechanism at the top had snapped and the torn and tattered blind had fallen to the floor. She'd stepped over it and locked the shop door behind her.

Honestly, what was Matt doing with the family business? She'd seen the shop through Jake's eyes as he'd looked around and embarrassment had heated her face as she'd taken it all in anew.

Embarrassment, as well as a riot of feelings that had surged through her from the moment he'd walked into the shop. Such a storm of feelings, she was going to have a serious rethink of her plans, if Jake Jones was moving back to town.

Her thoughts were tumultuous, tripping over each other, and exposing feelings that she'd hidden away for a long time. The feelings that had stopped her from having any successful relationships at university, and when she'd started work at her first school. Every time she went on a date, she compared the guy to Jake, and the bottom line was—no one ever measured up. She knew her brothers were the same. In their thirties—well Donny was almost there—and not a serious relationship to be seen. The attitude of their father had probably talked them out of ever settling down and having their own family.

It was crazy, but after so many failed attempts at relationships, Jenni had decided to focus on her teaching career and forget about meeting anyone. If it happened one day, well and good; if it didn't she'd be a career teacher and work her way up to a promotion position.

The plans had been there, but a permanent job hadn't eventuated. There were too many graduates looking for jobs in the city, and finally, she realised if she wanted a job, she would have to go bush.

But she hadn't told her family about the job yet. That was going to be a surprise for Mum.

Her stomach was still churning and her hands shaking as she closed the front door of the McDougal family house on the river. Even though they were in the tropics, the wind that came off the water in winter could be cool at night. Her hands were red and chapped from being in ice all day and she didn't think she'd ever get the smell of the fish from her fingers.

As the door clicked shut Matt's voice came down the hall. 'Is that you, Mum? Where did you put my good denim jeans? I need them to go out to the poker game with the boys at the pub.'

Jen pulled off her backpack and put it on the table inside the door as her eldest brother strolled down the hallway.

'Oh hi, Jen. I thought you were Mum home for her break.'

'Don't you 'hi Jen' me, you louse.' The temper that had been building in her chest ever since Jake Jones had pushed open the door of the fish shop burst out in one angry torrent.

'How dare you leave me in the shop all day? I had things to do and a Skype meeting with the education board that I had to cancel. I'll never work there for you again! Is that clear? I'm over it, Matt I've been home less than twenty-four hours, and I've spent nine of them in the stinking fish co-op.' Jenni's voice got louder as she let out her feelings.

'Whoa, calm down.' Matt held his hands up. 'I'm really sorry. I've just got back. I'm sorry you had to spend the day there, but I got tied up, honestly, sis.'

'Yeah, with a woman, Mum reckons.' Jen put her hands on her hips. 'And just how old are you, Matthew McDougal? Mum is still washing and ironing for you and putting your clothes away?' Once she'd started Jenni couldn't stop. 'I'm sure I'm adopted. Between the behaviour of the three of you and the way Dad treated Mum— God rest his soul— there is no way I'm related to any of you. No wonder poor Mum—'

Her oldest brother's hands descended on her shoulders and his voice was quiet. 'Jenni. Just calm down. I'm sorry. I should've rung you but the solicitor called me and he managed to squeeze me in. I was all afternoon in his office.'

Jenni sniffed and looked at him suspiciously. 'Mum said it was something to do with salt.'

Matt wrinkled his forehead for a moment and then he burst out laughing. 'I can assure you I had no time for any 'salt'. Look I'm really sorry I stuffed up your day, but why are you so upset? It's not like you at all, sweets. I've never heard you yell before. Is that what school teaching has taught you?' His grin was wide as he stared down at her affectionately

Jenni ducked from beneath his hands and pushed past him. She walked down the hallway, not able to help herself from stomping on the bare wooden floorboards. It was a satisfying sound and one that she'd used a lot when she was angry with their father in her teens. Pulling out the old kitchen chair, she flopped onto it. 'Put the kettle on and I might forgive you.' She ran her hands over the red laminate of the kitchen table. Nothing had changed in this room since she was a child. It just looked a bit older and worn these days.

Matt shot her a look, walked over to the stove and picked up the ceramic kettle off the hob before crossing to the sink and filling it. 'Tea or coffee?'

'Coffee, please.' Jenni sat back and looked around. Mum had always done her best to keep the house nice, but before Dad died, any spare money had always gone back into the business. By the look of the fish co-op—she hadn't seen any of the charter boats yet—she wondered how much money there was to go into the business—or the family house— these days.

'The place looks run down,' she said.

Matt nodded. 'There's not a lot of spare cash these days, sis. The house is the last on the list. We could really do with a new boat, especially with the new company coming into town. What Mum earns goes towards the rates and the upkeep of the old place, but it's never enough.'

Regret shot through Jenni. It was hard that Mum had to keep working. She'd worked in the shop when Dad had been alive, and now she was working at the pub, cooking for the tourists.

She screwed up her nose as Matt leaned back against the sink and looked at her. 'Money's tight, but we do what we can.'

'Did you say you were going to a poker game?' Jenni asked with a frown.

'Yeah, there's a few deckies in town who like a game. We play every Monday night.'

'For money?' Jenni couldn't help the suspicious note that crept into her voice.

His lips were set in a straight line. 'No, Jen. Not for money. You don't need to worry. I didn't inherit Dad's gambling habits.'

'Sorry.' She propped her chin in her hand as Matt turned and lit the gas. 'I noticed how old the shop was looking too.'

'It's been a very quiet season. But now the grey nomies have started to arrive, business at the shop and on the charters will pick up. It always does. We'll be okay.'

The kettle came to the boil quickly on the gas flame and Matt filled two mugs with instant coffee and poured the hot water in before he crossed to the old rusted Kelvinator fridge to get the milk out.

'Ta.' Jenni nodded her thanks as he put the mug in front of her. He sat beside her and gestured over to the stove.

'Mum's left a casserole in the oven. She always cooks for whoever is home before she goes to work.' To his credit, he did look a bit sheepish.

'Really, Matt? Mum's still got the three of you at home.' She shook her head. 'How old are you? Donny will be thirty next birthday, and you and Dane are already in your thirties. And you're all still home and poor Mum is cooking, cleaning and washing for you? It's a bit rough.'

'Mum doesn't mind. She said she likes having the company. A couple of times we talked about moving out and she didn't like the idea. Although lately—

Matt paused and scratched his chin.

'Lately what?' Jenni picked up her mug and took a sip.' Her hands had finally stopped shaking, and calm had returned. If anything, she was cross with herself for her overreaction to Jake, and her outburst with Matt.

Although he could have rung me to say he was going to be late.

'She has been getting out and about a lot more in the past few months. She never used to go anywhere much at all.'

'Doing what?' Jenni frowned. Mum had always been too busy for the social events in town.

'She goes to the different clubs at the pub through the week. She's been playing darts, and she's joined the historical society. The other night she was talking about taking a bus trip across the Savannah Way all the way to Broome.'

'Really? Good on her.'

Matt shook his head. 'The problem is I don't know if we can afford it.'

Jenni stared at him in disbelief. 'Are you for real, Matthew? After what Mum has done for you, you can't even help her out with a holiday? And she's cooking at the pub at night too?'

'Look, Jenni. You've been away. You don't know how tight we are. Insurance costs for the boats and the cost of fuel have skyrocketed over the past few years. Between charters, Dane and Donny work over on the ships, while I man the shop.' Matt's dark brows lowered in a frown. 'And now our biggest worry is the rumour that the new charter business will start up on the river this season.'

Jenni put her mug down with a thump. 'That rumour appeared in the shop this afternoon.'

'What?' Matt's eyes were wide and he put his mug down and leaned forward. 'You mean they're here in town already? I haven't seen any ads up on the notice boards yet.

'Jake Jones is back in town. On one of the flashest boats I've seen here for a long time. I don't think it's the type of business where they'll be putting photocopied black and white ads up in the caravan parks.'

'He's come back to the Bay to work?'

'No. It's *his* company. Or so he told me this afternoon. And by the look of the boat, and the swish shirt and logo, it's going to make it hard for us.'

Matt's smile stunned her. 'That's great. I'm really pleased he's made a success of his life. He always was a good guy.'

A good guy?

'And it doesn't bother you that he's come back to town to take a share of the tourist trade?'

'No. If it has to happen, I think it's great that it's Jake. At least it's someone we know and we can work with him. Like I said he was always a decent guy.'

'You've got a very short memory. What about what he did to us? It doesn't bother you how he left town?'

Matt stared at her over the rim of his coffee mug and his gaze was level. 'I think Dad can take a lot of the blame for what happened and the way you reacted.'

'Jake *stole* from us, Matt. We trusted him. Dad gave him a job, and he *stole* from the very hand that fed him.'

She didn't even mention that Jake's deception had broken her heart. He hadn't been the person she'd thought he was. But her brother wasn't going to let it go.

'I always believed if Jake took that money, he had very good reason to. His mother did it tough, and he adored her—'

Jenni snorted. 'Yes. So much that he didn't even come home from Europe for her funeral.'

'Don't be so judgmental. I know he broke your heart when he took off, but I'm sure he had his reasons for not coming home.'

'He didn't break my heart.' Jenni picked up her mug and stood. 'I'm going to have a shower. I smell like fish.'

'Jen?' Matt's voice was soft. 'Don't be hard on Jake. Give him a chance.'

Jenni stood in the kitchen and stared long and hard at her brother before she shook his head. He'd always been the soft one of the four kids. The eldest, but he'd provided a good role model for being calm, and holding the legendary McDougal temper under control.

Although rather than emulating her big brother's behaviour, it was the memory of Dad's red face and raised hand that helped Jenni control hers when she felt it building. Genes were strong, but not strong enough to make her cruel.

And she knew her brothers were the same. All three of them.

'No, Matt. I won't. He let me down. It was obviously in his character, and he won't have changed. I'm just surprised that you're not more upset about him coming to town. It's going to impact on our business.'

'*Our* business?' Matt fired up for a change and Jenni took a step back. 'First time I've ever heard you interested in *our* business.'

'Oh, go take a flying leap.' Jenni threw her mug in the sink and it clattered against the metal. Matt muttered something under his breath as she walked out, but she didn't go back to hear what he said.

'And Jen?' Matt called after her. 'Do you really want to know what 'salt' is?

She poked her head back around the door. 'Yes, what was Mum on about?'

His grin was wicked. 'Sex at lunchtime.'

Jenni giggled as she turned for the hallway.

'*Oh, Mum!*' she thought.

Chapter Five

Jake leaned on the wheelhouse on the top deck and watched the moon rise. The high-pitched whine of the osprey across the river rose to a wavering squeal as another osprey approached the nest. He watched the interaction until the second bird flew away. He lifted his beer and took a long draught.

Being back home was strange.

Gus had gone down to the cabin for an early night, as he had a six a.m. start to meet the helicopter. Jake had opted to stay up on deck for a while, and he was using the time to try to get his thoughts in order. Sitting on the leather bench seat on the deck of his luxurious charter boat, and looking back at the house that he'd grown up in was a strange feeling. It was as though his past and current lives were running in parallel. If he closed his eyes, the sounds were the same as the nights he and the McDougal brothers had gone fishing around the point in the small launch that Dane had bought and done up. They'd always been complacent about crocodiles, and now as an adult, Jake shook his head, thinking how lucky they'd been as they'd spent so much time on the water. He was the same age as Donny McDougal, and it was Donny who'd brought him home from school to play on their first day in kindergarten.

Jake could still remember an overheard comment at a school swimming carnival one summer when Helen McDougal had cheered for him in a race.

Something like *'that Jones boy isn't good enough for the McDougal family.'*

Mum had heard it too, and he could still remember the pride on her face when he'd won his first place ribbon, but he could also remember the hurt that was in her eyes when the comment had been made in the silence before the applause for the winners. Old Mrs Jackson from the bakery had a loud voice.

But he'd never felt second best with the McDougal family. From Helen or the three boys. He'd been welcome in their home and was almost a fourth son in the family right through primary and high school. Hell, there'd even been a spare bed for him in Donny's room.

And Jenni. He'd never felt second best with her either. He pushed her from his thoughts. Last he'd heard—he'd kept in touch with the news before Mum had passed away—Jenni had moved to Brisbane.

He'd assumed that she would have been married, and had a couple of kids by now.

If Jake had known she was living here at Second Chance Bay and working in the family business at Karumba, he might have reconsidered setting up his business here.

It was Jenni whose opinion had mattered the most. It always had. The comments of the townspeople, and the judgment passed on him there he could handle. Although he did know that was why he'd come back to town, to prove to the critics that he'd made it.

Stupid really.

Probably most of those who had judged him at the time were long gone. And ironically the one person he wanted to prove himself to was the one who could never know the truth. He wouldn't do that to Jenni.

A light flickered across the shore at the wharf up from the pub. As he sat there, the low putt-putt of an outboard motor reached him.

'Ahoy, there. Anyone on board?'

With a grin, Jake put his beer on the table and walked to the back of the boat.

'Sure is, but don't you go scratching my baby with that heap of shit you call a boat.'

Matt McDougal stepped from the dock onto the back of Jake's boat. He looked around appreciatively and whistled before he held out his hand. 'Welcome home, Jonesy boy.'

Jake looked at Matt's hand for a moment before he took it. Matt's grip was firm, and even in the shadowed moonlight, Jake could see his grin was wide.

And welcoming.

Some of the heaviness that had been in his chest all day lifted.

'Wanna beer?' he asked.

'I thought you'd never offer.' Matt followed him up to the top deck and looked around while Jake pulled a beer from the deck fridge and handed it to him.

Matt shook his head as his gaze travelled slowly over the top deck of the boat. 'You've come a long way, mate. Jenni tells me you're our new opposition in the Gulf.'

'Maybe not so much opposition.' Jake nodded. 'I was going to come and see you guys tomorrow. Are you all still in the business?'

'We are. Dane and Donny are out on charters this week. Donny's round the west of Darwin, and Dane's up near Weipa. And yes, it'll be good to chat. We'll be picking your brains.' Matt sat back and looked at Jake. 'You've done well for yourself, mate. I'm really happy for you.'

'I appreciate your words, and your welcome, much more than you'll ever know, Matt.'

Even though Jake was Donny's age, he and Matt had formed a close friendship in their teens.

'Don't expect it from all of us. Mum'll be fine and the boys will come around. Jenni's the one who holds the grudge.' Matt looked at him curiously. 'You know even though it was my father, I never believed what he said. Or if there was any truth in it, I knew you would have had a damn good reason.'

Jake shook his head. 'It's not something I'm going to talk about, mate. It's not a time of my life I like to remember, but a lot of years have gone by, and everything's changed. For all of us.'

Matt laughed. 'Maybe for you, but not so much for us, Jonesy.'

'I was surprised to see Jenni here. She's working in the business? I never thought she would.' Jake popped the top of his beer.

'Oh hell, no. I'm in the bad books because she was filling in for me for a couple of hours today, and I got held up in Normanton. She ended up working in the fish shop all day. She only arrived home from Brisbane last night.'

'So she's only visiting?'

'Yeah. She doesn't come home much. She left town a while after you did.'

'Husband and kids?' Jake kept his voice casual.

'Nah, she's a teacher and a career person through and through. She reckons she loves it, but Mum worries about her. Reckons she's not happy living away, but that's mothers for you.' He put his beer down. 'I'm sorry, mate, that was insensitive. I went to your Mum's funeral.'

'Thanks. I appreciate that. I knew you would. I didn't have the money for the airfare back from Europe. She lost her battle with breast cancer when I was still a lowly deckie. I talked to Mum every day she was in hospital in Normanton, and I know she understood. But it was still really tough, not being here for her.'

'Yeah, it would have been. She told me you used to ring her every night.'

Jake lifted his head. 'You visited her in hospital?'

Matt nodded. 'Mum and I used to take it in turns.'

Jake shook his head as his throat tightened. 'And you drove all the way to Normanton to see her? She never said.'

'Of course we did. I guess she didn't want to bring up the McDougal name to you.' Matt looked away. 'Sad thing that, when there's bad feeling between good people.'

Jake ignored the lump that had formed in his throat, but in that moment, he knew he'd been right to come home. He cleared his throat and took a swig of beer. 'I'm going to do the old place up and move in.'

'That'll take a while.'

'It will, but I'm going to settle here. I'm home now.'

'For good?'

Yep. For good.'

Matt lifted his bottle and clinked it against Jake's. 'In that case, welcome home again. There's going to be a lot of people happy to see you here. Your business is going to be good for the Bay.'

A lot of people? He knew one who wouldn't be happy.

But Jake didn't put what he was thinking into words.

Chapter Six

A week went by before Jenni saw Jake Jones again. Her temper had been short and her mood irritable when she thought about Jake being back in town. What gods were laughing down at her? Ten years, and they'd hit town in the same week?

She'd managed to—almost, anyway—forget him over the past few years, and now he was back on her radar she couldn't stop herself thinking about him.

Seeing Jake again brought what had happened slamming back into her thoughts, and she wasn't happy. Her life had been settled and she was on the path to doing what she wanted to. And she had been happy doing it. She'd been happy about coming home, but now his presence had tainted that.

Tainted. That was exactly the word. What Jake had done before he'd left town had tainted everything.

Jenni spent the past week on tenterhooks, sure she'd run into him somewhere in the small town, but he'd kept a low profile. Or maybe it was because she didn't leave the house much. The fancy boat had passed the house a couple of times as it purred smoothly up the river, but she'd ignored it.

On Friday afternoon, Mum had raised her eyebrows. 'Haven't you got something nice to do, love?' she asked as she tried to fill the kettle while Jenni washed up. 'It's lovely to have you home, sweetheart, but you need to get out of the house. Surely there's someone you want to catch up with? Have a coffee with some of the girls, maybe? Go for a run? Do you still jog and do those triathlon things?' Mum's eyes had narrowed. 'You're still too thin. I'll have to fatten you up a bit.'

Jenni shook her head. 'I still run to keep fit, but no competitions lately. I've been too busy with school stuff. I don't

think any of my friends stayed in town. They've all moved away.'
The one person she'd spent most of her time within the last two
years of school was the one person she had no desire to catch up
with.

'Why don't you go down to the dock and wait for your
brothers? Matt called a few minutes ago and said they've radioed
in. They'll be coming through the heads any time now. They'll
both be pleased to see you.'

'I will. I thought they'd be later than this.' Jenni drained the
sink and wiped her hands, hiding a smile when a look of relief
crossed Mum's face. She knew Mum hated anyone else in her
domain. 'I can't wait to see the boys. It's over two years since I
last saw them.'

'Well, get your skates on because they'll dock in about fifteen
minutes. Tell them I've got the night off. I'm just about to put a
roast on so we can all have dinner together.' Mum blinked a tear
away. 'It's the first time you've all been home together since your
dad went.'

Jenni crossed the room and put her arms around her mother.
'I'm sorry, Mum. I've been slack.' She bit her lip as she hugged
Mum close and decided to break her news. 'But I've got some
news. I was going to make it a surprise when the truck arrived.'

'Truck?' Mum looked up at her, a frown creasing her brow.
'What truck?'

'The truck with all my stuff in it. I've given up my apartment
in Brisbane and everything's on the way home. I've got two terms
at Second Chance Bay High School in the English department.'

'Oh, my goodness!'

Jenni smiled as her mother let her go and jumped up and down
on the spot, before grabbing her in another huge hug. 'Oh, my
stars, that is awesome.'

'I thought you'd be happy.'

'I am but the timing is a bit hard. I've got some news too.'
Mum stepped back and looked at her and her smile faltered.

'News?'

'Yes. I'm going away too. But at least you'll be here to look after your brothers,'

Jenni put her hands up. 'Whoa . . . let's backtrack a little here. First off where are you going?'

'I'm going to Broome with . . . Rick.'

'Rick from the pub?'

'Yes, he's opening a pub over in Broome too, and he invited me to go for a bit of a holiday with him.' Mum's face flushed.

'You cheeky thing. Are you seeing him?'

Her mother folded her arms. 'Yes, I see him every night when I cook at the pub.'

'You know what I mean.'

The blush deepened. 'Yes, I guess you could say we're "seeing" each other.' Her mother's forehead creased in a frown. 'Do you mind, love? The boys are okay with it. They like Rick. Her cheeks flushed. 'I—um—sometimes stay the night at his place.'

Even as surprise coursed through Jenni, she shook her head. 'Of course I don't mind, you silly thing. You deserve to be happy, Mum. It's a long time since Dad went.' She doubted that Mum had been happy before he went, but that had never been talked about.

'So yes, I'm going away for a while. Rick wants me to stay over there for six months, and help get the pub bistro set up.'

'And he'll be there too?' Jenni nudged her mother with a cheeky smile.

'Yes, he will.' Mum cleared her throat. 'And now that you're home, it solves my biggest problem. I was worried who was going to look after the boys.'

'Mum!' Jenni put her hands on her hips and her voice was a splutter of disbelief. 'If you think I'm going to look after three grown men and tell them where their jeans are and serve their Weetbix out for them each morning, they are going to be very disappointed. Very, very disappointed.'

'I know I've spoiled them.' Despite her words, Mum's smile was still wide. 'It hasn't hurt them.'

'Spoiled them? I pity the poor women they end up with. If they ever do get married. Because you know what, Mum? If you keep making it so good at home, they are going to turn into three crusty old bachelors and stay here forever. It will do them good to look after themselves while you're away. I'm really happy that you're doing it. For your sake too.' She shot a sidelong glance at her mother. 'And I like Rick too. He's a good man. I always knew he fancied you.'

'Oh, get away with you.' Mum picked up the vacuum cleaner again but she was smiling. 'Get over to the dock or you'll miss the boats coming in. Apparently, they've had good trips and they're loaded up with fish and happy guests.'

'That's what we want to hear. Return customers. Matt said it's been quiet.'

'It has, but we can talk about that later when you're all home for dinner. Now get yourself off to the boats!'

'Yes, Mum!' Jenni hurried down to her room—the room that was the same as when she'd left. Her favourite childhood books were still in the shelf at the head of the bed, and her bride doll was in pride of place on the chair beneath the window. How many nights had she lain in bed and dreamed of her own white wedding? Jenni gave a huff of disgust and pulled out a pair of long cotton pants and a clean T-shirt. It would be cool down on the dock if the wind blew up.

***

Jake and Matt sat on the fence near the public boat ramp where the charter boats moored offshore, watching the activity on the water as they waited for the two McDougal boats to come home.

'Mosquito fleet's starting to come in.' Matt nodded to the continuous fleet of ten-foot tinnies that were heading back into the river mouth. A procession of four-wheel drive vehicles grew longer as the drivers backed them down the ramp as they took turns to retrieve their boats.

'I'd forgotten that term,' Jake said with a laugh. 'All the retired blokes who go out each morning to catch a feed. There mustn't be many fish out there today. They're coming in early.'

'Nah. There's always fish.' Matt glanced down at his watch. 'It's almost beer o'clock. The happy hour groups will be starting to gather in the caravan park soon. The fishermen will just have time to clean their catch, and then pull up a chair and a beer. '

'Look at us.' Jake laughed as Matt stared out into the Gulf. 'Can you remember when we were kids and heading past this spot in the launch? We used to laugh at the old blokes sitting here watching the boats come in.'

'We're just a couple of *older* blokes now, mate. Not too old.' Matt pointed past the channel markers a couple of kilometres past the river mouth. 'Here comes Donny now.'

Jake narrowed his eyes and nodded as he made out the shape of the boat familiar to him from his teenage years. The *Sally M* had been an old boat then, but she still had class. At thirty-three metres, and sleeping thirty- four with private en suite facilities for each cabin, she was a grand old lady. When she was built, she'd been one of the largest charter boats in Queensland. He'd helped the McDougal boys—and Jenni—clean her between trips and earned himself some pocket money. He was looking forward to stepping onboard and running his fingers over the beautifully polished timber inside the saloon. Even though he'd skippered some beautiful boats in Europe, they'd all been slick and modern; the *Sally M* was stylish, but he did notice she looked a bit rundown.

'It'll help you buy some fishing gear, son,' old Bill McDougal had said when he'd offered him the job. Jake had agreed but every cent had gone to Mum. Money had been short in the old house on the river.

Jake shut down the line of thought. If he let himself dwell on past events, it sat in his chest like a stone.

Am I crazy to have come back here?

No matter how many friends he'd made in the Mediterranean, how many charters he'd skippered, or how much money he'd made, happiness had eluded him there.

He sat back and watched as the *Sally M* approached the dock. Sitting here bare-footed in the sun, in his old cut-off denim shorts and a plain white T-shirt, contentment filled Jake and he began to think he'd made the right move, no matter what his doubts were. He'd shed the white linen shorts and the polo shirt with the company logo because there was no one to impress today. He stared over the water; the only person he wanted to impress would probably prefer the old Jake anyway.

Or no Jake.

'Who's minding the shop?'

The very person he'd been thinking about walked up and stood behind her brother. Jenni gave Jake a cool nod and then turned to Matt with a smile. 'You playing hooky again, Matthew?'

'No. Maisie from the caravan park is minding the shop while I help unload the fish. Donny said they've got a huge catch on board. How do you fancy helping us freeze some of it down later? I've got a flash new cryovac machine.'

'Ergh. No thank you.' Jenni tilted her head to the side and chuckled. 'Not the same Maisie from Melbourne who lived in Toorak Lane every winter when we were growing up? Maisie with the blue rinse?'

'The very same,' Matt replied. 'But the years have moved on and she's moved sites over the past couple of winters.'

Jenni's peal of laughter warmed Jake's heart, but he clenched his hands as he looked up at her.

'Tell me she hasn't moved to Dunrootin Lane?' she asked with a pretty smile, a smile that made Jake's heart speed up.

'So you haven't forgotten what they used to name the streets in the caravan park?' Matt looked at his sister with a frown. 'That's good because you've been gone way too long, Jen.'

'Well, I'm back now, and no, I haven't forgotten.' she said quietly as she kicked at a stone and avoided Jake's gaze. 'I'm going to wait down on the boat ramp. It's warmer down there.'

Jake tried not to stare as Jenni walked down the concrete ramp across from where they were sitting. She was still slim and lithe and the sun glinted on her hair that reached halfway down her back. Her shoulders were straight and she carried herself confidently. While her back was turned to him, he drank in his fill.

Matt's low voice pulled him from his need. 'That was interesting.'

'What?'

'The way Jenni said she was home now. Did you get the impression that she meant she was home, rather than just visiting?'

'Sorry, I wasn't paying much attention.' Jake pointed to the boat that was almost in front of them. 'She's still a beautiful boat.'

'A bit long in the tooth, and the upkeep costs are getting worse by the year, but yes, she's a beauty.'

'Do you ever go out on charters?' Jake turned back to Matt because while ever he was looking at the approaching boat, Jenni was in his line of sight.

'No. Would you believe the one time I went I got seasick? Not a good look for a skipper. So, I get to run the land part of the business. The bookings, the finances, the orders and the fish and prawn sales side of things.'

'So, you get the worry without all the fun?' Jake cut straight to the chase.

'Good to talk to someone who understands. The rest of the family reckons I'm a whinger.' Matt ran his hand through his tousled curls. The wind had picked up and as Jake looked back at Jenni, she was standing on her tiptoes, holding her hair with one hand. From where he was sitting, it was like looking at the eighteen-year-old girl he'd fallen in love with. She looked no different as she stood there, obviously excited about seeing her brothers.

'A whinger?' He turned his attention back to Matt. 'In what way?'

Matt sighed. 'Because I'm always on about money, Donny reckons I'm a tight arse, but the only outgoing money he sees is when he fills the diesel tanks up.'

Jake sat quietly for a minute. 'If I can I'd like to help. I know my leaving was . . . difficult . . . but I'd like to help out if I can.'

Matt's voice sparked with interest. 'In what way, mate? How can you help our business?'

'Well the *Sally M,* and also, the *Elsie'*—the other boat had been named after the matriarch of the family when Bill McDougal had started the charter business back in the eighties— 'are much bigger than my two boats. I'm thinking of an arrangement where we combine charters and you provide the mother ship, and my boats can go out deep and wide for the game fishing.'

'It could work. But I'd have to get the others to agree.' Matt held Jake's gaze steadily. 'And I'll be honest with you. You might not get the same welcome—or enthusiasm— from Dane and Donny. But I'll work on them.'

'Or Jenni,' Jake said glumly.

'You've still got it bad for her, haven't you? Even after all these years?'

'Yeah, you'd think not seeing her for so long would have cured me, wouldn't you?'

'Not to mention all those hot French chicks.'

Jake laughed. 'I was a dull boy over there, all work and no play.'

'No play?' Matt asked, his grin wide. 'None at all?'

'Well, maybe a little.'

Sometimes he'd tried to get Jenni out of his head. How long did it take to fall out of love with somebody? The old maxim, they were meant for each other had stayed active way too long. Part of his reason for coming home was to get Jenni McDougal out of his system.

To come back to the Bay, and live here without her. Settle down and accept she was gone from here and gone from his life. And what did he come home to? Jenni in town, and the same feelings surging back.

Bloody ridiculous.

Ten years.

One look at her, and Jake was right back where he'd been when her father ran him out of town.

In love and not able to do a thing about it.

There was only one answer. Immerse himself in work here like he had overseas.

But the little voice inside niggled at him.

Maybe you can change her mind.

Maybe he could show her the man he was without her knowing the truth of ten years ago?

***

Jenni stood on the boat ramp, waiting for the boats. She stood up and down on her tiptoes and grabbed for her hair again as another big gust of wind lifted it. She was conscious of Jake sitting on the fence not far behind her.

A strange feeling gripped her. Seeing him out of the swish charter boat uniform, and back in his old clothes, it was as though her old Jake was back with her.

Scrap that, not *her* Jake. No matter how hard she'd tried over the past week, he had stayed in her thoughts, and she knew she had to do something about it.

If she hadn't signed the contact with the education board for the two terms of work at the local high school, she would have gone.

Fled town like Jake had.

Her emotions were in turmoil. When she'd crossed the road to the boat ramp and spotted him sitting beside Matt, her fingertips had tingled, and her heart had sped up. She'd stood behind them for a moment, watching the wind ruffle Jake's hair, and feasted her eyes on the broad back beneath the snug-fitting T-shirt. No matter what she knew about Jake Jones, her body wouldn't stop the traitorous reaction. After a couple of minutes Jenni swallowed and walked across to them.

Moving down to the boat ramp had been a stupid move because Jake was behind her now, and she could feel his eyes on her. Maybe if they'd had closure when he'd fled town, maybe if they'd had a conversation, she wouldn't feel like this.

There'd never been any closure. One minute, they'd been inseparable, and then the next minute he'd gone.

Her family had been shocked by his actions, but Dad had been hard the afternoon he'd dropped the bombshell.

'Jake stole from us, Jen love,' he'd said the afternoon he came looking for Jenni. She'd been down at the boat ramp, where she was standing now as the memories bombarded her.

'I never trusted him,' Dad went on. 'He fitted too easily into our family, and he thought he was one of us. Blood always tells, and none of the Jones family was ever any good. I was a fool to take the boy in and trust him.'

'What? What did he do?' Jenni's world had shifted in that moment.

Even as she thought of it ten years later, her breath hitched and her stomach churned as her father stared at her, his eyes hard.

'He's been taking some of the takings from the fish shop very day. Two thousand dollars all up. I've been watching him. I thought our till was down a bit so I tallied up the takings. I caught him at it today.'

Jenni had shaken her head as she stared up at her father. 'No. I don't believe it. Jake would never do that.'

'Well, you have to, love. He's admitted it.'

'I want to go and talk to him.' She'd pulled away from her father's grip as his fingers had circled her wrist. 'Now.'

'You can't. He's leaving.'

'Leaving?' Confusion ran rampant through her as Jenni had put her hand to her stomach, thinking she was going to be sick.

'The sergeant gave him a warning and he's driving him to Normanton tonight. I told him if he left town, I wouldn't press charges.'

'What about the money?' Jenni had barely been able to get the words out.

'I let him keep it. Maybe it'll give the boy a start.' His voice was gruff and Jenni stared at her father. Dad never gave anything to anyone; it was a good thing to do in a horrid situation to help Jake out. A turmoil of thoughts had whizzed around her head and finally disappointment and disgust had settled in her chest.

To this day, Jenni couldn't reconcile the Jake she'd known—and loved—with a man who would steal from her family, and then leave town with the proceeds.

Matt had always refused to believe that Jake was guilty, and he and Dad had had a strained relationship until the day their father had died.

Jenni glanced behind her. Matt and Jake were deep in conversation, as thick as they'd always been. A ripple of doubt, with a smidgeon of guilt thrown into the mix, ran through her. Matt had stayed loyal to Jake the whole time, and welcomed him back to town.

Why had Jake left town?

Because he was guilty.

That was the only explanation for him leaving so suddenly.

Chapter Seven

Donny came in first, and the horn of the *Sally M* tooted when he spotted Jenni on the concrete ramp. She ran across the soft sand and around to the dock where he was berthing the large vessel.

'Jen!' Once the ropes were secured Donny jumped over the side of the boat and hugged her. 'Welcome home, sis. It's about time you came to visit.'

She landed a kiss on her brother's unshaven cheek. 'You look like a hobo, Donny.'

'We've been busy catching fish. Just as well you're home; we'll need a hand to clean them all.'

Jenni pulled a face at him, and stood with her arm linked through his as their older brother, Dane, brought the second boat in.

It took an hour for the guests to disembark, and Jenni smiled as her brothers handed out large polystyrene boxes of fish to the guests. Contrary to Donny's words, she knew the fish would have been cleaned and then frozen down in the big freezers on the boats, ready for the guests to take their catches back to the southern states.

Matt came over and waited as a small crane lifted off the last big boxes of fresh fish, ready to go the shop.

'Just as well there's a crowd in town,' he said.

'A bit too much of a crowd,' Donny murmured, looking back to where Jake was sitting on the fence.

Jenni stared across to where Donny was looking. She wasn't alone in her opinion of Jake Jones coming back to town.

##

Three hours later, the atmosphere in the McDougal kitchen was noisy and happy. Donny and Dane had showered and shaved; Mum bustled about serving up a baked dinner, a satisfied expression on her face as the conversation between her four children became lively.

'I'll give you a hand, Mum.' Jenni walked over to the sink where Mum was draining the veggies, but her mother waved her away.

'No, you stay and talk to your brothers. This is nothing. I'm used to serving up for a hundred at the pub.' Jenni looked back as Dane stood behind her and rested his chin on her shoulder and they watched Mum deftly drain, stir and season. It was a bit quieter away from the table, where Donny and Matt were in the midst of a heated discussion about finances.

'Already.' Mum rolled her eyes as she looked at her youngest and eldest sons as Matt put his beer bottle down heavily on the table.

'Oh, yum. Is that Karumba Pub peas, I can see?' Dane reached past Jenni and picked a cooked pea out of the saucepan.

Mum slapped his hand away. 'Yes, they are, but you can wait for your dinner, young man.' She laughed as she stared up at him. 'Just because you've grown so tall, doesn't mean you lose your manners.'

'And *bejesus* cauliflower too? Oh, Mum, I love you.' Dane reached over again and filched a baked potato out of the tray, and got his fingers slapped for that too.

'*Bejesus* cauliflower?' Jenni screwed her nose up. 'Is that something new on the pub menu?'

Mum shook her head with a laugh. 'No, but your brother has been eating at the pub a bit.' She winked at Jenni. 'Might have something to do with a certain waitress here, methinks.'

Dane shook his head. 'Nope, it's the fabulous food there. That's all.'

'So, tell me about these veggies,' Jenni asked with a laugh.

'Yeah, so you can cook them for us when Mum goes off on her travels.'

Jenni whacked him on the shoulder. 'I'm not cooking for anyone. Or if I do, we'll take it in turns.'

'Sugar, soda and salt in the peas, Jen,' Mum said. 'Makes them sweet and keeps them green.' She laughed again. 'And the short order cook before me said the only way to cook cauliflower was to cook the "bejesus" out of it, and your big brother loves it like that.'

'Soft and runny, yum.' Dane gave a satisfied sigh.

Jenni smiled as she looked around at her family. It was so good to be home. Life had been lonely in her apartment in Brisbane.

Mum pointed to the cutlery drawer. 'You can set the table now, Jen. 'It's almost ready.'

As Jenni turned to open the drawer, she froze as Mum called over to the table. 'Matthew, did you invite Jake?'

'I did, but he said he didn't want to impose.' Matt shot a glare at Dane, and Jenni felt him stiffen beside her.

'Good,' he muttered beneath his breath.

Mum turned around slowly. 'I heard that, Dane. And I'm disappointed in you. What sort of welcome is that for a man who's come back to town, and has no one here of his own?'

Dane shrugged but his voice was terse. 'So why did he come back?'

'That's his business and not ours.' Mum put the saucepan on the sink with a clatter. 'Matthew, you get over next door and tell Jake to get himself over here quick smart. I've cooked enough for him too. The poor boy's been over there by himself for a few days.'

As Matt nodded and headed out the door, Mum leaned back on the sink and folded her arms. 'And I expect the three of you to be polite and welcoming. I thought I brought my children up to be kind. And forgiving.'

Dane went to speak and obviously thought better of it. He reached out and raised his eyebrows at Jenni as he took the knives and forks from her hands.

Donny obviously felt he could put his opinion across. His voice was quiet and calm. 'I think to be fair, Mum, that Dane is thinking of Jenni's feelings.'

Their mother shook her head. 'Jenni's a big girl now. She doesn't need anyone speaking for her.' She raised her eyebrows. 'Do you, Jen?'

Jenni shrugged as Dane had. 'It's only dinner. I'm sure I'll survive one meal in Jake's company.'

'Just watch the silver,' Dane muttered as he crossed to set the table.

It was going to be an interesting meal.

She just had to survive it.

*****

Jake argued, but Matt wouldn't listen. 'No, mate. I told you before, it's a family dinner.'

'You're invited.'

'I'm not tidy enough.'

'You'll do.'

'Just let me get changed then.' Jake headed across the deck, but Matt was close behind him.

Before he knew it, he was being dragged off the boat, in the direction of the McDougal house next door.

'I'm not going back without you. Mum will have my hide if I do.'

'Yeah, what about the rest of the family?' Jake could feel the tension building in his temples. He could deal with the fallout—it might be ten years later than he would have liked—but he worried about the impact on Jenni. They hadn't had a real conversation for ten years, let alone sat at a dinner table together.

In the house of his accuser.

'At least let me get changed, Matt.'

'Nah. You're fine as you are. Better than the corporate gear. Although I'd like to see Donny's face when he sees your boat.'

'Let me at least grab a six-pack.' Jake turned back to the boat.

'No, Mum's ready to serve up. Come on.'

'What did you say about Donny's face?' he asked as he trudged reluctantly behind Matt.

'He'll be green with envy. He wanted to upgrade the boats before Dad died, but Dad wouldn't have a bar of it. And then when he was gone, we could see why. The finances weren't there.'

'I'm impressed that you've kept the business going, between the four of you.'

'The three of us,' Matt replied. 'Jen has nothing to do with it. She won't even take her dividend from the family company each year, not that it's much. She insists that it goes back into the business.'

They reached the gate in the fence all too quickly. The McDougal house was out of sight from his place, around the bend in the river, away from Jake's home and jetty. So at least he hadn't had to see Jenni coming and going all week as he'd worked on *Moonshine*.

Matt obviously sensed his discomfort. 'It's okay, mate. We're all grownups now.'

Jake swallowed. 'Yeah. That we are.'

Matt pushed open the kitchen door and as Jake followed him in, the conversation came to an abrupt halt.

Helen McDougal walked over, untying her apron and put it on the duck cupboard next to the door. Jake smiled as he looked at the old cupboard that was supposed to hold shoes, but in the times that he had visited had had a plethora of what everybody dropped as they came in from outside.

He stood back looking at the collection of screwdrivers, keys, loose change and clothes pegs, and strangely he relaxed. Nothing had changed. As he looked across at Helen's big smile, the tension eased even more. Helen held her arms open and he folded her in a hug.

'You've grown up, Jakey.'

'I hope so, Helen.' Damn it, his voice was shaking and he could feel moisture building behind his eyes. He blinked it away before he embarrassed himself.

Jenni was standing by the fridge, a jar of sauce in each hand. He nodded at her; even if her mother expected him to hug Jenni, she'd made sure her hands were full. He knew her well.

Dane and Donny stood. He sensed the smiles were forced, but they each held out a hand in turn and shook his firmly.

'Sit down, everyone. It's all served up.' Helen gestured to the chair near the door. 'You sit there, Jake. Where you always did.'

The reference to the past killed the conversation again, and there was an awkward silence around the table as everyone took their seats. Thank goodness for Helen, who chatted as she carried the plates over to the table and placed a loaded dinner plate in front of each of them.

Finally, Donny spoke. 'Can I get you a drink, Jake? Beer? Soft drink? Water?'

He looked at what everyone else was drinking and nodded. 'A beer would be great, thank you.'

'So Jake, tell us all about your travels.' Helen's voice was bright as she gestured for them all to start eating.

Jake picked up his knife and fork. 'Not so much travels. I've been in the one spot for the last eight years. In the marina at Monte Carlo.'

'Half your luck.' Donny's voice held a note of curiosity. 'I've seen photos of some of the boats over there. Mega millions.'

Jake nodded as he sliced the succulent pork. It was a long time since he'd sat at a kitchen table and had a home-cooked meal. The first two years after he'd left Karumba had been spent in a variety of cheap boarding houses on the north Queensland coast as he'd completed his courses and worked on the boats. 'Yep, there's some money over there, that's for sure. If you ever wanted to travel, you'd have no trouble getting a job over there. They love the Aussies. We've got a reputation for having a work ethic.'

'Maybe one day.' Donny nodded.

Jake looked up surprised as Jenni spoke quietly. 'That's one place I'd like to go. France. Ever since we had Mrs MacLean in high school teaching us about French culture, I've wanted to go there. Paris in the spring is on my bucket list.' Her voice was dreamy. 'One day.'

Jake looked over at Helen as relaxation settled in his bones. The conversation was flowing around him, and there were lots of smiles. 'Thanks for the invite, Helen. It's a lovely meal.'

'So Matt tell us you're back to stay, Jake?' Dane's voice was careful.

Jake picked up his beer and took a sip before he answered. 'Yes, I'm home now.'

Okay, in for a penny, he thought. 'I've already mentioned it to Matt. I was going to come across and see you. To ask to meet with you all. I've got a business proposition you might be interested in.'

'Why would we want to go into business with you?' Dane was unsmiling. Jake looked up and caught Jenni looking at him intently. Warmth crept through him before she masked her expression and then dropped her gaze.

'The new legislation is going to open up Australian waterways to a lot of high-end competition. You're going to have to be able to offer something special if you want to keep the customers coming to you.'

Dane and Donny looked at each other before they turned to Matt. 'What legislation?'

Matt shrugged. 'I don't know. What are you referring to, Jake?

'I saw the headline on the ABC news online this morning. I knew nothing about it either, but it's going to have a huge impact on charters around the country.'

The three McDougal brothers frowned together, and Helen and Jenni exchanged a glance.

'What's happening, Jake?' Jenni's voice was soft.

He put his fork down and pulled out his phone. 'Excuse me for doing this at the dinner table, Helen, but it's pretty important.'

She nodded. 'Go ahead, Jake.'

He read aloud the news headline that had caught his attention that morning.

'International superyachts set to be attracted by possible tax break and 'virgin' cruising grounds.'

'Tax break?' Matt's frown increased. 'What sort of tax break?'

'Well, if I understand it properly—I've been away for a long time—under current laws, foreign-owned yachts that want to travel to Australia and operate charters have to pay the ten percent GST.'

Matt nodded. 'That's right. The way it stands now, anyone from overseas who wants to charter in Australian waters has to pay the GST on the value of the boat.'

Dane chipped in. 'An owner sends his super yacht out and it might be worth a hundred million … so he's got to put ten million on the counter for the government before he can do anything.'

'That's the way it's always been, and it's made our fishing and cruising grounds not viable for international companies.'

Jake kept reading from the small screen in front of him. 'Charging the GST on a charter, instead of the yacht's value, would open up Australia to international vessels that traditionally operate in luxury hotspots such as the Mediterranean and Caribbean.'

Dane pushed his plate aside and picked up his beer. 'Holy hell. That's going to be huge for us. First I've heard of this. How the heck will we compete?'

'They say the legislation will be through in a couple of months.' Jake looked up and held Dane's eyes steadily. He was the brother who would need the most convincing. 'That's why I talked to Matt the other day. I've got a business suggestion that will position you uniquely up here.'

Dane's voice was full of suspicion. 'What would you want to help us out? Why don't you just want to take your cut of the business?'

'Two reasons.' Jake's throat was suddenly dry, and he picked up the carafe of water in the middle of the table. He filled his glass and drank before he answered, aware of five pairs of eyes on him.

'Because, it will also benefit my business, and—' he paused and looked at each of them —I owe this family.'

Jake was satisfied to see the flush that tinged Jenni's cheeks.

Chapter Eight

It was close to midnight when Jake finally left. Dane had thawed, and the conversation had been animated as they'd discussed the change in the charter boat legislation. Jenni had helped Mum clear the table and do the dishes and then helped serve up homemade apple crumble and custard. Jake had been polite, but distant, the couple of times she'd spoken to him. Now Jenni stood in the shadows by her bedroom window until he was out of sight. She wrapped her arms around herself not knowing how she felt.

Well, okay, she knew how she felt. She'd wanted to run after Jake, and have him hold her in his arms and kiss her like he'd used to. It was time to admit that to herself. Heck, he'd only been here seven days. Why had he really come back to the Bay? There was nothing here for him; his life in the Mediterranean must have been exciting. Way more exciting than a small backwater like Second Chance Bay would ever be.

International charter takeover or not.

She stared through the window and put her hand on the cool glass. The night was dark and the sky was brilliant with diamond stars. Memories overwhelmed her.

The first time Jake had kissed her, it had been on a clear winter night just like this one. Next to the gate he'd just closed behind him as he'd headed back to his flash boat.

It had been Mum's fortieth birthday, and the party had been in full swing. They'd managed to slip away from Dad's eagle eye. If Jenni had heard him say once that she was too young to have a boyfriend, she'd heard it a hundred times.

Besides he had nothing to worry about; she and Jake were only *friends*. Jake was a better friend to her than any of the girls at school; they loved the same things. She would walk along the river bank with him for hours chasing crabs—and avoiding crocodiles—and talking. Talking about his plans to build a life on the water, talking about her desire to study to be a teacher.

He treated her like one of the boys and his company was easy. Jake didn't know the thrill that went through her whenever he held her hand, or put his arm casually around her shoulders. To Jake, Jenni was a mate—simply another one of the McDougal boys.

Unable to settle, Jenni reached for a jacket and opened the sliding door that led from her bedroom to the verandah. She was too restless to sleep. The house was quiet; she could just hear the murmur of Mum's voice. She smiled; Mum had said she was going to make a phone call.

It was good to see her happy and making plans for the future. Mum had done it tough when Dad had been alive. Their life had been hard and rough; Mum deserved to have some happiness. She's been a fabulous mother to them, and everything she'd done had been for the four kids. Mum had sacrificed a lot for her family.

It was time she had time for herself. Even though Jenni had loved her father, she knew he had been a difficult man for Mum to live with. His boats had come first, his mates at the pub, his gambling, and then Mum and the kids came a sorry last. It had been sad for all of them when he'd died in his late fifties, but a life of hard drinking and hard living had caught up with him.

Her three brothers were good men. Growing up the way they had, had made them determined to live good lives. The only thing that Jenni worried about now was why they were all still living at home.

Each of them had had relationships, but like her, she suspected that they too had trust issues.

With a shrug, Jenni stepped out to the verandah and welcomed the fresh air.

The night was still and there was no moon, and it wasn't too cold so she left her jacket unzipped as she walked towards the water. Even though it was winter, she still kept an eye out for snakes. As she got closer to the McDougal jetty, she could see the lights of Jake's boat around the bend. His silhouette passed by one of the windows on the top deck as she stood watching, and a shaft of longing for the old easy days ran through her. When life was uncomplicated, and everyone got on. When there was no shadow from the past hanging over them. Jake stepped out onto the deck and held the railing staring in her direction. Even though it was dark and she knew he wouldn't be able to see her, Jenni stepped behind the clump of bushes at the side of the path.

Wide awake, she stared at the water; she knew that she was going to have trouble falling asleep tonight.

What had Jake meant when he said he owed the family?

Was it an admission of guilt? When he'd fled that had been enough of an admission for her. Her father might have been hard but he'd never lied to her.

Could she find it in herself to forgive Jake? Maybe he hadn't changed like she thought he had. Maybe circumstances had forced him to take the money from the shop.

Tears ached in Jenni's throat and she shook her head.

No.

No matter what had motivated Jake back then, she could never forgive him.

Dishonesty was a trait that she couldn't accept.

Even if she still cared about him. Even if he still made her heart sing.

He was not the man she'd thought he was. He never had been, and he never would be.

***

Jake couldn't sleep.

He was wired. Talking to the McDougals about the things they could do if they formed a partnership had been received so much better than he'd imagined in his wildest dreams. Even Dane had come around and shaken his hand as he'd left the McDougal home a couple of hours ago.

Jenni?

Jenni had been a different matter. Even at the end of the night, when they'd been relaxed, she'd been aloof. When he'd said goodbye, her eyes had been downcast and he knew that she didn't want him there.

She didn't want him in their home.

She didn't want him in Second Chance Bay.

She obviously didn't want him in her life.

Well, she was just going to have to get over it; he was here to stay.

He lay on the deck and looked up at the stars, cursing the man who had taken Jenni from him as he thought back.

##

February 2008

'Jake, come in.'

Jake stood outside the door of the office at McDougal's Fish Co-op. He knew the shop well; he'd been working there since he was sixteen. Mrs McDougal was behind the counter and she smiled at him absently as she bagged the fresh prawns that had just come in on the afternoon trawler.

'I'll give you a hand with that after Mr M speaks to me.'

Her smile had been distracted and sad. She'd obviously known what was about to ensue.

Jake had walked into the office and respectfully taken his cap off. As he held it by his side he glanced down at it— a navy blue cap with the McDougal logon on the front. He'd been lucky that the McDougals had taken him under their wing when he'd made friends with Donny at school.

'Sit down.' There was no welcome in Mr M's voice.

Jake frowned as he sat down. Maybe Mr M wasn't happy that he was heading off to college for a few weeks for some intensive training for his coxswain's certificate. He'd offered to make up the hours in the shop by doubling up before he went, and when he came back so that the boys were free to deckie on the family charter boats. Maybe he was embarrassed because he'd overheard some of the conversation with that sleazy guy who'd come in demanding to see Bob yesterday afternoon. Jake had ended up going outside when the conversation from the office had been heated. Luckily there were no customers in the shop. The guy was carrying on about paying debts as Jake had pushed the door open and gone outside for a while to give them some privacy.

The guy had stared at Jake and given him a mouthful as he'd left a few minutes later.

'What are you staring at, boy? You make sure your old man pays his debts or there'll be trouble.'

Jake had shrugged and gone back into the shop. He served for the next hour and then balanced the till before he left the cash in the bank bag in the drawer under the counter for Bob to collect on his way out.

He sat there and Bob McDougal stared at him over the desk, tapping a pen on the wooden top. Finally, he reached into the drawer and pulled out his chequebook.

'I'm not going to beat around the bush,' he said.

'In what way, sir?' Jake's mother might have been poor, and a single mother, but she'd taught her son respect and good manners.

'You've been seeing our Jenni.'

'Seeing?' Suddenly he swallowed; he intended to marry Jenni McDougal when he had enough money, and when he had his own business behind him. But not before then.

'My wife saw you.'

'Saw me?'

'Last month at her birthday party.' McDougal glared at him and Jake lifted his chin. They were nineteen years old and he'd done nothing wrong.

'You were kissing my daughter at the gate between our two properties when you snuck out of the party.'

It was the first time that Jake had kissed Jenni, and it had been a special moment, and he didn't appreciate it being sullied by being spied on, and by being accused of sneaking around.

He wasn't a kid to be chastised. He lifted his chin and held her father's gaze steadily.

'Yes. I kissed your daughter. But as we are both adults, so I don't see a problem with that.'

'I took you on because I thought you could do with some pocket money. It wasn't an invitation to infiltrate yourself into my family. My daughter is not going end up with river trash.' McDougal's voice was as cold as the ice in the cabinets in the room beside them.

Jake stood, pushing the chair back as hot fury flooded his veins. 'I beg your pardon?'

'You heard me, boy. River trash. The Jones always have been and always will be. You will not taint my daughter with a connection to your family.'

Jake stood there unable to believe what he was hearing. He opened his mouth but McDougal yelled at him before he could speak.

'Sit down and listen.' The words were spat at him.

McDougal opened the cheque book and wrote quickly. Jake stayed standing, the only noise in the room apart from the blood surging through his temples was the scratching of the pen on the paper. McDougal stood, ripped the cheque from the cheque book, and shoved it at Jake.

'Take this, and leave town. I don't want to see you around here—or around any of my kids again.'

Jake stared down at the cheque that was now in his hands unable to believe what he'd just heard. The bell on the shop door tinkled as he stood there.

Two thousand dollars.

'Take it and get out. And don't mention it to anyone or you'll be sorry. Go and do your course, and get a job in a different town. Second Chance Bay is not for you.'

Jake had slowly lifted the cheque as McDougal stared at him, his face red, and the smell of alcohol wafting on his breath across the desk. He'd held the man's gaze as he'd torn it into small pieces. Holding his hand above the desk Jake let the scraps of paper flutter down to the desk.

'Don't you ever speak to me like that again, and don't you ever try to buy me out. I won't be working here again until you apologise for the way you spoke about my family.'

Even if he'd known what was going to happen, he wouldn't have reacted in any other way.

Jake had pushed the chair out of his way, turned on his heel and shoved the door open.

He ignored the customers in the shop and the offer of bagging prawns was long forgotten as he ran for the dock, and jumped into his small aluminium tinnie.

He crossed the river to go home to their old house at Second Chance Bay to lick his wounds.

River trash.

Old man McDougal would pay for that.

Chapter Nine

Jenni pushed open the door of the fish co-op and the bell jangled above the door. Matt had gone back to Normanton to see the accountant, but this time Maisie from the caravan park had been available to take over for the day. Jenni was here to relieve her for a lunch break because Mum was busy packing. Now that everyone was home, she and Rick had decided to set off sooner. Rick had turned up the other night towing a brand-new off-road caravan that had been delivered from Brisbane on the back of a huge truck.

'He's obviously got a quid. Owns a few pubs in the north,' Matt said to Jenni as Rick led Mum to the van, his hands over her eyes. A lump filled Jenni's throat as she watched Mum giggle like a teenager.

'She's so happy. It wouldn't matter if he was broke,' she said with a smile.

'True, but Mum's had enough years of that,' Matt said. 'It's time she got a bit spoiled.'

They followed the couple to the van and smiled as their mother exclaimed over the luxury interior.

'Oh my God, look, there's even a washing machine,' she cried as they poked their heads around the door. Rick had smiled as Mum looked around inside, and then he beckoned to Jenni and Matt. He stepped along the footpath away from the van.

'I want to head off earlier than we'd planned. I know you've just got home, Jenni. Will it work okay with you guys if we leave next week?'

Jenni nodded. 'Of course, it will. We're all grownups now.' She put her hand on Rick's arm and reached up to brush his cheek with a light kiss. 'Thank you, Rick. Mum is so happy.'

'I'm a very lucky man. Helen is a good woman.' He lowered his voice. 'And I plan to make an honest woman of her, so who do I ask for permission in the family?'

'Permission for what?' Matt said blankly.

'For permission to marry her, of course!'

Happiness ran through Jenni and she hugged Rick.

'Don't say anything; I'm going to surprise her tonight.' Rick's grin was wide.

'Well, of course, you have permission. I'm the eldest and I say yes.' Matt shook Rick's hand. 'Absolutely yes! I'm very happy for you both too.'

Rick had done the deed, and of course, Mum accepted and was now sporting a massive engagement ring, and busily packing the caravan.

Jenni sighed as she crossed to the counter. Mum was just bubbling with happiness.

'Hi Maisie.'

'Young Jenni! I heard you were home.' Maisie's hair was silver and purple as it had always been, but the lines in her face were a little deeper.

'Not so young anymore.' Jenni walked around and hugged the elderly woman who had befriended the family before Jenni was born. It was over thirty years since she and her husband had first made the trek from Melbourne to Karumba for their annual winter holiday.

Jenni took a deep breath of fresh air as she walked behind the counter. The ever-present smell of nicotine, and Avon perfume was as strong as ever.

'I've missed you, love. Are you home for a visit? Or home to stay?'

'I'm not sure yet.' Jenni changed the subject before she had to answer more questions. 'I hear you've finally moved sites.'

She was answered with a cackle that quickly turned into a smoker's cough. When Maisie recovered, her grin was wide. 'Yeah, love, since my Jack passed away my fun days are over. You heard right though. I've moved the van down to Dunrootin' Lane the past couple of winters.'

Jenni shook her head with a wide grin. 'It's been called that so long they need a street sign up.'

'Nah, a lot of the old codgers find it offensive, they don't know how to have a good laugh at themselves. Now, I'll go and have myself some lunch and a smoke over at the pub. What time do you want me back?'

Jenni shook her head. 'Don't worry about it. I've got nothing else to do. I'll take over for the afternoon if you like.'

'Ooh, you're a good girl. I'll go and play the pokies for a while. If I have a win I'll split it with you.'

'No need.'

Maisie refused to take any money when she filled in at the shop. She always said that it was her daily entertainment talking to the grey nomies as they rolled into town, and always bought fresh prawns on their first day in Karumba. She slipped the plastic apron off and passed it over to Jenni. 'They tell me that nice young man of yours has come back to town too. Is that why you came back?'

Jenni forced out a laughing response. 'Jake Jones? Oh heavens, no. I didn't even know he'd come back. I haven't seen him since I left.'

'I hear he left his fancy boat in France to come back and work with your brothers.

Jenni played dumb and widened her eyes. Honestly, this town had a grapevine like nothing she'd ever seen anywhere else. 'I think Jake's boats are too flash for us.'

Maisie tapped her nose. 'Wouldn't hurt you blokes to have a flash boat.'

'It's up to the boys what they do.' Jenni shrugged. 'I'm here to teach.' She looked at the display cabinet with a grin. 'And to serve prawns when my brother heads out of town.'

'If Matt ever decides to go on the boats, you might find yourself in here full time. It'd be better than being in a classroom with a heap of kids all day. Anything would be better than that in my books.' Maisie's cackle filled the air as the door shut behind her, the smell of Avon perfume lingering.

'There's no chance of that ever happening,' Jenni muttered.

The bell over the door tinkled again and she looked up hoping it might be Matt home early.

Her breath caught in her chest as her gaze encountered the sexy hazel eyes of Jake Jones.

***

'Hi Jenni.' Jake closed the door behind him. 'I was hoping to see Matt.'

She shook her head. 'I'm sorry. You're out of luck. He's gone to Normanton for an appointment.

'Damn. I've got a problem I was hoping he could help me with.'

'Oh?' Jenni was looking past him at the door as though she was hoping he would use it. Her voice was cold and disinterested, and Jake's temper began to simmer.

Who did she think she was to treat him as though he was the river trash that her father had called him ten years ago?

Jenni wasn't the same person she'd been back then. Jake bit down on the cross words that threatened and crossed to the counter. He stood there quietly looking at her until Jenni finally looked at him.

'So, what's the problem?' she said.

'My other boat is on the way down the Gulf, and I'm down a crew member. I was hoping that I could borrow one of your hostesses for my first charter in a few days. I know the boys haven't got another charter for a couple of weeks.

Finally, the bland look left her face as one eyebrow quirked, but her mouth was still set in a tight line. 'You know more about what's happening with our bookings than I do.'

'I wouldn't say that,' he said. 'And I didn't know I'd be down a crew member till Gus rang me just now.'

'Gus?'

'My other captain. And a good mate of mine too.' Jake leaned against the counter. 'I interviewed in Darwin before we headed over here and I was all set, but one of my hostesses broke her arm yesterday. The seas were rough on the way across from Bathurst Island, and she slipped on the wet deck.' Jake ran a hand over his short-clipped hair. 'I want this first charter to be perfect, Jen. It's important to me.'

She nodded and her voice thawed a little. 'I'm sure it is.'

'So, I'm after a hostess. Do you know who works for them? Anyone local or do they fly in?

'A hostess?' Jenni smiled at last. 'What does a hostess do?'

'Serves the meals, clears the tables, services the cabins. Oh, and does the guests' laundry. And works behind the bar and tallies up the drinks every night.'

'Hm, really? I think you might be used to a different level of service in your European marinas.' This time it was a chuckle that bubbled out and Jake relaxed a bit more.

'Dane and Donny and the deckies do all that,' Jenni said. 'And the guests wash their own clothes. At least we offer a washing machine and dryer on the boats. Our charters are rough and ready. For the true fishermen, not for someone looking for a fancy five star holiday.'

'So they're not going to be able to suggest anyone by the sound of things. Damn.' Disappointment ran through Jake. 'Maybe I could find someone in town? Backpackers?'

Jenni shook her head. 'The town's changed Jake. All old locals and grey nomies now. We don't get many backpackers up this way. It's too far off the beaten track and there's not a lot of entertainment at night. Even the Animal Bar is a quiet place for a drink these days. The attraction of the wild and unruly in that famous song has long gone.'

'I'd forgotten about that Red Hot Chili Peppers' song. We thought back then it'd put our town on the international map. Do they still bolt the furniture down in case of bar fights?

Jenni shook her head. 'No. I think if you go there now, according to Maisie you might find a few old locals having a quiet beer or playing the pokies. The town has really changed, Jake. Are you sure you want to start your business here?'

'I'm home, Jenni,' he said simply. 'This is my dream. This is why I've worked so hard over the past ten years.' He looked at her curiously; she obviously wasn't happy about him being home and he wanted to reassure her. 'I'm not going to be competition to your family's business. I want to add to it and I want to help out.'

'So you say.' Her shoulders were straight and her demeanour was still stiff, despite the occasional smile and chuckle.

'Well, you're going to struggle. Matt can't even get a casual to work in the shop. There's only Maisie.'

'And you.' His voice was glum. An idea began to flit through his head as he stared at Jenni. 'When do you start at the school?"

Her eyes narrowed. 'Who told you I was working at the school?'

'Matt, I think it was. Your brothers are all proud of you getting an education, and being a teacher.' Jake pushed himself away from the counter. 'So am I.'

Jenni didn't answer but he noticed the flush tinge her cheeks pink. She wasn't as aloof as she was making out.

'So when do you start?'

She shrugged. 'When school goes back in three weeks. I'll only be working at the local school for a little while. And then I'll go back to Brisbane. That's my home now.' She lifted her chin and her gaze was steady.

A burst of warmth fired in Jake's chest, and moved down to his belly as her blue eyes held his for a long moment.

'So, you're at a loose end for the next couple of weeks?' he said. 'How would you like to come out on *Moonshine* for a five-day charter? Help me out, and we could spend some time getting to know each other again.'

Jenni didn't answer for a moment, but Jake held his breath as the tip of her tongue came out and she moistened her top lip.

'Not really. Do you really think I'd work on *your* boat?'

The warmth inside him changed instantly from desire to anger.

'Why, Jenni? Aren't I good enough for you?' His voice was curt as hurt slammed through him

'I didn't mean that.'

'Didn't you? Sure sounded like it to me. Echoes of the past, hey?' He turned on his heel and called over his shoulder as he pushed the door open. 'Get Matt to call me, if it's not too much trouble in your busy schedule.'

Chapter Ten

The door closed quietly behind Jake and Jenni's hair fell over her face as she lowered her head. She gripped the counter so hard her knuckles whitened, and guilt ran through her. She had been overly rude, and she knew that she'd hurt Jake's feelings. He'd never had that attitude of not being good enough before he'd left. Maybe coming back to town had made him realise he'd done the wrong thing.

Not only by the McDougals but also by the values that she thought he held.

Jake Jones had to have a reason for coming back to town, and she didn't trust him. All this talk of working with her brothers and helping out the family business made no sense.

Why would someone who was obviously as successful as he was want to come back to Second Chance Bay and work with the very people he'd done the wrong thing by?

There was something not right about the whole thing, but there was no way Jenni was going to sit back and let Jake hurt her family again.

And for all his soft looks, and his "I'm proud of you," she wasn't going to let him get close enough to hurt her again.

No way.

Jake Jones could remain at a distance, but by God, she was going to find out why he was here.

The shop was empty so she grabbed a bottle of water from the drinks cabinet and headed out the back.

A stupid move. As she lowered the water bottle, she stared down at the dock. After Mum's party, the afternoons Jake had been in the shop, and Dad had been safely out in the Gulf fishing, Jake would ring up the till and close up. Jenni would wait and they'd sit on the dock together and watch the sunset. No matter how long you lived at Karumba, the stunning sunsets were different each day. There was always a group of tourists at the pub on the point watching the fishing boats come home and enjoying the sea breeze under the lovely cool shade of the coastal almond trees. Jake and Jenni had spent so many afternoons of that last year before life had changed, sitting on the dock waiting for the sun to set in a spectacular golden ball over the silver waters of the Gulf.

She couldn't help smiling as she remembered Jake would count down as it got lower and lower, and the instant the sun slipped behind the horizon, he would hold her close and kiss her.

But only if Dad's boat was out of sight. It was crazy, but Jenni knew deep down that Dad wouldn't approve of them being in love.

Because she was in love with Jake Jones and in that last year, they had planned a future together.

Young love and foolish dreams. That's all it had been. She had been naïve and vulnerable. The only thing she was grateful for was that she'd never slept with him.

Coming home had raised so many different memories. Things that she could put aside when she was in Brisbane, but being back here, there was a happy memory everywhere she turned.

If she could discover why Jake was really here, maybe she'd be able to move on. Maybe she could finally get over him, and be happy.

Ten years was way too long to mourn over a lost relationship. Jenni knew it had made her bitter, and the way she'd argued with her brothers since she'd arrived home was a sign that she needed to lift herself.

She was turning into a shrew.

"My tongue will tell the anger of my heart, or else my heart concealing it will break." When she'd taught *'Taming of the Shrew'* to her English class last term, she knew that described her so well. She had to learn to temper her words. Her broken heart was long ago and in the past.

From now on she'd make an effort to be pleasant.

To everyone.

##

'Two more days, and we'll be on the road.' Helen wiped a hand over her weary face as Jenni walked into the kitchen. 'I'll be glad to take a break.'

Jenni looked around the kitchen and then back at her mother. Casserole dishes covered the benchtops and a huge pot of something delicious was bubbling on the stove. The oven was glowing red, and the smell of cakes baking mingled with the stew.

'What are you doing? You do know you can cook in the caravan?' Jenni walked over and kissed her mother's cheek before she peeked in the pot on the stove. 'You told me it had an oven too, didn't you?'

Helen waved her hand before she turned back to the sink. 'No, this is for all of you. You'll be busy when you start at school, and you've probably forgotten the boys' favourite meals. Dane likes curry, Donny prefers chilli and Matt—'

'Whoa. Stop right there.' Jenni put her hands on her hips and stared at her mother with disbelief, but Mum kept talking.

'And Matt has a sensitive stomach, so just plain casserole for him. He always has had, but you probably didn't know that. And when you iron their jeans, Matt doesn't like creases in his, but the other two do.'

The front door opened and Jenni waited until the footsteps came down the hall. Matt poked his head around the doorway and smiled.

'How was the shop this afternoon, Jen? Busy?'

He walked into the kitchen, followed closely by Dane and Donny. Matt opened the fridge and pulled out three beers.

She stared at her three brothers and her eyes narrowed. Before she could answer they all sat down at the kitchen table and popped open the tops of their stubbies. Her hands clenched as she walked across and stood behind Matt's chair.

'So how should I know that? Didn't you think Maisie was going to be in the shop all day?'

Matt raised his beer. 'I knew you'd stay there after she went for lunch and then I saw her old Datsun at the pub in town.'

Remember, I am not going to be a shrew.

Jenni's voice was very controlled as she regarded her eldest brother. 'So you know me well, do you, Matt? And what about you pair? Do you know how rude you are?' She looked at Donny, who had the grace to look a bit ashamed. Dane was looking down at his beer. 'Maybe Mum who's been slaving over a hot stove all day, so you can eat while she is a thousand kilometres away, would have liked a drink too? Maybe I'd like a beer. You should be over in the animal bar at the pub, you've got no manners!'

Matt stood and clomped to the fridge. 'Would you like a drink, Mum? Sorry.'

'No, I'm fine, thank you.' Mum frowned at her. 'Jenni, what's got up your nose? You've been cranky ever since you came home. Are you feeling well, love?'

A ripple of guilt ran through Jenni. Yes, she had been cranky ever since she'd come home. Bickering with her brothers, and being oversensitive. The not-be-a-shrew affirmation hadn't lasted long.

'I'm sorry,' Jenni said quietly as she took the beer that Matt held out, and pulled out a chair. 'You sit down, Mum. I'll wash the dishes while you have a break.'

'We'll do it together.' Mum stood behind her chair.

Dane looked at Donny, and then they both looked at Matt. 'We'll do the dishes while you both sit down,' he said

By the look on Mum's face, it was the first time that had happened for a long while.

'Thank you,' she said slowly. 'And okay, I will have a wine.' She turned to Jenni. 'Now madam, tell me why you're so upset with your brothers.' Mum hadn't called her madam for years, and the guilt settled more heavily in Jenni's chest. Maybe she should have stayed in Brisbane and looked for a job in another rural area. But the thought of coming home had seen her through a couple of difficult terms at the inner-city school where she'd been a contract casual teacher.

'I'm sorry. You all wore my temper. I'll keep it in check from now on.' Jenni held up a warning finger. 'But that still doesn't mean I'll be cooking and washing up and ironing your jeans for you when Mum goes.'

'We don't expect you to,' Dane said. 'We are quite capable.'

Jenni made a sound a cross between a snort and a laugh. 'I'm pleased to hear that. Besides I won't be here for a week after Mum leaves.'

'Where are you going?' Mum looked worried. 'You haven't changed your mind about working at the school, have you?'

Jenni shook her head. 'No. I'm going out on Jake's first charter as a hostess.' There was no need to tell them she'd just decided that.

Mum choked on her wine, and a flurry of suds landed on Matt's face as he dropped the pan he was scrubbing.

'What?' Dane's voice was quiet. 'Why would you do that?'

'Because I'm the only one in this family who seems to be concerned about what Jake Jones is up to. Why is he so fired up to work with you three? I don't believe a word he says when he reckons he's here because he owes us. So, I'm going to see what he's up to.'

Chapter Eleven

Dane had looked thoughtful when Jenni had asked about Jake's motives, but Matt and Donny had sprung to Jake's defence.

'For goodness' sake, Jen. What's your problem?' Matt shook his head. 'Give the bloke a chance, he's been bloody generous with what he's offered us since he hit town.'

Jenni shook her head. 'No one does things like without a good reason.' She jumped as Mum put her wine glass down with a thud.

'I'm going to bed. I'm tired. Your dinner is on the stove.' She looked at Jenni. 'Would you please put the leftovers in the casserole dishes and put them in the freezer.'

Jenni and the boys were quiet as Mum put her glass in the sink and left the kitchen without a backward glance.

'Now look what you've—'

'Matt. Button it.' Dane's voice was low and firm. 'Everyone just pull back and be a bit thoughtful.'

Matt ran a hand through his tousled curls. He was the only one of the four who had inherited Mum's thick dark curls and her soft nature. 'I'm sorry. I think we're all tired and a bit stressed. But I just want to say one thing.' He turned to Jenni. 'If you insist on going out on Jake's boat, you think long and hard about why you're doing it. If you have an ulterior motive, it's not the right thing to do.'

'I'll be helping out,' she said quietly. 'He came to see you today because his hostess has a broken arm. He actually *asked* me to do it.'

Matt raised his eyebrows. 'I suppose that's okay then.'

After dinner was over and the kitchen cleaned up, her brothers headed to the lounge to watch the news. Mum's door was closed and Jenni stood outside for a moment, tempted to knock but there was no sound coming from inside.

She needed to tell Jake she was going to accept his offer before he changed his mind or found someone else. If her brothers were going to be so trusting, it was up to her to make sure that they were not going to find themselves in something they weren't prepared for.

Jenni closed the front door quietly behind her and headed across the yard. The gate opened with a creak and she paused as she looked at the jungle of long grass on the other side of the fence. As she stood there wishing she'd brought a pair of boots she spotted a flattened path where Jake had made his way over to their place. Slipping through the gate, she glanced across to the old Jones' house. Eerie shadows darkened the verandah on this side, and as she paused there was a scurry of movement in the long grass near the door. Jenni put her head down and followed the flattened grass towards the water, trying not to think of the creatures that could be around.

The boat was in darkness and she wondered if Jake was out. But as she stood there, a light flicked on the upper deck, so she swallowed and walked the last fifty metres to the jetty.

She shook her head. The jetty didn't look safe. The posts were rotten, and it sagged lower on one side.

Why on earth had Jake moored the luxury boat here?

The river was dark and shadowy, and as she approached the jetty, there was a swirl in the water just to her left. She jumped and picked up the pace. When she'd been a kid she'd seen crocodiles climb the high bank and bask in the sunshine on the grass flats above the river; surely they'd not be up here at night?

Not willing to take the risk, she put her head down and ran the last few metres to the timber jetty.

'Jake?' Her breath caught as a bright beam of light was directed her way. 'Are you there?' she called out.

'Jenni?' Jake stepped off the boat onto the dock and walked towards her. 'What's up? Everything okay?'

She nodded, suddenly feeling awkward. 'Yes, I just wanted to talk to you about what you said this afternoon.'

'Yes?' His voice was wary.

'I've decided to help you out. If you still want me to. With the hostess position, that is. I mentioned it to Matt and he said'—Jenni crossed her fingers behind her back— 'that he didn't know anyone.' She had mentioned it to Matt, and that's what he would have said if they hadn't descended into an argument, but she still felt guilty bending the truth. She wasn't being entirely honest, but Jake certainly didn't need to know her reasons.

***

Jake was trying to act low-key. When he'd spotted Jenni coming towards the boat, his heart had sped up. He tried to talk sense to himself and remember the reception he'd had from her since he'd arrived.

'Yeah, sure. Let's talk. But not out here. Come aboard.' He held out his hand. 'Take my hand. Watch where you step; a lot of the planks are rotten. I'd hate to see you end up in the water. I need to get some light rigged up here before the others arrive tomorrow.'

He ignored the twitch as the nerves in his arm jumped when Jenni's cold fingers took his. He led her along the wharf to the far end where Moonshine's stern was protected from hitting the jetty by an inflatable barrier. 'I actually just saw a big croc surface close to the boat.'

'I heard it.'

She let go of his hand as soon as she stepped aboard. Knowing the rules of a boat, she bent down and slipped her thongs off.

83

'Let me put some lights on and then we'll go and sit inside. It's a bit cool out here on the water tonight.' He looked back at her as she followed him quietly. 'I'm pleased you came over, Jen.'

She nodded as he flicked on the bank of lights that lit the saloon and the middle deck. Jenni's indrawn breath was satisfying. Her eyes were wide and round as she looked around, and Jake was grateful that he had taken such care in choosing the interior for the boat. His gaze followed hers and he saw his boat through fresh eyes. The cream-colored drapes that covered the large windows facing the side decks were open so he crossed the room and pressed the switch and they slid closed quietly. Plush burgundy leather sofas that would seat a crowd of eighteen people comfortably formed two squares around the two circular glass coffee tables. On the front wall was a long timber bench where Jake had been working on his laptop when he'd heard her approaching. Fully expecting Matt, he'd been taken aback to see Jenni approaching the jetty.

The windows facing the bow were set high in the wall and curved around to follow the semi-circular shape of the front deck. Moonlight poured in and reflected on the crystal lamp on the bench beneath the window. Jake crossed over and gathered his papers together and put them in a folder, and closed the computer as Jenni watched quietly.

'I was just working on a logo for the bookings website,' he said. 'My web designer has suggested "Exotic Fishing in the Tropics" for a tagline. What do you think?'

Jenni shrugged but he noticed interest flare in her eyes before she looked away. 'Sounds fine to me.'

'Would you like to have a look around the boat before we talk? You can decide then if it suits you.'

Jake couldn't believe that Jenni had come over to say she would help him out. If she was serious, he'd play it cool, but inside he was turning somersaults at her offer. One, because he really needed someone, but second, the thought of having Jenni on the boat with him for five days—even though there would be others around—would give him an opportunity to show her that he was still the guy she'd always known.

It would be hard; there was no way he would ever tell her or any of the McDougal family that Bob had set him up. The man was dead and gone, and it wouldn't be fair to the family to taint their memories of him. There would be nothing to be gained by it. But by his behaviour, and his hard-earned success, Jake knew he could show Jenni that he was a decent, honest and trustworthy man.

At least that's what he hoped for.

Maybe there was a chance that they could revive the feelings that they'd once had for each other, because he'd known the minute that he'd seen her—closed face, cold reception and all— that she was still the person that he had loved. They might have been young, but the feelings that he'd had for Jenni had been strong. Jake had never experienced it again, no matter how hard he'd searched for love in the last ten years.

One look at Jenni, and he'd known she was still in his heart— where she'd always been.

'Yes, I would.' She nodded and looked around and her voice thawed. 'This is really lovely, Jake.'

Hearing her say his name in that slightly husky voice warmed his heart.

He held out his hand and was surprised when she took it again. 'Come on then, I'll give you the grand tour. And then can I offer you dinner? I was about to stop and eat. Or have you eaten?'

One side of her lips lifted in a quirky smile. 'Sort of.'

'Sort of?' Jake tried not to stare too hard at her face. She was still beautiful; her eyes were bright, and her dark lashes lowered as she shook her head. Her high cheekbones held a tinge of pink, and he wasn't sure if it was the sun, or being with him that had caused the slight flush. He could only hope.

'Don't ask. I was busy fighting with the boys. Poor Mum got upset and went to bed, so I didn't feel like eating.'

Jake laughed. 'You lot never change. I thought your Mum would be used to your bickering by now. I got so used to you all fighting when we were kids, I could ignore it.'

'But that's the point. We're grown up now. We should be more mature and be able to get on without arguing all the time. Although—her lips quirked again—'the boys were in the wrong and I gave them a serve about making so much work for Mum.'

'It's families, Jen. It means you care about each other.'

'Maybe. It's just that we never agree. On anything.'

Jake's voice was quiet. 'Enjoy it. I was always envious of you being part of a large family when I was a kid. I guess I tried too hard to be a part of it.' He didn't want to say too much, but this was an opportunity not to be passed up. He could start letting Jenni know the truth without telling her the details. 'But no matter what happened, I'll always be grateful to your family for the start I got in life.'

Things were getting too serious, so he shook his head and smiled down at her.

He tugged on her hand. 'Follow me.

Showing off the rest of *Moonshine* was satisfying. After seeing the guest accommodation, the staff cabins, the stainless-steel commercial galley, and the wide fishing deck, Jenni even asked to see the engine room. Everything he showed her was new and sleek and spotlessly clean.

'And a lazerette storage area too! She's beautiful, Jake. You've done very well for yourself. Is the other boat the same?'

'A little bit smaller. This is the one I'll live on until I get the house done.'

'The house?'

He gestured to the shore. 'Mum's house. I'm going to do it up and live there. That way if the two boats are out on charters, when I hire more skippers, I'll have a home base.'

'Oh. So you are serious about settling back in the Bay?'

'I am.' He grinned and tried to lighten the heavy atmosphere that seemed to keep coming back. 'Now while we talk about the hostess job, let me feed you.'

She held up her hand and shook her head. 'No. I'm fine. Just give me the details. That is if you still need me.'

Jake nodded. 'Oh, I do. And I'm grateful for your offer. I accept.' He stared at her and this time she held his gaze. 'But I must admit I'm surprised, Jen. I thought you weren't too interested when I mentioned it this afternoon.'

Her glance flicked away from his, the tip of her tongue appeared and his interest quickened. He knew her so well still; she was lying to him about something.

'Oh, I thought I'd help out. It'll be nice to be out on the water again. And the main thing that decided me is that Mum will be gone and the boys will have to fend for themselves.' Her smile was forced. 'And this is certainly a better option than the poor old tired *Sally M.* Have the boys seen the boat yet?'

'Not really, Matt had a quick squiz before I came over for dinner. Dane and Donny are coming over tomorrow.'

Her eyebrows rose but she didn't say anything.

'Now before we talk, I'm going to get my dinner. I'm starving.'

'Okay. That's fine.' Jenni looked at Jake with a frown as he crossed to the door that led out to the lower deck.

'Come with me. It's still in the water.'

##

Jenni held her breath as Jake leaned over the bow; if he leaned any further he'd go head-first into the dark water. Her fingers itched to go over and hold his hips to keep him balanced

87

like she would have done once. The tide was roaring in and the water was swirling around the boat, and it moved a little on the mooring. She stared as he straightened up. He pulled in the crab pot, and his biceps bulged and she couldn't help lowering her gaze to the strong thighs encased in snug-fitting jeans.

Jenni's mouth dried and she fought licking her lips again as he turned to her, a triumphant grin lighting up his face. She was going to have to put a stop to these physical reactions if she was going to be spending five days—and nights— in his company.

'Two beauties! Look at these, Jen.'

She crossed the deck and leaned on the rail beside him. Two huge mud crabs were clicking and moving in the trap he'd pulled in. Their dark shells glistened green and dark blue in the moonlight as they snapped and tried to escape. Their walking legs, covered with lightly patterned dots, were getting caught in the mesh of the trap as Jake held them up.

'They're huge! I'd forgotten how big crabs get up here.'

'These are the biggest I've caught yet.' His grin was cheeky and a ripple of warmth ran down Jenni's spine as he held her eyes with his. 'I haven't been able to help myself. I've had crab for dinner every night—apart from your Mum's baked tea—since I arrived. The seafood in Europe is very different to here.'

'Is it? I hope you're not too hungry because they're going to take a while to cook and cool down before they'll be ready to eat,' she replied.

Jake's teeth flashed in the moonlight, and she couldn't help thinking what a good-looking man he'd become.

'This is the third lot of booty for the night. The others are cooked and cooling down in the fridge. I was going to drop in some crabs for your mum. I remembered how much she loved them when your brothers and I used to go crabbing. Her chilli crab was to die for.'

'And me,' Jenni said softly. 'I used to come with you too.'

'Did you come with us? I don't remember.' Jake's face screwed up in a frown as he tipped the crabs into a large bucket.

That was like a dash of cold water, and the happy warmth that had begun to envelop Jenni disappeared. She watched as Jake cleaned the deck down with the towel again. No wonder the place looked so good; Jake had cleaned up every drop of water that had splashed from the trap and the bucket. It was a wonder he was going to take them into the galley and cook on that pristine surface. She couldn't help but compare it with the McDougal boats. The metal rivets on their decks had rusted from years in the salt water, and the decks were stained with the evidence of the many fish caught during hundreds of charters. Dad hadn't been too particular about the upkeep of the boats as long as there was beer on board, fish to be caught and paying customers.

'I also bought a feed of Gulf banana prawns off the trawler this afternoon. Can I tempt you? I won't feel right eating in front of you.'

Jenni smiled ruefully. 'And I suppose you went to the trawler because the witch in the fish shop was so cranky.

He shook his head with a laugh as he stowed the crab trap in a hatch, and then reached for a large towel to wipe off the side of the boat. 'Okay, she might have been a bit unfriendly, but I wanted to go and catch up with the guys on the trawlers too. '

'I'm sorry.' Jenni kept her voice quiet. From now on, she'd make a supreme effort to be pleasant.

Get thee behind me, shrew!

She'd be the smiling hostess, no matter how hard it was. If Jake trusted her, she could get to the bottom of why he was home.

'That's okay, Jen. It's been a long time.'

Chapter Twelve

If anyone had told Jenni that she'd be sitting on a luxury cruiser beneath a full moon with Jake Jones eating huge Gulf prawns a week after she arrived home from Brisbane, she would have said they were crazy.

But here she was, sitting at a polished timber table, eating off fine gold-rimmed white china, as prawn juice ran down her fingers. She nodded her thanks as Jake picked up a linen serviette and passed it to her. As she wiped her hands he stood and cleared the dishes away.

'So tell me more about the trip. Where's the charter going? How many guests, and what sort of clothes do you want the hostesses to wear?' she asked.

Jake rinsed his hands at the sink and came back over and sat down across from her. 'Before we talk business do you want to go and have a wash?' Jenni nodded and stood, trying to remember where the closest bathroom was.

'Use the powder room off the deck. It's the closest.'

'Thank you.' Jenni went out onto the deck, looking for the door Jake had pointed out when he had given her the tour. A cool breeze had sprung up and the temperature had dropped a few degrees, and she pulled her light cardigan round her shoulders. Pushing open the door, her eyes widened and she shook her head as she entered the spacious powder room.

Gleaming white basins and fuchsia-pink guest towels lined the back wall. She bit back a grin, wondering if it would look like this after a few fish had been caught on deck and the guests came down here to clean up. At the same time, she marvelled at how well the boat was set up and how well it was kept. Jake was here alone this week, so he must keep it like this. He could teach the McDougal brothers a thing or two.

Soon it would be her job. For a moment she wondered if she was being foolish. How much would she be able to find out while Jake was busy with charter guests and she was working to keep the boat cleaned, and the guests happy? She straightened her shoulders as she washed her hands; she would do it.

A sweet fragrance drifted in the air, and her eyes opened further as she turned and spotted the fresh white Asian lilies in a glass vase on the table beside a pile of thick white towels. As Jenni looked back at the oval gilt-edged mirror, she started with surprise. Her cheeks were flushed and her eyes were bright. She looked . . . animated.

With a frown, she wiped her hands, before rinsing her face and patting it dry. She ran her hand over her hair, smoothing back the loose tendrils that had come out of her ponytail. She straightened the towel on the rail and headed back to the dining room.

It was time to get to business.

##

Jake insisted on walking Jenni back to the house after they had made the arrangements for the charter. It would leave in three days when the guests arrived by light plane. It was the same day that Rick and Mum planned to head west.

'Call over and pick up your uniform when the other boat comes in tomorrow. And you can meet the other crew members too,' Jake said.

As they reached the gate, he put out a hand and touched her arm lightly. 'I really appreciate what you're doing, Jen. You've got me out of a fix.'

She cleared her throat and went to step back, but Jake circled her wrist gently with his fingers and tugged her closer.

'Not a problem. You want to help us, I can repay the favour,' she said and tried to smile. Her heart was thudding as his fingers slid down and held her hand.

He shook his head. 'Nothing to repay, and speaking of that, I hope you understand I'll be paying you for the trip. It's not a favour.'

'I don't expect to get paid. You don't have to. I'll enjoy being on the water.' She lifted her eyes and despite herself, she knew her expression was almost coquettish. It was the reaction to his fingers brushing gently on her skin. 'And I'll enjoy getting to know you again, Jake. Find out all about your plans here.'

'And I will too. Enjoy getting to know you.' Jake leaned over and brushed his lips over her cheek and Jenni froze. Before she could pull back or speak, he'd let her go and turned to walk back through the gate.

Jenni stood and watched until Jake was at the jetty. He turned back and waved before he disappeared on the deck. She opened the front door and headed to the kitchen. She was wide awake, and her thoughts were in turmoil.

For someone who was here with an ulterior motive, Jake was just *too* nice. He'd welcomed her aboard, he'd shown her around and he'd answered all her questions openly and without hesitation.

The main thing that she'd been wondering about, and that she'd thought was too gauche to ask was where the hell had he got all his money from?

He'd left here ten years ago, with nothing. Now that she'd seen the boat—and there was another one, she realised that Jake's boats were worth millions. They were like nothing that Second Chance Bay had ever seen before.

She went to switch the kitchen light on and jumped as someone moved near the table.

'Oh Mum, you scared me,' she said as the light came on. 'Couldn't you sleep?'

'No. My head was full with what I've got left to do.' Her mother shook her head. 'I heard you go out, and I waited for you to come in. I need to talk to you.'

'Over a cuppa?' Jenni asked with her head on the side.

'Sounds good.'

Jenni stood by the stove as the kettle boiled and she poured the water into the pot. She lifted down two fine china cups and saucers and took the milk from the fridge.

'I've missed you, Jen. Having a natter with the boys over a cup of tea wasn't like having my daughter home. And now you're here, and I'm heading off. Murphy's Law, isn't it?'

Jenni pulled out a chair and sat down and watched as her mother picked up the pot and spun it around before she poured the tea.

'You'll be back before you know it.' A frown creased her forehead. 'Unless Rick wants to stay over there?'

'No, he assures me we'll come back here, as soon as he gets the pub up and running and gets good managers in. This is home. For both of us.'

'So when's the wedding? I hope I get to be bridesmaid.'

'Not for a while. I want to get used to being a part of Rick's life first. By the time we get married, you'll probably have kids who can be page boys and flower girls.'

'That could be a while,' Jenni said as she sipped her tea.

'Am I right in thinking you've been over to see Jake?' Mum's voice was cautious.

Jenni lowered her gaze and nodded. She knew she'd upset Mum when she'd said she was going to find out what Jake was up to.

'He's a good boy, Jen. And I'm very pleased he's done so well for himself.'

Again, she nodded, sipping her tea so she didn't have to answer, but there was no stopping Mum.

'I hope you sorted things with him and you've gotten over this silly idea that Jake is on some sort of vendetta. He doesn't have a dishonest bone in his body, you know.' Mum stared at her and her eyes were intense. 'You do know that, don't you?'

Jenni knew she'd upset Mum enough tonight, so she nodded. 'I do. He's a good man,' she said softly. She was pleased that she did because Mum visibly relaxed. Her shoulders eased and she rested her chin in her hand.

'Oh, that's so good. I can go away and not worry about you. It was making me feel ill, actually. I'm pleased you sorted it out. I hoped he'd tell you the truth.'

Jenni didn't know what her mother was talking about, so she nodded again and then reached for the packet of biscuits in the middle of the table. 'Tim Tam, Mum?'

'Why not? Now tell me all about his boat and where you're going to.'

It was after midnight by the time they stopped chatting, and Jenni smiled as Mum hugged her good night.

'It sounds wonderful, and I'm sure you'll have a fabulous time out there. Text me some photos, won't you?'

'I will. And you send me some of your trip west.'

They walked up the hall together, and Jenni opened her bedroom door. 'Night, Mum. Sleep well.'

'I will now,' her mother said with a smile.

Jenni closed the bedroom door and leaned her back against it. *What a night.*

Sitting chatting with Jake as though nothing apart from the role of the hostess was on her mind, and then convincing Mum she didn't have a vendetta going against Jake had been exhausting.

Jenni yawned, but there was one more thing she wanted to do before she went to bed. She crossed to the desk and booted up her laptop, hoping the intermittent internet service was working tonight. Dane and Donny were online gamers, and she could barely get her email to download when they were online. But the house was in darkness, so she assumed they'd gone to bed. The connection was fast and she opened up a search engine and typed in Jake Jones wondering how many there would be in the world.

To her surprise, her Jake—*no, not my Jake*—the Jake she was looking for came up in number one position in the search results.

Jenni read the first article, her eyes widening. By the time she'd scrolled through at least twenty articles, she was even more convinced that Jake was up to something.

And then she searched through the images. A strange feeling settled in her stomach as she flicked through photo after photo of Jake, each time with a different beautiful woman in evening dress on his arm.

She swallowed.

And I sat there tonight on his luxury boat in a pair of faded jeans and a ratty old cardigan.

The bylines under the photos referred to him as the "outback playboy from down under", and "Aussie millionaire" was peppered through some of the articles.

Aussie millionaire!

She kept reading, trying to get some clue as to where Jake had made his money, but there was nothing.

The next page she clicked on was "Exotic Fishing in the Tropics", the tag he'd mentioned tonight. Her eyes almost popped as she went to the booking page and read what the charter fee was per person for a five-day charter.

Almost twenty thousand dollars per angler!

Two hours later, Jenni had exhausted every search avenue. She'd even found Facebook references to Jake in her searching. A photo of Jake in a bar in Monte Carlo, looking no older than when he'd left here. She checked the date; he would have been twenty-two when it was taken.

Me and my deckie mates, the friend who'd posted the photo had tagged it. *Outback Jake.*

A deckie wouldn't have made the money that Jake would have needed to get those two boats. The boats with the fancy china, and the best of everything.

From Outback Jake to Outback playboy.

Jenni dropped her head in her hands.

The only thing she could think of was that Jake had come by his wealth dishonestly. There was no other way he could have afforded those luxurious boats.

Maybe something had happened and he'd fled the Cote d'Azur like he'd left town here.

But why was he here?

Her thoughts went round and round in circles. She threw herself onto her bed and closed her eyes, but her sleep was broken by dreams.

Dreams where Jake was holding her in his arms and telling her he was sorry.

Chapter Thirteen

The night before *Moonshine* and *Starshine* were due to leave on their respective charters, Rick decided to hold an impromptu farewell at the pub. He and Helen were leaving on their trip tomorrow, the same day the charters were heading out into the Gulf.

Not only did Rick invite half the town; he invited Jake and the crew from his boats.

Jake arrived late with Gus; they'd been filling the fuel and water tanks of both boats over at the main dock in town. Then Jake had insisted on a final walk through the two vessels, to make sure that everything was perfect. As they walked along the river to the pub, Gus shook his head.

'Was everything to your satisfaction, *sir*?' His eyes glinted as he chuckled.

Jake nodded. 'It was. There's only one problem.

Gus turned with a frown. 'What?'

'My other skipper is a smart arse.'

Gus laughed as they waited for a space to clear as a crowd jostled to get through the opening in the fence. 'Someone has to keep you in line.' He looked around at the dozens of people under the trees. 'Jeez, this is some big party for a small town.'

Jake shook his head. 'No. Most of these people are tourists here to take photos of the sunset. They'll disappear the instant it drops below the horizon.'

The tiki torches along the edge of the river bank flickered in the early evening breeze as the sun sank lower. Dozens of photographers stood with cameras poised, several even had tripods set up. Gus and Jake waited until there was a gap in the crowd and then Gus pointed to a table at the edge of the open-air bar. 'There's the crew over there.'

The indoor section of the pub was packed, and Jake spotted Rick serving behind the bar as they made their way across to the table.

'Hey, guys.' Jake slid onto the bench seat opposite Claudette, the hostess he'd hired for *Starshine*. It was a small charter world; he'd been pleased when she'd turned up to be interviewed in Darwin. A few years ago, he'd worked with the young Frenchwoman on a charter to Nice, and he knew she had a great work ethic. She'd often mentioned wanting to work in Australia, and during the interview, she'd told Jake she'd followed her dream after a couple of years in the Caribbean. She'd been in Australia for almost a year working in the Whitsundays and had agreed to do Jake's first charter, and then she was flying back to Europe because her visa had expired.

'The French accent will go down well with the clients,' Gus had said when he'd first met Claudette and then he'd winked at Jake. 'Not to mention, she's drop dead gorgeous.'

'She's also an excellent worker,' Jake had said. 'And a top person too. A great sense of humour.'

Gus had sighed. 'My perfect woman.'

'Hey, Jake, Gus.' The two men on the opposite side of the table greeted them both before Gus headed for the bar. Ryan and Cade were both highly experienced deckies who'd come with great references. Ryan had worked out of Darwin, but Cade had worked around the world for different charterers.

'All set for departure tomorrow?' Cade asked.

Jake nodded. 'All good.' He looked around. 'Where's Tony and Jonathon?'

'They're in talking to the chefs in the kitchen. Apparently, there was a delivery of fresh fruit and vegies here today, and they're doing a deal for some extra fresh provisions,' Ryan replied.

Jake leaned back and nodded as Gus put a schooner in front of him. 'Thanks, mate.' He was very satisfied with the crew he'd hired. A chef, a deckie and a hostess for each boat would ensure that the charter ran smoothly. All they needed now was for the guests to fly in tomorrow and his new business would be up and running.

He was nervous. A whole new venture into an area that he was familiar with shouldn't have fazed him, but the investment in setting up the boats and moving to Second Chance Bay had been significant. He'd breathed a sigh of relief when the first two charters had filled within two days of advertising.

'Stop looking so worried, Jake.' Gus held his beer up. 'Cheers, mate, and congratulations on your new venture. It's going to be great.'

'I wish I had your confidence, mate.' Jake stared into his beer and Gus shook his head. 'It's a bit like pre-wedding jitters, isn't it?'

'Who's getting married?'

Jake looked up at Matt who was standing beside him. 'Hi, Matt. No one is. Gus is just giving me a serve because I'm nervous about the first charter.'

'It'll be great. The whole town's talking about it, and how good it is to see you bring your business to town.'

'Really?' Jake moved along so Matt could sit down on his left.

'Yeah. You're a hit already.' Matt put his beer on the table. 'Looks like you've got a top crew too. Your two chefs are in there helping Mum.'

'Helping?'

'Yeah, it's really busy in there and they've both pitched in and helped. Community spirit already.' He looked at Jake with a slight grin. 'You want to watch your new hostess too. One of the chefs was seriously chatting her up in the kitchen.'

Jake looked over at Claudette who was deep in conversation with Ryan and Cade. He frowned. 'My hostess?'

Matt laughed. 'My sister, you boofhead. You know Jenni? Your other hostess.'

'Oh.' Heat rose up Jake's neck. 'Why should I watch her? You mean because there shouldn't be romance between the crew? I've made that clear in the staff procedures. I don't care what happens on shore, but nothing once we're on board.'

Matt shook his head. 'God, you're thick, mate. I meant you had some competition.'

Jake didn't answer for a moment. 'I wish, Matt, but she can't stand me. I was surprised when she agreed to help out.'

'She'll come round. Jenni's done it tough the past few years. She put herself through uni, there was no money when Dad died, and she worked two jobs at night for a few years. Then she's only had contract work since she graduated. Not a bad thing though. I've got a feeling she'll stay here now.'

Jake shook his head. 'She told me she was going back to Brisbane.'

'A bit of self-protection there. She's not as immune to you as she makes out.'

'We'll see.'

'Speak of the devil.' Matt gestured across the bar area. Jenni was making her way over to their table. Jake was pleased; he'd been busy since *Starshine* had arrived and she hadn't been over to meet the crew yet, although it sounded like she'd already met Tony and Jonathon tonight.

He narrowed his eyes; his two chefs who were walking very close to her.

Jake ignored the surge of jealousy that ran through him when Tony reached across and took Jenni's arm. She stopped and turned to him with a wide smile.

Wake up to yourself, he thought. He should be pleased his crew were all getting on well.

Very well, he thought as Jenni's laugh reached them. He hadn't heard that for a long time.

The three were still laughing as they reached the table.

'Hi. Looks like you three have already met.' He moved out from behind the seat and stood next to Jenni. 'Jenni. Meet the rest of the crew. Ryan and Cade are our deckies, and Claudette is the other hostess. And this is Gus.'

As Jenni lifted her hand in a friendly greeting her perfume wafted around him. Despite the cool breeze, it was hot in the crowded area, and she had dressed accordingly. A pretty pink dress draped her soft curves and he was hard-pressed not to stare. Her lips were glossy with some sort of pink stuff, and she'd done something to her eyes, and they looked even wider than usual.

Her cheeks were rosy and her smile wide; he had to concentrate on not reaching out to pull her close to his side. His heart ached for what he'd lost.

Ten years of their lives wasted. All he hoped was that he could convince Jenni that he still loved her, and that he was worth loving back.

He was. And he was going to do his best to convince her of that.

***

Jenni looked at Jake as he sat down and everyone moved along the bench seat so she and the other newcomers could slide in. As she paused, the other places were taken so she had no option but to sit next to him.

Look on it as a positive, she thought; she could see him in action with his crew before the charter began and see what made him tick.

101

Stupid. I know what makes him tick. I just need to reconcile that with what happened and what he is now.

The conversation was animated and Jenni sat back and let it wash around her.

'So you have the charter route planned, Jake? The weather gods have been kind?' As Jake leaned forward to answer Cade, his leg pressed against Jenni's and she stiffened. She was right on the edge of the seat with no room to slide along, and if she swung to the side, it would be obvious that she was uncomfortable. She sat perfectly still and tried to ignore the little frissons of trembling nerve endings that were firing up with the pressure of Jake's leg against hers.

'Yep. We're going to head out to Sweers Island to start and then we'll head out deep and *Moonshine* will follow the western side of the Gulf over to Limmen Bight. We've got an ornithologist on board who wants to look at the birds there. Gus will head deeper and take the serious fishermen out deep for the last three days.' Jake turned to Jenni. 'I had an enquiry from a scientific group for a similar trip to the bird islands but I've passed that on to Matt. I think your boats could handle the bigger groups.'

'Oh,' she said.

'Yes, I know your brothers haven't ventured away from fishing charters before. There are some great opportunities for scientific trips and some educational government tenders to apply for.'

'I'm sure Matt was pleased.' Jenni smiled but her heart wasn't in it.

Why is Jake so goddamned determined to help my brothers out?

'Yeah. I think he was. We've got to help each other out in this business.'

'That's a generous attitude,' she said carefully as he looked down at her. Jake's eyes were bright and he looked relaxed and happy.

'Jake's always gone out of his way to share his knowledge since I met him.' Gus was looking at them curiously. 'He's done himself out of a bit of business though because he's willing to share.'

'Is that why you came home?' she asked.

'No. I came home for lots of reasons but that wasn't one of them. There was still plenty of work over in the Med.'

She waited for him to elaborate, but Jake turned to Tony. 'When are you loading the supplies onto the boat? The chopper for the first guests for *Moonshine* arrives at ten thirty in the morning. I'd like to have it all stowed by ten at the latest.'

'No problem, boss. Matt and Dane are helping me bring the stuff over from the cool room in the fish shop and Helen's sending the fresh produce over from the pub first thing.'

'Good. 'He nodded. 'Gus, you're all set? Is there anything the crew need to know? If we have a bit of a Q and A now, we can settle back and enjoy the night.'

'No, we're all good. Still embarking at five p.m.?'

'Yep. Tide's good for that.' Jake turned to Jenni. 'Your uniform was okay?'

He'd sent it back with Matt yesterday afternoon. Jenni had tried it on and it had fitted perfectly. Knee-length navy shorts and a white collared shirt with the *Moonshine* logo, as well as a cap with *Moonshine* embroidered on the brim. Jake had also sent a message to say any colour white-soled shoes would be fine.

'Yes. All good. What time do you want me there tomorrow?'

'Sorry, I thought I'd already told you that. If you can be there at eight, Claudette will take you through the procedures for meeting and greeting and getting the guests settled. We'll give them lunch on board, and then Cade will do some fishing talks in the afternoon.'

A tendril of excitement began to unfurl in Jenni's chest. If only she was going on this trip purely to work. Without her ulterior motive of sussing Jake and his motives out, she could really enjoy the week. It had been a long time since she'd gone out on a charter. When she was in her mid-teens, Dad had let her go on a couple of fishing charters on *Elsie.*

In the days when Dad had been happier and hadn't carried that dark look and bad mood on his shoulders.

Now that she was an adult and knew the financial difficulties that a business could face, she could understand more why Dad had changed. The financial pressures must have become burdensome. All she could remember was Mum looking worried, and Dad spent a lot of time at the pub in town. It had been a relief to leave and head to Brisbane to get away from the tense atmosphere, especially when Jake had left, and she no longer had anyone to talk to about the situation.

When he'd been out on the water, Dad had been happy. He knew where the fish were—the locals used to say the McDougals could smell the fish on the wind and knew where to go to get the best catch. That was one of the reasons their charters had been the most popular back in the early days.

Jenni swallowed as the excitement dissipated and a heavy sadness settled in her chest.

Why was she doing this? Mum was about to leave and the boys were doing okay. She should just go back to Brisbane and pick up her old life.

Jenni jumped as Jake's breath warmed her cheeks as he leaned closer and spoke quietly.

'You okay, Jen? You're not worried about working on the boat, are you?'

She shook her head but as she went to speak the noise of the conversations rose around them.

'Too noisy,' she mouthed back.

Jake nodded to the shore. 'Come for a walk with me.'

Reluctance warred with her desire to go with Jake, but it would have looked strange if she'd refused. Jenni slid out of the bench seat and waited for Jake to follow. He led the way past the low fence and the coastal almond trees. The sun was hovering over the horizon and a burst of golden light spread over the dark blue water. The red and green channel lights flickered in the distance and the lights of the McDougal croc tour boat winked as it headed back to the dock. Dane and Donny had taken an early tour out tonight so they could get back for Mum and Rick's farewell.

They reached the sand and stood looking over the water. After a moment of silence, Jake reached out and took Jenni's hand and she caught her breath.

'Is everything okay, Jenni? You looked really worried back there. You'll be fine.' He chuckled. 'I'm not a hard taskmaster, and anything you need to know, just ask me.'

'No, I'm looking forward to it.' She decided to be honest with him, it wouldn't hurt. 'I was thinking about when I used to go out with Dad on the charters when we were in high school. Back in the good old days.'

Jake dropped her hand and turned back to look at the water. 'Yeah, the good old days.'

She was surprised to hear the cynical tone in his voice. Before she could answer, the PA system crackled and Rick's voice came over the speakers.

'I'd like to welcome everyone here tonight. After dinner, I've got some thank yous to make and we've got some celebrating to do, and I'd like to get my lovely lady out of the kitchen sooner than later, so if you haven't ordered your meal yet, please come on up and place your orders now.'

'Come on.' Jenni turned to go back but Jake's hand fell gently on her shoulder. She turned back slowly. His face was in the shadows, his head silhouetted by the great orange ball of sun on the horizon.

'Wait.' His voice was soft. 'Watch the sunset with me first. Like we used to.'

'No, Jake. We need to order. Rick wants Mum out of the kitchen.' Her voice was harsh. If Jake had taken her in his arms and counted down the sunset with her, Jenni knew she would have cried.

Cried for what they had lost, and for what they had become.

She turned on her heel and left him on the sand, watching the sun slip below the horizon—alone.

Chapter Fourteen

Despite being confident that she could handle the hostess work, Jenni wiped her hands nervously on her shorts as Jake turned *Moonshine* towards the main dock in town. He'd been quiet since Claudette had gone back to *Starshine* and both boats had left the dock at Second Chance Bay and headed to the port in town. The smaller boat was following *Moonshine* along the river.

Jenni had checked the guest rooms, set the tables for lunch, and put the fresh flowers that had been delivered onboard this morning into each of the cabins, as well as the saloon and the dining areas. As they approached the public dock, her eyes widened. A small crowd of people stood next to a minibus with the *Moonshine* and *Starshine* logos sign written on the side, along with a background of blue water and jumping fish.

A bus just for the short trip from the airport three hundred metres away? *Just how rich was Jake?*

The playboy description she'd seen on the internet and the pictures of him in evening dress came back into her mind. She'd been softening towards him ever since her harsh dismissal of him at sunset last night. Guilt had rippled through all her night and she hadn't slept well. It had lasted through the speeches Rick had made, through the congratulations to the older couple on their engagement, and when Mum had come up and hugged her and wished her a good trip.

When Mum had turned to Jake and hugged him, she'd heard her say, 'Look after my girl.'

Dane and Donny and Matt had been in fine form, and each of them had bought Jake a beer until he'd held up his hand and said, 'soda water for me for the rest of the night. I'm skippering tomorrow.'

Why is it only me who can see Jake for what he is?

Why was the rest of her family falling over themselves to be nice to him, and to listen to all of his suggestions?

Mum had hugged her tight this morning after they'd shared a pot of tea at daybreak in time for Jenni to walk over to the boat.

'You look nice in your uniform, love.'

'Thanks. I look the part anyway,' she replied with a laugh. Matt poked his head around the door with a yawn. 'How long till you both leave?'

'I'm going in ten minutes,' Jenni replied.

'Rick's picking me up at seven.' Mum lifted the pot. 'Want a cuppa?'

Matt nodded. 'I'll tell Dane and Donny you're both about to go.'

Sitting at the kitchen table with Mum, and her three brothers in their PJs made Jenni smile, even though she knew Mum was heading a few thousand kilometres away from them. After the pot was drained and almost a whole loaf of bread had been toasted and demolished by her brothers, Jenni stood. Her small bag was packed and waiting by the door.

'Enjoy yourself, pipsqueak,' Matt said. Donny and Dane echoed his comment, with their mouths full.

'Enjoy cleaning those fish,' Donny said.

She dropped a kiss on the top of his head as she walked past. 'I do it better than you anyway.'

Mum had followed her outside and held her arms out for a hug. 'You have a great time, darling. And Jenni, can I ask you just one thing?'

Jenni smiled and nodded. 'Of course.'

'You be nice to Jake, okay?'

She'd nodded jerkily.

'Cake's out of the oven.' Tony's voice interrupted her thoughts and she forced a smile to her face. She'd been disappointed when she'd realised Tony was the chef on *Moonshine;* he'd been a little bit too friendly and familiar last night, and she hoped he knew that once they were on board, there was a rule for staff behaviour.

'Thanks. I've got the coffee pots on and the table's set for lunch. The coffee tables are ready for morning tea to be served.'

'Interesting mix of guests.' Tony nodded to the wharf as Cade jumped off the bow and secured the ropes to the bollards. He waited there until *Starshine* eased in on the other side of the dock and secured her ropes too.

Jake helped Cade lift the gangplank down before he walked onto the jetty. Jenni watched as he shook the hands of the men, and smiled as he took the hands of the only two female guests who stood at the back of the group. For a moment she thought he was going to kiss their hands, and she smothered a laugh. He wasn't that European.

'I'm looking forward to the charter,' Jenni replied. 'I hope they're not too hard to please.'

'If you have any problems, don't hesitate to ask. I'm happy to help you with anything.'

She went to say thank you, but then Tony added. 'You know where my cabin is.'

She nodded briskly. 'If I have any questions, I'm sure Jake will be happy to answer them. He's already offered.'

Tony's eyebrows rose. 'Whoops, am I poaching on the captain's territory?'

Jenni held his gaze and didn't confirm or deny his assumption. It might make life easier if Tony thought that she was involved with Jake. Everyone knew they'd known each other for a long time. She walked to the deck where the gangplank joined the boat and watched as Jake directed the guests to the respective vessels. Claudette was standing at the top of the gang plank on *Starshine* and she gave Jenni a wide smile as the first guests headed to each boat.

Jake walked ahead of them and Jenni stood back as the six guests for *Moonshine* boarded. Tony and Cade came and stood beside her.

'Welcome aboard everyone. I'd like you to meet our lovely hostess, Jenni, our fabulous chef, Tony, and you've already seen our deckhand, Cade in action. Because we're such a small group, there's no need for name tags.' Jake turned to the crew. 'I'd like to introduce our guests to you.'

Jenni put her hands behind her back. For some silly reason, her hands were shaking as Jake did his professional spiel; he had a commanding presence.

'Professor Jim Ramsey, and his wife, Leonora.' The professor and his wife smiled as Jake introduced them.

'And this is Greg Saunders, Pat Andrews, Alan Ward, and last but not least, Ken Erikson.'

As the four men returned the greeting, Jake stepped back. 'I'm off to the wheelhouse now. Jenni will show you to your cabins, and then morning tea will be served. I'll be back down to join you for any questions you may have.' He glanced at Jenni and she nodded.

She'd familiarised herself with the cabins that had been allocated and stepped up to the professor and his wife. 'If you'd like to follow me, I'll show you to your cabins first. Cade has already put your bags in there for you.'

Once the guests had been shown to their various cabins—each of the men had been allocated a single cabin—meaning Jenni had five cabins to service twice a day, she hurried back to the saloon. Tony had put a plate of warm scones covered with a tea towel on each coffee table along with single plates of freshly made carrot cake with cream on the side.

'Yum, smells great,' Jenni said as she checked the coffee pot.

'There's plates served out in the galley for you and Cade. The captain will have his with the guests. Come and have it now, you've got time for a quick cuppa before they come up.'

Jenni grabbed a coffee and hurried to the galley, one eye out for the appearance of the first guest. Tony took her through the procedure for the serving of the cold platters for lunch and she was pleased to note his new professional distance.

As long as he doesn't say anything to Jake about thinking that he and the new hostess were an item.

Leonora Ramsey walked along the deck past the open galley window. Jenni drained her coffee, dabbed at her mouth with a serviette and hurried to the door. 'Great cake, thanks Tony.'

***

Jake watched as Jenni served and cleared away lunch. Her movements were deft, and she was professional as she engaged the guests in friendly conversation. After the guests left the dining tables to go back to their cabins, he sought her out in the galley. His eyes narrowed as he stood at the door. Jenni and Tony were standing close to each other, deep in conversation. Her smile was wide and natural as she looked up at the chef, and Jake waited until she went back to the sink before he walked in.

He injected a bright note into his voice. 'Thanks, both of you. Great lunch, and nicely served.'

'Thanks, captain. Would you like to look at the menu for dinner? I was just showing Jenni which wines to chill.'

Jake shook his head. 'No need. I have every confidence it will be excellent, thanks Tony.' If there was one thing he knew was important, it was to show his crew he had confidence in them.

Tony nodded and went back to the cool room.

'Jenni. Could you come up to the wheelhouse for a moment?'

Jake was angry at himself. It was stupid to be jealous because Jenni was talking to Tony. She was simply doing her job, but he couldn't handle the thought of her being interested in someone else. It was something he was going to have to get over, because if anything, the longer he'd been in town, Jenni's attitude to him had

111

cooled even more. He stepped back and gestured for her to precede him and followed her up the polished timber stairs to the top deck.

'Have a seat, please.' He pointed to the second swivel seat next to his.

'Is there something wrong, captain?'

His eyes narrowed at her tone. It was very different to the friendly way she'd been speaking to Tony a few minutes ago.

'No. I just wanted to check that you were on top of everything, Jenni. Any questions? Problems? You know what you have to do for the rest of the day?'

Jake stared past her to the jetty.

Jeez, he was going about this the wrong way.

'Yes. I'm fine. Claudette was thorough. I know where everything is, and I know what needs to be done.' She lifted her face to his and a glimmer of a smile appeared. 'In fact, I don't think I'm going to be very busy, am I? Once the cabins are serviced in the mornings, there's not a lot left for me to do apart from the meals.'

Jake let himself grin. 'You could help Cade with the fish filleting.'

'If there's any fish caught.'

'Don't you worry about that. My charters will be renowned for the fish we catch.' The atmosphere lightened as Jenni's laugh filled the wheelhouse.

'Don't tell me the boys taught you how to smell the fish out?'

Jake shook his head. 'No, I have to be honest. Today's technology is probably better than that.' He pointed to the large screen of a state-of-the-art fish finder on the console.

'That's cheating.' Jenni shook her head. 'Not as good as the old ways.'

'I guess I have to agree, and that's why I want to support the boys with your charter boats. There's a lot of fishermen who prefer to chase the fish without modern technology.'

Her expression clouded for a fleeting moment, before she looked back at him. Her voice was low and intense. 'Don't get me wrong, Jake. I appreciate what you seem to want to do.'

Seem to. He lifted his chin and waited for her to continue.

'You seem so keen to help the boys build our charter business back up.'

He nodded.

'But what I don't get is why you would want to?'

Jake kept his voice controlled. They were getting too close to what he didn't want Jenni to know. 'Can't the why just be that I want to share my skills with people that I grew up with? Men who I respect and admire? Men who taught me a lot over the years before I left?'

The last three words hung in the air between them. Jake would never tell Jenni why he'd left town. If she ever came to trust him, it would be without knowing why he had.

He didn't want to burden her with the truth.

Chapter Fifteen

The sun was low in the sky as *Moonshine* left the dock and led the way to the river mouth and the two motor cruisers made their way out into the Gulf. Jake slowed down each time one of the mosquito fleet boats came in through the heads so the wash of the cruiser didn't reach the small boats. Jenni stood on the bow and waved as they passed the sand bar where Dane and Donny had a full complement of guests out watching the sunset. As they waved back, Jake tooted the horn above. Their guests were all up on the top deck with their cameras.

Jenni moved back to the saloon. As soon as the sun slipped out of sight it was time to serve the pre-dinner drinks and canapés that Tony was preparing in the galley. As she hurried around to the passageway that ran along from the bow to the stern, she caught her breath as Jake's hands grabbed her shoulders before she ran into him.

'Sorry, I wasn't watching where I was going.'

'All good. I saw you back there. I was coming down to watch the sunset with you.'

Heat rose up Jenni's neck as Jake's hands continued to hold her gently.

His voice was low. 'We need to get this sunset watching organised. I'm not going to give up, you know, Jen.'

She frowned at his enigmatic words. 'Give up on what, Jake?'

'Convincing you to watch a sunset with me.'

She shook herself from his grasp and pointed to the sun as it hovered above the horizon. 'I'm here, you're here. The sun is setting. You can't get more organised than that. Excuse me, Jake. I have canapés to put out.'

Jenni's breath caught as Jake's fingers tightened and he looked around. The guests were up top, Tony was in the kitchen and there was no sign of Cade. He lowered his head closer to hers and before she could step back, his lips brushed her cheek, just above the corner of her lips.

Jenni put her fingers to her cheek as he stepped away.

'Now we're organised. And I'm happy. Think about that, Jen.'

Before she could answer, Jake turned and hurried back to the wheelhouse, where he'd obviously left Cade.

She was thoughtful as she walked to the saloon. Maybe that was the way to find out what he was up to.

Respond a little bit, and get his trust.

Jenni nodded. It couldn't hurt as a strategy.

And it could be pleasant, said the little voice deep in her heart.

##

Dinner was a noisy affair. The more wine Jenni served, the louder a couple of the younger customers became. Ken and Greg insisted on tipping Jenni each time she poured a glass of wine for them, and there were several of those poured before it was time to serve dessert. She hurried into the galley with the cleared dishes from the main course.

'Tony, do you have a spare jar or a plastic container?'

'Sure.' He opened a cupboard next to the cool room and passed her a tall plastic jar with a red screw top lid. Jenni dug into her pocket and pulled out the six fifty-dollar notes that had been slipped to her during dinner.

She shook her head as embarrassment flooded her. 'I'm not used to this tipping business. It really makes me uncomfortable.'

'It's the way the charters work, sweetheart. All over the world, so don't be embarrassed. It's an endorsement of the great job you're doing. You should know that.'

'It's an indication of how much they're drinking. I feel like giving it back to them in the morning,' she said with a rueful smile as she dropped the notes into the jar and screwed the lid tight.

'Surely you're used to being tipped?' Tony asked as he added a scoop of ice cream to each bowl and then put a fresh mint leaf on top.

Jenni shook her head as she put the jar back into the cupboard. 'This is the first commercial charter I've done at this level of luxury. Or should I say with this level of client. I'm used to working on my family's boats.' She didn't see the need to tell him she was actually a teacher, and doing a favour for Jake.

'Just do the job and smile. I think that younger pair are "fly in fly out" miners. I heard them talking on the deck before. They'll be single and have plenty of disposable income.'

Jenni sighed as she picked up the first two desserts that Tony had plated to take into the dining room. 'I'll try to get used to it.'

The two men were speaking loudly as she placed the dessert plates in front of the professor and his wife. As she turned to go back to the galley for the rest of the desserts, Jake walked down the staircase from the upper deck and glanced over to where the two young men were getting louder.

Jenni paused. 'Would you like your dinner served now, captain?'

Jake turned and held her gaze steadily. 'That would be good, thank you, Jenni.'

As he walked out, she noticed that he went to sit at the table where the two young guys were sitting. The other two older fishermen were sitting with the professor and Leonora.

She asked Tony to serve Jake's dinner and then loaded up four dessert plates and headed back to the dining table, pleased to hear that the conversations had returned to a normal conversational level of sound, as Jake steered the conversation to the fishing tomorrow. When she placed the dessert in front of Ken, he reached into his pocket and she held up a hand.

'No, thank you. It's fine. My pleasure.' She hurried out of the room and back to the kitchen, but caught Jake's frown as she turned to the door.

'Jake's dinner is right to go,' Tony said.

'I'll be straight back for it.' Jenni said as she picked up the last two desserts. 'But I think I'm trouble.'

Tony looked at her curiously. 'What did you do?

'I held up my hand and said not necessary when Ken went to pull out another note for another bloody tip.'

'Customer is always right, sweetheart.' Tony flicked a tea towel over his shoulder.

As she picked up the desserts, Jake's cold voice reached her. 'Tony's right. The customer is always right. What was that all about? The 'it's my pleasure.'

Temper began to simmer in Jenni's chest. Less than twenty-four hours on the boat and she was already regretting it. With her mouth set, she put the plates down, and strode to the cupboard, pulled out the jar and held it up.

'This is what it was all about, *captain*. It mightn't bother you if *customers* want to throw fifty-dollar notes away—three hundred dollars' worth in one meal—but it sure bothers me. If this is what luxury cruising is, you can give me the *Sally M* charter any day.'

While she stood there and eyeballed Jake, Tony disappeared into the cool room.

'I'm sorry. I can understand why you feel uncomfortable. That's a bit over the top.'

'Do you really think that, or are you just saying it to make yourself look better, Jake? It's all about the money for you, isn't it?' Jenni's voice rose in volume and pitch. 'Well, you know what? I don't think the McDougal family needs that sort of help.'

Jake's eyes widened and a dark flush stained his cheeks. 'We'll talk about this later. I'll take my dinner in and you bring the rest of the desserts. They'll be waiting for them.' He waited for her to pick up the desserts before he came into the galley. Jenni had to brush past him on the way out and she could feel the tension in his body. She looked up and could see a muscle twitching in his cheek.

Jake picked up his dinner and by the time he followed her into the dining room, he was smiling and his body was at ease.

Even his body can lie, she thought.

Four more nights.

Four more nights of putting up with Jake Jones and his bloody boat.

Chapter Sixteen

Jake waited until the guests had left the dining room and headed out to the deck. Professor Ramsey and his wife had declined the offer of coffee; they were going to have an early night, but the other four had decided to have a night fish as soon as *Moonshine* stopped travelling.

'We'll pull up for an hour or two,' Jake said. 'I'll send Cade down to rig the lines for you after I go up to the wheelhouse.' He would have preferred to travel a bit further, but as he'd told Jenni earlier, the customer was always right and they were here to please. The weather forecast was good—no wind— so they might as well take advantage of the calm conditions and fish while they could. 'I'll get Jenni to bring your coffee out to you on the deck. A rule on my charter, guys, no drinking on deck while you fish. It's not safe.'

Jake went back to the galley. Tony and Jenni were talking quietly but stopped and looked up as soon as he appeared in the doorway.

'Coffee for the guys out on deck, please, Jenni. They're going to fish for a while. No more alcohol to be served tonight. When you do that, can you bring me a coffee up to the wheelhouse please. Black with two sugars.'

Jenni nodded and turned her attention back to the sink.

'You can knock off after that. The coffee cups can be brought in when you set up for breakfast in the morning.'

'Okay, I'll be up in ten. I'll just finish up here, if that's all right?' She lifted her chin and met his gaze steadily, but her cheeks were tinged with pink.

Jake nodded. 'That's fine. Take as long as you like. I'll be up there for a few hours.'

Jenni frowned. 'All night?'

'No. Cade will take over at midnight. We should be at Sweers Island by then.'

He went up the wheelhouse using the outside stairs so he could check on the two younger men on the way. They'd sobered up a bit once the fresh salty air had hit them, and the four men were sitting quietly on the fishing deck on the stern.

'Good luck fishing, guys. If you'd like your catch cooked fresh or frozen down to take home, we can do either. Just let Cade know your preference. He'll look after you.' Once he was confident they were all fit enough to be safely out on deck, Jake ran up the stairs and relieved Cade.

'We're pulling up to fish for an hour. We'll anchor here; it's not real deep so we won't need much chain.'

'Rightio, skipper,' Cade said. 'I'll head out to the bow. Are you ready now?'

Jake nodded. 'Yep, give me five to check the radar and call *Starshine*.'

He checked the radar and made sure they weren't in a shipping passage, and once he was sure it was clear around them, he radioed Gus and explained they were pulling up to fish for an hour.

'We're about two nautical miles behind you, boss. I think we'll keep going. We've got a quiet group on here. They all went to their cabins after dinner.'

'A bit of a rowdy crew here, but harmless. Like throwing their money around, though. Cashed-up miners.' He looked up as there was a movement in the doorway. Jenni was standing there with a mug of coffee in her hand. She went to put it on the table and leave but Jake held up his hand for her to wait.

'I'll call you in the morning to see where you are. Forecast is looking good, and there's not many boats out here.'

'Roger, boss. Over and out.'

He hung up the radio mike and swung around on his chair. 'Thanks for the coffee, Jen. Appreciate it.'

She nodded and stood there quietly.

'Oh, for goodness' sake, stop looking at me as though I'm the devil incarnate.' Jake ran his hand over his head in frustration and closed his eyes for a minute. When he opened them, Jenni was sitting on the chair next to his, staring ahead out to sea.

'Just wait there while Cade puts the anchor out. We need to talk.'

He cut the engines and waited for the boat to stop, and then he stood and signalled to Cade. The deckie released the brake on the gypsy and the anchor chain rattled out. Jake watched the depth indicator and indicated with hand signals to Cade when enough chain was out. Finally, Cade locked off the brake and put the devil's claw on a chain link. He stood there for a moment, one foot on the chain feeling the tension until the anchor took hold and then he gave Jake a thumbs up.

'Thanks, mate,' Jake said when Cade came to the wheelhouse door. 'Four of the guests are waiting on the aft deck for you. Just an hour's fishing, and then get some sleep. I'll see you at midnight. We might do some drift fishing tomorrow if it's quiet.'

Jenni sat there quietly, but when he turned from the door, Jake noticed she was looking at the instrument panel.

'You haven't forgotten what the fishing is like out here then?' she said.

At least she was talking to him.

'No. Once learned never forgotten.'

'What was it like in the Mediterranean?' Her voice sounded interested, and Jake didn't think she was just filling in time.

'Why do you ask?'

'Just interested.' Now her voice was wary as though she'd overstepped some hidden mark.

'The fishing, or the work, or just being there?'

'All of the above, I guess.'

Jake sat on his chair and ran a quick eye over the instruments before he spoke. 'An honest answer?'

'Yes please.'

'It was lonely to start with, and then it was bloody hard work.'

'To start with?'

He nodded. 'After the first three years, and they were hard years, I got used to it. Mum died, and I couldn't afford to come home. I didn't think I'd ever—'

Jesus. He must be tired; he'd almost said he'd never forgive her father for running him out of town.

'Ever what, Jake?' Her voice was soft.

'Ever forget not being here for Mum when she was sick.'

'It would have been hard. I was away when Dad had his heart attack too. I never got to say goodbye.'

'I'm sorry.' Jake leaned forward and took one of Jenni's hands between his. 'Jen?'

'Yes?'

'Can we start again? Can we forget everything that's happened and just pretend that we are getting to know each other now? Let the past go?'

'Maybe.' Her eyes were downcast, and the lights from the instrument panel flickered over her face in a macabre shadow.

'I'm sorry I was short with you over that tipping business. It's been a while since I've had to deal with something like that, and I didn't handle it well. I'll have a word with them if it's making you uncomfortable.'

'With the cashed-up miners?'

He detected a note of disbelief in her voice, but he nodded. 'Yes.'

'If that's what you want. I thought that you'd want as much money out of this charter as you could get.'

Jake looked at her and he wrinkled his brow in a frown. 'Why would you think that? The tips go to the staff. Usually, we pool them and divvy them up at the end. Or that's what happened in Monte Carlo. This is my first trip out here, remember.'

'Tell me more about your time over there. Did you ever get to Paris?'

'I did. It's a beautiful city.'

'One day,' she said softly. 'Now tell me why you really left?'

'Left there, or left here?' He stared at her but she wouldn't meet his eye. 'I'll never forget not being able to talk to you before I left Second Chance Bay.'

She lifted her head. 'Your actions decided your path, Jake.'

'I guess I'll always be guilty to you then.' Weariness flooded through him. 'We've got a big day tomorrow. Go to bed.'

He couldn't even bring himself to her name. Without another word, or even a glance in his direction she picked up his empty coffee mug and left.

Jake stared out over the sea for ages. The moon had risen and a silver path danced on the low waves. The occasional whoop from the aft deck indicated that there were fish being caught but after an hour, the noise stopped as Cade wound up the fishing.

He decided to stay on the anchorage until dawn; he was in no mood to look for uncharted reefs. It wouldn't matter if they arrived at Sweers Island a few hours after *Starshine*. Picking up the mike, he called Gus so he wouldn't worry when they weren't behind them.

The night was quiet; there was nothing apart from the slap of the waves on the hull and the clank of the anchor chain on the bow. The current gurgled quietly as it rushed past the hull, mirroring the thoughts that rushed through Jake's head. But unlike the current, they had no direction.

How the hell had he ever thought bringing Jenni on the boat was going to put him in a better light?

From her attitude tonight, it was obvious that he'd been judged and found wanting.

Jake dropped his head in his hands as he sat out the watch until Cade came to relieve him at midnight. The sad part was, no matter how Jenni looked at him or how she reacted to him, he couldn't stop caring about her. He knew underneath that cynical exterior was the young girl he'd fallen in love with. Hell, he was even more attracted to the feisty woman she was now.

The question was: what could he do about it? He shook his head as the night closed in around him.

There was nothing he could do.

The only thing that would convince her that he was a decent guy was to tell her the truth about her father and what he'd done, but that would destroy any chance of them ever being together.

Shit, what had been the point of him coming home?

Maybe he'd pack up the boats and head back to France.

At least he was respected there for what he'd achieved.

Chapter Seventeen

Jenni lay in her bunk in the cabin on the bottom deck and sleep eluded her. The sadness in Jake's voice and the despair in his expression had almost brought her undone. She couldn't understand him. He had what he wanted; what more could he want?

Why did he look and sound so unhappy? After an hour the rocking of the boat in the gentle swell hadn't helped her get to sleep. She lay there wide awake staring at the moonlight playing across the ceiling.

No matter what had happened in the past, she had to forgive Jake. Seeing him so unhappy was awful; she couldn't cope with it. From tomorrow, she'd change her attitude and be kind to him.

At least she could do the right thing. Watching Jake and trying to figure him out wasn't going to work. Her feelings for him were still there. Okay, they were hidden under years of resentment and bitterness, but the more time she spent with him, the more that was rolling away. She'd never met anyone else who made her feel like he did, no one else who she worried about when they were sad.

I guess that's what love is, she thought, finally admitting it to herself.

She'd loved him when he'd left and that was why it had left such a mark on her soul. And she still loved Jake Jones.

Tomorrow was a new day. There were four days ahead to get themselves sorted.

Jenni rolled over and thumped her pillow, but there was a smile on her face as she drifted off to sleep.

***

Just after dawn at first light, the engines fired and Jenni woke as the boat began to move. She pulled over her phone and looked at the time; it was almost five thirty and she had plenty of time before she was due up in the galley. She lay there for a moment and then decided to get up. Maybe Jake was back in the wheelhouse; she knew from her time on Dad's boat that a watch was not supposed to be more than four hours. She smiled; Jake would follow the rules; she did not doubt that.

With a smile, and feeling happier than she had since she'd come back to Second Chance Bay and first seen Jake, Jenni climbed out of the bunk and had a quick shower in the small bathroom attached to her cabin. She pulled out a clean shirt and gathered yesterday's clothes to run through the washing machine, reminding herself to offer to wash the rest of the crew's clothes. Yesterday's desire to leave the boat and go back home had gone, and the day ahead beckoned with promise.

But her smile didn't last long after she arrived on the top deck. Jake was in the wheelhouse and when she waved good morning, he scowled and turned his head away. Okay, she could cope with that; she'd been in a similar mood for a week or more.

Leonora Ramsey was already in the saloon, and Jenni quickly gathered up the tray of coffee cups that the fishermen had left on the table.

'Good morning,' she said with a bright smile. 'Can I get you a coffee, Mrs Ramsey?'

'Leonora, please, and that would be great, thank you.'

'I won't be long.'

Tony was already in the kitchen chopping up fresh fruit for a fruit salad. 'Morning, sunshine,' he said. 'You look bright and happy this morning. You must have slept well.'

'I did, actually,' she said. 'Before I forget, throw your clothes into the hamper up on the main deck, and I'll put them through the machine and dryer for you.'

'Thanks, sweets. Can you do me a favour if you're going that way?'

'Sure,' Jenni nodded as she got the coffee machine going. 'What do you need?'

'Do you know where the lazerette is?'

'Yes, the bit up the front under the wheelhouse?'

'Yep. Aft of the wheelhouse,' he said with a smile.' If you're up that way, there's a big bag of muesli just inside the door. Could you be a love and grab it for me?'

'I'll just wait for the coffee to perk and I'll take one up to Jake if he's still up there.'

'I'd say he will be because young Cade was snoring fairly well in the cabin next to me when I came past. They stick rigidly to their four-hour watches by the look of things. Jake is a good skipper.'

Jenni grinned.

Good, the first chance to make amends to Jake.

She poured two coffees and took one into the saloon to Leonora with a small dish of pastries. 'Breakfast will be on in an hour or so. This should keep you going.'

Leonora looked up from the bird book she was reading. 'Thank you.'

Jenni carefully navigated the stairs as she carried up Jake's coffee.

Black with two.

The sea was a little rougher today and she hung onto the rail with one hand as she went up to the top deck. As she stepped out of the stairwell, she looked ahead. They were approaching a small island. Whitecaps dotted the sea between the boat and the land, and it rocked slightly in the long lazy swells that were under the short choppy waves.

'Morning, captain,' she said brightly.

Jake turned and his face was set. 'Thank you, just leave it on the table.' He turned away and Jenni stood there for a moment before she realised he wasn't going to say any more than that.

With a shrug, she looked around trying to remember where the hatch was that led to the lazerette storage area Jake had shown her the night he had taken her on the tour of the boat. She leaned forward and looked past the wheelhouse but couldn't see it. Finally, he turned.

'Was there something else?'

'Um, the storage area? You showed me a hatch that led to it the other night?'

'Down on the aft deck.' His voice was short and he turned back to the instrument panel.

'Thank you,' Jenni muttered heading back to the stairway.

She found the hatch, retrieved the muesli and delivered it to Tony. By the time she had a load of washing on, and returned to the galley, the appetising aroma of bacon and eggs filled the middle deck.

'I'll just set the tables.' She hurried into the dining area, and quickly laid out the cutlery and plates.

Just as well I got up early, she thought. Being a hostess was a lot more time-consuming than she'd thought it would be. But Jenni was enjoying it so far today, despite Jake's bad mood.

Meal preparation on the *Sally M* and the *Elsie* had been a lot more casual—more along the lines of every man for himself. But then she reminded herself that guests on her brothers' boat didn't pay the exorbitant price that guests were paying on *Moonshine*.

A tendril of doubt began to unfurl and she pushed it away. Today was the day to give Jake another chance. She swallowed and carried the meals into the dining room. Everyone was quiet this morning, and the men barely noticed her, apart from a quick nod of thanks as she put the plates on the table.

No stupid tips this morning, she thought thankfully.

Breakfast was served and cleared away quickly as the island approached. Not far away, *Starshine* was moored on their port side.

Professor Ramsey, and his wife had opted to go ashore and Cade was taking them in the rubber tender. The other four men were fishing off the aft deck, and Jake had come down from the wheelhouse once the anchor was set.

'When you get the cabins serviced and after morning tea, I'll get you to give me a hand down here, please.'

She nodded and hurried off. If it put Jake in a better and more approachable mood, she was happy to help with the fishing. By the time the beds were made, the washing was in the dryer and the bathrooms wiped over, it was morning tea time.

Cade had returned in the tender and was helping out on the aft deck, rigging lines, and baiting hooks. When Jenni went to the aft deck after morning tea had been brought out, and then tidied up, Jake shook his head. 'It's fine. We don't need you now. Cade's back.'

She got the impression that she had taken longer than he'd expected but was determined not to let it worry her; she was here as a hostess and she was doing the duties as directed. Heading to the galley, she poked her head in to see if Tony needed a hand with anything but he wasn't in there. With a shrug, she headed back to the dryer, took the clothes out and folded them, and then put them in the crew cabins.

When she came out there was a lot of noise down on the fishing deck. Curiosity got the better of her, and Jenni ran lightly down the stairs. She stopped at the bottom in time to see Ken's rod bent double and him digging his heels into the deck as the momentum of whatever was on the end of his rod pulled him forward.

Jake looked over and saw her and the smile that crossed his face was spontaneous. Jenni grinned back.

'Can you give us a hand now, Jen?' he called across the deck. 'We've got a bit of a tangle down the back on the lower deck and we need to clear it before the fish goes around there.'

Jenni let her gaze follow to where Jake was pointing. Greg and Pat had their lines tangled and the final mess was tangled around the railing on the starboard side. She nodded and gave Jake a thumbs up, and hurried down to the lower deck. As she leaned over the railing and reached for the tangled line, she heard the tender. Cade had collected Professor Ramsey and Leonora from the island and was approaching the cruiser.

Everything happened at once. The huge fish that was pulling Ken's line headed beneath the back of the boat, and the calls from the upper deck were louder as he fought to keep it. As Jenni watched the line bobbing in the choppy waves, a couple of black fins cruised between the approaching tender and the back of the boat as the sharks picked up the frantic movements of the fish as it fought for its life.

'There it is!' Ken's voice was loud as she stood there holding the tangled lines and looking up, and the silver glint of a massive northern blue fin tuna broke the surface briefly before it headed back under the water. As Ken disappeared around the port side of the boat, she caught a glimpse of two more large sharks hanging around.

Game fishing at its best.

Jenni had forgotten how much she enjoyed being out on the water and seeing the thrill of the catch. The fishermen would be happy. She climbed over onto the duckboard at the back of the boat as the tender approached. By the smiles on the Ramseys' faces, it looked as though the bird watching trip had been successful too. Catching Cade's attention, she pointed up to the fishing deck and he nodded and throttled back the small outboard. After a minute of idling at the back of the boat, Jake called over.

'All clear now.'

Cade gunned the outboard, and when they reached the back of *Moonshine*, he threw the rope to Jenni. The waves were getting choppier as the wind picked up.

Professor Ramsey stood and jumped onto the duckboard next to Jenni as the tender bobbed in the waves. Cade held his hand out for Leonora to take hold and Jenni leaned forward ready to help her on board. As she stepped out of the tender, a large rolling swell caught the tender and slewed it to the side.

Jenni watched in horror as the woman slipped between the tender and the back of the boat, and disappeared into the oily dark water.

Without a second thought, she kicked off her canvas shoes and dived into the water, aware of Cade reversing the tender away from the boat.

Trying not to think of the sharks that she'd seen only a few moments ago, she dived beneath the back of the cruiser and opened her eyes. The current was strong and the salt water stung her eyes. She trod water and looked around. Leonora was already about five metres away from the back of the boat.

Jenni pushed to the surface and pointed to where Leonora was trying to swim against the current. 'Cade, she's over there and drifting away! Quick!' she yelled.

Taking another deep breath, she dived beneath the water.

Chapter Eighteen

Jake's blood turned to ice as Jennie disappeared beneath *Moonshine*. He knew she was a strong swimmer and that she was confident in the water, but she had a huge vessel to contend with, an unpredictable current and the sharks that he'd spotted as the fish thrashed in the water.

'Cut your line,' he yelled to Ken as the four fishermen looked over at the water in horror.

Jake ran down the steps pulling his shirt over his head, and kicked his shoes off before he jumped over the stainless-steel rail between the deck and the duckboard.

All he could think about was losing Jenni. He'd watched in disbelief as Leonora had fallen between the two boats and he'd known what Jenni would do even before she'd kicked off her shoes. She'd had no hesitation diving in. It was no one's fault. Cade had followed procedure; it was the rogue wave that had caused the woman to slip.

Cade had the tender idling about ten metres away from *Moonshine* and as Jake went to dive in, he saw Cade reach over the side of the tender. Jake's breath caught and he watched as the deckie lifted the dark-haired woman into the inflatable boat. Seconds later, Jenni pulled herself over the side and put her arms around the woman who was sitting on the middle seat. Cade gunned the throttle and the tender surged towards the back of *Moonshine*.

'Thank God.' Professor Ramsey supported himself on the railing as the tender approached. Jake put his hand on the man's shoulder. 'We'll get them on board, and see if we need to get medical attention. There's a small medical clinic on the island.'

'As long as we don't have to go in that small boat again,' the older man said.

'No, they'll come out to us if we need them.'

Cade approached slowly and they all watched the swell as it rose and fell a metre at a time. It had come from nowhere. Half an hour earlier the sea had glassed off, and there had been no wind.

Just the unpredictability of the sea.

'Now!' Jake yelled and he jumped into the tender as Cade brought it in close. The other men, including Tony, had come down to the back of the boat, and they helped Jake lift Leonora across from the rocking boat. Her husband put his arms around her and buried his face in her sodden hair.

'God, sweetheart. That was too close for comfort.'

'I'm alright, 'she said, although her teeth were chattering. 'Wet and cold, but I'm not hurt.' She turned to Cade and Jenni who were still in the boat. 'Thank you.'

Tony stepped forward with a blanket and assisted the couple to the bench seat on the aft deck, and the other men moved away to give them space. Jake sat with his arm around Jenni and waited for the rolling swell to pass. She looked up and met his gaze and held it as they waited for the boat to stop rocking. Finally, the sea flattened and she jumped from the tender to the duckboard.

Jake followed her and held out his arms and she fell into them. They stood there for a moment, Jenni's wet cheek against his bare chest.

'Don't you ever frighten me like that again, Jenni McDougal.'

She shook her head against his chest as she took in slow deep breaths.

'Are you okay?' he asked as he finally released her. 'I'm going to have to go and see to Leonora.

'I'm fine. Just a bit shaken now that it's all over. Those sharks had me worried.'

'I want you to go up to my cabin and have a shower. Get warm. There's a spare robe in the cupboard behind the door.' Jake took her chin gently between his still-shaking fingers and looked down at her. Her eyes were dark and wide, and her wet eyelashes were clumped together but she was still beautiful. 'And then I want you to stay there and wait for me. Okay?'

She nodded, compliant for once. 'Okay,' she whispered. The look in her eyes gave him hope.

He kept hold of her with one arm as he turned. 'Tony, can you please help Jenni up to the master cabin while I look after Mrs Ramsey?'

'Sure, captain.'

'And then come back down and help Cade with the tender.'

'I'm fine,' Jenni protested. 'I can get there myself.'

Tony shook his head as Jake handed her over. 'Captain's orders, Jenni.'

***

As Jenni stood under the steaming hot water in Jake's bathroom reaction set in. Her legs were shaking, and she was shivering. It took a long time for the chills to pass; every time she closed her eyes she could feel the rough skin of the shark brush against her leg.

Maybe she wouldn't tell Jake that it had been so close to her. It had brushed against her leg just as she'd pushed herself into the inflatable boat.

Finally, she switched the taps off and stepped from the shower, wrapping herself in a thick fluffy towel. Now that she was warm and dry—and relatively calm again—she felt silly being up here and waiting for Jake as he'd instructed.

As she thought about going back to her own cabin, the door opened and Jake stepped inside. He shut it quietly behind him and leaned his back against it. His eyes were dark and hooded as he looked at her. Another shiver ran down her spine but this time it had nothing to do with fear or being cold.

'Jenni.' Jake's voice was low as he stepped over and took her arms. There was something in his voice that shook her as he linked his arms around her waist. Suddenly the robe seemed thin.

'I love you.'

She widened her eyes and her heart set up a thudding in her chest as she stared at him, her mouth dropping open.

'I've always loved you, Jen. From the time we were teenagers, and the whole time I was away from you.' Jake rested his forehead against hers. 'I never realised what it meant that I hadn't told you and that I was away from you all of that time. Not until you disappeared under the boat, and I thought I'd left it too late.'

Jenni pulled her head back and stared into his hazel eyes. She was so close she could see each gold fleck in his irises. His eyes were deep, and held something she hadn't seen for a long while. 'Jake, it's just a reaction. You're making more of the accident than you should. I was fine.' Suddenly she remembered Leonora. 'What about Leonora? Is she okay?'

'She's fine.'

'That's good.' She felt self-conscious having him so close. Shivers ran up and down her spine. She could smell his masculine smell and his hands were warm on her waist.

'They were both in the saloon having a brandy as I came up here.' He pulled her closer and his voice had steel in it. 'I know I'm probably scaring you because I don't know if you're ready for this. To hear what I want to say. What I have to say.'

'I think you've already said it.' Her voice shook as she looked up at him and something let go inside her heart as it beat painfully in her chest. She wasn't game to let that tendril of hope take root.

'Jenni?' The steel in his voice had been replaced by soft persuasion.

'Yes?'

'Can I kiss you?'

She answered with her lips instead of words, lifting her face to his.

Damn the consequences, damn the reason she was here. Jake was all that mattered. If she was honest with herself, he was all that had ever mattered.

Nothing else did. His actions as a teenager had set them apart, a fall off the path that she would have preferred he'd stayed on, but she could forgive him for that. He'd said that he loved her, and she knew she still loved him. She always had.

His lips were gentle at first, and Jenni sighed against Jake's mouth as he slid his hands beneath the robe and linked them around her back. Now his hands were burning hot against her skin as his tongue played along her bottom lip. As she opened her mouth to speak, he pressed his mouth harder on hers.

'No words,' he murmured against her lips. 'Not yet. Just feel with me.'

Jenni closed her eyes. It did feel so right. It was like coming home to the place she knew she'd always wanted to be. Her throat tightened and her eyes pricked with tears.

Happy tears.

She opened her eyes and pulled back. A smile was playing around Jake's lips and he pulled her even closer to him.

'Do you think you need to lie down?'

'I think I do.'

##

An hour later, Jake propped his head on his hand and looked down at Jenni. She was pressed against him from shoulder to toe, and her soft skin was warm against his. He'd left the boat on the anchor and once he'd ensured that Leonora was okay, he'd asked Cade to take the watch while he checked on Jenni. Tony was keeping an eye on Cade for him too because it had been a frightening experience for the deckie.

Jenni's cheeks were flushed with a rosy tinge and her eyes were heavy and slumberous as she looked back at him. Her warm breath puffed against his lips as he leaned down to kiss her. The last thing he wanted to do was leave her in his bed alone. But he was the captain and duty called.

She knew him too well.

'Duty calls?' she asked and as she stretched the sheet slipped off her chest, exposing a temptation.

He bit back a groan. They had waited a long time to sleep together, but it had been worth the wait. Lowering his head, he kissed her again, and reached down and grabbed her hand as her fingers trailed down his stomach, heading lower. . .

'Not again, you witch.'

Her giggle filled him with joy, an even deeper feeling than the physical expression of their love had given them.

'The witch from the fish shop. Are you sure you've made the right choice, Jake?'

'Oh, I'm sure. And I'm going to show you again later tonight.'

He sat up and swung his legs over the side of the bed. 'But you're right, duty calls. I have to go and relieve Cade. Tony said he can fill in for you tonight.'

Jenni sat up and pulled the sheet up. Her hair fell around her face, but she smiled as she looked up at him. 'Don't be silly. A bit of a dip in the Gulf? You run down and get my clothes for me, and I'll have a quick shower.'

'I'm going to have a quick one too.'

She raised her eyebrows and slid out of the other side of the bed. 'I'm going first.'

Needless to say, Jake was late relieving Cade from his watch.

Chapter Nineteen

The days passed quickly—way too quickly for Jenni. The days helping Jake make the charter successful were fun and she'd picked up the routine easily. Tony and Cade were good to work with, and she gradually learned how a tight crew worked together and helped each other out.

And looked out for each other.

The guests had settled into the routine, and many fish were caught. Once they'd left *Starshine* at the island, and headed over to the Limmen Bight, the sea was smoother and Leonora had been confident enough to go ashore in the tender again.

But it was the nights that were unforgettable. Jake had insisted that she move into the master cabin with him.

'It's not a problem,' he assured her. 'For all the guests know, we're a couple, and like you said, even Tony picked it up even before we knew it ourselves.' He had taken her to delightful places every night, and there hadn't been much sleep between watches.

'A skipper needs to get more sleep, wench,' he said one night as he fell into bed at midnight.

The hardest part had been the night watches, when Jake had left their bed every four hours to go on watch. But they hadn't done much talking, and Jenni was uncomfortable about that. There were things she wanted to say to Jake, to clear the air. If they were going to make a go of their relationship, there had to be honesty between them.

Complete honesty.

On the last night on board, Tony cooked a special dinner. A sumptuous feast of freshly caught coral trout, and potato bake. Jenni had helped in the galley during the afternoon while Jake was on watch as they headed back towards the coast after they'd caught up with *Starshine*. She'd learned how to make crème brulee and had eaten too much licking out the bowl as she and Tony had laughed together in the kitchen.

'Next charter, I'll share my secret cheesecake recipe with you,' he said as she whipped the cream for the dessert.

Jenni shook her head. 'This was a one-off,' she said. 'I was just helping out. 'I start a job at the local school in a couple of weeks.' She stared out the open window to the sea; the thought of going back to being a teacher didn't appeal at all.

'That's a shame. You and Jake work really well together.' Tony opened the stove and glanced at her as he slid a loaf of bread in to warm. 'I thought you'd been doing this for a long time. You're a natural.'

'I love it. I think the sea is in my blood.'

'So why don't you think about staying?'

'You know,' she said thoughtfully. 'I might just think about that.' The thought of Jake going off on week-long—and sometimes longer charters—wasn't one that appealed. The thought of starting at a new school suddenly appealed even less. Maybe after the two terms, he'd take her on the boat as a hostess.

As long as they were still together.

Great sex was one thing, but they needed to talk. Jenni needed to tell Jake that she had forgotten and forgiven what he'd done. She loved him and didn't want to lose him again, but Jenni needed to know how he had been able to afford his boats.

Whatever Jake Jones had done, she would live with, but had to know the truth.

Dinner was fun, and the atmosphere was light. Jenni took a meal up to Cade in the wheelhouse and he nodded with a smile. 'Smells great, thanks.'

'Jake said to tell you he's going to relieve you early, so you can come down and have a couple of drinks.

Cade put his thumb up. 'Beauty. He's a great skipper. One of the best charters I've ever worked on.'

'He is,' Jenni agreed as she left the wheelhouse. Jake *was* a good skipper. He was a people person; firm with the crew, and he was great with the guests. The six on board had already promised to book another trip.

'Return customers, that's what we want to see.' Jake put his arm around her as they walked up to the wheelhouse to take the eight p.m. watch.

'Careful,' she said balancing the two dishes of crème brulee in her hands.

They relieved Cade and Jake checked the instruments before he turned to his dessert. The vessel was travelling on autopilot until they came within sight of the coast.

All was quiet apart from the scraping of spoons on the plates for a few minutes.

'Tony was a great find,' Jake said as he put his empty plate on the bench top. He looked at her with a smile and held his arm out. Jenni put her empty dish next to his and squeezed onto the narrow seat beside him. 'It's been a great charter.' He dropped a kiss on the top of her head.

'In many ways,' she said. 'Except for Leonora going overboard. But even that had a happy ending. They said they're going to come again so no hard feelings there.' She looked up at Jake. 'Tony asked me if I was going to come again. It got me thinking.'

'Overrated, that is,' Jake said with a smile.

'What is?'

'Thinking,' he said. 'I'd much rather do this.'

Jenni shivered when Jake's lips found that sweet spot at the side of her neck. She sighed and leaned into his embrace. After a moment, she spoke again. 'Seriously though, I do want to talk to you.'

'So what were you thinking about? I'll behave.' Jake stood and moved across to the other seat.

'Aw, you didn't have to do that.'

Jake sat back and folded his arms with a smile. Jenni looked at him, still unable to believe that they were a couple.

'So talk to me. I'm listening.'

'You might not like what I'm going to say.'

'Try me.' His smile made her insides curl, and Jenni reached out one hand and put it on Jake's firm thigh.

'That's not going to help me concentrate. Or are you trying to distract me?'

'What would you say if I thought being a hostess was a job I'd like to do again?'

'Really?' His grin was wide. 'I'd say you're hired. Next question?'

As she went to speak, a buzzer sounded and Jake leaned over and flicked a switch. 'Okay keep talking, but I have to drive the boat now. We've passed the waypoint where we come off autopilot. Rightio, you've got most of my attention.' He looked forward watching the water ahead.

Jenni put her head down. 'Jake? I think we need to be honest with each other. I was angry at you for a long time when you ran away, but I want you to know that I'm sorry for turning you away when you came to see me that last night.'

'I understood that. Eventually.'

Jenni looked up. Jake's jaw was set and a muscle twitched in his cheek as he stared ahead. He nodded without looking at her. 'Go on.'

'I want you to know that I can forget about what you did . . . and that . . .' She swallowed and bit her lip.

'And that?' he said.

'That I forgive you.'

Again, the muscle in his cheek twitched. 'That's very kind of you.' All humour had left Jake's voice and a strange feeling settled in Jenni's stomach.

'I know you must have had a very good reason.'

Jake sat still and looked down at the screen, not speaking as he entered coordinates onto the screen. Finally, he turned to her. 'I'm very pleased that you think that. Is there anything else you want to say?'

'Yes.' Jenni swallowed again wondering how best to phrase her next question. 'You want to be with me, don't you, Jake? Like this isn't just a fling. We are . . . together?'

He reached out and took her hand and relief rushed through her. 'That's what you're worried about?'

'Some. But there's one more big thing I want to ask.' She relaxed as his fingers stroked her hand. 'I want to know . . . I need to know how you bought the boats. Where you got the money from?'

His hand let go of hers and he gripped the helm with both hands. When he turned to her, his eyes were shadowed. 'Why, Jenni? Do you think I stole . . . again?'

'I just want to know how you afforded all this.' She waved a hand around at the boat. 'They must be worth millions.'

'They are.' He nodded tersely. Flashing green and red lights flickered on the water ahead. 'I have to concentrate on steering us in now. Go to bed, Jenni. I'll talk to you later.'

Chapter Twenty

Five hours later Jake sat at the control panel in the wheelhouse staring ahead as *Moonshine* approached the mouth of the Norman River. Was it only a couple of weeks since he and Gus had arrived and travelled up the river to Second Chance Bay? He shook his head, it was ironic really, the name of the bay; he'd kidded himself he could have a second chance with Jenni, but he hadn't factored in her lack of trust.

Not that he could blame her really.

Cade had come up to relieve him on watch but he'd sent him away. 'We're not far off the coast. I'll do all night,' he'd told the young deckie.

Cade yawned and nodded before he headed back to his cabin. Jake sat there thinking. Over the years, he'd thought that Jenni would have quickly realised that he wouldn't have done what her father had accused him of. Hell, he'd even regretted listening to her father's threats and leaving town that day.

Now ten years later, she still thought he'd taken the money. And she was prepared to forgive him?

Well, she could take her bloody forgiveness, and leave him in peace.

He didn't need her. He wasn't good enough for her.

The problem was, what was he going to do? If she was going to stay in town, he didn't want to be there.

He might love her, but he couldn't be with someone who would doubt him so readily.

I just want to know how you afforded all this, she'd said.

Jake dropped his head onto the helm and tried to deal with the emptiness that sat hollow in his chest.

If there was no trust between them, there was no future.

***

Jenni lay in Jake's bed and waited for him to come down from the wheelhouse. She knew Cade was due to relieve him at midnight and she lay there awake and worrying when Jake didn't come. No, she was worried before then. The look on Jake's face had been bitter, and his voice had been cold.

She was sorry he'd reacted like that, but she wanted honesty between them. If he wasn't prepared to be honest and talk to her, there was no future for them.

He hadn't answered any of her questions, and she was pretty sure he wasn't going to. It was almost light when she drifted off to sleep, only to be woken by her phone buzzing as it came back into range. She glanced at the clock, it was just after five, and she was still alone in the bed.

There were a few text messages from Mum, telling her about the trip, and how much fun they were having. A couple of happy photos of Rick and Mum standing next to the van brought a smile to her face, but it disappeared quickly. After pulling on her shorts and shirt she had a quick wash and pulled her hair back into a ponytail. Tony was already in the kitchen, and had started cleaning out the freezer.

'Do you ever sleep, Tony?' she asked forcing a smile to her face.

He shook his head and flicked a curious glance her way.

Jenni was absolutely miserable inside, but she was determined not to go up and see Jake. If he wanted her to know the truth, he could come and see her. He could make the first move.

He was the one in the wrong. He'd always been in the wrong.

Breakfast was served and cleaned up. Three hours later, farewells had been made Jenni's misery trebled as the guests disembarked. *Starshine* was a couple of hours behind them, so she decided to stay on board so she could say goodbye to Claudette. *Moonshine* was berthed at the public dock in town.

Working her way along each deck, she stripped the beds in the cabins and cleaned the bathrooms. Not sure what to do with the linen and towels—she had a feeling that it would go to the local laundrette—Jenni finally went in search of Jake.

She went slowly up the stairs to the wheelhouse, but it was empty. Cade had driven the bus to take the guests to the airport, and Tony was still in the galley. She went up to the master cabin and tapped on the door and when there was no answer she pushed it open quietly.

Maybe Jake had gone for a sleep?

But the cabin was empty. She walked back down to the galley, her sadness increasing with every step. 'Tony, have you seen Jake,' she asked quietly.

'I think he went for a walk. I saw him head towards town about an hour ago. Everything okay, sweets?'

Jenni shook her head and felt stupid when her eyes filled with tears. 'Do me a favour, Tony? Say goodbye to Claudette for me and say thanks for the help she gave me. I've got a few things I need to do in town and at home.' She blinked and smiled at the chef. 'Thanks for a great trip. I learned heaps. I'm sure I'll see you around town.'

'Or on your next hostess stint?' Tony put the dishcloth down and crossed the galley to the door. He opened his arms and hugged her. 'You take care of yourself, love.'

Jenni nodded and picked up the bag that she'd left near the back of the boat. With one last look at *Moonshine*, she put her head down and headed for the fish shop; she would borrow Matt's car and drive home across the bridge.

##

Jenni had managed to be bright and bubbly when she went to get Matt's car keys. Luckily the shop had been full and she'd said a quick hello, yes it was great, and I'll see you later, as she took his keys and hurried out. She was worried she was going to run into Jake, and the way she was feeling she didn't want to see him.

Not now, maybe not ever.

The house was empty without Mum, and there was no sign of Dane and Donny. She'd been so preoccupied in town, she hadn't even noticed if the two McDougal boats were in the river. She threw her bag into the laundry and kicked her shoes off. The house smelled musty and she walked into the kitchen expecting to see dirty dishes everywhere, but to her surprise the sink was clear.

Maybe the boys had been eating out. After filling the kettle and putting it on the gas for a coffee she didn't really want, Jenni wandered aimlessly around the house, opening windows to let the fresh air in.

Could she have handled the way she confronted Jake any better?

Or any worse?

She groaned and pushed open her bedroom door. She frowned as she noticed a buff-coloured envelope propped against her pillow. Picking it up, she turned it over. Her name was written on the front in Mum's loopy writing.

She walked back to the kitchen and put it on the table while she made her coffee. Pulling out a chair, she sat down and lifted the flap on the envelope.

The letter inside was from Mum, and Jenni's mouth opened as she quickly read what her mother had to say. She dropped the letter after she finished reading it before picking it back up and reading again slowly this time, trying to absorb the words on the paper.

Jen sweetheart,

This is hard to write but I have given the situation a lot of thought over the years, and again more so since you and Jake both came home to Second Chance Bay. I hope you will find it in your heart to forgive me. I know that you and Jake belong together, and

Grief for the years that had been lost due to her father's lies filled Jenni until she thought she would burst. She picked up her coffee and focused on taking slow sips as she calmed herself.

Grief for the lonely death of Jake's mum, with her only son thousands of miles away across the sea.

Grief for the ten years she could have been with Jake.

Grief that her father would lie to her.

And worst of all, anger with herself that she could have ever believed Jake guilty of a crime he would never have committed.

And then she'd made it so much worse by saying trust was necessary to their future. She had demanded trust from Jake, without offering it in return.

No wonder he didn't want to be with her. No wonder he didn't want to speak to her.

Jenni put her head down on the table and cried for what she'd lost.

Chapter Twenty-One

The second weekend after the *Moonshine* charter had returned Jenni sat at the desk in her bedroom. It was the same desk where she'd done her homework in the days she'd been a student at the school where she was starting work tomorrow. She traced her fingers around the faded blue ink of the heart she'd drawn on her desk the week before Jake had fled. Two Js entwined in a circle inside the heart. The ink heart had always been hidden under a pile of books in those days; she'd been too shy and sensitive to risk Mum or her brothers seeing it.

Jenni stood with a sigh and left the desk clear as she placed the folder and textbook into her briefcase. Her future was uncertain; once the two terms were up—and she knew they were going to drag—she'd look for a job somewhere else.

It was the least she could do. Jake deserved to succeed in town, and if she hung around, he would always be reminded of the past and how no one—scrub that—how *she* hadn't trusted him. She closed her eyes thinking of the hurt in his eyes when she'd asked him about how he'd afforded the charter boats.

No trust. There was no true love without implicit trust.

For the first few days she'd hoped that maybe Jake would seek her out, but she knew him well. He was hurt and she had let him down. He would leave again; she had to tell him she was the one leaving this time. It was the only thing she could do to make up for her lack of trust.

Moonshine had disappeared, and she was scared Jake had left already because of her. One night a week after she'd come home Matt had stared at her as though she was crazy, when she finally summoned up the courage to mention Jake. The boys were watching the news; she'd offered to cook and Matt had wandered into the kitchen.

'You okay, sis?'

'Yep.'

'Ah, finally she speaks,' Matt said. 'We thought you had the shits with us, but we did tidy up before you came home.'

'You did.' Jenni ran the hot potatoes under the cold water for the salad she was making. 'Matt? Do you know where Jake and *Moonshine* have gone?'

He looked at her curiously. 'Yeah, they went straight out on another charter, the day after you came in. Didn't Jake tell you he was going?'

She shook her head. 'No. We didn't part on the best of terms.'

Matt shook his head. 'Jeez, you give that poor guy a hard time. How the heck did you both survive five days in each other's company?'

Heat raced up Jenni's neck and her cheeks burned. 'Very well, actually. Until I stuffed it up on the last night. I told him I forgave him for taking our money and then I asked him where he got his money from.'

'Jeez, Jenni. You sure know how to kick a guy.' Matt came over and put his hands on her shoulders. 'And did he tell you about his father? More to the point did he tell you about our wonderful father and what he did?'

'No. But I know about that now. About Dad lying. But how did you know about Jake's father?'

'Jake told me about his inheritance before you went out on the charter. But I also know he worked hard to get where he is today.'

Jenni frowned. 'But if he's on a charter, who's his hostess? Claudette was leaving as soon as we came in.'

Matt shrugged. 'As far as I know, Gus and Ryan went on the charter too. *Starshine's* around at the public dock, so I guess they did. A hostess doesn't have to be a woman, you know.'

'I know that. I wasn't thinking. I could have gone out again,' she said softly. 'I could have told him I was sorry. But I don't think he'll ever forgive me.'

Tears welled in her eyes, and Matt held his arms open for a hug. 'He'll come around, pipsqueak. 'He loves you. You'd have to be blind Freddie not to see that. The boys and I have bets going on how long it will take you two to realise that.'

'Really?'

Matt grinned. 'Don't worry, the odd bet with a brother is not gambling.'

'I know that.' Jenni lifted her chin as resolve filled her. 'No matter what happens, I have to tell Jake I'm sorry.'

***

'So what's crawled up your butt this trip?' Gus stared at Jake after he'd spoken sharply to Ryan when he spilled a bucket of water on the aft deck. 'You've been very short with the crew a couple of times. Not a good look, mate.'

'Nothing for you to worry about.' Jake turned from Gus but the older man's hand landed on his shoulder before he could walk away.

'When something impacts on the crew, and has you looking sour for ten days, I think it is.' Gus dropped his hand and his expression was sympathetic. 'I'm about to relieve Cade in the wheelhouse. You grab us both a coffee and come up. Ryan's got the fishing under control.'

Jake looked across at the aft deck; the fishermen had lines out and they were chatting. Ryan was on hand for any problems that might come up; it was a small charter with some serious fishermen who knew what they were doing and needed little assistance. They'd caught so many fish the men had already booked another trip for next Christmas.

He turned back to Gus. 'All right. Give me ten minutes.'

151

'And bring a couple of pieces of that cake that Tony was baking. Smelled pretty damn good. With cream and ice cream, please.'

'At this rate, we'll all put weight on.' Jake laughed as Gus walked up the stairs.

'But Tony's a bloody good chef. You hang on to him,' the older man called back.

Jake followed Gus's instructions and ten minutes later he pushed open the door of the wheelhouse with his shoulder, balancing the tray holding the cake and coffees.

He placed it carefully on the top of the console. 'I apologised to Ryan on the way up.'

Gus looked up from the chart he had spread out on the bench along the side of the small room. 'Good.'

Jake sat on the swivel chair in front of the helm and stared at the water. There was no wind and the expanse of flat silvery-blue sea stretched unbroken to the horizon. A huge flock of migratory birds created a shadow on the deck as they flew over *Moonshine*.

'Variegated whimbrels,' Jake said.

'Smart, aren't you?' Gus said with a grin and Jake couldn't help smiling back.

'Leonora Ramsay told me what some of the migrating birds were called.'

'It's good to see you smile. Now tell me what's wrong. Woman trouble, I'm guessing?'

Jake nodded.

'I thought so. One minute you and Jenni were all lovey-dovey, and then you haven't spoken her name once since we've been on board. She went very well as a hostess, I hear.'

'She did.'

'And?' Gus stared at him and Jake shrugged.

'It's a long story, mate, and it goes back ten years. In a nutshell, Jenni's father accused me of stealing money from their shop and ran me out of town. Jenni believed him and that's the end of the story.'

'Doesn't sound like it to me.'

'Okay. So then she wanted to know how I afforded the new boats.'

'And did you tell her?'

Jake lifted his head and stared at Gus. 'No.'

'So you let her assume that there was something underhand there?' Gus ran his hand over his grizzled face. 'Jesus, Jake. Of course she did. How long ago was it? Ten years? She would have been just a kid.'

'She was nineteen and we were seeing each other.'

'So of course she would have believed her old man. Did you deny it then?'

Jake shook his head. 'I tried to see her the night I left but she shut her bedroom window in my face.'

'So let me get this right. You were accused. You left town under a cloud. You come back a millionaire?'

'I guess so.' Jake picked up the coffee mug.

'And then when she asks you where you got your money, you didn't tell her about your own father? You let her think there was something shonky about your actions.'

'She should have trusted me.'

'Maybe she should have, but you didn't help the situation when you could have, did you?'

'I guess not.'

'It comes down to two things, Jake. Actually three.' Gus sat on the chair beside him and reached for his coffee. 'The first two are communication and honesty.'

'What's the third?' Jake was beginning to feel a bit better, listening to Gus's take on the situation.

'The most important one of all. Do you love Jenni?'

Chapter Twenty-Two

Jake brought *Moonshine* into the dock at the old house. The river was a deep green and the current swirled along the mangroves as the tide pushed in. The sky was clear, and the afternoon was warm, and he let that lighten his mood.

He loved Jenni McDougal and he wasn't going to let her go. They'd work it out. He would tell her the truth about his inheritance from his father. The inheritance had set him up and provided the deposit for him to go into business with his two silent partners and purchase his boats. He could deal with her thinking that he'd made a mistake as a young boy, so she didn't think badly of her father.

He changed from his uniform and slipped on his denim shorts and a clean T-shirt before he picked up the papers that he'd printed out in his cabin and put them in an envelope.

With a steady step and hope in his heart, Jake jumped off the boat onto the path, and headed for the McDougal house. The windows were wide open, but all was quiet. He walked around the back and tapped on the kitchen door.

There was no answer, so he pushed the door open and looked in.

She was sitting at the table, a mess of papers and books on the table top. As he pushed open the screen door Jenni looked up, her eyes red-rimmed and her cheeks wet with tears. Jake's heart almost stopped. He hurried over and crouched down beside her.

'What's wrong, Jen? Is everyone okay?'

She shook her head from side to side and didn't speak.

'Tell me, sweetheart. What's the matter?'

Her eyes welled with fresh tears and she looked down as one plopped onto his hand. Jake reached up and wiped the tears away with his thumb.

'Jake.' Her voice was husky. 'I'm sorry. I honestly didn't know, but I should have believed you. I should have trusted you. That's what it's all about, isn't it? I failed you. I let you down. And because of that and my father, you weren't here to look after your mum when she needed you most. I know what my father did. He lied to cover up his own failings.'

Jake pulled her to her feet and held her close rocking her, murmuring soothing sounds until she stopped crying.

'It's okay, baby. I'm sorry I left without seeing you, but all the anger of those days came back. I didn't think I was good enough for you.' Never would he tell her that her father had called him river trash and that had stayed with him for years. The irony was that his own father had come from a huge cattle property in Central Queensland.

Nowhere near a river.

'Oh, Jake. We've lost so much time. How can you ever forgive me? And my family?'

'There's nothing to forgive, babe. But there's two things you have to know. It's not about trust, it's about honesty. Three things actually.'

She lifted tear-filled eyes and pressed her lips to his mouth. 'You don't have to explain anything.'

'Yes.' He nodded. 'I want to tell you. My father didn't know about me until after Mum died. He'd been up here on a holiday, and I was the result of a summer fling. Mum knew he loved the land, and she didn't want to leave the sea, so she didn't ever tell him about me. She chose to be a single mother. That's something I have to deal with. But she contacted him when she was dying and then when he died, it turned out he left me a sizable chunk of money, and I bought the boats with it. I have a couple of partners too. You'll meet them soon.'

'Are they coming on a charter?'

Jake laughed and shook his head. 'No sweetheart, you're going to meet them on our honeymoon.'

'Honeymoon?' Her lips tilted in a watery smile, but his Jen was back.

'Shouldn't there be a proposal before a honeymoon?' she said.

Jake sat her back down on the chair and dropped to one knee. He held her eyes with his and put his right hand on his heart.

'Jenni McDougal, I've loved you since the first minute I saw you. You are in my heart, and you will be there while ever I have breath in my body. Will you marry me?'

Jake's eyes moistened as she reached down and put her hand over his heart. 'Jake Jones, I love you more than life itself. I always have, and yes, I promise to love you forever.' Her face broke into a beautiful smile as she leaned down and rested her forehead against his. 'I don't think we need anything more formal than that, so tell me about this honeymoon.'

'Oh yes, we do, your brothers would be after me, if there was no wedding.'

'Okay, that's true.' Jenni watched curiously as Jake pulled out the envelope he'd put into his pocket.

He handed it to her. 'I thought you might like to see Paris in the spring.'

Jenni's eyes widened as she opened the envelope.

'Oh my God,' she squealed. She waved the airline tickets in the air, and her delighted cries coupled with the slamming of a door and heavy footsteps as her three brothers walked into the kitchen.

'Hi Jake, good to see you're back. And to see you smiling for a change, Jenni,' Matt said as he went to the fridge. 'What's for dinner?'

Jake laughed at the look on Dane's and Donny's faces as Jenni replied.

'Ah, I think we might have snails and frogs' legs.'

'And French champagne,' Jake added as he pulled Jenni into his arms. 'We have something to celebrate.

He couldn't see the look on his future brothers-in-laws' faces as Jenni's lips met his, and quite frankly, Jake Jones didn't care.

THE END

Book 2
Her Outback Protector
Don's story

Annie Seaton

Dedication

This book is dedicated to Ian, my patient husband.
It was written very quickly, and he cooked while I wrote!

Acknowledgments

A special thank you to:
my wonderful editor and critique partner, Susanne Bellamy, and
my eagle-eyed proof-reader, Roby Aiken

Chapter 1

As the small plane banked to the right, Claire Templeton leaned forward and pressed her face to the window. For the first time in three days of travelling and gradually changing her appearance in cheap motel rooms, a glimmer of confidence began deep within her.

Brisbane to Mackay. Mackay to Cairns. Cairns to Mt Isa.

And now, the final leg of her trip to Second Chance Bay at the base of the Gulf of Carpentaria was almost over.

Maybe she'd done it. Claire hoped she had; her future depended on it.

She jumped as the pilot's voice cracked into her headphones. 'You're in luck today, folks.'

The plane was small, and he handed each of the three passengers a set of headphones as they boarded in Mt Isa. It suited her; it meant she didn't have to interact with the other passengers, although they both looked harmless enough: an elderly woman clutching half a dozen Myers shopping bags and a young man who had gone to sleep as soon as the plane had taken off. He didn't stir as the pilot's voice droned on.

'We're over Burketown now, and you can just see the tail end of the Morning Glory. She's late today. Usually passes over Karumba before dawn but if you look to the east'—he turned back to see if they were doing as he instructed— 'you can see those lovely big rolls of cloud.'

Claire peered at the cloud formation. It looked like long rolls of cotton wool. Not very wide but stretching as far as she could see. Quite impressive.

'The Morning Glory is unique to the Gulf of Carpentaria. It's not very wide but can stretch — sometimes in an almost perfectly straight line — for a thousand kilometres from one side of the gulf

to the other. Bloody awesome, it is. I never get tired of seeing it.'
He turned again and caught Claire's eye with a grin because she
was the only one paying attention to him. 'They say the old
codgers in the Burketown pub can smell it coming.'

Claire nodded and gave him a polite smile before she looked
back to the window.

The plane began to descend, and she turned her attention to the
narrow river snaking through the wetlands beneath them. A silver
ribbon caught the early morning sun; to her deep satisfaction, there
was no sign of habitation below.

Claire had researched her destination very, very carefully.
Second Chance Bay was a place few people visited; it had little to
attract it unless you were a fisherman, and she was highly unlikely
to run into anyone who had heard of her.

Or so she hoped.

The last three days of keeping her head down and waiting for
someone to recognise her had been exhausting. With a contented
sigh, she sat back and ignored the churning nerves in her stomach.

Her new life was ahead.

The airport was tiny, a small fibro shack with a flat roof, and
apparently, with no one manning it. The pilot taxied the plane to
the gate near the fence before he climbed out. He came around,
opened the door and lowered the steps. Claire waited until he'd
helped the older woman down and watched as she walked over to a
waiting car. The young man bounded off with a 'thanks, mate' to
the pilot before Claire unbuckled her seatbelt and stood, bending
her head low as she stepped through the narrow doorway. Her
hands shook, and she took a deep breath as a blast of moist,
cloying heat almost took her breath away.

The pilot stood at the bottom of the steps and lifted a hand to
help her, but she waved him away politely.

'Just the one suitcase?' he asked.

Claire nodded. Looking around, she wondered which way she'd have to walk. There was no taxi service at the airport, but she knew a general store was about a hundred metres away where she could call a taxi to take her to Second Chance Bay. If there wasn't one available, she would walk. It was only about three kilometres along the river to the small house she'd rented on the north shore; that would be her first obstacle overcome.

She shook her head with a slight grin. No, not really the first, probably the hundred and first obstacle that had confronted her over the past three weeks, but she had to let all that go now.

'Are you getting picked up, love?'

'I'm fine, thank you.'

He handed her the suitcase. 'I've got to get going. I've got a fishing charter out of Normanton mid-morning. Taking a group out to Sweers Island.'

Even though she didn't want to engage, Claire's natural politeness kicked in.

'It was a very pleasant flight. Thank you for pointing out the cloud.'

'You here for long?' He looked at her curiously, and she immediately regretted her comment.

'Just a short visit.'

'So I'll see you on the Sunday flight?'

She shook her head. 'No, we're driving to Darwin.' The more of a false trail she could leave, the safer it would be on the slim chance that someone did track her to this isolated bay. The blasted media were so persistent, as she well knew.

'Okay, then. Have a good trip. Bloody hot up there this time of the year.'

Claire nodded and picked up her suitcase. He was right. Even though it wasn't far past eight a.m., the sun was beating down on the top of her now-blonde hair. The breeze picked up the loose strands and blew them across her mouth. At work, she'd kept her hair up in an elegant chignon and rarely wore it down. That had become her signature look, and the studio had hired Marnie, a hairdresser, to look after her styling once the show had taken off. She stopped, put her suitcase down, pulled a scrunchie from her pocket, and tied the loose strands back; it was difficult because the new style—thanks to manicure scissors in a motel room—had left it a long, shaggy cut of different lengths. Marnie would groan if she could see it now.

Once her hair was tied back as best she could, Claire pulled a baseball cap onto her head and picked up her bag before stepping out to the gate in the fence. A flat, wide road ran parallel to the water, a few houses were edging the road that headed down towards the general store. She could see the store sign at the front. When she heard the plane taxiing out to the runway, she stopped beneath a tree with wide, spreading branches and dug into her handbag for her sunglasses.

The road was deserted, and the only sounds were the whoosh of the tiny waves breaking onto the sand across the road and the occasional sound of a motor as boats headed out into the Gulf.

Claire gripped the handle of her suitcase and set off with a determined step.

***

Don Douglas turned onto the road that led down to the general store at Karumba Point. Dane and Matt had laughed at his new strategy, but he'd argued with them.

'It's worth a try. I'm sick of the bloody employment agencies sending the wrong people out there. What do they think we need up here?'

'Settle down, mate. It's not a drama. If we can't get someone in time, I'll come with you on this trip, and Jenni can come and help too.' Jake had a solution; his lateral thinking had seen him make his first million before he'd come home to Second Chance Bay before his thirtieth birthday.

'I don't expect you to bail me out, Jake. What about little Leni?'

Jake and Jeni's two-year-old loved being on the water, but it wasn't the place for a child out in the Kimberley wilderness. His brother-in-law, Jake, had been a godsend to the family since he'd come back to the Bay. He'd bought into the family business, and the old McDougal boats, the *Helen M* and the *Elsie,* had been refurbished. The fishing business had been so good over the past two seasons Don had been able to take out a business loan and follow his dream, setting up on his own. He'd bought a classic old boat built by the well-known boat-building family who'd been building craft in Brisbane for over a hundred years.; He'd refurbished her for two years in his downtime, hiring contractors for the bigger jobs, but had enjoyed restoring the old timber in the saloon and cabins himself. Within a few months on the water, the *Kimberley Adventurer* was fast building a reputation as one of the top cruises in the northern waterways.

He advertised it as the classic adventure tour and had been attracting the wealthier end of the tourist population. That's why he was fussy about the crew he hired. The employment agency in Darwin didn't get it.

Don had thrown the two applications they'd sent into the bin. 'It's not even worth a reply email. A Dutch girl who doesn't speak English and has no experience, and a sixty-year-old man who wants to fish when he's not on duty? Jesus, give me a break. All I want is a hostess. Someone reliable with a bit of class. Someone who can talk to the passengers. Is that such a big ask?' He folded his arms and shook his head. 'So, I'm trying the locals. Maybe one of the school leavers this year. If we can find a local, that would do the trick. And it would be sustainable.'

Jake had shaken his head, but Matt, Don's brother, laughed, putting the thoughts of the family into words.

'Mate, we have a population of five hundred in Karumba and sixty-two in Second Chance Bay. You know most of them anyway, so what's the point of putting an ad up in the local store? You could think about it all week and finally realise there's no one suitable here.'

Don slammed the door of his old Toyota ute and strode to the general store. He walked into the crowded shop and stood at the back near the postcard stand waiting as the three staff behind the counter dealt with the breakfast orders of the crowd from the caravan park next door. Finally, there was a lull, and Pammy, the store owner, waved him over.

'Good to see you, Donny McDougal. Can I do you a bacon and egg roll? With barbeque sauce like you like it?' Her grin was wide.

'Why not.' Don smiled back. 'You got a minute spare, Pam?' Pam Harris had run the store for as long as he could remember.

'For the best-looking man in town, course I have, love. Come outside, and I'll have a quick break. Fleur, a bacon and egg roll for one. On the house.'

She pushed open the door and led Don over to the faded pink umbrella shading the green plastic table and chairs at a precarious angle.

'Fleur,' he said with a grin. 'A backpacker?'

Pam shook her head. 'No, my sister's daughter up from Brisbane. She needed a job.'

'That's what I wanted to ask you.' He held up the small white card he'd filled out. 'I'm after staff.'

'Bloody hard up here, mate.' Pam lit the cigarette and blew out a plume of smoke. Don held his breath until it wafted past.

'It is. I've got a tour leaving next Thursday, and I need a hostess.' He gestured to the shop. 'What's Fleur's background?'

Pammy shook her head, but a grin spread across her tanned face. 'You're not poaching my staff. Besides, I'm keeping an eye on her. She got herself in a bit of trouble in the city.'

'Fair enough. Can I put this up on your noticeboard?'

Pammy reached out and took the card. She squinted as she read it aloud.

'Host/Hostess wanted for touring the waterways of the Kimberleys on a ten-day wilderness tour. Preference given to an applicant who is seeking a permanent job. Classic boat, with luxury inclusions, sleeps eighteen guests, chef on board. Day trips on excursion tenders and helicopter. Local knowledge preferred but not essential.' She stubbed her cigarette in the glass ashtray on the table. 'Jeez, Donny boy, you've hit the big time. Sounds pretty swanky. Luxury inclusions, hey?'

'I had to take out a decent loan to set it up that way.'

'I'll bet.' She looked up ruefully. 'Just as well I'm not charging you for your brekky. And here I am, not able to afford a decent umbrella.'

Don laughed, and a cheeky grin wrinkled Pam's face. 'You're doing okay,' he said.

'I am, but while ever that umbrella puts up some shade, I don't need to waste money on a new one, do I?'

'You're tight, Pammy.'

'But I'm doing well. Listen, I might apply for your job, Donny. Right up my alley, hey?'

'I couldn't afford you. You've got your own little gold mine here.'

'Yeah, it's doing pretty good. But I tell you what, I could do with a holiday.'

'Grey nomie season is almost done.'

She nodded and lit up another cigarette, and Don moved his chair back a fraction. He wasn't a snob, but a bottle-blonde-haired sixty-year-old with a chain-smoking habit wasn't who he was after, no matter how good a person Pammy was.

'Yep, they're starting to move out. Just the stalwarts left down in Dunrootin' Lane down the back of the park.'

Don chuckled. He loved talking to Pammy; you were always guaranteed a smile, and she was a hoot when she'd had a couple of wines at the pub. 'Yeah, our season's almost done too. Fish have been scarce this last couple of weeks; the wet's building early.'

'The glider group's coming into town to ride the Morning Glory next week, and then I'll take a break, I think.' She shot him a glance before she turned away and blew the smoke over her shoulder. 'I was serious, Donny. If you want a hostess, I can do it.'

'Thanks, mate. But you need a break; it's been a busy winter in town.' What he didn't say was that the type of clientele who paid upwards of twenty thousand dollars for ten days of cruising had high expectations. And that was why he didn't want Jake and Jenni to help him out. The age group on the charter wouldn't appreciate a two-year-old in the small confines of the luxury charter.

'Okay. You're a thoughtful bloke, but—' Pammy stopped talking as she gestured up the road. 'There you go. You've put out the call, and here comes someone new to town. The universe is looking out for you, Donny.'

Don looked to where she was gesturing with her cigarette. A slim young woman was walking along the other side of the road, past the pub, pulling a small, wheeled suitcase behind her.

'Give me your card. I'll stick it in the window and bring your brekky out. Want a coffee to go with it?'

'How about one of your legendary chocolate milkshakes?'

'With malt?' she asked.

Don nodded. 'Yes, please.'

'Done.' She pushed the chair in and Don looked up, watching curiously as the woman approached the store. Her head was down, but occasionally, she would lift it and look around, scanning the road and the houses around her as though she were looking for something. As she turned onto the path towards the store, she lifted her head and looked directly at him. He nodded and smiled, but she put her head down and didn't respond.

With a shrug, Don picked up the Normanton weekly newspaper from the table; maybe it was worth putting an ad in that paper. Spread the net to the next town.

The woman carefully placed her suitcase outside the door, and the bell jangled again as she pushed the door open. A waft of icy air blew out of the shop past him, along with the aroma of frying bacon. Don rubbed the back of his neck, and his fingers came away wet with perspiration; the season was heating up early. He'd checked the charts; the weather next week was shaping up to be good for the tour.

Ten days on the water with three side trips to local waterfalls and a helicopter trip to a spectacular gorge. He enjoyed the scenic trips rather than the fishing these days; the clients were wealthy and usually easier to please than the fishermen who were chasing the big catch. Organising them and liaising with National Parks and the indigenous owners of the area took up a lot of his time, and he'd even thought about hiring an admin assistant. If he continued as skipper on each charter—Dane was his back-up in case of emergency—he was going to have to move across to Wyndham for the whole season next year.

He grinned ruefully. Apart from the year he'd spent at maritime college in Tassie gaining his master's qualification, he'd always lived in the family home.

It was time to spread his wings.

Pammy came out and placed a wrapped-up burger, and a milkshake in an old-fashioned anodized container in front of him. 'I didn't know if you were in a hurry or not.' She gestured to the window with a smile. 'Your ad's up. And you already have some interest.'

Don leaned forward and looked around Pammy. The woman was standing at the window reading the card. As he watched, she pulled out a small notebook and wrote something down. The phone number, he assumed.

'Told ya.' Pammy's smile was gleeful.

'Not a local?' he asked.

She shrugged. 'Haven't seen her around before.' She chuckled, and her laugh was deep and husky. 'And the suitcase is a dead giveaway, ya dork.'

'True.'

'Do you want me to tell her that you're the one doing the hiring?'

Don looked back inside but the woman had disappeared into the shop. 'Why not? I'm getting desperate. If I don't get someone in the next day or two, I'm going to be serving meals, clearing tables and running the bar as well as skippering the charter.'

'Leave it with me, lovely.'

Don waited as Pam went back inside. It was only a minute or so before the bell jangled again, and the blonde-haired woman walked out. She removed her baseball cap and tipped the huge sunglasses onto the top of her head. 'You're Don McDougal?' Her voice was soft, and Don had to lean forward to hear.

Don put the milkshake down, pushed the chair back and stood. 'I am.'

'And you're the one hiring for the charter in the window inside? Is it filled yet?'

He smiled. 'That job card literally went up about a minute before you walked inside. So no, not yet. Are you interested?'

'Perhaps. I'd need to know what skills you require. And also'—she dropped her eyes and broke eye contact— 'I might not be able to get references in time.'

This time, when her hand rose to tuck her hair back, he noticed the slight tremor in her fingers.

'Sit down. We can chat about it now.' How lucky was he? If she turned out to be suitable, he could go home and stick it into his brothers. He could tell by her words that she had class.

Don walked around the cheap plastic table, pulled the other chair out and waited until she sat.

'Thank you,' she said. 'I guess I'm about to be interviewed, but I haven't had time to get nervous.' She lifted her head and smiled, and Don stared. When she smiled, her whole face lit up, and her green eyes glowed with life.

'Two-way street. I can answer your questions first to see if you think it might suit you.' He looked curiously over at the suitcase. 'You've just arrived in town?'

'I have. I came in on the morning flight from Mt Isa.'

'Do you have accommodation booked?'

This time, her nod was slow, and she dropped her gaze again. Don's eyes focused on her lips.

'Yes. Not really holiday accommodation. I'm renting in the next town. I came here to see if I could call a taxi to get me there.'

'The next town?' he said with a frown. 'Normanton?'

She looked up again, and the clarity of her eyes struck him again. 'Second Chance Bay.'

'It's not quite a town,' he said slowly.

'I know,' she said simply.

There was silence for a few seconds and she gestured to his burger. 'Please don't let me keep you from your breakfast. It'll be getting cold.'

'Are you eating? Can I get you a coffee?'

'A coffee would be good. Thank you. Flat white.'

Don stood and walked into the shop again, pleased to see the crowd had thinned. He'd been too busy reading the paper to take notice of the comings and goings of the customers. Pammy was standing at the sink, one hand in soapy water, the other holding a coffee.

'A flat white for the lady, please, Pam,' he called above the radio that had been turned up louder.

Pam nodded to the other girl who moved quickly to the coffee machine. 'I'll bring it out to you.'

Don opened the door, and his eyes widened when he took in the empty chair. He swivelled around; the suitcase had gone too. With a shrug and the fleeting thought that he mustn't have measured up, he picked up his burger. The disappointment that ran through him was surprising. It didn't have so much to do with filling his hostess position but more about satisfying his curiosity about the pretty woman moving to Second Chance Bay.

The coffee came out at the same time as the suitcase wheels grated on the gravel path at the side of the shop, and the mystery woman reappeared.

'I needed a wash.' She gestured to the facilities between the shop and the caravan park. 'I didn't like to leave my bag out here, but I guess it's a bit different to the city.'

'You could leave your bag on the side of the road all night, and it would still be there in the morning. It's a pretty safe place here.'

On the land, anyway, he thought. Before Don could stand, she gestured for him to stay where he was and sat opposite him again. He smiled as he settled back and quickly demolished the small burger. He picked up the napkin and wiped his mouth and the barbeque sauce from his fingers. Pammy was always heavy-handed with the sauce.

'Let's start again.' He held his hand across the table. 'I'm Don McDougal, owner of the *Kimberley Adventurer*. I live around in Second Chance Bay too.'

Her hand was cold in his, and he could feel the slight tremble in her fingers.

'I'm Claire. Claire…Templeton. And I was intending to look for a job in a few days. I just didn't expect to find one on offer so quickly.' She flicked up the sunglasses again and put them on top of her head. Reaching down into her bag, she pulled out a pair of thick, dark-rimmed reading glasses and put them on.

Putting her bag on the floor close to her chair, she sat straight in the chair and regarded him, tension obvious in every line of her body.

'Please don't be nervous. We're very casual up here.' Don tried to put her at ease.

'Thank you.' Her stiff shoulders seemed to relax slightly, but she tugged back the hand that he'd forgotten he was still holding. Her fingers were long and narrow, and her skin was soft.

'Well, Claire, let me tell you a little bit about our family business. My brothers, my sister and her husband, and I have a few boats up here, so we hire a lot of staff. Unfortunately, the hostess I'd signed on for the cruise starting next week called yesterday and said her partner wasn't happy about her being on a boat with a male skipper.' He shook his head. 'I don't think he understood what a big vessel we're on. We've got half a dozen crew and eighteen passengers. Anyway, it doesn't matter. The bottom line is that I'm down a hostess. And I need to find one fast.'

'What sort of work does a hostess do?' she asked.

'Um.' Don tried to gather his thoughts. 'A bit of everything. Services the cabins, serves the meals, clears the tables, and most importantly, tallies up the bar bill for the guests at the end of the charter.'

'Okay, that sounds like something I could handle.'

'What sort of work do you usually do?'

The expression that crossed her face was hard to pinpoint.

'Oh, a bit of this and a bit of that. I waitressed when I was at … when I was younger. I know how to make a bed, and my maths skills are top-notch. I can certainly tally up a bar bill.' Her voice held a tinge of amusement. 'But like I said before, I don't have any references. I also don't have any paperwork to give you.' Her shoulders lifted in a small shrug. 'The rest of my stuff will arrive later. So I'll understand if you want to pass.'

Don looked at her for a long moment, and she held his gaze. The maritime workers that passed through the north were often itinerant and had few qualifications. Usually, it was word of mouth from skipper to skipper, and he'd only had the occasional experience with a deckhand who wanted to smoke a joint on deck at night. He didn't care what they did on land, but his boat was drug-free. Her expression was open, and her eyes were clear and steady.

Even if she had no references, he had a good feeling about her so far.

'Do you know your tax file number?'

Claire shook her head, and Don tapped a finger against his mouth and thought. 'Okay … I guess for the first trip, we could pay you cash in hand. I don't usually do that, but I do need to get this sorted quickly. How would you feel about that?'

'Whatever suits you. Um, would I have to cook?'

'No. We have a chef on board.'

She nodded. 'Good. That's one thing I don't do well.'

Don narrowed his eyes. From a couple of minutes of conversation, he'd got the impression of a well-spoken, intelligent woman. It sounded like there were a few things she could do well, and again, Don wondered what she was doing here in this frontier town.

She had *class*.

'Okay, have a think about it and you can let me know what you decide later today.'

Claire picked up her coffee and closed her eyes as she sipped. Her face was finely structured, and there were shadows beneath her eyes, but despite her fragility, Don sensed a quiet strength. He couldn't figure out how he knew that, but he was sure of it.

Mystery woman. The north attracted all types, many running from broken relationships. He glanced down at her fingers, but she wore no rings, and there was no tell-tale white mark on her ring finger. Although her skin was so fair, it would be hard to see.

She placed the cup carefully back onto the saucer and stood. 'I have your number. Is there a public telephone in Second Chance Bay? I don't have a mobile, and there's no phone connected at the rental.'

'How about I show you?' Don grinned. 'If you can stand getting into my fish-smelling ute, I can give you a lift to the bay. You could wait hours for the taxi to come over from Karumba town. And then you still have to get the public punt across. And no, there's no phone over there.'

'The public punt?' Her forehead wrinkled in a frown.

'Yes, the punt to cross the river. That's how you get across if you don't have your own boat.'

'Oh.'

'There's no bridge. It was washed away in the wet last year, but it will take a population explosion over at the Bay for it to be replaced, and I can't see that happening this century.'

Claire looked at him carefully, without speaking, obviously weighing up the alternatives.

'Plus, the chance of Joe—the taxi driver—being sober when he gets here isn't something I'd like to put money on,' Don added with a grin. 'The call for taxis in town is minimal, and Joe's usually in the pub.

'Oh. Okay then. Thank you. I'll accept your offer.' She bent and took the handle of her suitcase before he could take it, and Don flicked a glance towards her as they walked to the ute. Her acceptance was in words only. Her body language was telling him that she didn't feel comfortable with the situation. She held her head stiffly and didn't meet his eye as he opened the door for her. Taking her suitcase from her, he swung it into the back of the ute.

Chapter 2

Claire stood on the porch of the small house and watched the sun disappear behind heavy cloud. After she'd unpacked, she sat on the soft sofa with her Kindle—the only electronic device she had with her. If she didn't have a phone or a laptop, she wouldn't be tempted to look at social media—or the news. The trolls on Facebook had been cruel when the program went to air.

And for days afterwards.

Combined with the media camped outside her house, it almost did her head in. Guilt had flooded through her to think that she had been a part of that madness for a few years.

A story at any cost. Don't worry about the truth, and don't worry about who you might hurt in the process. As long as the audience numbers were there and the ratings stayed up, the bosses were happy.

Social media was a cruel thing.

She surprised herself by falling asleep before she'd read one chapter of her book and slept soundly. The dreams that had haunted her sleep for the first couple of weeks seemed to have gone, but sometimes she had trouble remembering what had actually happened and what she'd dreamed.

It was mid-afternoon by the time she woke, and Claire had stretched like a cat. Relaxation filled her, her limbs were loose and fluid.

Lightning flashed in the distance and it energised her. She took a deep breath; there was rain in the air. On the annual summer holiday at the farm, her grandfather had taught her how to smell rain coming, as well as the other signs that a farmer knew presaged rain. Snake tracks in the dirt meant the snakes were on the move, and rain would always follow. She looked around nervously. Snakes up here would be very different to snakes in the outback of New South Wales where Claire had researched a program. Big and venomous. The program also looked at snakes in the tropics, and the images stayed with her.

The house was set back from the river that she'd crossed in Don McDougal's boat this morning. The clouds had come in as she'd unpacked the few belongings from her suitcase and scoped out the house. There had been clean sheets in a linen cupboard that smelled of mothballs, and she'd made up the bed. The house was austere, but the basic necessities were there. She had somewhere to cook, sleep, eat and wash—and that was all she required.

And somewhere to hide and lick her wounds. Metaphorically,

Not with a healing tongue, but with some rational thought; this was a place to get her head together. Taking a job up here would also focus her attention away from the past few weeks, and that was a good thing.

Claire couldn't believe that she'd made such a basic mistake when she'd rented the house; there was no way to get to Second Chance Bay by road. She had assumed that there would be a bridge over the river.

All roads—all two of them from the main town of Karumba and the road from Normanton—ended on the eastern side of the river. *That* hadn't been mentioned by the owner of the house. She'd made her enquiries, booked the house from a generic email address, and had paid six months' rent by bank cheque. There wasn't a great demand up here for rentals, and she hadn't had to supply rental references. Getting supplies in would have to be a priority tomorrow; she hadn't liked to ask Don to wait while she bought some groceries.

Claire didn't ask anyone for anything. She hadn't before, and she wasn't about to start now. She'd been let down too many times, and the last time she had been let down, it had left her life like a train wreck.

Forcing her thoughts away from her job and her life in Sydney, she focused on the rumbling of her stomach.

The squashed muesli bar and the apple in her handbag would have to do for a meal tonight. Tomorrow, she'd get herself back on the public punt and find a grocery store within walking distance. As well as food, she had to buy more hair bleach; she only had one packet left, and she didn't imagine they'd be calling into shops on the charter. It sounded like the local taxi wasn't an option. At least it wasn't far to walk from the house to the punt; Don had pointed out the jetty as they'd motored across the river.

'We can get isolated here in the wet if the river floods.' He stood at the back of a small aluminium boat as he steered towards the shore. His mid-brown hair was longish, and the breeze lifted it. The sun reflected off his sunglasses, but she knew that he was watching her.

Claire had perched at the front, her handbag on her lap, and her fingers gripping the handle of her suitcase. She wasn't used to boats but wasn't going to mention that, in case it jeopardised her chance at this hostess job.

If I decide I want it.

She knew her eyes were wide, but she'd have to learn how to pull herself across the river at the public crossing when she wanted to go back. How hard could it be? It was something she was going to do first up tomorrow; new experiences were ahead of her, and that would be the first. She blocked the thought of what the rest of the experiences would be; once the social media furore had settled down, she was going to have to find a new career.

Media was behind her, and she'd never go back to it.

A small boat whizzed past them and the wash rocked theirs slightly and she grabbed for her handbag as it slipped. She clung to it tightly; if she lost her bag, she'd be in all sorts of trouble; she would have to find somewhere safe in the rental to leave some of her money. It was encouraging to hear Don say it was a safe place to live.

He had said most of the locals who lived on this side of the river had their own boats. Claire knew she'd have to learn how to get across; finding another place to stay wasn't an option.

'How often does the river flood?' she asked as he'd pulled up at a small jetty; she'd told him the address she was looking for.

'This is the address you gave me. It's the Dundas house.' He pointed to the house as the motor idled. 'The last moderate flood was about ten years ago, but the biggest, the last major flood was in 74. Before I was born. Don't worry. At worst we get cut off from across town for a few days, so you always need to make sure you've got a good food store in the pantry. In the wet season that is.'

'The wet season's coming up, isn't it?'

'It is.' He looked at her curiously. 'It will start to build in six weeks or so. We've also got to watch for flooding from cyclones that can come from the west and the east. Even though we can get across to town by boat when the flow slows down, sometimes the roads from Karumba and Normanton to the south can be closed for a couple of months. How long are you staying up here? Not over the wet season?'

Claire had considered her answer carefully. She had an answer prepared for most questions, and most were far from the truth. But she had to rethink, because if there was a job going, and an ideal job on a boat far from anyone in the isolation of the Kimberley wilderness, she wanted it.

She spoke slowly. 'I guess it depends on how much work I can get up here. I may move on to Darwin in a few weeks. Or maybe not.'

Don had helped her out of the boat and carried her suitcase along the jetty. He'd waited at the gate as she'd tried the key to the rental, and she had turned with a nod when the door unlocked.

'Good to see someone here. It's been empty for a long time,' he said, pointing to the north. 'Our place is another six houses along this way around the bend in the river. If you need anything this afternoon—come around. You can't miss it. There's a big white boat called Moonshine moored at the jetty on this side of our place. Anyway, come around later when you're settled in, and let me know if you want to talk more about the job.' He waved and began to walk back to the boat; the grass was long, and Claire had worried about snakes as she'd crossed to the gate. At least someone had mown the grass, and the gardens and lawns were neat.

Don stopped and called out to her from the end of the jetty. 'But I will need to know in the next twenty-four hours, so give it some thought. The job's yours if you want it.'

Now Claire stood watching the rain, the welcoming glow of the lights from the cottage a soft, cosy yellow behind her. But she preferred to stay out here while she decided what she was going to do. It didn't matter if she let the job on the boat pass; she had enough cash to do her for a while before she moved on again.

She let out a soft sigh. How long before she would get over what had happened and re-enter the real world? She'd have to work again. Her parents had left her the house, but the upkeep was expensive. She had a small nest egg of savings back in the bank, but it would only last six months or so at best unless she could find a job while she decided what to do. She didn't want to rush in and sell the house as a knee-jerk reaction; it was where she'd grown up, and it held too many memories to sell.

Yet.

The best decision she'd made was to come up here to the Gulf and give herself time to think. Growing up in the city, the ocean had always fascinated her, and even the smell of the salt soothed her. She had all the time in the world; she had nowhere to be, and no one was expecting her. Until she ran out of cash, this job was something she'd have to think about carefully. It all depended on who was on this charter. What if they were from Sydney? Even though she'd changed her appearance, she was still recognisable. The media wouldn't be fooled by blonde hair and big glasses.

But the job on the boat was enticing; especially the thought of being paid in cash. That could extend her stay here by a few months. Claire had left her plastic cards, her social media accounts and her mobile phone in the safe at her house.

No one could find her here. Her phone and her spending couldn't be tracked.

She knew from personal experience—and was now ashamed—that she, too, had used those things to track someone they'd wanted to interview on the program. It wasn't hard to get the information by paying for it, even if it was a grey area of the law. Shame prickled at her neck. Getting the next story, having the biggest story, had seen ethics put aside sometimes.

Maybe while she was here, she'd use this time to write an article or maybe a book. About going off the technology grid and eschewing social media. The more she thought about the idea, the more excitement niggled at Claire; it would give her a purpose, and it would let her stay here for longer. Maybe by the time she'd done that, things would have settled down, and she would be last week's news.

When the rain stopped, she'd go around the river and see Don.

***

The rain was falling heavily when Don went outside to light the barbeque. He waited until the hotplate was smoking and then put four large pieces of marinated steak on to grill. Matt and Dane would be home soon, and it was his turn to cook. They could argue over the extra piece of steak. And they would argue. Three brothers living in a house together led to some arguments; it was just like when they'd been growing up, but at least they'd grown past wrestling on the lawn.

Poor Mum. He could still remember the day she'd put the hose on Matt and Dane when they'd been pummelling the crap out of each other after an argument about who'd caught the biggest fish.

With a wry grin, Don went back inside and brought out some sausages that had been thawing in the fridge. That was the easiest way to save an argument. But no matter what the dynamic was, theirs was a close-knit family, and he knew his brothers would lay their lives down for him if it ever came to that.

That's what came of having a liar and a gambler for a father. He pushed those thoughts away. No point dwelling on the past.

Dad had been gone for a few years now, and Mum had a happier life.

Don stood at the edge of the covered verandah, watching the rain tumble down. He must have jinxed the weather by talking about rain and floods to Claire. She was a strange mix, independent and private, but with an air of fragility. As far as he'd gleaned, she was going to be living alone in the old Dunstan house. It had been empty for a couple of years since old Ma Dunstan had passed away, and her grown-up kids had come up from Melbourne and tried to sell it.

Caitlin Dunstan, now obviously a mover and shaker in the Melbourne real estate world, had forgotten her Second Chance Bay roots, along with any knowledge she may have had of the real estate market—or lack thereof—in the Bay. He'd smiled when he'd overheard her telling Mum that if it didn't sell in six months, they'd Air BNB the house.

Six months later, the solid old cottage got a lick of paint, the old furniture was taken to the tip at Karumba, and some basic furniture and linen and new crockery were put in. Not surprisingly, as well as not being snapped up for sale, it also hadn't had one visitor in the eighteen months since it had been listed on the holiday site.

Until mystery woman Claire Templeton had turned up yesterday.

But her motivation was none of his business. If she wanted the job on the *Adventurer*, it would solve his immediate problem, and she could learn as she went. He wondered who she was. Not just a beautiful woman with shaggy, long blonde hair and pretty green eyes. Even though her manner had been subdued, Claire's eyes had been full of life. A couple of times, he'd seen them spark, and she'd gone to say something but had thought better of it and lowered her gaze.

A mystery woman indeed.

Don was used to noisy, chattering women. His sister, Jenni, and his mother were both chatterboxes, and the house had been blissfully quiet since Jenni had married Jake, and Mum had set off on her grey nomie travels with her new partner, Rick. Don lived with his brothers, Matt and Dane, in the family house where they'd grown up. He was happy there; it was a comfortable bachelor household. The football volume on the television, the dirty dishes in the sink, and the occasional line of empty beer cans along the bench on the weekend didn't bother them.

He'd thought about inviting Claire over for a barbeque, but when he'd considered the state of the house, he'd hesitated. Maybe another time; he didn't want her to think he was a slob. Not until she'd accepted the job anyway.

Despite her reticence, something had stirred inside Don as he'd looked at Claire and dropped her off at the Dunstan house.

An unfamiliar man-woman response.

A response that he'd not had since he'd had a brief fling with a backpacker he'd met in Darwin last year. He shook his head; he hadn't thought of Elke for months. It had been fun, but there'd been nothing in it, and she'd headed back to Sweden, happy to finish her travels down under. If Claire was going to come and hostess on the boat, he'd make sure to keep his distance; it caused too many problems getting involved with staff, and that was a rule they'd all agreed to and stuck to firmly. Jake and Jenni had been different. Don smiled as he thought about how they'd got together when Jake had come back from Europe a couple of years ago. Sometimes, when he went over to visit Jenni and Jake—they'd built an incredible tropical house on the point north of Karumba— he envied their happiness. Having a partner in life, someone to share things with, would be good. Little Leni had completed their happy family; Don loved playing with her when he went over to visit between charters.

Jeez. He shook his head again before he bent down to turn down the heat on the barbeque as the meat began to sizzle, more than a little disgruntled. What was bringing on all these happy family thoughts? He couldn't ever do that; he spent too much time away to have a home base and a family who would expect him there to mow the lawn and dry the dishes.

So why couldn't he get Claire Templeton out of his head?

The front door slammed, and footsteps pounded on the timber floor down the hall that ran through the centre of the old Queenslander. The fridge door squeaked loudly as it always did, and after a couple of minutes, his oldest brother, Matt, poked his head around the back door. 'Up for a beer, Donny?'

'Yep. I was waiting for you to get home. Where's Dane?'

'He's gone to the pub for dinner. He's got his eye on the new waitress.'

'Lucky her.' Don shook his head as Matt came out holding two cans of beer. He tossed one to Don. 'I knew you'd be up for a beer. It's been hot today.'

'Yeah, one of the others will warn her he's a love'em and leave'em guy,' Don said. 'He won't be late.'

'To be fair, Dane was with Nicki for a while before he lost interest.' Matt pulled out one of the wooden seats around the outside table. He shoved aside a pile of newspapers that had built up since they'd last eaten outside.

'I don't think it was so much he lost interest. I think she moved on because he spends so much time away on the boats.' Don's words echoed his earlier thoughts. 'Doesn't go with happy families.'

'Jake and Jen do okay.' Matt nodded before he tipped his beer up. 'Yeah, but I get what you mean. Same goes for you too. I think you and Dane are both going to turn into cranky old bachelors.' He gestured to the untidy area around them. A couple of shovels leaned against the back wall of the house, and half a dozen fishing nets stretched along between two poles. 'Two cranky old codgers living in a pig sty.'

'What about you, bro? I haven't seen you settling down.' Don pulled a face. Matt was right; it was time they had a bit of a clean-up around the place. Although they were all busy with the business, Matt had done the books and run the office for the past few years. Since Jake had come on board and Don had branched out into his Kimberley adventure charter business, there was never enough time to do much more than sleep and eat in the family house.

'Huh, I spend all my time in the co-op trying to balance the books. All right for you two. You get to meet all the ladies out on the charters.' Matt shoulder-bumped him on the way past. 'So what's going on the barbie?'

'I pulled some marinated steaks out of the freezer.'

'Sounds good. You found a hostie yet?'

'Maybe. I was half tempted to ask her over for dinner, but—' he gestured around the undercover barbeque area.

Matt grinned. 'She must be pretty hot to consider inviting her home. That's not like you.'

Don shook his head. 'No, she's actually a neighbour, and she doesn't know anyone in town. She only arrived here this morning. Moved into the Dunstan place around the bend, and she's looking for a job.' He frowned as the aroma of the cooking meat tickled his taste buds. 'Damn. I should have invited her.' He passed the barbeque tongs over to Matt. 'Do me a favour. Flip those steaks over, and then clean up around here while I'm gone.'

Matt watched him with surprise as Don hurried into the house.

Chapter 3

Absorbed in her thoughts as her pen flew over the paper, jotting down her ideas, Claire jumped when someone knocked loudly on the door. Apart from the occasional call of a bird, since the rain had stopped, the air had been quiet and still. She stretched as she stood and realised she was starving. Making her way to the front door, she smoothed her hands over her loose hair, still not used to having her hair out and over her face. As she passed the mirror, she glanced at her reflection. She still wasn't used to being blonde either; it was going to take some time to adjust.

Pulling the door open cautiously, she looked out onto the porch. It was still light enough to see Don McDougal standing there watching the river. The rain might have cleared away, but it had left a damp and heavy humidity behind. As she'd watched the sun set over the township on the other side of the wide river earlier, perspiration had trickled down her neck. Luckily, she'd found a small water-cooled evaporation unit—albeit old-fashioned, but still effective—in the laundry and had dragged it into the kitchen.

Don turned to her as she stepped out onto the porch.

'Hi Claire, I didn't mean to hassle you so soon.' His smile was wide, and her heart gave a big kick; the black T-shirt clung to broad shoulders and outlined strong biceps. Claire had always been a sucker for muscular arms. A reluctant grin lifted her lips. One of the half-hour programs she'd done had been in a male gym, and the team back at the station had teased her mercilessly, knowing her fascination with muscles. Back in those days, she'd shared her thoughts.

Her grin faded. And look how that had come back to bite her. Her voice was shorter than she'd intended as she stared at him. 'Hassle me?'

He folded his arms across his chest, and heat warmed her cheeks as her eyes lingered on his arms and shoulders.

'I realised that you probably had no food here, and Second Chance Bay isn't the most cosmopolitan place for eating out.'

No man should fill a T-shirt so well. Or have a sexy, deep voice.

Claire folded her arms as long-dormant quivers tugged at her.

'In fact, if you've had a chance to explore, you'll know there's nothing on this side of the river. It's purely residential.' He unfolded his arms, and her mouth dried as her eyes came level with his chest. 'And unless you had a stack of groceries in that small suitcase, I'm guessing you haven't had dinner?'

She nodded before she could help herself and then waved one hand. 'It's okay; I have a couple of snacks in my handbag.' She looked across at the river, now dark and swirling. 'I certainly won't be going back across the river to eat out. I'm fine. I'll go across tomorrow and get some supplies in.'

'Please come and join us. We've got a barbeque happening a couple of hundred metres away.' He lifted his head and sniffed. 'I can even smell the onions cooking from here. That's how close our house is.'

'I—' Claire's mouth watered as she smelled the enticing aroma.

'Now, don't say no. There are only the two of us, and we're used to cooking for five, so we have way too much food. And we'd love to have company.'

'Five?'

A wife and three children?

Before Claire could protest, he held out his arm. 'Come on. You're fine as you are, and by the way, there's no need to lock your door at Second Chance Bay.'

He stood there with his arm crooked, while Claire tried to think of an excuse, but she couldn't come up with one.

'That's very kind of you. Thank you.' She turned to the door. 'But I will get my keys and lock the door.'

When she came back out, Don was standing on the front lawn, and she was relieved when he didn't hold his arm out again.

'It's not far up to our place.'

Claire walked beside him. The grass wasn't as long as she'd thought it would be, and there was a well-worn path along the bank of the river.

'That's Jake's boat. He's my sister's husband. He moors it here because they live out on the Gulf and it's more sheltered from the weather upriver.

Claire widened her eyes as she saw the boat that Don was pointing out. The boat was a huge luxury motor cruiser and would rival any of the million-dollar boats in Sydney Harbour.

'Is your charter boat like that?' If it was, she'd give even more serious consideration to the job.

'No. *Adventurer's* a lot bigger than *Moonshine*.'

'Bigger than that?' Her eyes were wide as she stared at the million-dollar cruiser. Who were these people? Multimillion-dollar boats in a backwater in a frontier town

'Yep, but not as luxurious.' Don held out his hand as they reached the next backyard. 'There's a bit of a jump across here. We keep meaning to fill it in, but none of us ever has the time.'

Claire took his hand, and his fingers were warm against hers as she jumped across the narrow ditch. She dropped his hand as soon as she was on the other side.

'She's a lot older than Jake's boat, but I've spent two years restoring her. She mightn't be as flash as some of the boats on the Kimberley waterways, but she's beautiful. A classic lady.' He held open the gate for her, but Claire hesitated.

What the hell am I doing? She'd broken the rule she'd followed for the past month. The rule that meant not getting involved with anyone. People who were going to ask questions about her.

Where do you come from? What do you do? Are you married?

But worst of all. *You look familiar. Don't I know you from somewhere?*

She'd changed her name. Taken off the pretentious double-barrelled Harris-Templeton when she'd left Sydney. In the media, she'd always used her second name—Sybil anyway—and along with Harris, it was a long jump to connect Sybil Harris with Claire Templeton.

Being Claire Templeton had solved a few problems; her passport and her credit cards were all under that name. Her work credit cards and her public persona had all been under Sybil Harris. For the first time, Claire wondered if she should have risked being recognised at the airport and fled overseas anyway. She closed her eyes as she remembered seeing the media circus on the news at Sydney Airport when a rumour had circulated that she was supposed to be flying to Japan. It had been news to her too; she'd been in a motel in the western suburbs of Brisbane when she'd seen the jackal media pack on the late afternoon news. They still made a story of it, even though she wasn't there, and watching them rehash the events of that night made her sick to the stomach.

'Claire?'

She lifted her head as the deep, sexy voice intruded on her thoughts. Don was holding the gate open, waiting for her to walk through ahead of him.

'This is our place.'

Claire shook her head. 'Look I really can't intrude on your family. Your wife won't want an extra for dinner.'

The rich, deep laugh sent the blood thrumming through her veins, as did his next words.

'Wife? I don't have a wife. You'll just have to put up with two blokes. Matt's my oldest brother, but we cook a good barbie between us. Plus, we'd love some company. We get a bit sick of each other, night after night. Besides, as I said, it's just the two of us tonight. My other brother, Dane, has gone across to the pub for dinner apparently.' As he spoke, that familiar Aussie smell of meat and onions frying on a hotplate drifted in on the slight breeze that had come up.

She had to eat, and the thought of a barbequed meal was certainly more appealing than the apple and squashed muesli bar that were waiting in her bag. It had been kind of Don to offer; he owed her nothing unless this was his way to entice her to take the job. She'd just have to be careful with what she said. Following him through the gate, she tried to remember what she'd told him earlier.

The grass in this yard was long, and the gardens along the fence were overgrown, weeds choking the flowers that poked their colourful heads above the lush green weeds. A variety of coloured crates leaned drunkenly against a small shed, and a couple of small wooden boats were upturned on the grass. Don led her around the shed to an undercover paved area where a tall man with dark hair like his was standing beside the barbeque, a pair of tongs in one hand and an empty tray in the other. Where Don was broad-shouldered, this man was long and lean.

'Great timing,' he said with a welcoming smile. He put the plate and tongs down and held out a hand. 'I'm Matt.'

'Hello.' Claire took his hand and shook it. 'I'm Claire. It's very kind of you to feed me.' She couldn't help smiling as he laughed and gestured to Don.

'Better than looking at this boofhead all night.' He gestured around to the barbeque table. 'A boofhead who owes me, little brother. Not only did I clean up out here, but I cleared the kitchen too.'

'I hope you didn't clean up on my account,' Claire said.

'I just did as I was told.'

Don's cheeks reddened as he looked at her. 'It needed doing. Working all the time, none of us notices how we let things go.' He moved his gaze across to his brother. 'Mum and Rick are due home next week, and someone needs to weed her veggie patch and mow the lawn, or she'll be after our hides.'

'Well, it won't be me,' Matt said as he loaded the meat and onions onto the tray.

'Looks like it'll be Dane because I'll be off on a charter.' They both chuckled as Don pulled out one of the chairs at the table and gestured for Claire to sit down. 'Matt, you keep Claire entertained, and I'll get the plates and salad.'

Claire swallowed as Matt took the seat opposite her.

'So, Claire. Don says you've moved into the old Dundas place?'

She nodded.

'And you're going to work on the charters?'

This time, her nod was hesitant at first. Technically, it wasn't a lie if she was going to take on the job with Don. She was sick of lies these last few weeks.

The silence that followed was awkward, but Matt filled it after a minute or two. 'There's plenty of work up here. Or at least there is in the dry season. Did Don fill you in?'

'Only on the job he's got coming up.'

Matt kept talking until Don came back out with a bowl of salad on a tray with plates and cutlery. He filled her in on the boats the family-owned, and the family. Guilt and frustration settled in her chest; she hated not being able to be honest.

'That sounds good. I'm seeing as much of the country as I can.'

As Don opened the tin of beetroot that he'd brought out on the tray, Matt looked at her quizzically.

'Have you been to the Gulf before?'

'No. I haven't.'

'You look familiar.' When he frowned and put his head to the side, nausea clawed at Claire's stomach. She put her hand to her face to reassure herself that she was still wearing her glasses.

Oh God, not already.

Matt shrugged. 'Maybe I've seen you down in Cloncurry. Have you been there?'

Mutely, she shook her head. Forcing brightness into her voice, she trotted out the words she'd used over the last month. 'They say we all have a doppelganger, don't they?'

Matt looked over at Don and laughed.

Don shook his head, but he was smiling. 'Don't even think about it, Matthew McDougal.'

'They reckon my baby brother here looks like that Scottish movie star. I can never remember his name, though.'

Claire looked at Don and this time she put her head to the side and couldn't help the grin tugging at her lips 'Oh yes. You could pass for Gerard Butler.'

'That's his name!' Matt slapped a hand on his thigh. 'And last New Year's Eve, Mum and Jenni put him in a kilt, and the girls went wild.'

'Yeah, at least I looked better than you did.' Don's voice held a chuckle. 'Mum hired everyone's costumes online, so we weren't allowed to refuse to get dressed up.'

Claire leaned back in the chair. Now that the attention was off her, she was slowly starting to enjoy herself. She nodded as Don held up a bottle of white wine that was on the tray. 'Just half a glass, thank you.' She turned to Matt. 'Are you going to tell me who you went as?'

'All right. I'll never live it down.' He rolled his eyes. 'I was a cartoon freak when I was a kid. Mum said I was easy to look after because all I wanted to do was watch cartoons. I loved the Flintstones, so she hired me a Fred Flintstone costume.'

'That would have been cool,' Claire said.

Don's grin was wide. 'It would have been, but apparently, the costume company didn't know the difference between Fred and the baby on the show.'

'Pebbles or Bamm Bamm?' Claire giggled.

'Oh, Claire. Will you marry me?" Matt put his hand on his chest. 'I've never met a girl who knew the Flintstones before.'

'That's because you go out with all the young ones. Pick someone closer to your age, and they'll know all the shows.' Don must have realised what he'd said, and Claire laughed at the horror that was on his face. 'I didn't mean you were the same age as Matt!'

'I loved my cartoons too,' she said. 'So, tell me what you wore.'

Matt looked sheepish. 'I spent the night in a green nappy thing, a girly top with bows, and a red wig with a bone through it.'

Don let out a hoot. 'And not only did he look sweet, but he also won the best dressed at the pub for the night.'

'Yeah, and all the girls were after Gerard Butler here, and I got to dance with Mum and all her friends who grew up with the Flintstones.'

'This was here? It sounds like it's more social than it looked when I arrived today. I only saw a caravan park and one small shop. The one where I met you, Don. I couldn't get over how deserted the streets were. The river was busier than the town.'

The joking conversation set the tone for the next hour, and Claire watched the happy banter between the two brothers as she cleared the plate of meat and salad that Don had served out for her.

When she was finished, she put her cutlery neatly in the middle of the plate and stood. 'Please let me help you wash up, before I go.'

'No.' Matt waved her away. 'It's my turn, and I cleaned up most of it before. I'll do it while Don sees you home.'

'I can find my own way back. I've taken up too much of your night anyway.'

'Mum taught us good manners. I'll walk you home.'

'Okay then. Thank you.' She stood, relieved that there hadn't been an inquisition. The two McDougal men had good manners.

Don stood and waited while she held out her hand to Matt.

'It was nice to meet you,' Claire said.

'And you too. I'll look forward to seeing you again.'

Claire tensed as she intercepted the look that Don shot his brother's way.

Chapter 4

Breakfast was a cup of tea, her apple and two stale biscuits that Claire found in an unopened packet of biscuits in the kitchen cupboard. The muesli bar hadn't appealed. The foray across the river to get food today would have to be her first job. Although after the fine dinner she'd been served last night, Claire wasn't hungry. Her appetite had fled a month ago, and her clothes were all a bit looser. She picked up her handbag, opened the zipper at the bottom of the bag, and pulled out a wad of cash before peeling off two fifty-dollar notes. That should see her out for a week or two. She took half of the cash and walked around the house looking for a hiding place, but the house was so sparsely furnished there was nowhere to hide anything. Her eyes settled on the open biscuit packet sitting on the table, and she pulled out the few stale biscuits and slipped a wad of notes at the end before pushing the biscuits back in and sealing the packet with a peg she'd seen beneath the kitchen sink. After putting the packet back into the bare pantry, he zipped up the concealed pocket and put the money in her small purse before hitching her bag onto her shoulder and slipping on her sandals. That way if the punt sank—God forbid—or her bag was snatched, she would have half her cash left.

It was time to see if she could manage the punt to get across the river to the store. As she was locking the door a shout caught her attention.

'Claire!'

She didn't have to turn to know it was Don's voice. Biting her lip, she stood and waited as he hurried along the path. The sun was already shining out of a deep blue sky, and there was no sign of rain—or even one cloud marring the blue perfection. The river seemed to be flowing more gently this morning, and it looked bluer than it had last night. Second Chance Bay had turned out to be a very different place from what she'd expected, but she was liking it.

'Morning, Claire. I'm sorry to bother you early, but I've had someone else call about the position. Because I offered it to you first, I wanted to be fair and give you the opportunity before I talk to them.' Don's eyes were friendly, and his tone was light.

Claire took a deep breath. She'd been toing and froing all morning and had changed her mind about three times. She swallowed and held his gaze. 'No. I understand. You have a business to run.' His gaze was intent as he waited for her answer. 'If you're happy to take on a pretty raw recruit, I'd be happy to say yes.'

Don's eyes were a bright blue, fringed by dark lashes, and Claire couldn't help holding his gaze. For some reason, he fascinated her. It wasn't just the good looks because there was no doubt he was a fine-looking man; it was more to do with his kind demeanour. His eyes held kindness and concern, and when she said yes, she was surprised to see satisfaction in them too. Deliberately, she shifted her gaze back to the river; it was safer than looking into those blue eyes for any length of time.

He nodded, and she glanced at him; a satisfied smile had settled on his face.

Damn, she hoped she hadn't made the wrong decision. Life was complicated enough without a good-looking guy on the scene.

'That's great. You've saved my skin.' His face crinkled in a smile, and his tone was relieved.

As her grandmother would have said, he was a gentleman. Over her years at the network, Claire hadn't encountered too many of them. She had also appreciated the obvious respect and affection between the two brothers last night. Respect wasn't something she'd seen a lot of since she'd started her career.

Before she could help herself, the words tumbled from her lips. 'Would you like to come in?' She glanced at her watch. 'A cup of tea while we talk about the job?'

'Were you on your way out?'

'I was heading across the river, but I've got all day and nothing to do, apart from please myself.' Her voice was bright, and she was surprised at how relaxed she was. She was feeling much more settled, and the bright sky and the warm breeze were adding to her serenity.

Not to mention the tall, broad-shouldered man who was standing beside her.

'Thank you. It's been a while since breakfast. Dane—my other brother— had me up at some ungodly hour. He needed a hand with one of our fishing boats. I've been across the river twice already this morning. So, thanks. A cup of tea would be great.'

He followed Claire down the hall and into the kitchen, and she gestured to the small table and two chairs under the window. 'Have a seat. I'll put the jug on.' She flicked the jug on and reached down for two cups. Luckily, there had been two small long-life milk in the cupboard. She bit her lip again. But no sugar.

'Um, how do you take it?'

'Black, no sugar.'

She poured the water for the tea and put the two cups onto a tray that was next to the electric jug. With a grimace, she crossed to the small pantry and took a couple of biscuits from the packet before putting it back on the shelf. A flush warmed her neck as she put some on a plate and put it on the tray. She carried the tray across to the table and sat down.

'I'm sorry. These biscuits are pretty stale. I'm looking forward to stocking the pantry.'

To his credit, Don picked up one of the gingernuts and bit into it. 'Just the way they should be. They're not teeth-breaking quality.'

Claire couldn't help the smile that crossed her face. 'I'll do some baking once I go shopping. I like to bake. My aunt gave me her old tried and true recipes.'

Where the hell had that come from? Why not tell him your life story!

Her neck heated, and she knew that the flush would have spread to her cheeks. The curse of fair skin.

'I'll look forward to it.' His voice was low, and his eyes held hers.

Claire folded her hands on the table and sat up straight. Her voice was brisk and business-like; she could do that easily. 'What do I need to know?' She lifted her chin. 'About the position, I mean. I'll understand if you'd rather have someone experienced and prefer to go with them if that's who's enquired.'

Don shook his head. 'No. It's yours. As long as you're free from next Monday for a bit over two weeks.'

'I am. Tell me more about it. When can I see the boat? To learn my way around.'

'Not until we get over there. We leave from Wyndham. Over in Western Australia. That's where the boat is.'

Claire felt her mouth drop into a round O. 'Western Australia? I thought it was a local charter.'

He looked at her curiously. 'No, this is the Gulf, the Kimberley, and my charters are at the top of Western Australia. Does that make a difference to you?'

'Oh. I've heard of them, but I've never taken much notice of where they were. I knew it was the north.'

'Let me tell you about it, and you can decide. I keep my boat at Wyndham, where we pick up the passengers. They fly in from Darwin on a light plane. We offer a ten-day cruise exploring between Wyndham and the Mitchell River, and visit King George Falls, Berkeley River, the Drysdale River and a few other well-known places.'

Claire pulled a face. 'I haven't heard of any of them.' She spoke quickly, so he didn't think she wasn't interested, because she was. 'But I'm happy to go there. I haven't seen enough of Australia.'

He looked at her curiously for a minute, and Claire remembered that she'd said last night that she'd been travelling around the country.

'Up here in the north, I mean,' she added quickly.

'Well, you're in for a treat.' Don picked up the mug and sipped his tea, looking at her over the rim. 'We usually do this charter after the wet when the falls are spectacular, but we've had enough rain this winter to keep them flowing, so we scheduled an extra cruise.' A proud smile lit up his face. 'The investment in the boat has been well worth it and the extra work I've had to put in. The demand for the cruise has been great.'

'So how do we get there? I haven't got a car.'

He waved a hand. 'Your choice. You can fly in with the rest of the crew if you want. We pay for the travel. They'll take the helicopter from Darwin, but getting to Darwin from here will take about three flights. Sometimes, you have to go to Brisbane and back up again. Or if you're happy to take a road trip with me, I'm driving over next Monday. It'll take a couple of days to get there. I just drive and sleep and hit the road fast. I've got some gear I need to take over to the boat.' He looked sheepish. 'And I hate flying, but that's between you and me. Don't mention it in front of my brothers.'

Claire couldn't help smiling. 'I understand completely. I hate it too. And I've had enough to do me for a while. As long as you're happy for me to keep you company, I'll take the road option with you. I've got nowhere else I have to be.'

And it would save being in airports and a city for the time being.

***

Don drained the last of his tea and stood, wondering why the hell he'd felt the need to boast about the charter company. *Frig it*, he'd sounded like a sixteen-year-old trying to impress the pretty girl at school.

Claire pushed her chair back and stood. 'What else do I need to know? What do I need to bring?'

'I suppose we should talk wages and paperwork.' Don named the daily rate for the hostess position, and she nodded.

'That's fine. But paperwork?' Her voice sounded nervous and she had her hands clamped together on the back of the chair. 'What sort of paperwork do you need from me? I'm travelling, and I don't have anything with me, really.'

'Just the usual. Address, next of kin and all that. I need it under Work, Health and Safety rules.'

'Okay. Will I do it here or when we get on the boat?'

'You said you were going across the river for groceries?'

She nodded.

'How about I take you over now, and we can do it all at the office at the co-op? I can get you a uniform too. It's just black shorts and a white polo shirt with the logo on it. And a pair of white-soled shoes.'

'Okay,' she said slowly but put her hand to her lips. 'I'll come now, but shoes are a problem. I don't have any suitable shoes for a boat.'

'What size are you.'

'A seven.'

'I'll see what Jenni can rustle up. We have a bit of stock for the crew at the office.'

'Thank you.'

Don held out his hand again. 'So we have a deal? I have a hostess?'

Claire put her hand out, and he held it. The minute her fingers touched his, he wondered if he was making a big mistake.

The barest touch of her skin against his sent his pulse skyrocketing. She must have been aware of his reaction because she pulled her hand away after a quick return grip and looked at him strangely. He'd have to put a lid on this attraction; she was going to be crew. But the warm feeling stayed on his fingers as she locked the door.

Don had moored one of the family boats at the jetty near the house, and he gestured to Claire to follow him towards the house rather than to the public wharf. She hesitated when he turned left at the path, and he hurried to explain.

'We'll take my boat rather than the public punt. I need to bring some stuff back over. And I can help you with your groceries.'

She was quiet on the way across, and Don wondered if he'd upset her in some way. Maybe she didn't like him taking over.

Half a dozen local fishermen were lined up fishing near the co-op and one of them came over and caught the rope that Don threw to him and tied them off to the bollard at the end of the wharf.

'Thanks, Wattsy. Caught anything?'

'Nuh, Donny. Just a way to fill in the morning while the missus babysits the grandkids.'

He stepped out of the boat and held his hand out to Claire, but she ignored it and swung over the side to land lightly on the wharf. She still didn't speak as she followed him up to the building. Dane was out on a day charter with Jake on *Moonshine*, but Matt would be in the office. Don had to hold back his groan when they walked through the door, and Jenni was at the counter.

Then he realised he was worrying over nothing. Claire was nothing more than the new hostess, and they were here to do business and find her a uniform,

Jenni raised one eyebrow as Claire stepped into the shop behind him.

'Jen, this is Claire Templeton. Claire's here to do the paperwork to come on the *Adventurer* next week. The other hostie couldn't come.' He turned to Claire who stood quietly beside the door reading the fish species poster as though it was of great interest. 'Claire, this is my sister, Jenni.'

Claire nodded and smiled briefly, and before Jenni could start the third degree—as she always did—Don opened the door to the office. Once the door had closed, he pointed to the chair in front of the desk. 'Have a seat. I'll just pull out the employment forms.'

'It's still cash in hand, the deal?'

He lifted his head from the filing cabinet drawer to look at her when she spoke. 'Yes, just for this trip. If you work out—it was time to sound like an employer, not the adolescent lovesick goon who'd taken him over in the past few hours— 'and you stay on for more trips, we'll put you on the books then.'

Chapter 5

The hostess's job was sorted; the uniform complete with three pairs of shorts and three shirts with the Adventurer logo on them, as well as a pair of new shoes had been handed over to Claire.

'We always keep a supply on hand. Especially the shoes. The closest shoe store is down in Cloncurry,' Jenni explained as she handed over the uniform pack after Claire and Don had finished the paperwork in the office. It hadn't taken long. Claire had filled in as much of the form as she could and put Aunt Bea as her next of kin. She left her address vacant, and when Don looked at her quizzically, she made the excuse of being between apartments as she travelled. There was no need for him—or anyone—to know that she was the sole owner of a house in a leafy and well-to-do suburb on the north side of Sydney Harbour. He also looked up surprised when she said she didn't have a mobile phone number.

Prevarication had become second nature to her, and Claire bit her lip, a little ashamed at how easy it was to avoid the truth. In contrast, she'd landed smack bang in the middle of happy family land, where no one seemed to have a cross word for anyone.

Jenni kept one eye on the cute little girl asleep in a porta cot in the corner of the store. She grabbed her brother's arm as Don went to walk over to the cot. 'Please don't wake her up, Donny. If she wakes up, that'll be the end of sleep for the rest of the day. We had a late night last night.'

'Out on the town?'

'No. Teething.'

Don grinned and hugged her as he turned away from the cot. 'The joys of being a mum, hey, little sis?'

'Yeah, and where would we go out on the town here anyway?' Jenni looked over at Claire with a smile. 'As much as I love living here, I do miss the shops and restaurants in the city. I lived in Brisbane for a few years after I finished uni.'

She looked expectantly at Claire, inviting her to chat, but Claire simply nodded.

'Just as well there are no shops here. My baby sister is a shopaholic,' Don said with a grin. 'You could always get Jake to move back to Europe.'

An emphatic shake of the head. 'No. We're here to stay. This is where we want to bring our children up. And besides, there's always online shopping, Donny boy.'

Claire was made aware again of the close relationship between the McDougal siblings. A past yearning to have family close to her age flooded through her. When she was a child, she hated having no siblings. Her only cousins—and as she'd grown up, she'd discovered that Ross and Elise were very distant cousins—had lived at Gilgandra.

The McDougals were so relaxed with each other. She imagined the other brother would be much the same. Something she had little—if any—experience with. Her parents had married late in life and had been in their forties when Claire was born. Both had passed in their early seventies, and the only family she had left now was Aunty Bea, her mother's younger sister.

Claire moved across towards the door as the siblings continued to spar. When she spotted the pile of women's magazines on a table under the window, her mouth dried, and she fought to control her breathing. The panic started as a knot in her stomach and began to work its way into her chest.

Anxious to leave, to get outside, away from people, Claire dropped her head and opened the door. The sharp clang of the bell over the door made her jump, and she glanced apologetically at Jenni, but the baby didn't stir.

'It's fine,' she said softly. 'Leni's used to that. It's only when her uncles tickle her that she wakes up.' The questions Claire had expected hadn't been forthcoming, but the calm that had filled her earlier today fled when she was in company.

How long would it take before this self-consciousness passed? Waiting for someone to say, 'Ha! I know who you are. And I know what you did. How could you be such a dreadful person?'

A shiver ran down her back as she stood in the doorway, waiting for them to stop talking. She swallowed and thought about just leaving, but her manners were better than that.

Aunty Bea had tried to talk sense into her before she'd fled Sydney. Claire had called in to see her at the aged care facility before she'd driven to Newcastle and left her car at a long-term parking station before catching the night train to Brisbane.

'Claire.' Her aunt's voice was calm, and her eyes had been sympathetic as she'd held Claire's shoulders with gentle hands. 'Stop taking it to heart so much. Everyone who knows you and loves you knows that you wouldn't have done it. You haven't got a calculating or nasty bone in your body.'

Claire had shaken her head. 'Aunty Bea, it was public humiliation, *national* public humiliation. I know it was a set-up, but no one else knows that, and I couldn't prove it. Even when I denied knowing anything about what happened, I wasn't believed. I came out of that night's program looking like the arch bitch of television.'

'Oh, sweetie. I do worry about you. You're too soft. You've never been any good at confrontation.'

'And I trusted others to do the right thing. Just like I was brought up to do.'

Her eyes filled with tears as her aunt brushed a gentle kiss on her forehead, and she was surrounded by the comforting fragrance of her familiar lavender perfume.

Now, her resolve strengthened as she stepped through the door of the co-op.

Get over it. Move on. Life goes on.

***

Don was surprised when Claire walked out.

Jenni shot him a look. 'Are you sure she's hostess material? She's very quiet.'

'She'll be fine. She just couldn't get a word in with you gas bagging.'

'Good references?'

Don shrugged.

Jenni rolled her eyes. 'You mean you've hired someone without references? Again? God, Donny, when will you ever learn?'

'Keep your voice down. You might as well tell the town.' Don folded his arms and glared at Jenni. 'And you'll wake Leni up.'

'I guess it's your charter. I hope you know what you're doing.' They both turned guiltily to the door as the bell rang, but it was an older couple coming into the shop.

Don lowered his voice. 'Claire had a barbeque with Matt and I last night, and I can tell she's a good person. I have no doubt about hiring her. She's keen, and she needs a job.'

'Why is she looking in Karumba? There's no work here.' Jenni whispered. 'Wait there.' She turned to serve the couple who had picked up a bag of fresh prawns from the fridge at the end of the counter. While she was serving and chatting—Don had been surprised to see Jenni there—he took the opportunity to leave.

Claire was sitting on a seat watching a ship go up river. The sun was high in the sky, and the fishing boats were coming in with the morning's catch.

'I didn't think this was an industrial port?' She turned and smiled at him, and the worry that Jenni had set churning in his gut subsided.

'It's not as busy as it used to be,' he said sitting beside her. 'The live export and the zinc have stopped now. It's just general cargo and fuel, and fishing products for export.'

'Different to what I expected. Anyway, thanks for the uniform and everything. I'll go and do my shopping now, and I'll see you next Monday,' she said.

Don frowned. 'I'll give you a lift to the town, and then I'll take you back across the river.

She shook her head. 'There's no need. I can manage.'

'Look, I've got nothing on until this afternoon when Dane and Matt come in on the charter. I'm at a loose end, and it's crazy for you to take the punt.'

She lifted her head and stared at him, and he could almost see the wheels turning in her head.

'I'm not your boss yet. Just a friend offering to help out. And while we're there, I can get some stuff for when we travel across to Wyndham next week.'

The smile that slowly lifted her lips was sweet. Her face lightened, and her eyes crinkled at the edges. 'In that case, I guess I have to accept.'

'I leave my ute parked in the shed behind the co-op. I'll go and get it. He gestured to the road. 'I'll meet you over there on the corner.'

By the time Don reached the shed and turned around Claire was standing on the corner. A slight breeze was blowing in from the Gulf, and her hair ruffled in the breeze. As she reached up to push it back from her eyes, her dress hugged her soft curves and she smiled at him again. He wondered if she realised how that gentle smile transformed her cool face into something softer. More approachable. He turned away, cursing himself for being attracted to her.

He had a two-thousand-kilometre road trip ahead in her company, not to mention ten days on the boat.

***

It was a couple of kilometres around to the main town, and Claire looked at the landscape with interest. Everything was so flat here; along the side of the main road, large birds stood in the water that filled the channel along the edge of the flat paddocks, poking their bills in and out of the water, searching for food. The IGA was in a short street with only a few shops. A bank, a real estate agent and a takeaway store completed the row of old buildings. A store with bakery on the sign was closed and, as she looked closer, the windows were boarded up.

Don followed her gaze as she parked the car. 'We've had a few shops close here as the population has decreased since the zinc mine closed. Bread and the newspapers are brought up from Normanton every day now.'

He came around and opened the door of the ute for her. Claire held her handbag tightly as she climbed out, thinking about what she had to buy.

At the front of the shop, four elderly men sat in a line on the bench beneath the window.

'Papers not in yet, Harry?' Don called as they approached.

'Nah, the bugger's late again. He'd better get here; it's past cuppa time.' Harry—Claire assumed he was the one who answered—looked at her curiously as she followed Don into the store. Heat ran up her neck as his next words followed them in.

''Bout time that McDougal lad got himself a woman.'

'She's a looker too. Bit skinny on it, though,' came the reply, followed by a hacking cough.

Don stopped near the grocery trolleys and shook his head. 'Sorry, a few old locals with no manners.'

210

She reached up and swapped her sunglasses for the spectacles she'd pulled from her bag. 'It's okay. I'm used to all types.' Claire reached for a second trolley, ignoring the stand of glossy gossip magazines beside the cash register that made her stomach plummet to her feet. At least she wasn't on the covers anymore. Self-consciously, she reached up and touched her hair, reassuring herself that she wasn't recognisable. 'So, tell me. What will I need to take in the way of food on the road trip? Will we eat at the motels or eat as we travel?'

'Ah.' This time, there was a dull flush on Don's cheeks. 'I should have explained the trip a bit better. There are no motels. We go bush along the Savannah Way.'

'Go bush?' Her voice caught in a gulp.

'Yeah, we'll be swagging it and cooking for ourselves. Don't worry about food for the trip. You just get whatever food you need for the house and the personal stuff you need for a few weeks, and I'll sort the rest.'

Chapter 6

Don *had* sorted the trip well. Just after dawn, four days later, they crossed the river in his boat to where his ute was parked at the co-op. Claire's suitcase was packed with her new uniform, her shoes and some of her clothes—and two bottles of hair bleach for touching up the regrowth.

With Don ferrying her across the river, she hadn't had to face the public punt, but it was something she had to learn to do on their return.

Nerves had skittered in her tummy all night, and she wondered if she was doing the right thing or if she'd just jumped at a chance to get further away. She couldn't hide forever; eventually, she'd have to resurface. There'd be media interest when they found her, but she knew how the news worked. By that time—a few months after the event, she'd be the mystery woman who had reappeared, and the focus in the media would have changed.

Claire well knew how fickle the media game was. Always chasing the next big story, the highest ratings, the most viewers. And it didn't matter who got trampled in the process. Now that she was on the other side, it was so much easier to see what a sham it was.

How naive was I to think I could make a difference to the world?

Her eyes were gritty when her alarm trilled at four a.m., and she'd stumbled into the bathroom, her head aching. Splashing water on her face, she tried to wake up and dispel the awful dull feeling that had stayed with her as she'd thought of the past few months.

Of course, Don had arrived early; when she'd heard the boat revving at the jetty outside the back of the house, Claire had her head in the laundry tub, washing her hair after touching up the regrowth again. If she'd known how hard it was to keep her hair blonde, she would have reconsidered dyeing it in Brisbane. But she hadn't been thinking straight then, and she was getting quite used to the ash-blonde colour. She hurried from the bathroom before he reached the front door, rubbing at her eyes. They were stinging from where the hair bleach had splashed up from the small sink.

Damn.

'You there, Claire?' His voice preceded a knock on the door.

'Won't be long. My bag's just inside the door. It's unlocked.' She wiped her eyes, switched on the hair dryer, and quickly dried her hair before plumping it up with her fingers.

Excited anticipation warred with the nerves in her stomach. A quick coffee and a Panadol had chased the headache away. She'd only seen Don once since he'd helped her carry her shopping a few days ago. He'd called in one evening as she'd been cooking biscuits to take on the trip to tell her when they would be leaving.

She hadn't invited him in, but his nose had twitched as the smell of baking wafted from the kitchen.

'That smells good.'

Heat had run up her neck. 'I thought I'd do some baking to take while we're travelling. Nothing like a bikie to go with a cuppa,' she said self-consciously. She didn't want him to think she was trying to score points or anything.

After three nights on her own with no computer or phone,c and no one to talk to, boredom had come screaming in, and she was thankful she had the road trip and the charter to look forward to. She'd walked along the river to the south, keeping an eye out for snakes—and other residents—but hadn't seen either. The punt was an intricate-looking arrangement of ropes and pulleys, and her stomach sank as she contemplated having to do that in the future.

What an isolated place.

'Well, that's what you wanted,' she'd muttered to herself as she walked along the mudflats to the south of the punt jetty. A variety of birdlife scurried ahead of her, and crabs skittered across the wet mud at the edge of the water.

It was peaceful, and she could feel herself healing. The upside was that calm had settled, and the fear of being recognised hadn't been a problem that was constantly with her. The other benefit was that she'd used the time to get some more words down, and that kept her grounded. She was rested and looking forward to something different.

The adrenaline-fuelled rush to get here had kept her hyped, but now she was settled; Claire wondered what she was going to do with her time when she was here in the house. There were only so many walks she could take before the river closed into thick bush at the south. She hadn't gone the other way as there were more houses to the north. And if she was honest, she didn't want Don to think she had gone looking for him. It must be the state of mind she was in; she'd never been attracted to someone so fast.

She jerked her thoughts back to the present and yawned as she hurried to the small living room. The door was open, and her suitcase was gone. 'I'll just get the stuff out of the kitchen,' she called as Don came back to the door. She hadn't been sure what to wear, so she had opted for a pair of long cargo pants, a T-shirt, and the sturdy walking shoes she'd brought from Sydney. She'd thrown them in at the last minute, unsure of what she'd need in the wild north. She certainly hadn't expected a two-thousand-kilometre road trip, sleeping under the stars in a swag.

With a rugged sea captain. A good-looking one. Not to mention one that oozed sex appeal.

'All ready?'

Claire nodded as she walked to the door. A Tupperware container full of assorted homemade biscuits was in one hand, and her handbag was gripped firmly in the other. She'd worried too much about leaving money in the house while she was gone, so last night, she'd shoved the notes into her handbag and zipped up the compartment. Hopefully, there'd be a safe or somewhere secure on the boat to put her bag while they were on the charter.

'You look the part.' Don looked at her, and there was a touch of admiration in his eyes.

'I hope I don't let you down.' She was nervous about camping out. There weren't going to be many places for rest stops on the road. The day he'd come to see her, Don had dropped in a book and a brochure for the charter, and she'd read them with interest.

There were two ways to go west, and he'd chosen the shortest, but the downside, as the book told her, was that it was a very rugged road. She'd felt like she was doing research for a program as she'd read the book. The Savannah Way was classed as an adventure drive and started in Cairns in the east and went through the savannahs of the Top End—thus the name, she thought with a grin—before ending at Broome in the west.

The photographs of gorges, rivers and waterfalls had piqued her interest. Then when she'd turned to the brochure her excitement had grown, pushing away further the dark thoughts that had dogged her for the last month.

'You'll be fine. Even though we're going to do it fast, you'll get to see a part of the country that few people see.'

Claire locked the door behind her, checked that her handbag was securely on her shoulder and looked up at him with a smile.

'Lead on, McDuff.'

'That's McDougal.' Don grinned back at her before he turned away to the jetty. As she followed him, Claire let her gaze wander over the broad shoulders and the snug-fitting jeans.

As they crossed the river, she focused on keeping her gaze on the mangroves along the north side past the houses. She pretended to be watching the pair of jabirus that were standing in the shallows.

This attraction to Don was something she was going to have to be very aware of. Careful that he didn't see her looking at him or daydreaming about him holding her.

She was here to work for him, and he was her boss. And she certainly didn't want any more complications in her life. She'd had enough already to do her a lifetime.

***

Don was carrying spare fuel, but he still stopped at Normanton to top up before they turned onto the Savannah Way.

'Every little bit counts when there's a long way between fuel stops.' He glanced across at Claire as they turned into the service station. 'Do you want to grab a coffee while we're here? This will be the last chance for real coffee until we reach Katherine the day after tomorrow.'

She shook her head. 'No, I'm fine, but I might just use the amenities.'

She slipped out of the car, those crazy large sunglasses covering half her face, the handbag that she always held close tightly beneath her arm and walked quickly across to the ladies' room that was separate from the service station main building. By the time, he'd filled the ute and paid for the fuel, she was back in the passenger seat, sitting low in the seat.

Don started the car, wondering for the umpteenth time what her story was. On the way down to Normanton, they'd chatted—or rather, he'd talked, and Claire had uttered the occasional yes or no in response to any questions he'd asked her. He was careful not to get personal; it was very clear that she wasn't prepared to share

216

anything. All he knew was that she was from Sydney and that she had a recipe book from her aunt.

But her life—and her problems—were none of his business.

He had a hostess for the charter; he had someone to talk to on the bloody long trip across to Wyndham, and an added bonus was that she was damn fine to look at.

Jeez, how sexist did that sound, he thought. Jenni and Mum would be right onto him for thinking that.

But hell, he was a red-blooded male, and of course, he appreciated a fine female figure. There was nothing wrong with admiring from afar; he knew how to keep his distance, and he didn't want to spook her.

From Claire's point of view, she was heading into the unknown, with a stranger she hadn't met a week ago, to a job that she hadn't even heard about a week ago, to a place she hadn't heard of.

If it had been his sister doing that, he would have told her she was foolish, but he sensed that foolish wasn't a word that applied to Claire Templeton.

'Would you like me to share the driving if you want a break?' Her quiet voice interrupted his thoughts as they turned off the bitumen onto the iconic road known as the Savannah Way. She rushed on. 'I know you wouldn't have anyone to share the driving if I hadn't come with you, but I'm happy to take a turn.'

Don nodded. 'I'd appreciate that. It'll get us there a bit faster if I can snooze in the car. We can drive later in the day.' He nodded ahead. 'We've got two hundred ks of dirt ahead, but once we get to the Gregory Downs turnoff, the road's sealed all the way to Burketown, and you can take over. You'll just have to keep an eye out for road trains because it's only a single-lane road.'

'I'm pleased you'll let me help.' Claire turned from the window. 'And you don't have to worry, I learned to drive on dirt roads in the outback.'

He nodded again, reluctant to ask any questions. Her privacy was something she hung onto like that damned handbag.

"Can I ask you something, Don?"

He changed back a gear as the road narrowed, and the ute juddered on the patch of corrugations. Dust billowed behind them, but he kept an eye ahead for anything coming towards them as the road levelled out again.

'Sure, what's up?' he said.

'You said you leave the boat over there. How come you live so far away?'

He shrugged. 'I ask myself the same question every time I do this trip, over and back. I'm going to have to seriously consider living over there.'

'Where's over there?'

'Probably Wyndham. But it's a small place. And I guess if I'm truthful—' he cleared his throat, thinking he was going to sound like a wuss.

'If you're truthful?' she prompted.

'I'd miss the family too much. Don't get me wrong, I'm not a sensitive new-age man or whatever the current term is. As much as we blue a lot of the time, I enjoy my brothers' company. And I am a quarter-owner of the company there, so I should be there to help.' He was thoughtful as he stared ahead for a few minutes before he glanced across at Claire. 'I'm thirty-two, and except for when I did my marine courses in Tassie, I've never lived away from Second Chance Bay. I guess that makes me sound pretty boring.'

Claire shook her head. 'No. Not at all. I think you're very lucky. If I'm truthful—'

Don eased back on the accelerator a bit, so he could hear her quiet words over the roar of the engine.

'Yes?' It was his turn to prompt.

'If I'm truthful, I'm envious of your family life. I've only met your brother and sister, but I've heard the way you speak of your mum and your other brother, and it's obvious that you all have a good relationship.'

'It wasn't always like that. Pardon my language, but our dad was a real bastard. I think since he died, we've all got a lot closer.' Don stared ahead and was surprised when Claire reached out and lightly touched his hand on the steering wheel. Her touch prompted him to put into words what he was thinking. 'I've always worried that his traits might have passed onto me. That's why I've never settled down with anyone.'

'Trust me, you have nothing to be ashamed of or embarrassed about. These days, you don't come across many people who care about others like that.' Her voice was tight, and her tone was cynical. 'You're a good person, Don. I can tell that.'

The more he got to know her, the more certain he was becoming that Claire was running away from someone.

An abusive partner?

It wasn't any of his business. He'd looked at her employee form, and it had the name of a person with the address of an aged care facility as the next of kin. He hadn't commented when he'd seen the bottles of hair bleach she'd bought, but as he thought more about it, he knew she was hiding from her past. His hand clenched on the steering wheel.

If someone had tried to hurt her, they deserved a thrashing themselves. He couldn't help the question that spilled from his lips. 'Do you have family back home?'

He glanced across, and he regretted asking as her hesitation became obvious. Her hands gripped the bag tightly, and eventually, she looked up at him just before he turned his attention back to the road.

'I only have my aunt. Aunt Bea, the one on my employment form.' She took a deep breath. 'She and Uncle Jack were out on a farm at Gilgandra, and I spent a lot of time out there when I was growing up. I've got a couple of cousins somewhere— and their kids— but I haven't seen them for a long time. Seeing you with your brother and sister brought home to me how much I missed out on not having a family. I'm an only child; the only company I had growing up was imaginary.'

He kept his voice light and tried not to sound like he was digging. 'One day, you'll settle down and you can create your own family.'

'Maybe one day.' Her voice was wistful rather than sad. 'The biological clock is ticking faster every day.'

'If it's not a rude question, how old are you?'

'Same as you. Thirty-two.'

Don was surprised; she looked much younger than he did, but before he could answer, his attention was drawn to the road ahead. A huge cloud of red dust ahead indicated a large vehicle was approaching.

He looked to each side of the road; there was a flat piece of cleared ground in the scrubby bush that had obviously been used as a campsite as wheel tracks went into it. He wrenched the wheel to the left and accelerated up the slight incline to the flat.

'Road train,' he said as they headed bush.

Claire turned around and looked through the window behind them. 'Holy shit!'

Don grinned as he did a three-point turn so they could go back onto the road. Red dust filled the air around them, and the smell of cattle on the truck pervaded the interior of the ute even though the windows were up and the air conditioning was on.

She shook her head as he backed up. 'That's a road train? I didn't like to show my ignorance. How long was that?'

Don looked down the road before he turned back onto the dirt. The back of the long high vehicle was disappearing down the road towards Normanton. 'Anywhere between forty and fifty metres long.' He grinned. 'Do you still want to share the driving?'

Claire let go of the bag and folded her arms. 'Give me some time to get over that awful smell and I'll think about it. What on earth is it? It smells like something died.'

'Cattle.' He looked at her curiously. 'You've never seen a road train hauling cattle before?'

Her eyes were sparkling now. 'No. You don't see that in the city at all.'

They set off along the road again, but the serious conversation had been interrupted by the road train. But as Claire looked out the window watching the landscape go by, Don felt as though he had got to know her a little more.

He reached down and turned the stereo on.

'If you don't like the music, just let me know. I'm a Johnny Cash fan. My family pays out on me.'

As the first song came on, she turned, and her smile was sweet. 'Love that song. Johnny Cash is one of my favourites, ever since I saw the movie about his life.'

A warm feeling settled in Don's chest as they headed west.

Chapter 7

As it turned out, Claire didn't drive that day. She was fascinated by the small settlements they drove through; it was a whole new world, nothing like the idealised outback she'd seen in the movies. Doomadgee was red dust and abandoned cars; small groups of aboriginal people stood looking curiously as they drove through.

So different to the city, Claire realised what a narrow existence she'd led; she had travelled widely overseas and had visited a few Australian cities with the program, but she'd never experienced anything like this remote country before.

'I guess I'm seeing the true outback,' she commented as they approached a wide river ahead,

'You are.' Don threw a quick glance her way. 'It can be a bit confronting at times. Wait until we get to Katherine.'

'It makes me feel as though I don't know my country at all.'

'You've never been north before?'

'Or to the outback.' She shook her head. 'No further west than Gilgandra or north of Brisbane. I went there for a conference once, so I didn't see too much of the city anyway.'

She could have kicked herself when Don replied with a question in his voice. 'A conference? That would be a new world to me. I've never been to one.'

'Pretty boring.' She injected disinterest into her tone. 'You haven't missed much.' She wished she hadn't mentioned Brisbane as the memories came flooding back. That had been the conference where they'd picked up the lead to the story that had eventually been her downfall.

It had also been at that conference that she'd first shared a bed with Ben, the program director. They'd been out for dinner a few times, and he'd been persistent about taking the relationship further. It had taken a while before she'd agreed to go out with him in the first place.

'No, Ben. We work together. Social life and work don't mix.'

He'd laughed and told her she was old-fashioned. 'This is the twenty-first century, babe.'

Maybe she was old-fashioned. Maybe she'd chosen the wrong profession.

No. Claire bit her lip as the ute slewed to the left in some loose sand; she had made a poor choice.

In her career, and in sleeping with Ben. It was all linked, and she hadn't realised and look where she had ended up now. But if old-fashioned meant caring about people's feelings, and not wanting to be in the limelight, that's the way she'd rather be.

Strangely, for the sort of job she had, Claire had hated being in the limelight. She'd seen her role as a different way of promoting social justice; it was why she'd studied law. The job had been everything she'd wanted to start with until the change of management last year. Ratings had always been important, but their reporting had held integrity before then. The show had won awards and they had been ethical.

Until the management change, ratings and advertising dollars took precedence over truth.

And then the program aired the week after she'd slept with Ben. Her world had come crashing down.

'Bulldust.'

'What?' Claire jumped and stared at Don with a frown, worrying for a moment that she'd spoken her thoughts out loud.

'That was a bull dust hole we just hit.' His frown matched hers. 'The road's worse than I thought it would be; we're going to have a slower trip than I hoped for. There's been a lot of cattle moved out here.'

She must have looked confused.

'Road trains,' he explained. 'They chop the road up, and the bull dust can settle into holes. You never know what's under the dust until you go down into one. I'll drive for the rest of today. I was going to try to get to Borroloola tonight, but that's still three hundred kilometres away. We'll have to camp at the Robinson River crossing instead.'

'Whatever you say, boss. I'm just following along.' She smiled. Even though she was feeling low, the conversation had pulled her out of those thoughts that sent her into a downward spiral.

'The next couple of days will be quicker. This is the only unsealed part of the road.'

'I'm in your hands.' Heat rushed up Claire's neck when he glanced over at her. The silence was heavy. After a moment, Don reached over and turned the stereo back on.

Claire turned back to the window, lost in her thoughts. But this time, it wasn't about work.

Don McDougal was hard not to think about.

***

The road was the worst that Don had seen it in the half a dozen trips he'd done in the past year. Road trains loaded with cattle and numerous grey nomies travelling the Savannah Way in the dry season had brought the road into a shocking state. He tried to hide his displeasure; the last thing Claire needed was a grumpy boss and a driver she had to spend the next two days and nights with. They'd stopped for a quick cuppa out of the thermos he'd brought, and he smiled when Claire had held out the Tupperware container.

'A melting moment or an ANZAC bikie?'

He'd had two of the freshly baked biscuits and then another two when they'd stopped for the sandwiches he'd packed early that morning.

224

The consolation was that once they reached Borroloola, the road was tarred; narrow but without the worry of washouts and bull dust. It made the thought of moving to Wyndham and basing himself on the boat between charters much more attractive. If the road stayed in this condition, he'd either have to consider going the long way across the Barkly Highway each trip or relocating.

So, if he moved, he'd be there by himself. It was time he was independent. Jake had lived in Europe for ten years, and it hadn't killed him. Being on the boat all the time and not travelling back and forth would give him more time to keep it in top condition. And more importantly, more time to focus on getting a permanent crew and not go through the dramas of getting deckhands, a chef and a hostess every trip. Matt and Dane would have to cope without him running the fishing charters.

How sad had he sounded when he and Claire had shared some stories? He was bloody thirty-two years old, and he'd made it sound as though he couldn't survive without his family close by.

Hell, the way she'd shared her childhood with him, she'd done that for most of her life.

So as soon as this charter was over, a move to Wyndham and living on the boat was a priority. He wouldn't have to face this treacherous road again. As he planned the year ahead in his mind, he took his attention from the road for a split second.

The steering wheel wrenched to the left, and he had to grip it tightly as the ute tipped into a large hole on the left side.

Claire screamed, and she bounced forward, her head almost hitting the windscreen, but her seat belt held her tight.

'Bloody hell!' Don held on for grim death as the ute tried to roll over to the passenger side. A loud clunk came from the suspension as something let go, and the vehicle sagged to the other side. The motor screamed, and he knocked it out of gear and lifted his foot from the accelerator, but the motor kept whining as it sunk into the deep hole. He killed the ignition and turned to Claire.

'Are you okay? Did you hit your head?'

'No, I'm fine. I just got a fright. What happened?'

She looked up at him from the passenger side, and Don realised how deep the ute had sunk on that side.

'More bull dust. If I'd known the road was this bad, I wouldn't have come along the Savannah Way.' Don pushed open the driver's door, and the ute creaked and rocked as he moved to get out.

Claire's eyes widened, and she reached down for her handbag that had ended up on the floor. 'Should I get out too?'

'Just stay there until I suss out the damage. There's no danger. We're not going to roll now.'

'But we could have?' Her voice trembled, and Don felt bad.

He reached over and put his hand on her arm. 'It's okay. I might have to change a tyre, and then we can find somewhere to camp for the night and get an early start tomorrow.'

He walked around to the passenger door and held it open while Claire climbed out. The ute was at a precarious angle, and some of the load in the back had shifted. Luckily he'd tied the jerry cans of fuel and water on securely, and they were still firm against the backboard.

'What can I do to help?' she asked. He glanced up from where he had squatted at the back of the ute.

'Just wait there for a sec. I'm going to have to get the ute out of the hole and then try to find somewhere to set up camp.' He stood and put his hands to his eyes. The sun was dipping below the row of paperbarks ahead, and he realised that they weren't far from the river crossing. He climbed back into the car and called out. 'Just wait over near that cleared patch.'

She stood back as he'd directed, and Don started the car and put it into low range. He backed it up as far as he could and then put the accelerator down, and the ute rocked from side to side as he cleared the hole. He drove down the road about fifty metres and then climbed out. He beckoned to Claire and hid a smile as she walked gingerly down the road, her eyes on the fine red dust in front of her. By the time she reached him, he had squatted in front of the front left tyre.

Her once clean shoes were red with dust, and he smiled as she bent and unrolled the bottom of the cargo pants and a puff of fine dust dropped to her shoes.

'Welcome to the Top End,' he said.

'Hmm. Are the Kimberleys like this?'

'Even better. There's still red dirt, but it's broken by spectacular gorges and waterfalls. Wait till we get to the Cockburn Ranges, and you see the western face lit up in a red glow at sunset. It's a magnificent sandstone escarpment that rises high above the surrounding plains. There's black siltstone embedded in the sandstone, and the stripe goes for hundreds of kilometres.' He stood and shook his head with a rueful grin. 'Listen to me! I've been practising my patter for the boat too much. I sound like a bloody tourist brochure.'

Claire held his gaze and he found it hard to look away. 'You make it sound beautiful.'

'It is a beautiful part of the world. That's why tourists pay ten thousand dollars a trip to see it.'

'I noticed on the brochure it's classed as a luxury holiday.' Her hands clenched nervously, and she bit her bottom lip. He'd noticed her do that a few times when she was out of her comfort zone. 'Where do most of the guests come from?'

'Mainly from the city. Sydney. Melbourne, Adelaide, and often from overseas.'

'Oh.'

Claire dropped her gaze and scuffed the ground with her boot.

'Well, the tyre's okay, and I can't see anything wrong with the suspension, so we'll head down the road away. The campsite's not far away.'

Chapter 8

Two hours later, they'd made a camp on a flat clearing a couple of hundred metres from the road. Don set up the swags and got a fire going while Claire got the eskies and set up a small camp table and two camp chairs that were on the back of the ute.

She stood back and took a deep breath as contentment filled her. The occasional car went past—but no more road trains, thank goodness—and no one else had camped near them. Lights flickered upriver a couple of kilometres, and on the far horizon, a bright light lit up part of the night sky.

'That's the aboriginal settlement over at Robinson River,' Don explained as Claire stared at the light in the distance.

Claire looked around nervously. The firelight lit up the centre of the camp, and Don had lit a camp light on the table, but dark shadows encroached on the edges of the camp, and the occasional rustle and crack came from the scrubby bush. She had put her handbag in the swag and zipped up the canvas.

'Is it safe to camp here?'

'Yes, it's all safe here. No one will bother us. If we were in Borroloola, we'd probably set up camp in a locked compound. There's a serious alcohol problem there that the community is working hard to control.'

She shook her head. 'No. I meant the wildlife, not people.'

As Don had set up the camp, she'd asked if they could camp closer to the river, and he'd led her over to a sign at the side of the road.

'Crocodiles inhabit this area. Attacks cause injury or death,' she'd read aloud. She jumped back as though they were going to come up the hill where the road went into the river. 'Crocodiles?' she squeaked. 'Here? We're way inland!'

'They're here. They follow the major rivers and floodplain billabongs into freshwater rivers, creeks and swamps, so we always have to be careful.'

Claire had backed away from the sign a few more steps and pointed to the swag. 'And you expect me to sleep in a tent on the ground where crocodiles roam?'

Don chuckled, and her temper burred.

'Don't laugh at me. I'm serious. Are there crocodiles where you take the charter?'

This time, he looked sheepish. 'Yes, but mostly freshwater. They'll bite if you step on them, but they won't kill.'

'Great,' she muttered. 'That's okay then; what's a bite between friends.'

She'd followed Don back to the camp and stood by him as he put the barbeque plate on the fire. Once the meat was sizzling, she went over and picked up one of the camp chairs and put it in the light of the fire. Don sent her a curious glance, and she pulled a face at him.

'At least I can see around me if I sit near the fire. Do you have a doctor or a nurse on this boat of yours?'

'There's no need. Most of the staff have emergency care and CPR. I noticed you did on your employee from.'

'I do, but I don't know that it extends to crocodile bites. You'd probably need more than a band-aid,' she said drily.

'I like this feisty Claire.' Don put the tongs on the table and headed across to the esky. 'I was starting to think you were regretting accepting the job.'

'Only in some ways,' she said slowly.

'Would you like a beer or a wine or a soft drink?'

'A cold beer would be great, thanks.' Claire watched the flames as they subsided into the coals. Shades of blue, yellow and magenta contrasted with the orange glow of the embers. She nodded her thanks as Don passed the cold can to her and pulled up the other chair near the fire.

'Penny for them?' he said softly.

***

Don settled back into the canvas chair and sipped at his beer, the cold a welcome relief to his parched throat. Red dust had surrounded them today, and the camping gear was covered in a fine film of red. He waited for Claire to reply, and for a while, he thought he might have overstepped the mark. She'd been much more relaxed this evening, joking about crocodiles and band-aids; He'd seen that spark in her personality that he'd suspected was underneath her cool exterior.

'Are you worried about the charter?'

When she lifted her head, the sadness in her eyes surprised him. 'Yes.'

He cleared his throat and pulled his chair closer. 'Look, I didn't want to cause you any worry, talking rot about crocodiles and stuff. I was teasing. We might see the occasional freshie, but we only swim where it's safe. Please don't worry.'

She lifted the can, and he watched as she closed her eyes and sipped. The silence was long.

Her voice was bleak when she finally spoke. 'I have a big favour to ask you. I'm sorry I can't tell you why, but I need to ask you something.'

'Okay.' His voice was wary. He didn't want to promise anything, but he'd consider whatever she asked.

'If anyone on board thinks they know me, would you tell a little white lie for me? Say I've been in the north for a few months. Only if they ask, that is.' Her voice rushed on quickly. It seemed as though once she'd started, she couldn't stop. 'Don't worry, I'm not

231

a criminal or anything. I haven't broken the law.' Her laugh was bitter as she lifted her head, and her eyes held his. 'That's quite rich, isn't it? I'm actually a lawyer.'

This time, his eyes narrowed. 'A lawyer?'

Claire nodded, and he couldn't look away as the tip of her tongue appeared and she ran it over her top lip. 'Yes, a lawyer,' she finally replied. 'I went to university straight out of school. Please just trust me when I say I have done nothing wrong. I just found myself in a situation where I was accused of something.' She waved one hand, and her beer tipped over in her lap. 'Oh damn.' She jumped up and put the can onto the table, and dabbed at her cargo pants with the bottom of her T-shirt. Don walked over to the ute and brought back a roll of paper towels.

'Here you go. Use this.'

'I'll smell like a brewery now.'

'At least it's better than a cattle truck.'

That got a quiet laugh from her. 'Please trust me when I say I'm not in the wrong. I'm just taking some time out. Lying low from the media and thinking about what I want to do with my life.'

'If the situation calls for it, I don't have a problem saying you've been up here for a while.'

'Thank you.'

He let it go at that as he turned to the barbeque. 'Time to eat, hey? How hungry are you?'

'Surprisingly, very hungry. I shouldn't be, I've barely used up any energy sitting in a car all day!'

'It's the fresh country air that does it, and anything cooked over a fire is always more appealing too.'

'Thank you.' Claire nodded as he handed her a plate piled high with steak and onions.

'There's some bread rolls in the esky if you want to make a burger?'

She shook her head, her mouth already full as she tucked in.

As they sat around the fire, the mood was relaxed. The tension had eased from her shoulders, and Don was able to get a laugh a few times as he told her anecdotes about the north.

The more she laughed, the more he dug deep for stories. 'You'll probably meet ol' Cruzer if you stay in the Dunstan house for a while. He'll come knocking on your door.'

'Ol Cruzer?' Claire leaned back in the chair, one hand on her lap and the other relaxed by her side.

'Yeah, he's an old fella who claims he was shipwrecked in the Gulf back in the sixties. He gets around in tattered old pants, no shirt and I don't think he owns a pair of shoes. He's harmless, but once he hears you're there, he'll come to visit, and bring you some of his speciality.'

'Fish?'

Don laughed. 'No.'

'Prawns?'

'No.' He watched her as he put one finger to her lip, and her eyes lit up.

'I give up.'

'Honey.'

'That's kind of him.'

'It is,' Don chuckled.' But you have to be careful not to spread it too thickly on your toast. 'Ol Cruz grows some "special" green plants out in the bush, and his bees live around the flowers. It's known locally as Happy Honey. Just a local myth, I don't think it could be true.'

Claire was still laughing as they stood and cleared away the dishes.

'I'll go down to the river and wash them.' Don gathered the dishes into a small plastic crate

'The river?' Her laughter died.

'Don't worry. I'm not going to do a Crocodile Dundee. I'll just fill the tub and come back up here.'

He looked down as Claire reached out and held his arm. A tingle ran up his forearm. 'Are you sure it's safe? Do you want me to come with you?'

Don went to say no but then thought twice. 'If you want to. Two pairs of eyes are better than one.' He regretted saying that a few minutes later as he stood at the edge of the river and shone his flashlight around. He reached back and handed it to Claire, who was standing at a respectable distance from the water.

He lowered the crate and it was almost full when the light flashed past him and hovered in the middle of the river.

'What's that?' Claire's voice was tight.

Don stood and lifted the crate, some of the water sloshing on his arms. He followed the direction of the beam where two red glowing eyes were highlighted in the middle of the river. 'Hmm, well that would be a crocodile.'

'Really.' This time, a squeal came from behind him.

'Yep.'

Claire shone the flashlight along the bank and her sigh of relief was loud. 'There's none on the shore.'

'No, and he won't bother us either. Come on, let's get back to the camp.'

As Don washed the dishes, Claire dried and repacked them.

'They won't come up here, will they?' She looked around nervously. 'Should we sleep in the ute?

'No.' Don hastened to reassure her. 'It's safe. We're far enough away.'

Claire didn't look convinced as she headed to the swag. 'Good night.'

'Sleep well,' he said. 'We've got a long day tomorrow.'

##

Don sat by the fire until the coals had burned to nothing. He kicked some dust over the embers and made sure that the fire was out. He left the side of this swag closest to the ute unzipped. It wasn't crocodiles that you had to watch for out here in the Savannah wilds. It wasn't unknown to have unwelcome visitors of the human variety sniffing around a vehicle in the middle of the night.

Thongs, fuel and beer.

On his first trip across the Savannah Way, an old shopkeeper in Borroloola told him those were the items most likely to be stolen on the back roads of the Top End. The fuel they were carrying was chained to the backboard, and the small amount of beer was locked securely in the ute, but he would still sleep lightly.

Thongs? He didn't wear them in the bush; they were for the beach. He lay there looking out at the night, but sleep eluded him.

He rolled over, punched his pillow, and then sat up.

Claire's words earlier in the night had stayed with him. He grunted and reached for his phone. There was service out here from the tower at the small settlement at Robinson River. Guilt settled heavily in Don's chest as he opened the search engine and typed in Claire Templeton. He justified the search to himself; Claire was in his employ and had admitted to him that there was an issue in her past.

No matter what she said, he had a right to know. His first responsibility was to the paying clients on the charter. He was the owner, skipper of the boat, and responsible for everyone on board.

If there was any chance that Claire's presence on the charter would cause a problem, he needed to know.

But you could have asked her and insisted that she told you, said the little voice from his conscience *instead of doing this surreptitious search.*

But he clicked the keys and scrolled through the hits.

Claire Templeton was a popular name, but none of the hits he opened were the Claire asleep in the swag next to his. An actor, a singer and an interior designer. He amended his search to Claire Templeton, the lawyer.

Jackpot!

There was a hit on *Linked In*. Don clicked on it and scrolled through, but the woman in the photo had long dark hair. He was just about to close it but changed his mind as he looked at the photo. His eyes narrowed as he looked at familiar eyes and the heart-shaped face.

It *was* Claire, but a dark-haired Claire without glasses. He remembered the packets of hair bleach he'd seen in her shopping bag when he'd brought her back across the river.

So big deal, said his conscience. Lots of women changed their hair colour on a regular basis; that wasn't a crime.

He quickly scanned the information in the post. She'd graduated with Honours from Sydney Uni and then gone to work at a prestigious law firm in Bligh Street, Sydney.

Hell, even he'd heard of that one. They were often mentioned on national news as handling high-profile cases.

However, there were no more links from Linked In, and no other sites listed with Claire.

He stared outside into the dark, his mind working before he typed her name and the name of the law firm in the search box.

Success again! A small article in a legal newsletter wishing her well in her new position as host of *Impact Australia* network news program. He frowned as he typed in her name and the name of the program and came up with a blank. The trail went cold.

Maybe she hadn't gone there after all.

Chapter 9

Claire lay on her back, listening to every sound coming through the thin canvas of the swag. Leaves rustled, and small animals scurried around. She drew her feet up as far as she could—not that anything could get into the swag, Don had assured her—but she still stiffened at every sound, imagining a crocodile creeping into the camp. As she lay there, her eyes quickly became accustomed to the darkness as pinpricks of moonlight shone in through the seams in the swag.

After talking to Don about the charter, and the type of guests who would be on it, she was feeling sick. How could she ever have thought she could come up here and stay anonymous? Any guest from Sydney or Melbourne would recognise her immediately, blonde hair or not. All it would take would be one phone call. Or one post on social media and the media would descend in their hordes.

It didn't matter where the boat was; they'd find the *Adventurer*, and they'd find her. Her breathing hitched, and panic built in her chest. Placing her hands over her mouth, she focused on breathing in and out. There was no way she could get out of doing the charter now; she should have stayed in the relative safety and obscurity of Second Chance Bay, but Don had been kind to her; she couldn't let him down.

What the hell was she going to do? He'd sort of agreed to say she'd been up there for a while—or had he? She couldn't remember their conversation as the panicked thoughts whirled around her head.

Her breathing evened out, and she closed her eyes as sleep eventually overtook her.

***

Don pushed open the flap and jumped to his feet. The scream from Claire's swag had turned his blood to ice.

'Claire, I'm coming. What's wrong?' He kicked his boots out of the way and reached for the zip on her swag. Cursing because he hadn't grabbed the flashlight, he reached out in the dark, trying to find where she was. His hands connected with soft curves, and he pulled back quickly.

'What's wrong?' he said again. 'Is there something in here?'

'I'm ok…okay.' Her voice was trembling. Don reached out again but kept his hands higher this time. He touched her shoulders, and even in that light touch, he could feel her body shaking.

'What's wrong, Claire?' He kept his voice soft and calm.

'I'm sorry. I was dreaming.' Her shoulders moved beneath his fingers, and the mattress rustled as she sat up. 'I'm sorry if I woke you.'

'I hope it wasn't about crocodiles?'

'No. It wasn't crocodiles.' Her voice was bitter and full of emotion.

Don sat there unsure of what to do. It wasn't really the right thing to hold her—as much as he wanted to comfort her—and she had withdrawn into her prickly shell already.

'If you're worried, we'll stop at Victoria River tomorrow night. We can get cabins there. It's pretty bas—'

'No. There's no need to change your plans just because of me. I'll be okay.' Now, her voice was brisk, and she moved away to the corner of the swag. 'I'm fine. Go back to your swag.'

'No. I can tell you're upset. I'm not going to leave you. I'm still worried that it was the crocodile eyes that set you off. How about a cuppa?'

Silence.

It seemed as though she was cross with him, and for a moment, Don wondered if she suspected he'd been Googling her.

No, she couldn't. But the guilt stayed with him, along with concern for the state she was in. Her vulnerability touched him deeply, and a surge of protectiveness consumed him.

'Well, I'm going to have one. I'll go and get the fire going.'

'Thank you.' The reply was so soft he hardly heard it. 'I've got some herbal tea bags in my handbag. They help me sleep.'

'Do you want me to get it out of the ute?'

'No. I've got it here. I'm wide awake now.'

Five minutes later, he had a cheery blaze going. Don filled the billy from the jerry can on the back of the ute. He didn't want to spook Claire by going down to the water's edge.

He glanced over at her, lit softly by the firelight as he hung the billy on the tripod. She had pulled her knees up to her chest in the camp chair, and her arms were wrapped tightly around them. She'd passed him the teabag and then put her bag into the ute as soon as he'd unlocked it.

'Don't forget to lock it again,' she'd said.

He'd looked at her curiously. 'Will do.'

The flames snapping, and crackling provided a soothing backdrop. Don glanced at his phone. 'It's almost dawn. How would you feel about a cuppa and packing up camp, and getting an extra early start?'

'That's okay. Whatever you want to do.' Her voice held little expression, and she stared at the flames.

Don couldn't help himself. While he waited for the water to boil, he crouched in front of her chair, but her eyes remained downcast.

He reached over and gently held her chin and tipped her face up. 'Claire, would it help to talk about what's bothering you?'

She held his gaze. The shadows beneath her eyes were darker than they had been yesterday, and he felt helpless, a feeling he wasn't familiar with.

'Look, I've been a sounding board for my sister over the years. I've got broad shoulders. If you want to talk, I can listen. And I won't share anything you tell me.' He tried to inject some lightness to dispel the heavy tension in the air. 'Some of the things Jenni told me over the years would make your hair curl.'

'You're a good brother. She's a very lucky girl.' Claire gave a quiet chuckle and cleared her throat, putting her hand up to her mouth, her fingers brushing his, and he moved his hand away. 'I'll be okay. There's nothing I can do apart from what I'm doing now. Circumstances won't change, but time'll go by and I'll get over it.'

'Get over it?'

She looked at him long and hard, and for a moment, Don thought he'd connected.

'Over what happened, and I'll get back to the real world.'

'As a lawyer?'

She shrugged. 'Who knows? I might like working on the boat. You might be stuck with me.' This time, the laugh that came from her lips was forced, and Don knew she was putting on a front. 'They say a change is as good as a holiday. Don't they?'

'You probably will fall in love with the life.' He lightened the conversation. 'There's nothing like being out under the stars, away out in the wilderness, and seeing the Milky Way in full splendour. The Kimberley will get a hold of you. That's another reason I'm thinking about moving across there.'

'You really think you will?'

'Yeah. At the end of this trip, I'll probably take the boat back to the Gulf and work on her over there. Spend some time with Mum when she gets home, have Christmas with the family, and then head back over to the Kimberleys.'

'What about the ute?

'It can stay at Wyndham. I'll need a work vehicle when I move over there.'

'So we won't be doing this drive back?'

'Probably not. I've got to put some more thought into it yet, but don't worry, we'll get you back to the Bay. Besides you might be over the Savannah Way by the time we get to the coast anyway.'

'So you won't have any charters over the summer?'

The billy boiled over, and the fire hissed as the water hit the coals. 'No, we can't charter in the wet. Too unpredictable.'

'How do you mean?'

Don glanced up at her as he poured the water onto their teabags. 'Swollen rivers, gushing waterfalls and tropical thunderstorms most afternoons. It's not safe.'

'It would be the best time to see it, maybe.'

'It is. And that's when the air tours get most of the business.'

'It sounds majestic.' Claire's voice was brighter now.

'That's a word that's often used to describe the tours. We've had some fabulous reviews on Trip Adviser for our charter.'

'Our? You have a business partner?'

'No. just a figure of speech. It's just me.' Don laughed and shook his head as he passed her the cup. She lowered her legs, and he smiled as she examined the ground before she put her bare feet down. 'You're really not used to the outdoors, are you?'

Her smile was bright, and he was pleased to see the sadness that had surrounded her seemed to have lifted. 'No, but I plan to change that.' She gestured around. The sun wasn't far off, rising, and the sky was getting lighter in the east. 'In fact, I already am!' She regarded him as she sat down and picked up his mug.

'You plan to travel around for a while?'

Again, that shrug. 'A few months.'

A comfortable silence descended for a few minutes as they drank their tea.

At least Claire looked a bit happier now. For a while, she'd looked like she was on the verge of tears. As the sky lightened the shadows lifted and her colour seemed to come back. She was a beautiful woman; green cat's eyes slightly tipped at the corners in a heart-shaped face with lips that were lush and full.

Kissable popped into his head.

As her cup moved to those lips, discomfort filled Don when he realised Claire was looking back at him. He dropped his gaze to his mug, but she reached over and put her hand on his arm. 'Thank you for being kind. I know I can be moody, but I do appreciate it.'

'Nothing more than any decent person would do,' he huffed. Don stood and tipped out the dregs of his tea before getting the thermos from the back of the ute. No point wasting the boiling water; it would do them as they travelled today.

Claire stood and stretched as he tipped the billy and poured the boiling water in. He dragged his eyes away from the strip of bare skin that appeared between her T-shirt and the waistband of her cargo pants.

The reaction he had wasn't one that a gentleman should have in the middle of nowhere with an attractive woman. He turned his back and stayed over at the ute pretending to check the ropes. By the time he turned back around, Claire had disappeared back into the swag.

***

As she sat in the swag and gathered her toiletries bag—not that she'd needed that so far—Claire thought about the stupid dream. It was the fright of seeing the crocodile that had given her the nightmare; the fright had stimulated her brain and set other thoughts swirling. Something about the dream tugged at her, but she couldn't remember what it was. All she could see was that poor man sitting in the interview chair. She pushed open the swag and carried the small bag over to the ute.

It didn't take long to pack up camp. Claire was learning new skills each hour that passed. Watching Don hang the billy over the fire and seeing how he held it to tip the water. Learning how to roll up her swag had been fun, but she'd been conscious of his proximity as he leaned over to show her how to pull the tags tight. He smelled good, fresh and clean, like washing that had come in from the sunshine. He'd put on a clean T-shirt, and Claire considered going down to the river and having a wash to freshen up.

She stood beside the ute as Don loaded the table and chairs. There was no point in being a coward; she was going to have to toughen up before she got on his boat.

With a determined and deep breath, she grabbed her soap and a face washer and headed for the small stand of trees. It was a far cry from any bathroom she'd used before, but she coped.

She came out of the small copse of trees and headed down the hill towards the water, keeping a wary eye on the grass and the loose, reddish sand at the edge of the river. As she paused a few metres back from the edge, a huge splash came from the other side. She jumped and put her hand to her chest, but the splash was immediately followed by the roar of an engine. She watched fascinated as a large four-wheel drive vehicle ploughed across the river, about fifty metres downstream at the crossing, with a huge arc of spray on either side. Waiting until it had disappeared up the hill, Claire looked around at the river before gingerly stepping to the edge. She bent down, her eyes fixed on the water in front of her. She widened her eyes; it was so clear she could see the flat brown stones on the bottom as the water trickled over them. It was only about twenty centimetres deep, nowhere for a crocodile to hide.

Feeling very brave, she leaned forward with her hands cupped and washed her face.

'You're getting brave.' Don's voice from behind brought a smile to her lips.

'I am. But you did come to guard me.' Claire gestured to the river. 'I didn't realise how pretty it was out here.' She shook her hands dry as she looked across to the other side. The sand there was not red and closer to the colour of sand that she was used to. A lush patch of bright green grass ran down one side of the small cove and into the water. The sun was getting higher, and sunlight sparkled on the water, which was flowing faster on the other side of the river. Small stands of shrubs with a pale pink flower edged the grass, and lacy cobwebs held tiny droplets of water like diamonds.

Don came down and stood beside her before crouching and washing his face and hands. His eyes glinted with mirth as she reached down and rinsed her face again.

'Are you missing a bathroom? There's a secluded copse over there.'

'I know.' She stood up straight and grinned at him. 'I already found it.'

'You're doing well.' He turned and held out his hand. 'Come on, we'll get going. About six hours more and the worst part of the trip is over.'

His fingers were strong and warm, and Claire didn't let go of them as they walked up the hill. A warm feeling curled in her chest, and she squeezed his fingers when they reached the ute.

'Thank you,' she whispered. Unable to help herself, she reached and brushed her lips across his cheek.

'What for?' Surprise crossed his face as she stepped back, but Don kept hold of her hand as she looked up at him.

'For being a good man.'

His laugh was self-conscious as he let go of her hand and flicked her cheek with a gentle finger.

'Thank *you* for keeping me company.'

##

By the time they'd done the third river crossing, Claire was enjoying herself. Looking up the middle of a wide river as the ute ploughed through metre-deep water was exhilarating. It was almost like being on a boat. As they went up the hill on the other side, she frowned. 'How come the motor doesn't conk out?'

Don grinned back at her and pointed to the funny black thing on the side of the windscreen. 'That's what the snorkel's for. It stops the engine ingesting the water.'

Claire shook her head. 'This has been an education so far. Does anyone ever float away?'

He nodded, and she widened her eyes.

'Often. Wait until you see the abandoned car wrecks along the side of the road from now to Borroloola. The retrieval of breakdowns keeps the local mechanic in business. Cars, camper trailers and utes—the road gets worse from here. The grader from Borroloola doesn't get this far out.'

'It's a whole new world out here.' She folded her arms. 'And I'm loving it more every minute.'

And it wasn't just because they were isolated and not seeing other people, taking away her fear of being recognised. She was enjoying being with Don and was gaining more respect for him each time he safely manoeuvred the car through deep ditches, washouts and bull dust, and through rivers.

I'm even getting the lingo right, she thought with a grin.

The fragments of that stupid dream in the early hours had finally left her, and she felt foolish for waking him up. When he'd come into the swag, and his fingers had brushed against her breast in the dark, a jolt of awareness had hit her. All she'd wanted was for his arms to go around her and comfort her. She'd been hyperaware of him ever since and hadn't been able to resist kissing his cheek. It had been tempting to brush her lips over his mouth, but she'd thought better of it. It was simply a thank-you kiss for a man who was showing her kindness and friendship. And a man who'd given her a job.

She had to remember that. Once they were on the boat, Don would be her boss.

Then, these stupid feelings that were building in her would have to be put aside. Don McDougal came from a different world than hers—not that she was sure what her world was like at the moment.

One consolation—as strange as it seemed—trying to put him out of her mind had taken the worry of what had happened in Sydney into the back of her mind.

She reached for the small pillow that Don had put on the seat and leaned her head against it as the landscape went by.

Chapter 10

They reached the small township of Borroloola in the late morning. As Don had said, they'd passed abandoned cars and trailers covered in red dust. They'd stopped once for a cup of tea and a snack, and she'd helped him hold the jerry can up and fill the fuel tank with diesel.

As they drove into the small town, Don turned to her. 'Do you want to stop? Do you need anything?'

Claire went to shake her head, and then she thought of Aunt Bea and how she'd be worrying about her. 'If you want to have a break, I wouldn't mind finding a public phone and calling my aunt if we've got time to stop.'

Don flicked her a glance. 'No need to worry about a public phone. You can use my mobile. I was going to call in at the mechanic and get him to put the ute up on the hoist, just to check the suspension. I can't see anything wrong, but that was a pretty loud bang when we went into that bull dust yesterday.'

'Thank you. There's service here?'

'Yeah.' He turned the ute off the main—now tarred—road and drove a hundred metres past some old houses until they reached a small row of shops. Claire was surprised to see many of the businesses were closed and the front windows boarded up. She pointed to a grocery store that had a high wire fence around it, with a gate at the front that was propped open. A group of children, surrounded by half a dozen mangey dogs, were playing on the red dirt.

'Why are the windows boarded up?' she asked curiously.

'There's a few social issues out here.'

She turned and watched as they passed more buildings with fences and boarded-up windows and it reminded her of a program they'd done on similar issues earlier in the year. She'd been nominated for the Walkley for that program.

Don turned into the workshop yard and parked the ute. Cars in various states of disrepair lined the cyclone fence, but the building was freshly painted, and the workshop area looked tidy from where Claire was sitting. A red kelpie came running out, barking madly. 'Don't worry about the dog. She's harmless.' He turned off the engine and leaned forward and pulled his phone out of his back pocket. 'Hopefully, Jim can look at the wheel straight up. Hop out and stretch your legs, it'll be a few hours until we hit the Stuart Highway.' He grinned, and the tanned skin around his blue eyes crinkled. 'Sick of being on the road yet?'

Claire opened the door and Don came around to her side. 'No. I'm not. It's a whole new experience.' This time she grinned up at him as she stood close to her. 'A walk will be good. Those ute seats get a bit hard after a while.'

'They do.' He handed her his phone and pointed to a takeaway shop a couple of doors further along. 'Coffee's not bad there if you want to get a couple after you make your call.'

'Thanks. How do you have yours?'

'Cappuccino with two sugars. Thanks.'

Claire reached in for her bag and hugged it tight to her chest with one hand, Don's phone in the other. As she walked away, he called out to her. 'Three two, three two, three two, to get into the phone.'

She waved in acknowledgement and headed for the store, deciding to order the coffee first. Pushing open the door, she stepped into the dark and cool interior, the smell of fried food overpowering. Despite the oily smell, she was surprised to see a display of freshly made sandwiches and homemade cakes in a small refrigerated cabinet next to the counter.

'What would you like, love?' A woman with a purple apron covering her dress and an immaculate hairstyle smiled across the counter.

Claire looked at the sandwiches. If she bought some lunch, it would save a stop in an hour or so to prepare something. So far, apart from a few homemade biscuits, she'd contributed little to the road trip.

She certainly hadn't been a fount of scintillating conversation or happy company, and she'd cut Don's sleep short with that stupid dream. The least she could do was buy him lunch.

'Two salad rolls, please, and two cappuccinos. To take away.'

'You in a rush love?' A waft of strong perfume came from the woman as she moved to the cash register.

'Not really. I've got at least twenty minutes.'

'I'll make you a couple of fresh ones. Those premade ones will be snapped up by the boys from the mine when they come in for lunch.'

'The mine?'

The woman laughed. 'You must have come in from the east.'

Claire nodded.

'Well, if you're heading west now, you'll get a shock, four-lane highway past the mine for quite a few miles. It's the boys from there that keep my shop going. And the grey nomies and the fishermen going out to King Ash Bay.' She picked up a couple of bread rolls and walked over to the bench. 'What about you, love? Where are you heading?'

'We're going—' Claire's breath caught as she looked down at her face staring up at her from the cover of a glossy gossip magazine.

SYBIL HARRIS FLEES TO THE COTE D'AZUR, the lead headline read.

'Um…to Wyndham.'

The woman chatted on about the coast, and the road, but Claire's ears were buzzing.

'I'll be back in a minute.' She pushed open the door and pulled out the plastic chair at the table outside the shop. As she tried to settle, she looked over to the workshop. The ute was now up on the hoist, and Don was talking to the mechanic.

The media were still on her case. She huffed a bitter laugh. At least they had her out of the country. Surprisingly, that thought calmed her.

She took a deep breath and took Don's phone from her pocket. Talking to Aunty Bea would help too.

She typed in the password and her eyes widened as the screen opened to Linked In. And a photo of her, taken when she worked at Baker and Baker in Bligh Street.

What the hell?

*****

The strut to the shockie had a slight bend in it, but Jim assured him that it would last the trip.

'No prob, mate. If you're in a hurry, just replace it when you get there. I haven't got one in stock, and it'll take a week or so to get one up from Melbourne. Even longer, probably.' He pointed to a Rodeo ute with a smashed back window. 'That poor bugger's been waiting three weeks for his new glass. He was loaded up with fresh meat and fruit to take out to Roper River, and his fridge was full. The missus and I ate salad for a week!'

Don paid the bill and then backed the ute out. Claire was walking back towards him carrying one coffee and a brown paper bag. He jumped out and opened the door for her as she crossed to the ute.

She shoved the coffee into his hand and threw the brown paper bag onto the seat before getting into the ute and staring

251

stonily ahead. She put her bag onto the floor, and after he'd closed her door and climbed into the driver's seat, she handed his phone back to him.

'Did you get onto your aunt?' he asked carefully as he started the car. As he looked over his shoulder to reverse out, he glanced at Claire. Her lips were set, and there were two spots of colour high on her cheeks. 'Everything was okay?'

'She's fine.' The tone was clipped. She gestured to the seat. 'If you're hungry I got you a salad roll.'

'Good plan, thanks. There's a nice grassy area at Cape Crawford. We'll stop there. It's about an hour away.'

As they drove along the highway, kindly sealed by the McArthur River mine, there wasn't a word spoken.

As the hour of silence passed, Don's temper built.

Talk about moody.

Even at her crankiest, Jenni would always say what was bothering her, usually accompanied by a good thump. Claire was obviously upset about something, but opposite to Jenni, it looked like she bottled things up.

He stared ahead at the road. You could cut the air in the ute with a knife. It was at least another ten hours to where he'd planned to stay tonight and then a relatively short trip across to Wyndham in the morning. He couldn't let it go; if Claire was going to be moody like this on the boat—for no good reason that he could see—he was going to have to speak to her. He wouldn't let her moods impact the guests.

And he wasn't looking forward to that.

But yet beneath his temper, there was a part of him that worried about her. It was because he found her so bloody attractive; he had to remind himself that the sad vulnerability might be calculated. Anyone who could switch moods like that had a problem.

He had to keep that in his head and get over the physical reaction to Claire.

But maybe she was frightened of something?

Just after eleven, Don pulled the ute up on the road outside the hotel at Cape Crawford. The grassy area was one of the nicest places to stop on the journey west, and the amenities were clean and open to travellers. Claire had the door open, her bag tucked beneath her arm, and was striding across to the building before he had turned the engine off.

With a shrug, he picked up the lunch bag and took it over to one of the tables sheltered by the huge trees. He put the empty coffee cup in the bin, sat down and waited for her to come out before he opened the bag. The silence was broken as a helicopter took off from the paddock beside the hotel. The hotel, the shack where the helicopter flights were booked for sightseeing over the Lost City, and half a dozen houses were the only buildings in the tiny settlement at the junction of the Carpentaria and Tablelands Highways.

A good ten minutes later, she walked across the grass and passed another coffee to him. Her hair was wet, and she'd changed her T-shirt. She must have made use of the public showers.

'Thank you.' He gestured to the bag. 'I waited for you.'

'I'm not hungry.' She sat and folded her arms, looking around at the picnic area.

'It's a good place to stop.'

When she didn't reply, Don reached for the bag and took out one of the salad rolls.

'If you're not going to eat, I'll put yours in the camp fridge.'

'Whatever.'

Don's family knew that it took a lot to fire his temper, but he knew they all would have recognised the set of his jaw and his slow movements as he put the bread roll back down on the paper.

'May I have a word?'

She lifted her chin and stared at him.

He stared back. 'I'm going to be frank here, Claire. Your moodiness is pissing me off. One minute you're telling me how "kind" I am and kissing me, the next minute, you're playing no speakies and sending me dagger glares every time I open my mouth.'

'I did not.'

'What? Kiss me or the filthy looks?'

'Not a real kiss.' Her chin was as high as his.

A real kiss was something he might try one day. Maybe that would stir up the calm and controlled Claire Templeton. He wondered what it would be like to peel away layer by layer and find the true woman beneath that exterior.

'As your employer, I have to say something. I can't risk you being like this on the *Adventurer*.'

'Like what?'

'Oh for Pete's sake, Claire, Like this! Snarky when you do deign to talk to me.'

'I can give you my word you I won't be snarky with the guests on the boat.' She moved across the seat closer to him and lowered her chin so they were almost nose to nose.

'Unless…'

Despite his temper, he couldn't help but notice the coconut fragrance coming from her damp hair. 'Unless what?' He held her gaze and didn't budge. It was hard not to let his eyes drop to her lips, which were millimetres away from his.

'Unless they stalk me on social media.'

He frowned. 'What the hell are you talking about.'

And then the guilt punched in as he remembered she'd used his phone at Borroloola. That's when her mood changed. When she'd come back from the shop and making her call.

'Fair enough.'

'Fair enough? That's all you've got to say.' Her face came closer, and he could smell peppermint toothpaste on her breath.

She turned her head to look past him and moved back a little.

He put one hand on her arm and cupped her cheek with the other. 'Tell me what's wrong, Claire?'

Her eyes met his again, and a sucker punch hit his gut as tears glittered on her long lashes.

'I'm sorry. I wanted to know more about you. You fascinate me, and I wondered if I knew any more about you, I could help.'

'You could have asked.' Her voice trembled.

'I did. A couple of times.'

Her soft sigh blew on his lips, and without thinking, Don dipped his head and laid his lips lightly on hers. She didn't move away. His fingers tightened a little bit on her face, and he lifted his other hand and cupped her cheeks with both hands. This time, the kiss was deeper… and longer. Relief flooded through him when her lips parted beneath his, and her hands crept around his neck.

Don's pulse hammered as her tongue brushed his briefly. Claire drew back and lowered her hand to his chest. He put his hand over it.

'I'm sorry for being so hard to get on with but seeing myself on *Linked In* on your phone brought me undone. And the magazine in the shop, and then Aunt Bea told me that reporters had been to the aged care home wanting to talk to her.' She lifted her head and her face was awash with tears.

Don reached out and used his thumb to stop another tear from falling.

Her voice hitched in a sob. 'And then to know that you knew all about me and hadn't said anything.'

'Whoa, Claire. I don't know *all* about you. Any more than what you told me. You were a lawyer. I don't know why you're up here, and I don't know why reporters would be trying to find you. Or what magazine you're talking about. I do know you're running from something, and in my defence rather than curiosity, it was more worry that drove me to look you up.'

She pulled back from him, and for a moment, he thought she was still mad at him, but she dug into her bag and pulled out a magazine.

'I saw it in the shop at Borroloola. It was the last one, so I bought it.' Her laugh held no humour. 'Not that anyone way up there would have recognised me off the cover.'

He held his hand out as she passed him the magazine and he looked down at a photo of a dark-haired Claire on the cover.

Chapter 11

'The *Cote d'Azur*?' Don lifted his head after he'd looked at her picture on the front of the trashy magazine. 'Second Chance Bay is a long way from the Mediterranean.'

Claire nodded. Don still had hold of her hand. He'd put the magazine on the table and so far, had only looked at the headline and hadn't opened it to read the article.

'And who's this Sybil Harris with your photo on a beach in France?'

'It's a photo of me, and it was taken at Ettalong on the Central Coast last summer. They've photoshopped me onto a French beach! The media will do anything to beef up a good story. Trust me, I've been there and, sad to say, part of a team that's done things that were just as unfair.' She took her hand from his and tucked her hair behind her ear. 'Sybil Harris is my work name. I thought it was better to change it for the show after being at the law firm.'

'You did leave the law firm and go to a television network.' He looked at her sheepishly. 'I'll be honest I did Google that.'

'It's okay. I know you were only trying to help. It's only been a few weeks since it happened, and I think I'm gradually coming to terms with it. My real name is Claire Sybil Harris-Templeton. Thank goodness none of them have discovered that yet.'

'Is there a chance they'll pick that up?'

'Probably. Maybe I was stupid to run away, but I was so upset about that poor man and all of the garbage that the media was making up that I couldn't cope with being in the city.'

'Changed your hair colour?'

She looked down and nodded. 'And cut my hair with manicure scissors in a hotel room. I was kidding myself. I still look the same, don't I?'

Don leaned back and looked at the magazine and then at Claire. 'There's a resemblance, but she—you—could pass for your sister. Or even just someone who looks like you.'

'That's a relief.' Her shoulders relaxed, and she smiled as he took her hand again. Holding Don's hand grounded her. She refused to think about the kiss they'd shared. 'I was worried back at the house when Matt said I reminded him of someone. You didn't seem to see it.'

'I've never seen'—he let go of her hand and flicked open the magazine— 'Impact Australia.'

'I was the host for six months.'

'I'm out to sea on charters most of the time, and to be honest, I hate the way television has gone lately. Stupid reality shows and the news reporting that's not even news.'

'I know. There are no standards. It's all about chasing the dollar these days. I'm sorry to say I was a part of it. I was very trusting and naïve. And I guess it was ego that kicked in when I was offered the job.'

'Tell me what happened.' His thigh was warm against hers as he looked at the article. Claire closed her eyes for a moment, savouring the pressure against her leg.

'It's a long story, and we should get back on the road. You said we've still got a lot of hours on the road today.'

'You're right.' He handed her the magazine and glanced at his watch. 'We will, but on one condition. You eat your lunch now, and then you can tell me as we drive.' He reached out and held her shoulders gently. 'But only if you're happy to tell me. I don't want to have forced you into it by that *Linked In* stuff.'

Claire dropped her head to Don's shoulder and it was like going home. His hand came up and cupped the back of her head and she breathed in the same fresh smell as she had early this morning. She closed his eyes again as his fingers gently smoothed her hair.

'I'm happy to. It will be good to share. I haven't told anyone else. Aunt Bea knows a little bit about what happened, but she thinks I've gone on a holiday to take some time out.'

'Okay. Come on, then. Eat up. I'll just go to the amenities, and then grab us another coffee before we go. You okay here by yourself for five?'

She nodded, feeling better than she had for a month. 'Of course, I am. I don't think there's a media horde hiding here. And Don? Thank you.'

'You've got to stop all this thanking me all the time, you know.' He grinned, and her heart gave a little kick. 'Wait until I get you on the boat, you'll see me in my true tyrannical form. Now eat your lunch, and I'll take you on another scenic tour of the Top End.'

Claire did as she was told and finished the salad roll. As she ate, she flicked through the magazine article. The story was so bad and so way off base she even smiled at times.

The mystery that everyone seemed to be reporting on now, was where had Sybil Harris gone? France? Morocco? New York?

I wish.

They didn't seem to be focusing on the show any more, that was old news.

Hopefully.

She shook her head as she took the scraps across to the bin.

Talk about gutter journalism, photoshopping an old photo of her and saying she was in France!

By the time Don came back and handed her a coffee, Claire was feeling a lot better.

##

'It happened on the program one night.' Claire looked across at Don and he reached over and squeezed her hand in brief encouragement. She looked down at her fingers when he let them go. How could a simple brush of skin against skin send a jolt though her whole body?

They were back on the road. A much better road, single lane, but at least it was tarred. She stared ahead, reliving the events of that night. 'I'd missed the staging meeting. They changed the time of the meeting, and the production assistant stuffed up and left me out of the email, saying it had been brought forward a couple of hours. I'd missed a couple before and it had been okay. As long as I had the running sheet and my research was up to date, I knew I'd be fine.' Claire pulled her knees up and hugged them.

'Could the lack of an email have been deliberate, do you think?'

Claire shook her head. 'No, Giselle is a top-notch assistant. She just about grovelled after the meeting when she realised it was her fault that I missed it.'

'Fair enough.'

'I should have been fine with what I had. It might sound like ego kicking in, but I was a damn good reporter. I was even nominated for a Walkley this year.'

Don whistled. 'Even *I* know what that is.'

'I went to introduce the guest, and when I read the teleprompter—that's the screen that flashes up the script between me and the camera—it threw me. As soon as I saw his name, I panicked. Inside anyway.' She bit her lip as she recalled Ross Timmins sitting across from her. 'He wasn't the guest that I'd been expecting. I managed to stay calm on the outside. He had such a kind face, and his eyes were sad.'

Claire had been expecting to ask some hard questions of the CEO of a charity where money had gone missing. The federal corruption agency had been investigating him, but the CEO had so far managed to evade any charges; she'd been surprised when he'd agreed to be interviewed. Unbeknown to him, the network had been given some crucial information, and that night's show was the night she was going to present that information to him.

And expose him.

On air.

In front of the nation.

Her stomach churned, and she felt ill. Instead, Ross Timmins had been sitting there.

'I had no idea who he was,' Claire continued as she brought Don up to speed. 'But I trusted my production crew and the research team, so I asked him the questions as they came up on the teleprompter. Questions about his young son and how he'd died. Questions that intimated that he hadn't done as much as he could have seeking medical treatment. It was loosely linked to the charity that was being investigated. I'll never, ever forget the look on his face.'

'So, what happened?' Don asked quietly.

'That's the problem. I don't know.' Claire dropped her gaze to her hands. She hadn't even been aware that they were clutched tightly in her lap. Her knuckles were white, and she eased her fingers apart and flexed them.

'We went to an ad break, and he collapsed in tears. Giselle and Ben ran over to him, and they had to help him off the set.' She closed her eyes as she remembered his stricken face. 'I was left sitting there stunned. I brought him to that state and on national television.'

'You didn't cause it. Your team did. Or whoever wrote the questions.'

'I should have been at the meeting. The crazy thing was that when they pulled up the teleprompter, none of the questions that I'd asked were there. My running sheet disappeared, and I had no proof that I'd been given the wrong questions.'

'You were set up.'

'I was. But even I started to doubt my recollection of what had happened when it hit the fan. I had no evidence of anything. I simply looked like a hard bitch. When I finally stood up, the network CEO was next to the camera with a face like thunder. Ben was there, holding his arm, holding him back. The boss looked like he was ready to attack me.'

'Then?'

'I got hauled into his office. I explained about the teleprompter and the running sheet, but he didn't believe me. It looked like I had gone out for glory off my own bat. Anyone who knows me knows I wouldn't have done that. Even Ben didn't support me.'

'Ben?'

'The director. We were sort of seeing each other.' Claire bit her lip and stared ahead at a large cloud of dust. 'What's that?'

'Cattle muster. They do it by helicopter out here.'

Having her attention taken away from the memory of that night helped her breathing return to normal.

'Did you lose your job? Is that why you're up here?'

'No. Would you believe the ratings went through the roof, and all of a sudden, I was a golden-haired girl.'

'I don't understand?' Don frowned as he slowed the car as a couple of horsemen waved at them.

'With the program and the station. The CEO ended up being delighted. I was even offered a bonus. It was the media that turned on me. I was made out to be the hard-nosed bitch who would do anything for ratings. Sybil Harris, arch bitch.' She shook her head as Don backed the speed off more as a mob of cattle appeared a hundred metres ahead. 'The headlines, the social media, the phone calls. You've got no idea what it was like. It was as though I was a criminal. They camped outside my house. I had to leave. I was mortified.'

'Have you quit?'

'No, I took a leave of absence. No pay. But my contract is up for renewal in a month.'

'Will the network renew?'

'Probably.' She shrugged. 'I don't know, but whatever they decide, I've come to a decision. I won't go back. It's not what I'd expected. It's not what I wanted it to be.' She turned to face him as Don turned the engine off. 'I don't know what I'll do yet. Job wise, that is.'

Hundreds of beasts milled in the paddock on either side of the road. The thudding of helicopter blades filled the air. Two horsemen were rounding up the stragglers that had broken out onto the bitumen road.

'I took that job because I thought as part of the team, I could make a difference. We did make a difference on a number of our reports, but this one's disillusioned me. I can't go back.'

'Not even to vindicate yourself and find out who set you up? Have you got any ideas?' Don reached over and put his arm around her, and she rested her head on his shoulder.

A fragment of memory flitted through Claire's thoughts, but she couldn't hold onto it.

'No.'

'It has to be someone on the crew. It shouldn't be too hard to work out.'

'Perhaps not, but I've taken the coward's way out. I'm not going back to Sydney until it all dies down.'

Chapter 12

As they turned onto the Stuart Highway and headed south for a short while before turning west again, Claire didn't stir. She'd been asleep for a while, obviously exhausted by going over what had happened.

Bastards, Don thought. It wasn't hard to see that Claire was a good person and that her motivation for taking the job had probably been idealistic. She'd been shafted, and the media had come in after her blood. As she'd said, anything to improve ratings; it was such an artificial world. Give him the freedom of the sea and the outback any day.

He glanced over at Claire again. Her lips were gently parted, her eyes closed, and her chest rose and fell with each breath she took. Her fingers held the pillow that she'd propped up against the window. When she'd yawned and dug out the pillow, Don had changed his mind about the route they'd take. It meant a rough road for a while but would cut a good three hundred and fifty kilometres off the trip.

Claire woke up as soon as they hit the dirt. She rubbed her eyes and looked around. 'Roadworks?'

'No. I've decided to take a shortcut. I'll head for Top Springs tonight, and it means we'll get to the boat a bit earlier tomorrow.

'You're the boss.' She rubbed her eyes again and stretched. 'How long was I asleep?'

'A couple of hours. How do you feel?'

'Much better. Thanks for being a sounding board.'

'My pleasure. Sorry, the ute's going to shudder for a while.' Don slowed down as they hit more corrugations. 'Listen,

I've been thinking about what you said the other day about being on the boat.'

'What do you mean?' Claire tipped her head to the side, and her hair fell over her shoulder. His fingers itched to hold her close again, and he looked away.

She was an employee, for God's sake. He shouldn't have kissed her back at Cape Crawford.

And now he had a dilemma. He'd shown her sympathy, he knew her story, and he'd given into the attraction he'd felt, breaking his cardinal rule of not getting involved with employees.

What he'd been thinking about broke that rule and every other one he'd ever made about dealing with staff.

He grinned ruefully. 'The favour you asked about me saying you'd been on the boat for months.'

'Yes?' she said slowly.

'The guests on the boat are usually wealthy, savvy businessmen and from what you've said about the high-profile show and the media circus afterwards, I think there's a pretty good chance someone onboard will see the resemblance.'

Her face fell. 'So, you're saying you don't want me on the charter?'

'No, I'm going to suggest something that should dispel any idea that you're Sybil—?'

'Harris,' she filled in for him.

'Yes, Sybil Harris.' He shot her a sideways glance. Her eyes were already on him.

'Tell me?'

'I will when we pull up for the night. Not long now.'

***

By the time they pulled up just before dark, Claire was feeling much better. Sharing with Don what had happened had been cathartic, and being able to be honest about the mutual attraction had taken away the emotional undercurrent from their conversation. This time, they worked well together. Claire knew what had to come off the back of the ute and managed to set up her swag.

'I'll do that for you,' Don said, but she knocked back his offer to help.

'No. I'd like to see if I can do it. There's a new me after today. I'm going to have a go at new things and take some risks.'

They'd had to stop for cattle a couple of times on the last leg of the trip. The last hundred kilometres had been flat and straight, and the road wasn't too bad. Red dust and dry yellow grass on each side, along with low scrubby trees. As they came into Top Springs, Don turned to her.

'There's a camping area at the back of the pub, plus some cabins. So, cabin or swag? Your choice.'

'Swag. There was no point bringing them on the ute if you were going to take a cabin. And I was comfortable last night.'

'Good stuff,' he said with a grin.' And the best part is, the pub does an amazing meal, and there's a camp kitchen too, so we won't have to light a fire.'

'What about crocodiles?' she asked, but her tone was joking.

Don spread his arms wide and spun around. 'Do you see a river?'

'Just checking.'

He reached over and helped her up as she stood up from pegging down her swag. 'Nightmares tonight?'

'I hope not.'

Once they were set up, Don pointed out the amenities block at the back of the hotel. 'Do you want to have a shower before dinner?'

'Do I have time?"

'Sure. I'll go in and book a table, and then I'll come back and wash some of the road dirt off too. Might as well make use of them.' He chuckled. 'Get value for our twenty dollars.'

Claire went to the ute and picked up her toiletries bag and towel. She opened her suitcase and pulled out clean underwear and one of the dresses she'd packed. Holding her handbag in one hand and clutching her towel, clothes and toiletries in the other, she walked across to the small amenities block.

It was basic but clean, and the water was hot. She stood beneath the shower and tipped her head back, rinsing the shampoo from her hair. Telling Don what had led to her arrival in Second Chance Bay had been cathartic, and she wondered what he was going to suggest. It was a worry that he thought she might be recognised, but she could simply shake her head and deny being Sybil Harris as she went about her new job on the boat.

A little frisson of nerves tugged at her as she turned the taps off and reached for the towel. Was she being naïve again?

\#\#

Admiration filled Don's eyes as Claire walked back to the campsite. She put her head down as the warm evening breeze blew tendrils of damp hair onto her face. She put her dusty clothes in the ute and tucked her handbag beneath her arm before she turned to him.

'I didn't realise how much dust had settled on me. The water was red!'

'You'll get used to it. It's one of the things that our guests comment on most when we go for the treks.' Don held the door of the hotel open for her, and Claire smiled as the cool air hit her face.

Surprisingly, the room was crowded, and there was a small queue over at the counter. Instinctively, she dropped her head and let her hair fall across her face.

What am I going to be like back in the city? she wondered. *Will my life ever be normal again?*

If anyone had told her a month ago that she'd be sitting in a pub on a dirt road in the middle of the Northern Territory and sleeping in a swag, she would have waved a dismissive, manicured hand.

Claire looked down at her fingers as they sat at the table. Her nails were clipped short and square now and unpainted. She hadn't worn make-up since she'd left Sydney.

But the change was good. It was as though she was morphing back into the real Claire Templeton again. A place where she was comfortable in her own skin.

'What would you like to drink?' Don nodded over to the bistro. 'We'll let the crowd clear before we order our meal.'

'Just a soft drink, thanks. Lime and soda will be fine.' She wasn't going to risk anything that might set off another nightmare tonight.

As Don walked over to the bar, her gaze stayed on him. A shame he'd added a button-through shirt to the clean black jeans he'd changed into. The muscles that his usual T-shirts clung to lovingly weren't as obvious tonight. But his height and broad shoulders and the way he held himself were just as appealing. Don was a strong man, both physically and character-wise, and Claire had appreciated the concern he had shown to her. She also appreciated what a fine-looking man he was. As he stood at the bar chatting to the barman, she wondered what his solution was going to be. When she'd thought that he was going to suggest that she didn't come on the charter, her first reaction had been disappointment.

Drumming her fingers on the wooden tabletop, she waited for him to come back with their drinks. By the time he walked back and placed her soft drink and a glass of beer on the table, her nerves were zinging.

'Thank you.' Claire picked up her drink and took a long sip as Don sat down. As soon as he'd had a drink, she sat up straight and put her hands on the table.

'So tell me this idea of yours. How do we get rid of any idea that I'm Sybil Harris.'

'Okay.'

She waited.

He put his beer on the table and leaned back in his chair. Fresh soap and a hint of aftershave wafted across to her, and she looked up. Don had shaved, and his tanned skin looked smooth. It was just as attractive as the dark stubble that had appeared over the past couple of days. Claire curled her fingers and dropped her head to avoid the temptation of reaching out and running her fingers along his chin to see if it felt as good as it looked.

Oh, for goodness sake!

'Okay …' His deep voice interrupted her thoughts as she chastised herself.

Claire lifted her head to meet this gaze. 'You've got me worried, Don. If you've changed your mind about me coming, I can get back to Second Chance Bay. I should have told you my story before we left.'

'No. It's fine. This is what I am proposing.' He chuckled, and Claire frowned.

'What's so funny?'

'I'm not actually proposing. That was a poor choice of a word.'

'What?' She stared at him, totally confused now.

'The whole crew on this charter is new. New chef, new deckhands'—he smiled— 'and a new hostess.'

'So your idea is…?'

'How would you feel about being Claire McDougal?'

'What?' If a jaw could drop, Claire's did.

Don put his hand up. 'Not in reality. Just for the trip. And it will explain why I'm teaching you the job from scratch. Most of the crew would expect that I'd have an experienced hostess on board. We'll tell the crew that I couldn't get one in time—they would have seen the recent ads at the agency in Darwin when they signed on—and that my wife of six months agreed to do it. Not only to help me out but also because she was missing me so much. Does that sound feasible?'

Claire sat back and crossed her arms as she looked at him, not sure what to think. 'So …' she said slowly. 'Would the skipper and his wife share a cabin?'

'If we wanted to be convincing, we would. But there's a small single bed in my cabin. And you will have the hostess cabin for your privacy too. The deckhand's and chef's cabins are at the back of the boat. The hostess is up by the wheelhouse, where my cabin is. Besides, most nights, I'll be up on watch, so you won't have to put up with my snoring.'

***

By the look Claire cast his way, she might have been thinking it was a ploy to get her between the sheets.

Don had standards. On his boat, and in his personal life. Okay, so he was attracted, but if she thought he'd try and pull that she didn't know him well enough yet.

Yet.

She cleared her throat as she shifted her gaze back to him. 'Okay. It sounds as though it's a good solution. I think?'

'Claire, I have a rule. Business and pleasure don't mix. Not while we're on the boat anyway.' He lowered his voice and reached for her hand. Claire watched as his thumb rubbed her open palm. 'But I'll also be upfront with you. In case you haven't noticed, I think you are a very interesting woman, and when we go back to the Bay, maybe we can explore our relationship a little more.' He laughed. 'Then again, you'll have seen me in action by then, and I'll probably yell at you a hundred times.'

'So, you'd yell at your new wife, would you?' Her tone was prudish, but it was tempered by a cheeky grin.

'It's good to see you smile, Claire. Really smile.'

'I'm happy for you to do that. If you're really sure. You don't owe me anything, you know.'

'I want to. It's a horrible situation for you to be in.

'I know. And I've handled it really badly so far.' She sighed. 'But I can see light at the end of the tunnel. I'll go back to Sydney, deal with the flack and try to discover who did this. Try to clear my reputation and move on.'

'Maybe the network already has. Have you heard from them since you left?'

'No. But I don't have a phone, and I didn't leave any contact numbers. Although Aunt Bea did say, the network had called her. I just wish they would leave her alone. She doesn't deserve to be pulled into this mess.' She held his gaze and squeezed his fingers.

'And neither did you. But you know what?' Her pretty lips tilted in a smile.

'What?'

'There's nothing like dumping your problems on a relative stranger to make you feel better. And I am feeling better with each day that passes.'

Chapter 13

The night spent at Top Springs and the road trip the following day were uneventful. Claire had no more bad dreams, and Don seemed a little bit more aloof since he'd shared his idea of pretending that Claire could pose as his wife. Dinner had been as good as he'd promised, and their conversation had been light, mainly information Don shared about how the charter would work.

There had been no more hand-holding or brushed fingers, and on the way back to the campsite, he had kept a distance between them.

With a brief good night, Don had waited until Claire was in her swag. She'd zipped it up and fallen asleep almost immediately.

Now, the signpost ahead said that Wyndham was only a few kilometres ahead.

'Not far off, now,' Don said as he changed back a gear.

Claire nodded and looked at the landscape flashing past. Salt pans that stretched as far as she could see to the west were edged by a low mountain range.

'This is the beginning of the Kimberley,' Don said. 'Spectacular landforms, deep rivers, salt pans and wetlands. And great fishing. Things unique to the north.'

'It's very different. The earthy colours are beautiful,' Claire added.

'Don't be put off when you see Wyndham. The town's had its booms and busts, and since the meatworks closed, tourism is one of the things that keeps it going. It's the only deep-water port between Broome and Darwin, and exports of cattle, nickel, iron ore & produce from the Ord River area do make it a busy little port.'

As they approached the port, she looked with interest at the wide expanse of brown water. 'It's so wide.'

'It's where the King, Pentecost, Durack, Forest and Ord Rivers all meet the sea.' Don laughed. 'Excuse my geography talk. I've used it for the talks I give on the charter.'

Claire frowned as a thought hit her. 'Will I be expected to know about the Kimberleys, do you think? Being your ... wife.'

Don shook his head as he turned onto a road that ran along beside the wide brown river. 'No. I'll make it clear that this is your first trip. But I suppose living at Second Chance Bay, you should know a bit about the Gulf.'

'Did I grow up there, or did I come there after we got married?'

The look on Don's face was comical and she chuckled. 'This was your idea, so you'll have to get used to it.'

'I know. We'd better get our stories straight.' He pulled up outside a high cyclone fence but kept the engine running as he opened the door. 'Tonight, when we're on the boat,' he said as he climbed out to unlock the gate.

They drove about a hundred metres along the river to a wharf. 'The *Adventurer* is on a floating pontoon at the end,' Don explained. 'To cater for the tidal flow and the wet.'

'This is where the guests get on?' Claire looked around. They'd come through the small township and had crossed through the port, and she hadn't seen any hotels. 'Where do they stay? You said it was an upmarket—'

'An upmarket charter,' Don finished for her. 'Yes, we are. The guests fly to Kununurra, and we coach them from there in an air-conditioned coach. Some come in from *El Questro* too. We've got tonight by ourselves, and then the rest of the crew will arrive in the helicopter tomorrow.'

'The helicopter?'

'Yes, that's a helipad you'll see on the top deck. We use the helicopter to go to the top of some of the waterfalls and for sightseeing. Then one day to get organised and the guests arrive in time for cocktails.'

'Who flies the helicopter?'

'Not me. I hate flying. We have our own pilot on board. Again, it's a new guy this charter. If you're lucky, he might give you a hand with the serving and clearing up. The last pilot was a great help. He hated sitting around doing nothing and pitched in to help wherever he could.'

A shaky feeling ran from Claire's stomach to her throat as nerves hit again. It was getting very real and very close.

'Um, you said cocktails? Will I be expected to make them?'

'You will. But don't worry, it's easy to learn. If you can follow a recipe, you can make a cocktail.'

'I hope so.'

Don's laughter was warm. 'Claire, stop worrying. You'll be fine. I wouldn't have asked you to do this if I'd thought you weren't up to it.'

'Can we have a practice?'

'We can. We'll work out a past for you tonight, and I'll teach you how to make cocktails. But don't worry. It's a set menu for dinner and cocktails on the first night. My special "Top Ender" cocktail, and then the guests usually move to wine.'

He parked the ute in a parking bay next to a small shed at the wharf. 'Here we are.'

Claire widened her eyes. She knew it was a luxury charter, but she hadn't expected a boat anywhere near the size of this one.

She stepped out of the ute and put her hand to her eyes. A sleek white hull, at least thirty metres long and with three decks reaching high, was moored at the wharf. The boat gleamed in the hot northern sun and oozed luxury … and money.

Don unlocked the door of the shed. 'I store the swags and camping gear in here, so leave your bags over there. I'll get this away and then we'll board.' He quickly unpacked the ute and then carried a small ladder over to the side of the boat.

'I was wondering how we get up there.' Claire pointed to the opening at the back of the deck.

'I'll climb onboard and then drop the gangway for you. It needs to stay down because the first food deliveries will be here late this afternoon.'

A few minutes later, he was up the ladder and unlatched a half-door that Claire hadn't noticed in the side of the deck. The steel gangway slid to the wharf with a clang, and Don came down. After he'd secured it, he picked up her suitcase.

'Ready to come aboard, Mrs McDougal?'

She nodded. 'The guests will call me Claire, I hope, because I'd never remember to answer to that.'

Once on board the boat, it was obvious that the vessel had been restored meticulously. Don had said on the trip across that he'd worked on it over a couple of years, and the boat was in top condition. The rails had been polished to a high gleam, and once they were inside the huge saloon on the middle deck where the gangway had been lowered from, it was obvious that he had fitted it out with quality inclusions.

'Welcome to my *Adventurer*. It'll be good to be back on board. I miss her when I'm over at the Bay.'

Claire took a breath and let it out slowly. 'Wow. This is just amazing.'

'Come with me, and I'll show you the cabins up near the wheelhouse. You can leave your stuff up there safely.'

Claire followed him up a set of polished timber stairs. 'Do you have a safe on board?'

He nodded. 'There's a safe in each cabin, and I've got one in my suite. Why do you ask?'

She patted her handbag with a wry grin. 'I've got a fair bit of cash in my bag, and it will be good to put it somewhere safe for the trip.'

'Sure.' He grinned. 'I've noticed you were very attached to it.'

She pulled a face. 'I don't have any of my credit cards with me. I was trying to stay incognito.'

At the top of the stairs, there were two doors and a narrow corridor leading to a huge, well-lit space. 'That's the wheelhouse, and the door on the left is my cabin, and the other is the spare, where the hostess usually stays.'

Claire wondered why the hostess had a cabin up here when the rest of the crew were elsewhere, but she pushed away the suspicion that jumped into her mind.

Don pushed open the door of the second cabin and put her suitcase inside. 'If you want to leave your bag in there while I show you around up here, it'll be safe.' She went to follow him in, but he put the case down and stepped back before she was expecting it. She was wedged in a narrow space between Don and the door.

'Sorry.' He was so close his breath was warm on her lips, and Claire fought the desire to reach out and hold his arms.

Get over it, she thought. *It's only because he's been kind.*

They did a sort of step left and step right, and then they were both back in the corridor, and there was space between them again.

He led her to the wheelhouse and pointed to the array of computerised nautical stuff on a wide bench that ran along a wide glass windscreen with a three-sixty view over the water. 'This is where I'll spend most of my time.'

Claire stepped into the large space. There was a door on each side that led out onto a narrow deck that appeared to run the length of the boat on each side. Don looked around as he crossed over to the bench and flicked some switches. 'We're still on land power, so I'll run the air to cool the boat down a bit.' He picked up a folder with a glossy blue cover and handed it to her. 'This might help you understand your role over the next ten days. There's a map of the boat and a guide to where everything is stored, too: linen and all that sort of stuff. It's Jenni's work. She said it would make it a lot easier for the staff when they were learning their way around the boat.'

'Thank you.' She took the folder from him. Already, she was feeling a distance between them. Rather than being her transport—and new friend— as he had been the past couple of days as they'd travelled forty-eight hours, Don was now the captain and, as such, her boss.

'So we've got some work to do today. But you've got two days to learn your way around and get the cabins ready for the guests.'

'Okay. I'll sit down and read it. It'll be good to get to work.'

'Great. I've got some calls to make, but first thing I think you should do is get to know the boat. While I make my calls, have a good look around. Explore the whole boat. In the cabins, the storage areas, and in the galley. Best way to get a feel for the *Adventurer*.'

He led her back downstairs and took her to the main saloon. 'Have a read of Jenni's guide, and when you're ready, have a wander around. I'll be on board most of the time if you've got any questions, but I've got to go up to the port office for a while now. Make yourself at home. There's plenty of water and cold drinks in the cool room, and there's a coffee machine over there.'

'Don?'

He paused and looked at her.

'I'm fine. You don't have to worry. You go and do whatever you have to, and I'll have a read of the manual and get my bearings.'

'Thanks, Claire. You're a champion. You still don't realise how much you've got me out of a fix.'

'Go. I'm sure you've got a lot to do!'

'Yes, ma'am.' He stopped in the doorway and his grin was cheeky. 'Keep that up, and no one will be in any doubt who the boss is.

Chapter 14

Sunset over the Cambridge Gulf—as Claire now knew it was called after reading the staff manual—was spectacular. The salt flats across the river glistened like diamonds and the hues of the sandstone cliffs behind them deepened to reds, oranges and golden brown. Not only did Claire now know the name of the gulf, but she also knew what every storage area on the boat held, where the washing machines and dryers were located on the back of the top deck near the entry down to the cramped cabins of the crew, and where the charter was going. She'd unpacked her suitcase in her cabin and hung up the shirts for her uniform.

She also knew the role of each crew member and the itinerary for the charter. She'd memorised a bit about each location so she could sound knowledgeable for the guests. If there was one thing she had, it was a good memory. As Don had said, the guests would board for cocktails the day after tomorrow, and then they would depart at approximately six-thirty. Dinner would be served shortly after leaving port, and then they would cruise overnight to the King George River.

That's when her work would begin. Until she got over the hurdle of meeting the guests, her nerves were on a fine edge. Keeping herself busy all afternoon had stopped her dwelling on the possibility of being recognised.

With a sigh, she watched as the sun slipped below the horizon in a stunning display of colours.

'I never get tired of the brilliant colours up here.'

Claire jumped when Don spoke. 'I thought you were still down on the wharf.' A delivery truck had been unloading up the gangway for the past hour, so she'd settled herself on the other side of the boat to stay out of the way.

'All done. Food's on board, and the alcohol. The cool room is chockers. Steve, the new chef, has done a great job with the menus and the orders. All I have to see now is that he can actually cook! Are you ready for a cocktail-making lesson?'

'I am.' She stood, and Don stepped back to let her go down the stairs in front of him.

'You've learned your way around,' he said as she led him to the bar at the back of the saloon on the upper deck.

'I have, and I know this is where the first-night cocktails are served before we head to King George River and wait for the tide to rise so we can cross the sand bar.'

'I'm impressed.' His eyes crinkled as he grinned at her, and those damn nerves in her stomach skittered all over again.

'And I also know that the cocktail we're about to make is called a "Top Ender".'

'Like I said, you're a quick learner.'

Claire smiled ruefully. 'You'd be surprised what I had to learn in my job, and how fast I had to absorb it.' She pointed to the bar stool. 'Sit down, Captain, and I'll make your welcome cocktail.'

Don shook his head with a big grin and sat on the chrome and black leather swivel stool.

***

Claire was smiling, and she looked more relaxed than he'd seen her, even though she was about to start charter work that was going to be arduous. Her blue eyes sparkled as she mixed the rum, pineapple juice, squeezed the limes and chopped the mint that he'd unpacked and stowed in the cool room on the bottom deck mid-afternoon. She'd been busy; he hadn't even seen her in the cool

281

room, but she must have scoped out the delivery when they'd finished.

With a flourish of her hand, she decorated the top of the cocktail with a sugared mint leaf on top of the shaved ice and handed it to him. 'Welcome aboard. I hope you enjoy your charter on the *Kimberley Adventurer*, sir.'

Don held her gaze as he lifted the glass to his lips and sipped. Without breaking eye contact, he leaned forward and slid another glass over. Claire's cheeks were flushed when he finally looked away to pour half of his cocktail into the second glass. He passed it to her and then lifted his glass to clink on the side of hers. 'Cheers, and welcome aboard to you, too.'

She lowered her eyes as she sipped, but the flush high on her cheeks stayed there. 'Thank you.'

Don slid off the stool and carried his drink across to the sofa under the window that looked out over the back deck. A jacuzzi spa was set at the far end. 'Come and sit where it's comfortable. It's probably the last chance we'll get to sit down for the next ten days.'

'The *Adventurer* is an absolute credit to you, Don,' Claire said softly as she sat beside him.

'Thank you. I'm pretty proud of her.' He sat back and closed his eyes. The long drive and the manual work this afternoon—not to mention the potent effect of a rum cocktail—had him fighting a yawn. He put his glass on the table in front of them. 'Now we have some work to do. But first, any questions or concerns you have about your role?'

Claire shook her head. 'I think I've got it all sorted.'

'I'll get one of the deckies to give you a hand with the cabins tomorrow.'

'I've already done them.'

'No, I mean with making up the beds and putting the towels and toiletries in there.'

'I've already done them. I found the list of names and which cabins they were allocated to, so I've already made them up. But I would like you to check that they're okay.'

Don stared at her. 'You're a wonder. But be careful.'

He regretted his teasing words as soon as her face fell.

'Be careful? Did I do something I shouldn't have?'

'No.' He reached out and took her hand in his. It was good to feel the soft warmth of her skin against his again. 'I meant if you work that fast, you'll have a job for life.'

He was rewarded with a wide smile, and her hand stayed where it was.

'All we have to do now is get our stories straight and invent a past,' she said.

He nodded. 'How about another cocktail and some nibbles to go with it?'

'Is that wise?'

He squeezed her fingers. 'A wine or a soft drink instead if you're worried about a headache.'

'Oh, what the heck,' she said. 'If we're going to be so busy, let's live dangerously.'

After the third cocktail, Don was feeling mellow—and hungry. They'd worked on a simple story. Claire was from Gilgandra in outback New South Wales—she knew the area where Aunt Bea had lived—and had met Don on a working holiday in the Gulf. They'd known each other for twelve months, had a whirlwind courtship, moved in together and married last winter. The hostessing story was what he'd suggested—she missed him too much, and they were going to live on the boat for the wet season.

A couple of hours later, Claire put her empty glass on the table and giggled. 'I'm starving, Captain. Is there anything to eat?'

'How about some fresh prawns? If we only have a few each, the chef won't notice that the order is a bit light on.' He winked at her.

Gawd, he'd winked at her like some sleaze.

'You're the boss, aren't you?' She winked back at him and then sat up straight.

And she winked back.

Damn the woman, Don knew when he was in trouble.

'Is there any fresh bread, or did you freeze it all?' Her words were clear, but the little hiccup that escaped from her lips made him smile.

'Come on.' He stood and put his hands out to Claire and pulled her up. She came up faster than he'd expected, and before he could step back, her soft curves pushed up against his chest as she looked up at him.

'Whoops, sorry. I forgot the rule.' Her breath warmed his lips.

'What rule?' he whispered.

'Um, wasn't there one about the captain and the crew?' Her lips seemed to be closer as he held her gaze. Her eyes were shining up at him, and a smile played about those pretty lips.

He sighed. 'I don't remember. Did I say there was?'

'I distinctly remember you saying there wasn't to be any freter … and frater … oh, you know what you meant.'

'Fraternisation?'

'Ye—' But the word was cut off as their lips met and clung. Don closed his eyes. He wasn't sure who'd closed the distance, but all he knew was that he was happy right where he was at that moment. The first time he'd kissed Claire, it had been driven by sympathy; this time, it had nothing to do with feeling sorry for her. It wasn't about anything apart from how much he wanted to hold her, to feel her lips against his.

He stopped thinking when Claire's lips opened slightly. She tasted of rum, and sunshine, and tropical islands. He could almost hear the music playing, and the palm trees rustling. Lowering one hand he slowly pulled her closer. She eased in against him, fitting as though she was made for him. A small sigh escaped her lips and he gently teased her lips with his tongue. Her arms wound around his neck and her soft curves pressed closer.

'Are you sure you want to eat?' he murmured against her lips.

'I … I'm—' She stiffened in his arms and pulled back a little. He opened his eyes as a voice called from the deck.

'Ahoy there. Is there anyone on board?'

Claire's eyes were wide as she stepped back, and her cheeks flushed. She put her hand to her lips and then smoothed her hair. Don tried to focus his thoughts as footsteps clattered up the gangway.

'Gidday.' A tall gangly guy with red hair stood in the doorway of the saloon. 'I saw the light on, so I thought I might be able to doss here tonight.' His accent was Scottish.

Don narrowed his eyes. 'How did you get through the gate?'

'I climbed over the fence. My gear's on the other side.' He walked in and held out his hand, shooting a curious look in Claire's direction, and Don bristled. 'I'm Steve Smyth. Your chef.'

'Ah.' Don blinked and held out his hand as realisation kicked in. 'Sorry, Steve, you threw me there for a minute. You can't be too careful. I'm Don McDougal, the skipper.' He glanced at Claire. 'And this is … my wife, Claire.'

'Sorry, I'm late. I got held up—not literally—I mean, I had bike troubles at Halls Creek, and I was late getting away this morning. I couldn't raise anyone at the caravan park up the road, so I was going to kip in a paddock, and then I thought I'd see if there was anyone on the boat. I thanked my lucky stars when I saw your ute there and the lights on.'

Don wondered what else he'd seen from the wharf, and then realised that he'd just introduced Claire as his wife, so it didn't matter. He shook Steve's hand and looked at Claire again. 'We were … ah … just about to cook some dinner.' He shot an apologetic glance at Claire. 'Sweetie'—the word felt strange as it came out— 'would you put the kettle on and maybe rustle us up some toast.'

The look directed his way was hard to read, but her words were even. 'Sure, darling. Nice to meet you, Steve.'

'You too, Claire. Is there anyone else on board yet?'

'No, the rest of the crew will be here tomorrow lunchtime. I'll unlock the gate for you. If you want, you can lock your bike in the shed, too.'

'Awesome.' Steve, the chef, beamed at both of them.

Claire headed towards the galley. Don frowned. Her voice was terse, and she didn't look back. 'I'm not hungry. I'll put the kettle on and slice some bread, and then I'll go to bed. It's been a long day. Good night.'

'Ah, okay. I'll get Steve settled in the crew's quarters, and then I'll be up once I secure the boat.'

She looked down as she walked past him, and Don stopped the groan that threatened to come from his mouth.

Something was wrong.

Chapter 15

Claire couldn't believe what had happened—or what had almost happened—in the saloon. Anger nudged rational thinking aside.

Pretend to be my wife? he'd said.

Pah! All along, Don had been playing Mr Nice Guy with the goal of getting her into bed. She'd been a fool to fall for it. Three drinks and all her self-protection had gone out the window.

So badly damaged by what had happened, Claire knew she'd given her trust too quickly, and way too easily. Not only had Don McDougal got a hostess on the cheap—and he was probably paying below award rates—he thought he'd got a bed partner for the duration of the trip. No matter what he'd said about doing the right thing.

Stupid, stupid, stupid. He'd been playing her the whole time, and she'd fallen for it. Show a bit of sympathy, share a gentle kiss, pull back and show more kindness. And then ply her with rum, and she'd been putty in his hands.

The worst part was, she'd wanted to go to his bed. Almost since the minute she'd met him. She'd never been attracted to a man like that before. Ever.

Fast and furious. A casual physical attraction. In different circumstances it might have been different. But as he'd said, he was her boss, and there'd be no relationship on board.

Not if she had anything to do with it.

As the effects of the three rum cocktails began to wear off, a headache began to niggle at her temples in a consistent rhythm. Apart from the nibbles that Don had dug out of the cool room, she hadn't eaten a proper meal all day, nor had she drunk enough water. She wrenched the tap on, filled the kettle sliced some thick, jagged edged pieces of bread, and put them on a plate next to the toaster. She opened the cool room and reached for one of the bottles of water she'd seen there earlier.

Don and Steve were down on the wharf, and she watched them for a moment before closing her eyes and rolling the cool bottle on her forehead. Claire knew she wanted more than Don was offering. His kiss had held a promise; he'd set her head spinning with that long, intimate touch of his lips on hers, and the way his hand had caressed her had left her with an unfulfilled ache. She sighed.

At the moment, she couldn't think clearly enough to know what she wanted.

But one thing was certain: she didn't need any more complications in her life. Ten days on the boat—it was too late to change her mind about masquerading as Don's wife. She'd already been introduced to the chef as the skipper's wife.

'Sweetie!' he'd said. *She'd give him sweetie.*

With her head thudding with pain and her mind spinning with thoughts of how much Don had disappointed her, she pushed open the door of her cabin, pleased that she'd made her bed up earlier. Slipping out of her dress, she kicked off the white-soled shoes she'd worn all day and lay back on the bed.

Claire dozed lightly for a short while until there was a soft tap on the door.

She rolled over and buried her face in the pillow. If she ignored him, he'd go away. She lay there holding her breath and sat up with a gasp as the door opened a little way, and a chink of light shone on her face.

'Claire?' Don's voice was soft.

'Go away. I'm asleep. Or I was.'

'I want to talk to you. I want to apologise.'

The last thing Claire wanted was a fake apology; he must think she was a soft touch. 'Okay, apology accepted.'

She blinked as the cabin light came on, and Don stepped into her cabin, shutting the door behind him.

'Do you mind? I am entitled to some privacy, and I believe this is my cabin?'

'I was worried you might be upset.'

'About what? Twigging to what you're really up to?

'What?'

'You know what I mean. I'm still here, aren't I?' She kept her eyes level with his. Pride helped her speak casually.

A muscle ticked in his jaw, and she knew he wasn't as calm as he was making out. 'I promised to help you out with your problem, and I'm a man of my word.'

She rolled over and turned her back to him. 'Please turn the light off on your way out before you shut the door.'

The door closed with a loud click, and she brushed away the first tear that rolled down her cheek.

***

Don was too angry to go to bed, and he headed into the wheelhouse. He and Steve had eaten a sandwich—prawns—and had a coffee, and Steve had apologised.

'I'm sorry, skipper. I'm knackered, I'm going to have to hit the sack.'

Don had shown him the cabin in the crew's quarters. And yes, as Claire had said, the beds were made up, and there were fresh towels in the bathrooms.

What the hell was Claire playing at? He'd had no intention of kissing her until she came onto him, and then he couldn't resist those soft lips. He'd made it quite clear where he'd stood all along, but she'd crumbled his defences.

And the rum hadn't helped.

Who knows where they'd be now if Steve hadn't arrived?

In bed in his cabin, he had no doubt of that.

Just as well that Steve had arrived when he had, and she'd chucked a hissy fit.

Let that be a lesson to you, he told himself.

Women and work do not mix.

##

Just as well, Steve was a chatterbox. The mood between Claire and Don was as distant when they both arrived in the galley at the same time the next morning. He stood back and gestured to the door. She stopped in the corridor.

'After you,' he said.

Claire put her head down and went straight to the cool room, and pulled out a bottle of water. Steve's cheery whistle preceded him along the corridor, and he walked into the galley with a smile as Don was filling the kettle.

'Leave that with me, skipper. I'll get some breakfast going for you. Nice set-up you've got here.'

Don nodded. 'Thanks. That'd be great. We've got a bit to do today.' He turned to Claire. 'Although you're pretty much on top of things, aren't you, love?'

'I am. But I'm sure I can find something to do.' She turned to Steve, and the smile she bestowed on him had Don narrowing his eyes as jealousy surged through him.

Bloody hell. He didn't need that.

'I can give you a hand down here, Steve. I've done all the cabins,' she said.

'Sweet, that'd be great. I want to rearrange the pantry and check off the order to make sure I've got everything I need before we leave port. I haven't been to Wyndham before, there's not a lot here. Any shops?'

Don nodded. 'There's a grocery store back in the first bit of town. Before you get to the port. Claire, if Steve needs anything, take the ute out of the shed. The keys are on the shelf in *our* cabin.'

'I will.' Her cheeks flushed, and he felt mean.

'What would you like for breakfast, you pair?' Steve poked his head into the cool room. 'How about an omelette?'

'I'm fine, thanks. I'll just grab a piece of toast later and a coffee from the machine in the bar,' Claire said. 'I'll be back down to help you in half an hour.'

She put her head down as she walked past Don, but she didn't meet his eye. He was still feeling cross with her and wanted to sort it out before the crew and passengers arrived, and they embarked on the charter.

'Thanks, Steve. I'll come back down in half an hour, too. An omelette sounds good.' He turned to the door and hurried after Claire.

'Wait up, Claire. I'll come up with you,' he called after her as she headed for the staircase leading up to the top deck. Her back was rigid as he followed her up the stairs, and she pushed open the door to her cabin. 'You'd better get used to going into *our* cabin before the crew are wandering around, if you want to stay as Claire McDougal.' His voice was harder than he'd intended, but he was still smarting from the smile that Claire had given Steve. 'And maybe less flirting with the chef would make being my wife more believable.'

She swung around and stared at him, two spots of colour on her cheek. 'What did you say?'

'You heard me.'

Claire folded her arms and stared at him. 'What is your problem?'

Don ran his hand through his hair. 'No, Claire. You're the one with the problem. All of a sudden, I'm the big baddie. Okay, so we had a few drinks, and I let my guard down, but remember it was a two-way street. You kissed me too.'

She put her head down, and he could see her lip quivering, but he didn't soften. 'However you feel about me—and you're sending mixed messages—we need to sort this out before everyone else arrives. Two things: no one's going to believe our story, and second, I don't want disharmony on the boat. You can feel what you feel, but keep it hidden. If you can't, you can get off now, and somehow I'll manage.'

Her head lifted, and he almost broke when he saw her eyes awash with tears.

***

'I'm sorry.' Claire kept her voice steady, even though she felt awful. 'I was in the wrong, and the way I spoke to you was unacceptable. I'll be polite from now on.'

Don shook his head and reached out, putting his hand on her shoulder as she stared at him. 'I don't want polite, Claire. And if you treat me distantly, it'll be as obvious as—'

'I said I was sorry. What I said was awful.' She shifted her gaze from his. 'It's no excuse, but at the moment, I've forgotten how to trust anyone. I thought about everything you said, and I know I thought the wrong thing.'

'And what was that?' His piercing gaze pinned her.

'I guess I thought that all you wanted was a bed partner for the trip. I guess I wondered why the hostess cabin was up here.'

He laughed, but it held no mirth. 'That's the way the cabins were when I bought the boat. Would you really like to be down in the crew's quarters sharing the bathroom with five blokes?'

'No.'

'And Claire, this isn't over between us by a long shot. But if you think I was only after sex, maybe you don't know me well enough. But I think we should call a truce and talk about this after the trip. What do you think?'

When he smiled at her, Claire managed to smile back. 'Okay,' she said softly. 'And please say you accept my apology?'

She was supposed to be an intelligent woman, but she'd let her emotions get the better of her, acting more like an insecure teenager.

'Of course, I do. I know what you've been going through, and I'm sure you're nervous about everyone coming on board.'

'I am. Almost sick to the stomach.' She took a deep breath. 'But with your support, I'll get through it.'

She looked at the hand he held out to her and was sorely tempted to take it. To go back to where they'd been last night, but she shook her head. 'I've got one small job to do'—she ran her hand along the top of her hair—' and then I'll be down.'

His brow wrinkled in a frown, and she pointed to her head again.

'My hair. I don't want a hint of dark roots growing through in the next ten days. Just in case anyone is suspicious.'

Don chuckled. 'Fair enough. How long will that take? I'll save you some omelette. You need to eat, no matter how nervous you are.'

'Thanks. I'll be down in half an hour.' Claire reached out and touched his cheek. Don hadn't shaved, and the stubble on his skin sent a small quiver shooting down her tummy. 'I'll see you down there.'

Chapter 16

The mood on the *Adventurer* the next night was jovial … for most of the crew.

So far, so good.

Sean, Haydn, and Travis, the three deckhands, were all in their early twenties and hadn't batted an eyelid or shown any interest when Don had introduced Claire as his wife and the charter hostess.

Derek, the helicopter pilot, a man in his mid-forties, with tanned and weathered skin, had looked at her curiously, and Claire's breath had caught. Eventually he'd looked away and made a comment to Don about it being a better boat than any he'd been on. They'd arrived in the helicopter, and it was now secured on the helipad. Uniforms had been issued, but the crew were in civvies tonight.

Don called a meeting for the whole crew before dinner once they'd settled in and checked out the boat. Claire sat on the sofa at the back of the timber-lined saloon where she and Don had drunk rum cocktails last night.

Was it only last night? It seemed longer.

'Welcome aboard, everyone. It's good to have you here. Beers are on me tonight, but as soon as the guests are on board, we have a no-drinking rule until the end of the charter. I hope the agency told you about that. I run a tight ship, and I'd appreciate you letting me know of any problems as soon as they happen.'

They all nodded, but Derek didn't look too impressed. Claire thought she was the only one who caught Derek's eye roll when Don turned back to the small bar fridge.

'Any questions, please hit me with them now. We're going to be busy starting tomorrow afternoon,' Don said.

Sean looked around and then put his hand up.

Don smiled. 'No need for a hand, mate. What do you want to know?'

Claire had already noticed that Sean was the quiet and serious one of the three "deckies" as they called themselves. It was a whole new world for her.

'What route are we taking, skipper?'

'King George River, the Drysdale, a heli-picnic at Toe River will keep you busy on the third day, Derek, and then the three of you will be full on with the fishing at the back end of the charter. We'll go across to Mitchell River and Surveyor's Creek.'

Steve grinned. 'One day I'll be rich enough to go on one of these trips as a guest.' He laughed and nudged Derek. 'Only problem is the meals wouldn't be as good as what I'd do.'

Derek looked back at him with his lip curled and Claire decided she didn't like him in that moment.

'Got tickets on yourself, mate?' he said.

'Nah, I'm just the best chef around up here these days. You can tell me what you think at the end of the trip.'

A good comeback, Claire thought. She caught Don's eye, and he held her gaze. They shared a moment of understanding. He'd picked Derek as a problem too. She hadn't realised how hard it would be getting an agency to organise staff that you were in close quarters with for the length of a charter.

'Good to hear, Steve. So far what you've produced has been great.' Don handed over the cans of beer he'd pulled out of the fridge.

When he went to hand one to Derek, the older man said curtly, 'I'd rather have spirits.'

Don raised his eyebrows as Derek crossed to the bar and took down a bottle of top-shelf whiskey.

'Okay, seeing it's the first night, spirits are fine.' He and Claire exchanged another look.

The conversation was social as they sat around the saloon. Steve finished his beer and went to cook, and Derek left with a sullen look when Don screwed the cap on the bottle and put the whiskey back on the top shelf.

The three young deckies laughed and joked as the aroma of pizza wafted through the saloon. Rather than messing up the dining room, they all moved out to the deck to eat when Steve called out that the pizzas were ready.

Derek came back up and looked curiously at Claire as he reached for a slice of pizza. 'You ever worked in Darwin?'

She shook her head as her stomach tightened. 'No, why?'

'Thought I knew you from one of the other boats or somewhere.' He narrowed his eyes, and Claire forced a cheerful note into her voice.

'Not me. I've never been to Darwin. What about you, have you been to Karumba? Maybe you've seen me there in the fish co-op. I help the family out when we're home.' She crossed her fingers behind her back. The first of the lies didn't come easily.

'Nah, never been there. You must look like someone I know.' He wiped his mouth with the back of his hand.

A real charmer.

'They say we all have a *doppelganger,* don't they?'

Don met her gaze and smiled. They'd had this conversation before he'd known who she was.

'A doppel what?' Derek said gruffly.

'A *doppelganger* is the German for "double walker",' Sean said. 'It means a person who looks incredibly similar to you.'

'Yeah, I knew that,' Derek said.

As they cleaned up after dinner, he disappeared leaving his plate out on the deck. Claire didn't hold any hope for Derek helping her with the meals when there were eighteen guests to look after.

***

Don followed Claire up the stairs after she'd cleaned the saloon and helped Steve in the galley. Even though she and Don had made their peace, she still felt uncomfortable around him, mainly because of the attraction she felt. Seeing him work today, and how good he was with the crew, and how deftly he'd handled Derek, just added to it.

Tonight, she'd moved her things into the master cabin in case anyone was poking around. She didn't trust Derek; a few times, Claire had caught him looking at her, and she didn't like the thoughtful expression on his face.

'Got a minute, Claire?' Don's voice was polite, as it always was now. She was pleased that he'd talked to the crew in his introduction about professional behaviour at all times because it let them keep a distance between each other that was professional, rather than the affectionate touching of a couple.

'Yes, sure.' She hid the nervous tone in her voice as she wondered whether he was coming to bed now.

He closed the door behind them and crossed to the large window that looked over the water to the mountains. It was late, and a few scattered lights of distant houses blinked in the darkness. Claire sat on the small chair that was in the corner of the cabin.

'What do you think of Derek?' he asked.

'He could be difficult, I guess.' Claire put her elbow on her knee and propped her chin in her hand. 'I guess it depends on what he's like with the guests. He's a bit gruff.'

Don sighed and leaned against the wall. He looked tired, and a wave of feeling rushed through Claire. 'He came highly recommended, but I think I might have been dudded with a less than honest reference. It happens up here. The less than scrupulous operators often pass on staff who don't work out like that. But a good pilot is scarce up here. They get snapped up.'

'It's too late to replace him now, isn't it?'

Don's hair stood up in untidy spikes when he rubbed at it. 'Yes, it is. I'll just have to keep a close eye on him. And I'm sorry, I don't think he's the kind to help you out when it gets busy.'

'I've already picked that. But don't worry. Steve's great, and it'll work out.' Claire pointed to the bed. 'You look really tired. Why don't you get some sleep? I'll take the small bed.'

'Thanks. This will be the last night that I'm in here. I'll be in the wheelhouse and on watch once we're underway.'

'All night?'

'Four hours on, and four hours off, but until I know that the deckies can do a proper watch, I'll stay in there with them.' He crossed the room and sat on the side of the bed and toed his shoes off. 'How are you feeling about tomorrow? Nervous?'

'Surprisingly, no.' And she was telling the truth. She was more nervous being around Don than with the thought of the guests arriving. 'The thing with Derek, it lets me practise what I'd say if it comes up. They all seem to have accepted we're married without a problem.'

'They've got no reason to question it.' Don yawned and lay back on the pillow. Within minutes, he was asleep. Claire had intended reading the book she'd taken from the guest bookshelf, but now that Don was out like a light, she let her gaze linger on his face.

Chapter 17

As the afternoon grew later, Claire's nerves were in a jumble. Steve's normal happy-go-lucky mood had snapped when she'd dropped the third cup on the galley floor, and it had broken.

'Shit, Claire, go and polish the windows or summat.' His Scottish accent broadened when he was upset. Everyone was on edge as they waited for the coach with the guests to arrive. Don had taken her through the guest list last night when he'd woken up, and there were only a couple from Sydney that she thought might know the program. But it was all an unknown. In the end, she calmed down, telling herself that worrying wouldn't change anything.

She hovered around the bar, polishing glasses—albeit carefully—and checked the bar fridge for the hors d'oeuvres that she'd brought out from the cool room. Steve said he'd have the hot food ready at five o'clock when the guests boarded. She had half an hour to change into her uniform, tidy her hair and put some lipstick—and her clear glass spectacles—on.

Don was in the wheelhouse, and she poked her head around the door. 'I'm just going into the cabin to get changed. Is there anything you need?'

Her eyes widened as he turned. He had changed into navy shorts and a white collared polo shirt, and a captain's hat sat on his head. His face was clean-shaven, and his hair was damp from the shower. Claire's heart set up a patter.

'No, all good here. The coach driver just radioed in, they're ahead of schedule. When you get changed can you please tell Steve they're about ten minutes away. I've let the crew know.'

'Ooh, I'd better get my skates on.'

'Are you okay, Claire?' Don's voice was low as he pointed to the window.

Claire stood on her tiptoes and pulled a face. Derek was sitting at the front of the boat under the windscreen. She leaned close to Don's ear, and a waft of woody aftershave tickled her nose. 'Eavesdropping?'

He nodded.

'Okay, sweetheart,' she said loudly. 'We're all good to go in the bar. The cold food's in the fridge, and the cocktail prep is done. Let's toast a successful trip when you come down to meet them.'

'Thanks. I'll meet you down there.'

Claire ran lightly down the stairs before she got changed. 'They're early, Steve. Ten minutes.'

'Rightio. I'll be ready. Thanks, luv.'

As she turned to go back upstairs, she came face to face with Derek. His face was sullen, and she stared at him. 'Is anything wrong?'

'Nothing that will concern you.' His mouth was set in a straight line.

She frowned. 'If there is a problem, you'd better tell the … you'd better tell my husband.' The words gave her a funny feeling as they came from her lips.

'Not worth it. He's already had his say.'

Claire looked after him as he slouched away and then hurried upstairs to get changed.

***

Don looked with pride at his crew standing in a row along the wharf at the base of the gangplank. Even though they were a new crew, they'd all co-operated. Hair was slicked back, and each one was in uniform and wearing the *Kimberley Adventurer* cap—even Claire.

Derek had even done the right thing and was standing at the far end of the row, not looking as morose as usual. Don let his gaze linger on Claire as he waited for the passengers to disembark the coach. He could tell by the set of her shoulders and her hands clenched by her sides that she was really nervous. But as soon as the coach doors opened and the passengers began to walk across the wharf, a wide smile settled on her face.

Don stepped to the head of the queue and beckoned Claire to come up and stand beside him. The coach driver and his helper directed the passengers over to the gangway before they unloaded the luggage. This was the slowest part of the whole routine. As usual, the passengers were excited and wanted to chat and exclaim about the boat—that always filled him with pride—but Don briefly introduced himself to each of the eighteen passengers before he turned to Claire, saying, 'And this is my wife, Claire. She'll be your hostess for the next ten days.' He held her elbow gently as she stood beside him, and for a moment, he could almost pretend what he was saying was true.

Finally, the last of the passengers were onboard, and Claire ushered them to the bar on the middle deck as Sean and Travis carried the luggage to the cabins. By the time Don reached the bar behind the stragglers, Claire had already made a tray of cocktails.

So far, no one had appeared to pay undue attention to her, but she kept her eyes down as she mixed the cocktails. The passengers were pretty much as he'd anticipated from the manifest. Five middle-aged couples were travelling together from the UK, two elderly couples were from rural Queensland, and the four he had worried about the most were executives from Sydney travelling together with the primary goal of catching fish. They were the most likely to recognise Claire if anyone was going to.

'Welcome aboard. I'll be back to chat in a while,' he said to each couple as he moved through the group as they settled in the bar and out on the back deck, but he had the four guys outside in his sights. Joining the group who already had their cocktails in hand, he took off his hat. 'Welcome aboard, guys. You're after fish, I'm told?' Placing his hat on the table at the back of the deck, he held out his hand to each man in turn. I'm Don McDougal, the *Kimberley Adventurer*'s mine, and I'm your captain for the charter.'

'Don.' One of the men stepped forward. 'You might not remember me. Jim Smith. I was on your charter out of Karumba six months ago. I had such a great trip, when I saw you had a Kimberley charter, I told the guys we had to come.'

Don looked at him closely. 'Hey, Jim! I do remember you. You caught that huge barra the day before we came in. Welcome back.'

'One point three metres.' He almost glowed with pride, and his chest puffed out as he held up his hand for a high five. 'You're a secretive bugger. You never mentioned you'd just got married when we were on the trip. Must have been about the same time. When was the wedding?'

Don swallowed. 'Well. You know how it is. I was busy on the boats.'

Jim turned back to the bar. 'You've done well for yourself, mate. Congratulations. Did Claire come to the wharf when we came in on that trip? She looks familiar.'

Don cleared his throat. 'Ah, probably. Anyway, let's hope for some great fishing over the next week. I'll introduce you to Derek, He's going to be taking you guys to some fantastic fishing spots in the helicopter.'

The men all clinked their glasses. 'That's what we're here for.'

Chapter 18

Claire relaxed more as each day passed. The passengers were not a bit interested in her, apart from the meals she delivered and the clean laundry she delivered to their rooms each day. To be fair, they were a great mix of people, totally focused on relaxation and sightseeing—and, in the case of the four men travelling together, catching the biggest, most elusive fish. All the guests were polite and friendly and not overly curious. She settled into a routine, surprised by how much she was enjoying the charter now that the risk of anyone recognising her was no longer at the forefront of her mind.

Each day, when they went off on an excursion, in the tender or by helicopter to a waterfall or a secret fishing location, they came back happy and hungry.

The job was full on. Claire changed sheets, washed towels, did the guest laundry and cleaned windows and then, three times a day would serve meals to eighteen guests and then cleared the tables when they were done.

Don took over the bar duties at dinner each night, and she was grateful for that.

'But you still have to tally up that bar bill at the end,' he said with a wink one night. 'That's in your role statement.'

'Thanks, boss,' she said with a smart grin as she wiped down the bar after another busy night. The last guest had gone to bed, and Don and Claire were alone in the bar; it was the first time she'd been alone with him since the charter had started.

Or, as far as she knew, she had. Now, she looked at him curiously. 'Have you had any sleep at all since we left?'

'I have, but I haven't slept as soundly as you. I was cuddled up close to you last night, and you didn't even stir.'

Her head flew up, and she gripped the wet sponge. 'You what? What do you mean cuddled up?'

'Sssh. Someone might hear you.'

When she saw the teasing glint in Don's eyes, Claire let fly with the sponge, and it hit him square in the chest. Liquid trickled down the front of his shirt, and she giggled when he shivered. But he moved quickly, grabbed her hand, and held the sponge over her head with the other one before she could move.

'Will I squeeze the water out or not?' he wondered aloud.

'Don't even think about it. It's stale beer, not water.'

Don pulled her close, and she was hard up against him. Sheer pleasure ran through Claire. For the first time in weeks, laughter—created by pure happiness—bubbled up from her chest.

'You are going to so pay for that, girl.' His voice was quiet but teasing. Claire stared up at him, and there was a moment when it was just them, lost in each other's eyes. His head came closer and she put her hand on his chest—his damp chest. A smile played about her lips, as his mouth came closer to hers.

'Come on, you two. Haven't yous got a perfectly good cabin on the top deck?' Steve yawned and scratched his head. 'I came up to check I turned the gas off.'

Claire jumped back, heat suffusing her face and neck, but Don kept his arm loosely around her shoulders. 'Claire has, but I've got to relieve Haydn on watch'—he lifted his arm and put his face near his watch exaggerating the movement so his cheek was pressed against hers— 'in three minutes.'

Claire stepped back as he lifted his arm, and she slipped beneath it. 'Well, I still have a load of washing to do and wait to put it in the dryer.' She wrinkled her nose. 'Fishing clothes.'

'Come up to the wheelhouse and talk to me while you wait.' Don ruffled her hair as he headed for the steps. 'I could do with some company.'

The contentment in his voice stayed with Claire as she wiped down the rest of the bar.

Steve walked past her with another yawn. 'See you in the morning, love. I don't know how you do it.'

'Do what?' Claire asked with a frown.

'Look so fresh after a huge day of nonstop work, and you're still going. It must be *lurve*.'

'Go to bed. You're talking rot.' But the smile stayed on her face after Steve headed down to the crew's quarters.

***

Don watched as Claire went back and forward along the deck at the side of the wheelhouse, down to the washing machines and back again.

Despite their worries, the charter had gone well. The crew were competent and cheerful, and even Derek had come around a bit, although Don didn't think he would hire him again. There was just something about him that didn't meld with the rest of the crew. They were halfway through the charter and tomorrow they would be cruising along the Hunter River, and Derek would take the passengers up to see the Jackson Falls from the air.

Not one person had commented on Claire's likeness to the missing television presenter from Sydney, and he'd seen her relax more as each day had passed.

'Do you want a coffee?' Her face appeared around the door.

'Are you going to have one?' he asked.

'No. I'm going to go to bed.'

'I'm fine. I've got some Coke up here.'

Claire stood in the doorway. 'Okay. I'll get those clothes out early. Are you going to get some sleep tonight?'

'Are you getting lonely in there?' He couldn't help teasing her and smiled when she pulled a face at him.

'Behave, Captain.' She stood in the doorway, looking out over the water as the boat cruised silently along the deep waterway.

Don turned the autopilot on before leaving the helm, and walked over to stand beside Claire.

'It's beautiful out here,' she said almost reverently. 'I had no idea how wonderful it is.'

'It certainly gets in your blood.' They stood there silently for a few moments looking up at the diamond bright sky.

'It's like black velvet. As though you could reach out and touch it,' she said.

'You've done really well, Claire.'

'I'm really enjoying myself.'

He hesitated. 'It might sound crazy, but there's a job here for you if you want it next season.'

'Thank you. That's the nicest thing you could have said to me.'

'So?'

She shook her head. 'So, I'll go back to Sydney and sort out my life, and then I'll decide what I'm going to do. I'll probably go back to practising law.'

'I'll miss you.' It felt natural to put his arm around her, and Don was pleased when Claire rested her head against his shoulder.

'You could always come down and visit,' she said quietly.

'Is that a real invitation?'

She nodded, and Don smiled. When she looked up at him, her eyes shone in the moonlight; it was hard to see her expression, but still, a shaft of need lodged in his soul.

'I'm really going to miss you,' he said.

Claire lifted one hand and cupped his cheek, and Don rested his forehead against hers.

'I'll miss … all this, too.'

He pulled back. Disappointment and an emptiness left a hollow ache in his gut. Turning to the helm, he spoke quietly. 'Go to bed, Claire. It's going to be a big day tomorrow.'

But neither of them knew what the day was going to bring.

Chapter 19

The need to tell Don that she didn't want to leave had been hard to ignore. When he'd asked her to stay, Claire had been so tempted, but it wasn't the right thing for her. What the right path for her in life would be, she had yet to discover. This respite—once the fear of being discovered by the media had disappeared when the charter had begun—was simply that. A respite—time to give some thought to her future.

She had to go back and resume her *real* life; this was an interlude, a time to regroup and get her head together. Claire had given a lot of thought to her priorities, and working on television was at the very bottom.

And besides, no matter how kind Don was, it was friendship, that was all. The thought of living up here and having a relationship with Don was a dream; he had offered her a job because she had suited his needs on the boat. No more than that, no matter how pleasant it was. She couldn't—wouldn't— give up her life in the city to move permanently to Second Chance Bay.

She rose early, stepped into the bathroom to take a quick shower, and put on her fresh uniform. Allowing herself a quick glance into the small alcove beneath the window at the back of the cabin, she could see that Don was asleep, his hands flung high on the pillow. She looked away quickly and ignored the ache in her heart.

She set the breakfast table in the small dining room at the back of the galley where the crew had their meals.

'Morning, Derek,' she said brightly. Even though his demeanour had improved, she still didn't like him as much as the other crew. Steve was a perfectionist, could be terse when he was under pressure at mealtimes, trying to get eighteen entrees and then eighteen mains out for the guests, but she liked him. The three deckhands were happy-go-lucky, but hardworking.

Derek grunted and continued reading without looking at her. As she pulled milk and fruit from the cool room, Steve wandered in, rubbing his eyes. 'Pancakes for you lot this morning; you're going to need the energy, apparently.'

Sean and Travis wandered in, dressed in their uniforms, ready to start the day; *Haydn must be on watch*, Claire thought, as she put the fruit juice and glasses on the table.

'Thanks, Claire,' Travis said.

Sean looked past her. 'We've already lowered the tender, skipper. I know you want to get an early start.'

Don walked in, his hair damp and a smile on his face. 'Morning all, and thanks Sean. Yep, this is our biggest day. All eighteen have chosen an activity today. Claire, I'll get you to go in the tender; there's a swimming hole under the waterfall, and four of the guests have opted for that activity.

'Um, crocodiles?' she asked.

Don laughed and shook his head. 'Nope. No crocs there.'

'How many coming with me, Don?' Claire had noticed that Derek never referred to Don as skipper or captain. Derek put the magazine down as Don glanced at the manifest.

'You've got ten today, so a few trips up before lunch would be great.'

'I'll take the tender to the swimming hole, and then when we get back, Trav will take the guys mud-crabbing.' Sean reached over for the magazine that Derek had put down.

Steve brought out a plate loaded with pancakes, but Claire shook her head and reached for the fruit. As she looked up Sean was looking at her curiously. He looked back down at the magazine and then up at her face again.

Claire froze; she looked at the front of the magazine, but slowly let her breath out when she saw it was an old one.

Sean put it flat on the table. 'Has anyone ever told you, you're a dead ringer for that reporter woman.'

Don stiffened across the table from her, but he casually reached across for the magazine. 'Yeah,' he said with an easy smile. 'I told Claire that the first time we saw her on TV on our honeymoon in Sydney. They could be related.'

'Are you, Claire?' Sean persisted.

She shook her head. 'No'—her voice croaked, and she cleared her throat— 'No relation.'

Derek reached across for the magazine. 'That's an old article. She's the one who's gone missing now. 'He narrowed his eyes. 'The network was offering a financial reward for anyone who spotted her.'

Claire laughed and hoped it didn't sound as artificial as it felt. 'They found her. Don and I saw a picture of her on a beach in France on our way over.' She smiled at Don, but it was a brittle smile. 'Half her luck. This husband of mine took me to Sydney for our honeymoon. I can only dream of the south of France.'

The conversation turned to the best holiday destination, but Claire still felt uncomfortable. Derek was quiet, and he'd pulled his phone out and was looking at it intently.

Don must have noticed too. He stood as soon as he'd eaten. 'Right, you lot. Time to get to work. Everyone knows the drill for today?'

'Claire?' Steve called out from the galley, and she stood and walked in. Tension filled her.

'Yes?' She poked her head around the door.

'There's a basket of cold drinks and morning tea packed. I'll get the boys to put it in the tender for you.'

The morning out in the tender was pleasant; the waterhole was crystal clear and cool, and Claire went in for a swim in the pool beneath the waterfall with the English couples.

'Bloody top stuff,' Reg, one of the husbands, said as he surfaced after diving in. 'It's going to be hard to go home to snow.'

Claire sat back on a flat rock shaded by the cliff, giving the guests time to have a long swim before she opened the morning tea basket. Sean had dropped them off and gone back to take the four fishermen to the crabbing creek. There was a two-way radio in the basket if they needed to contact the mothership.

She looked up as Derek flew over in the helicopter. They were so low she could see the delighted expressions on the faces of the guests as they flew over. Twenty minutes later, they flew back the other way.

'Morning tea's on, folks.'

She poured out the tropical juice that Steve had packed and unwrapped the tea towel that held fresh-baked muffins. As she put the plate in the middle of the rock, the loud thudding of a helicopter filled the air. She looked up as a helicopter swooped low over the waterfall; it wasn't the one from the *Adventurer*.

'Busy around here this morning,' Reg commented as he reached for a muffin.

Claire nodded but was distracted when the radio crackled soon after. The helicopter from the boat passed over again, heading west, and she had to walk away to hear what was being said. So much for a quiet morning on the water. There was a huge boab tree about fifty metres away, and she wandered along the edge of the waterhole towards it until the noise of the helicopter had receded.

'Claire, here. Over.'

'Claire, it's Don.'

'What's up?'

His voice was low and urgent. 'There's a bit of a situation here. Sean's coming back to collect the group, but I want you to stay there. Get yourself out of sight as soon as you can. Over.'

Claire's blood ran cold. 'What is it? Over.'

'We're about to get visitors. A television network helicopter from Darwin just radioed the boat. I guess it's about you. Shit, I'm sorry, Claire, but I'll deal with it. Just stay out of sight, okay? Over.'

'I will. Over.' Her voice was resigned, and, strangely, she accepted the situation. It had only been a matter of time until it came to this.

'Wait there. I'll come and get you when it's safe. Over and out.'

She dropped the two-way to her side and walked back to the group. 'Sean's on his way back,' she said brightly, trying to think of a reason why she wouldn't be going in the tender. 'Um, there's another group coming, so I'll stay here and wait for them.'

Sean looked at her curiously when the passengers clambered into the tender, and she stepped back. 'You coming, Claire?'

'No. Don's coming out with another group. I'll wait here.'

'Unusual for the skipper to leave the boat.' He gunned the small motor and the front of the tender lifted as they headed down the river. After a few minutes, they rounded a bend and were out of sight.

He was right. Don must be worried if he was leaving the *Adventurer*. Her heart thudding and her knees trembling, Claire stepped back and looked around. The high cliffs rose majestically above her, and the small waterfall trickled down the rock face to her left. A narrow track led to the top of the cliff, and she headed for it, determined to get out of sight. From up there, she would be able to see what was happening on the *Adventurer*. If the helicopter went over again, there were plenty of stands of trees for her to hide in. But she was worried that they'd already probably spotted her as they'd headed towards the boat.

By the time she reached the top, the sound of a helicopter approaching had her looking for cover. She peered through the foliage and let out a sigh of relief; it was Derek and the helicopter from the boat, but still, she stayed out of sight until they had passed over.

Claire reached the top of the cliff and looked out to the north, shading her eyes with her hand; the river wound lazily into the distance, but it was very different to the sheltered waterhole below. The *Adventurer* was moored in the middle of the wide channel, and another helicopter hovered above the boat. Even from this distance, she could see the spray misting from the churned-up water. She turned back to the river that eventually fell over the cliff and down to the waterhole below. Small rapids tumbled along the rocks upstream.

She drew a sharp breath and froze as something moved in her peripheral vision. Turning her head slowly, her heart pounded, almost in time with the fast-approaching helicopter.

Three large crocodiles were sunning themselves on a flat rock, almost at the top of the waterfall and only thirty metres away from where she was standing. As she watched, one slid lazily into the water, and she backed away silently to the track. Suddenly, the thud of the helicopter surrounded her, and she looked up as a man leaned out and pointed at her. The chopper turned and headed for the flat ground next to the waterhole below. Claire had no choice but to go back to the track; the crocodiles were between her and escape.

She bit her lip and prepared for the confrontation that had haunted her for the past month.

Chapter 20

Don quietly briefed Sean when he came back with the guests. Sean's eyes widened as Don headed for the tender.

'You're in charge until I get back,' Don called out. 'Let Steve and the other guys know what's going on, but, mate, if that grey chopper comes back before Derek does, stand on the helipad with one of the others and don't let it land again, okay?'

'Yes, skipper.'

Don jumped in the tender and headed upriver. One hand gripped the side of the tender as he pulled the starter cord. His knuckles were white, and he rolled his shoulders, trying to ease the tension.

The situation with the reporters on the media helicopter had been ugly. They'd landed on the boat's helipad without permission, and he'd confronted them.

'What the hell do you think you're doing?' he'd yelled over the noise of the rotors. Finally, they'd stopped and two men in suits had climbed out.

Don had stood with his arms folded and his jaw set. 'I have our chopper about to come in and land, so unless there's an emergency, you need to leave now.'

His worst fear was confirmed when the taller of the two sauntered over to the deck.

'We're here to interview one of your guests,' he said.

Don played dumb. 'Yes, who? Is there a problem?'

'Sybil Harris.'

Don frowned and shook his head. 'No one of that name on board. You've got the wrong boat, mate.'

The reporter shook his head. 'Nope, this is the one. Maybe you know her as Claire Templeton.'

Don called his bluff and shook his head. 'Nope. Please move that chopper off my boat, I've got one coming in now.' Right on cue, Derek's bird appeared over the cliff face two hundred metres away.

Don had no doubt that it was Derek who'd alerted the media, and they'd turned up bloody quick. At least they couldn't talk to him; while they were on the helipad, he couldn't land.

'We'll be back.' Frustration laced the guy's voice. It looked like he'd thought he had a scoop, or whatever they called it.

They'd climbed back in and taken off immediately and headed upriver. Derek landed the helicopter carrying the guests as soon as they were clear. He avoided Don's eyes, as the next guests had climbed into the chopper.

Derek would keep until Claire was safely back on board.

The tender was at top speed as he whizzed up the Roe River towards the swimming waterhole. As he rounded the last bend, the grey chopper took off from the clearing.

Shit.

Scanning his surroundings, Don eased back the motor, but there was no sign of Claire. He pushed the boat into the small bay and jumped out, quickly securing the anchor to a rock.

'Claire!' Don cupped his hands around his mouth and yelled. The noise of the chopper was fading in the distance, but there was no answer. There was a small opening behind the waterfall. If Claire was hiding in there, she wouldn't be able to see or hear him. Forcing himself to be calm, he clambered over the large rocks and then climbed the five metres up the cliff face.

Even though the waterfall was running at a trickle, the water was cold. Don stepped through the misty curtain.

'Claire!' He looked around the small space as his eyes became accustomed to the darkness, but it was empty.

He ducked through the water again and back outside and called again, but all was quiet.

Surely those bastards wouldn't have forced her into the helicopter?

Surely, she wouldn't have gone with them willingly.

Don stood and stared around him. The landscape was quiet and still.

Claire was gone.

Despair rocked him to the core as he realised how much he cared for her.

In the two weeks since she'd wandered into the courtyard of the store, he'd felt sorry for her, and he'd been sympathetic to her plight. He'd given her a job, and over that time, he'd learned who the real Claire was.

Now he knew what Jenni had meant when she'd told him when he met the right person, he would fall hard and fast.

And he had.

He loved her.

Don pushed himself to his feet, scanning the flat landscape around him before he got back into the small boat. Just as he was about to start the motor, he narrowed his eyes; there was a track heading up to the top of the cliff. He hadn't noticed it on previous visits. The gravel crunched beneath his feet as he jumped out of the small boat.

Small rocks tumbled from above as he ran towards the cleared scrub.

'I thought you said there weren't any crocodiles here.'

Relief flooded through him. He stopped and waited as Claire jumped down off the end of the track. 'There's not,' he said. 'They don't body surf down waterfalls.'

'Well, they're up there,' she said. 'And I hope they stay put.' Her voice trembled as she walked over to him.

Don opened his arms, and she stepped into them without hesitation.

Thank God. He dropped his head and rested his chin on her hair.

'Why are you here? Why didn't you stay with the boat?' she said.

'Because I needed to make sure you were okay.' His voice was muffled against her cap. 'I couldn't see you. I thought those guys had taken you with them in the helicopter.'

'I'm okay. I hid on the track, but they didn't come after me.' She shook her head. 'I knew they'd seen me coming back down because they turned around and landed down here. I took off when I saw those crocodiles.' Her eyes held his, and the smile that spread slowly on her face told him everything he wanted to know. 'I hid behind this huge tree trunk and stayed put. I know their type; they wouldn't climb up a steep hill like that one. They'll doctor up a photo somehow, now they know I'm here.'

Don watched her face as she smiled up at him. 'I thought I'd lost you, Claire. It was the worst moment of my life.'

'I'm here, and you're stuck with me.' Her eyes were shining as they held his. 'Now tell me what you mean exactly by *lost* me?'

***

Claire lifted her face to Don's; the expression on his face was the only thing that mattered to her now. It was more important than any of the situation that had brought her so much stress. But that situation had brought her to Don.

Lost me? She didn't think he was talking about losing a member of the crew. Or she hoped he wasn't.

'I hadn't thought it through.' His arms tightened around her, and happiness settled in her chest. 'I should have known they'd go looking for you. I'm sorry they've found you.'

Her voice was calm as she held his gaze. 'I don't care about them. All that energy I've wasted worrying about being in the news and magazines, it doesn't matter, does it? It's not important.' Claire didn't care anymore about those two journalists—or whoever it was who had spotted her and leaned out with their huge telephoto lens—or what they thought about her. 'I do think they took a photo of me from up there.' The chopper had swooped up the cliff face and hovered over the flat rock where the crocodiles were basking in the sun.

Don cupped her face in his hands and lowered his face to hers. 'So the whole world will know where you are now; how do you feel about that?'

'I don't know that anyone apart from the media will be terribly interested in telling the truth. But I'm *very* happy with where I am right at this moment.'

'So am I.'

Don had left the *Kimberley Adventurer* to make sure *she* was okay. By doing that, he's shown that she was important to him. Claire knew now she'd placed too much importance on the past and the events of the last month. None of that mattered. Don cared for her, and he put her welfare first. He'd left the boat in someone else's charge, and he'd come to find her himself. He could have sent one of the deckhands, but he hadn't, and that told her so much.

Don wouldn't let her down, and she hoped it was because he cared for her as she did for him. It was all about trust.

'Thank you.'

'What for?' His voice burred against her cheek.

'For showing me what matters.' Claire lifted her arms and put them around Don's neck, and his lips slid slowly along her cheek.

'You're right, Claire. I have to show you …' he said as his mouth moved closer to hers.

She frowned and looked around. 'Show me?'

'How fast … and how much I've fallen in love with a certain green-eyed blonde.'

Claire smiled when his lips found hers.

Epilogue

Two months later

The *Kimberley Adventurer* approached the mouth of the Norman River. Don stood behind Claire, his arms linked loosely in front of her. Sean had stayed on board when he'd left the boat in the marina at Darwin and flown to Sydney with Claire.

'Nervous?' Don's breath warmed her cheek as he lowered his head and brushed a kiss across her cheek.

'Very,' she said.

Don's chest vibrated against her back as he chuckled. 'This is from the woman who just took on the biggest television producer in the country, told him to get the media to back off, and informed him who'd set her up.'

'That was different. This is your *family*.'

If it wasn't for the nerves playing havoc with her, Claire would have been totally content. Thanks to a directive from the owner of the network, she was no longer in the sights of the media. Don had been with her every step of the way. They'd gone to Ben's house, and Claire had fronted Giselle, who'd moved in with Ben when Claire had left town.

Even though Giselle denied that jealousy had motivated her actions, she had admitted to setting Claire up. The network wasn't doing anything about it because the ratings had gone through the roof, and Giselle had kept her job.

The producer had begged Claire to sign another contract, but she'd looked at Don and smiled. 'Thanks for the offer, but no. I'm going back into law. I'm setting up my own business in the north.'

'You've already met half the family: Matt and Jenni. And Leni.' Don let go of her and called to Sean, pointing to the wharf near the building that had **McDOUGAL'S FISH CO-OP** on the rusty roof. 'Over there, mate.'

'Yes, but when I met Matt and Jenni, I was just the new neighbour, only in the Bay for a few weeks.'

'And when you meet Mum and Rick, and Dane and Jake, you'll be the new lawyer in town.'

Claire was quiet as the boat approached the wharf, where a group of people and a small girl were waiting.

'And the new daughter-in-law and sister-in-law.' Claire looked down at the new rings on her left hand, still unable to believe that she and Don had married in Sydney before they'd flown back to Darwin. They'd toured from Darwin to Broome in the *Adventurer* after they'd returned, and she'd had the best honeymoon anyone could wish for.

Who needed the south of France when you had Don McDougal for a husband?

Don took her shoulders and turned her around to face him. His blue eyes shone as he looked down at her. Claire's chest swelled with love for this man—her man—and all her nerves disappeared as he smiled at her.

'Stop worrying, sweetheart.' His words vibrated against her lips as he sealed his words with a gentle kiss. 'How could they not love you?'

THE END

Book 3
Her Outback Haven
Dane's story

Annie Seaton

Dedication

This book is dedicated to the Finlays—David and Maria, Rex and Denise—
fishing buddies we met at Karumba, and now lifelong friends.

Chapter 1

'I won't be long, little mate.' Dane McDougall pushed the bowl to the back of the ute tray and tickled under the pup's chin. 'A takeaway hamburger for me, and we'll have an early night ready to hit the road tomorrow.' He slammed the door of his Land Cruiser ute that he'd parked outside the pub. Dane was late, and he knew that his brothers would be impatient because they hated eating after dark. After a hard day on the boats and in the fish co-op, they were always ready to eat early. He reached into the esky, popped the top off a water bottle and filled the pup's water bowl. Bits was tied securely onto the back of his ute, with plenty of rope to move around.

It would suit him just fine to make his announcement and get out because he knew that he was going to cop some flak from his family.

Jake—his sister Jenni's partner—had guaranteed the loan, and he was the only one who knew what Dane had done, and he'd promised not to tell Jenni. Once Jenni knew any family news, she thought it needed to be shared with the other siblings, but until the deal had been finalised, Dane wanted it kept quiet.

It had been signed, sealed and delivered in the solicitor's office in Normanton this afternoon. The best part was that Mum and her partner Rick were home from their caravan travels for a while and had taken over the management here at the pub in Second Chance Bay. Dane knew he'd always been Mum's golden-haired boy—he'd helped out with his brothers and sister when Mum had done it tough, and she would back him against his siblings. Unfair advantage at times, but hey, his mother was savvy.

With a final pat on Bits' head, he strode through the pub and outside to the family's usual table at the back of the grassed area overlooking the water. It was about ten minutes before sunset, and the tables were almost empty as most of the patrons—always the grey nomies and the occasional younger backpacker—jostled for the best spots over at the edge of the grass to catch a photo of the sun setting over the Gulf of Carpentaria.

Dane stood there and looked to the west. The early evening sky was magnificent, and it looked like Mother Nature was going to celebrate with him. Shards of gold, overlaid with deep violet, lit the sky, and the sea held a silvery hue near the shore, deepening to burnt orange as the huge golden orb headed slowly for the horizon. He couldn't keep the smile from his face as he walked over to join his family. Excitement zinged through him, and he felt lighter than he had felt for a long time; it was hard to keep the grin off his face. He slowed his pace, shoved his hands in his pockets and reduced his walk to a casual stroll as he crossed the lawn to the table.

Jake was sitting behind Jenni and had his hands looped loosely over her pregnant tummy. Jenn had her head back on Jake's shoulder as they watched the sunset, at the same time keeping an eye on two-year-old Leni as the small girl played in the children's playground only a few metres from the table. They needn't have worried as Mum was over there on Nanny duty.

Don, the brother closest in age to Dane, and his partner, Claire, were sitting and talking quietly at the end of the table. As Dane approached, Don reached up and pulled Claire closer and brushed his lips over hers.

Dane shook his head.

What the hell was happening to his family? You'd think Cupid had visited.

Not for me, he thought.

He'd had a brief relationship last year with Nicky, a girl he'd gone to high school with, but all she'd wanted was the wedding ring and the noose around his neck. *And* for him to support her with all her family problems, he'd helped out as best
328

he could and then moved on. Nicky and the whole family had left town last Christmas and moved down to Richmond and they'd lost touch.

Matt, the oldest of the four siblings at thirty-five, walked out of the bar with a tray of drinks, followed closely by Rick. 'I knew you'd be here soon, so there's a beer here for you too, bro,' Matt said.

'Thanks, I'll return the shout next time because I'm not staying long tonight.' Dane followed them and sat on the long bench seat at the end of the table.

'Why not? It's Friday.' Matt nudged him as he put the tray on the table. 'Hot date?'

'Nope, just a little pup who wants to go home to his bed. I have an early start tomorrow.'

'Early start?' Matt frowned. 'We've got no charters on, have we?'

'No, but I've got a road trip.'

'I didn't know that.' Matt sounded peeved.

Dane reached for his beer and his voice was as dry as his throat. 'Last time I checked I wasn't aware I had to report in.'

'Jeez. Don't get your knickers in a twist. I just thought there must have been a charter I'd forgotten.'

'Nope, no charter until next Saturday. I've got a bit of a drive ahead of me tomorrow.'

'I thought you went to Normanton today?' Matt stared at him and grinned. 'My God, Dane McDougall is leaving the Bay twice in one week. You having a mid-life crisis or something? I know, there's a woman involved.'

'Don't be a smart arse.' Dane knew Matt was trying to get a rise out of him.

Don slid along the bench and joined in the conversation. 'Who's having a mid-life crisis?'

Dane rolled his eyes. 'No one.'

'Where're you off to then?' Matt looked at him curiously, and Dane understood why. It was rare for him to leave town by road; his journeys were usually by boat, out to the Gulf and work-related.

He sat back and sipped his beer with a satisfied smile. 'To my new property.' He caught Jake's eye and smiled.

'What new property?' Matt and Don spoke together, and Jenni turned around. Her question followed immediately.

'Dane McDougal, you've always been the quiet one. What new property?'

'I'll tell you all about it when Mum comes back to the table. Then I can answer all your questions in one hit.'

Matt reached up and scratched his head. 'And what pup are you talking about?'

'My new boy. He's called Bits.'

##

Dane realised that he wasn't going to get away early like he'd wanted. By the time Mum brought Leni back to the table and greeted everyone, the rest of the family took their time ordering their meals, and they didn't beat the tourist rush to the bistro after the sunset.

Jake called to him from across the table. 'You should know this family well enough by now, mate. You're not going to get away with a hamburger and an early night. It's Friday night.'

'True.' Dane shrugged and turned to Matt. 'Order me a T-bone and chips while I go and get Bits. I can tie him up at the edge of the grass and keep an eye on him.'

Fifteen minutes later, the pup was asleep on Dane's boots under the table, the meals had been ordered, everyone had a drink, and Leni was sitting on Mum's lap at the end of the table.

Matt turned to Dane. 'Now we want to hear what you've done and all the details.'

Dane smiled. He loved winding Matt up; he was so serious. It must be the accountant's genes in him. Or the oldest brother responsibility kicking in.

'Well, when I was in Normanton today, I parked behind a ute, and there was a cage in the back full of all these cute little dogs. They all looked lonely and I couldn't resist. Bits and I were made for each other.' The smile threatened to turn into a full-blown grin; he could almost hear Matt's teeth grinding.

'No, boofhead, not the dog. The new property you've bought. Is it in Normanton?'

'Nope.' Dane picked up his beer and sipped, enjoying the chorus of groans from his siblings.

'Come on, Dane,' Jenni said with a teasing smile 'Spill! This is exciting. Getting ready to look for a bride and settle down on a quarter-acre block, are you?'

Dane spluttered into his beer. 'No way. Just because you lot are all lovey-dovey lately doesn't mean I have to do the same.'

'Dane, stop being such a torment,' his mother said, but her smile was affectionate. 'Tell us what you've done.'

'I'm starting up another business.' He looked over at Matt and Donny. 'And before you get worried, I'm not going anywhere. I can link into our charters, and I think it should supplement it well.'

'So, what else do you know about besides fishing?' Matt stared at him again, and this time, his frown was pronounced.

Dane sat back and folded his arms. 'Jeez, I'm overwhelmed by all of this confidence in me.'

'Be nice, son. We all just want the best for you.' His mother's voice held a little bit of censure.

Dane turned to her as surprise filled him. 'I thought you'd at least be on my side, Mum.'

'There's no sides,' she said. 'We all want to support you in . . . in whatever it is you've done. I trust all my children to make good decisions.'

Jake leaned forward. 'There's no need for anyone to worry. Dane's seen a great business opportunity, and I've backed him.'

Three stony faces looked back at him, unimpressed that Dane had shared with Jake, the brother-in-law before he'd shared with them.

'So, are you going to put them out of their misery?' Mum asked.

Dane sat back and folded his arms to match those of his siblings. 'I've bought some land a hundred kilometres up the coast.'

'Land?' The look on Matt's face was almost comical. 'How's that going to supplement the fishing?'

'I'm going to build a fishing lodge. Just south of the aboriginal land at Staaten River. A luxury, exclusive lodge.'

Matt nodded slowly. 'Not a bad idea. Could work.'

'We've talked about it for years, and I heard that Bobby Foley was selling his land, so I made an offer, and he jumped at it.'

'So, have you seen the place yet?' Don asked.

'No, that's where I'm heading tomorrow. I'm going up for a couple of days. I need to look at the logistics. Things like getting the builders in, not to mention getting the frames of the buildings up there. It's a long way in, on a bad track, and it's going to be expensive. And don't worry, Matt, I'll be back in time for the next charter.'

'I'm not worried about that. I'm just wondering about the wisdom of buying a place sight unseen.'

'And from Bobby Foley,' Don muttered.

Dane shot him a look.

'I didn't think there was a road across to the coast around the Staaten National Park area,' Matt said.

'Not a good road, just a four-wheel drive track, but there's an airstrip. The track turns off at Dinah's Creek near the cattle station and goes south of the river to the coast. Bobby assured me it's passable with a high four-wheel drive most of the year. He was in Normanton yesterday when I signed the contract.'

'If you do go ahead with it, you could ship the building materials down from Weipa, and there are a lot of tradesmen up there too. It wouldn't be far for them to come down by boat on their days off.'

'That's what I thought,' Dane said. 'Most of the tradies in Weipa are there to make a quick buck before they head south again. They'd jump at a weekend job.'

Matt screwed his mouth up. 'So, how long is the cooling-off period for the property? Will you have time to see it and get out of the contract if it's no good?'

Dane shook his head slowly. 'There were others interested, so it's been rushed through. We settled this afternoon.'

'You've settled already? Sight unseen?' Matt's voice rose almost to a squeak. 'Are you serious?'

'Oh, for God's sake, Matt. Stop carrying on like an old woman.' Dane flicked a glance at his mother. 'Sorry, Mum, no offence meant.'

'And none taken because I'm a long way from that.'

'Calm down, Matt. Let him tell us about it.' Don's voice was even, but Dane could see the furrow in his brow.

'It's fifty acres with deep-water frontage near the existing house. The wetland system inland is one of the last wild river systems in the world. It'll position the business for unique environmental trips too. The migratory bird life there is amazing.'

'Does anyone live close to it?' Jenni asked.

'No, there's just the rough fishing camp with limited facilities at Dinah Creek about fifteen kilometres inland, and there's a small aboriginal settlement about sixty kilometres north.'

'Sounds isolated,' Matt said, but he looked a bit less worried. 'I'm not going to ask you how much you paid for it, but—'

'Good, because it's none of your damn business.'

'But,' Matt continued as though he hadn't been interrupted. 'What sort of condition is the house in? Can you do it up, or is it a knock-em-down?'

'That's what I'm going up to see. I'm thinking if it's in a fit state to live in, I could let the builders stay there instead of camping out while they build the new lodge.'

Don nodded, and Dane waited.

'Well, I think the idea's got merit. We could do a charter and combine the Gulf fishing with barra fishing in the Staaten River. And, like you said, we could venture into ecological and birdwatching trips, too. It's pretty much untouched.'

'Thanks, Donny,' Dane said.

'No, don't go thanking me. I've still got reservations. If Bobby Foley's involved, there'll be a scam somewhere. Are you sure it's his to sell?' Don asked.

'Yes. I know what he's like, so I asked the solicitor to double-check. Apparently, the house was an outpost of a small mission back in the early 1900s. The Anglicans had a mission up at Kowanyama, and Bobby said there's an old church there too, but it's a ruin. It's been in his family since the 1940s. He grew up out there and they worked on the cattle station.'

'Well, I think it sounds fabulous.' Mum leaned over and squeezed his arm. 'I'm proud of you, Dane.'

Chapter 2

Nicole peeked in on Binnie; she was sound asleep in her bed on the enclosed veranda, and as always, the surge of love that filled Nicole's chest as she looked at the child was physical. Plump cheeks were pink from the hour they'd spent building castles in the sandpit before lunch, and dark lashes framed eyes shut tightly as the beautiful little girl slept.

Leaving the door ajar, Nicole hurried around to the other side of the verandah. She barely spared a glance for the silvery blue sea or the deep clear sky, her thoughts were already on the order she had received last week. A light breeze blew in from the water, keeping the temperature to a reasonable level; she wasn't looking forward to the heat and humidity that was only a couple of months away. Their first summer last year in the Gulf had been a shock, but after a few months, they had both acclimatised. One thing, there was never a shortage of tank water, and she and Binnie had spent many an afternoon in the plastic blow-up pool in the shade around the back of the house under the brilliant red Poinciana tree.

Binnie should sleep until four, so it would give her a chance to get started on the new commission. Nicole paused by her supplies table under the shuttered windows that faced the Gulf. A bag of untouched clay sat there, and her ever-present guilt kicked in. She should have been working nights to get the Information Centre order done. The deposit had been much needed, and the balance of the payment would see them through the next few months. It was almost time for a trip to Normanton to stock up the pantry.

The clay sat there looking at her accusingly.

'All right, all right, I'm coming.' She crossed to the table and picked up the bag of kaolin clay. It would be much easier not to have to mix her own, but moist clay weighed a lot more, and she couldn't afford the shipping these days. She was just lucky that she'd had some of her equipment in Laura's car before—

Nicole pulled a shutter down on those thoughts. She'd followed the advice of her high school art teacher, and she was happy with where she was now.

Where *they* were now.

'Life can be like a lump of clay; if you don't mould and shape it into something, it will sit like a lump on the table until someone does something with it or throws it away,' Mrs Hart had said. Her lessons had never been boring, and she had recognised Nicole's talent and had nurtured her. Both artistically and as a life mentor through a difficult time.

'Extend yourself. Don't be boring. Clay is never boring. There's always more to explore and more to create. Life is like pottery; a great adventure as deep and broad as the earth that the clay comes from.'

Nicole knew she'd thrown away her life by making wrong choices. Her only regret was that she couldn't contact Mrs Hart and let her know she was okay now. It wasn't worth the risk.

But having Binnie in her life had come from that wrong choice, and she would go back and make the same decisions again for that very reason. Maybe her later decisions would have been different. Binnie's confidence had gone ahead in leaps and bounds over the past year; the isolation had healed them both.

Almost.

Nicole lifted the scales from the shelf behind her main work table. The downside of working with dry clay was the mixing, and she couldn't afford a clay mixer. It meant that she didn't need to work out to stay fit; even though she was thin, the muscles in her arms were stronger than they'd ever been in the days when she'd paid a fortune for membership at the flash gym in Melbourne.

She paused as she opened the plastic bag and tilted her head. A frown pulled at her forehead as she let go of the bag and crossed to the louvre window beside the door. Dust was hanging above the road as a vehicle approached the turnoff to the driveway to the house.

Her hand went to her pocket, and her breath stilled; the car keys were still on the kitchen table at the back of the house. She usually made sure they were in her pocket.

I've become too complacent.

The old Subaru she'd changed Laura's car for in Gympie on the trip north was locked away in the shed at the side of the house. Nicole hurried quietly through to the kitchen and picked up her keys and purse, ready to grab Binnie and flee to the shed if it became necessary. It had been weeks since the last vehicle had gone past the house, and she'd been relieved when it hadn't stopped but continued south, the roof basket of the off-road vehicle filled with tents, jerry cans and fishing rods.

Tiptoeing to the front door, she glanced along the western verandah as she stood there. Binnie was still asleep; she'd rolled over, and her face was buried in the pillow.

At least the house looked deserted from the outside. The mess in the yard and under the house bugged her, but she'd always figured it was safer to leave it like it was.

Neglected and looking as though the house was unoccupied. Although with squatters around, that was a risk in itself.

She stood there and held her breath again as the rising dust came closer to the gate.

Keep going, go past, keep going, she willed the vehicle. Biting her lip, indecision filled her; stay in the house, or grab Binnie and sneak down the back stairs to the shed?

The white four-wheel drive ute slowed and turned into the gate, and her stomach clenched. She gripped her keys tightly and waited, with the occasional glance at Binnie as the ute approached the house and slowed. Her leg muscles tightened as she got ready to run, and a bead of sweat rolled slowly down her forehead.

The ute came closer, and she clenched her jaw until a small measure of relief lightened Nicole's worry. She could see the logo on the side: **McDougal Fishing Charters-Second Chance Bay.**

She'd heard of them, and they were more likely to be here for a reason that had nothing to do with her. As long as she and Binnie stayed silent, and they didn't come to the house.

Nicole's breathing eased, but she stood silently behind the closed door, taking care to step back into the shadows where she couldn't be seen. With a bit of luck, whoever it was would walk down to the water and not stay too long. Mr Foley had told her it was a deep-water frontage, great for launching fishing boats when she'd signed the lease, but no one had turned up with a boat in the months since they'd arrived.

The car pulled up with a crunch of wheels on the gravel driveway at the front. She pressed herself against the wall, keeping her gaze on Binnie as a door slammed.

She slept on without a murmur, and Nicole stood silently.

Waiting. Waiting for the tread of footsteps on the rickety double stairway at the front of the house.

But there was nothing. No sound. No footsteps. No voices.

She leaned forward and looked through the half-closed louvres. A tall man with broad shoulders was bending down to something at his feet, a fair way from the house, halfway between the vehicle and the water. She put her fingers on the glass slats and stared; his back was to her and he was too far away to see her even if he did turn around. She narrowed her eyes as a high-pitched yip reached her, and then the man walked slowly away, holding a lead. A tiny little black ball of fur plonked its bottom in the middle of the path and the man stopped again. He was close enough for her to hear his chuckle as he tugged on the lead.

'Come on, Bits. Don't tell me you're scared of crocodiles. Fine fishing companion, you'll make.' His words drifted across through the window as he called to the dog. After a few seconds of non-cooperation on the dog's part, the man walked back, bent down and scooped the pup into his arms and walked towards the shoreline.

Nicole was relieved, but she still didn't want him to know that there was anyone living in the house.

Fishing. But why was he here? So far away from Second Chance Bay.

As far as she knew, no one knew they lived here, except for Mr Foley, their landlord; he'd promised to be discreet when she had asked him not to mention she was living here. Each time she went to town, she went to a different store and didn't get into conversation with anyone.

Tried to look like a tourist.

The highest risk was picking up her supplies at the post office, but she always had them sent with the instruction to be collected at Normanton Post Office, which ensured her anonymity.

No address on record, and she'd gone back to her mother's maiden name. The only problem was it made it difficult to sell her pieces because she'd been so well-known as Nicoletta Spagnolo—Bruno had insisted she use that name as he was sponsoring her—when she'd won the first award. It had meant starting from scratch here as Nicole Curtis, but the commissions had been coming slowly as she'd emailed various catalogues from a generic email account that gave her anonymity. And Bruno had been so self-centred that he'd never even met her mother or asked about her, so he wouldn't know the name.

She hoped.

Nicole leaned forward and waited. The man spent a long time down at the water's edge, looking along the beach, and Nicole relaxed a little as she walked to the back of the house. Binnie was still asleep, so she made her way to the kitchen, where she could get a better view of him as he walked further away from the house. She frowned as she went into the large open kitchen; she'd forgotten she'd left the window open, so the breeze would flow through the house. It was too late to close it now; that would just draw his attention. She watched as he picked his way along the shoreline, getting further away from the house with each step.

Her heart was still beating fast, and a dull ache tugged at her chest.

Please hurry up and go, she begged silently. The tension kicked back in, and Binnie would wake up soon. She didn't want her to be frightened; it had taken months to win her confidence after—

Tears welled in Nicole's eyes; she wouldn't go there.

***

The deep-water frontage was much better than Dane had expected. A small jetty built out into the middle of the bay would cater for boats the size of Jake's *Moonshine* and *Starshine* with no trouble at all, even if the tide was low. The water was deep enough to take a commercial vessel to consider Matt's advice and ship the building equipment in by boat. Much of the Gulf was shallow, as many skippers found when they came aground on sand shoals in seemingly deep water.

It was only a kilometre or two from here to the mouth of the Staaten River, and the river was deep and wide. Up in the Kimberleys, where Don had worked charters recently—and where Don had met Claire— the accommodation was inland, and the guests had to be taken to the boats by coach. Dane decided to go and find the airstrip here after he checked the house out.

So far, it was looking great, and he was happy with what he'd paid for it, now that he'd seen that the land around the house was high and well away from the wetlands.

Excitement filled him; the same old fishing charters they'd been doing since their father had established the business in the eighties had become routine and monotonous. Now Don had his charters up in the Kimberley, and Jake's boats had added an upmarket edge to the existing charters out of the Bay. Dane had been taking out the original family boats—the *Sally M,* and the *Elsie* were both tired and in need of refurbishment—and he was ready for a change too.

This was an ideal location; he could picture the buildings set back a little way from the water. They could fly the guests into the airstrip, cater for them at the lodge and take them out on a day trip. He'd install a commercial kitchen in a separate building and hire a good chef. If he was going to do this, he'd do it well. With Jake as a silent partner and his local fishing knowledge, Dane knew he could make this an upmarket luxury adventure experience.

Next stop was the house; the main question would be— demolish or refurbish?

He turned to head back to the house; the keys to the front door were in the ute.

His neck prickled, and he stopped and looked up; a curtain was blowing at an open window. For a moment, it had looked as though someone was standing there. He shrugged, put Bits down when he started to whimper, and walked back to the ute, keeping his eyes on the house.

It was an incredible building; maybe he *would* keep it. A Queenslander with a magnificent red tree in full bloom overhanging the rusted roof sat close to the beach. The grass was long around the house; broken and rusted tools were scattered around the front yard, and old pieces of machinery were under the house. It looked as though no one had lived there for years. Old cane furniture sagged on the verandah that wrapped around two sides of the house. Lace curtains filled the two front windows, and a small tree had pushed through the railing on the old-fashioned staircase that came down from the verandah in a line with the front door and then split to the left and right.

He wondered what he would find inside, mostly rats and bird droppings with that window open, he guessed. It would have been a magnificent house in its day, but it would take a lot of money—and work—to restore the place to its former glory.

Dane looked up as a loud creak pierced the stillness of the early afternoon. With a frown, he stared at the house as the front door opened.

Bloody hell. There was someone inside!

Squatters. He'd soon move them on.

He stood there frowning as a small girl ran down the stairs and hurried towards him, a wide smile on her face as she headed for Bits.

'Binnie. No! Come back now!' The cry was shrill and loud.

Dane looked back to the house. A slightly built woman with fair hair was hurrying down the side of the stairs closest to where he stood with Bits.

The puppy yapped as the little girl crouched down beside them and held her hand out. She giggled when Bits' wet nose touched her hand, and when his little pink tongue licked her fingers, she giggled again.

'Hello. Are you Binnie?'

The little girl looked up at Dane with wide eyes. The woman hurried across and reached down, and took the little girl's hand. She pulled her away and gently pushed her behind her.

'How do you know her name?' Her voice was soft, but her gaze was like steel as she stood protectively in front of the child.

Dane straightened his shoulders and stared back at her. She was almost as tall as he was. 'I didn't. I assumed that was her name because you called it from the steps.'

'I want you to leave our land now.'

'Your land?' Dane stared at her. It was like one of those westerns he'd loved as a kid; all the woman needed was a shotgun on her shoulder pointing at him, and the image would have been perfect.

'Yes.' She folded her arms and glanced nervously back at the house as though she was measuring the distance to get away from him. 'My husband is asleep. He . . . he went fishing all night. Drive out quietly, so you don't wake him up. Come on, Binnie.' She reached down and picked the child up and turned back to the house.

'Wait.' Dane put his hand out, and the woman jumped as his fingers brushed her shoulder.

She turned slowly.

'Mrs. . .?

'Curtis,' she said.

'I'd like to speak to both you and your husband. Together.'

'Why?' Her voice was wary. When she glanced back at the house again Dane realised it was fear that filled her eyes. Her shoulders were stiff, and her jaw was tight.

He stepped back and put his hands up. 'I'm sorry, Mrs Curtis. Let me start again. My name is Dane McDougal. We have a fishing charter business at Second Chance Bay.' He gestured to the ute. 'As you can see on my vehicle.'

'Why do you need to talk to me? To us, I mean?'

'Because I was told that no one lived here and that this house—my house—was empty.'

'Your house?' She shook her head. 'It's not your house. We live here.'

'You're squatting.'

343

Her voice rose as she stared at him. 'No! We're not squatters. We rent off Mr Foley. He's the owner.'

Dane nodded. 'Mr Bobby Foley *was* the owner. He was the owner before he sold me this land and this house. So, I need to speak to both you and your husband about vacating the premises as soon as possible. I'm the new owner, and I have plans for the house.'

To Dane's utter consternation, her eyes filled with tears. The woman—Mrs Curtis—bowed her head and put her free hand up to her face.

'No.' Her cry was full of anguish.

Chapter 3

Nicole had no doubt that Dane McDougal of McDougal Fishing Charters was telling the truth. She also had a three-year lease signed and a receipt showing she had paid for the rental of the house until the end of next year.

Embarrassed by the tears that had sprung to her eyes, she brushed away at them with one hand. Binnie wriggled in her arms and grunted.

'Go upstairs, Binnie. Wait for me on the verandah.' She slid down Nicole's legs and walked across to the stairs.

Nicole smiled at Binnie to dispel the obvious tension. No matter what the little girl lacked, she was observant—and obedient.

Usually.

The man waited until Binnie had climbed up the steps with a wistful look back at the puppy.

'Can we go inside? Or perhaps I can wait on the verandah while you get your husband.' He ran a hand through his hair as she watched him, his frustration obvious.

'Please give me a moment while I get Binnie a drink. She's not long woken up.' Nicole shook her head. She hadn't realised that Binnie could reach the door latch. Horror flooded through her at the thought that she may have wandered outside one night. Although it was beautiful in its isolation, the property was fraught with danger. Nicole could live with the huge spiders that sometimes found their way inside, but she was always very wary of the snakes and the crocodiles that she knew were out there. For someone who'd grown up in the city, she was very proud of how she'd coped up here.

So far.

Even during the category one cyclone that had threatened last year, she'd managed to cope and kept them safe.

Safety.

That was all she needed. As time passed, the threat from Melbourne would pass.

It would.

'So?' The man's voice was quiet.

He was staring at her with a strange look on his face.

'I'm sorry, what did you say?'

'Can I wait on the verandah while you get your husband?'

Nicole bit her lip, wondering what to do.

Or say.

'Yes, please come up to the verandah.' She strode towards the house and hurried up the stairs ahead of him. Gesturing to the small cane setting near the door, she watched as he followed her up the stairs. 'Please take a seat. It's stronger than it looks.' As much as she hated to offer, good manners prevailed. 'Can I offer you a cup of tea?'

'Thank you, that's very kind,' he said.

She waited until he sat at the table, pushed open the front door and took Binnie inside. She sat her at the kitchen table and crossed to the camping fridge.

'You stay there. Mummy was worried when you opened the door.'

Binnie nodded.

Nicole reached for the juice and the carton of long-life milk. 'Juice or milk?' She held them both up. Binnie pointed to the juice, and Nicole reached for a plastic mug. Once she had put the drink in front of Binnie and added a couple of biscuits to a plate on the table, she turned and filled the kettle, her mind working furiously.

Could she believe him when he said that he hadn't known she was here? How could Mr Foley have sold the house and not mentioned it was tenanted? She frowned as she waited for the water to boil. To be fair, she had asked Mr Foley not to tell anyone she was here, but she also hadn't expected that he'd sell the house.

Panic clawed at her stomach, and as Nicole reached up for the cups and teapot, her hands were shaking. There was nowhere to go, and they couldn't move because there was no money. They had enough to buy groceries and pay the car registration and insurance when they came due. The rent included the electricity, and the deposit on the recent commission had been enough to order the clay.

The credit on her internet dongle had run out, and she'd not been able to check her email for two weeks; that was on the list when they went to Normanton next week. The library internet was free, so she'd decided to use that from now on.

The kettle whistled, and Nicole poured the boiling water onto the tea bags. Adding sugar and milk and another plate of biscuits to the tray, she turned to Binnie. 'When you finish your drink, you can go and play for a little while, but I want you to stay inside. Okay?' She reached down and hugged the little girl, burying her face in the sweet-smelling hair.

'Okay?' she repeated when she stood straight.

Binnie nodded.

'I'll talk to the man and have my tea, and then I'll call you. You stay inside until I call, and then you can say goodbye to the puppy. Right?'

Again, the sweet nod. Nicole's heart clenched; she would give anything, do anything to hear that sweet little voice again.

Damn you, Bruno Spagnolo.

She crossed to the cupboard where she kept her papers and pulled out the informal letter that had served as a lease and the handwritten receipt showing she had paid three thousand six hundred dollars for three years rent. It was probably the only place in Australia where you could rent a house for twenty-four dollars a week. She put it on the table in case he insisted on seeing it.

She might not be able to do anything about Binnie not talking for twelve months, one week and three days—the date was fixed in Nicole's head for life—but she would fight tooth and nail to keep a roof above their heads.

A roof for which she had paid good rent.

***

Bits had gone to sleep in Dane's lap, and his fingers smoothed the little pup's coat while he waited for the woman to come out of the house with her husband. All was quiet, and he could hear no voices. Finally, the door opened, and she emerged carrying a tray set with two cups, a pot of tea, a sugar bowl and a jug of milk.

She set it carefully on the table and pulled out the other chair, her head down. There was no sign of the little girl—or a husband. Dane glanced at his watch. He had intended to travel down to the campground at Dinah's Camp and sleep in his swag after he'd checked out the house, but if he didn't get going soon, it would be too late to travel there. He didn't know the road well enough to traverse it in the dark. He looked at the tray and then up at Mrs Curtis.

'Is your husband still sleeping?'

Her reply was quiet and surprised him. 'Do you have any identification to prove you are who you say?'

Dane stood, put Bits on the chair and pulled his wallet from his back pocket and removed his driver's licence. He passed it over to her. 'Photo ID.'

She took it from him, and he was surprised again to see her hands shaking as she looked at the photo and then up at him. She passed it back without a word. He returned it to his wallet and then to his pocket and sat down again, leaving Bits on the other chair. He hadn't stirred.

She lifted the teapot and filled a cup with a hot, strong brew just as he liked it.

'Milk? Sugar?' She tipped her head to the side, and it was as though they were having a normal, friendly afternoon tea.

An eerie light surrounded them as the sun went behind a cloud, and the wind whistled around the corner of the house from the sea. Some loose sheets of iron banged above their heads. There was no sound or sign of life from inside.

When she had poured her tea, she pushed the plate of biscuits towards him, but he shook his head.

'Maybe the pup would like one.'

Dane smiled and reached for a biscuit and put it beside the pup. Bits' nose twitched but he stayed asleep.

'Thank you, Mrs Curtis,' Dane said. It was obvious that his presence had unsettled her, so he waited for her to start the conversation. It was a strange setup here.

She sipped her tea, and he waited her out. Finally, she put the cup on the table and looked at him. Her skin was fair, like her hair, and there were a couple of fine lines around her eyes. Her hair was pulled back from her high forehead in a ponytail. Her blue eyes were tired and fringed with long lashes, but it was the shadows beneath them that he noticed more.

'Please call me Nicole.' She lifted her head, and his gaze brushed her long and slender neck. 'I'm not going to beat around the bush. After I tell you why we *must* stay here, I'm going to beg. If I tell you the truth, I hope that you'll allow us to stay here for as long as I've paid the rent.'

Dane went to speak, but she put a shaking hand up. 'Please hear me out. There's one thing I need you to promise me. What I am going to tell you has to stay between us. No one else can know we're here.'

'I'm not sure if I can promise that at this point.' Dane held her intent gaze. He was used to the various characters who came and went in the Gulf. For those who wanted to disappear, it was a wild frontier where it was very easy to drop out of society. 'Tell me why you're here.'

'Binnie and I live here by ourselves. I have no husband. There is no one asleep inside, like I said before. It's just the two of us.' Her voice was matter-of-fact, but her eyes were sad. 'We're here so I can keep Binnie safe.'

Dane couldn't help interrupting. 'There's just the two of you, way out here? On your own?'

She nodded.

'But that's *not* safe. What if you had an accident? Or you or your child got sick? It's hours from Normanton to here. Do you have a car? Or do you travel by boat?'

'I know. I have a four-wheel drive in the shed over there.'

A frisson of sympathy niggled at his chest, but Dane pushed it away. He'd got too close to Nicki's family issues—it must go with the name; her full name was Nicole too—and he'd pulled back before he'd become too involved. But her family issues there had been nothing as serious as a woman and a child living so far from anywhere. Alone.

'Okay, I understand that you seem to want to disappear, and I'll accept that. But why can't you move somewhere else?'

'In one word? Money.' She shrugged, but her dark brown eyes remained on his. 'I've paid rent for this house until the end of *next* year, and I have a lease signed by Mr Foley. I can show you. I shouldn't have to leave. And the bottom line is I can't afford to leave. So I'm begging you to let us stay.'

'Yeah, Bobby Foley. I'm sorry to be the one to tell you, but he's one of the greatest con artists in the Gulf. He neglected to tell me that the house had tenants when he sold it to me.' Dane shook his head as frustration filled him; he'd always been a soft touch, but this was a situation where he was going to have to be firm. 'Look, Nicole, I'd love to help you out, but the bottom line is, I have business commitments. I've taken out a substantial loan to develop a business based here, and like you, there is one word for me to consider too. *Money.* I can't afford to wait until the end of next year before I build the lodge and get my business up and running. I need to see a return on my investment.'

Her shoulders went rigid, and a wave of fear crossed her face. He was horrified when her eyes filled with tears, and she put a shaking hand up to her face. Dane was a sucker for tears, he always had been. Jenni had known how to get her own way when they were kids, but this time, he knew the tears weren't put on. The woman was clearly terrified.

'Look,' he said gently. 'I know you said there was a money issue, but what if I found you somewhere to live back in Second Chance Bay? I know where there's an empty house. My brother's partner was living there for a while, and now it's empty.' The Dunstan house had been vacant since Claire had moved in with Donny.

'But it's in a town where there are people, and people are curious about where you come from. I can't afford for that to happen. She lifted her head, and her face was stark with an expression that was hard for Dane to understand. 'I have to stay here.'

Her expression broke his heart.
Grief? Fear?

Chapter 4

It was strange to be sitting on the verandah and having a conversation with another adult. Nicole could count on one hand the number of conversations she'd had over the past year.

With adults, anyway.

Although she made sure that she spoke to Binnie constantly, and she knew the little girl understood her, her speech had not returned. She could follow Nicole's instructions, and sometimes, it appeared she was going to speak. Then, her little face would cloud over, and she would close her lips tightly. Her development was normal; Nicole had read all the articles on loss of speech due to trauma at the library, and she prayed that one day, the words would come back. In the meantime, they took one day at a time, and she was reassured by Binnie's development and her ability to understand what Nicole was saying.

She didn't need a child psychologist to tell her what had caused it.

The day that Binnie had stopped talking remained etched in her memory. She shivered; even thinking about it filled her with terror.

It could have been Binnie. It could have been her. Or both of them.

'Nicole?' The deep voice was gentle as it pulled her from her thoughts. 'Are you with me?'

'I'm sorry.' She took a deep breath, trying to calm herself, but the events of the afternoon and the fear that had filled her when he'd driven up the drive were hard to shake. 'What did you say?'

'I said, why can't you afford for people to see you?'

'I meant risk, not afford. But please don't worry, Mr McDougal, I'm not a criminal.'

'It's Dane.'

'Then don't worry, *Dane*. Like I said, I'm not a criminal.' Nicole picked up her teacup and stared at it so she didn't have to see the expression that she imagined would be on his face.

'But you're hiding?'

'I am. We are. We have to.'

There was silence between them for a while, and finally, he let out a sigh. 'Look, I know you're entitled to privacy, but if—and only if, I am going to consider letting you stay for a while, I need to know more.'

'Fair enough,' she said.

'I mean, is it going to impact on my land or my business if what—or who—you're so scared of finds you? I need to know.'

The buzzing in her ears should have warned her, but Nicole pushed herself up from the chair as her heart began to beat furiously. Her mouth dried, and the last thing she was aware of was Dane lunging for her with his arms held wide.

***

Dane pushed the door open with his shoulder, aware that the little girl was inside somewhere. He'd known Nicole was going to faint as soon as she'd stood; her face had gone chalk-white, and her eyes had rolled back in their sockets. He'd been fast enough to catch her as she'd crumpled back down towards the chair. He'd scooped his arms beneath her legs and made sure her head was supported by his shoulder before he headed for the door. She was a featherweight, and as he carried her, he could feel the gauntness of her frame that he hadn't noticed under the loose trousers and long shirt before she'd ended up in his arms.

A surge of sympathy stuck in his throat.

What a life.

Hiding out here, with just a small child for company, it had to be a domestic violence issue.

'Binnie,' he called softly. 'Are you there?'

The small girl came down a long, dimly-lit hallway that led to the back of the house. Her eyes widened when she saw him, and she backed away, her eyes wide. She pressed herself against the wall and put her hands over her face.

'It's okay, sweetheart.' Dane kept his voice soft and even. 'Mummy was feeling a bit sick, and I'm taking her to the sofa to lie down. Can you show me which room is the lounge room?'

As the little girl pointed to the door to his left, Nicole began to stir.

'Wha—' She stiffened in his arms as her eyes opened, and she looked up at him.

'It's okay. You fainted. I'm just looking for a sofa to lie you down.'

'We don't have one,' she mumbled as she blinked a few times. A little bit of colour had come back into her cheeks and he could feel the steady beat of her heart against his arm. 'Just our beds.'

'Which room?' he asked, keeping an eye on Binnie as she crept cautiously towards him. He didn't want to scare her.

'The bedroom. Across the hall.' Nicole's voice was still weak, and Dane changed direction, following her instruction. He pushed open the door and as he walked in, there was a sharp tug on the back of his long-sleeved shirt at the same time a little foot kicked his leg.

'Put her down. I want my Mummy. Now.'

He looked down as Nicole pushed at him, her hands strong. 'Oh my God. Oh my God, Binnie.' Her voice shook, and tears spilled from her eyes. She pushed herself away from Dane, and her feet went to the floor.

'What's the matter? Are you ill again?' He tried to hold her, but she turned away. She shook her head and dropped to a crouch, her arms going around the little girl, her chest heaving with sobs.

'Binnie, oh Binnie. Say it again.'

'Don't let the big man hurt us.' The little voice was quiet but shaking.

Regret pierced Dane's chest as he stood there, unsure of what was happening. He didn't want to move and frighten the little girl any more than she was; she was obviously terrified. He looked around the room as Nicole rocked the small girl in her arms.

Two single mattresses lay side by side on the floor near the window, and a suitcase and three boxes sat in a neat line along the wall. His eyes narrowed as he took in the spartan nature of the room. He hadn't taken any notice of the rest of the house as he'd carried her inside.

Nicole's little girl was still clinging to her, and he stepped back to give them privacy. The little girl's arms were tight around her neck, and Nicole had her face against the small head.

'I'll wait in the kitchen,' he said quietly. Nicole lifted her head, and the expression on her face wrenched at his heart. It was full of joy, but tears were rolling down her cheeks. There was something going on here that he didn't understand.

Chapter 5

Nicole's legs trembled as she walked along the hall, holding tightly to Binnie's hand. The joy of hearing that little voice for the first time in over a year lightened her step and pushed away the immediate worry of potentially losing the house. Dane McDougal was a kind man, he had shown that in his concern for them already.

Maybe they could talk, *really* talk. Maybe he would understand.

He was standing at the window looking thoughtful as he stared out at the Gulf. The light was fading quickly as it did in the tropics and she flicked the light switch on.

'How about another cuppa?' she said brightly. 'My mum always said it was the cure for all ills.'

'Thank you. That would be good. Are you feeling okay now?' He walked across to the table and two chairs, and for the first time, Nicole looked at him as he pulled out the chair and sat.

Really looked.

He was a tall man with a rugged face, clean-shaven, but obviously overdue for a haircut. Mid-brown hair tipped with blond brushed his collar. Her eyes travelled down to broad shoulders; his hands were strong, and a flush of warmth travelled up her neck as she remembered being in his arms.

'Mummy?'

Nicole's smile was so wide it tugged at her cheeks. 'Yes, sweetheart.' She was still holding Binnie's hand.

'Can I have some juice, Mummy? Please.'

She let go of her little girl's hand, and her fingers caressed Binnie's hair before she crossed to the small camping fridge in the corner of the large room. 'You can have whatever you want today.

It's just a shame we're due for a shopping trip. We need to have a celebration tonight.'

Dane's hands were flat on the table as he leaned back in the chair. She was conscious of him watching her every move, but she felt comfortable in his presence. She had gradually gotten used to having another person inside the house with them. 'While I get our drinks, how about you show Mr McDougal your drawing.'

She smiled as Binnie walked purposefully around the table and gathered her precious colouring book. For a child her age—she would be five in February—she was already showing artistic talent passed down from Nicole. The back of each colouring page was filled with her little drawings.

Nicole's breath caught as Binnie spoke clearly. 'This is a cow, and this is a boat.'

Dane lowered his head and looked at each page. Nicole turned away, biting her lip to hold back the emotion and filled the kettle again. Once she had herself under control, she said, 'I'll just go out and get the tray.' She didn't want to tell him she had only two teacups. When they fled Melbourne, she left with only the clothes on their backs, some of her tools, her purse and Laura's car. After three weeks of driving as far away from Melbourne as she could get, they'd ended up in Normanton. Once they had found the house to live in and had paid the rent, Nicole had been very frugal with what was left. The tea set comprising a pot, two cups and the milk jug and sugar basin had been a one-dollar find at the op shop in town, along with a few other basic necessities the day they had passed through Normanton on the way to the house.

Listening to Binnie talk to Dane as she showed him her drawings were incredible. Maybe it was having someone else in the house that had unblocked whatever it was that had been holding her silent. Maybe it had been the shock of Nicole fainting, it was hard to guess, although she knew full well the cause of Binnie's silence. Goosebumps crept up Nicole's arms. She put the cups into the sink, rinsed them, and then emptied the tea leaves into the bucket.

As she turned to the window, she was taken aback by how dark it was. 'Where has the day gone? It's teatime, young lady.' She swallowed and looked at Dane, framing the question she didn't want to ask. 'Would you like to stay for dinner? I'm afraid we're having fish. You probably get sick of that.'

He hesitated for a moment, and then he smiled. 'Only if you will let me contribute. I have a fridge the same as yours'—he gestured to the camp fridge— 'in the back of the ute. 'More food in it than I'll eat in a couple of nights.'

'Where are—were—you going to stay tonight? We've really held you up here.'

'I was heading for Dinah's Camp, but if you don't mind, I'll drive up to the other end of the beach and camp out in my swag. It's a bit late to drive across the wetlands. I'd hate to go off the road into the soft ground.'

'You're most welcome to bunk out on the verandah tonight. I'm very grateful for your help today. More than you'll ever know,' she added quietly looking at the top of Binnie's head. 'Why don't you go and get whatever you want to heat up while I bath this little one, and cook her some eggs.'

'Mummy?'

Nicole fought the lump in her throat; she'd shed enough tears today to last a lifetime. 'Yes, sweetie,' she replied as Dane stood.

'We didn't get the eggs from the chicken pen today.'

'You have a chicken pen?' he asked. 'I didn't see it.'

'It's about a hundred metres through the bush. I built it up high on stilts, and we have a small veggie garden there, too. Just enough to keep us going between visits to Normanton. Along with the fish we catch, we're pretty self-sufficient here.'

He shook his head as he headed for the door. 'You are.'

Nicole stood staring at the door for a long time after it closed behind him.

##

Dane took his time at the ute to give Nicole time to bath Binnie. Before he'd come outside, he'd checked to make sure the colour had come back into her face, with no chance of her flaking out again. She'd jumped up suddenly; maybe it was lack of food that had caused her to faint. He frowned, trying to remember what they had been talking about when the colour had left her face. He'd asked her what impact it would have on his business if whoever she was hiding from turned up.

The look of fear that had crossed her face in that instant had stayed with him. It was clear she had good reason for hiding herself out in this wild country. Dane shook his head as he pulled out the slide under the camping fridge. It wasn't safe—a woman and a small child out here, no matter what they were hiding from.

What if there was an accident? Or if one of them got sick? Snake bite? What if Nicole cut herself while she was building chook pens or something? She could bleed to death and leave a small child out here alone.

He shook his head again, unable to believe the risk she was taking. He couldn't condone someone living out here like that now that he owned the place. It would be irresponsible.

There was no medical facility within a hundred kilometres. The odds of something happening out here were high. Plus, some rogue characters made their way to the Gulf and squatted in empty houses. Nicole had been lucky that he'd turned up and not someone with fewer scruples.

No, he couldn't allow her to stay here. Whatever her problem was, it wasn't any of his business. He'd do anything he could to help them move on, but he wouldn't sleep at night knowing there was a woman and a small child out here on a property he owned.

360

Dane turned his attention to the plastic containers in the small fridge. One was labelled "Curried Chicken" and the other "Beef Goulash". Knowing his mother, there would be enough in each to feed an army, let alone one woman. Hell, he'd pulled in fish that weighed more than she did.

He pulled out the gas bottle with the heating ring on top and tipped the beef into the small saucepan he used for his camp cooking. Once it was heating, he dragged the swag off the back of the ute and set it up away from the house, well away from the water. He wouldn't impose on them, and he didn't want to get too friendly. He'd turn the conversation to them moving out after they'd eaten, then he'd hit the sack and leave at first light tomorrow.

Damn. He frowned as he looked around. It was too dark to have a good look at the site now and think about where to position the lodge and the jetty. He'd have to stay for a while after sunrise in the morning. But once he'd sorted the tenancy situation out tonight, there'd be no need to see Nicole again tomorrow. He'd reimburse her the rent from the day of settlement and then follow it up with Foley back in Normanton.

He should have known the sale had gone too smoothly. Foley was the biggest scammer in the north.

The smell of aromatic herbs pulled him from his brooding, and he opened the packet of instant rice and stirred it in. After bringing the stew to the boil and letting it bubble for a couple of minutes, he turned the gas off, picked up the saucepan, and headed for the stairs. Nicole had switched on most of the lights, and that surprised him, but he guessed she thought if there was anywhere around tonight, he was here to deal with them.

He stared at the house. How the hell had she lived out here for over a year? If Binnie was going to be five, she'd have to go to school soon, so that was another persuasion he could use. A child that age needed stimulation from being with other kids.

Yeah, and you'd know, wouldn't you, he thought. Until Jenni and Jake's Leni had arrived a couple of years back, he'd had nothing to do with kids.

Ever.

The house looked less in need of renovation with the soft lights shining from the inside. It was a graceful old homestead, and he stood back and had a good look at it. The basic structure seemed good; the roof was rusty but maybe a coat of paint would fix that. It all depended if it leaked or not, but he could check those details with Nicole.

Before you evict her.

Dane took a deep breath and held the hot saucepan carefully as he crossed to the house yard and then climbed the steps. 'Dinner's ready,' he called out cheerfully as he tapped on the door with his free hand.

'It smells good.' The quiet voice came from a chair at the side of the verandah facing the water. He wondered how long she'd been sitting there watching him set up camp and cook.

'If you've got a couple of plates and two forks, we're set to go.'

Nicole reached behind her, and a light came on. The table where she was sitting had been laid with a plain white cloth. Dane smiled as he noticed the small jar filled with wildflowers in the centre. A plain glass carafe of cold water and two small glasses completed the setting.

'Very swish,' he said with a smile. 'I hope the food does it credit.'

'It smells good,' she said. 'Thanks for sharing your dinner. I hope it doesn't leave you hungry.'

'There's probably enough for leftovers tomorrow too.' He held the saucepan up. 'This is hot. Will I put it on the cloth?'

She laughed and shook her head. 'It's not a cloth; it's an old bed sheet. The table's old, and it's covered with paint and lumps of clay, so I covered it up.' As Nicole pushed her chair back it caught on a loose board and Dane reached over to grab it while juggling the hot saucepan. She reached out at the same time, and their fingers brushed. He caught the chair, but she pulled her hand back swiftly as though she'd been burned.

'I'll get a couple of bowls. Have a seat.' Her voice was quiet as she headed for the door.

Dane waited until Nicole entered the house and then he pulled out the chair opposite hers. Sitting there gave him a view along the verandah towards the back of the house. As far as he could see in the dim light, the floorboards were in good condition, and there was no obvious rot in the timber. The little paint that was left on the verandah posts was faded and flaking off. The vertical slats beneath the railings were bare of paint and had weathered down to bare wood. He looked out to the west; considering the weather would come howling in from the Gulf, the exterior condition of the house wasn't too bad.

He wondered what the interior was like. Craning forward in his chair, he could see through the open door of the room at the end of the verandah. With a frown, he stared at the equipment that filled the space.

It looked like some sort of workroom and he wondered whether the equipment was Nicole's or if it had been there when she took up the lease. If that was the case technically it would belong to him. More junk to clear out.

The door to the house opened with a creak and he turned around. It was hanging off one hinge, one of the things that needed immediate attention, if he was to be a landlord for the short time she'd be there.

'Is there anything else that needs fixing?' he asked as she walked back to the table. 'As your landlord, however temporary, I'm happy to see to that, and anything else I can fix with a few tools.'

'There's no need,' she said with a gentle smile. 'It's fine. I would've done it myself, but I haven't got any tools.'

'I'll sort it in the morning. Has Bobby Foley been up to check on the place while you've been here?'

'I told him there was no need.' She put her head down and fiddled with the cutlery.

Dane gestured with his head towards the end of the verandah. 'Is he using it for storage?'

'No, that's mine,' she said slowly. There was silence and then she continued. 'It's an excellent space for me to work. That's another reason why this house suits us very well.' Her chin came up and determination filled her eyes as she held his gaze. 'I can keep an eye on Binnie while she plays, and when she's asleep I'm still within hearing range.'

'What sort of work do you do?'

The tip of her tongue appeared between pink lips as she stared at him. Pale blue eyes surrounded by blonde lashes narrowed and a frown wrinkled her brow.

Dane waved his hand. 'Sorry, I'm probably asking too many questions. I don't mean to pry.'

'It's all right. I'm a potter. It's not a secret.'

He was getting used to the soft gentle tones of her voice. 'What sort of things do you make?'

'All sorts of different pieces. But mainly large commissions.' She shrugged ruefully. 'That's the only problem with being out here. It's a bit hard to get the heavier pieces to the post office and freight them down to the city. Not to mention expensive.'

'I guess there would be quite a few things that would be hard about living out here.' Dane was still having trouble coming to grips with the fact that Nicole and her little girl had lived out here for over a year. He'd seen many squatters and itinerants pass through in the years he'd worked on the waterways of the Gulf of

Carpentaria. It was hard not to pigeonhole them into a stereotype, but they were usually a bit rough around the edges and most had attitude. Men and women.

Nicole had a gentleness to her. He could imagine her in a fancy restaurant or a flash house in a big city, not that he'd had a lot to do with either of them. She held herself gracefully and her movements were slow and considered.

Class.

That was what she had; she oozed class.

Now her slight shrug was hard to define as she held his gaze in the dim light. 'I like it out here. It suits me very well.'

'Well, it's not the time to talk about that. Let's eat while it's hot and then we can talk business afterwards.'

'Let's.' Nicole nodded and reached for her fork. She lifted a forkful to her mouth and closed her eyes. 'This is absolutely delicious. You're a good cook.'

'Well, I could try and get brownie points, but I can't take the credit for cooking that stew, although I can barbeque a mean steak. As much as I hate to admit it, my mum cooked it for me.' To his surprise, heat ran up his neck and into his cheeks and he covered up his embarrassment with a chuckle. 'A bit like having my lunchbox packed.'

'You're very lucky,' she said. 'I don't have my parents anymore.'

She looked down at her meal and a wave of sympathy ran through Dane as she spoke quietly. 'Binnie is my only family these days,' she said quietly. 'That's why it doesn't matter that we live out here.'

'Well, I can think of several reasons why it does, but like I said we'll talk about it later. Let's not ruin the meal.' He picked up his fork and they ate quietly for a few moments.

Nicole reached for the carafe of water in the middle of the table and lifted her eyebrows at him as she held it up. He'd packed a couple of beers for the nights he was away but left them in the esky when he'd come over here. It just didn't seem right, fronting up with a beer in hand. It wasn't a social occasion.

'Yes, please,' he said.

'And don't worry,' she said with another one of those pretty smiles. 'I boil all the water out of the tank. The one time I climbed up and lifted the roof of the tank to check it, I was horrified.'

'Some wildlife?' He quirked an eyebrow as he kept his gaze on her face.

'Lots of wildlife! Luckily, we hadn't drunk any water before I checked. Now I always buy water when we go to town. But we've run out, so I am double boiling at the moment.'

'Do you shop in Normanton or Weipa?

'Normanton.'

'How often do you go to town?' he asked.

'About every eight weeks or so. Our food usually lasts that long and we've got pretty good at catching fish.' She looked past him towards the workroom. 'I've been trying to get some more work done to put in the Information Centre there, but I'll have to go to town before I get the last few finished. Supplies have run too low.' She turned her attention back to him and smiled, and his insides gave a funny little squirm. 'And thank you again for dinner. It's pretty good to be eating something apart from fish.'

'What sort do you catch?' he asked.

Nicole laughed, and the sweet sound rippled through the still evening air. The squirming in Dane's gut turned into a surge of warmth, as the happy expression stayed on her face. The wariness that had been there, to begin with, had disappeared, and she seemed more comfortable with him being there. He found it hard to look away from her.

'I don't know the name of them. We just eat the same sort all the time. I was careful the first time we ate it, and when it didn't make us sick, we kept eating them. That's one thing up here, there's plenty of fish to catch.'

'Have you ever had troubles with crocodiles at the shore?'

She nodded. 'I've seen them up the beach a few hundred metres away, but I've never seen any near the house, but I'm really careful. Binnie gave me an awful fright today, opening the door. She'd never done that before.'

'Where is she now?' Dane asked.

'She went to sleep as soon as she'd eaten.' Nicole lifted her head and her eyes gleamed brightly in the dim light. 'It's been a very big day for her. I'll tell you why later.' She raised the glass to her lips and sipped the water.

Neither spoke for a while and the silence lengthened; it was obvious that she was searching around for something to say. Dane waited her out. She was going to be upset when he told her she was going to have to move out.

So,' she said finally. 'Tell me about your business. All fishing?'

'Yes, we have a family business based down in Second Chance Bay. My oldest brother manages it. Matt looks after the accounts and the fishing co-op side of things. My sister, Jenni, and her partner, Jake, have brought in a couple of new boats, and my other brother Don and his partner, have an exclusive charter business up in the Kimberley.'

'Wow, it sounds like a very big concern. What do you do?'

'I'm a simple fisherman. I take the charters out.' Dane put his glass down. 'My father started with a single prawning boat back in the eighties, as well as starting up the fishing co-op where we still sell the prawns at the Bay. We all grew up surrounded by fish and prawns.' He chuckled. 'And would you believe Jenni, my sister, hates fish?'

'I can.' She laughed with him. 'I can truly sympathise with that after only a year of living on it.'

367

'It's only been the last two or three years that we've diversified, and all of a sudden everybody seems to have their part of the business, so I decided it was time for me to find my own.' He gestured around. 'So, I bought this. I'm building a fishing lodge here. I'll be working with Jake and Jenni and bringing their charters here. But we'll talk about that later. You know all about me, so now tell me a little bit about you.'

Her face closed, and her lips set. 'There is nothing to tell,' she said. 'Binnie and I are living here. We are quite happy and I'm doing my pottery. End of story.'

Dane let that one go; he knew he'd overstepped the mark with his direct question.

'I have some fresh figs inside and I made some custard for Binnie's dinner if you'd like some dessert.'

'That sounds great, thank you. Can I help you clear the table?'

'No. You stay there. I'll take them in.' Nicole picked up the two empty bowls and the cutlery and walked inside. She was very finely built and if he was reading between the lines right, she was thin from not eating enough. There was not a lot of money to spare.

He was going to find out why she was here; if he was to have any chance of convincing her to move, he needed to know what she was so scared of. Surely there were authorities to deal with this sort of thing, and refuges where they could be safe before women and children started a new life.

Hell, how could he suggest ways of helping Nicole when he knew so little about what services were available? One thing he did know after only a few hours; he wanted to help her, but he felt useless. His life revolved around boats and fishing. His awareness of social services was limited to what he'd seen on the television news.

Dane's thoughts whirred away, and he shrugged. His mother always told him he got too involved in caring about others. He'd always been the one who'd brought home the stray kittens and dogs, not to mention the new kids who'd turned up at school and had no friends.

So, he cared about the underdog. There was nothing wrong with that. People might think he was too interested in others' lives but that's the way he was, and it wasn't just curiosity.

The door opened, and Nicole walked out carefully holding a small chopping board covered with fresh figs. He jumped up and took it from her.

'Thank you. I'll just go and get the bowls and the custard.'

It was only a few seconds before she was out again. Her smile was wide as she sat down opposite him again. Dane got the impression that she was trying to be much more social too.

'Thanks again for the meal,' she said brightly. 'It was very tasty. You'll have to tell your mother what a good cook she is.

'Don't worry about that,' he said with a smile. 'Mum cooks at the local pub at Second Chance Bay and the nights that she's on, all the locals come out for dinner. Perhaps next time you come down to Normanton you could come up to the Bay.'

He sensed her withdrawal immediately.

'We go straight down and come straight back,' she said. There was silence again and this time it lasted longer. Eventually, Nicole passed him a bowl and gestured to the fruit and the custard.

'Thank you.'

They ate in silence, broken only by the clinking of the spoons on the bowls. When he'd finished, Dane pushed his plate to the centre of the table. 'Would you like me to help you wash up before we talk business?'

She lifted her head and stared at him. 'No, let's talk business now. I'll clean up after you go.'

Chapter 6

'Okay,' Dane said as she held his gaze steadily. 'I guess we need to talk about how long it will be before you can move out.'

Nicole swallowed and tried to stay calm. Their safety and their future depended on the outcome of this conversation; she had to convince him. 'I've paid rent and I have a lease.' She tried to keep her gaze steely, but her voice wavered.

'And *I* own the property and I have plans for it.' Despite his words, Dane's tone was conversational and held no threat. 'I'll do everything I can to help you find somewhere else,' he said kindly.

Nicole looked at him and she put her hands on the table with her palms facing up. She had to convince him to let them stay here. 'It's a very difficult situation for me. The bottom line is I can't afford to move. I have no money and until I get paid for the commission that I'm working on now, I simply can't move.'

'I'll go and see Bobby Foley and get your rent refunded. How would that be?'

'That would be a maybe. A very slight one,' she said slowly. 'But I'd rather stay here, for quite a few reasons. Surely I have some legal right if I've paid rent in advance and have a lease?'

'How long did you say you paid rent in advance?'

'Three years.'

'Wasn't that risky, giving him so much money? What if your plans changed?'

Her voice was bitter. 'Oh, there's no worry of that happening.'

'And how long have you been here already?'

'We've been here a year, so I'd need to be refunded two years before I could even consider moving.'

'I'll go and see him, and I'll get your two years' rent back.'

She nodded. 'That's fair. And then you keep it and I can stay here.'

'No, I'll give it back to you and you can move. I know a couple of rentals down at the Bay.'

Nicole shook her head. 'We won't be moving to a town.'

'Second Chance Bay is barely a town,' he said.

'No.' Her voice was fierce, and she saw the surprise flare in his eyes. 'Read my lips. We will *not* be moving.'

Dane leaned forward in his chair, and for a moment she thought he was going to reach out to her, but he ended up clasping his hands on the table. 'Okay. Let's be truthful here. If you want me to consider your reason for staying, you have to tell me why.'

She squeezed her eyes shut and shook her head. 'I can't talk about it.' Nicole was physically incapable of recounting "it". 'All I can tell you is that if we move there's a chance that our location will get out. Nobody can know that we're here. Nobody.' As much as she tried, she couldn't stop the trembling despair that broke her voice. She leaned forward and held her head between hands that wouldn't stop shaking. 'I don't want to talk about it. Please don't make me think about it.' She couldn't look at him. Her vision was starting to go silver at the edges.

'Oh no, you don't. Don't you go fainting on me again.' Gentle hands pressed the back of her neck and pushed her head down between her knees. A wave of nausea rose from her stomach, and she gagged.

'It's okay.' His voice was soft and gentle, and she took a deep shuddering breath as the urge to vomit passed. Her arms and legs were shaking, and despite the heat of the night, goosebumps pimpled her skin.

***

Nicole's reaction to his questioning left Dane startled. He knew her distress was genuine, and she wasn't putting it on.

'It's okay. Ssh.' He tried to soothe her by rubbing her back and the feel of her sharp shoulder blades beneath his hand was depressing. 'I won't make you do anything that puts you in danger. I promise. Please calm down. Okay?' He kept his voice low and even.

Gradually her trembling stopped, and she lifted her face. She was close enough that her breath warmed his cheek. He opened his arms as Nicole sat up straighter and she leaned into them. Her head fell onto his shoulder, and her deep shuddering breaths filled the quiet.

'Today was the first time Binnie spoke since it happened. It's the first time I've heard her little voice in twelve months.'

'It's okay, Nicole.' He pressed her head against his shoulder, wondering what had happened with Binnie, but reluctant to ask. 'You're safe.'

'That's how bad it was.' Another shuddering breath. 'He'll kill us if he knows where we are.'

'No one knows you're here. You're safe. I won't let anyone hurt you. Or Binnie.'

He felt her relax in his arms slightly.

'Thank you. It's the first time anyone has cared.' She shook her head and her hair brushed against his face. 'But not because they didn't care, because nobody knew.' The last word was a whisper.

'You look exhausted. Go inside and freshen up, and I'll make you a hot drink. And then I think you should go and get some sleep.' He kept his voice gentle. 'When you're in bed, I'll go down and get my swag and I'm going to sleep on the verandah. Is that okay?'

She nodded. 'Thank you.'

##

373

Dane woke with a start as the early morning bird song filled the air the next morning. Bits was still asleep snuggled up against his back. He had stayed awake most of the night, listening for any sound inside, but once Nicole had gone into the bedroom carrying the cup of tea he'd made, all had been quiet. He'd finally drifted off after four a.m.

He sat up and rubbed his hand over his chin. A shave and a shower were needed, but that would have to wait until he got home. Unzipping the swag, he climbed out. The pup followed him and ran down the stairs to the grass.

'Good boy.' He crossed to the edge of the verandah and gripped the railing, grimacing as the timber crumbled beneath his hand.

Hmm. What he'd feared

But that was the least of his worries this morning. He had to figure out what to do with Nicole, the tenant who looked like she had to stay in his house until her situation was sorted.

The door opened, and he swung around. Nicole stood there. She wore a pair of jeans, a close-fitting white T-shirt and a mutinous look on her face. 'What time are you leaving?'

He drew himself up to his full height and stretched. His T-shirt rode up his front and he tugged it down. Her gaze followed it and for a moment the determined look on her face wavered.

'Leaving?' he said. 'If you'll let me have a quick look inside the house, I'll be on my way.' He couldn't help himself. 'As long as you're okay for me to go?'

'Of course.' Her voice was clipped. 'I'm fine. We're fine. Just forget all that last night. I'm embarrassed. I lost control and it won't happen again.' She folded her arms across her chest. 'Give me five minutes and I'll take Binnie down to feed the chickens. You can have a look around while we're gone.'

Before he could reply, she turned, disappeared through the doorway and the door closed in his face.

Dane ran his hand through his hair. *Well, that went well*, he thought.

He rolled up his swag, pulled his boots on and took it back to the ute. The only thing he didn't have was the camp saucepan; he'd collect that when he had a look in the house.

He grimaced again; it felt a bit intrusive, looking through the house while Nicole wasn't there. Shaking his head, he talked sense to himself.

It's your house, and you still need to sort out this situation. Just because you have an unexpected tenant you don't want—even if she has a past that's damaged her—you've still got the lodge and the loan to consider.

He heard a door close as he loaded the ute and looked up.

Nicole and Binnie were heading along the shoreline to a small stand of trees.

With another shrug, he called to Bits and walked back up the stairs.

Chapter 7

Binnie was playing quietly on the verandah with a lump of clay that Nicole had taken from her workroom. She was sitting there making a small puppy, talking quietly as she played. Now that Binnie had spoken, it seemed that the dam had broken, and she'd been chatting to Nicole nonstop since they'd woken up this morning. It was the one thing that was helping Nicole to stay calm.

When they'd come back from the chook pen, Dane had been waiting on the verandah, the small pup in his large hands.

'Thank you. I've had a good look through. The house needs some work, but I don't think it's too bad. Thank you for letting me take a look.'

'Not a problem. It's your place, after all.' Her tone had been bland, and he'd shot her a curious look.

'I'll hit the road now,' he said.

'I'll just get your food container,' she said. He gave her another strange look and she wondered why. When she came back from the kitchen, he'd gone down the stairs and was waiting by the ute.

No matter what he said, she wasn't leaving. It was bad enough having to go into Normanton every couple of months. The problem was he owned the house.

How many years would they have to hide? How the hell could she spend the rest of her life like this?

There was only one answer. Until Bruno Spagnolo stopped looking for them. And she knew that would be never.

Nicole sighed as she walked down the stairs to say goodbye to Dane.

'Binnie, do you want to pat Bits before we go?' he'd asked with a smile that Nicole tried to ignore. Not only was Dane a kind and decent man, he was also handsome, and when he smiled his face lit up. She wouldn't let her gaze linger on his strong shoulders and long legs.

Binnie ran happily down the stairs, with a loud, 'Oh, yes please!'

Nicole waited on the small landing where the stairway split into two and watched carefully. One thing that she had been worried about—and had watched for carefully each time they went into town—had been Binnie's response to men, but it appeared there was no problem. She waved goodbye to Dane and asked him to bring Bits back for another visit.

Maybe she'd blocked the memories as Nicole had tried so hard to do.

Unsuccessfully.

Nicole sometimes thought she needed to go to counselling, but that would open up a whole legal minefield. Because she'd never reported what she and Binnie had witnessed, she was probably liable in some way. Grief clogged her throat and she cursed Dane McDougal for visiting and putting her in this position. For bringing those memories to the surface again.

Binnie held the little pup to her chest and buried her face in the soft dark fur. 'Goodbye, little puppy,' she said quietly. Tears pricked at Nicole's eyes.

What was Binnie missing out on, being out here in the sticks by themselves?

Maybe it would just be easier, and better for them both, to pack up and go before Dane came back. Nicole bit her lip.

It would be if she had money. Plus, there was no way of moving the equipment that she'd gradually got into her workroom over the past year. She had to be strong and get through this. She'd survived before and found them a place to live. Until Binnie was due to go to school she'd hoped they could stay here.

That in itself was going to be a problem when birth certificates and legal documents were needed for enrolment. But that was a few months away; she'd cross that bridge when they came to it. Until then they would've been right if the house hadn't been sold.

She drew herself straight as the last whirls of dust blew away from the road and the sound of the ute disappeared. She'd nodded to him when he'd said goodbye and the concern in his eyes had almost weakened her resolve to be distant this morning.

Embarrassment flooded her at the thought of how she'd lost it last night. The memories had taken over and for a while, she thought she couldn't bear it. Being held in Dane's arms had provided a safe sanctuary she hadn't wanted to leave.

His warmth, his manly smell, and his strong arms, not to mention his kindness, had made being in his hold a very attractive place to be, but Nicole had forced herself to move away. Dane McDougal probably thought he'd arrived at the crazy house.

After she'd disappeared into her room with the cup of tea he'd made for her last night, she'd lain there for hours reliving the memories. Strangely it had strengthened her and when she'd woken up this morning it had been easy to remain distant and formal. Dane had obviously sensed her withdrawal, but he'd been kind as he'd said goodbye.

'I'll go and see Bobby Foley on the way back to the Bay,' he'd said. 'And I'll be in touch.' He hadn't said how that communication would occur; Nicole knew he'd have to come back but she pushed away the anticipation of seeing him again. 'We'll talk soon.'

With a nod, she waved one hand as he opened the car door and put the pup inside. She couldn't afford to get close to anyone. There was danger down the path. Her knuckles were white as she grabbed the timber railing; there was only one thing she could do.

She had to get to work and make as many pieces as she could and get some more money together.

'Come on Binnie, we'll boil a couple of those eggs for breakfast.' Nicole waited until Binnie put the clay in the sun to bake and smothered a smile as she saw the three-legged dog. Once the eggs were on the stove she crossed to the workshop and picked up her purse.

She pulled out her business Mastercard and stared at it. There were ten thousand dollars in that account and the card had three months left on it before it expired.

The problem was, Bruno would be watching the transactions on her cards.

With a determined shake of her head, she held the card, ready to put it into the back of her purse. As she held it, she stared at the name on the card.

Nicoletta Spagnolo. That Nicole had never legally existed, but with his connections, Bruno had been able to get a card in the name he had given her.

Who was she these days?

Nicole Curtis, the woman hiding in her outback haven?

Nicoletta Spagnolo, the well-known potter?

Or the woman she was: Nicole Smyth—her birth name. The woman she'd lost sight of over the past three years, since that fateful day that her sister had met Bruno.

The day that their lives had changed forever.

The meeting that had resulted in the loss of her sister's life.

***

In the end, Dane didn't travel any further. He didn't go to Dinah's camp as he'd intended, and he didn't head to the small settlement of Kowanyama. His research trip had been hijacked, although he had scoped out the land and the house, and he knew it was suitable for the lodge he intended to build. Instead of visiting the two settlements that were easily accessible from the house on the coast, he was keen to get back and see Bobby Foley and sort out this rent situation. He should have known there'd be some sort of complication, dealing with that scammer. The locals said he'd rip off his own family if there was a quid to be had. Although that was the oldies in town who said that; Dane doubted that many of the young ones would even know what a quid was. He'd front Foley first, and if he had no joy there, maybe he'd go back to see the solicitor before heading to the Bay.

Nicole had been distant this morning, but he could understand why. It hadn't bothered him. Beneath her terse and quiet exterior, he'd sensed she was embarrassed about opening up to him, and even more so for collapsing into his arms last night. Even though she hadn't told him exactly what the problem was, the depth of her fear and distress was obvious. She'd opened up his protective streak and his money was on domestic violence; Dane couldn't understand how a man could hurt or threaten a woman and a young child.

He could just hear Mum now.

Another stray, Dane? But after he went back to the Bay, when he'd sorted out Foley, he was going to sit and have a good talk to Mum. Her advice was always spot on, and hopefully, she'd have some ideas, because he had none. The situation had to be dealt with, but sensitively. Nicole had said that Binnie hadn't talked for a year. What the hell were they hiding from?

He could still feel Nicole's slight body in his arms and remember the fresh soapy fragrance of her hair as she put her head on his shoulder. As he'd held her close he knew that he'd given her some measure of comfort, and by God, she'd needed it.

How could he possibly leave a woman and a young child out there on his property? But short of packing her up and taking her to town, he couldn't force her to leave and come to town with him. There were a few empty houses at the Bay; as the original settlers had aged and moved on few young people wanted to live on the side of a river where their house was only accessible by boat.

He frowned; not being able to afford the move didn't matter. The rents were cheap, and he could help her move. It was the fear that gripped Nicole when he'd discussed her moving that was the impediment.

Dane was itching to get his hands on Bobby Foley and he'd be threatening him with all sorts of breaches of tenancy law if he didn't refund her rent.

The road condition deteriorated as the corrugations deepened and he turned his attention to his driving. Frustration niggled as he had to slow his speed; he was keen to get back home and make a plan. He hit the audio button on the dashboard and waited for the music to distract him. None of it took his attention from the problem that was pressing on him, and he hadn't even thought about the house or the lodge. All he could think about was a beautiful sad woman who had touched his soul.

Chapter 8

Bobby Foley lived on the other side of Normanton, and Dane detoured around the town and turned into the old place where the Foleys had lived for the past twenty years. Rusted car bodies, overturned boats, tattered prawn nets and empty fishing crates littered the front yard, the long grass growing through the various rubbish.

Foley had had a go at everything over the years, from prawns to charter fishing, to selling real estate. It appeared his latest moneymaking scheme was being a landlord.

Dane slammed the door of the ute after he made sure that the window was down for fresh air for Bits who was asleep on the front seat. He stepped through the bits of rubbish, ran up the steps and pounded on the front door.

'Foley! Are you home?' he yelled as he pounded a second time.

Quiet. Silence. No movement.

Not even one of the dozen or more dogs that usually lounged around the yard were there to bark at him. Dane knocked again but there was still no answer. Finally, he gave up and walked back to the ute. As he opened the door a car backed out of the garage next door.

Old Harold Johnson stuck his head out of the car window. 'Foley's gone, mate.'

'What do you mean gone?' Dane walked over to the fence.

'He left town in a hurry last weekend.' The old man chuckled. 'I'm betting Bobby overstepped the mark just one too many times. There were a couple of big brawny blokes here looking for him after he left on Saturday.'

'Damn.' Dane stared at the house. 'Thanks, Harold.'

'The local cops are looking for him too, so I don't think he'll be back in a hurry. I hope he doesn't owe you money because you won't ever see it again.'

'No, nothing major, just one of his usual scams. Thanks, mate.' Dane lifted his hand and waved as he walked back to the ute.

He drove through Normanton looking at it through different eyes, wondering what it would be like to be Nicole, being in a tiny town and scared of being seen. She'd be much safer over at Second Chance Bay.

He drove past the Purple Pub and the replica of the world's largest recorded crocodile. Killed by a single shot in Normanton in the 1950s, the creature's nickname was Krys and measured in at more than eight-and-a-half-metres. A ripple of fear ran through Dane; all he could see was Nicole standing on the shore fishing as a croc lurked in the shallows. Or Binnie playing in the yard as one spotted her with dark beady eyes.

He thumped the steering wheel in frustration and Bits looked up at him and whimpered.

'Sorry, pup. We'll be home soon.'

The trip back to the coast was quick and he pulled up at the pub in less than an hour, hoping that it was a day for his mother to be there.

The chances of talking Nicole into moving to town were zero. 'Bloody hell,' he muttered. 'What are we going to do, Bits?' Mum's car was in the carpark around the back of the building, so he gathered Bits under his arm and headed for the back door of the pub.

'At least we'll both get a good lunch.'

***

After Binnie had eaten her breakfast, Nicole tidied up the kitchen. She'd gaped when she'd opened the camp fridge and seen

384

the food containers stacked inside. For a moment she smiled; Dane McDougal was a kind man. But then, common sense kicked in; he wanted something from her.

'Come on, Binnie, you can play on the veranda. 'I've got some work to do, and then we'll have to go to town in a few days.'

Thanks to Dane's kind food donation, they could put the trip off and she would have enough time to finish the pieces for the gift shop.

But Dane being kind to her didn't mean she was going to trust him.

As well as being a kind man at first, Bruno Spagnolo had been charismatic. Laura had fallen under his spell and married him after a whirlwind three weeks. Nicole suspected that Bruno being happy to take two-year-old Binnie on too was the catalyst for her single-mother sister to fall in love with the older man.

But Nicole knew she was as much to blame as Laura. Bruno's charisma and his interest in her work, and his conviction that he could launch her on the Melbourne art scene, had sucked Nicole in too.

Even when he'd suggested—firmly—that she take Spagnolo as her artistic name—because of the connection he'd said— he had been so persuasive that she and Laura hadn't seen a problem with it. The only thing she drew the line at—much to his displeasure—was refusing to move into the nineteenth-century Italian Renaissance mansion he owned at Malvern.

'But, *Bella,* ' he'd argued, 'there are fifteen bedrooms and you will have your own wing. I will set up a studio for you. You will be company for my Laura and our Binnie'—Nicole had blinked at that— 'when I am away on business.' Bruno was always overseas on business although the nature of his business was a mystery to Laura.

It had taken over a year for the truth to begin to surface; strange comments overheard by Laura from some of the businessmen who Bruno hosted in their home raised suspicions. The gradual isolation of Laura and Binnie from their friends and their old life always had a logical reason given by Bruno.

His possessiveness of Nicole, as his protégée, became overwhelming, and the day that a very distressed Laura had called her to come over was the same day that Nicole had decided to go back to her name and break ties with her overbearing brother-in-law. But it had been a year since Nicoletta Spagnolo had hit the Melbourne art scene. Galleries, exhibitions and invitations into the closed ranks of the art world. She had decided to go back to using her name and had planned to tell Bruno that night.

If only they'd seen the truth earlier, she thought ruefully as she lifted her hands off the wet clay. She stood there and watched the wheel go around and was surprised when a tear plopped on the table.

If they hadn't been so naïve, Laura would still be alive, and Nicole wouldn't be in hiding, fearing for her life and that of her niece. She wiped a hand covered with wet clay over her face. There was no point dwelling on what might have been.

She'd done her best, and they had to look forward to the future.

There was work to be done. She switched the kiln on to heat and tried to focus on the day ahead.

##

Three days passed, and Nicole knew she couldn't put the trip to town off any longer.

The food Dane had left had been delicious and much appreciated. Although seeing Binnie's excitement at homemade biscuits and cake had been depressing. Nicole realised what a plain diet they had survived on over the past year. They couldn't live on eggs and fish for the rest of the week, plus they were down to the last carton of milk. She worried about using the tank water for Binnie even though she boiled it twice.

If the water was off…

That's the last thing I need. Her greatest fear was that *she* would get sick and that Binnie would be left here alone. No one would ever know; it was a horrifying thought that made Nicole's blood run cold. There wasn't even phone service for her to call for help. At least Dane McDougall knew they were living out here and now that made two: Mr Foley and Dane McDougall. *At least that was someone,* she thought. When she got a bit more money together she'd get one of those satellite cases that gave you phone service out in the wilderness. At the moment food was the priority, with nothing spare for luxuries.

'Come on, Bin, we're going to go to the shops today,' she said early on Friday morning.

Binnie jumped up and down with excitement. 'Can I get a new toy, Mummy? Can we go to the library?'

Guilt flooded thought Nicole. Binnie had missed out—and was still missing out—on the normal things that a small child should experience each day. Could she have handled this situation better? Should she have gone to the police?

No. Fleeing had been the only solution. Some of Bruno's "acquaintances" had been policemen. Others had been thugs and even worse, she knew that some of them had been criminals. To this day, she couldn't understand the attraction that Bruno had held for her and Laura.

'Can I find someone to play with in the town, Mummy?'

Even Binnie calling her Mummy made Nicole guilty. She'd figured it was safer when they were travelling if anyone they encountered thought that they were mother and daughter.

The biggest guilt trip of all was that she had never asked Binnie if she remembered what had happened. The longer she left it, the more Laura became a memory and one that she wasn't sharing with Binnie.

Surprisingly, Binnie had had no nightmares, and she had never mentioned the day they had left Laura at the mansion. It was as though Binnie had blocked out the memory, and if that made her happy, that was the best way to handle it. It was better than the alternative: that she remembered what they left behind them that afternoon. It was only the lack of speech that had been an indicator that she did have memories.

Since she had started talking five days ago, she hadn't stopped. It was as though the little girl was trying to make up for those lost months. Nicole jumped when Binnie tugged at her T-shirt.

'Can we go and visit Bits, the puppy, too?' she said softly. Nicole was amazed each day by Binnie's fluency and comprehension.

'Not this visit, but we might get you some new pencils and a colouring book.'

'And a toy dog for me to cuddle?'

'I think we could manage that. Come on, we'll go and pack the car, and then you can put your pretty dress on.'

Nicole sighed. That was something else to put on the list today; a trip to the op shop. Binnie was growing fast and needed new clothes. They had a lot to do, and it would be late by the time they got back.

Maybe, if they were quick, she should go up to Second Chance Bay to the fish co-op and see if she could see Dane. Maybe they *could* look at the houses there that he'd talked about. She didn't know if he actually worked there, or maybe was out on the boat. It wasn't worth the risk of driving all the way, and him not being there. She suspected that it was a fair drive up to the Bay from Normanton, and she couldn't afford to waste the fuel. Or spare the time.

Why did she want to see him anyway?

Because he was good to you, her conscience chimed in. *The least you can do is visit and say that you're okay and thank him for being so kind.*

No, they wouldn't be doing that, she said to herself.

Wait and see until you get there. Maybe. You'll get a good amount for the pottery bowls.

No!

The one thing that Nicole wouldn't admit to herself was that she couldn't forget being in his arms.

It took almost an hour to load the car. Nicole had carefully wrapped all the blue bowls with the swirl of water in the glaze in bubble wrap that she'd saved from the last trip. The woman at the Tourist Information Centre in Normanton had said that the bowls had been very popular and that they would take as many as she could supply. The tourists loved them as they just had a small "Normanton, North Queensland" etched on the side of the swirl in fine print.

She had three dozen made so that should pay enough to let them do a good grocery shop and buy some things at the op shop. Hopefully, they might have a little toy dog and some coloured pencils there. Every dollar saved meant they could buy more food and stay away from town longer. Nicole glanced down at her purse wondering if she should risk using the card and draw some money out. Maybe just before Binnie went to school they could go somewhere far away from here and use an ATM, but anywhere in Queensland was too close to where they were. She didn't want Bruno Spagnolo to have any idea that she was in the north of the country.

If she knew somebody who lived in Western Australia or Tasmania she could post the card and get them to draw some money out and post it to her. She did have an old friend in Perth and her address was still in her purse. She shook her head.

It wasn't worth the risk.

'Come on, Bin, get your shoes on. We're going to town, sweetheart.'

Chapter 9

'Hi, Mum.' Dane leaned over and kissed his mother's cheek as he walked into the large commercial kitchen at the back of the pub on the point at Second Chance Bay. 'Rick working?'

'He went to help Donny with the boats for a while. He'll be back about ten. Jake said you went straight out on a late-booked charter as soon as you got back the other day. We weren't sure when you'd be back.' Helen crossed to the cool room and pulled out three heads of lettuce. 'Be a love and wash your hands and break these up for me. I'm running late with Rick gone. Then you can tell me all about your new place.'

'I haven't had a chance to get my head around what's happened, with Jake grabbing me as soon as I hit town.' Dane crossed to the sink and scrubbed his hands with the anti-bacterial wash. 'Yeah, there's a lot to tell.'

'Oh, no, don't tell me it was no good? I was worried about you buying it from Bobby; he's been no good since primary school. He used to steal our lollies way back then.'

Dane chuckled as he reached down to the stainless shell shelf for a colander, put the lettuce in and then turned the tap on. He leaned back against the workbench and folded his arms as his mother sliced tomatoes. 'Actually, the house is surprisingly good. There's just a slight complication.'

'What's wrong? Is it going to cost more than you thought to get it going?'

'No, the business side of things is all good. It's going to be a perfect location for a lodge. Have you ever been that far north, Mum?' He reached over and picked up a cherry tomato and popped it into his mouth.

Helen slapped his hand away as Dane reached for another tomato. 'Those lettuce are ready for your attention now. And no, I haven't been up there. So, what's the problem?'

Dane began to break the lettuce into leaves and put them into the bowl Helen had placed beside him. 'It's a beautiful old house, and I think with a bit of attention it could be a feature of the lodge. An old Queenslander in surprisingly good nick.'

He stared across at the large window that framed a view of the Gulf to the north. When Nicole had taken Binnie away from the house the day he'd left, he'd had a good look through, but it had been hard to focus on the things that he should have looked at. The more he'd walked through the rooms, the more he'd realised how tough they were doing it. It was like a monastery. The rooms were empty, apart from the two mattresses, the suitcases and the boxes he'd noticed when he'd carried Nicole into the bedroom. In the kitchen, there were two bowls, one frypan, and a small saucepan. He'd opened the cupboards to see if there was any water leaking in the kitchen, and they had all been empty. A plastic crate held a small amount of food and long-life milk, and he frowned.

Before he'd looked at the rest of the house he'd hurried out to the ute, taken everything he had out of his portable fridge and brought it inside. A strange feeling had lodged in his throat as he opened the fridge and filled it with the food. It had been almost empty.

Not sympathy, but more concern for the dire situation that Nicole and Binnie were living in and had been for more than a year.

'Dane?' Mum was staring at him with a frown on her face. 'What's wrong, love? You look worried.'

'I am,' he said. 'Someone is living in the house.'

'What? Bobby didn't own it?'

'Oh, yes, it was his to sell and now it's mine. There's no problem there. He just "forgot" to mention there was a tenant.'

'They'll have to move on then.' Helen picked up the knife and sliced the cucumbers at a speed that fascinated Dane.

He watched for a moment and then turned his attention back to the lettuce. 'It's not going to be that easy, Mum. It's a woman with a young child, and it broke my heart. They have very little food and no money, but she refuses to move. She said she has a lease for almost another two years.

'Easy fixed. Bobby Foley will have to reimburse her rent and she'll have to move on.'

'That's the logical solution, but there are complications.'

Mum shook her head. 'Isn't there always with some of the people who come up here?'

'I think Nicole and her little girl are hiding from her husband. She was terrified when I said she'd have to leave. She was so upset when I asked her what had happened, that she fainted.'

'Another stray for you to collect, son?' Helen walked over and put her hand on his shoulder. 'Did she tell you what happened?'

'No, she was very private, and I sensed when I left that she regretted telling me the little that she did.'

'You can't take it all on board, you know. There's many out there who need help.'

'I know, Mum. But I can't stop thinking about her.'

'The Dustan place is empty. She could move in there.'

'I suggested that, but she's adamant about not coming into a town. She's seriously frightened.'

'If it's that bad, surely the police could be involved? An AVO?'

'I don't know. She's got to come into town for supplies soon—although I left all the food I had for them—and I'll try and catch her then.' He put the last of the lettuce leaves in the bowl. 'She does pottery and she sells her pieces in Normanton. I saw

393

some of her work when I was looking through the house. Dark blue pieces with a water pattern in them. She's very good.'

Helen looked at Dane for a moment and then crossed to the big cupboard where the plates and bowls were kept. She opened the door and pulled out a bowl.

Dane's eyes widened. 'That's one of Nicole's.'

'I bought a set last week when I was in Normanton. I use these for the individual salad. I'd like to meet her. I've asked Jill to see her about a set of speciality plates. Nicole Curtis, Jill at the shop said her name was.'

'That's her.'

'So, what are you thinking about doing?'

Dane ran his hand along the back of his neck. 'I don't know. It's hard. I'm keen to get work started there, but I also don't want to evict her. One thing she'd done there is set up a workroom with her equipment. But the other problem is the little girl. She's almost five and she'll have to go to school soon.'

'You need to go and see Bobby Foley and get her rent back.'

Dane huffed. 'Yeah, I tried that. He's left town.'

'Again,' Helen said dryly. 'He'll be back.'

'Yeah, maybe so, but that doesn't solve my problem.'

'I'd like to place a large order for here. I'm refurbishing the restaurant.'

'That's great. It would sure help Nicole money-wise.'

'I wouldn't be doing it out of charity, she's a very talented young lady. I remember seeing similar work at an exhibition in Melbourne when Rick and I were travelling, but I can't remember the potter's name.'

'Melbourne? I wonder?' Dane mused.

'Do you think it would help if I came with you next time and spoke to her? Reassured her and gave her some options?'

Dane shrugged. 'It's worth a try, I guess.'

'Okay, let me know when you're going up next and I'll roster myself off for a couple of days.'

Dane moved around the bench and hugged Helen. 'You know what, Mum?' he said with a smile. 'I think I know where I got my "looking after strays" habit from.'

'Get away with you, son.'

Dane picked up another tomato and popped it into his mouth as he left to go back to the co-op. He wanted to pick Matt's accountancy brains.

***

There hadn't been much rain since the last time they'd been to Normanton and the road was dry the whole way. The corrugations weren't too bad and there was no traffic on the track from the coast to the main road that joined Weipa and Normanton. Once they turned off the track onto the main road, Nicole's nerves kicked in. They were out in the world now, passing other cars and heading to a town of over one thousand residents. Still small, but there was always the possibility of seeing someone she knew.

And being recognised.

The main road was in worse condition than the track because of the constant traffic and trucks that chewed the road up. She glanced into the back seat of the Subaru to make sure that the box of pottery was strapped in securely. She smiled as she turned back to the road. Binnie was fast asleep, clutching the one tatty soft toy she owned.

The town was quiet and there was a space outside the Tourist Information Centre. Nicole parked and sat in the car for a few minutes getting her courage up. She looked up and down the street, but there was only an elderly couple walking away from where she'd parked. With a deep breath, she reached over and shook Binnie gently.

395

'We're here, sweetheart.'

Binnie waited on the footpath while Nicole carefully lifted the box out. She held on to the edge of Nicole's T-shirt as they walked into the building

'Oh, hello.' The woman greeted them. 'I was hoping you'd come back soon. I have some news for you.' Her smile was wide, but Nicole looked around nervously as she placed the box on the counter.

'News?' she asked hesitantly.

'Yes, not only have we sold out of your bowls, I have an order for you too.'

'Oh, thank you. Jill, isn't it?'

'Yes, Jill. That's me. Anyway, the manager at the pub at Second Chance Bay wants to order a set of speciality plates. If you're ever up that way, you could call in. I reckon you'd get a big order if Helen could meet with you. She's after a range with a fish on the plates.'

'Oh, that does sound interesting.'

'Can you do it? I can tell Helen, or if you could go and see her, I'd say it would be worth the drive.'

Nicole bit her lip. 'Actually, I'd already thought about going up there today. I have a …friend …up that way.'

'Where do you live?' Jill lifted the box off the counter and took out one of the wrapped bowls.

Nicole waved her hand casually. 'Oh, we move around a bit. At the moment, we're just visiting. We've moved down near Cloncurry, but we won't be there long.' She hated telling lies, but no one—apart from her previous and current landlord—knew where they lived.

'Must be hard to do your work, moving around.' Jill smiled as she unwrapped the bowl. 'Oh, Nicole, these are even prettier than the last ones.'

'Thank you. I was pleased with them too.'

'And the good news is, we put the prices up a little bit, so I can pay you a bit extra for both consignments.'

Nicole couldn't help her smile; the day was shaping up well.

'That's so kind of you.'

'We're a "not-for-profit" organisation. And we volunteer here at the centre. I'm pleased I was on today when you came in.'

'Is there a grocery store up at Second Chance Bay?' Nicole asked. She could do the shopping there and drive straight home after seeing the manager.

'Not in the Bay itself, but there is one at Karumba on the way in. It's a couple of kilometres from Second Chance Bay on this side of the river. Sometimes I go up there to shop myself. The fresh fruit and veggies come in on the boats at the wharf, and the groceries are a bit cheaper because they don't have road freight added.'

Nicole nodded. 'Decision made. I'll go up there, and I'll see Helen while we're there.'

Jill went to the till and pulled out an envelope. 'This is the extra money for the last delivery'—she peeled off some extra notes— 'and this is the payment for today's delivery. I'd be happy to see another order from you in another month or so if you're up this way again before you move.'

'Thank you, I hope I'll be able to drop in again.' Nicole shrugged. 'But who knows, my husband's work is itinerant, and we could move at the drop of a hat.'

'Well, I do hope to see you again.' Jill turned away as the door opened and another customer walked in.

Nicole swallowed as she put her head down and took Binnie's hand, clutching the notes and the envelope in the other. 'Bye, Jill.'

She hadn't handled that well. One minute she said she'd go up to Second Chance Bay, and the next she'd said that she may not be around due to her "husband's" work. But Jill hadn't appeared to see anything strange with her response.

She let out a happy sigh as they walked outside. 'Let's go shopping, sweetie. I think we can afford to buy you a brand-new toy today.'

Less than half an hour later, Nicole and Binnie were back in the car, with a new soft toy, some pencils and a bag full of clothes for Binnie. The little girl was holding the toy close to her chest; she'd insisted on the black dog, even though it hadn't been as pretty as the others.

'Bits the second,' she announced with a wide smile.

A surge of love hit Nicole squarely in the chest and she reached over to the back seat and squeezed Binnie's little hand. 'Bits the second, it is, sweetheart. You are such a good girl for … Mummy.' Her throat clogged and she swallowed.

The road from Normanton to Karumba was narrow, but to Nicole's relief, it was tarred. She'd filled up the car with petrol at a garage at Normanton and parted with two precious fifty-dollar notes. It was only an hour later as they approached Karumba and she drove through slowly looking for the grocery store so she could stop there on the way back after she'd seen the manager at the hotel at Second Chance Bay.

She found the small IGA supermarket and took note of where it was before she followed the signs to the next town. The shoreline was flat and identical to the coast up at her house. The Gulf stretched out in a silver sheen to the horizon, but here, unlike where they lived the water was dotted with many small fishing boats. A large container ship was making its way towards the river mouth.

It was a strange feeling seeing so much activity after their self-imposed solitude. Nicole followed the road until she reached the end. A small hotel with a blackboard sign at the front saying "Bistro Open" sat at the end of the road. Just before the driveway to the hotel, another road turned to the left and she slowed the car. The road followed the river inland. About a hundred metres along the riverside of the road was a building with **McDOUGAL'S FISH CO-OP** on the roof. A rush of excitement at seeing where Dane's business was based zinged through her blood, but she tried to ignore it. She was here to see the manager about work. If she happened to bump into him while she was here, so be it.

Who are you kidding? said the little voice on her shoulder.

Along the wharf between the hotel and the co-op, several boats were tied to mooring posts. She drove into the car park of the hotel and parked the car. She pushed her now full purse into the small handbag and swung it over her shoulder before she undid the seatbelt on Binnie's car seat.

Squaring her shoulders she walked across the bitumen with Binnie holding her hand and pushed the door of the hotel open. To her relief, it was almost empty. It was eleven o'clock and they were ahead of the lunch rush. A couple of older men sat at the end of the bar nursing beers, and low conversation came from the gambling alcove to the right.

The barman flashed her a welcoming smile. 'Morning. What can I do for you two lovely ladies? Lunch orders don't start until eleven thirty.'

Nicole smiled and bent down to Binnie. 'Would you like a special drink? A red one.'

Binnie nodded, and Nicole straightened and smiled at the barman. 'I'll have a small fire engine drink please.'

'And for you, love?'

She shook her head. 'I'm fine, thank you. I was hoping to see someone called Helen. She's the manager?'

The barman chuckled and shook his head. 'She'd like to be. And she thinks she is most of the time, but I'm the manager of the hotel.' He held out his hand across the bar. 'I'm Rick Curtin. Helen is my partner—in life and work. What can I do for you?'

A flush ran up her neck as she shook his hand. 'Ah, the lady at the Information Centre at Normanton said she was interested in some more of my plates.'

'Ah, so you're the mysterious potter.'

Nicole swallowed. 'Mysterious?'

'Helen's been trying to find out how to get in touch with you since she bought those bowls, but neither Mr Google nor the information centre staff could help. She'll be very pleased you've called in.'

'Is she here?'

'She'll be back very soon. She just went down to the co-op to get some prawns. Garlic prawns are on the menu today. You should try them. Her speciality.' He put his fingers to his mouth in an Italian gesture and a shiver ran down Nicole's back.

It reminded her of Bruno. She put her head down and spoke quietly. 'We'll take Binnie's drink outside and wait for her to come back. Thank you.'

He crossed to the post mix and mixed the drink quickly. With a flourish, he put an umbrella on the top and smiled over the bar at Binnie. 'One fire engine.'

Nicole went to get her purse out, but he shook his head. 'Don't worry about it, love. On the house. It's a business meeting after all.'

'Thank you.' She picked up the drink and took Binnie's hand, and they went outside. There was a large tree shading half of the lawn near the water, and they settled at one of the wooden tables. The garden area was deserted, the quiet only broken by the low throb of a motor as a small boat sped past on its way out to the fishing grounds.

Nicole drew in a deep breath of fresh air. Today, calm had descended upon her and the extra money from the Tourist Information Centre, and the possibility of another job had filled her with hope. Being in town wasn't spooking her as much as it had on previous visits, and Binnie was chattering away to her new toy in between slurping her drink through the straw.

Maybe she would go to the co-op and see if Dane was there. But what was the reason to go and see him? What would she say? Maybe another thanks for his visit? She should have thought to pack the food containers that he'd left. but they were sitting on the benchtop back at the house. Or maybe she could ask how he had gone with Bobby Foley?

Binnie was playing quietly with her new toy. Nicole sat and stared at the water and enjoyed the unfamiliar serenity until the dark thoughts crowded in.

Chapter 10

It had been one of those black days in Melbourne when you needed a scarf around your face, and knee-length boots to keep your feet dry and your legs warm. The sort of clothes that Nicole hadn't worn for a couple of years. They hadn't needed winter clothes in since they'd travelled north and then settled on the Gulf. She could give Binnie's away; she'd well and truly grown out of them. She frowned; the op shop at Normanton wouldn't be interested in them, and besides, she didn't want to open any conversation about where she'd lived before. So, the old clothes would stay in the box.

The weather on the day that Laura had called her had been particularly bleak. At first, Nicole had considered not going over to her sister's house, but Laura's voice had held desperation and Nicole had detoured to the mansion on her way to the office where she was working as a temp between the pottery classes she ran at the local college.

Binnie had been crying in the background as Laura had begged her to come. 'Nikki, please, I need you. I'll tell you all about it when you get here.' So, Nicole jumped on the tram after ringing the office. That was the end of another temp job; not that she'd minded because she hated working on cold calls for the various companies that used the temp agency. It wouldn't be for much longer because her art was finally starting to make her a steady income, thanks to Bruno introducing her to the Melbourne art scene. Once she had fifteen thousand dollars in the bank, she was going to work full-time in the studio that he had hired for her. And she intended to pay back every cent that he had spent setting her up, despite his dismissal of her intention.

'*Bella*, it is for you. I have plenty of money,' he'd said constantly.

Laura's Prado was in the driveway and Nicole remembered that Laura had picked up a new kiln for her and it was still in the back. There was no sign of Bruno's car. Nicole had been relieved; even though her sister's husband had sponsored her career, she didn't like the way he operated. She didn't like the way he was gradually taking over their lives. Maybe it was okay for Laura; she'd married him, but the way he was trying to control Nicole's career was unnerving. He'd even told her last week that she was to leave the temporary job that she hated, but she had emphatically refused.

'How do you think it makes me look, Nicoletta?'

She squared her shoulders and stared at him. 'My name is Nicole, and my working has nothing to do with how you "look", Bruno.' Laura stood behind him shaking her head, with a worried look on her face, but Nicole had argued until Bruno had stormed out.

Laura had put her face in her hands and when she'd finally lifted her head, her voice trembled. 'You shouldn't have done that, Nikki. Binnie and I will pay for it.'

'Laura, if it's that bad, leave him. Come and live with me.'

Laura had simply shaken her head. 'I can't. You don't understand. But please, Nikki, please apologise to him when he comes back.'

So, to make it easier for Laura, she did.

And Bruno had been happy again.

Since he'd married her sister two years ago, Nicole had seen her sister's vitality drain away. She'd given up her career as a librarian at the university, and eventually, Laura stayed at home all day with a three-year-old child. Even though Binnie wasn't his child, Bruno didn't agree with daycare.

'A mother's place is with her child,' he said often. 'And we don't need that small salary that you get for all those hours. Nicole knew what salary Laura had been on as a graduate librarian, and it wasn't small by anyone's standards. Eventually, she gave in and resigned from her position and was dependent on Bruno for money.

On that fateful morning when Nicole knocked at the door, there had been no answer. At first, she'd thought that Laura wasn't home, which was strange because she begged her to come over, and she rarely left the house.

And her car was in the driveway. Maybe she'd taken Binnie to the park for a walk?

She was about to turn around and head to the studio where she had some pieces waiting in her workroom for her attention when the door opened.

Laura reached out and grabbed her. 'Quickly. Come in.' Her sister's voice was full of urgency. Once they were inside, she burst into tears and Nicole grabbed her.

'Laura, what's the matter? Where's Binnie? Is she okay?'

'Yes, she's fine. For the time being.'

'What do you mean?' Nicole gripped Laura's hands, surprised by the level of her distress.

'I'm leaving him, Nikki. I can't stay. The things I found out, all those things that I suspected, they're all true. I married a criminal.' Her hands were shaking as tears rolled down her face. 'And not only a criminal. He's a murderer. I know it's true. I overheard a conversation and he knows that I did. I'm so scared. As soon as he went out, I packed the car, and I want you to drive. I'm too upset. I've got to get out of here.' She dug in her pocket and handed Nicole the car keys. 'You go and get Binnie while I get my handbag from my room. She's in that cardboard fort you built in her playroom. Poor little pet overheard our argument, and she scarpered in there. It's her safe place, I think. She'd been spending most of the day in there lately. There is no way Bruno is going to stay as her stepfather. I don't want her tainted by his world.'

Nicole looked at Laura; there was a small suitcase on the floor beside her. She put a shaking hand to her mouth. 'God, Laura. I can't believe it. Where are you going to go?'

'I don't know. I'll hide out somewhere for a while and then decide. I've been squirrelling some money away.'

'He's not going to let you go easily, you know.'

'I know, that's why we have to go now. Hurry, Bruno'll be back soon—' Laura stopped, and her eyes widened as she tipped her head to the side. 'Oh God, that's the garage door now. He's home already. Quickly, go and hide with Binnie. Keep her quiet. Bruno doesn't know she goes in there. As soon as he goes upstairs we'll leave.'

'He'll see your car's out there.'

'I'll tell him I got it out for you to borrow.'

'But will he see your suitcase in it?' Nicole's arms were covered with goosebumps, despite her thick jumper.

'I don't know. But at least he won't know you're here yet. Quickly, go and hide. Now.' Laura's whisper was ragged.

Nikki reached out and grabbed her sister and held her close for a few seconds. 'It'll be okay, Loz. I'll look after you. Don't worry, as soon as he's gone we'll leave.'

Every day that had passed since that morning, she had been thankful that she had hugged her baby sister before she'd gone into the playroom.

Chapter 11

'Hello. You must be Nicole.'

Nicole turned with a start; anyone could have walked up to them without her noticing as she'd relived the past; she had to be more vigilant. Thinking about that day had brought the crushing fear back.

She stood and held out her hand, not surprised to see it was shaking. 'Yes, I am. And you're Helen?'

'Yes, I am. Helen McDougal. I'm so pleased to finally meet you.'

Nicole's thoughts scattered. *McDougal?* Suddenly she remembered that Dane had talked about his mother cooking at the hotel; she hadn't given it another thought.

'I believe you met my son, Dane, a few days ago.'

'Yes. I did.' Her voice was flat. Who else had he told that she was here?

Helen must have read her mind. 'Don't worry, he's kept your presence in the house private. I only know about you because he told me about your pottery, and I asked about what he was going to do at the house. And I'd already bought the bowls and I put two and two together. And don't worry, Dane is very discreet. Sit down, I'll go and get us a drink.' She turned to Binnie. 'Would you like another drink, sweetheart? Rick said you had a fire engine before.'

Binnie turned wide eyes to Nicole.

'Would you like one?' Nicole asked.

The little head nodded vigorously. 'Yes please.'

'What about some lunch for both of you? Maybe some hot chips for your little girl, and I've just made a big pot of garlic sauce for garlic prawns?' Helen smiled. 'It was very convenient you being out here. I've left Rick peeling the prawns. That's one job I hate! I'd rather scrub a grill than peel them.'

'Thank you, but we won't have time. I still have to shop for our groceries, and I want to get back before dark. So just a quick chat.'

'I can have a meal ready in a few minutes,' Helen said persuasively. 'The sauce is ready. And it's on the house for a friend of Dane's.' No matter how much Nicole protested, Helen insisted, and she gave in eventually.

'Well, thank you. I appreciate it.' She looked at Binnie was a smile. 'And so will Binnie.'

'My pleasure.' Helen went to walk off and then turned. 'Dane is coming for lunch too. When I went to get the prawns and told him about the garlic sauce, he said he might wander over. He'll be very surprised to see you here.'

Nicole nodded. She didn't know what to say.

'Stay out here. I'll eat with you too. The crowd won't arrive for another hour.'

'Crowd?' Nicole's throat dried.

'Just the grey nomies from the caravan park. Today is the day I have the ten-dollar special. It gets them in every week.'

'Oh.' Nicole searched around for a reason to leave but couldn't think of one. 'We'll have to be very quick though. We only have half an hour or so.'

'Well, I'll get cracking,' Helen said. 'We'll talk orders while we eat.'

***

408

'So you think your plans for this lodge will come off after being up there to look at it.' Matt leaned back in his desk chair and put his feet up on the corner of the desk.

'Yeah, it's going to be good. I need to talk to some builders here and at Weipa to figure out the best way to do it.' Dane respected Nicole's privacy; he wasn't going to share that she was up there with anyone other than Mum. 'But I do want to talk to you about the best way to set up the finances and the company before I start.'

Matt's face lit up. Finance was his speciality and Dane often wondered how bored his oldest brother got spending his days sitting in the office at the fish co-op. Maisie still ran the shop most days, but occasionally Matt would have to come out and serve. Dane couldn't have stood being stuck in a building day in and day out. Being on the water was his choice and he loved every minute of it. This new venture had fired him with excitement. Once he sorted out Nicole's situation, he could focus on the construction. And he wanted that to commence sooner rather than later.

Matt pulled a foolscap pad and pen over in front of him. 'Let's talk some figures. You're going to have a good running cash balance if you make this a luxury adventure trip and charge accordingly, so an offset loan is the way to go. So what—'

Dane's phone trilled, and he pulled it from his shirt pocket. 'Excuse me.' He frowned as he glanced at the screen. 'It's Mum.' He clicked the answer button. 'Hi, Mum, what's up? Do you need more prawns?' A smile spread across his face as he listened. 'Fabulous, I'm on my way. Don't let her leave.' He went to disconnect but Mum had more to say and he listened. 'Okay. I was coming there anyway. Got it.'

Matt looked at him curiously as he stood and pushed the chair in. 'Her?' he asked.

'A friend of mine is up at the pub for lunch. I'm going to go and catch up with her.'

'I'll come with you. I wouldn't mind a feed of Mum's garlic prawns. I can almost smell the sauce from here. I'll see if Maisie'll hang around for another half hour or so.'

Dane hesitated. 'Ah, do you mind if I go by myself? My friend is very shy.'

'Okay.' Matt looked surprised. 'Who is she, and where did you meet her? I've never seen you so keen to go and see someone.'

'Long story and one I can't share yet. I'll bring you back a feed of garlic prawns.'

Matt nodded and sat back behind the desk. 'I've probably got enough to do here anyway. Has Jake told you we've been talking about replacing this old shed with a modern building?'

Dane paused in the doorway. 'No, he didn't, but it's a great idea. We might even get Jenni helping out more if we get a new building.'

Matt laughed. 'You think?'

Dane shook his head. 'No, you're right. She still hates the smell of fish. Thanks, Matt, I owe you one. Gotta go. We'll have a beer tonight.' He took off without a backward glance and jumped in his ute to drive the hundred metres to the pub to save time. He was terrified that Nicole would leave before he got there. She was skittish enough to take off.

As he parked, he could see Nicole and Binnie sitting at the table where the family usually sat. He locked the ute and sauntered across the lawn.

'Well, hello, you pair. This is a nice surprise. Did you hear on the grapevine that Mum was cooking garlic prawns today?'

Nicole's cheeks had a slight flush on them as she looked up at him. Her voice was soft and gentle as always. 'Would you believe I forgot you said your mum was the cook here? I came up to see the manager about an order for some of my pottery, and she knew who I was.' She looked at him from beneath her lashes. 'And she knew where I was living.'

He looked down as a little hand tugged on his jeans. 'Where's Bits the first?'

Dane crouched down, his eyes at a level with Binnie's. 'Bits the first?'

She held up a black stuffed toy. 'This is Bits the second. He wants to meet his brother.'

'Well, I'm sorry.' Dane pointed across the river. 'See that white house over there with the dark roof?' Both Binnie and Nicole followed the direction of his finger. 'That's my house, and Bits the first'—he flashed a grin at Nicole and was pleased to get a smile in return— 'is asleep in his bed.'

'Can we go and see him, Mummy?'

Dane stood up as Nicole answered. 'No, sweetie. We won't have time. We have to do the grocery shopping and get home before dark.' She turned to Dane. 'Thank you for leaving us your leftover food. It meant I had time to finish my work and bring it down this trip.' Her eyes lit up as she held his, and small wrinkles fanned at the corner of her eyes as her smile grew. 'They took it all, and now your mother wants to buy some plates too.'

A surge of warmth centred in his chest as she held his gaze for a long time, and he found it impossible to look away. 'I think you'll find she wants more than plates. I think she's going to keep you busy.'

'That's what I like to be. Busy,' she said softly.

'Here comes lunch,' he said. 'I'd better go order mine.'

'No need, Dane,' Mum said with a smile. 'I saw you pull up and you have a large serve here on the tray. I hope it's okay, Nicole, I did some chips and chicken nuggets for Binnie.'

'Thank you. You're very kind.' Dane noticed the tremble in her voice and wondered how long it had been since she'd encountered kindness.

The plates were offloaded, and Binnie looked at her meal. 'My mummy used to cook me chicken nuggets when I was little.'

Dane was surprised to see the flush deepen on Nicole's cheeks, and she looked down quickly. 'Do you want tomato sauce, Bin?' she said, and her voice was husky.

'Yes, please. My other Mummy, I meant.' Binnie persisted. 'We loved chicken nuggets.'

His mother reached for the dish of sauce she had on the tray to cover the awkward silence that followed. Nicole was staring at the little girl with a look of horror on her face.

'Here you go, especially for you, Binnie,' Helen said before she turned to Nicole. 'Nicole, I have a big favour to ask you, and Dane, it impacts on you too.'

Nicole lifted her eyes to meet Helen's and Dane was surprised to see a sheen of tears in them. She blinked, and it disappeared, and he wondered if he'd imagined it.

'On me, Mum? he asked.

'Yes.' Helen shot an apologetic look at Nicole. 'I was planning on coming up your way with Dane, the next time he went up there to meet you and to talk to you about the order. I'd like a whole set done, and with the lunch rush about to start, I don't have time now.'

'So, what's the favour' Nicole asked quietly. Dane glanced at her left hand with interest as she caressed Binnie's back.

Strange. She hadn't stopped touching Binnie since the little girl had made the strange comment.

'I was hoping to persuade you to stay the afternoon and night at our house over at the Bay. It's private if you're worried about that. I know Matt's going down to Cloncurry to stay overnight, and we could talk at length, and do some designs.' She looked over at Dane. 'And I know that Dane would like to talk some business with you too.'

'That sounds like a plan,' he said. Nicole was staring at him, and her expression was hard to read. 'What do you think, Nicole?'

Chapter 12

Nicole didn't know what to say. Her newfound serenity had fled when Binnie had dropped the clanger about her "other" Mummy. Her stomach was still clenched, and she was just going through the motions of eating the meal, delicious as it was.

'I've got to go and put some more rice on,' Helen said. 'It looks like the bistro is about to get busy. Like I said, you're most welcome to stay at our place. Have a think about it and let me know in a while.'

'Is that where Bits the first lives?' Binnie said around a mouthful of chips, and Nicole's stomach muscles tightened even more. To Dane's credit, he didn't buy into the conversation. For the first time in a week, Nicole had the awful thought that it would have been better if Binnie hadn't been talking.

As the thought crossed her mind, guilt flooded through her and she came to a snap decision. 'I think we could manage that, especially if Bits will be there.' She turned to Dane and noted the surprise on his face. He'd expected her to decline the offer.

He nodded and smiled. 'Bits will be there, and I'm sure he'd love to see you again, Binnie.'

The little girl picked up another chip. 'Well, that's settled then,' she said with a nod.

Nicole's mouth dropped open, and her lips tilted in a half smile as she locked gazes with Dane. 'Where on earth does she pick up these expressions?'

He shrugged. 'Television?'

She shook her head. 'Binnie hasn't seen any television for a while.'

'Just a smart little button, then,' Dane said.

Nicole looked at Binnie thoughtfully. 'She's taken more on board over the past year than I realised. When she wasn't talking

413

I'd have long conversations with her, and it looks like she was taking it all in.'

Helen came back and placed a carafe of water and some glasses on the table. 'I thought three red drinks might be a bit much.'

'Thank you,' Nicole said. 'And Helen? I'll accept your offer. Thank you. It'll be good for Binnie to have some company other than me too.'

Helen glanced at Dane and a look passed between them. 'I don't know how you'll feel about this, but my daughter has a little girl a bit younger than Binnie. How would you feel about Jenni and Leni coming over to the house this afternoon? The girls could play while we talk about the design I'd like you to try.'

Nicole bit her lip. 'You are all being extremely kind and thoughtful. I guess that would be fine. But,' —she looked around anxiously at the crowd beginning to drift out to the tables in the garden— 'is it okay if we leave now?'

Dane stood and gestured to her bowl. 'Would you like Mum to put that in a takeaway for you?'

Nicole put a hand on her stomach. 'Oh no, but thank you. I've had plenty. Binnie's finished too. Come on, Binnie, it's time to go.' She looked across at Helen and spoke quickly as she stood and grabbed Binnie's hand. 'Thank you for the meal, I'll see you later.' The more people who walked out of the pub, the deeper her anxiety grew. She picked up the toy from the end of the table, and took off, almost dragging the little girl to the car.

***

Dane raised his eyebrows at his mother before he followed Nicole to the car park. By the time he caught up to her, she had the little girl buckled into her car seat. She stood straight and closed the door, dragging in deep breaths.

'This was so not a good idea,' she said shakily. 'I need to go home.'

414

He couldn't help himself. Dane put his hands on her shoulders—thin frail shoulders—and held her gently, but firmly. 'I want you to take one slow deep breath, and then breathe it out. There's nothing to be afraid of.'

Her face changed in an instant. 'Nothing? What would you know about what I have to be scared of?'

His fingers still gripped her shoulders. 'Look around you, Nicole. We are the only ones in the car park, and no one within sight is paying us any attention. You're okay. Binnie's okay. You're safe.' Gradually her breathing evened out, and her shoulders relaxed beneath his hands. This time he held his breath as she lowered her forehead to his shoulder. 'It's just so hard. I don't know how much longer I can do this.'

He lowered his hands and laced them loosely around her waist and she didn't move away. 'Just stay calm. I'll keep you safe, I promise.'

And in that instant, Dane realised how much he meant that. This gentle woman and her little girl had touched something deep within him; a part of him that had never kicked in before. He cared about what happened to them; and not only that, he cared about how they felt. He wanted Nicole to be happy. To smile and laugh and live life without being scared.

Gradually she pulled back and looked up at him. 'I'm okay now. Tell me where I have to go to get to this place of your Mum's.'

'Are you right to drive?'

'I am.'

'Then jump in and follow me. We haven't got far to go.' He winked at her and ran across to his ute. By the time he was inside and had it in reverse, she'd started the car and followed him when he drove out onto the road. Less than a hundred metres on, he swung into the vacant block beside the co-op and waited for Nicole to park beside him.

He expelled a sigh of relief as she did. Until the last moment, he'd still wondered whether she would follow him. He walked over to the car and stood by her open window. 'Anything you need tonight, or anything valuable, bring with you. It's usually fairly safe around here, but you never know.'

While she got Binnie out and filled a small bag from the car, he went down and checked the boat. He'd hate it to be the one that was always full of smelly crab and fish traps, but he was in luck. Matt had brought the newer one over this morning.

Binnie's eyes were wide as he led them down to the shore and helped them climb in. 'It's the only way we can get to Second Chance Bay,' he reassured Nicole. 'It's not a thriving metropolis.' She was quiet as they quickly crossed the river and he swung the boat into the jetty at the back of the house. Mum was going to call into the co-op and make sure Matt was still going to Cloncurry, so Nicole wasn't overwhelmed by too many members of the family turning up.

Jenni would come over after Leni had her afternoon sleep. He jumped out and looped the rope around the post and then held his hand out for the bag that Nicole clutched on her lap. At the same time, he reached down and put one arm beneath Binnie's legs and swung her out of the boat. Her giggle made him smile.

'You go and wait by the gate and call Bits and I'll help Mummy out.' Dane held out his hand. Nicole reached up and took it and he helped her out.

'Thank you,' she said dropping his hand as soon as she landed lightly on the timber jetty.

Binnie had already found Bits standing at the gate wagging his tail. She was on her tippy toes trying to reach over the gate. Dane scooped her up and lifted her over onto the newly-mown grass and she lay on the grass beside the pup chattering away.

He turned to Nicole. 'It's never the right thing to say to a lady, but you looked tired.'

'I must admit not having to do that drive back this afternoon is a relief. It's been a big day.' She stared at Binnie and spoke almost beneath her breath. 'An emotional day.'

'How about I show you the guest room, and make you a cup of tea, and you can have a rest. I'm happy to keep an eye on Binnie. Unless you want her to have a sleep too? Mum'll be over about three and you'll have a couple of hours before she goes back to cook tonight.'

'I don't think there's much chance of a sleep with Bits the first around.' She smiled, and he ignored that feeling that settled in his chest every time she did. 'I think Bits number two has been forgotten.

Dane looked down at her as she watched Binnie play with his pup. 'She's a good kid, Nicole. You've done a fine job with her, considering how you've been living by yourselves.'

'Thank you. Instead of me having a rest, put that cuppa on, and I'd like to talk to you about the house.'

He opened the back door and led her down the hall. 'Binnie will be fine in the backyard. It's fenced, and I locked the gate.'

He gestured to a chair next to the kitchen window where she could see Binnie playing with Bits. 'Tea or coffee?'

'Coffee, please. Instant is fine.'

He made the coffee and sat on the other chair near the window. At least since Mum and Rick had been home from their travels, she'd organised a woman to come in and keep the house tidy. When he and Donny and Matt had been living together last year, it had turned into a bit of a pigsty, and Mum had roasted them when they'd come home in the caravan.

'Did you see Bobby Foley about getting my rent back?' Nicole cut straight to the chase.

Dane shook his head. 'No. He's left town.'

She nodded briskly. 'Well, that's easy then. We stay there.'

'Whoa. Not so fast. I have a business to build up there. One of the reasons I wanted you to come to the Bay was to see how private it is living here.'

'No.' Her voice was quiet and despite the negative word, it held no nastiness. Just stubbornness.

'Okay. Consider this. Please.' Dane's frustration was growing at her refusal to consider an alternative. 'You're wanting to stay there because it's private and inaccessible, and you don't have to see anyone apart from when you come to town. Is that right?'

'It is. And I've paid three years' rent.'

'So how private is it going to be when I bring builders and tradesmen in to build the new cabins, and to do the house up.'

'I don't think you can do that without my permission.' Nicole's tone was sweet, but her gaze was like steel. 'I have a rental agreement, and I've paid my rent.'

'So, would you give me permission?'

Her voice was soft. 'I really can't answer that. I'd have to think about it.'

Dane bit back his growing frustration. He was caught between a rock and a hard place. He was keen to get his project started, but he was very aware of the fragility of this woman. And damn it, he'd worried about her non-stop since he'd left her at the beginning of the week 'So how long do you think you'll need to think about it?' He ran a hand through his hair. 'Look, Nicole, the last thing I want to do is make it hard for you. I guess from what I'm seeing you've had a pretty hard time, but you know you can't spend your entire life hiding in the wilderness.'

She lifted her chin. 'If I decide to it's my business and I can do whatever I see is best for Binnie and me.'

'But don't you think you might be seeing it from a narrow point of view? In the time you've been up there, your world has shrunk to the place that you live in. How many people do you see?'

She stared at him. 'None.'

'How many friends are you in contact with?'

'None.'

'What about family?' He kept his voice quiet as he sensed she was getting angry, but damn it he wanted to push her buttons to get a reaction. She was always so soft and gentle, it brought him undone. She must have the patience of a saint.

'Binnie is my family.' Her voice caught on the single word and she dropped her eyes. Dane felt like a heel and he thought carefully before he spoke again.

'What about Binnie's schooling? What about her interaction with other kids? With other adults?' He kept his tone conciliatory and patient.

Nicole lifted her head and her eyes were dark and bleak. 'You think I don't worry about that every day? You think I'm without feeling?'

'No.' Dane reached over and took her hand between his. Despite the warmth of the afternoon, her fingers were like ice. 'I think you are a very special person in a difficult situation. And I'm grateful that I picked Foley's place to buy and met you both. I want to help you, Nicole, and I hope that you'll let me—and my family—into your lives.'

He looked up from their clasped hands to see a solitary tear rolling down her cheek. Dane let go of her hand and stood and opened his arms. Nicole rose slowly and stepped into his embrace.

Chapter 13

Dane looked up as the front door opened just after three o'clock. His mother walked in carrying a thermal food bag, with Jenni and Leni close behind. He put his finger to his lips and pointed to Binnie and Bits who were curled up asleep on the sofa beside him.

'Ssh,' he whispered.

'Sweet little pet,' Helen said with a smile.

'She went to sleep watching *Sesame Street*.' He shook his head. 'Poor little mite was fascinated by the television. She kept walking up to it and putting her hands on the screen.'

'Where's Nicole?' Helen asked quietly.

'She was tired, so I offered to look after Binnie while she had a lie-down.'

Jenni stared at him, her expression one of amusement.

Dane stood and walked to the kitchen and they followed him down the hall. 'So what's that look for, little sister?'

Jenni shook her head. 'Is this my big brother here? You usually run a mile when there are kids around. And you offered to babysit? This must be some woman you've brought home.' She crossed to the biscuit jar and took out a biscuit and settled Leni on the floor.

'Keep your voice down, Jen. And I haven't brought anyone home. Nicole is here to have a meeting with Mum about her pottery.'

Jenni's response was between a snort and a laugh. 'Sure, she is. I can see the look on your face when you say her name.' She smiled. 'My brother has finally been hit with Cupid's arrow.

About time! I'd given up on the three of you until Donny met Claire.'

'Jenni.' Dane's voice held a note of warning. 'Put a lid on it. Nicole's not travelling well, and I don't need you in here opening your big mouth and—'

'Stop it the pair of you,' Helen said quietly. 'Jenni, stop teasing your brother and Dane, you stop biting. Now I'm going to put the kettle on. Dane, you go and tap on the door and let Nicole know I'm here and then the two of you can take the girls and Bits for a walk while we talk about the set I want and see if she can make it for me.'

Dane did as he was told, and Jenni took Leni's hand and followed him out of the kitchen.

'Sorry,' she said quietly.

'It's okay, Jen. It's complicated, but it's not my story to tell. I'm pleased you came over. It'll be good for her little girl to have a playmate for a while.'

'Where do they live?'

Dane shook his head. 'If she wants you to know, Nicole will tell you. You go and introduce the girls while I get her.'

He walked to the room at the end of the hall. It had been Jenni's room when the family had all lived at home, and now it was the spare room for guests. Not that he and Matt ever had anyone stay since Mum had moved out with Rick, and Don had moved in with Claire. He tapped lightly on the door and waited.

There was sound of movement from within and the door opened. Nicole poked her head around it. She smoothed a hand over her tangled hair. Her cheeks were pink and flushed and had more colour than Dane had seen in them yet.

'Is your Mum here?' she asked quietly.

He nodded. 'She's in the kitchen. Did you have a bit of a rest?'

'I did. I went out like a light, thank you. What about Binnie? I hope she wasn't too much trouble.'

'The last I looked, she and Bits were both fast asleep on the sofa. My sister's in there now.'

'Thank you. I usually sleep lightly because I'm always listening out for her.'

Dane looked at her and it was hard not to reach out and touch her flushed cheek. Her eyes were heavy-lidded, and as he watched, she rolled her shoulders.

'I feel the best I've felt for ages.'

It was good to see her smile. He had to bite back the words that rose to his lips.

You look beautiful, he thought.

'That's good,' he said briskly instead. 'Come down to the kitchen when you're ready. Mum's put the kettle on. She's got a couple of hours, I'd say, so hopefully, you can get it all organised and ready for you to go home tomorrow.'

As he turned to go, Nicole reached out and touched his arm. He looked down curiously, unused to the zing that fired his nerve endings at her touch.

'Thank you.' She lifted her hand, turned away, and shut the door.

Dane was thoughtful as he walked back to the living room.

***

Why did I have to go and touch him, Nicole thought as she quickly washed her face in the bathroom adjacent to the bedroom. She ran her fingers through her hair; her hairbrush was in her handbag in the living room. Biting her lip, she stared at herself in the mirror. It was time to distance herself from Dane; it had been stupid to accept the offer of staying here overnight. She'd seen the look on his face; she was *not* going to become dependent on another man. It had been foolish to reach out and touch him; she didn't want to give him the wrong idea.

At least he was transparent; his motivation for helping her out was clear to her. The pair of them living on his property was the impediment to him following through with his business plan. At least Dane seemed upfront and honest.

Nicole had never figured out Bruno's motivation for getting so involved in her life; both professionally and personally. After he'd sponsored her as an artist, it was as though he thought he'd owned her. The doubling up of being his sister-in-law as well after he'd married Laura had seemed to cement that perception in his mind. Nicole knew she couldn't forget that, and she couldn't afford to let someone else try and control their lives.

No matter how much Dane McDougal—and his mother—wanted to help her, she would not let her guard down. No one ever did anything for no reason; there had to be something more there. They wanted something from her. She straightened her shoulders and headed for the kitchen. Maybe it was simply to have her move off his place, and maybe it was as simple as a set of dishes, but in her experience, nothing was ever simple.

Binnie's giggle reached her as she went down the hallway, and then Dane's deep tones and an unfamiliar voice. His sister, she guessed.

Way too many people getting to know them.

She bit her lip again; Nicole had intended being cool and distant when they talked about the order, but by the sound of the voices and laughter coming from the direction of the kitchen, it was going to be hard.

Why, oh why did I agree to this?

Because the money from this order will make a difference, common sense chimed in. *It will give you money to put aside for when you have to move on.*

And that day wasn't far off.

Nicole took a deep breath and walked down the hall and into the kitchen. A young woman with blonde hair was sitting at the table with a child on her lap, and Binnie was sitting on the chair beside them.

Helen looked on with a smile as Dane stacked a pile of plastic containers into a tower until a gentle nudge from Binnie had them all tumbling down to the table. Her little laugh was infectious, and Nicole couldn't help the smile that pulled at her lips. Dane had his back to her, and her gaze lingered on the muscles that rippled in his back as he lifted his arms to stack the containers again. He was a strong man, both inside and out, and held way too much appeal for her.

Be wary, she told herself.

'Fourteen, fifteen, sixteen . . .' Binnie counted, and Nicole raised her eyebrows in surprise.

Dane turned around as she stepped around the table. 'Binnie learned to count to twenty when *Sesame Street* was on before she had her nap.'

Nicole reached over and smoothed Binnie's hair back from her face. Her eyes were bright, her cheeks were rosy and there was a big smile on her face; so different to her normally serious little face.

Regret tugged at her. Binnie hadn't ever counted for Nicole, but she couldn't tell the two women it was because she hadn't spoken a word until ten days ago since they'd fled from Melbourne.

What sort of mother—carer—would that make her look like? As Dane had said before she'd gone for a sleep, what sort of life was she providing for Binnie?

A *safe* one, she thought to herself.

Helene interrupted her thoughts. 'Nicole, this is Jenni and my granddaughter, Leni.'

Nicole forced a friendly smile to her face. Her social skills were very rusty. 'Hello,' she said.

'Come on, girls. We'll go outside and play for a while.' Jenni looked hesitantly at her. 'If that's okay with you, Nicole?'

'That's fine. I'd like to get straight into talking business with your mother.' She knew her voice was cold; she didn't know how she felt about Binnie taking so easily to these strangers. If anything, a little seed of jealousy had sprouted, and that made her feel awful.

'A cup of tea or a cold drink while we chat?' Helen asked.

'Stay there, I can look after myself,' Nicole said briefly. She crossed to the sink, picked up a tea bag and put it in one of the cups that were there. After pouring the hot water into the cup, she waited while Jenni led the two small girls to the door.

'You too, Uncle Dane. You can come and play, too.'

'Yes, Uncle Dane,' Binnie parrotted. 'I want you to come too.'

Uncle Dane! The jealousy grew another couple of tendrils.

'I'll see you in a while, Binnie. You be a good girl.' That was a silly thing to say. Binnie was always perfectly behaved, but the little girl barely glanced at her as she ran from the room.

Helen and Nicole were left sitting at the table.

'So, Helen.' Nicole picked up the teacup and tried to keep her tone business-like. 'Tell me exactly what you have in mind.'

Helen leaned back and smiled, and Nicole was struck by what a fine-looking woman she was for someone with four—that's how many Dane had mentioned, she thought —grown children. Her face was unlined, and her expression and her body language spoke of someone who was very content.

The older woman put her cup down and reached for the pencil and pad that was on the table beside her cup. 'Since Rick and I have been managing the hotel, we've tidied it up considerably, and business has improved. The restaurant has always done well, but we've started to build it up even more. We're going to expand the seating area outside, and Rick's going to put in a platform with a telescope to view the sunset.' Helen chuckled. 'After all, that's what most caravanners do the long trek up here for. The sunset and the prawns. Rick's looking after the outside improvements, and I've been tasked with making the restaurant more upmarket.'

'In what way?' Nicole asked, impressed by Helen's enthusiasm.

'We've already replaced the tables and chairs, and a new menu board is about to be delivered. I would like to have a dresser displaying your pottery, and I'd like to have a set of plates and bowls and platters all in the same colour and same design.' She gave a small chuckle. 'I don't know how hard it would be, but I had an idea for having a fish-shaped plate with the flat bit at the end in deep blues and greens.'

Nicole watched, impressed at the speed and quality of the drawing that Helen produced with the pencil. She nodded. 'Yes, I could do that.'

'Great. I wasn't sure if you'd have the equipment you need out there.' Helen looked at her curiously.

'It's taken me a while, and I had to get it delivered to the post office when I could afford it, but I'm fairly well set up now.' There was no point trying to hide it, Helen knew she was living out on the property that Dane now owned.

'And I guess that's one of the reasons you wouldn't be too keen on moving?'

'Yes.' Nicole's reply was non-committal.' If she and Binnie did move, she'd have to leave much of her equipment behind because it wouldn't fit into the Subaru. She wouldn't get a truck out there, because there would always be a paper trail to where she'd moved.

Now that she knew Dane, maybe if she did leave, he could store her extra gear somewhere.

Nicole shook her head. *No,* she wasn't going to depend on anyone.

Helen's voice softened. 'It must be hard living out there by yourself with a small child.'

Nicole lifted her chin. 'No. We do very well.'

'That's good then.' Helen obviously sensed that she didn't want a heart-to-heart or a shoulder to cry on. That suited Nicole just fine because she knew if she started to talk, she'd probably break down. She reached over for the pad and held out her hand for the pencil. 'May I?'

Helen nodded and passed the pencil over.

'Now how many of each would you like?'

The pen was poised above the pad, but there was silence from Helen. Nicole glanced over; the older woman was staring at her with sympathy in her eyes.

Nicole straightened her shoulders. Her nerves were already stretched tight and she didn't want sympathy that would push her over the edge. She was away from her comfort zone, Binnie was out of sight and with strangers, and all she wanted was to be at home in her haven in the wilderness. She looked down and began to make a list to give her something to focus on.

Plates.

Platters.

Bowls.

'I guess about a hundred plates and bowls, to begin with. And say a dozen platters. Is that too much for you?'

Nicole couldn't believe the numbers that Helen said. She'd be working day and night to fill the order, and she would have to get a lot more clay in, plus extra liquid glaze. Excitement curled in her stomach at the thought of the size of the order. It would keep her busy for at least three months with those quantities. And it would give them so much extra money for security.

'No, that's fine. I can manage those numbers.'

'I've got some magazines in my bag with some examples of what I like. I'll give them to you to take with you. Now you do me up a quote and give me your bank details and I'll pay a fifty percent deposit. I know you'll have to buy a lot of material.'

Nicole looked up and nodded. 'Thank you. I'll get the quote sorted tonight, and I'll give it to Dane to give to you later. But Helen'—her voice shook as she thought that this might be the death knell for the order— 'I only accept cash. Will that be a problem?'

Helen frowned for a moment and then shook her head. 'That's fine. I'll get around it.' She held out her hand. 'So, we have a deal?'

Nicole relaxed as she took Helen's hand and shook it. 'We do.'

Chapter 14

Helen and Jenni left together at about five. Binnie and Leni had played together happily on the lawn as the adults sat outside watching the sun lower towards the water.

'I'll look forward to hearing from you, Nicole. I'm excited about this.' Helen passed the magazines over as they were leaving. 'I almost forgot these.'

Dane, Nicole, and Binnie walked down to the jetty with them, and Binnie jumped up and down waving as Jenni steered the boat across the river.

'It would be hard to get used to, having to come home by boat,' Nicole said as the boat headed for the other side.

'In the wet season or at flood times, it can be challenging. There was a bridge years ago, but it washed away in a flood. The population over this side had dwindled so much, they figured it wasn't worth replacing it,' Dane said as they walked back towards the house. 'But we all grew up here, and Mum ran the household and the business singlehandedly after Dad died until Matt was old enough to take over.'

'How old were you when your Dad died?' she asked curiously.

'I'd started work, and Jenni had just finished high school.'

'That would have been hard for your mum.'

Dane shrugged. 'In some ways, it was easier for her. Dad wasn't an easy man to live with.' He reached down and swung Binnie up onto his shoulders. 'Let's race Mummy to the gate.'

Nicole walked slowly as they ran ahead, Binnie squealing and giggling. It made her smile, but it made her sad too. It was going to be hard for Binnie to go back to just her company after the full day they'd had. It was hard to believe it was only this morning they'd set out. She frowned. As well as the grocery shopping, she still had to go to the library at Normanton to check her email. She'd order the extra clay and glaze online, ready to be picked up the next time they came to town.

'Penny for them?' Dane's deep voice made her jump and she looked up. He was standing there holding the gate open for her.

'Sorry.' She picked up the pace. Binnie was running for the swing that hung from a large tree near the side fence. 'I was just thinking that I forgot to go to the library today.'

'You like to read?'

'I do, but it was to check my email, and now I'll have to place some orders too. For your mother's work. I said I'd do up a quote and give it to you.'

'You're very welcome to use my computer.'

Nicole smiled. 'That would be great if you're sure it's okay. It will save me time tomorrow.'

'How about Binnie helps me get some dinner ready while you do what you have to? There's a printer there too.'

'Thank you.'

Five minutes later, Nicole was set up at his desk. Dane had logged on for her, and she was ready to place her order. It was the only thing that worried her about ordering, but it would take a deep search by Bruno to find the address for the delivery of any goods she used PayPal to pay for.

She hoped.

As Nicole paused, the computer clicked onto the screensaver and she sat watching the photos that rolled across the screen. Many photos of Dane at various ages were interspersed in the collage of family snapshots. The other two boys looked like him, but Dane was the best-looking of the three. There was a photo of him hauling a huge fish into a boat, wearing a pair of board shorts. His chest was bare and bronzed and muscled.

She knew she was gaping, but Nicole's mouth dried, and she stared at the photograph until the next one rolled over.

Enough of that!

She opened Google and searched for a new supplier of the material she needed. She always used a different one so the order was a one-off. It didn't take long to find the products she needed; she ordered the quantities she'd worked out in her head and went to the shopping cart to finalise the payment. Her fingers slowed as she entered Nicole Curtis, care of Normanton Post Office, and then entered her PayPal account details.

A sick feeling lodged in her stomach. Every time she placed an order she worried that Bruno was watching. Maybe her faith in the privacy of information was naïve.

Once she'd placed the order, she quickly typed up a quotation for Helen and printed it out on the laser printer beside the computer.

Oh, how she'd missed the ease of technology at her fingertips.

The order was complete, she turned back to Google and logged into her account.

There were three new emails, and she clicked on the inbox to open them. The first two were delivery notices for the last two orders that she had already collected from the post office and the third . . .

Oh my God. She drew in a sharp breath.

The third made her heart pound.

How dare he? Did he think she was a gullible fool?

Nicole stared at the screen until her vision blurred. There was no way on God's earth she was going to open that email. Her heart beat so hard that she put a hand to her chest and fought down the nausea that was clawing at her throat.

Bruno would know if she'd opened it. She'd used the "show this has been read notification" herself, and she knew that if she clicked on it, Bruno would know she was accessing her email

Her hands were shaking as she read the subject line one more time.

Please open this. It's Laura. I need to talk to you.

Nicole reached for the mouse to close the screen, her mind whirling and her heart pounding. It was as though Bruno was in the room with her and fear iced in her veins.

***

Binnie had lined up a row of frozen chips on the oven tray and was counting them as Dane prepared the meat that he had taken out to barbeque. His mother had dropped in a couple of salads and a small cheesecake, and he'd opened a dip and found some fresh crackers in the cupboard. He wasn't sure whether to offer Nicole a wine or not.

As he turned the oven on, he heard the study door close, followed by her footsteps on the wooden floorboards of the hallway.

'Here comes your Mum,' he said to Binnie, but she was focused on her task on the table. He remembered what she'd said about her "other" Mummy and wondered what she'd meant. Dane looked up as Nicole walked into the kitchen.

'Just about ready to cook,' he said as he turned around. He frowned; her face was pale, and her lips were colourless.

'Everything okay?' he asked casually, not wanting to make a fuss.

She nodded, and then shook her head and gestured to Binnie.

Dane nodded, understanding that she didn't want the little girl to see she was upset about something. 'How about a wine? I

433

think you've earned one today, snaring such a good order. And a lemonade for this one to join in the celebration.'

Binnie looked up. 'Yes, please!'

Nicole nodded. 'That would be good.' A little bit of colour had come back into her cheeks, but her lips were still bloodless. 'Thank you.'

'A red or a white?' Dane crossed to the dresser and took out two of the good glasses that Mum had left here.

'Red please if we're having steak.' Nicole leaned over Binnie and ruffled her hair. 'I could hear you counting. You've learned a lot today.'

'Can we get a TV at our house, Mummy? I could learn lots of numbers.'

Nicole nodded. 'Maybe we can, but we'll have to buy DVDs because there won't be any television reception out there.'

Dane had picked a bottle of red off the wine rack near the door as she'd been talking to Binnie and opened it. 'You might be surprised, you know. There are some repeater towers all the way up the coast to Weipa and I know we often pick up television reception on the boat when we're up around Staaten River which isn't far from where you are.'

'Don't be silly,' Binnie said. 'Boats don't have television.'

'Oh. Yes, they do, Miss Big Ears.' Dane looked up and held Nicole's gaze as he answered the little girl. 'One day you can come on my boat and I'll show you. It has lots of things on it that will surprise you.'

'Tomorrow?' she asked hopefully.

Nicole dropped her eyes from his, and Dane turned his attention to pouring the wine. He couldn't get used to the feeling that ran through him when he looked into her eyes. It was a soppy, gooey feeling in his stomach, and he wasn't sure about it. All he knew was that he found her damn attractive and wanted to keep her safe. It would be good to see those shadows leave her eyes and see those pretty lips tilted up in a smile more often.

'No, we have to go home tomorrow.' She lifted her eyes to meet Dane's again. 'But definitely another time.'

Good, that gave him a little bit of hope.

Hope for what, he wondered?

'Maybe I could give Binnie a quick shower while you cook the barbeque? We bought some new PJs for her today.'

'Sure. Just help yourselves. There are clean towels in the cupboard in the main bathroom. I've got some sausages to cook for Binnie. Is that okay?'

He was pleased to see that Nicole's colour had gone back to normal when she nodded.

'That's fine. And we do owe you for your hospitality and what you've done for us.'

Dane shrugged. 'I'd be cooking a barbie anyway, and Mum would have sent the salads over, so it's no extra work. Besides, I've got a few days between charters, and it gives me something to do. Not to mention good company.'

She smiled that gentle smile that sent his gut all warm and tight as she took Binnie's hand and led her to the bathroom.

##

An hour and a half later, Binnie was tucked up in bed in the guest room, and Dane and Nicole were sitting out on the back porch watching the river change colour as the night closed in. There was a myriad of coloured lights blinking out in the Gulf tonight; Dane was surprised to see the number of fishing boats that were still out there. The small boats, referred to by the locals as the "mosquito fleet" usually came in with their catch before sunset. But it was a pleasant night, the air was warm and there was no wind, and he assumed the fish must be biting.

Nicole had been quiet during dinner, but Binnie had chattered nonstop as they'd eaten the steak and sausages that he'd cooked on the outside grill. She'd sat back and listened as he'd answered the myriad of questions that Binnie posed to him, and he had to remember that it was only a short while ago that she'd started to talk again, according to what Nicole had said the night he'd stayed at the house with them. That had never been mentioned again, nor was there a mention of the "other Mummy" comment.

For the first time, he wondered whether Nicole had done something wrong, but the thought was fleeting. He knew instinctively that she was a good person, and he trusted his judgement.

'Would you like another glass of wine?' He held up the bottle and she jumped when he spoke. Her brow was furrowed, and she was staring into the growing darkness.

She nodded and held her glass out.

'You look like you've got the weight of the world on your shoulders,' he said as he poured the wine.

Nicole held the glass up and the ruby red liquid caught the light of the citronella candle he'd put on the table to chase the mosquitos away. A gentle sigh puffed from her lips, but she didn't answer.

'A problem shared is a problem halved, they say,' he said quietly.

She stared at him and her eyes glittered. 'You know, Dane, if you thought I was emotionally unstable, I could understand why.'

'I don't think that at all, Nicole. I know you wouldn't be living up the coast with Binnie unless you had a very good reason. I know a lot of women live in fear from problems with relationships.' He leaned forward and took her hand. 'Domestic violence can be dealt with. You've taken the first step and taken yourself away from the situation, now you need to get help to deal with it. No matter what the circumstances were, you didn't deserve it.'

The laugh that came from her lips was like nothing he'd heard before; it was full of bitterness. 'If only it was that simple. I have to stay strong for Binnie and I have to be brave.'

'Did something happen this afternoon? When you were on the computer?'

Nicole nodded. 'I can't talk about it. I shouldn't even be here with your family.' She waved a hand and a few drops of wine spilled onto her lap, but she didn't notice. 'The more people that know who we are and where we are, the more chance there is of us being found.' Her voice was harsh. 'And that can't happen. Ever.' Her eyes were bleak as she stared at him. 'I wish you'd never bought that house.'

'But I did, and I'm here with you. And by God, Nicole, I want to help you. I want to make sure that you and Binnie are safe.'

She jumped to her feet and the glass of wine went flying. 'You can't help us, Dane. No one can.'

Nicole hurried across the lawn to the gate, her movements jerky and every line of her body tense. Her breath was loud as she drew in deep ragged breaths. Dane walked over slowly not wanting to spook her. As he drew closer, he could see her body trembling, and he put his hands gently on her shoulders.

'Nicole. Please. You can trust me. Let me help you.' Her frail shoulders were rigid under his touch until she sagged beneath his hands and he caught her before she fell. She turned and buried her face in his T-shirt.

Dane knew at that moment that he would do anything to protect this woman.

Once she started talking, she relaxed into him and the words flowed.

He held her close as his horror grew.

Chapter 15

Over in the corner behind the fancy dolls' house and expensive toys that Bruno had insisted on buying for his stepdaughter was a small fort made from old cardboard boxes. Nicole had made it for Binnie one day when she'd been babysitting, and the little girl loved it. They had painted it grey and looped a string of flags made from coloured paper around the cut-out turrets. The door was a piece of cardboard that had been cut from the side of a box and taped to the doorway that Nicole had made just big enough for her to crawl through and follow Binnie into the little castle. Small slits were cut in the cardboard at Binnie's eye level, so she could see out. Her little niece loved playing in it and every time Nicole came to visit, Binnie insisted on sitting in there and listening to the fairy stories that Nicole made up for her.

Laura had told her on the phone last week that Binnie had even taken to having her afternoon naps in there.

The sound of the door opening and Bruno's loud voice had Nicole scurrying across the room. She got down to her knees, crawled through the small opening, and pulled the cardboard door shut behind her. Binnie was sitting in there and she opened her little mouth wide to say hello, but Nikki put her finger to her lips, shook her head and whispered a very quiet 'shush' next to her ear.

'Laura!' Bruno's loud voice came through the closed playroom door. 'What do you think you're doing?'

Laura's response was quiet, and Nicole couldn't make out the words. She reached out her arms to her niece and the little girl snuggled into them and hid her face in Nicole's chest as the shouting got louder. Binnie's body was stiff, and Nicole rubbed her hand over her back in soothing circles. The little girl had heard this before; Laura had told Nicole that Binnie was crying in her sleep and had begun to wet the bed at night.

'Tell me where you were going.' More yelling came from the family room and Nicole closed her eyes wishing that the little girl didn't have to hear the angry words. The sooner they got out of here the better.

'You bitch, how dare you accuse me. You have no idea what you're talking about, you stupid woman.' There was the sound of a slap and Nicole tensed as Laura screamed.

There was silence and she held her breath until the soft tones of Laura's voice came through the closed door.

'Where's the kid?' Bruno yelled.

Finally, Laura yelled loudly, and Nicole knew it was for her benefit. 'Stop yelling, Bruno. She's up in her room asleep. You'll wake her.'

'Don't you yell at me, you bitch.' Another slap. 'Why is your car outside? Where do you think you're going?'

More muffled words.

'Nicoletta? Why does she need your car? I offered to buy her one, but she is another stupid woman. What is it with your family?'

The sound of loud footsteps came through the closed door, and then a dragging sound followed by a crash.

'I'm not a fool. Where do you think you were going?'

'I wasn't going anywhere. The suitcase has old clothes that Nikki was going to take away for me. You are so generous, Binnie has too many. I thought they could go to one of the charities.'

A slap and another scream. Tears began to roll down Nicole's cheeks as she heard her sister begging. She pressed Binnie closer to her chest.

'No, Bruno. Don't hurt me.'

Binnie's little body was shaking in her arms and Nicole moved her hands over the little girl's ears.

'You're lying to me again, Laura. You were leaving me. I won't let you leave. Why is your suitcase in your car? Do you have too many clothes too, lying bitch?'

Laura's scream turned Nicole's blood to ice. 'Don't touch me. No! Don't touch me.'

Binnie started to whimper, and Nicole let her go for a minute. She held the little girl's gaze and put her finger to her lips. 'We have to be very, very quiet and then we will go and help Mummy. Okay?'

Nicole pulled her close and put her hands over Binnie's ears again as the yelling intensified; she was terrified that Binnie would start crying, and he would know that Laura was lying. But Bruno was yelling, Laura was screaming, and Binnie stayed silent.

'No, no no! My baby. Think of my baby!'

Her last scream made Nicole's blood run cold and she fought the faintness that threatened. She had to protect Binnie, whatever happened.

A shot rang out in the next room, and there was a loud thump.

Nicole's vision pricked with white lights, but she fought it as she held Binnie to her. Bile rose in her throat and burned as she swallowed it down.

The silence from the room beside them was more frightening than the yelling that had preceded it. Binnie was silent and stiff in her arms.

The door opened, and Nicole froze. She closed her eyes and held her breath; there was no sound for a few seconds. Binnie was stiff in her arms and didn't make a sound.

After a moment the door closed again, and the footsteps receded.

Time ceased to have any meaning, and Nicole didn't know how long she sat there gripping Binnie to her. When she looked down, Binnie's eyes were closed, and her breathing was even. She'd found her release in sleep.

Nicole reached into her pocket and pulled out her phone and dialled the first two zeros of triple zero ready to push the last one if she needed to call emergency.

The garage door opened and there was a squealing of tyres and the throbbing tones of Bruno's sports car as he backed out of the driveway.

In the months afterwards, Nicole realised that she had known what she would find in that room. Somehow, she crawled out of the fort, clutching Binnie to her chest and the little girl stayed asleep. Slowly and quietly, Nicole crossed the room, opened the door, and stepped into the living room.

The shock of seeing Laura, her only sister, her only family, lying on her back on the floor in a pool of blood, her eyes wide open, was a sight that she would never forget as long as she lived.

She held Binnie with her face pressed tight to her chest, ran over to Laura and bent down. One side of her sister's face was covered with blood. With shaking hands, she pressed her fingers to the side of Laura's throat, feeling for a pulse.

Nicole let out an anguished cry and Binnie woke up and began to scream. She tried to shield the little girl, but her scream rang around the room. 'Mummy, Mummy. I want Mummy.'

As Nicole pressed the third zero, those words were the last words Binnie spoke until the day Dane McDougall came into their lives.

Chapter 16

Dane's arms held her close and Nicole felt safe for the first time in many months. She gripped the sleeves of his soft T-shirt and kept talking.

'I strapped Binnie into Laura's car and we drove for six hours. I stopped in a small country town across the border, filled up the car, and went to the ATM. I drew out as much money as I could. I did that for the next few days until I realised that it was giving Bruno a trail of where we were going. I started to pay cash for everything, and I didn't draw any money out again.'

His chest vibrated against her cheek as he finally spoke. 'What about the police? Did you go to the police at all?'

She shook her head. 'There was no point. I knew what Laura had told me over those past few weeks. She married a criminal. Bruno was involved in the gang warfare in Melbourne and she said he bragged that half the police force was on his payroll. He would have known very quickly that I must have been in the house and that I knew that he . . . I knew what he did to Laura.'

'And you think he's been looking for you ever since?'

'Of course, he has. Binnie and I could send him to jail if we went to the police. But I never knew who he had in his pocket. So, it was safer to leave.'

She stepped back and looked up at Dane and the expression in his eyes rocked her to the core. 'You . . . you believe me?'

'Of course, I do. I've seen your fear, and I've seen your strength. You are one amazing woman to have carried that with you … for how long?'

'Fourteen months.'

He gathered her close in his arms again, and she rested her head on his strong shoulder. 'What happened today to upset you?' he asked quietly.

'He emailed me. He pretended to be Laura.' Her voice hitched with a sob. 'My dead sister. That's the sort of bastard he is.'

Dane took a deep breath. 'I want to help you through this. I want to help you get back into living a real life. Not hiding out.'

'Why would you want to do that?' Nicole bit her lip. 'I'm sorry. Since Bruno, I don't trust very well. He sucked in both Laura and me; he took over my life as much as he could. It was as though he got glory from my exhibitions. He even made me change my name to his; he convinced me it would open doors. He was probably paying for those doors to be opened and I fell for it.'

'Will you trust me? How can I convince you that I mean you no harm and that I don't want anything from you?'

'Not even your house and land that we're stopping you develop?'

'That's the last of my worries at the moment, Nicole. I'm going to track this bastard down, and we'll make sure that he gets what he deserves. If you won't let me do it for you, let me do it for Binnie.'

She was quiet for a moment as she thought of what this man was offering.

Finally, Nicole stood on her toes and rested her cheek against Dane's. 'Thank you, she whispered.

##

After they crossed the river the next morning, Dane insisted on following Nicole's Subaru in his ute. Not only into Second Chance Bay where he helped her do the grocery shopping, but then he followed her the eighty kilometres back to Normanton. To her shock, he'd then insisted on following her car for the whole six-hour journey until they arrived in a convoy back at the house on the Gulf.

'You don't have to follow us,' she'd protested as they'd sat at his kitchen table eating breakfast, with Binnie happily drawing between them. A couple of times their gazes had connected, and Nicole had dropped hers. Something had changed between them; after sharing her story with him last night, she felt very close to Dane.

And she felt lighter.

For the first time, she began to think that maybe there was a way out of this horrid situation that she had been trapped in for more than a year.

He'd simply smiled and nodded. 'Yes, I do.'

But his decision to accompany her on the journey home had been made after she'd refused point blank to look at the vacant house a few houses along from his place. 'Not yet, Dane. Maybe one day, but I'm not ready yet.'

He'd listened, but then he'd insisted on doing the trip with them.

'Haven't you got to work?' she asked.

'Not for another two days.'

In the end, she'd given in, but it had been good to know he was travelling along behind them all the way. Binnie had kept twisting around in her car seat and had given a running commentary on how close Dane was to them for most of the trip until she fell asleep just before they turned off the main road.

Their house and the surroundings were deserted—as they should be. Dane parked behind them and came across to the car. He opened the back door and smiled as he looked in at Binnie.

'Do you want me to lift her out while you open up the house?' he whispered.

'Yes please.' Heat ran up Nicole's neck as she preceded him up the stairs. It was a very domestic situation. She unlocked the door, and Dane took Binnie over to the mattress on the floor and gently laid her down before pulling the light cotton sheet up over her.

A strange feeling ran through Nicole as he brushed his fingers lightly over Binnie's rosy cheek before he stood up and walked back to the door where she was standing.

'Come and I'll help you unload those groceries,' he said. 'And then I'd love a cup of tea.'

She smiled. 'I'll put the kettle on before we start.'

It didn't take long to unpack the car. As she began to put the food into the cupboards Nicole frowned and put her hands on her hips. 'I didn't buy these chocolate biscuits, or muesli bars, or a block of chocolate.'

'My treat.'

'You didn't have to do that, Dane,' she protested.

'I just wanted to make sure you had some good stuff to eat when I call in next week.'

'Next week? You don't have to do that.' Despite her words, the thought that he'd be back soon made her happy.

'I'll be coming by sea. We've got a three-day charter up here.'

'But you won't bring anyone ashore with you, will you?' Her eyes widened at the thought of strangers coming ashore.

'No. I won't. We'll moor around at the mouth of the river where the fishing is, and I'll come around in the tender'.

'Won't you be needed?'

He grinned, and the flash of white teeth in his tanned face and the sparkle in his eyes sent a shaky feeling right through Nicole.

'I'm the skipper. The deckies can cope for a couple of hours without me.'

She nodded. 'Ah. I know nothing about boats.'

'We'll have to remedy that, won't we?' There was a promise in his words and the trembling crept lower, down between her thighs.

'Maybe.'

'That's better than a no.' His grin got wider. 'When do you think your order will arrive at the post office? I was thinking I could collect it for you, to save you a trip down.'

Nicole shrugged as she put the last of the groceries in the cupboard. The camping fridge was full too. 'I haven't used that supplier before, so I don't know. The post office has been good. They know I'm out of town—but they think I'm down on the Cloncurry road—and they hold my deliveries until I get into town to pick them up.'

'How the heck did you get all of that equipment up into your workroom?' He gestured to the room along the verandah.

She chuckled. 'With a lot of improvising. I pulled the kiln up with a couple of ropes; the rest I managed to carry up the steps and push along the verandah.'

'You amaze me.'

Nicole looked up and their eyes met and held. She looked down as Dane's hand reached for hers and he pulled her slowly towards him.

She didn't—couldn't—resist.

Her gaze stayed on their joined hands and her heart rate kicked up a notch as his other hand slid around her waist. Heat warmed her cheeks as his head lowered to hers and his breath whispered on her cheek.

'I'm going to look after you, Nicole. And not because I think it's the right thing to do. It's because I want to spend more time with you. Get to know the *real* you, the happy vibrant woman who is behind this fear that you carry with you.' The warmth of his lips touched her cheek. 'What do you think of that?'

She couldn't think. Her brain had gone to mush along with the rest of her body. And then his lips slid along her cheek to the corner of her mouth. Butterflies were running rampant in her stomach and sending exquisite quivers down lower.

'You're not playing fair,' she murmured.

'I'm just thankful that there's a little girl asleep in your bed, or I'd be playing a lot harder. This is a promise, Nic.' His lips closed on hers, and a warm liquid sensation flooded through her as she joined him in the moment.

She lifted her arms and put her hands at the back of his neck, pulling his head down harder. The kiss deepened as his tongue played along her lips, and she opened her mouth to welcome him in.

Eventually, Dane was the one to pull away. 'Like I said, this is a promise. I know we've only just met, but I know I want you to be a part of my life.'

Warm shivers fired in her stomach as his hand caressed her arms. His touch was pure magic, and she'd never felt anything like it before.

'I'm going to have to go to get back before dark,' he said reluctantly. 'But I bought something for you when we stopped in Normanton. So, I don't have to worry quite so much about you.'

'Show me,' she said softly.

His arms went around her waist again as his lips returned to hers. Nicole closed her eyes and a soft chuckle puffed out of her lips. 'I didn't know you could buy that at a shop.'

Dane stepped back, and his face was flushed, but his eyes were happy. 'Minx. I'll be back in a minute.'

Nicole stood with her fingers against her lips, willing her heart to slow down. Her thoughts were scattered, but it was so good to feel something other than fear. She watched as he went to the car and then bounded up the steps two at a time.

'It's only a cheap one, so don't go saying you won't accept it. You can give it back to me when you move out of here. It's in my name so there's no fear of it being linked to you. Okay?' He pulled his hand from behind his back and handed her a small mobile phone. 'It didn't cost much more than flowers and chocolates, but I'll get them next time.'

She reached her hand out for it. 'I won't say no. Thank you. Will it work up here?'

In his other hand, he held a black case. 'It will with this. This little device turns it into a satellite phone. We use them on the charter boats and they work like a dream.'

'And that was more expensive than flowers and chocolates, I'd say?'

'That one was more along the lines of dinner at an expensive restaurant, and we'll do that one day. I promise.'

'Thank you.'

Dane slapped his hand against his forehead, but his grin was wide. 'Is this Nicole who's standing in front of me? She's not arguing?'

Nicole shook her head and held out her hand for him to hold it. 'Do me one favour, Dane?'

'Yes?' His eyes were dark.

'Call me Nic. I liked it.'

Chapter 17

The week passed quickly and despite an early restlessness, Nicole and Binnie settled back into their routine. Binnie chatted more and more each day, and the only thing pressing on Nicole was the fear that one day she would ask about Laura. She had memories, and the mention of her "other" mummy, stayed with Nicole. The pottery was coming along well, and she'd been able to fire and glaze a dozen plates with the clay that she had already had on hand.

She lifted one to the light. The blues were beautiful, with a touch of deep green as she tipped it to the side. Hopefully, Helen would be pleased with them. As she picked up the brush and painted the glaze on the side of the last plate for the day, her thoughts turned to Dane and his family.

Well, not turned, she admitted to herself. Dane McDougal had been in her thoughts—both sleeping and waking—since he'd left five nights ago.

At first, she'd tried to resist thinking about him and then had let her thoughts explore the unfamiliar feelings that he'd raised in her. In her twenty-five years, she'd had two boyfriends and had slept with only one of them in the first year she'd gone to art college.

But the feelings that ran rampant through her at Dane's touch, at his look, at his cheeky grin, and even thinking about him, were feelings she'd never experienced before.

She tried to analyse them, but couldn't, because every time she thought of them, Dane was in her head and the feeling came back.

She thought of his family and wondered why they were so keen to help her, be kind to her, and look out for her. It was not what she was used to. She and Laura had fended for themselves since their mother had passed away when Laura was in her last year of high school and Nicole had been at art college. Neither of them remembered their father; he'd left when Laura was two.

Their mother's family had left Mum well off and that inheritance had passed down to the two girls when she'd died; they'd never wanted for anything.

Nothing, except normal loving relationships, like she'd now seen in Dane's family. No wonder she and Laura had been ripe for Bruno's picking.

Laura would never have the opportunity of having a loving relationship, and she wouldn't see her beautiful little girl grow up A tear splashed onto her hand and Nicole wiped it away on her shorts. She stood staring out at the sea and vowed that she would provide a normal family life for Binnie. The fact that Dane's face sat squarely in her thoughts didn't surprise her.

Nor did it bother her.

But it was early days. She would wait and see what developed.

##

It was late in the afternoon and Binnie had woken up from her sleep, and it was almost time to cook their dinner. Nicole was feeling stronger; they had more food in the cupboards and camp fridge than they'd ever had, and they hadn't had to catch fish since they'd come back. She smiled as she had to move the block of chocolate in the fridge to reach the sausages she'd thawed for dinner.

An unfamiliar sound drifted in the window as she went to turn the gas on, and she paused.

'Bin, turn the light off, please.'

Binnie did as she was instructed immediately. They'd played this game before. Nicole walked over in the dark and took

450

her hand. 'It might be time for a game of hide and seek,' she said quietly.

In the event of an emergency, she'd found a perfect hiding spot in the house, and she and Binnie had practised hiding in there. Nicole had made it a game to see how long they could be silent. No matter how unlikely it seemed that Bruno would find them, she always believed that he would find them one day.

She took Binnie to the side of the old gas range and watched as she crawled to the alcove behind it. 'Mummy's just going to look out the window and then I'll come in too. Now you be quiet and count like you've learned to, under your breath. Okay?'

The last view of Binnie was chubby little legs and a shorts-covered bottom crawling along the side of the stove.

Nicole crossed to the window and stood to the side. It was a motor that she could hear, and it was getting louder.

Like a motorbike. She shuddered. Bruno had ridden a huge powerful motorbike when he'd first taken Laura out.

The sickness began in her stomach, and she pushed her fist against her mouth as she peered through the window out to the road at the end of the driveway.

But there were no lights sweeping the night sky. As she turned back to the kitchen, flickering light to the north caught her attention. There was a large boat with red and green lights moving along the front of the bay. As she stared at the horizon, her eyes still adjusting to the dark, a smaller light moved into the shore. A flashlight danced on the water close to the edge of the bay.

Dane?

Nicole moved silently to the alcove. 'Stay there till I come back. Okay, Bin?'

'I will,' came the whisper, 'but now you've made me lose count.'

'Start again,' she whispered.

Nicole used the door at the back of the kitchen to go out and stand in the shadows on the veranda. Her heart was beating a low and steady beat, but her senses were on high alert.

She was fairly sure it was Dane, but until she was sure, she wouldn't show herself.

The sound of a metal hull scraping up the rocky beach broke the still night air.

The small yip that followed brought a smile to her lips.

It *was* Dane, and he'd brought Bits with him.

Her eyes adjusted to the dark, and she watched as he secured the small boat to a tree, holding Bits with his other hand. Her stomach curled with anticipation as he strode towards the house.

Before he reached the top of the stairs, she stepped out from the shadows.

'Hello, Dane.'

'Oh, thank God.' He put the pup down and it was only two steps until he reached her and took her in his arms. His hands were shaking as he held her close and he buried his face in her hair.

'It's okay. I heard the motor, so I hid Binnie. It's okay, Dane. We're here and safe.' It was so different to be reassuring him for a change.

His voice was rough. 'I thought you'd left. When the house was in darkness, I was sure of it.' His lips pressed against hers in a desperate kiss. 'I thought you'd left. I thought I'd come on too strong and fast.'

'We're here. If we were going to leave, I'd tell you.'

'Promise?' His lips were firm and cool against hers as he elicited the promise.

'I promise. Why were you so worried?'

'Because I've been trying to call you on that phone for the past two nights and it rang out.'

Nicole looked up surprised. 'It hasn't rung.'

'Has it gone flat?' Finally, a hint of a smile in his tone.

'I don't know. I left it on the bench and I haven't looked at it again. I did plug it all in like you showed me.'

Dane took her hand and they walked inside. Nicole flicked the kitchen light on and bent down. 'We have two visitors, Bin.'

There was a squeal and a chuckle at the same time. Binnie's squeal as Bits sniffed out her hiding spot and Dane's quiet chuckle behind her. 'It's flat.'

Nicole swung around. 'But it's plugged in?'

'It is, but the switch has been turned off.'

'Oh,' she said sheepishly. 'Sorry, it's ages since I had a phone, and besides no one was going to ring us.'

'I tried.'

'Oh.' Nicole crossed to the stove. 'Come on out, you pair. We have to get some dinner on for our visitors.'

'I hope that's an invitation,' Dane said.

'Do you have much time?'

The slow lazy curl of his lips sent a quiver darting straight downwards. 'I'm on watch at midnight.' He looked down at his wristwatch. 'And that is a whole six hours away.'

***

Nicole had cooked a pasta dish with sausage and garlic, and to cater for the third person at the table had thrown a salad together. Binnie and Bits were fast asleep on the mattress in the bedroom; he'd helped her drag the other one out of the bedroom and into the living room. He leaned against the wall with his legs stretched out in front of him. After comparing each other's weeks, the conversation turned to more general topics.

'I can't believe you've never been out to sea,' he said shaking his head. Nicole was leaning back against his chest and each time she spoke her head moved and her fine hair tickled his chin. His arms were looped around her, and he was trying to keep the conversation going because all he wanted to do was kiss her senseless.

If he was honest, that's not all he wanted. But with a young child in the house, it wouldn't be right.

And it was too soon.

Dane was in the middle of asking her a question when Nicole moved suddenly. One minute he was chatting away and the next . . .

He swallowed as she turned quickly and straddled his thighs; he stared into the heavy eyes of a woman oozing sex appeal.

'Um, what are you doing?' he managed to choke out as her hands slipped beneath his T-shirt.

'Something I've been wanting to do for the past two hours.' Even her voice was different—low and throaty.

God help him. Her knees were on either side of his thighs and she was moving even closer. He swallowed as the blood surged through his body. 'Binnie?'

'Is sound asleep.'

'You're not playing fair.' He could barely get the words out as the blood left his brain and travelled elsewhere.

'Fair or not doesn't matter. This is what I want. What we want?'

With a groan, he moved quickly and rolled over so that Nicole was lying beneath him. The smile on her lips was wide as he lowered his mouth to hers.

Chapter 18

Nicole hummed under her breath as she worked on the first platter early the next afternoon. Despite the late night, she'd woken early. Dane had left with about ten minutes to spare before he was due on watch. Neither Binnie nor Bits had stirred as Dane and Nicole showered together just before midnight, their laughter and talking kept as low as possible.

She had walked him to the small boat, despite his protests about crocodiles, but had given in and stood well away from the shore as he'd pushed the boat into the water.

But not until he'd kissed her thoroughly first.

'I'll be up in three days,' he promised. 'Hopefully, your clay has arrived, and I can bring it with me.'

'Wait until it comes before you make the trip,' she said.

'No. I'll want to see *you*. Don't argue.'

'Yes, sir,' she'd said with a smile that didn't want to go away.

As expected, Binnie squealed with delight for a good half hour when she discovered Bits had come for a visit. Now she was curled up with him and having her afternoon sleep; Dane had left Bits behind saying it would keep the little girl entertained while Nicole worked.

She picked up a piece of sandpaper and worked away at the rough spots that had remained on the platter after the firing. With a grunt of satisfaction, she held it up; the shape was perfect. Now to get the glaze on; it might be best to leave it until she'd woken Binnie and Bits and they'd had their afternoon tea.

As Nicole mixed up some cereal for the pup and Binnie, the combined yips and squeals were so loud, she almost missed the phone ringing.

'Ssh.' She picked up the phone with a smile, expecting it to be Dane, but it was a woman's voice.

'Hello, this is Jill from the Tourist Information Centre. Could I speak to Dane please?'

Nicole hesitated. 'I'm sorry. He's not here at the moment.'

'Is that you, Jenni? I'm after your Mum.'

Nicole muffled her voice and put her hand half over the phone. 'Sorry, not here either.' She should never have answered the phone. Whoever he'd bought it off must have recorded Dane's name as the owner and passed it on.

Small towns!

'Okay, love. Can you tell her to call me, please? There's been a fellow here a few times, looking for that potter lady. Nicole, I think her name is. He's been persistent, and he's just left. I said that your Mum will know where to find her.'

Nicole's blood ran cold, and she dropped the phone without replying.

Two people knew where to find her. Dane and *his mother.*

She closed her eyes and put her hand to her mouth.

Was it Bruno? How had he tracked her? The only way she could think was through her PayPal account and that had led him straight to the Normanton post office. Would he have come himself, or would he have sent one of his thugs?

Panic built in her chest as her thoughts skittered around. Her pulse was racing, and a sharp pain was building at the base of her throat.

They had to leave.

Now.

Before Helen told him where to find her. As far as she knew, Helen knew nothing about Bruno or Laura. Dane was at sea and couldn't help her, but all she wanted was to talk to him and tell him why she had to leave. She couldn't contact him without going through his family, and she didn't want to raise an alarm with anyone else.

If Bruno came here, they'd be sitting ducks and she well knew what he was capable of. Dane knew how dangerous he was and—

Nicole bit back a groan as Bits ran into the kitchen closely followed by Binnie.

Damn, she was going to have to take the dog with her. The chickens were all gone, and she didn't have to worry about them. A snake had got to them while she was at Dane's place last week.

She took a deep breath and began to plan their escape.

***

One of the passengers had taken ill, and Dane had decided to cut the trip short. It was a family group who'd booked the charter, so they were all happy to go back to Second Chance Bay while they sought medical attention for the oldest member of the family who had suffered stomach pains. He wasn't sick enough to be medi-vacced off the boat but was too sick for the trip to continue. Dane had radioed ahead to Matt and let him know they were coming in, and Matt and Jake were waiting at the dock with the paramedics when he brought the *Elsie* down the river in the afternoon.

It took less than half an hour to disembark the passengers. He walked into the office with Matt and Jake while the deckies scrubbed down the boat and offloaded the rubbish.

'A couple of days off again, hey mate?' Jake said. 'You've had it easy over the past couple of weeks. How's the new place going? Jenni said you've been up there a couple of times.'

'Yeah. It should be good. I'm still thinking about what to do.'

'Want some company next time you go up? I wouldn't mind having a look.'

'Yeah, sure.' It was easier to agree now and come up with an excuse later.

Matt went across to the small fridge and opened the door. 'Beers?'

Dane held his hand out for a beer, but Matt paused. 'Oh, I forgot. There was a message for you from Mum when you were coming through the heads.'

'What about?'

Matt shrugged. 'I don't know. She said to tell you it was urgent, and it was something to do with a Nicole or some name like that.'

Both Matt and Jake's mouths dropped open as Dane pushed past them and ran for the door.

'I didn't know what to say, love.' Helen was in the kitchen at the pub basting a roast that had been cooking for a while by the delicious aroma that pervaded the dining room. 'I knew I couldn't say too much, so I said I'd get back to him. He's a very nice man.'

Dane snorted. 'Not from what I've heard. What did he say his name was?'

Helen turned to the bench and dug into her handbag. She read the card before she passed it to Dane. 'Gareth Scholes. He's from Melbourne. He said it's imperative that he speak to a Nicole Smyth. When he described her I knew it was your Nicole.'

'Smyth?' Dane looked down and read the card. 'Where's he staying?

'In the motel next to the airport. Maybe she's come into some money or something.'

'Maybe.' Dane didn't want to frighten his mother. 'I'll go and see him.'

***

It only took an hour to pack what Nicole needed to take with them. Lifting the camp fridge while loaded had been impossible, and it added an extra ten minutes while she unpacked it, carried it to the car, and then reloaded it. Binnie's eyes were wide, and her bottom lip quivered.

Bloody heck. She was so intuitive.

'We're just going on a little trip, sweetie, so get your pencils and your Bits Two.'

'What about this Bits? Can he come too?'

Nicole nodded. 'Now hurry up and go and get your things. I've packed your new clothes and we'll get going.'

As she drove south she worried about what to do. She only had a thousand dollars in cash, not enough to head off and set up somewhere else. Maybe she could just lie low for a while. As far as she could make out, whoever was looking for her was in Normanton. If she took the turn off before town, she could bypass Normanton and head for the Bay, drop Bits off, and maybe—if the offer was still going—take up the offer of that house that Dane had wanted to show her. She and Binnie could get the boat over and stay inside and no one needed to know they were there. It wasn't an ideal solution, but it was the best she could come up with, with limited money.

The problem she had to overcome was that Dane wasn't onshore for another two days. She bit her lip as she took the turn north of Normanton and headed for Second Chance Bay. There was a motel up the road from the pub near the airport. She would see if they had a vacant room and then drop Bits off with Helen.

And hide.

***

Dane sat in the conference room at the front of the hotel and shook his head in disbelief as he stared at the man opposite him. His mother had been right; Gareth Scholes was a good man and his motivation came from a place that Dane had never imagined.

'At the pub up the road, you say. Now?'

Gareth nodded. 'Yes. So, are you prepared to tell me where Nicole is?'

Dane ran a hand through his hair. 'I need to talk to her first. I tried to call her, but she's not answering her phone. 'I'll have to go and get her, but we won't be back until tomorrow.'

'So, you're not prepared to tell me where she is?'

He shook his head. 'It's not up to me to make that decision. Mate, you've blown me away by what you've told me. Tell me, how did you track her to here?'

'An eBay order. A PayPal payment and a delivery to the post office at Normanton. And then we tracked the pottery order to the pub here via the Tourism Office.'

'So much for privacy these days. Nicole had reason to be scared.'

Gareth frowned. 'I'll be honest with you, Dane. I'm not an investigator or anything. Just someone with IT skills who knows how to hack into systems. For the right reasons.'

Dane heard a car door slam and he automatically glanced at the window. The hair on the back of his neck stood to attention and he widened his eyes as he stared. He half stood, and the chair fell to the floor behind him with a crash. Gareth turned and followed his gaze.

Dane ran for the door, closely followed by the other man.

Nicole had just opened the front door and climbed in, and now her dark green Subaru was heading up the road towards the hotel.

'Bloody hell, we need to catch her,' he yelled. 'Where's your car? I walked down from the pub.'

Gareth ran beside him to the car park adjacent to the small airport.

***

There had been a room at the pub for two nights and then Nicole decided she'd reconsider her options when Dane came home. First job was to drop Bits off, and then park the car around the back of the motel and hide out. She felt conspicuous in her car. Although the sun had set, it was still light enough to see. Too many people knew it was hers. They had enough food to bunker down in the motel for a week if need be. She parked at the side of the hotel and grabbed her bag. There was too much money in there to let it out of her sight.

Before Nicole could get out of the car, Binnie had wriggled out of her seat, picked up Bits and pushed open the door. She was weaving her way through the tables towards the one on the lawn where they'd sat last time.

'Binnie, wait.' She put her head down and took off after the little girl and the pup.

In one instant her world went crazy.

She'd almost caught up to Binnie and Bits when Dane yelled out her name. 'Nicole?'

At the same time, Helen walked out of the kitchen, and her eyes were wide as she gestured to Dane.

Fear twisted Nicole's insides as a woman screamed from the table beside her; she turned slowly as the woman lunged for Binnie.

'Binnie, Binnie,' the woman sobbed as her arms went around the little girl and Bits took off.

Their little girl.

Her little girl.

Dane caught her as her knees buckled and she looked into the face of her sister.

'Laura?'

461

Epilogue
12 months later

Nicole held the plate up to the light and frowned; there was a hair from the paintbrush set in the glaze. With a soft sigh, she put the piece on the table on the side of the verandah. It had to be perfect for every order she did. Near enough wasn't good enough.

It was a glorious day on the Gulf. A huge flock of magpie geese had flown over at dawn, heading for the wetlands down near the river, and woken her in time to see the Morning Glory roll cloud. It had been spectacular this morning and had filled her with inspiration for a new series of bowls. Now the only sound was the rhythmic banging of hammers at the far end of the beach as the builders finished off the last of the lodges.

It had taken Nicole a few months of Binnie not being there to get used to the quiet. Sometimes, she still caught herself wondering what she'd cook her little niece for dinner, but those days were getting few and far between as the weeks passed. She had plenty to keep her occupied. New commissions, new lodges, and a man she loved more as each day passed.

Jake's *Moonshine*, with Dane onboard, was due to dock at the new jetty in an hour. Even without the lodges being open—the grand opening was next weekend—the charters had been full, with a waiting list for bookings stretching months ahead. The familiar frisson of excitement as Dane's homecoming grew closer started in her toes and worked its way up to her heart. This afternoon, the workers were catching the boat back to Weipa and a weekend of solitude, with just the two of them here to wander around their new resort, beckoned.

'We'll make the most of it this weekend, sweetheart, because the lodges are fully booked for six months after the opening next weekend,' Dane had promised as he'd left on the boat with Jake five days ago. 'And I've got something to run by you and we need time to talk it over.'

Nicole had been curious, but he hadn't said any more.

Everyone was coming up for the grand opening, and it still surprised her how quickly she'd become used to being a part of Dane's family after almost eighteen months of living in the wilderness alone with Binnie.

Gareth, Laura, and Binnie were flying up next Friday for the grand opening and she was looking forward to seeing them. Laura had met Gareth at a bereaved parents' group—she had believed that Bruno had found Nicole and Binnie after he'd shot her. It had been Gareth who had encouraged her to search for them, and he had helped her for the six months until he'd tracked Nicole's PayPal transaction.

The day that Laura arrived in Second Chance Bay was imprinted on Nicole's memory forever. The sheer happiness of seeing her sister alive and well, with only a small scar where the bullet had scarred her forehead to remind her of that dreadful day, had overcome all Nicole's fear, and the difficulty of being with people. Hearing that Bruno had also died that day—a shotgun death after a gangland drug deal gone wrong—had filled her with sorrow. Not for his death, but the fact that she'd left Laura, thinking she was dead when she'd needed her most, and then taken Binnie from her mother for over a year.

And she hadn't needed to.

By the time Laura had regained consciousness in the hospital, Nicole and Binnie had been long gone.

Gareth had shaken his head when they had all settled down that day. 'You did a damn good job of hiding and keeping her safe, Nicole. It's taken me six months to find you.'

'I'm so sorry, Laura,' she'd said. 'I couldn't feel your pulse and I thought the worst. I called triple zero and got Binnie out of there before he came back.' Her control had slipped, and she'd sobbed. 'I didn't know what to do. I should have stayed with you.'

'But Bruno might have come back, and then where would we have been?' Laura had wrapped her in her arms. 'You did the right thing, honey. You called emergency. And having Gareth help me this year has had a happy ending.' She looked at the man standing beside her with a wide smile. 'We're getting married next year, and now we have Binnie, we can be a family.'

Rather than hiding away in a motel, the night at the hotel had turned into a celebration as the rest of Dane's family had joined them.

Nicole headed for the shower in the newly refurbished bathroom in the beautiful old house. When she'd agreed to move in with Dane after she'd come back from Melbourne—she'd only lasted there for three weeks—he'd organised to have the house renovated, and they'd moved to the house at the Bay for three months.

The graceful old Queenslander that Nicole told Laura was her outback haven, was now painted in a soft white and had a new roof. As well as a new kitchen being installed, the interior floors had been polished, and Dane had replaced the verandah floor, railings, and stairs so that they looked the same as the original design.

But the best part was the new studio at the end of the verandah, next to the office that Dane had added as the reception area for the new lodges.

As she dried her hair, the loud blast of *Moonshine*'s horn rang across the water. Quickly pulling on a short floral dress, Nicole closed the door behind her and ran down the stairs.

The workmen had packed up their gear and were waiting to board as the boat came to the wharf. Dane was standing up at the wheelhouse and she smiled when he blew her a kiss. She waved back and waited for the boat to dock.

Dane and Jake walked down the gangway together and after greeting the workers, Dane hurried across, lifted Nicole from her feet, and kissed her. 'I've missed you, Nic.'

'It's been a long week here, too,' she said linking her arms around his neck.

They stood close together as the workers boarded the boat.

'We'll see you in a few days for the big weekend,' Jake said as he walked back up the gangway. 'Apparently, Helen's got the catering under control, according to Jenni.' He gave them a wave as the deckie undid the ropes. 'See you soon.'

Dane and Nicole walked to their house hand-in-hand. Streaks of gold, overlaid with indigo lit the sky, and the sea faded to silver near the shore, deepening to burnt orange as the sun sank slowly to the horizon.

As they reached the bottom of the staircase, he turned to Nicole. 'I can't wait any longer. I've been practising this for five days and I'm so nervous I need to get it out. Now.'

Nicole frowned. 'What's wrong? Practising what?'

Dane put one hand gently on each side of her waist and stared down at her. 'I met a beautiful woman on this very spot a year ago. She was Nicole Curtis and then I found out she was really Nicole Smyth, after she'd been hijacked for a short and forgettable time as Nicoletta Spagnolo.'

Nicole smiled. 'Confusing, wasn't I?'

Dane reached into the pocket of his shorts and pulled out a black case. 'I've thought of a way to get rid of all of that confusion, Nic.' He flicked open the case and Nicole stared at the beautiful ring that was nestled in dark blue satin. A pink diamond winked up at her.

'I found the ring I wanted in a catalogue, and Donny collected it for me from the Kimberley diamond store last week and gave it to Jake who brought it up to me from Second Chance Bay.'

'A ring?' She swallowed.

 'I'd like you to be Nicole McDougal. What do you think?'

She smiled as Dane took the ring and slipped it onto her finger

'I love you, Nic.'

Nicole reached up and held his loving gaze as she gently pulled his head down towards hers. No more words were necessary as the sun slipped below the horizon in a glorious flash of gold.

THE END

Book 4

Her Outback Paradise

Matt's story

Annie Seaton

Chapter One

'Omigod, omigod, omigod!' Sara Sweeney squealed and twirled in the tiny kitchen of her granny flat and then squealed again when the phone fell off the kitchen countertop, landing with a crash on the faded pink tiles. 'Sorry, Caro. Are you still there?'

Sara picked up the phone and pressed it to her ear, but she could only hear static. Hurrying to her bedroom, she tipped the contents of her handbag onto the bed, looking for her mobile.

'Damn, damn, where is it?' As Sara spotted it, the ACDC song she'd downloaded for her ringtone filled the small room, and she grabbed for the phone.

'Caro? Sorry, I forgot I was on the landline and I dropped it and I've killed the phone. Did you say what I thought you did?'

The calm tones of her friend's voice assured her that she had heard her right the first time. Sara flopped onto the bed and put her hand on her chest. 'That is awesome! When did you make up your mind?'

'About three o'clock this morning. I figured there was no point staying here.'

'True.'

'My contract is ending, and well—as you know—it's not really a place I want to be.'

'I know, sweets. Even though the Barossa Valley is a beautiful part of Australia, you've done it tough here.' Sara jiggled her feet on the end of the bed. 'Oh. My. God. I can't believe it. You're coming with me to Second Chance Bay! You know how excited I am about finally going home.'

'I do, but slow down. I'm just going there to check it out first. I haven't agreed to the contract yet. Sar?' Caro's voice was quiet. 'I want to ask a favour.'

'Shoot, love.'

'You don't start your job up there in the medical centre for a few weeks, do you?'

'That's right, I have a wonderful month of no work after I finish up with Roger the Dodger.'

There was silence at the other end, and Sara waited. Caro was her exact opposite: calm, considered, and quiet, while Sara knew she rushed at life. Like a bull in a china shop, as her grandmother had often told her when Sara was growing up. It would be so good to see Nan when she got back to the Bay. It had been way too long; it would be so good to be home at Second Chance Bay.

'I was thinking about taking a road trip,' Caro finally said. 'I'd like to take my own vehicle up to Queensland. It sounds as though some of the roads up there are rough.'

'You can say that again,' Sara replied. 'You mean a road trip up to Second Chance Bay?'

'Yes, how would you feel about travelling up with me by road instead of flying up? I was thinking about taking the longer route. Taking a trip up through Alice Springs and stopping to have a look at Uluru and Kata Tjuta on the way.'

'Of course. I'd love to. It'll be great fun. And I've never seen the Red Centre either. I've always flown out to Mt Isa to go home.'

'Excellent.'

'It's an awfully long way though. Are you sure you want to be on the road for that long?'

'It's over three thousand kilometres, but you know what, Sar? It's about time I got out of my rut and did something exciting.'

'And I'm happy to share the driving.' Sara jumped off the bed, crossed to the window, and looked out at the gloomy sky. 'Where will we stay? There are not many motels along the way.'

'Well, speaking of adventures. I was thinking about taking a couple of swags and some camping gear. What do you think?'

'I think it sounds like a top idea! When will we leave?'

'As soon as my contract is up.'

'When do you finish at the practice? Same time as me?' Sara went to her desk and looked at the calendar that was propped up on her small dressing table.

'Yes, same as you. This Friday. Roger wanted to take us both to dinner on Saturday night to farewell us both, but I told him we would be gone. I hope that was okay. Even if you don't come with me, it gives you an out.'

'Good. The less time I spend in his company, the better!'

'I was thinking about leaving as soon as possible, taking my time and having a good look around.'

'Well then, we need to get organised. I told Mrs Digby that I'd be leaving the flat early next week, but luckily, I haven't booked any flights yet.'

'It's going to be fun, isn't it?' Caroline's voice was quiet, and Sara frowned. It would be fun, and it would do Caro a power of good. She already had some ideas about how to cheer her up when they arrived in Sara's hometown. Sara crossed her fingers that she could make it so welcoming that Caro would take the contract she'd been offered as resident doctor at the medical practice. Sara was starting there as receptionist and clinic sister in a month. Sara crossed her fingers that she could make it so welcoming that Caro would take the contract she'd been offered as resident doctor at the medical practice. Sara was starting there as receptionist and clinic sister in a month. It would be great to have Caro in the practice. While she'd loved working as receptionist for Dr Rose before she'd moved away, he could be a bit of a stick in the mud when it came to making the workplace a bit of fun.

He was middle-aged and devoted to his career. On the rare occasion that he smiled, he wasn't a bad-looking man. Dr Rose kept himself fit and trim and apparently was the local table tennis champion these days, according to Nan.

'I think we need to get together as soon as we can and start planning this trip.' Sara looked at the mess of the small amount of packing she'd done. At least if she was in a vehicle, the packing would be way easier. A couple of boxes would hold what she wanted to take home, and she'd leave the rest for Mrs Digby, her landlady. She was going home to stay after eight years away.

Home. Finally.

'A good idea. What are you doing now?' Caro's voice interrupted her planning.

Sara grinned. 'I was supposed to be packing, but let's meet somewhere for coffee and get this trip organised.'

##

Sara was surprised when Caro suggested that they go out to one of the vineyards outside the small town of Tanunda, where they both lived. Caroline was not usually one to socialise, but Sara was already planning to work on that when they arrived at Second Chance Bay. The trip would be an excellent opportunity to get to know Caro better, and learn what she liked to do. Also, Sara knew there was some mystery in the doctor's past. She always seemed very sad, and maybe moving to Second Chance Bay would give her a new perspective. Sara had never asked what had happened; maybe the trip would lead to some heart-to-heart conversations.

She grinned and thought of her grandmother.

Yes, Nan, I'm still Mrs Fixit, she thought. I'm just no good at fixing myself.

'I'll pick you up, and I'll drive because I'm on call at the hospital tonight. They do woodfired pizza and red wine out at the Italian one,' Caro said.

'Sounds perfect!'

Half an hour later, Sara slipped her warm coat on over her jeans and jumper and ran out to Caroline's four-wheel drive. A slight shower had left the grass wet, and she shivered as she opened the door. The heater was on in the car and it was toasty warm.

'Mm, bliss. A much better way to spend a Sunday afternoon than packing,' Sara said as she secured the seatbelt. 'I can't wait to get back to the tropics.'

Caro nodded. 'It is.' Her cheeks were pink, her eyes bright, and she looked happier than she usually did. She looked curiously at Sara. 'You really are excited about going back to your hometown, aren't you?'

'I'm excited about going home.'

'What's so special about it?'

Sara considered her words carefully. She really wanted Caro to take the position at the local clinic, and she didn't want to discourage her. At the same time, she didn't want to build up any false expectations and have Caro disappointed when she arrived at the Bay.

Sara was receptionist and clinic nurse at the local medical practice and had befriended Caro when she had arrived there as a locum twelve months ago. The doctor Caro had replaced hadn't returned, and she'd ended up signing a twelve-month contract. Dr Roger Dolman—Roger the Dodger to Sara—was a difficult boss, but Sara knew it wasn't her place to warn prospective staff that the work environment could be unpleasant. She'd learned to cope with it, and it was a job in a pleasant area that paid the bills. It had always been a temporary stop for Sara as she worked her way home to Second Chance Bay.

The vineyards were a great place to live, and there was always plenty to do and see, but nothing compared to the outback paradise of home.

Over the months, and to her credit, Caro had handled Roger well, managing to fend off his advances—never inappropriate, but always on the edge—without jeopardising her job. Dr Dolman knew how hard it was to get doctors in the country and was on his best behaviour—most of the time. Caro and Sara had formed an alliance, and the crusty old bachelor boss had taken the hint and stopped asking each of them out.

'It's a quaint little town on the Gulf of Carpentaria.'

'Quaint?'

'Maybe not quaint like the pretty little towns down here in the Barossa Valley. Maybe unique is a better word than quaint.'

'You have me intrigued.'

'It's a very small town, but in winter, it fills up with retirees and tourists from the southern states. They chase the warmth. Our climate is fabulous.'

'Hot in the summer though?' Caro indicated to turn onto the main road.

'We have air conditioners.' Sara flicked a sideways glance at Caro. 'I'm so looking forward to this trip. It's a great idea to drive up.'

Caro nodded. 'I figured it was a way to have a holiday and see the country. I'm so pleased you've agreed to come with me.' She changed back a gear as they slowed behind a truck. The vineyards were bare and grey beneath the heavy cloud, but Sara had lived in the Barossa Valley for two years after—

Nope, don't go there.

The car hummed smoothly along the bitumen, and soon they turned into the little boutique winery south of town. 'I figured if I get called into the hospital while we're eating, it's close enough for you to get a taxi home.' Caro parked the car and reached over to the back seat for her jacket.

Sara shivered again while she waited for Caro to button up her jacket. The wind had picked up, and it felt like it was blowing off the Antarctic. 'You won't need that up at the Bay,' she said with a grin.

'I'm looking forward to heading north,' Caro said. They walked into the cosy restaurant and snagged a small table next to the open fire.

'Coffee or wine first?' Sara glanced at her watch. 'It's after three.'

Caro smiled. 'It's a winery. I can have one glass. I need it to warm up.'

Soon, they were settled, and Sara leaned back in her chair and looked at the bright flames crackling in the hearth. 'That's about the only thing I'll miss about here. I do love to sit in front of a fire.' She chuckled. 'Sometimes in winter when we have a barbie at home, we light a bonfire, but that's as close as we get.'

Caro lifted her wine glass, and the firelight caught the ruby red liquid.

'And the afternoons at the vineyards,' Sara added. 'I've been to some great concerts since I've been here.'

'Tell me how you ended up in the Barossa Valley. It's a long way from the Gulf of Carpentaria.'

Sara lifted her wine and watched as it caught the firelight too. 'The warts and all story? I guess we've got time.'

As she leaned forward to begin her story, a shadow fell across the table, and Sara looked up.

'Well, blow me down. Sara Sweeney, as I live and breathe!'

'Maisie! What a surprise. I thought you'd be up in the Bay.' Sara smiled at the older woman. Maisie had been a regular visitor to Second Chance Bay every winter for as long as Sara could remember.

'I came here from Melbourne on a bus trip with some other old boilers. I'm flying up to the Bay in a couple of weeks. I leave my van up there these days. I'm getting too old and doddery to tow it all the way from the bottom to the top of the country. I thought it was you, Sara. What on earth are you doing down here?'

'I live here,' Sara replied.

'Married? Kids? Partner?' She flicked a curious glance at Caro, and Sara bit back a smile.

'No. None of that. I'm a career girl these days.' She turned to Caro. 'Maisie, this is my friend and colleague, Caroline. Caro, this is Maisie, who's known me since I was a kid.'

'And a pretty kid she was.' Maisie shook her head. 'You broke young Mattie's heart when you left the Bay, Sara.'

Despite her chuckle, something thick lodged in Sara's throat. 'I'm sure it wasn't a broken heart.'

Maisie nodded. 'Oh yes, it was. The poor boy is still single.'

Sara swallowed and forced a smile to her face; for a moment, going home lost its appeal. 'I'm sure Matthew McDougall is still enjoying life as much as he ever was. And the poor boy can't be that far off forty. I'm thirty-five.'

Caro smiled over at Sara. 'Sounds like you've got a reason to go home?'

Sara pulled a face at her. 'Don't you start.' She looked up at Maisie. 'Caro and I are about to take a road trip. I'll be back at the Bay in a month. I'm coming home to work at the medical surgery, and Caro might be going to work with Dr Rose.'

'You're a doctor, love?' Maisie stared at Caroline, and Sara could see that she had gone up in her estimation.

'I am, and Sara has enticed me to visit the Bay.'

'Best place in the world.' Maisie's blue-rinsed hair bounced as she nodded. 'I'll see you both soon, then. Nice to meet you, Doctor.'

Sara giggled as Maisie went back to her table. 'You've hit the big time, but be warned. Second Chance Bay will know all about you by the time we arrive now that Maisie knows you're coming.'

Caro leaned forward. 'Now tell me about this guy whose heart you broke.'

Chapter Two

Two weeks later

Matt McDougall opened the door of the rusted refrigerator in the small kitchenette. It had sat at the back of the tiny room in the family fish co-op since he was a kid. He'd opened that fridge probably five times a day for the past fifteen years, ever since their father had died. His accountant's brain kicked in as he reached in and pulled out the carton of milk.

Five times a day, multiplied by three hundred and sixty days—the family business only closed on public holidays—multiplied by fifteen years. He closed the door harder than he usually would, and the milk slopped out of the carton onto his hand.

Damn.

His already-strange mood deteriorated further. Twenty-seven thousand times he'd probably opened the door of that bloody old Kelvinator fridge. The jug boiled and he poured the boiling water onto his coffee bag.

Why did he have to be the one who worried about money?

He could have bought a new fridge anytime over the past couple of years, and why was he letting it worry him so much today?

Jake's flash charter boats, Matt's little brother, Donny's new luxury boat out in the Kimberley rivers, and his other brother Dane's fancy new lodge up in the Gulf probably all had good coffee machines, and here he was in a run-down old building with a coffee bag, boiling an old plastic jug.

The rest of his family were settled—in great relationships and financially secure—and he'd let himself get stuck in this old building, worrying about the dollars, when there was no longer any need to. It was time to stop burying himself in the business and do something about it.

But what did he want to do? The one woman he might have settled with had left him—he'd made sure of that—and up until now, he'd been content to stay looking after the finances of the family fish co-op, and then as his siblings expanded their interests into other areas, he'd naturally overseen the finances.

Jake was married to Matt's sister, Jenni, and Matt adored his niece, Leni. Now, there was his nephew, Callen, a relatively new addition to the family. Donny and Claire were working in the Kimberleys in Western Australia, and Dane and Nicole were up at Staaten River, adding two more lodges to their thriving business.

Matt winced as the steam from the jug burned his wrist, and when the coffee was a decent strength, he lifted the bag out and threw it in the sink. As he walked back into this office, the bell above the door tinkled, indicating a customer, and he turned and headed out into the shop.

Not only did he look after the accounts for the family businesses, but he was also expected to serve bloody prawns.

'Bloody Nora, Matthew! Is the milk in that coffee sour? It must be by the look on your face.'

Matt smiled, and his smile was genuine despite his bad mood. He put his coffee on the counter and hurried around to the other side.

'Hey there, Miss Maisie. You're back, so it must be winter down south. Give me a hug!'

The older woman hugged him back. 'Bloody heck, Matthew, you're getting more like your father every year.'

'Maybe I look like him, but I'm not like him.' Matt's voice was terse as his bad mood came rushing back.

'Of course, you're not. But you sure have a look of him. How's your Mum?'

'She's well. She and Rick are away in Europe.'

'Oh, the lucky duck, but she does deserve it after all she went through.'

'She does.' Matt didn't need reminding of that, and he frowned as he observed the curly, blue-rinsed head of hair. 'Now, what's this I hear about you moving to the best site in the caravan park.'

Maisie pouted, and her gravelly voice rasped out. 'Now, who the friggin' heck told you? There's no secrets in this bloody town!'

Matt tapped the side of his nose. Maisie was a character and her language was often as blue as her hair. 'I went over there looking for you last week. I thought you'd be due to arrive soon. Kev told me that he'd put you on the site at the end of Toorak Lane. The one with the best view of the water.'

'Yep. Old Sheila McIntyre went into a home after her Jimmy carked it.'

Matt swallowed a smile. 'I'm sorry to hear that.'

'Gawd, I'm not,' Maisie said. 'She was a right bitch, and she thought she was the queen of the park. She'd only been coming up for twenty-five years. I beat her by two years, but I still got relegated down to Dunrootin' Lane when my Reg died.'

'Ah, the social politics of a caravan park. But I guess you're the new queen now?' Matt reached for his coffee.

Her nod was definite, and her smile smug. 'I sure as tootin' am. We're going to get rid of that stupid bridge game they were playing and go back to a decent round of poker every afternoon.'

Matt chuckled. 'Maisie, it's so good to have you back.'

'So why were you looking for me, love? You need a hand in the shop?'

Maisie had helped out in the shop when she came up from Melbourne for as long as Matt could remember. She was great with the grey nomies, and they usually ended up spending more than they intended.

'If you're free.' He grinned and winked. 'Although you're now a woman of power . . .'

'Don't be bloody stupid. Go and make me a coffee, and I'll put an apron on. Might as well start now. You look like you need cheering up.' She looked around. 'Are you here by yourself these days? Is that why you were looking so bloody miserable when I walked in? Where's that pretty young girl who was here last winter? I had high hopes there.'

'What girl?' Matt took a sip of his coffee. 'I don't remember.'

'Well, I guess you didn't score then.' Maisie's husky laugh rumbled through the shop. 'Or if you did, it wasn't memorable.'

Matt shook his head. 'You're incorrigible. It's good to have you back, Maisie. How many hours work do you want?'

'I'll just go outside and have a ciggie before I start. I'll have a think about the hours.' She pushed the door open, and the bell jangled again. 'White with two sugars if you've forgotten, and none of that fancy bag stuff. A heaped teaspoon of International Roast'll do me.'

Matt grinned as he went back into the kitchen and flicked the jug on. He reached up and pulled out the tin of coffee that had been in the cupboard since last year when Maisie had worked in the co-op and was pleased that it hadn't solidified. He'd get a fresh one when he went to the shop. Maisie's two major pastimes were coffee and her beloved ciggies; it was a wonder she was still healthy.

By the time Matt had made the hot drink as directed and gone back into the shop, she was behind the counter kitted out in the yellow plastic apron; the smell of cigarettes had wafted in with her.

'Thank you, sweets. You're a treasure,' she said. 'Now tell me all about the family and what everyone's up to.'

Matt filled Maisie in on where everyone was, and that Mum and Rick were due back at the end of winter. 'They've been overseas a couple of months. Mum said she wanted to do one of those river cruises.'

Maisie nodded. 'Best thing she ever did was hooking up with that Rick. He was a good catch. If I'd been a few years younger when Reg died . . .'

Matt tried not to choke on his coffee. He swallowed and smiled at her. 'I'm sure you would have given Mum a run for her money.'

'That I would.' Maisie reached under the counter and pulled out a fresh packet of the white paper that they wrapped the prawns in. 'You go and get back to work in the office. I'll take over out here.'

As Matt turned to go back to his desk, she called out to him. 'Oh, I forgot to tell you who I bumped into a couple of weeks ago. Guess!'

Matt shook his head. 'I have no idea.'

'The new doctor who's going to work with Doc Rose. I'd heard the Doc was thinking of getting a second doctor in town.'

'I heard that too. It's been busy since the mine expanded. There are new families arriving in town each week. I know he was worried about getting someone to come to the Bay. Anyone from down south thinks we're too far away from everything.'

'Best place in Australia if you ask me. If it wasn't so bloody hot in the wet season, I'd move up here for good.' She looked at him intently. 'And you'll never guess who's coming with the new doc.'

'Who?' Matt was already thinking about what he was going to do first. Jake had asked him to get some prices on some new fishing reels for Moonshine, and Dane was waiting for him to mail the latest building quote for the new cabin at the lodge up to him.

'She's coming home.'

Matt screwed his nose up. 'Sorry, you've lost me.'

Maisie shook her head and spoke slowly. 'Sara Sweeney. She's coming home.'

Matt stood still and a strange feeling washed over him. For a moment he didn't say anything, and he tried to clear his expression because he knew how savvy Maisie was.

'Sara? She's with the new doctor?' The thought of Sara moving back to town with a partner was one that didn't sit comfortably with Matt, even though he had no right to feel that way.

He and Sara Sweeney had had a pretty hot and heavy relationship when she'd lived here, and he'd known that Sara wanted to settle down. She'd been after the engagement, the white wedding, the kids and the house, and the whole thing, but that was the one thing he hadn't been able to give her.

Eventually, she'd got sick of waiting for him to settle down, and moved to Adelaide. It had been the best thing for both of them.

'She was with the new doctor. They were planning a Thelma and Louise.'

Matt scratched his head. 'Maisie, what are you talking about? What's a Thelma and Louise?'

'Honestly Matt, you're such a typical man. You don't listen. It's a road trip.'

'Oh,' he said, none the wiser.

'I saw them in a winery.'

'Who? Thelma and Louise? Who are they?' Matt stared at her.

Maybe it wasn't such a good idea to hire Maisie. What would she be now? Heading for her late seventies. Was this the first sign of dementia kicking in?

'You think I've lost the plot, don't you?' Maisie laughed as she looked at him. 'I was on a bus trip to the Barossa Valley and they were there at a winery. Sara and the new doc are driving up from Adelaide, like Thelma and Louise in that movie.'

'Oh. It's Sara's who's coming home then. For a visit? Or to stay?' Matt didn't know how he felt about that. But he knew it would be hard to see Sara with a partner.

'Does she have any kids?'

'Who? The new doctor or Sara?

Matt frowned. 'The new doctor is a woman?'

'Yes. Sheesh, it'd be hard for a guy to do a Thelma and Louise.' Maisie put her hands on her hips. 'I've got the DVD in the caravan. I'll lend it to you.' They both looked up as the bell above the door tinkled and three couples walked in. 'You go and work, I'll look after the customers.'

'Thanks, Mais. You're a great help.'

'No wuckers, mate.'

Matt rolled his eyes and walked to his small office as Maisie greeted the customers. 'What can I do for you, love?'

He sat at his desk for a long time before he turned his computer on. Sara Sweeney coming home raised a whole heap of memories. Funny that he'd been thinking about her before Maisie had arrived.

A tiny little burst of happiness settled in his chest. Maybe she was home to stay?

Matt shook his head and pushed the excitement away.

It didn't matter how long Sara was coming home for; it wouldn't make any difference to how he felt. Matt didn't intend settling down with anyone.

Ever.

Not even the woman he'd once been in love with.

Chapter Three

'And you just upped and left?' Caro said as she slowed down behind the van ahead of them as they approached the Northern Territory border. Being on the road and spending many hours in a car together had moved Sara and Caro's professional relationship to a friendship. Even though they'd worked together for a year and been out for coffee a few times, Sara hadn't known much about Caro's past, and she hadn't shared her story yet. There'd been a few hints, but Sara hadn't pressed her. If Caro wanted her to know, she would share when she was ready.

In the two weeks on the road, Sara had shared her story with Caroline.

Well, half of it.

Caro had been curious the afternoon they'd met to plan the trip and had asked about Matt after Maisie moved away from their table.

Sara had been vague. The first of her two big hurts still sat deep within, and seeing Maisie had raised a lot of memories. Twice in her life, she'd been rejected, and it had taken her to thirty-five to regain her confidence and have faith in herself. She hid her lack of confidence behind a ditzy exterior and always put on a happy face. No one would ever have guessed that a shy woman with low self-confidence hid beneath those colourful out-there outfits, crazy red curly hair, and loud jokes.

'I did. I could see us going on like that for years. Matt was happy with his life the way it was, and his brothers were the same. They lived for their fishing'—Sara chuckled— 'I mean Dane and Donny did. Matt got too seasick to go out on the water. He ran the business side of things, and I guess he probably still does. Three bachelors, ripe for the picking but too involved in their business to have any time for anything else.'

'And you wanted different things?'

Sara nodded as Caro pulled out to overtake the long caravan in front of them. She waited until they were around it and had pulled into the lane ahead. 'I did. Back in those days, I thought I wanted marriage and kids, but I guess Matt did me a favour. I guess we just fell out of love—or I did anyway.' She crossed her fingers. 'We were probably too young.'

Caro flicked her a glance. 'I thought it was only a few years ago. You couldn't have been that young.'

'True. It was eight years ago.' Sara pulled a face. 'After I left and I thought about it, I knew that it wasn't that. I mean, I was twenty-seven, and Matt was thirty. When I pushed, he said we had plenty of time.'

'And you could hear the biological clock ticking?'

'I could. And there were so many girlie flicks out then about that. I guess I let them bother me too much. When I raised it with Matt, I knew I was wasting my time and he didn't want me, so I left the same week, rather than wait and get hurt.'

'He told you that he didn't want you?' Caro reached over and turned the music volume down as she waited for Sara to answer.

'No, not in so many words. I knew he was making excuses, so I decided to go.'

'What did he say?'

'I didn't tell him I was going. I haven't seen him or talked to him since I left.'

'And he's still single?'

Sara shrugged. 'Apparently. But listen, Caro, don't go getting any ideas. I'm over Matt McDougal and he did me a favour. He really is a lovely guy. I wasn't the right woman for him.' She looked sideways at Caro. 'Now if he's still single . . . maybe . . .'

'You'd have another go?'

'No! I meant you might like to meet him.'

Carolyn shook her head emphatically. 'No chance. I'm up here to work and—'

She bit her lip as she focused on the road.

'And?' Sara asked

'And to recover from a similar experience.' Caro laughed. 'I think our experience with the opposite sex went a long way to helping us deal so firmly with Roger.'

'He was harmless. It was his persistence that was annoying.'

Caroline shook her head again. 'No, Sara. It's never harmless. We could cope with his insistent behaviour because we had maturity and experience on our side. Imagine if someone with no self-confidence started working for him.'

'I don't have that much self-confidence, you know.' Sara looked down at her hands clenched on her lap. 'A couple of years ago I had the same experience as I did with Matt, with another guy and it left me pretty fragile. I made up my mind when I moved to Tanunda; I was meant to stay single. For a long time, I really believed I wasn't good enough for anyone. And now I've accepted my time's passed. I'm happy being by myself. My confidence is back, and I'm looking forward to going home.'

'Sure, there's no chance of rekindling that relationship? Maisie said you broke his heart.'

The sound that came from Sara's mouth was a cross between a snort and a laugh. 'Now that I don't believe. Now I've shared with you, you can tell me your story.'

Caro changed back a gear and slowed down as a huge road train appeared on the horizon. 'God, I hate those big trucks. They shake the car.' She was quiet until the truck with the triple trailer passed them. 'Are you happy to stop for the night at the roadhouse across the border? Or do you want to drive for a while?'

'Let's stop. I had a look at the map, and it's a long way before the next roadhouse. Almost to the Uluru turnoff.' Sara was sick of being in the car, although the prospect of another night of rolling out her swag on red dirt didn't appeal greatly either.

'Okay, we're almost there.' Caro glanced across at Sara. 'And over a wine, I'll tell you my story. It's not so different from yours, but I was a lot older. My biological clock had already run out.'

They were quiet as each was lost in their thoughts for the next half hour. Talking about Matt had helped Sara realise that she was over him. It had taken a long time, and then, when she'd met Jeff, she'd believed she was ready for another relationship. She bit back the sigh that rose in her chest. She thought it had been hard when Matt had rejected her. The fiasco with Jeff in Adelaide had turned her off relationships for life. She wasn't destined to be a wife and mother; it had taken some getting used to, but she'd accepted her life as a single woman, and she'd learned to be happy.

Sara reached over and turned the music up again. 'I think we need some happy music.'

They both laughed when the next song came on.

'Who needs the Bee Gees singing about being alone!' She searched her phone. 'Let's have some Pink!'

***

Ever since Maisie had told him that Sara was on the way home—and she didn't have a partner—Matt had been restless. On the first Saturday in July, after hectic days in the co-op and hectic nights trying to get the tax for four businesses up to scratch, he was pleased when Jenni arrived at the shop just before closing with Leni holding one hand and a pram being pushed with the other.

'Uncle Mattie.' The little girl ran through the door with a squeal and launched herself into Matt's open arms. 'We's having a barbie. Can you come?'

Matt squeezed her and dropped a kiss on the top of the blonde curls. 'I sure can. I need feeding. Your poor Uncle Matt has been working so hard he forgot to eat.'

Jenni pulled a face at him. 'More likely, you were too lazy to cook. Besides, Jake said he saw you having dinner at the pub the other night.'

Matt shook his head. 'One night at the pub and I'm the talk of the Bay. Jeez, you've gotta love this town.' He ruffled Leni's hair as he put her down. 'You tell your Mummy to be nice to Uncle Matt. I've been working my butt off, Jen.'

'And you think we've all been having a holiday?' I haven't seen Jake for fourteen days straight. He had two back-to-back charters.' Jenni folded her arms. 'Do you want to come over for dinner, or are you too busy being the family martyr?' Her tone was sharp, and it hurt. Jenni had always been the one to tell it how it was.

Matt ran his hand through his hair; he was in need of a haircut. 'Of course, I'll come and I'm sorry for being a grumpy bum. It's been a busy week. I didn't get the Boyle girl to come in after school because Maisie's back in town and was going to give me some hours, but she only turned up once. I've been flat out in the shop.'

'Maisie's in the hospital.'

'What?' Matt stared. 'Is she okay?'

Jenni nodded. 'I'm sorry. I thought you knew. Lurline on the desk at the hospital said she'd call you because Maisie asked her to let you know she couldn't work for a few days.'

'I would have gone straight over if I'd known. 'Matt glanced at his watch. 'Is she okay? What happened?'

'She had a fall.' Jenni put her hand up. 'Don't worry. It wasn't her age or anything. Apparently, someone had dug a hole at the side of the amenities block and hadn't roped it off. Maisie tripped and fell in the dark. She's okay, but they were keeping her in for a few days until the swelling in her ankle went down, seeing she's by herself in the park.'

'Poor old love. I wonder if it's too late to get flowers at IGA? I'll go over and see her after I close up.'

'That'd be nice. Give her my love. And Matt, if you go to IGA can you get me a big tub of coleslaw for tonight, please? The others are all in town.'

'What others?'

Jenni shook her head. 'For someone who supposedly runs the business, you don't have a clue! Your brothers are both in town. And Claire and Nicole too.'

Matt's face lit up in a smile. 'That's great. It's ages since we've all been together.'

He looked up at the clock. 'I'm going to close up now. What time are they arriving?'

'They'll be here soon.'

'Right. I'll go across river and have a shower and then see Maisie on the way to your place.'

Jenni turned as she reached the door. 'And one more thing. Tonight is a family occasion. No business talk. Okay?'

He nodded. 'I can do that. I'm looking forward to catching up with the boys.'

'If Jake gets home in time.' Jenni held the door open with her hip as she ushered Leni in front of the pram.

'You okay, sis?'

'I'm fine. I'll see you in a while. Don't forget the coleslaw.'

Matt would never admit it to anyone, but he'd always been a little bit jealous of his brother-in-law. Jake Jones had travelled and lived in France and came back to Second Chance Bay. By then, he had come back mature, experienced, and very wealthy.

Matt felt guilty—Jake was an all-round nice guy. But Jenni was his baby sister, and they'd been close. Now that she was with Jake, he and Jenni weren't as close as they'd been growing up, but he still watched out for her.

And now that Dane and Donny had their partners, Matt spent a lot of time home alone in the old family house. That unfamiliar restlessness tugged at him.

Maybe it was time for a change.

He nodded as he got ready to lock up the shop. It was time for him to leave town. There was a big wide world out there, and it was time to go and find it.

And if he wasn't here, he couldn't be tempted by Sara Sweeney.

Chapter Four

The smell of steak and onions enticed Matt as he pushed open the gate of Jenni and Jake's new house on the point north of town. Jake had come back to the Bay, having made his fortune on the Cote d'Azur, and then made peace with the family, married Jenni, and gone into partnership in the charter side of the business.

Jake and Jenni had been high school sweethearts, but Matt and Jenni's father had caused trouble between them and Jake had fled town not long after he'd left school. Not the only trouble the old man had caused. The rest of the family seemed to have forgotten about it, but it was the one thing that Matt would never forget, and it was the one reason that he would never settle down and have a family of his own. The others hadn't seen what he had growing up; being the oldest by a couple of years had meant that he'd seen more of how their father had treated Mum.

Jake and Jenni's new house was spectacular—a long way from the old timber house where the McDougal siblings had grown up. The house where Matt now lived by himself. The two storeys had a sloping roof and wide shady verandas that wrapped around the four sides of the house, which was painted in a soft grey. But despite its grandeur, it was a home. Comfy and colourful hammocks swung in the breeze on the first level, and Leni's trike and assorted toys covered the lawn. The house was welcoming, and Matt knew that their mother loved visiting here too. The last email had said how much she was missing them all, but Matt knew it was more the grandchildren that Mum missed.

Jenni's home oozed love and family, and when everyone was in the Bay, the family gathered here, but it wasn't often enough. Matt looked out to the Gulf and smiled. Three large vessels were moored close to shore. Jake's boat, *Moonshine*, was out there, and Donny, Dane, and their partners had arrived by boat too. Matt quickened his pace, keen to see his family.

Laughter and voices reached him as he walked around to the large expanse of lawn at the back of the house. He smiled when he reached the outdoor kitchen that looked over the Gulf. He was relieved to see Jake had his arm looped around Jenni's shoulders and Dane and Donny were leaning against the fence, each with a beer in hand. There was no sign of Claire and Nicole, but he could hear voices coming from the kitchen.

The long table was covered with a colourful cloth, and he placed the bag he was carrying on the end.

'Hey, big brother.' He grinned as first Dane, and then Donny, enfolded him in a bear hug. Their father might not have been demonstrative, but Mum had ensured that the brothers were not shy about showing affection. Jake left Jenni and came over and thumped Matt's arm.

'Hi, big fella, I hear you've been busy.'

Matt nodded. 'And you too. Charters have been good so far by the look of things?'

'It's been a great start to the season. Lots of visitors in town.'

'Us too,' Donny said. 'I'm thinking about getting another boat. We've turned away heaps of bookings because we're full up. It's kept us busy, but now that Claire—' He broke off and grinned.

'And now that Claire?'

Donny shook his head. 'I'll wait until she comes outside.'

'The lodge is full too,' Dane said. 'We've had to hire more staff.'

Matt was pleased for them, but that glimmer of disquiet that had dogged him all week flared up again. He sat in the co-op day in, day out, while his brothers were out experiencing life. He pushed the thought away as Jenni took his arm.

'Did you get the coleslaw?'

Matt nodded and pointed to the chiller bag on the table. 'I got some fancy cheese and olives too. And there's a couple of bottles of wine in the bottom.'

Matt nodded as Jake held up a can of Coke. 'Yes, please.'

'Thanks.' Jenni tipped her head to the side and tucked her hair behind her ear. Matt thought she looked tired. 'Did you go and see Maisie?'

'Yeah, briefly. She was holding court in the hospital foyer on a pair of crutches. Doc Rose was rolling his eyes. She was telling everyone about the new doctor and how pretty she is.'

'What new doctor?' Jenni shook her head. 'Of course, Maisie would know what's happening before anyone else in town.'

Matt hesitated. Of all his family, Jenni was the one who knew how badly he'd stuffed up with Sara. He should have been honest with her, but he'd known her so well she would have talked him around. That last night, Sara had tried to talk to him; he'd been deliberately distant, and he knew he'd hurt her.

The next day, she was gone, and he'd never heard from her again. Matt had been sad, but it had been for the best. He'd convinced himself that if Sara had really loved him like she'd always said, she wouldn't have left without saying goodbye, and she would have tried harder.

But that had been stupid. Even though it had been the outcome he'd wanted, he'd been bloody hurt, but the only one who'd ever guessed was Jenni.

If he'd had his time over again, he might have done things differently, but deep down, Matt knew it was for the best. It was what he'd wanted and how it had to be.

He looked up as his two sisters-in-law came out of the kitchen. Dane and Donny had hit the jackpot there, as had Jake with Jenni.

He hugged Claire first and smiled as she stepped back. 'You're looking exceptionally well.' He glanced across at Donny. 'Is there any news I should know?'

Claire's fair skin coloured, but her smile was wide. 'Just that you're going to be an uncle again.'

Matt dropped a kiss on her cheek and then turned and shook Donny's hand. 'That's fabulous news.' Before he could turn back to greet Nicole, Dane held his hand out too. 'You might as well get it all over at once, Matt. Nicole and I have news too.' Dane's voice was husky as he smiled at his wife.

Nicole reached up and hugged Matt. 'Yep, another family member on the way here too. We called Binnie this afternoon, and now she wants to come back and live with her auntie and uncle.'

'Then you'd have your hands full.' When Nicole had first moved north, her small niece had lived with her in the old rundown house up the coast where they had now built their upmarket fishing lodge. Matt shook his head. 'Gawd, two more babies on the way. Mum will be beside herself. Rick won't get her away again for a while.'

'Yeah, we did a three-way Skype the other night. There was lots of champagne flowing on their cruise by the time we finished. They're going to extend the trip a bit so Mum can have a couple of years at home. She won't leave the babies once they're born.'

Jenni sighed and pushed her hair back again. Matt frowned as he noticed her hand was shaking. 'Leni keeps asking when Nanny will be home. It's hard with her away with a new baby here.'

Dane and Donny went back to the barbeque to help Jake, and Matt turned to Jenni. 'You okay, Jen? You look tired.'

Her eyes welled as she looked at him. 'I'm just run down. Looking after the two kids, trying to keep the house in order, and

I've had some sort of virus. I haven't felt well for a couple of weeks.'

'Have you been to see Doc Rose?'

She shook her head. 'No. I haven't had time.'

'Call me. I can come and sit with the kids.'

She waved a hand. 'I'm fine. I just need a good night's sleep. Jake's home for a few days now.'

Matt put his arm around her. 'You take care of yourself, sis.'

'I will. Now tell me how Maisie knows all about this new lady doctor we're getting?'

Matt swallowed and looked over the top of her head. 'Apparently, she ran into them in the Barossa Valley.'

'Them? We're getting more than one new doctor?'

'No. A friend of hers is coming with her.' He lowered his voice. 'Sara is coming home, Jen.'

Chapter Five

Next to the site Sara and Caro were allocated at Kulgera Roadhouse was a fire pit in an old truck rim. It was full of white ash and looked like it was well-used.

'What do you think?' Sara looked at the small pile of twigs beside it.

'I think a fire would be good.' Caro pointed across the narrow road behind the camp area. 'The girl in reception said there's plenty of wood in the bush if we wanted a fire. We have to collect it ourselves.'

'Let's go. We can set our swags up once we get the fire going.'

Sara and Caroline headed into the bush, keen to warm up. They'd both been surprised at how cold it was out in the desert. The days were warm and sunny, but the temperature plummeted to below zero during the night.

'Thank goodness we both have warm sleeping bags.' Sara shivered as they headed into the bush with a couple of bags to put the wood in. They didn't have to go far; there was plenty of fallen timber just behind the fence.

'You can tell you're from the tropics.' Caroline was still in a short-sleeved T-shirt and shorts.

'I never got used to the cold,' Sara replied. 'I'm so looking forward to getting back home.'

'You really have decided to stay there?' Caroline said as she bent to pick up a small dead branch.

'I have. Nan's getting on, and it'll be good if I'm around to help out when she needs it.'

'Did you tell her you're coming home?'

'No, I wanted to surprise her.'

Caro looked at her with a frown. 'Will you stay with her? If she's not expecting you?'

'I'll stay for a short while until I get my place. I like living by myself.' Sara pointed to a dead tree on the ground at the side of the sandy track. 'And Nan'll be home. She never goes anywhere.'

'Do your parents live there?'

Sara shook her head. 'Gosh, no. Dad got out of the Bay when he went to uni and never went back. I lived with Nan from when I was fourteen when Dad got his first posting overseas. Dad's a diplomat and now he's at the embassy in France. They've been there for a few years. I don't think they'll come home even when he retires. They've bought a small cottage in a gorgeous little village called St Paul de Vence in the south of France. I'd love to go there one day, but just for a visit. The photos Mum sends are gorgeous.'

'It's a very beautiful village.' Caro's voice was wistful. 'It's in Provence.'

'You've been there?'

'I have. I got engaged there.'

Sara paused as she went to pick up some kindling. 'Engaged? I didn't know you were— or had been married?'

'We didn't get married. Dylan proposed in Paris, and I said yes in St Paul de Vence a couple of days later.' Caro held out the bag for the kindling.

'You had to think about it?'

'You should know me by now, Sara, after working with me for a year. I don't rush into decisions. That's why I'll visit Second Chance Bay before I decide to take the contract they've offered.'

'Fair enough.' Sara tried not to sound too curious, but she couldn't help asking. 'How long were you engaged?'

'Two years. I left him in Melbourne last year to come to Tanunda.'

'We make a good pair. What happened?'

As the two women broke branches off the dead tree, the top edge of a full moon appeared over the tree canopy to the east. They both stood there quietly as it rose until the heavy golden orb hovered over trees tinged purple by the sunset.

'I love the outback,' Sara said quietly. 'It makes everything else seem insignificant.'

'It does. To answer your question, our situations were a bit different. Dylan didn't like that I was in a medical practice. He wanted me to go into research like he was.'

'He mustn't have known you very well. You are a fabulous practitioner. One of the best doctors I've ever worked with. You're patient and compassionate and your patients all love you. Even the grumpy old men! That's why I'd love to see you take the contract at Second Chance Bay. Doctor Rose is a nice man and I'm sure you'd enjoy working with him.'

Caroline looked away, and Sara caught the glint of a tear. Maybe it was best to change the subject.

'I think a full moon deserves a glass of Tanunda port around the fire. What do you think?'

'I agree.' Caro put the bag down and stared at the moon for a moment before she turned back to Sara. 'Thank you for being an ear, Sara. Leaving Dylan was one of the hardest things I've ever done. I loved him, and I thought he loved me.' She turned away again to look at the moon. 'A sight like that moon makes you believe in romance, but I learned the hard way. There is no happy ever-after romance like the movies. Not for some of us, anyway. Dylan fell out of love with me. Once I told him I would be staying in practice, the last few months together were like living in an apartment with a stranger. We stopped doing things together, and he shut down. I stopped asking where he was when he was away all of the time. I never thought that he would cheat on me, and when he finally asked me to leave—'

'He told you there was someone else?'

'No. He told me he had simply stopped loving me and that it was time for me to move out. He said it was because I wouldn't listen to him, that if I loved him, I'd do as he said. It was his apartment, so I had no choice.' Her eyes filled with tears, and she brushed at them angrily. 'It toughened me up, Sara.'

'Oh, Caro, I'm sorry.'

'Even the last time he held me, I still loved him, even though he'd broken my heart. He held me close, and his lips brushed the top of my head, but I didn't cry. I packed my bag with my clothes, and I left everything else there, including the ring he'd bought me in Paris. I couldn't stand to stay any longer than I had to. It was awful.' Caro started walking, and her movements were jerky as she bent and picked up small branches. She stopped and stared at Sara. 'You know what? I'm forty-five years old, and I'm sick of being careful. I will take the contract at Second Chance Bay. What you've said about it being a good idea is enough for me. I'll email Dr Rose later.'

'Are you sure? That's fabulous!'

Although Sara was surprised at Caro's sudden mind change, she was happy. She could see Caroline living at the Bay, and Sara would do her best to help her find happiness.

'Now let's get this firewood and go back and have a wine to celebrate my new job.' Caro smiled, and Sara felt as though their friendship had reached a new level.

'Sounds good to me.'

##

Once they had a cheery blaze going, Sara headed over to the amenities block for a shower while Caro sent the email accepting the contract. The amenities block was basic but clean, and as she stood under the steaming hot water, Sara thought of ways to keep Caro at the Bay now that she had committed to the job. She was a fabulous doctor and wonderful with all her patients—from small children to the elderly. She would be an asset to the community. She was sad for her but determined to help her get over her broken heart.

When they arrived at the Bay, Sara had every intention of seeking Matthew out so she could make it clear that they could be friends. She owed him an apology; leaving like she had, and never contacting him had been rude. An over-the-top kneejerk reaction. She knew she'd placed too much importance on getting married; she thought she'd loved him, but if she really had, could she have left like she did?

Yes, a small voice whispered. You were hurt.

No, logic chimed in. You've managed your life very well without Matthew McDougall for the past few years. Rarely even thought about him.

Rubbish, said that small voice. You still think about him every day. And that had been the problem with the relationship with Jeff. Maybe he had sensed that she wasn't totally committed to him, but he'd never said anything about that before he'd left her.

He'd left her.

Sara hadn't been as upset as she had been when she'd left Matt, but Jeff's rejection had made her realise that she had to learn to be happy spending her life alone.

And she had been happy at Tanunda. She'd got her head together enough to accept that it was time to go home to the Bay. Second Chance Bay, where she had such happy memories.

Sara turned the shower off and reached for the towel. She was destined—and content—to spend her life alone. She could suit herself where she went and what she did. Maybe once she'd checked that Nan was okay and got Caro settled at the Bay, she could go to France and visit Mum and Dad for a while.

If Matthew was still single, he might be an incentive to get Caro to settle there. She could be the right woman for him. A little bit older, but maybe . . .

Water droplets sprayed through the air as Sara shook her head with a laugh, but there was no mirth in it. She'd had success in setting up a few friends as couples since she'd left Second Chance Bay with her own broken heart. It was time to pull back.

Love and let live.

Whoops, shouldn't that be live and let live?

By the time Sara had dressed and walked back to the campsite, Caro had put her laptop away and was sitting beside the fire.

'How about a real celebration?' she said. 'I checked out the roadhouse when I booked in, and the pub meals look okay. Let's eat inside tonight. My shout.'

'Sounds good to me,' Sara replied. The thought of cooking another meal and washing up camp dishes and pans in the cold air and red dirt didn't appeal.

They walked over to the log timber building and pushed open the door. The room was warm and inviting and to their surprise, they snagged the last available table near the fire. The room buzzed with conversation, and Sara looked around with interest. Older caravanning couples sat at the tables, a few backpackers and a large group of ringers and cattle workers lined the long bar.

Sara grinned and pointed to the ceiling; a collection of Aussie flags, hats, baseball caps and different coloured bras hung from the slatted timber. 'Interesting collection.'

'Welcome to the outback.' Caro grinned. 'I've read about the collections in some of these roadhouse outposts. I'm looking forward to seeing the termite mounds that the backpackers dress up too.'

'You'll see them on the way to Second Chance Bay.' Sara looked up as a couple of guys stood at the side of the table.

'Do you mind if we share your table, ladies? Last seats left in the house?' A tall guy in a khaki work shirt stood beside the bench they were sitting on.

'Sure.'

As Sara and Caro moved along, a guitar chord reverberated through the room as the night's entertainer began to play; it was too loud to get into a conversation with the newcomers at the other end of the table, but the girls were far enough away from the speakers to still be able to chat.

'Different to the city,' Sara said.

Caro nodded. 'It is. It doesn't have that polished veneer that you see in city bars. This is a true snapshot of outback life.'

'I love it. A bit of a wild frontier feel. It's so Australian, it reminds me of home. There's a similar roadhouse on the back road on the way into Normanton too.' A huge wave of homesickness engulfed Sara. It had been a long time since she'd let herself think of the Bay because the memories had made her sad for such a long time. Now, the anticipation of returning to the town where she'd spent much of her life excited her. In a couple of weeks, she'd be home and would see Nan. It had been way too long; a twinge of guilt coursed through her. It had been ages since she'd called her grandmother for a chat.

'Tell me about the Bay.' Caro's grin was wide. 'I guess I should find out more about the place I've just committed to for a year. Dr Rose replied immediately, and he seemed pleased that I accepted the job. I guess I'll have to find somewhere to live when we get there.'

'That won't be a problem. There's quite a few empty houses,' Sara said. 'It's an aging population, or it was when I left. The younger ones move to the city, and sadly, the elderly die.'

'That'd be right.' Caro pulled a face, but there was a smile there. 'Now I've accepted the contract, you tell me the negatives! So, what's the positives?'

'Oh, the Bay is a beautiful part of the world. Wait until you see the Morning Glory cloud for the first time. The town is right on the Gulf of Carpentaria and there's a wonderful river full of birdlife and the odd crocodile, if you like wildlife spotting. It's so interesting. I love wandering along the riverbank.'

'I'll pass on the crocs, I think.'

'The tourist industry is buzzing, and you can always get fresh fish and seafood.' Sara looked down. 'That's what Matt does. Or at least he did while I was there.'

'A fisherman?'

'No, he's an accountant. He looks after the books and the fish co-op for the family. It was Matt who told me we lived in an outback paradise. "Outback paradise right on the silvery sea", he used to say.'

'He sounds like a romantic?' Caro's glance was quick but curious.

Sara shrugged. 'I guess he was in some ways. I'll never forget the day we went out on his family's charter boat. As soon as we were out of sight of land, he was so seasick. His brother taught me how to fish, and I caught the biggest fish of the day.' The noise of the room faded as Sara looked at the fire and remembered that day. Matt had spent the trip in the cabin—and the toilet—but even though he'd known he would be seasick, he'd wanted to take her out to sea. When they'd got back to the shore, he recovered almost immediately. Back then, she'd been in the spare room at Nan's house, and Nan had been away on a trip.

Matt had been pale, and she'd made him lie down on her bed. One thing had led to another and—'

'Which way are you heading?'

Sara jumped as the deep voice interrupted her daydream. The music had stopped, and the guy in the khaki work shirt had moved up the bench closer to her. His thigh pressed hard against her leg, and she moved away.

'Oh, we've come up from South Australia, and we're heading to Queensland,' she replied without being specific. They'd heard a few horror stories on the trip about some less-than-savoury characters in the outback. 'What about you?'

'We're not travelling at the moment. Me and my mates are helping with the mustering out at Avonlea Downs for a couple of months. We're helicopter pilots, and we do the circuit in the Territory.'

'Interesting.' Sara looked across at Caro and wondered if she was happy to be talking to the other guy. She appeared relaxed, so Sara settled back in her seat. It was funny, but she felt as though she needed to look out for Caroline, even though Sara was ten years younger than Caro.

The guy leaned closer, and she caught a whiff of aftershave. 'How about I buy you a drink, lovely lady?'

She lifted her half-full glass of wine. 'I'm all good, thanks.'

With a shrug, he stood and headed to the bar and was soon talking to a couple of the backpackers that Sara had noticed earlier.

She closed her eyes and went back to her happy memories.

Chapter Six

Three weeks, four days, and three thousand kilometres after leaving Tanunda in South Australia, Caro and Sara drove into the small town of Normanton, an hour south of Second Chance Bay on the Gulf of Carpentaria. Sara knew that she'd been quiet since they'd turned north at Cloncurry onto the Burke Developmental Road. For some reason, her stomach had been in knots and the closer they got to the northern coast, the more it clenched.

'Slow down here.' She finally broke her long silence, and Caro shot a swift glance in her direction.

'Are you car sick? You're awfully pale.'

'No, I'm fine. I was just going to point out . . . look. That's the croc I was telling you about.'

'Oh my God. It's huge.'

'"Krys the Croc" is a replica of the world's largest recorded crocodile. It was killed here more than fifty years ago.'

Caro shivered. 'And you've been telling me for the past month this is a good place to live and work?'

'Don't worry. It's safe. I've only seen a few crocodiles at the Bay.'

'Huh, only a few, hey? Thanks for the reassurance.' Caro flicked the indicator on and pulled over into a vacant car park. The red dust-covered vehicle barely drew a glance from the passers-by. 'According to my Nav Man, we're less than an hour away from your home. So how about a coffee, and you can tell me what's been bothering you for the whole morning?'

'Sounds like a plan.' Sara unbuckled her seat belt and opened the door. 'Let's go look. I used to know where the coffee shops were in Normanton, but it's been a long time. My first job after I left TAFE was in the surgery here.'

They walked along the street and Sara watched the people she passed in the street. Normanton was the closest administrative centre to Second Chance Bay, and there was a good chance of running into someone she knew.

Not that they'd recognise her. She still had the curly auburn hair of her twenties, but these days, it was a lot longer, and she'd let the curls grow into spirals. In her time at the Bay, she'd lived in jeans and T-shirts and not the preferred primary coloured stripes that she favoured these days. She looked down with a grin at her purple tights, lime-green short skirt, and yellow and red striped T-shirt.

No, no one would recognise this Sara Sweeney.

'Love it,' Caro exclaimed as she stopped at the front of a small shopping arcade.

Sara grinned as she looked at the sign outside the shop. The "Local Drips" coffee shop was an addition to the town since she'd left. 'Looks good to me.' She followed Caro inside and they sat at a table near the window.

A smartly dressed waitress was at the table within seconds, a pencil hovering above her order pad. 'What will it be, girls?' she asked.

'Lunch?' Caro raised her eyebrows at Sara.

'Sorry, it'll have to be something readymade from under the glass. We close in fifteen. It's Saturday.'

'Is it?' Sara and Caro looked at each other and laughed.

'Sorry, we've been on the road for weeks and lost track of the days.'

'Half your luck,' the waitress said.

Caro jumped up and went across to the refrigerated glass and called over to the table. 'A salad sandwich?'

Sara gave her the thumbs up. 'And a flat white for both of us, thanks,' she said to the waitress. As she waited for Caro to come back to the table, the door opened, and she looked up.

'Oh, my goodness!' Sara jumped to her feet and rushed across the room as Caro looked at her with a frown.

'Jumpin' Jehoshaphat, Sara Sweeney. As I live and breathe!'

Sara grabbed her grandmother's arms and then happy tears filled her eyes as she hugged her. She sniffed. 'What are you doing in Normanton, Nan?'

Her grandmother's face split in a wide grin, and she put a hand up to her neatly permed curls as Sara led her over to the table. 'What am I doing in Normanton? I think you'd better answer that one first, missy. What are you doing in Normanton? And more to the point, without telling me!'

'I've come home, I wanted to surprise you.'

'Surprise me! You've given me a bloody heart attack.' Nan's face wrinkled as she frowned. 'And your timing is bloody awful, Sara. Why didn't you tell me you were coming? How long are you staying?'

'Why is it awful?' Before her grandmother could answer, Caro came back to the table. 'Nan, this is my friend, Caro. She's going to be the new doctor with Doctor Rose. Caro, this is Nan.'

Nan reached out her hand to Caro. 'I heard a new doctor was coming to town. Welcome.'

'Thank you. It's lovely to meet you. Would you like a tea or a coffee?'

'Please call me Ellen. A pot of Earl Grey would be good, thank you.' She stared at Sara, and her frown deepened. 'Now tell me what's happening.'

Sara smiled. 'I've come home to stay, Nan. I'm going back to work at the medical practice as s receptionist and the clinic nurse.'

'Well, that's wonderful to hear. I'm pleased you're here to stay, and I won't miss you.'

'Miss me. Where are you going?'

'I'm going on a cruise to New Zealand with my cousin, Alma. I caught the morning bus down here, and I'm catching the two o'clock coach down to Cloncurry and then flying to Brissie from the Isa tomorrow.'

'Well, I'll be here when you come back.'

'Good. Where are you staying?' Nan pulled up a chair and sat down.

'Um, your place?' Sara tipped her head to the side and then frowned as Nan shook her head slowly.

'Sorry, love. You should have let me know.' She tapped her lip with one finger. 'You haven't changed, have you?'

'Sorry?'

'Never organised. All you had to do was make one call. I've got house sitters in for a month. I won't be back until next month. A sweet English couple are looking after Jed for me.'

'Jed? Who's Jed?' Sara was getting confused and a little worried.

'Jed is my dog. He's a beauty. A rescue dog,' she said proudly.

'Oh well, no matter.' Sara waved a hand. 'I'll find somewhere to stay. There's always rentals.'

Nan shook her head. 'It might be harder than you think. Since they extended the zinc mine, and there are a lot more ships coming to the port, there's been an influx of workers. The rental market is tight in the Bay these days.'

'Oh.' Sara turned to Caro. 'I'm sorry. In my usual way—it sounds like I've given you some wrong information.'

'It's all right. Dr Rose said there's a flat at the back of the doctor's residence if I want it. You can stay there with me if you like until—'

Sara shook her head. 'It's too small. I know that flat. It's okay. I'll find somewhere.'

She ignored Nan's eye roll. Her self-esteem didn't need a battering.

##

Two hours later, Sara's complacency had all but disappeared. They'd seen Nan off on the coach and then driven to Second Chance Bay. As they'd driven past the sand flats and the wetlands on the southern side of town, the silver sheen of the Gulf glinted in the distance.

Caro had been quiet.

'Are you okay?' Sara had asked as Caro peered ahead at the narrow road into town.

'It's different to what I imagined.' Caro slowed the car as they entered the sixty zone. A faded sign hanging at an angle welcomed them to Second Chance Bay, and Sara looked around with fresh eyes. The town looked sad and neglected. As they passed the first residential streets, the yards were unkempt, and the grass was long, growing high along the sides of the upturned fishing boats. A couple of old rusted utes sat on the side of the road—one with four flat tyres and the other sitting up on bricks with no tyres at all.

'It's okay,' Sara said brightly. 'It's a shame that this is what you see when you drive in, but it gets better when we get over to Sunset Point.'

To her relief, the residential area over at the point was still well maintained, and Caro had visibly relaxed as they'd pulled up outside the small medical centre. Unlike Sara, Caro was organised and had rung Dr Rose from Normanton. He had told her to come straight to the centre, and he'd meet her there.

'Let's see if we can find room for you in the flat,' Caro said as they pulled up outside the old house.

Sara shook her head. 'No, honestly, it's tiny, and you won't want me underfoot while you're settling in. It's okay. I've got friends in town'—she crossed her fingers behind her back— 'if

510

you're happy for me to borrow the car while you meet Dr Rose, I'll get myself sorted and then drop it back. Is that okay?' She hid the tension that was building in her and smiled.

'Of course.'

As soon as they opened the gate, Dr Rose stood at the door and his smile was wide. To Sara's surprise, he hugged her in welcome and she stepped back to introduce Caro, feeling a little uncomfortable. Roger the Dodger had left a legacy, and she knew that was unfair because Hector Rose was a good man.

'I am delighted to meet you, Caroline.' He clasped Caro's hand, and Sara smiled. She had never seen the doctor so animated, but to be fair, it had been a long time.

Once the introductions were done, Sara left Caro at the surgery, where Dr Rose was going to show her around the medical rooms and the flat, and she headed along to the point.

The sea was flat and silver, and Sara wound down her window and took a deep breath. The salt smell and the sound of the birds wheeling above the boat ramp soothed her. Three small boats sat in the middle of the river, and the horn of a large ship boomed a warning as it entered the river.

I'm home to stay, and I'll see this every day.

A reluctant grin tugged at her mouth. *Once I find myself somewhere to live.*

You're a ditz, Sara Sweeny, she thought.

But a ditz who'd come home. And was very happy to be here.

She'd just have to dig into her nest egg and pay for a room at the motel along from the caravan park. Parking the car, Sara took a deep breath and headed for the office on the other side of the road.

Chapter Seven

On Saturday afternoon, as Matt was closing up the co-op, the phone rang. He hurried back into the office to answer it. Maisie had worked a couple of hours this morning—her injured ankle had healed—and it had given Matt a chance to catch up on the accounts. He looked up at the clock; he didn't fancy going home to an empty house. Maybe he'd go over to the pub for a quiet drink and a game of pool.

'McDougal's Fish Co-op,' he answered.

'Matt, it's me,' Jenni said. 'Have you got any plans tonight?'

'I was thinking about going to the pub.' Matt grinned. 'But it'll probably end up just the usual, a night at home by myself in front of the footie.'

'Half your luck. I'd give anything for a night of peace and quiet.'

'What's up, Jen? You need a babysitter?'

'No, we're having a barbeque. Again. Donny and Claire have been up at the lodge with Dane and Nicole this week, and they're all coming back to town tonight. Jake's invited them all for a barbie. I have to go shopping as soon as the kids wake up from their nap. And, of course, they're both having an extra-long one today.'

Matt frowned; Jenni usually loved company, but she didn't sound impressed.

'So you come over too.'

'Okay. Where's Jake?'

'God knows. Probably down fiddling with one of the boats.' Her voice was short, and Matt thought she sounded as though she was on the verge of tears.

'Right. How can I help? How about I do the shopping?'

'Thank you. That'd be great. It's all right for Jake. All he has to do is light the damn barbeque.'

Now Matt was worried. In the five years that Jake and Jenni had been together, he'd never once heard her criticise her husband, and that was the second time in one phone call.

'Leave it with me. I'll shop and don't you worry about any of the food.' Matt softened his voice. 'I'm worried about you, Jen. Go and have a lie down with the kids and have a rest.'

'I haven't got time. The place is a pig sty.'

'Jen. It's only us. Family. You know? We don't care what your place looks like.'

'Well, I do. I'll ring Jess at IGA and tell her I'll email an order through. All you'll have to do is pick it up.'

Matt gave up. 'All right. I'll have a shower here. I should have some clean jeans out the back. I'll be there in an hour or so. Okay?'

He frowned as the phone disconnected without Jen answering.

##

An hour later, he pulled up outside Jenni and Jake's house at the northern end of the Bay. Callen, the baby, was screaming, and every so often, Matt could hear Leni's sobs between the screams. He quickly grabbed the pack of meat and the groceries that Jenni had ordered and hurried to the front door. When he rang the bell, Jenni yelled from upstairs.

'Come on up, Matt, I'm just getting the kids in their PJs.'

Walking across the wide expanse of glossy white tiles, he went into the kitchen and put the bags on the bench and the meat in the large double fridge in the butler's pantry before running lightly up the stairs.

'Everyone decent?' he called from the end of the hall.

'Yes. We're in Leni's room,' Jeni replied. The crying had stopped, and he walked tentatively to the bedroom, pleased to hear a loud giggle and then Jenni's soft voice crooning to the baby.

'Uncle Mattie, Uncle Mattie. Come and play dolls with me.' Leni stood at the door in her pyjamas, her golden curls damp and clinging to her forehead. Jenni was in a chair by the window, breastfeeding Callen, their ten-month-old son. Matt smothered a grin. The baby wasn't wearing any clothes and Jenni pulled a face as she nursed him.

'The little monkey decided he was starving and couldn't even wait for me to get a nappy on him,' she said. 'He was screaming like a banshee.'

'I heard him. You're game to nurse him like that while he's feeding.' Matt chuckled. 'I'd hazard a guess? In one end and out the other?'

Jenni pulled a face. 'I've already been peed on . . . and worse today. Don't ask.'

'I won't. I couldn't do it. I'll stay an uncle, thanks. That's much easier, isn't it? How's the prettiest girl in the universe?' Matt bent down and picked up Leni. 'And my favourite girl.'

'She's very sad.' Leni's eyes were wide. 'Mummy didn't have time to dress my dolls with me. Callen was crying for his milk. Will you help me, Uncle Mattie?'

'Just for a minute because I'll have to go and get the barbeque going and the chairs put outside to help Mummy.' He glanced across to Jenni as he sat on the floor next to Leni. 'Heard from Jake?'

'Yes. Dane had a problem with one of the boats, so he'd gone up to meet them. They'll be a bit later getting here, so it gives me a chance to get the kids fed and in bed.' She smiled up at her big brother. 'Thanks for coming to help, Matt. I appreciate it. I'm sorry I was cross before.'

He waved one hand and took the Barbie doll that Leni passed him with the other. 'We all have good and bad days, Jen. I've been a bit down this week too.'

Jenni lifted Callen onto her shoulder and patted his back. 'What's wrong with you?'

Matt shrugged as he pulled the frilly dress onto the doll and handed it to his little niece. 'I don't know. A bit restless; the others are all doing interesting stuff, and I'm stuck in the office most of the time.' He forced a grin to his face to lighten the atmosphere. 'You know what I did today?'

'What?'

'I worked out how many times I've opened the door of the fridge.'

'Ooh.' Jenni shook her head. 'That's way sad, Matt. I think it might be time for a change.'

'That's where my thoughts were heading.'

Jenni crossed to the change table and tucked a nappy under her arm on the way. 'I get what you're saying, but you do know how much the boys appreciate what you do, don't you? All of them. You're indispensable to all the businesses, Matt.'

'I know. I guess it was—'

'Hearing that a certain lady was coming back to town?' Jenni's gaze was sharp. 'Be honest.'

Matt pulled a rueful face. 'I wouldn't admit it to anyone else, and don't you say anything, but yes, Sara coming back to town has thrown me a bit.'

Jenni walked to the door. '*I'll* throw her if she comes anywhere near me.'

Matt shook his head. 'No, don't you say a word.'

'Matt, I saw how upset you were when she left. And she never once had the courtesy to contact you or tell you why she did. And I'll talk to her if I want to.' Matt had spilled his guts to Jenni one night a few months after Sara had left. It was before she'd moved back to the Bay and had been teaching in Brisbane.

'Jen. Don't.' Matt's voice was firm and full of warning. 'Promise. Or I'm going home now, and you can do all of this by yourself. There's stuff between Sara and me you didn't know. Leave it.'

'Oh, all right. But I don't have to be friends with her.'

'No, you don't, but do remember I'm all grown up now. And you don't know what happened between us, but Sara going was for the best.' He pushed to his feet and ruffled his sister's hair as she walked past him with a sleepy baby in her arms. 'But I do appreciate the support. Come on, Leni. You can help me get the party ready.'

By the time the two boats were moored in the bay at the front of the house, the two little ones were in bed and asleep, Matt had marinated the steak, and the barbeque was alight. Jenni had made a salad and set the table, but Matt pushed her into the chair and poured her a wine when she said she had a load of washing to put on.

'Sit down, for goodness sake. It'll wait until tomorrow.'

'True.' She frowned when Matt passed her a glass of white wine. 'I haven't been drinking while I've been breastfeeding Callen. He might sleep extra well tonight if I have a drink.'

'One won't hurt, will it?'

'No.' Jenni shook her head. 'All good. And Matt, thanks for coming over. I really appreciate it.'

Voices and laughter reached them as Jake, their two brothers, and their partners walked along from the dock. Jenni lifted her face for a kiss when Jake came through the gate, and Matt was pleased to see the look of concern on her husband's face.

'I'm so sorry that I left you with all this, sweetheart. I'll stay home tomorrow and give you a hand.'

'It's okay, big brother Matt did it all. The only thing we haven't prepared is dessert.'

Claire smiled and lifted the Tupperware container she was carrying. 'The new boat has an incredible galley, and Nicole and I baked a dessert on the way down the coast. Lemon meringue cheesecake made with bush lemons from the lodge.'

'I found the recipe in this week's New Idea. I picked it up at the hairdresser,' Nicole said as she walked across to them.

'Yum, we're set then.' Matt crossed to the barbeque. 'You all go and have a wash, and I'll get the meat cooking.'

'Okay, thanks, mate.' Dane and Donny slapped him on the shoulder as they headed inside.

As Matt lifted the cover a sharp gust of wind blew in from the sea and caught the edge of the oval metal lid. It slammed down hard at an angle onto the hot barbeque plate, and Matt jumped as pain sliced through his right hand.

Jenni jumped up and hurried over to where he stood, grasping his fingers with his left hand. 'Let me see. Have you burned yourself?'

As Matt shook his head, a wave of nausea washed over him. Blood was running down his wrist and dripping onto the path. 'Um, I'm pretty sure I've sliced the top of my finger off.' He looked down at the barbeque and had to close his eyes.

Jenni's scream was shrill. 'Jake! Come quick!'

Chapter Eight

Sara had been in luck. The hotel on the point near the small town's airport had one room left, and she booked it for two weeks. Paid the first week and hoped she might not have to stay here for the full time. She'd had enough motel stays in her travels to know what soulless places they were.

The girl on the desk looked at her curiously but didn't ask any questions. Sara recognised her; she'd been a couple of years ahead of her at school.

'We serve breakfast in the dining room from seven until ten, and if you want a night meal, you have to go across the road to the hotel.'

'Thanks.' Sara nodded and took the key that was being held out to her.

'Did you go to school here?' The woman's curiosity finally got the better of her. 'You look familiar.'

Sara nodded. 'I did. For a while.'

'Back on a holiday, hey? Not much of a place to visit these days.' The lips turned down into a dissatisfied pout.

'You think?'

A nod. 'What is there to do here for two weeks? Unless you like to fish?'

Sara grinned, although she was wondering why such a negative person was at the front desk of the only hotel in the Bay. 'I do, but I'll be too busy working to find time to fish. I'm starting work at Doc Rose's next week.'

'Oh wow, are you the new lady doctor we've all heard about? We didn't know it was someone local coming home.'

'No. not me. I'm the receptionist and nurse.' Sara leaned against the counter. 'But the new doctor is here too. We travelled up together.'

'Well, welcome home.' The girl, Jan, according to her name tag—her name had escaped Sara— leaned forward. 'I remember you. You went out with that sexy Matt McDougal for ages.'

Sara nodded without speaking and picked up her purse from the counter. 'Thank you. I'm pleased there was a room.'

The door squeaked as it closed behind her. She made her way to Room Sixteen and opened the door. The generic dull brown bedspread, the plastic jug, two white cups and saucers, and the obligatory packet of milk coffee biscuits faced her.

With a groan, she chastised herself once more for not ringing Nan to make sure she could stay there. Anyway, a couple of weeks—or maybe four—would go fast, and she'd keep herself busy at the surgery and showing Caro the sights.

For the first time, a little glimmer of doubt surfaced.

Was coming home to the Bay a backward step?

Sara mused as she drove back to the surgery. Even though she'd made friends in the towns she'd lived in when she'd studied for her nursing qualification and worked in various medical practices, she'd never felt at home anywhere. The feeling that had overtaken her as they'd headed into the Bay earlier was enough to reassure her that this was where she wanted to be.

She grinned. Even if she had to stay in the old hotel for the first few weeks. It was her own fault; she should have told Nan she was coming home.

She looked at the Gulf as she drove Caro's car back to the surgery. The sea was a deep blue today as the wind blew in from the west. As she drove past the airport runway, a flock of Burdekin ducks waded in the sandy low tide shallows. Many species of migratory shorebirds came all the way from the northern hemisphere to breed in the wetlands and roosted all the way up the coast on the tidal mud and sand flats. Sara had spent many weekends birdwatching with Nan.

Contentment seeped through her; despite what Jan in reception had said, Sara knew she would have no problem filling her days at Second Chance Bay. She parked at the medical practice that fronted the small cottage hospital. As the permanent population of Second Chance Bay was less than five hundred, the hospital was more of an extension of the medical practice. These days, it was part of the North West Health Service area, but the locals had voted to keep the heritage name of Second Chance Bay Cottage Hospital. There was a wing with a small aged care facility, staffed twenty-four hours a day, but most patients were taken by ambulance into Normanton, where there were visiting specialist services. The closest major hospital was at Mt Isa, over five hundred kilometres away.

Sara's job at the medical practice wouldn't be busy, but the work would be varied. She'd worked here before, so she knew what to expect. Sara had really enjoyed working with Caro in Tanunda, but she wondered what the doctor's impressions of the small facility would be. In one way, she was pleased that Caro had accepted the twelve-month contract before they had arrived, as the town—or the practice—

might not meet her expectations.

She turned Caro's four-wheel drive—still covered with red dust— into the small car park at the side of the building, pleased to see that Dr Rose's vehicle was still there. She stepped from the vehicle and made her way to the side door where Dr Rose had taken Caro. As she reached up to push the side door open, a white twin cab ute accelerated around the corner, engine roaring. Sara waited as it swung into the car park beside Caro's four-wheel drive.

Her heart skittered a tattoo of beats as the tall man stepped out. For a moment, she'd thought it was Matt, but then she realised it was one of his younger brothers. He ran over to Sara, his face wrinkled in a frown.

'Is that Dr Rose's car? Is he here?' His voice was urgent.

'Yes, he's inside, showing the new doctor around. Is there an emergency? Shall I get him?'

'No, I'll go. My brother is better off staying in the car until we know if they can help him here or not. He ran to the door, pushed it open, and ran inside, calling out. 'Doc Rose?'

Without hesitation, Sara hurried across to the car; she could assist until the doctor came out.

A blonde woman climbed out of the back seat of the vehicle.

'Sara?' she said with a frown. It was Jenni, Matt's little sister. Her face was pale, and she had dark shadows beneath her eyes.

'Hello, Jenni. Yes, it's me. What's wrong? Can I help?'

Jenni's voice shook. 'Matt has cut the top of his finger off. He's in the back with Donny. What should we do? Bring him in? Or take him to Normanton?'

Sara fought to control her reaction. Her heart pounded, and her mouth dried as she went across to the car. She recognised Don, Matt's brother, sitting in the back seat. He was holding Matt's arm up high above his head.

Sara put her head in the open window. 'Good, keep it elevated, and if you can, get some pressure on the wound.' She swallowed as she looked across at Matt. 'Are you in much pain? Matt, or do you feel as though you're going to pass out?'

'I'm okay.' Steel blue eyes held hers, and her breath caught.

'Good. Do you have the rest of the finger?'

Donny nodded. 'Yes. It's packed on ice in a plastic bag. We weren't sure whether to come here or drive straight to Normanton.'

'On ice or in ice,' Sara asked with a frown

'No, it's not touching the ice. Thank God for Google.'

'Good.' Sara nodded. Her nerves were a jangled mess. Seeing Matt for the first time in so long and knowing he was hurt was surreal. 'You're in luck. You've got two doctors and at least one nurse here this afternoon.'

Jenni took her arm and pulled her aside. 'I Googled fingers as Dane drove. Matt's only got a limited amount of time before it's too late to save the finger.' She put a trembling hand to her mouth. 'He was so calm.'

'That's good, and you're right, we have to be quick. But let's leave it to the medicos. Here comes Dr Rose now.'

Caro glanced at her as the two doctors hurried towards the car. 'Sara, there's no nurse on duty. Can you go in and prepare the surgery for a wound cleanse, please?'

'I can.' Sara nodded and headed for the door. She tried to push away the thought of Matt being in pain. She knew that the doctors wouldn't give him anything until they'd assessed the wound.

By the time she'd found what she needed and prepared a tray in the small consulting room, the door opened. She was surprised to see Matt walk in, supported by a brother on each side. Caro and Dr Rose were close behind them.

'Thank you.' Dr Rose glanced at Dane and Donny. 'We'll examine Matt now while you wait in the waiting room. I think you need to keep an eye on Jenni; she looked as if she was about to faint. I'll get Sara to come out and check on her once we look at this finger.'

'I'll go out to the truck and get the ice bag,' Don said.

'Good.' Dr Rose nodded as the two men left the room.

'Sara?' Matt looked at her curiously. 'You're qualified now?'

She nodded. 'Yes. An RN.'

'Well done.'

The surge of pride that ran through Sara was incongruous to the situation. She glanced at Matt as Dr Rose helped him onto the bed. He seemed more interested in her being a nurse than he was in what the two doctors were doing.

Dr Rose and Caro went to the basin and sterilised their hands. Sara stepped back as Caro turned on the big light above the bed, and Dr Rose unwrapped the bandage that someone had put on the wound. She took the chance to look at Matt.

Really look at him. Sara fought back the tumultuous feelings that churned in her stomach and sent butterflies running to every nerve ending in her body.

Why did she feel like this? It was as though the eight years since she'd last seen him didn't exist. And that was not good.

She wasn't going to risk her heart again. It wasn't emotion or any leftover feelings; it was pure nostalgia with maybe some hormones thrown into the mix. Matt was still a very good-looking guy.

Sara turned away and busied herself at the surgical tray until the door opened, and Don poked his head around. 'Here's the . . . here's Matt's—'

'Thank you,' she said briskly and placed the plastic bag on the tray. She wasn't squeamish usually, but she was unable to look.

'Perhaps you could go and check on Jenni now, nurse.' Dr Rose glanced at her. 'Are you feeling all right? You're a bit pale.'

'I'm fine. My red-headed complexion.' Sara forced a smile before she slipped out to the waiting room. Jenni jumped to her feet and put her hand to her head as she stumbled. Her two brothers caught her and helped her back to the chair.

'I'm sorry. It's all right. I'm okay.'

Sara didn't like her colour. Jenni was pale, but each cheek held a bright red rosy patch. 'I'll get you some water.'

'Thank you. Is Matt okay?'

Sara nodded. 'The doctors are with him now. You did well getting him here. How long ago did it happen?'

Dane shook his head. 'It'd be less than half an hour. We just put a pressure bandage on it and jumped in the car. We should ring the others and let them know the doctor was here.' He turned to Jenni by way of explanation. 'Jenni's husband is there with the two children and our partners stayed there too. I told them not to go anywhere near the barbeque. It was the wind blowing the lid that did the damage. I can't believe that it did so much damage.'

'Ah.' Sara nodded as she crouched in front of Jenni with a plastic tumbler of water. She was trying to process the changes in the McDougal family since she'd left.

'You're Sara Sweeney, aren't you?' the other brother, Donny, said. 'You used to come to our place with Matt.'

'Yes. I've moved back home to the Bay to work.'

'I thought I knew you. You've been gone a while,' he said.

Jenni lifted her head and stared at her, and there was something unknown in her eyes. 'Things have changed since you left.' She lifted her chin higher and her voice wasn't friendly. 'A lot.'

'I'm sure they have.' Sara put her hand on Jenni's forehead. 'You're running a temperature. I think you should see the doctor when they've sorted your brother.'

Jenni moved away. 'I'm all right. Matt's the one everyone should be worrying about. It's my fault. He came over to help when I rang him. That stupid barbeque.''

'It was a freak accident, Jen. No one's at fault. We just have to wait and see if they think they can save it. And if there's time to get to wherever they would do it. Probably Mt Isa.'

'Or Brisbane,' Donny said.

For a moment Sara debated whether to say what she was thinking, and what she knew, but it wasn't her place to say. It was up to Caro and Dr Rose.

'If you're sure you're okay?' she said to Jenni.

The response was clipped. 'I'm fine.'

Sara turned away and opened the door of the examination room. The two doctors were at the end near the sink, talking quietly, and Matt was still lying on the bed, his eyes closed.

Dr Rose looked up and beckoned her over.

'We've given him a sedative. I know you're not officially on duty until the week after next, and I'd like to thank you for stepping in today. Are you feeling all right?''

'I'm fine.' She forced a smile; seeing Matt lying there injured was hard.

'What about Jenni?' he asked.

'She said she was fine, but I'm not sure. I didn't use a thermometer, but I think she could be running a temperature, and she seemed unsteady on her feet.'

'I'll tell her to make an appointment to come and see me later. I have another request for you. Caroline and I have discussed it, and with Caroline's experience in microsurgery, we've decided to operate here. Matthew's chances of keeping his finger will be much better than the time it would take to fly him to Brisbane. There appears to be little damage to the bone and the tendons, and we have the equipment here to operate.'

'I'm happy to perform the reconstruction,' Caroline said. 'And Dr Rose will do the anaesthesia. It all depends whether you're happy to assist, Sara?'

'Of course I am.' Sara didn't hesitate.

'Good.' Dr Rose said. 'Let's get started.'

Chapter Nine

The wave of pain drilled through Matt's fingers, up his wrist, and into his shoulder. He clenched his teeth and fought it. He drifted off to sleep to blessed relief and slept until a shadow fell across the bed. He opened his eyes, and for a moment, he thought he was dreaming.

It was like the recurring dreams he'd had for years. But now it was the real Sara standing there, looking down at him with a strange look on her face.

'I'm pleased you came home to me, Sar,' he whispered. Her face faded, and he drifted back off. When he woke next time, the new lady doctor was standing beside the bed.

She smiled down at him as she picked up the chart from the foot of the bed. 'Good morning, Matt. I'm pleased to see you awake. I'm Dr Morton.'

He nodded and gestured to the cup of ice at the side of the bed. 'Is it okay if I have some ice?' His voice was raspy.

'You can. You can even have some breakfast if you feel like it.' The doctor passed the small cup over to him.

'Where am I?'

'You're at Second Chance Bay in the hospital. We operated here.'

'I thought I'd dreamed it. So it's all over and fixed?'

'It is.' She shook her head, and relief flooded through him as she answered. 'You didn't dream it. You were very lucky that Sara and I arrived in town today. If you had to cut your finger off, you picked the best day for it.' Her laugh was musical and sweet, and it calmed him. 'Microsurgery was my specialty when I trained. Your injury was very clean, and it only took a couple of hours to get you sorted.'

'You've saved my finger then?'

'We're confident that it's going to be fine. Being your little finger meant there were fewer nerves to repair, but you're going to be in a bit of pain for the first day or two, and you must keep that hand elevated. But there's no reason why you can't go home tomorrow. Antibiotics will keep any infection at bay, and luckily you had a clean straight-cut injury, your nerves may start to re-join in as little as three to seven days.'

Matt looked over as the door opened. He held his breath as Sara appeared in the doorway.

'Is it okay if I come in?' she asked.

Matt nodded. 'Yes.'

Sara walked over to the bed and stood next to the doctor. 'Hello, Matt,' she said softly. 'How are you feeling?'

'I'm good.' He nodded again. 'Welcome home. I hear you're home to stay.'

She shook her head. 'I haven't decided yet. Just for a visit at this stage.' He didn't miss the curious look the doctor shot Sara's way.

'Anyway,' Sara said. 'I came to make sure you'd met Caro.'

'Caro?' He frowned.

'Me. I'm Caro,' the doctor said. 'And Sara's friend. We've just done a road trip right up the centre together to get here.'

'Ah, the Thelma and Louise.'

Sara's nose wrinkled into that cute button-shape that he'd seen many times before. A tug of nostalgia took away the ache in his hand briefly.

'Thelma and Louise?' she asked.

'Maisie told me it was a movie. You should have told me you were coming home, Sar.'

'I should have.' This time, her smile was rueful. 'And I should have told Nan I was coming home too, and then I wouldn't be staying at the hotel.'

'Plenty of room at the McDougal house these days,' Matt said.

Jeez. Matt couldn't believe he'd said that.

'Oh, I wasn't angling for an invitation, Matt. Nan's got someone staying at her place while she's away. The hotel is just a temporary measure.'

'The offer is there.'

Bloody hell. Next thing he'd be proposing.

Sara looked at him with a smile and it seemed forced. 'Thank you. Look, I'm sorry we lost touch, Matt. I was going to come over and see you.' She gestured to his bandaged hand. 'Before this happened, anyway.'

'I'll leave you two to catch up. I'll call in a bit later, Matt.' Caro nodded and walked to the door.

It was clear Sara didn't want to stay. Matt gestured to the chair at the side of the bed, and her eyes widened like those of a rabbit caught in the headlights.

'Sit down. We've got a lot of catching up to do.'

She hesitated and then sat stiffly in the plastic chair. 'Come on, Sar, we can be friends. Lots of water under the bridge in what? How many years?'

'I forget. Probably seven or eight.'

He held her gaze as she lifted her head, and her eyes were bright.

'We can be friends,' she said. 'I'd like that. That's why I was going to come and see you— to clear the air. It's too small a town to have any awkwardness. I guess we'll be running into each other most days.'

'We will.' He kept his voice soft. 'It's been a long time since you left—' Matt bit off the "me" just in time. 'And I was surprised when you left so suddenly, but it was for the best for you.'

'It was.' She nodded and looked down at her hands folded in her lap.

'This town was too small for you. And you wouldn't have been able to do your nursing if you'd stayed here. You've achieved a lot, Sar.'

Neither of them mentioned the conversation they'd had that last night. Matt wondered why it was so easy to remember every word eight years later.

'Tell me about the Bay, Matt. About your life. I see the rest of your family is settled with partners and kids. You?'

There was no way he was going to tell Sara that even though he wouldn't settle into a relationship the few times he'd been on a date, he couldn't get past the memory of Sara, and he'd given up going out.

'Me?' Matt winced as he shrugged, and the pain shot down to his fingers. 'You know me. Too busy working for there to be time for anything else.'

She nodded, but she was quiet.

'The business has expanded, and it keeps me busy. I'm there by myself most days. Maisie's just come back for the winter, and she'd been doing some hours for me.'

'Will she work for you while you're off?' As Sara leaned forward, a spiral of red curls fell over her face, and she pushed it away. He remembered running his fingers through those tangled curls.

Matt's mouth dried as Sara stared at him. 'Could you pass the water, please?' he managed to choke out.

He sipped through the straw, and the iced water eased the ache that had suddenly lodged in his throat. 'I won't be taking any time off. I can operate a computer and type into a spreadsheet one-handed. The doc said I can go home tomorrow.'

'Fair enough.' She stood. 'I should go and let you get some rest.'

Matt held out his good hand and took hers before she could move away. 'What about you, Sara? Is there a significant other in your life?'

She hesitated for a moment and then nodded. 'Yes, I met Jeff about four years ago.' She tugged her hand away. 'I really must go. I have things to do. Take care, Matt.'

Chapter Ten

Sara was out of breath by the time she'd walked back to the hotel.

Truth to tell, she had nothing to do. It had been too hard sitting one-on-one with Matt, and she'd had to get away.

Sitting there beside him as he'd lain on the bed, his strong profile turned to her, she had realised how foolish it had been to come back. Her feelings for Matt hadn't changed one bit. She'd had to clench her hands in her lap. The need to reach out and gently brush the hair back from his face had been overwhelming.

Coming home was very different from what she'd imagined it would be.

She went to bed early and tossed and turned in the hard bed all night.

##

'Hi, Sara. Come in. I've just boiled the kettle.'

Sara pushed open the door of the small flat at the back of the medical surgery. She wrinkled her nose. 'Have you been baking already, Caro? Or is that delicious smell wafting over from the hospital?'

'I did some shopping, and I felt like cooking. So there's a raspberry and coconut slice almost ready to come out of the oven.' Caro bent down and opened the oven door a little bit. 'Yep, almost done.'

'Yum. Count me in.' Sara pulled out the stool at the kitchen bench and looked around. She knew this apartment well; she'd often used the kitchen when she'd worked as a receptionist in the practice before she'd moved away. 'You've settled in okay by the look of things.'

Caro had flair and the small kitchen bore the evidence of her homemaking skills already.

'I have. I'm so pleased that you told me about Second Chance Bay. I've had a lovely welcome. Dr Rose is a sweetie, and I love the cottage hospital.'

Sara bit back a smile. A sweetie was the last term she'd use for Dr Rose. He was a serious man who rarely smiled. 'And you haven't even seen the medical practice in operation yet.'

'No. I'm looking forward to that next week.'

'Have you got everything you need here, or do we need a trip down to Normanton?'

'I'm pretty right. I went for a walk around to the IGA yesterday afternoon and got the basics. It's a friendly town; I had quite a few chats on the way home.'

'It's not every day the town gets a new doctor. You'll be welcomed with open arms.'

Caro nodded. 'And it's not every day you get to operate in the hospital the same day you arrive in town.'

'True. Matt was very lucky we arrived yesterday. It's such a long way to the next big hospital he probably would have lost the top of his finger.'

Caro smiled. 'On the way back from the town centre I called into the hospital to see him. Matt McDougall seems to be a very nice guy too.' The glance she shot towards Sara was curious.

Sara nodded and she knew her voice was hesitant. 'Yes, Matt is a good guy. But don't go getting any ideas, Caro. He's not the man for me. We had a good talk and cleared the air. We decided we can be friends.'

'Are you sure?'

'Yes, I am. I've been there. Been there, done that.'

'Got the T-shirt.' Caro's dry comment made Sara smile. She already seemed happier than she had been at Tanunda.

'I could have. It's time to get on with life. I'm home where I wanted to be. We've ironed out any awkwardness, and it's all good.'

'If you're sure. So if you have had a talk and you're going to be friends— again that curious look—'you'll be fine about going around and dressing his finger at his place when he goes home?'

'Not a problem.'

'It's healing well and I'm happy to send him home later today on the condition that he gets his finger dressed. He can't do it himself, of course. Matt said that his brothers are heading back home now that they know he's okay, and Jenni is busy with her children.'

'Of course. It's also part of my brief as clinic nurse. So just tell me what you want me to do there and how often.'

'Okay, I will. We'll leave it bandaged for the first few days, but I'll send the dressing kits and the saline solution home with him when he leaves. I'll get you to check on him once a day. Just to watch for infection and temperature.'

Sara nodded as the timer on the oven rang. 'Morning tea time.'

Caro picked up an oven mitt, opened the oven door, and slid out the slice tray. As she placed it on the wooden board to cool, she glanced at Sara. 'Speaking of Jenni, I'm going to try to see her this week. Do you think she'll make an appointment to see me or Dr Rose? She certainly didn't look well.'

'She's not happy with me. I picked that up loud and clear. But that's understandable. I guess the family thinks badly of me for leaving Matt. From what Matt said, he was pretty peed off, but, hey, that's the way the cookie crumbles.'

'You're very blasé about it, Sara.'

'Caro, it was eight years ago. A lot's happened since then. I've had one serious relationship. I've had different jobs and lived in some interesting places. I've got my qualifications. You can't go back to the past.'

'I guess you're right,' Caro said as she brought the kettle back to the boil.

This time, it was Sara who looked at Caro curiously. 'You know, Matt McDougall might not be a bad way for you to fill in your year in town.'

'You just leave me alone, Sara Sweeney. I don't need anyone organising my social life or my love life. The kettle's boiled. Do you want tea or coffee?

Sara looked at her thoughtfully as she poured the water into the teapot. If Matt took Caro out, it would take any attention off her. She'd feel more at ease, Jenni might stop being so cross, and the locals wouldn't wonder what was happening between her and Matt.

Yes. Sara nodded to herself as Caro pulled out two white mugs. It was time to pull out her matchmaking skills.

##.

Sara walked to the hospital mid-afternoon. Caro was already there meeting with Dr Rose, and Sara glanced at the four-wheel drive they'd spent the last month in. She smiled; Caro had been busy; as well as baking and making herself at home in the flat, and looking after a patient, she'd still found time to clean the car. The paintwork was gleaming, and only if you looked very closely could you see a trace of red dust in the wheel hubs. The interior of the car was empty and the swags and camping gear had been stored somewhere.

Sara pulled a face. While Caro had been energetic, what had she been doing? Walking around town feeling sorry for herself.

Second Chance Bay hadn't changed much in the years she'd been gone. The streets between the Gulf and the small shopping centre were bare of grass since the dry season had arrived. Grey sand added to the depressing vista of houses with faded paint and sagging guttering. She walked past Nan's house and was pleased to see that the grass was mowed and the garden was tidy.

She pushed open the door of the clinic, and the smell of freshly brewed coffee wafted out. Dr Rose had always been a coffee connoisseur and it would be a bit better than the coffee that had been delivered to her room this morning. The sachets of Black & Gold coffee on a tray with a pot of lukewarm water didn't quite make it.

Sara knew she had to get herself set up; there was no reason why she couldn't go and shop. No reason apart from being organised, and that's what she'd always found hard to do. Caro was already organised, and had her apartment sorted; she should take a leaf out of her book.

Maybe when she got settled at Nan's, she could get her thoughts together a bit better, although living there would be a temporary measure. She frowned as she walked into the office at the back of reception. There was no reason why she couldn't find a place to live now. She'd go and see the council office today. The Bay was too small to have a real estate agent. Or it used to be— maybe she could ask Matt.

If the truth be known, she'd spent too much time thinking about Matt McDougal for the past twenty-four hours. It was only the worry of what he'd done to his hand, she rationalised. Nothing more.

And if you believe that, you're off with the pixies.

'It's only that I haven't seen him for a long time,' she muttered. 'And I'm worried about him.' Sara jumped as Caro walked into the room.

'Who are you talking to?' she asked, looking around

'Um. No one.'

'Matt is right to go home this morning.'

'Is he getting picked up?'

'No, he said he's right to take himself. I questioned that, but he assures me he doesn't have far to go.'

Sara put her hands on her hips. 'He mightn't have far to go, but did he tell you he has to go home by boat?'

Caro screwed up her nose. 'By boat?'

'Yes, Matt lives on the other side of the river, and there's no bridge.

'Okay, I'd better make sure the dressing has a plastic cover to make it waterproof.'

'It's not only that. He's not going to be able to start the runabout one-handed.' Sara sighed. 'I'll take him home.'

'Are you right to do that, Sara? Do you know what to do? What sort of boat?'

'It's an aluminium runabout. Or it used to be. There's probably a new one these days. I've been over to the other side of the river many times. I haven't forgotten how to start Matt's boat. Or if he's got a new one, it won't be hard to figure out.'

'You're certainly full of surprises, Sara.' Caro shook her head and then said briskly. 'Okay. He's right to go. Hector and I have already seen him.'

Sara smothered a grin at the "Hector". She'd never heard Dr Rose referred to by his Christian name by any of the locums before.

They walked together from the surgery into the small cottage hospital.

Caro smiled. 'I already love this place. It's going to suit me very well.'

Sara nodded. 'It's only early days yet. You might find it boring after a while.'

'I'm sure I won't. Hector was telling me how busy it's been since the mine expanded. New families in town, and the days are always busy.'

'Different from when I was here before,' Sara said. 'Nan said there were new people in town.'

Matt was sitting on the side of the bed, fully dressed, as the two women walked into the small ward. He was the only patient in the small hospital.

'So I hear you're going home today.' Sara avoided his eye and looked at the wall above his head.

'Yes, this morning, according to both the docs. I'm just waiting for the all-clear.'

Caro nodded. 'You're right to go. Sara will be coming to your place to change the dressing every day for the first few days.'

Matt nodded slowly. 'Can't I do it myself?'

'Not one-handed. And I'd be more comfortable for Sara to check it every day. Infection at this stage could compromise the healing.'

Matt didn't look too impressed as he stood. His hand was elevated and strapped in a sling against his shoulder. 'Fair enough.'

Caro left them, and Sara leaned against the doorframe with her arms folded. 'So you're ready to go?'

'Yes.'

'And how do you intend doing that?'

Matt lifted his chin and held her gaze. 'The same way I have for the past thirty-plus years.'

She huffed a sigh. 'I'll take you. Have you got any gear to take?'

'I'm fine, Sara.'

'I don't think so. How are you going to start the boat? You seem to have forgotten very quickly that you've just had half your pinkie finger sewn back on, Matt.' She stared at him, and a ripple of nostalgia ran through her as he held her gaze steadily. 'I'm taking you. It's already sorted with Caro. Unless one of your family is coming to take you over?'

'No. And I'm quite capable of getting myself home.'

'I'm sure you are. But while you're under my watch, I'll take you.'

'Not yet.' Matt grunted as he walked to the door. 'I was going to go to the co-op for a while.'

'What?' Sara stared at him in disbelief. 'In the fish co-op? What for''

'Working in the shop.'

'Serving food?' Sara stared at him

He nodded stubbornly. 'Someone has to do it.'

'Well, Matt. That someone isn't going to be you. For several reasons. Risk of infection to you. And hygiene. You'll have to call someone in or close the shop.'

##

Matt went to fold his arms and winced as his arm brushed the bandaged hand against his shoulder. Frustration rose from his gut and he tried not to get cross. He and Sara were standing in the small garden at the front of the medical clinic.

'Bloody stupid accident,' he muttered, digging into his jeans pocket for his phone. 'Excuse me for a moment.' This time Matt's temper rose as he tried to hold the phone and put his password in at the same time.

One-handed.

He flicked a glance at Sara as she cleared her throat. 'And you thought you could go to work? And then drive the boat?'

'Don't be a nag. Can you put—' He broke off as he remembered.

'Can I put what?'

'Can you put my password into my phone please, and then dial Maisie. She's in the contacts. Under M.'

'Sure.' Sara held her hand out, and he passed her the phone. 'What's your password?'

'260884.' Heat warmed his neck, and he lifted his chin. 'I never changed it. Couldn't see the point in remembering a new one.'

Sara typed the numbers—her birth date— into the locked screen without commenting. Knowing that her birthday was Matt's password was strange. She didn't know what to think about that. A few seconds later, she passed the phone back, and he held it to his ear.

'Maisie? Hi, it's Matt.'

'Hello. What's up?' Her gravelly voice sounded as though he'd woken her up, and Matt glanced at the time.

'I was hoping you'd be able to work today.'

'It's Sunday.'

'Yeah, I'm sorry, but I've had a bit of an accident, and I can't get there.'

'Bloody Nora. You must be half-dead if you're not going in. What's wrong? You never miss a day's work!'

'Long story, Maisie. But I'm okay. Just a problem with my hand. Can you work? Even just a couple of hours to freeze yesterday's fresh prawns.'

'I'm sorry, Matt, I can't. I'm down in the 'Curry for the day. There's a poker tournament at the bowling club.'

'No matter. I'll sort something. Have a good day and good luck.'

'Thanks, love. I'll be back late tonight, and I'll come and give you a hand tomorrow.'

Matt disconnected the call with his thumb. He was going to have to call Jenni. She hated working in the co-op and hadn't worked there since before Leni was born. He handed the phone to Sara again. 'Sorry, Sar. I feel so bloody useless. Can you dial Jenni, please? She's in contacts under JJ.'

Sara took the phone back and obliged.

It didn't pick up for a few rings, and Matt was waiting for voicemail to kick in when Jake finally answered.

He sounded short of breath. 'Hey Matt, how are you today?'

'I'm on my way home or about to be. Is Jenni handy?'

'Sorry, she's still in bed. She had a bad night with Callen, and I'm minding the kids this morning. She woke up with a headache, so I've sent her back to bed. I'm going to take the kids out for the day and give her a bit of a break. Can I help?'

'No, it's okay. What about Dane and Donny and the girls? Have they left yet?'

'Yeah, they went at first light. They said to tell you to get better quick.'

'Thanks.' Matt went to scratch his head, and the sling tugged. 'Tell Jen I'll catch up with her tomorrow. Have a good day with the terrors.'

'Bye, mate. And listen, I'm bloody sorry about your finger. I've chucked that lid out. I didn't realise it was dangerous.'

'It was just an accident. I'm on the mend. I'll see you through the week, Jake.'

'See ya, mate.'

Matt put the phone down and took a deep breath. 'Sar? I'm really sorry but I need a big favour. A really big favour.'

Her smile was tentative as she looked across at him. 'Okay, shoot.'

'If you come over to the co-op with me, I promise I'll sit away from the counter and any seafood.' As he watched he saw the faint trace of a blush on her cheeks. 'I won't go anywhere near the product. I need you–'

'You need me to freeze down yesterday's prawns?'

He nodded sheepishly. 'Um, yes and the fish. We had a big delivery yesterday, and the day was quiet.' He rushed on as she stared at him. 'I'll owe you big time. I know you don't like the touch and the fishy smell.'

'It's okay.' She looked away, and her voice was cool. 'I've done it before. I think I can remember what to do.'

'I'll take you out for a meal to say thank you.'

She shook her head. 'There's no need for that. A favour between friends. Come on. It'll be a yuck job but the sooner I get it done, the sooner I can get you home and you can lie down. You've just had surgery, Matt. You need to take care of yourself.'

'Okay. I'll do whatever you say. And thank you.'

'Are you right to walk across to the co-op, or do you want me to go back and get a wheelchair?'

'Bloody hell, Sar. It was only my finger. I'm not crippled.'

Chapter Eleven

Sara deliberately walked slowly as they crossed the road at the corner up from the hospital. The fish co-op was only one block from the medical rooms and hospital, but she didn't want Matt to overdo it. It was less than twenty-four hours since he'd had a general anaesthetic.

'I guess I'd better think about getting a car if I'm going to stay up here,' she said before she thought.

'Is your partner going to move up here?'

Sara groaned inwardly. How was she going to get out of this one?

'Um, yes. Eventually. Probably.'

Matt glanced at her as she walked along beside him. 'What does he do? What did you say his name was?'

'Um, Jeff. He's in finance.'

'Not a lot of call for that up here.'

Sara thought quickly this time. 'He's an investment banker in Melbourne. He'll probably retire before he comes up. So, it will be a while before that happens.'

'What? When he's sixty?'

'No, um, sooner than that.'

'And he's going to come with a view to staying here without even seeing the place first? It's not exactly got the Melbourne coffee shop scene I'm sure he's used to. How old is he anyway?'

'About your age.' Sara crossed her fingers behind her back. The chances of Jeff ever meeting Matt were zero, so she could embellish the truth a little. He was actually a couple of years younger than she was and that had been much of the problem.

'Ah, for a while, I thought you'd found yourself a sugar daddy.'

Sara refrained from stamping her foot on the paved path that ran along the front of the hospital. 'Come on. Let's get this done, and we can get you home. I have other things to do.' She strode ahead towards the corner near the river.

Truth was, she didn't have anything to do. Until she found a place of her own or Gran came home, she was stuck in a bit of a no-man's land. The hotel room was not actually a place where she wanted to spend her day.

She could go start looking for somewhere to live. That would fill in the rest of the week until she began her job at the practice.

Matt caught up to her and walked along quietly beside her; the silence was a little bit uncomfortable.

Sara swallowed. It wasn't his fault. She was the one who'd come home, and it was up to her to make it work. They'd already decided they could be friends, but the tension in her had been caused by the conversation about Jeff. That had been stupid. She sighed as they reached the co-op.

'Don't worry, it won't take long. I was thinking as long as you do the prawns for me, I can give the fish away to the charter company for burley.' Matt reached into his pocket and pulled out a set of keys.

Sara shook her head as she opened the door for him. 'Sorry. It's not that. I'm happy to help, and I'll do whatever needs doing. I was just thinking about finding somewhere to live. Who looks after the rentals here now? Is it still the council office?'

'No, that closed a few years back. The council operates out of Normanton now.'

'I guess I need to go down there to buy a car anyway. Two birds with the one stone and all that.' Sara stepped in as Matt held the door open with his good hand. 'Thank you.'

'The mine does it now. There's an office over in the old town. They do the rentals for the new families that move in. I'm sure if they had anything, they'd let you look at it. But there's not a lot available at the moment.'

'Yeah. Gran said there were a lot of new families arriving in the Bay.'

'The mine's been good for the whole town. Even our businesses. The young blokes are cashed up and they take our shorter charters out to the Gulf on their days off.'

'That's good to hear.'

'It is, but there was a lot of resistance at first to the mine expansion from the older residents. But they can see now what good it's done for the town.' Matt nodded as he lifted a stool from behind the counter and put it over near the door. 'Is this far enough away to be hygienic?' His grin tugged at Sara's heart. Talking to him was like old times, but in those days, he would have held her hand as they'd walked. She swallowed.

Leave it.

Her voice was businesslike. 'It is. You sit there and tell me what to do.'

Matt leaned against the wall and obliged. 'In the fridge on the back wall, there are two large bags of fresh prawns that were delivered fresh yesterday. They came in on the trawler about midday, so they're still fresh enough to freeze down.' He pointed to a large double-door fridge cabinet beside the window. 'And there's a roll of large freezer bags on the cupboard next to it.'

Sara nodded as she lifted out the roll of bags. 'Okay. I've got them.'

'Bring them over to the counter, and then bring one bag of prawns over at a time.'

Sara opened the fridge, and the salty smell of fresh seafood met her. It wasn't too bad. The fridge was neatly arranged, and the contents of each shelf were labelled. The two bags of prawns were on the bottom shelf in a large blue tub. She picked up one bag and carried it over to the counter while Matt watched.

'Tip a good lot on the scales and get it as close to a kilogram as you can.'

'I'll have a wash before I start. Same bathroom?'

He nodded.

Sara walked towards the office and pushed open the door to the bathroom. Nothing had changed; the room was clean and tidy, with a blue towel hanging next to the wash basin. She quickly washed and dried her hands and walked back to the shop area. Matt was looking out the window at a car that had pulled up. He pulled a face.

'Customers. They saw me through the window as they drove past. I'll put the closed sign on the door. I don't usually worry about it as we're open most of the time.'

'No. Leave it. I'm happy to serve if you tell me what to do. Silly to turn away business.'

'Thanks, Sara. I really appreciate it. I feel so bloody useless. My little finger, for goodness sake! Who'd have thought that could incapacitate a bloke!'

'It'll be healed before you know it.' She put on a stern face.' As long as you do as you're told and look after it.'

'Yes, Sister Sweeney.' Again, that grin that made her tummy all squirmy.

The bell above the door tinkled, and a young couple came in with a small boy.

Sara stood behind the counter. 'Morning,' she said brightly.

'Hello.' The man stepped up to the counter. 'I was after some bait. We're taking our son fishing.'

Sara glanced over at Matt. 'Bait?'

He went to stand, and she shook her head. 'Uh uh. You tell me.'

'The freezer cabinet next to the door,' he said as he turned to the guy at the counter. 'What sort of gear have you got? And are you going out in a boat or from the shore?'

The guy laughed. 'This is our first time. We bought a plastic reel and hand line at the IGA store, and when we went down to the river, we realised we needed something to put on the end.'

'To catch the fish,' the boy said.

'We've just moved here,' the young woman said, 'and we have no idea what we're doing. We're from Brisbane, and Danny has started work at the mine.'

'Okay.' Matt nodded. 'A bag of small prawns will do the trick, Sar. Top shelf, left basket.'

She found them and carried them to the counter.

'Watch out for your dress, there's an apron folded on the shelf underneath the register. Sara reached down and slipped the yellow plastic apron over her head as the man walked over to Matt with the little boy. The woman stood at the counter and pulled out her purse.

'I'm just filling in for today,' Sara said. 'I've just moved to town too.'

She wrapped the prawns and noticed a price list stuck to the side of the register. 'That will be six dollars-fifty.' The woman handed over the right cash and Sara put it on the front of the till before she wrapped the frozen prawns in the white paper that was beneath the counter.

'Where are you from?' the young woman asked.

'Originally from here, but I've been away for a long time. Matt hurt his hand, and I'm helping him out.' She grinned and caught Matt's eyes as she looked across the room.

'You're doing well, Sar. I might hire you.' His eyes were alight with humour.

'Sorry, I've already got a job.'

'Where do you work?' The woman held out her hand. 'Sorry, I'm Marcy. We haven't met anyone yet. We've only just arrived this week, and Danny started work the next day.'

Sara took her hand and shook it. 'Hi. I'm Sara, and that's Matt.'

Matt nodded at them both and lifted his sling. 'Sorry I can't shake hands, but good to meet you.'

'And this is Justin,' Danny said.

'Hello, Justin. How old are you?' Matt asked.

'I'm six and I go to big school now,' Justin replied. The two men started a conversation as Sara handed the bait over to Marcy.

'Where do you work, Sara?' Marcy asked again.

'Sorry. I start at the medical clinic next week.'

The young woman looked shy. 'You're the first person I've met so far. Maybe . . maybe you'd like to have a coffee one day? Or maybe we could all have lunch one weekend?'

'Oh. Matt and I aren't—'

Matt looked up. 'We'd love to have lunch with you both one weekend. Sara has just moved back to town and we're getting reacquainted.'

Heat ran up Sara's neck. Things were moving a bit fast, although the "getting reacquainted" that Matt talked about was certainly not the way her imagination had been going. She would have to put a brake on her thoughts.

'That'd be great,' Danny said. 'That was my only worry with bringing the family up here. It's such an isolated area, and most of the workers at the mine are single guys.'

'We both grew up here, and it was okay, wasn't it, Sar?'

She nodded. 'It's a great place to live. I've come back home for good.'

Marcy looked curiously from Sara to Matt. 'I'm going to try and get some work while Justin is at school, but I know it will be hard in such a small place. If you hear of anything, I'd appreciate it.'

Matt caught Sara's eyes and smiled at her.

Damn butterflies. They were tromping around her stomach now.

'I know where there's a job going,' he said.

Marcy's eyes widened. 'You do?'

'It might not be what you wanted, but the hours will fit. What did you do before?'

'I was in retail. I worked in an electrical appliance store in a suburb in outer Brisbane. I was on the counter, but my main job was doing the accounts. I have references.'

'When can you start?' Matt asked with a grin.

'What here? In the fish shop?' Marcy's eyes were huge now as she turned to her husband.

'If you're happy to work with seafood.'

'Oh wow, yes. Oh, Matt, thanks so much. What a day it's turned out to be. I can start as soon as you want me. Justin goes to school tomorrow, so I'll have to take him and get him settled in the morning and then I'm free until three o'clock.

'Perfect. I'll see you after you drop him off.'

Sara cleared her throat. 'Perhaps Maisie could show Marcy what to do.'

Matt chuckled. 'I didn't think of that. It might get confusing.'

Marcy frowned. 'Confusing? Is it still okay?'

This time the chuckle turned into a laugh as Matt stood and crossed to the counter. 'I meant having a Maisie and a Marcy working on the roster.'

Marcy put her hand to her chest and let out a relieved sigh and then she smiled. 'Not to mention Matt!'

Matt held out his left hand and squeezed Marcy's. 'I'll see you here in the morning, and yes, I'll get Maisie to show you the ropes. I can spend the day in the office. Is that okay, Sister Sara?'

'I guess it is.' Sara couldn't help the smile she gave him. 'As long as you rest today.'

Matt rolled his eyes at her and returned the smile.

The butterflies started their clodhopping again, and Sara knew she was in trouble.

Chapter Twelve

Their boat trip across to the small residential section on the west of the river was uneventful. The aluminium runabout dingy was the same one the family had used when Matt used to take her across when they'd been seeing each other.

'How's your Mum?' Sara asked. 'You've never moved out of home?'

'No, I haven't.' Matt chuckled as she steered the boat across the river. 'But Mum moved out. I'm the only one who lives there now. Pretty boring, hey? A man of my age still living in the house where he grew up.'

'Not boring at all. It's a lovely old place, and I know how much you loved living here on the river.'

Sara glanced down at Matt when he didn't reply. She was standing at the back of the boat holding the tiller. It was a lovely morning and the river was flowing sluggishly. On the far bank away from the houses she could see a pair of jabirus standing in the mud flats. The sun was glinting on the shallows, and as she watched one of the birds leaned forward putting its bill into the water and stood motionless waiting for the opportunity of snaring a fish.

Matt's voice was quiet, and Sara had to lean forward to hear him over the sound of the motor. 'I've been thinking of that a bit lately.'

'And?'

'I think it's time for a change. The others have all got their businesses set up and going well. They're based here and away. Jenni's busy with the kids, and Jake has a great business going. Did you know when he left here after school, he went to the French Riviera?'

'No, I didn't.'

'And Dane and Donny have their businesses, so I've been feeling a bit—'

'A bit what?'

'Staid and stagnant, I guess. I'm thinking about moving. Trying something new.' Matt stood as the boat approached the shore. 'If you pass me that rope, I can throw it on the post one-handed.'

Sara picked up the rope, leaned forward and passed it to him. Her fingers brushed his, and she turned back to the motor, ignoring the little thrill that ran up her arm. Matt's words about moving away were some she would have to remember. He hadn't been prepared to settle down with her eight years ago—she hadn't been what he wanted—and now it looked like he was going to leave town. If he did move away it would make her life a bit easier—emotionally, that was.

He threw the rope to the post and snagged it perfectly. Sara cut the engine, and the boat rocked slightly on the wash that followed them in. She sat on the wooden seat in the middle and waited for it to stop.

'Stay there. I'll get out first and then give you a hand to get out. The last thing you want is to fall on your hand. It would undo everything Caro did,' she said.

Aware of his proximity, she held her dress close to her legs as she stepped up to the wooden jetty that was at the back of the McDougall house. Holding out her hand, Sara braced herself for Matt's touch, and as soon as he was safely on the jetty, she let go.

Stupid butterflies in her tummy.

'Caro seems like a nice woman,' Matt said as they walked together towards the back gate. 'Have you known her long?'

'She's a lovely person and a fine doctor.' Sara was pleased to hear that Matt was impressed with Caro. It was one step in the direction of getting them out on a date. 'We've worked together in the Barossa Valley for the past twelve months. I was at the practice when she arrived, and we hit it off straight away. I really enjoyed travelling up here with her.'

Matt stepped to the side so she could open the gate to the garden at the back of the house. Sara held it open for him, but he stopped and looked at her.

'You worked in the Barossa Valley? Isn't that in South Australia?'

'Yes, why?'

'I thought you said your partner was in finance in Melbourne. I assumed that's where you lived. That's where you moved to when you left here, wasn't it?'

Sara nodded and closed her eyes as she walked through the gate. How the hell was she going to explain that?

'Yes, it was. How did you know that?'

'Your grandmother told me.'

'Oh.'

Matt walked next to her and all was quiet as he waited for her answer.

Finally, he stopped at the back door. 'I'm sorry. I'm probably being too nosy.'

Sara simply shrugged. It was too hard to answer without telling more lies, so she changed the subject. 'I've lived in a few places. Where are you thinking about moving to?'

This time, Matt shrugged. 'Hard to say. I've got to give it a bit more thought. But it's good to have someone listen to my whining. I haven't mentioned it to anyone else.'

'My pleasure. It's hard to know what you want sometimes. I've been there. I'm happy to be your sounding board.'

As they stood at the door, Matt reached over and took her hand with his uninjured hand. He held it as they stood there, and Sara looked at the ground.

'Thanks for seeing me home, and thanks heaps for wrapping up all those prawns. I got Dan's number, and it would be nice to welcome them to town. What do you think about going to the pub for lunch one day next weekend if it suits them?'

'Sounds like a plan. I'll invite Caro too. Then they'll know someone else in town.'

'Excellent. I'll give Dan a call.'

She nodded and pulled her hand away. 'You take care of yourself. Go and have a lie-down, and don't do anything. Have you got something for dinner tonight?'

A strange look crossed Matt's face, and he shook his head. 'No, but I can open a tin of something.'

'You most certainly will not! I'll bring something over later. I have to take the boat back to get home, so it leaves you stranded. I didn't think of that. Not that you could drive it anyway.'

'True. I guess I'm dependent on you.' Again, the look on Matt's face was strange and Sara wondered if he wanted her to come back or not.

'I'll get a hamburger and drop it over, but I won't stay,' she said.

'If you're sure it's no trouble?'

'This week is fine because I'm not at work. You should be right by next week.' Sara turned away. 'I'll come back at six. Promise you'll rest?'

'I promise.'

As she went to walk back to the boat, he called out to her. 'Sara?'

She turned slowly. Matt was still at the door watching her, and Sara smoothed her hands over her dress nervously.

'Yes?'

'Thank you for looking out for me. And thank you for listening.'

And that made her feel even worse about lying to him. She lifted her hand in a brief wave before she hurried back to the boat.

***

Matt stood at the door until the sound of the motor died, and the boat was moored safely across the other side of the river. As Sara got out of the boat and tied it to the wharf, she didn't turn around. Her yellow dress clung to her thighs as the wind whipped up, and he stifled a groan.

What the hell was he going to do?

One look at Sara Sweeney, one afternoon in her company, and the feelings he'd held for her came rushing back.

No, they hadn't come rushing back, he reminded himself. They'd never left him. He'd just learned to push them away as he'd tried to forget about her.

But her return was timely.

He'd been thinking about going, and now he would. Staying away from Sara was necessary. She was the one person who had come close to breaching his determination never to marry.

Matt closed the door and walked to his bedroom. He lay carefully on the bed with the sling, holding his injured hand firmly to his chest. He closed his eyes and tipped his head back.

He loved Sara Sweeney. He always had, and he always would.

Matt knew he had to remember his vow. He had a temper like his father had—but he had managed to keep it under control as he'd got older. But it still simmered beneath.

With a deep breath, he cast his mind back to his teens. He was the oldest of the four McDougals, and he wondered sometimes if he was the only one who remembered what their father had been like.

A gambling and abusive drunk.

He knew that Jake hadn't liked Dad and that he had caused the fracture in Jenni and Jake's relationship, which had seen Jake leave town.

Dane and Donny had spent a lot of time at sea on the other boat to Dad, and he wondered if that was how they had stayed out of his range. But Matt had been the one in the fish co-op and the office during his teens and his early twenties before Dad had died. He remembered one time that Dane had threatened to take Dad out the back and deal with him. Dad had come home drunk and given Mum a mouthful and thrown his dinner on the floor.

'What's this shit, woman? A man'd be better off having a feed of prawns at work instead of coming home to this mush.'

But their father had laughed at Dane and gone to bed and passed out.

Like he did most nights.

Mum had blossomed after Dad had died. She was happy.

Matt knew he was the one who carried the scars of his childhood—both physically and emotionally. He knew that he'd been the only one who'd copped a flogging when he was little; Dad had stopped when Matt grew tall and filled out. The one time he'd gone to hit Dane, Matt had been about twelve, and he'd stepped in. But Matt still had the scars to show what he'd grown up with.

No one—not even their mother—talked about their father these days, and there were no photos of him in the house.

And that says it all, Matt thought.

The next time he was tempted to touch, kiss, think about, or even be in Sara's company, he'd remember the scar on his stomach, the one where Dad had kicked him and broken his rib because Matt had forgotten to lock the door at the co-op one Saturday evening.

When he and Dad had arrived on the Sunday morning to an unlocked door, his father had been suffering from too many beers the night before. He had pushed Matt over and then kicked him while he was down.

'Don't you ever forget to lock that door again,' he'd bellowed.

Matt had managed to work all morning to keep the peace, and it was only later that night, when he was having trouble breathing, that Mum had taken him to the hospital. He'd told the doctor back then that he'd tripped and fallen on the corner of his bed. Mum's expression had been full of anguish, but she'd stayed with Dad.

No. He shook his head as he lay there.

He would never take the risk of being like his father. It was safer to be alone. It was bad enough that he looked like him, and he was terrified that he'd inherited that gene for drinking and gambling.

And violence.

Sara Sweeney was safe. It was good that she had a partner. Another reason to stay away from her.

Matt lay there and vowed that he would get over Sara. He knew how close he'd come to succumbing the night eight years ago when she had hinted that she wanted to marry him. He had been so close to taking her in his arms and saying that's what he had wanted too.

But he'd managed not to, and the next morning, she'd left town.

And he vowed that he would leave the Bay at the end of the year. It would give him six months to find an accountant who could take over, tell the family it was his time to follow his dreams and think about where he wanted to go.

The problem was he had no idea where he'd go or what he'd do.

Matt lifted his arm, put the back of his hand over his eyes and tried to sleep.

Chapter Thirteen

Sara left the boat at the back of the McDougall's fish co-op and hurried back to the medical practice to see Caro. She knocked on the door of the flat, but there was no one there. With a frown, she went to the door of the medical practice, but it was closed and locked; there were obviously no patients for the afternoon's surgery with Dr Rose. There was no one at the hospital, so she went back out to the street and stood undecided. She had nowhere to go until she went back across the river later with Matt's hamburger.

Even that in itself proved problematic. So far her return to Second Chance Bay had been very different to what she'd expected. No grandmother home, nowhere to live and then Matt McDougall and his accident.

It would be rude to run in with his dinner and then leave, even though she'd said that was what she would do. He'd probably need a hand to cut it up and then wash up afterwards. As much as she didn't want to go back to Matt's, she knew she would take her dinner too and stay there for a while.

Matt McDougall terrified her. Not once in the two years that she'd been going out with Jeff—they'd never lived together—had she experienced that yearning that she did when she was in Matt's company. The need to look into his eyes, the desire to reach up and touch his face, to caress his hair, or to simply lean against him.

The simple act of being with Matt made her happy. A different type of happiness than any other she'd experienced in her life.

A unique emotion: a feeling of completion and anticipation at the same time.

The memory of that simple physical relationship made her feel sad. No longer could she freely touch him or put her arms around him. The desire to touch him when they'd been at his house had made her fingers ache and tingle.

The memory of being with him, when they'd slept together, was one that she pushed right away. There was no going back to those heady and happy days.

The thought of Matt leaving the Bay filled Sara with confusion. If he left, she wouldn't have to deal with him making her feel like this, but the thought of him going away and not seeing him upset her. It was as though the past eight years hadn't happened; she felt exactly the same way she had when she'd been here.

Whoa, girl, hold your horses. Nan's voice was so clear in her head, it was like she was out on the street with her.

Sara shook her head as she thought about how upset she'd been the night Matt had rejected her. And Nan had been upset too and had encouraged her to get away.

'But I didn't think you'd go away for so long,' Nan had said when the first year had passed.

Focus on that and forget all this squishy tummy, lovey-dovey feeling.

It was lust, pure and simple. Matt was a good-looking guy. She hadn't been on a date, let alone had sex, for well over a year. She and Matt had been very compatible—in all ways—and that's why she'd thought there was a future for them.

For Matt, it had obviously been sex and nothing more. He'd never considered a future together.

So why was she letting herself get so taken with him again?

Because you're a fool, she thought.

Sara straightened her shoulders and set off for the small business district in the centre of the original township of Second Chance Bay. From this moment on, she was going to stop fluffing around. She was going to stop daydreaming about Matt McDougall and a totally imaginary future.

He hadn't wanted her before, and neither had Jeff.

No one had. She'd tried not to let it bother her, but her parents had even left her when she was only fourteen. There'd never been any mention of her moving to Europe, and luckily, Nan had wanted her.

About the only person who ever had.

Sara had hidden her pain behind a bright and ditzy exterior for a long time.

And she was tired of pretending. She was going to go and find somewhere to live and make a future for herself. A happy future, here in her hometown.

And when she bought Matt's hamburger, she'd drop it off and then go straight home.

There was no need for manners. He could wash up when his hand was better.

The new Sara had been born.

##

Half an hour later, Sara's mood had lifted. Even though it was Sunday, the mine office had been open.

'We have to be here, in case of emergency,' the admin officer explained. There were two rentals immediately available; both on this side of the river, and both with reasonable rent.

'If you're keen, you'll have to put an application in today, Sara, because they'll be snapped up. It's really unusual for us to have any empty houses, let alone two at once. Normally, we wouldn't consider someone who doesn't work at the mine, but as you are a health professional and will be providing a service to our workers—indirectly—I'm happy to let you apply.' The administration officer gave her the addresses and two keys on the proviso, and she would return them within an hour. 'The second house is actually for sale, so I can only give three months lease at a time on that one.'

'That's fine for me to start with.'

Sara set off full of enthusiasm, and she didn't think of Matt for a full hour.

Well, maybe half an hour, but it was a start.

The first house near the shopping centre was too big for one person, so she headed off to the second house. As soon as she walked into the street, she knew which house it was going to be. She'd walked past the gorgeous little cottage every day when she'd gone to high school. It was ten years since she'd left, and Mrs Plummer had been elderly then.

According to the mine guy, the elderly woman had gone to an aged care facility in Normanton close to where her two children now lived.

Sara stood outside the house and smiled. It was exactly as she remembered it. The gardens were full of colour, flowers nodded along the inside of the front fence, and the lawn was green. Huge trees ran down each side inside the fence line, providing shade for the gardens that ran beneath the windows. The house was an old Queenslander with a central staircase that ran up to the front door. The windows were still covered by the lace curtains she remembered from high school.

Sara ran quickly up the front steps and put the key in the door. It opened with a creak, and the sweet smell of lavender greeted her. Even though she'd loved the house as a teenager, she'd never been inside, and she wasn't disappointed with what she saw.

The carpet was a soft grey with a burgundy rose pattern. There were a few pieces of furniture left in the house, enough for the essentials. The bathroom had the original 1950s basin on a pedestal in a deep pink, with a matching bathtub. The kitchen was quaint, and the house was high enough to see the river and catch the breeze.

Sara stood at the window and looked to the west. If she stood on her toes, she could see the McDougall house.

Enough. Stop it, she chastised herself.

One more quick walk around, with a brief stop at the overflowing bookcase in the living room, and she locked the door and hurried back to the office.

'I'll take it,' she said as she handed over the keys.

'Which one?'

'The smaller one. The house on Rosedale Street.'

'Excellent.' He found the required paperwork, and Sara pulled out her Visa card. Within ten minutes, she had leased a house for three months.

'If I have anyone wanting to look through it for purchase, I will always give you at least two days' notice.'

'That's fine,' Sara said. 'I'll be at work in the daytime, and I'm not a messy person.' She turned to leave, and a thought struck her. 'How much is the house?'

The figure that he named was less than half of what she expected, and Sara was thoughtful as she walked out of the office.

It would be manageable, and the price was so low it would barely mean a loan. Sara had saved hard over the past few years, always knowing that one day, she would need to purchase a house of her own.

She left with the key clutched tightly in her hand, keen to get to the motel and check out. She'd only paid a week upfront and was happy to forgo that to get out of the boxy motel room. The rest of her things were in Caro's shed, and she wondered where Caro was this afternoon.

Sara walked back through the small shopping mall and was about to cross the road when she spied Caro through the window of the only coffee shop in town. She changed direction and across to the café. As she opened the door, Dr Rose walked out and Sara was taken aback when he gave her a dazzling smile. She ordered a cappuccino at the counter before she made her way to the table where Caro was sitting with papers spread out in front of her.

'Feel like some company?' she asked.

Caro looked up with a start. 'Sure, grab a seat, just let me clear this away.'

'What are you doing?'

'Just filling in all the forms for the medical practice and the hospital. I've signed the contract, and this is all the other stuff. Honestly, it gets worse every year. It was easier to do it when Hector gave it to me, rather than take it back home.'

'Weren't you at the hospital?'

'Yes, but he had the paperwork at his place, so we came here for a coffee and went through it.'

'Sounds like you're getting on well.'

'Yes, he's going to be a good boss, and he's really pleased to have another doctor on board. He just got called over the wharf. You know, since the mine expanded, he's been on call seven days and nights a week!'

'He will be pleased to have you here then.' Sara looked up as the waitress brought her coffee over. 'Thank you.'

Caro looked at her curiously. 'You said Hector was here when you were here before?'

'Yes, he's been here for about twenty years.'

'Oh. Does he have a family here?' Caro toyed with the spoon on her saucer.

'He was a bachelor when I left here. I haven't heard of any change. Why?'

'Just curious. He works very hard.'

Sara smiled. Maybe there was a new incentive to keep Caro in town.

'How did you go with Matt? You didn't overturn the boat or anything?' Caro shook her head. 'I can't believe you took him home in a boat. How on earth did you manage that?'

'It was like riding a bike. It all came back.'

'How was he feeling?'

'He's okay, but I think I'll have to watch him. He thought he could work at the store on the way home, but I sorted him out.'

Caro laughed as Sara told her about selling the bait and wrapping the prawns. 'There's no doubt about you, Sara. You can lend yourself to any situation.'

'Oh, and we met a new couple in town, and Matt organised a dinner at the pub. He said to bring you along too.' Sara crossed her fingers behind her back.

'Nice. I'm really settling in. It feels as though we've been here a week, not a day and a bit!'

'I know, and I've found myself somewhere to live already.' Sara picked up her coffee. 'And you know what? As crazy as it sounds—'

'Crazy?' Caro grinned. 'Sara Sweeney doing something crazy? Never!'

'Don't be mean. Anyway, as I was saying before I was rudely interrupted, I think I'm going to buy the house.'

'Buy it? Are you that sure you're going to stay in town?'

'I think so.'

'Buying a house is a big step for only "think so".'

'Okay, I know so. I'm home. I'm settled. Matt and I have sorted out the past, and we're going to be friends.'

Caro looked at Sara over the top of her glasses and didn't say anything for a moment. 'Okay. I guess you know your heart. But be wise.'

##

A few hours later, Sara called in at the pub, and as she stood waiting for her order to be taken, her thoughts buzzed to and fro.

Will I get one or two?

It was early, and there were only a few people out in the beer garden, which would fill up as the sun set. It was an iconic spot for taking sunset photos, and Sara and Nan had often come down to watch the spectacular colours when she'd lived here.

She was still considering her options when the waitress came to the counter.

'What can I get you, love? Eat in or takeaway?'

'Takeaway please.' She swallowed and came to a decision. 'Two hamburgers. One with the works and one plain, and a large chips please.'

'Be about ten minutes.' She took Sara's money and handed her a slip with a number.

Sara walked out onto the grass and sat at one of the wooden tables beneath the big tree. The muted noise coming from the pub faded. It was quiet outside, and only the noise of the small boats returning from a day of fishing broke the silence.

She took a deep breath of the fresh salty air and looked out over the silver water of the Gulf. She loved this town, and she loved being near the water.

And she adored that little house, and she didn't want anyone else to live in it.

If she bought it, it would be a good reason to stay in town. Nan wasn't getting any younger, and she would love to have her only grandchild close by. Before she could change her mind, she pulled the mine agent's card from her purse. She dialled his number on her phone, and it picked up immediately.

'Hello. Mr Ryan? It's Sara Sweeney here.'

'Hello, Sara. Everything okay with the house?'

'Yes. Very okay. I wanted to make an offer on it.'

'Oh. That's good.'

Sara offered a figure ten thousand below the asking price.

'I'll get onto the vendors and get back to you by tomorrow.'

'Thank you.' Sara smiled as she disconnected and hoped that the offer would be accepted.

As she walked along the riverbank towards Matt's boat, she shook her head, but her smile was wide.

What the hell have I done?

Chapter Fourteen

Matt dozed on and off all afternoon. Sara filled his thoughts when he was awake, and when he slept. The sleeping dreams were more explicit than his waking thoughts and brought back memories of the six months that they had been together. It was hard to let go of that sweet feeling of contentment as he lay there staring at the ceiling.

The light was fading when he woke for the third time. His mouth was dry, and his head and arm were aching. When he stood, the room spun, and Matt grabbed for the table next to the bed. He sat on the edge of the bed until his head stopped twirling, and then made his way slowly and carefully down the hall to the kitchen.

Pulling out a chair he moved it one-handed to where he could see the back gate. It wasn't long before the sound of the boat's motor drifted across the water and in through the open window. Sadness filled him as Sara appeared at the gate and walked slowly along the path to the back door.

He loved her so much it was almost impossible to bear. He put his hand to his head and covered his eyes as the last of the afternoon light seared into his brain. That was why his eyes were wet. Angrily he brushed the back of his hand across his eyes and by the time she pushed the back door open, he had regained his composure.

'Matt,' she called quietly as she stood at the porch inside the back door. 'Are you awake?'

'I'm in the kitchen, Sara.'

No more Sar. It was too intimate.

Sara stepped into the kitchen and took one look at him before throwing the plastic bag onto the bench. She hurried across to the table and put her hand on his forehead.

'You have a temperature.'

'I feel like crap.' His voice was croaky.

'Have you taken anything?' Her hand was cool on his forehead.

'No, I just woke up and came into the kitchen.' Matt was disappointed when Sara moved her hand away.

'I'll get you some paracetamol to bring the temp down. Any other symptoms?'

'A headache and a bit dizzy when I got up.'

'Any pain in your hand?'

'No more than there was.'

'That's good.' She rummaged in the bag that was hanging on her shoulder and pulled out a slide of tablets. 'We'll get your temp down, and I'll call Caro.'

'No need for that.' Matt shook his head. 'I'm fine. I must be. I'm hungry. I can smell hot chips.'

'And we both know your weakness for hot chips,'

Their eyes met and held, and an uncontrollable surge of need ran through Matt. He reached up and took Sara's hand, and slowly pulled her close. He leaned his head against her stomach and closed his eyes. She stood beside him and didn't move. Her unique perfume surrounded him, and the warmth of her body soothed him. After a moment, she lifted her hand and softly caressed his hair. The contentment and yearning that flooded through him was stronger than it had ever been, in reality or in his dreams.

'I'm sorry, Sar.' His voice was husky, and his throat ached. 'I'm so sorry.'

'What for, Matt?' Her voice was a whisper.

He shook his head. 'I'm just sorry.'

She seemed to understand because she stayed there with her hand on his hair for a long time.

***

The grief in Matt's voice was clear. Sara knew that he was apologising for what had happened before she'd left town, but she didn't know how to respond. It wasn't fair to push him while he was unwell, but a tiny glimmer of hope flared in her chest as they stood there.

Eventually, she lowered her hand and moved away. He lifted his head and stared at her, and she was taken aback to see the moisture clouding his beautiful blue eyes.

'I'll get you a couple of tablets.'

He nodded, and the strange moment was broken. She turned her back and walked to the sink, sensing that he needed to compose himself. She automatically opened the cupboard where the glasses were kept and pulled out two glasses. After filling both at the sink, she crossed back to him, placed one glass in front of him, and handed him two painkillers.

As Sara crossed back to the sink, she worried about Matt. He was obviously feeling unwell to show his vulnerability— she knew it had always been there— but he'd always been the strongest, oldest sibling. He'd run the business, she'd seen him care for his mother when their father had died suddenly, and he'd looked out for the family.

She picked up the glass of water and drained it and then reached for two plates. When she turned back to the table, he was watching her carefully and she smiled.

'Do you feel a bit better now?'

'I do.'

She lifted out the larger burger and placed it on the plate. She looked around for the knife block that had been on the bench in the days she had spent many meal times here, but it was gone.

'Where's the knife block?' she asked.

'Mum took it with her when she moved in with Rick.

'Rick?'

'Mum's partner. Or fiancé, I should say. They're in Europe at the moment.'

'I'm pleased your mother has found a new partner.'

'She's very happy.' He pointed to the drawer beneath the window. 'There's a sharp knife in there.'

Sara opened the drawer and picked up a serrated knife. She carefully cut the large burger into four pieces and managed to keep it all together.

'Don't forget my chips,' Matt said with a cheeky grin.

'Who said they were for you?' she replied.

Matt's eyes were brighter now, and the dull flush on his cheeks had faded. She tipped a good serve of the chips onto his plate and then sat down.

'What about you?' he asked. 'Where's yours?'

Sara picked up the bag, took out the smaller burger and put it on the plate. 'I'm not really hungry. I had coffee and cake at the shops with Caro not that long ago. Oh, and I told her about dinner at the pub, and she was keen.' She stared down at the plate. The main reason she had invited Caro to dinner was to push Matt and Caro together. But now she wasn't so sure.

Matt had confused her. His determination to leave town, and his strange apology a minute ago; she didn't know where she stood with him.

'Your chips are getting cold.'

Sara picked one up and chewed it to keep him happy.

'What are you thinking about, Sara?' he asked.

Sara forced a smile to her face and looked at him. 'I was wondering if I over-shopped today.'

'Is it possible to over-shop in Second Chance Bay? Last I heard, the last dress and shoe shop closed a few months back.'

Sara picked up another chip and looked at it thoughtfully. 'No, I really shopped. I think I bought a house.'

Matt put the second quarter of his burger down and stared at her.

'A house? Why would you do that?'

'Because I'm going to stay here.' A frisson of nerves jerked through her body and Sara swallowed.

In for a penny and in for a pound.

Matt had been honest with her. This skirting around the truth wasn't the best way to move back to town. He'd been clear that they could be friends, and friends were honest with each other.

It was time.

Sara put the uneaten chip back on her plate. 'I'm going to be honest with you, Matt. You've been upfront with me.' When she looked at him, he looked over her head and a muscle jerked in his jaw. 'I've been a little bit loose with the truth.'

She sat up straight, and this time, he met her gaze.

'Jeff and I split up before I moved to Tanunda. I just didn't want you to think I came back here to try to pick up where we left off.'

He nodded and spoke slowly, but it was impossible to read his expression. 'I see.'

'I've decided to stay here. I've got a great job. Nan needs me, and I love the Bay. I'm here to stay. When I saw Mrs Plummer's house was for sale, I couldn't resist.'

Again, the nod. 'I'm really pleased for you, Sara.'

No more, no less. No, "I'm really pleased you're staying."

Matt picked up the next piece of his burger, and his focus was on that. Disappointment shimmied through Sara.

But really, what had she expected? Did she think Matt would declare his undying love and fall to his knee and propose?

She bit back the sigh that threatened to rise.

Of course, he wouldn't. He didn't love her, and he'd simply needed comforting before. He was unwell.

'Do you have a digital thermometer here?' she asked.

Matt shook his head. 'No.'

'How do you feel now?'

This time he smiled. 'Better. My headache has gone, and I don't feel as doughy. All I needed was chips.'

That sexy smile sent a shaft of longing through Sara, and she knew she had to ignore it. She couldn't spend the rest of her life like this.

'I'm not hungry.' She stood and pushed her chair in. 'Leave the plates and scraps. I'll sort it out when I come back tomorrow to look at your finger. You look much better. For a while there, I thought we were going to have to go back to the hospital.'

Matt frowned. 'It's getting dark. I'm not happy about you going across the river in the dark.' He glanced up at the clock on the wall. 'And the tide will have turned. It's going out, and it'll be flowing fast.'

Sara bit her lip. Matt was right; she hadn't thought about it being dark when she went back. 'True,' she agreed.

'Stay the night. There's plenty of spare rooms these days.' Matt stood and as he did, he put his hand to his head.

Sara reached out to him. 'What's wrong? Are you ill again?

'Just a bit dizzy when I stood up.'

'Okay. It's probably best that there's someone here with you. How the heck did your mother cope when she had four small children!'

'There was a bridge back in those days.'

'Okay. I think you should go back to bed. Have you had enough to eat?'

'Probably too much.'

'Do you . . . um . . . need a hand to wash or anything?'

'Or anything?' Despite his dizziness, Matt's smile was cheeky.

He grabbed her hand and pulled her closer, unable to resist.

'Blame it on the fever.' He lowered his head and Sara widened her eyes as she realised his intention. Before she could move away, Matt's lips captured hers. His hand was gentle on her waist as he kissed her softly, and before she could respond he lifted his head, and his eyes were shadowed.

'Good night, Sara. We'll talk in the morning. Honesty deserves honesty back.'

Chapter Fifteen

Matt slept deeply and dreamlessly. He was woken at first light by the sound of his phone ringing. He reached over to the bedside table before he realised he'd left it in the kitchen. Pulling on his jeans over his boxers he padded softly down to the kitchen.

Sara was already there, sitting at the table; she was dressed, and her usually wild curls were neatly tied back.

'You're up early. Did my phone wake you?'

'No, I was already awake. I was coming to check on you and then go across river before the tide starts going out.' She gestured to his phone on the table. 'Your phone rang, but I didn't like to answer it.' She seemed tense, and he worried about last night. He shouldn't have kissed her, but he'd been unable to resist.

'Yes, it woke me up. Excuse me for a moment.' Matt picked up his phone and looked at the time. It was still before six a.m. There was a missed call from Jake.

Strange.

He turned to Sara. 'Would you like to make us a cuppa before you go? I just have to make a call.'

'Is everything okay?'

'I hope so.'

As Sara filled the electric kettle, Matt returned Jake's call, and Jake picked up instantly.

'Jake, you call—'

'Matt.' Jake's voice was quiet. 'We need you.'

'What's wrong?'

Sara lifted her head and looked at him. Matt stared at her as he listened to Jake, and his blood ran cold.

'Have you called the others?'

'Yes, they're on their way.'

'What about Mum?' Matt asked.

'I don't know what to do there.'

'Okay, we'll talk about it. Jake, I'm on my way. Stay calm, mate.'

He put the phone down and took a deep breath. 'Don't worry about the kettle, Sar. I'm going to get my shirt and shoes. We have to go to the hospital.'

'What's happened?' Sara crossed to him and stood close.

'It's Jenni.' Matt's voice cracked and he swallowed. 'She was ill through the night and complained of a severe headache. Jake couldn't rouse her this morning. He called triple zero and she's at the hospital. He needs someone to look after the children. It looks like the RFDS might fly her to Mt Isa. They're on the way now.'

'Let's go.' Sara switched the kettle off. 'Get a shirt and whatever you need. Do you want me to lock up?'

'No, it'll be fine.'

'I'll wait for you at the gate.' She picked up her purse and was out the back door as Matt ran up to his room and grabbed a shirt and his wallet. His thongs were at the back door— they'd do.

***

The sky was beginning to lighten, and scudding clouds ran across the half moon. The wind whistled eerily through the mangroves, and the mournful cry of a plover reached them from the point.

'Are you okay to steer in this wind?' Matt asked as Sara climbed into the boat.

She was a little nervous but more worried about Jenni. She nodded.

'Yes, I'm fine.'

Matt was in the boat and sitting on the front seat before she could even offer to help him in. His face was grim, and he stayed quiet as she steered them across the river.

'Pull in at the co-op,' he said. 'My ute's there, and the keys are under the seat. It'll be quicker.'

Sara did as he instructed and was at the side of the boat, ready to help him up on the higher wharf on this side of the river. He gripped her hand firmly but let go as soon as he was steady on his feet.

'Thank you.'

They ran to the ute, and Matt opened the driver's door and went to jump in. Sara didn't say anything; it was only a block to the hospital, and he could steer one-handed.

'I'll put it in drive,' she said. 'Tell me when you're ready.'

He started the engine and nodded; she slid the shift into drive. It was only a minute or so before Matt parked in the small car park outside the medical surgery.

'I'll come around and open the door. Just wait,' Sara instructed.

She opened the door for him, and Matt took her hand as they hurried into the hospital. The main door was unlocked, and a woman was sitting on the seat nursing a baby. A little girl was playing with the toys in the corner of the waiting room. She looked up, her tired face lined with wrinkles and Sara realised it was Maisie who she'd last seen in the Barossa Valley.

Matt touched Maisie gently on the shoulder before he walked over and picked up the little girl.

'How's the prettiest girl in the universe?'

'Uncle Mattie.' The little girl planted kisses on Matt's cheek. He smiled, but Sara knew it was hard for him.

'My Mummy's sick.'

'I know, sweetheart. The doctors will look after her.' He crouched down beside her as he put her back down near the toys and stayed there as she picked up a puzzle.

'Hello, Sara,' Maisie said quietly. 'I didn't realise you'd arrived.'

'I've been here a couple of days,' Sarah said. 'I start at the medical practice next week. Has the doctor seen Jenni yet?' Sara didn't like to go in. It wasn't the right thing to do.

'Doc Rose is with her now. And Jake. The poor guy is a mess. I'm just so pleased he thought to call me. I'm only a hundred yards down the road. I met him when he followed the ambulance in his car.'

The door opened, and Sara looked up as Caro walked in.

The doctor's eyes widened in surprise when she saw Sara sitting next to Maisie. 'Sar. I'm pleased you're here. Can you wash up and come in, please? Hector called me and I stopped in at the motel to collect you.'

'I was over at Matt's. He wasn't well last night, so I stayed to keep an eye on him.' Sara sensed Maisie's curiosity but didn't explain any further.

Caro stood and went over to Matt, and their conversation was quiet. Maisie looked down and rocked the baby, who was asleep in her arms. The mood in the room was sombre.

Sara followed Caro into the hospital. 'Why did you need me? '

'Hector asked if you would go on the plane with Jenni to Mt Isa.'

Sara nodded. 'Of course.'

'Her husband will be there too, and you can monitor her vital signs.'

'It's not an RFDS plane?

'No, it's the air ambulance from Mt Isa. They were short-staffed, and I said either you or I would go with Jenni. Do you need to get anything? It'll be here shortly.'

'No. I'm fine. I've got my phone in my bag. I don't need anything else.'

Caro reached over and squeezed her hand as they headed for the sink. They could hear Dr Rose's quiet voice coming from the end of the room.

'Hector suspects meningitis, but until the bloods come back and they do a spinal tap, we won't be sure.'

'Is she very bad, Caro?' Sara kept her voice quiet.

Caro sighed. 'It's not looking good.'

Sara's eyes filled and she blinked away the tears. 'I knew she wasn't well on Saturday when I saw her.'

'Don't beat yourself up. No one could have known this would happen. Jake did the right thing. He called triple zero.'

As they stood there, a plane flew low over the hospital. 'There it is now. Hector wants to see you before you go.'

Sara nodded. In less than an hour, the lives of the McDougal family had been thrown into turmoil, and she prayed that Jenni would recover.

She was loved by so many people.

Chapter Sixteen

Jenni's battle was long, and she was still in danger three days later when Mum and Rick arrived in Mt Isa.

Matt's finger was healing— Sara had met him at the hospital twice to dress it and had kept him up to date on his sister's condition. On Thursday morning, she'd called into the house where Maisie and Matt were staying with the children. After she left, Matt sat at the table with his head in his hands. Caro said Jenni still wasn't responding.

'They're doing all that they can, Matt, but she may have to be airlifted to Brisbane.'

'Uncle Mattie!' Leni's screech around midnight on Thursday night pulled him out of his thoughts, and he ran down the hall to the little girl's room, but Maisie was already there.

They had been a strange duo, caring for the children, but Maisie had been a trooper. Dane and Nicole had been delayed by the bad weather that had closed in just after the air ambulance had taken off for Mt Isa. Jenni had been extremely lucky to get there.

Donny and Claire had arrived and stayed with them at Jake and Jenni's house for one night before they all agreed it would be best if they went down to the Isa to be there for Jake.

Matt hadn't spoken to Sara, and he'd tried not to think about her; they had bigger problems to deal with. For the first time, he was beginning to wonder if his determination to stay alone was the right path to follow.

It was not the time to think about it, but he missed her dreadfully. He hadn't seen Sara since she'd left the waiting room at the hospital. Just a brief glimpse as they'd wheeled Jenni out to the plane. Jake had run in and hugged each of the children before he left.

Matt had enveloped him in a hug as Jake had walked out with tears running down his face. 'Look after my sister, mate. Tell her I love her.'

Jake had nodded and hurried out.

Now Matt picked up Leni and held her close. The sweet smell of his sister's little girl almost brought him to tears. He'd never thought he wanted a family, but the events of this week had given him a whole new perspective on life.

When it was over—and he prayed that Jenni would come home well—Matt had decided to go outback. It was where he had done his best thinking years ago, and it was where he was going to go when this was all over.

The co-op had been shut all week, and in the scheme of things, it didn't matter. He had some big decisions to make.

His breath hitched as Leni's lips brushed his cheek. 'Don't be sad, Uncle Matt. Mummy just got better. I dreamed'd it.'

'That's lovely, sweetheart.' Matt's voice was thick.

Maisie looked at him as his phone rang in his pocket, and she held her arms out for the little girl.

Matt's breath hitched as he looked at Jake's caller ID, and he walked into the hall. He hadn't spoken to Jake for three nights; Donny had been keeping them informed each time there was a change in Jenni's condition. Unfortunately, she had deteriorated over the past twenty-four hours.

'Jake?'

Matt closed his eyes at the silence at the other end of the phone, and then there was the harsh sound of Jake crying.

His world fell to pieces around him as he waited. 'Jake? Tell me.'

***

Sara's phone rang at midnight as she tried to sleep. She had a room in the nurses' wing of Mt Isa Hospital. Jake had refused to leave the hospital. For a moment, she thought it might be Matt; he hadn't called, and she didn't think it was right to call him when the family was so worried. There would be time one day to see what he wanted to be honest about. She reached for the phone and listened.

A moment later she was pulling her clothes on and running to the intensive care ward.

Helen and Rick met her at the door of the waiting room; they had arrived this afternoon, and the family had invited Sara to meet them for coffee in the hospital dining room, but Jake had stayed with Jenni.

Tears ran down Helen's face as she reached for Sara. Donny and Claire were sitting near the door. Donny held Claire close.

'Oh, Sara.'

Sara hugged the older woman as she clung to her.

Chapter Seventeen

Two days later, Sara was on her way back to Normanton. Matt's mother, Helen, and her partner, Rick, had booked a flight and insisted that she accompany them.

'It's the least we can do, Sara,' Helen had said. 'You've been an amazing support to the family. And not only as a nurse but as a friend.'

As they waited for the plane in the small regional airport, Sara scrolled through the many text messages that she'd ignored over the past week. One message brought a smile to her face.

Helen looked at her. 'Good news?'

Sara nodded. 'I am now the almost owner of Mrs Plummer's house in Rosedale Street. My offer has been accepted.'

'That's another cause for celebration.'

'It is. I'll have a high tea, and you're all invited. As soon as Jenni is well enough.'

Jenni's recovery from bacterial meningitis had been nothing short of a miracle. She had regained consciousness just before eleven o'clock that night, and her temperature had dropped almost to normal within an hour. Jake had been with her when she had opened her eyes and smiled at him and asked where the children were.

'That's wonderful news,' Helen said. 'So you're staying? Your grandmother will be pleased.'

'She will,' Sara said. Helen had not mentioned Matt at all.

Dane picked them up at Normanton and hugged Sara. 'It's good to see you, Sara; it's been a long time.'

'Too long, Dane. But I'm home now.'

Dane walked over and hugged Helen and then pulled her aside for a quiet word.

All Sara heard was him say. 'He just said he needed to get away.'

'That boy,' Helen muttered.

Sara had hoped that Matt would be waiting for them, but there was no sign of him when Dane dropped her at the motel.

'Sara, we'd love you to join us for dinner tonight if you're not too tired?'

Sara nodded shyly. 'If you're sure. I don't want to intrude.'

'Don't be silly. Come to the hotel about six.'

She waved as the car drove off and headed back to the brown room of the hotel.

Her phone rang before she had the door open.

'Welcome home, Sara. How about a coffee when you're settled?'

Sara looked around the depressing room. 'I've got a better idea. How about you bring your car and help me move?'

##

Caro obliged, and by mid-afternoon, they were sitting at the table in Sara's soon-to-be-house sipping tea out of fine bone china. One of the cupboards had been full of china and ornaments and Sara hadn't been able to resist.

'I love this house, Sara. I can see you settled here for a long time.' Caro looked at her from beneath her lashes. 'Have you talked to Matt yet?'

'No. I . . . um . . . I thought I might go over to the co-op before it closes and say hello.'

Caro shook her head. 'The co-op's still not open. Hector told me Matt's gone away for a while.'

Shock ran through Sara. 'Away? Before Jenni comes home?

Caro nodded. 'Apparently. His brother is going to open the co-op on the weekend, and his sister-in-law is taking over looking after the kids. They seem like a lovely family. Very close.'

'They are. I wonder where Matt's gone.'

'You're still in love with him, aren't you?' Caro reached over and touched Sara's arm.

She nodded. 'Silly me. I am. And I think he knows it. That's probably why he fled town. Before I could come back and make a fool of myself.'

'I doubt it. I saw the way he looked at you. He cares about you, Sara.'

'He may care about me, but he doesn't love me.' Her breath hitched, and she bit back the next words before she made a fool of herself.

Unlovable Sara.

'Don't give up. Fight for him.'

Sara shook her head sadly. 'You can't make someone love you.' She jumped to her feet. 'Come on, let's get this unpacking finished, and then I'm going out for dinner. Do you want to come? I'm sure the McDougalls wouldn't mind.'

Caro shook her head, and her smile was secretive. 'I already have a date.'

Sara's mouth dropped open, and she shut it quickly. 'A date? Who with?'

Caro blushed as Sara looked at her. 'Dr Hector Rose.'

Chapter Eighteen

Matt's finger ached as he lifted the swag out of his ute. Dr Caro had been insistent that she tape his finger up seeing he was going out of town for a few days.

'You keep it clean, Matt, and keep taking those antibiotics as a precaution.'

'Yes, doc,' he'd said.

He'd gotten sick of explaining why he was going away. All he'd say was that he needed some space. Caro insisted on knowing exactly where he was going.

'The last thing your family needs now is another incident.'

He'd told her his destination, but no one could talk him out of going away.

Matt needed to do some deep soul-searching, and he had a favourite spot up the coast north of Jenni and Jake's house. His own outback paradise.

Jenni's illness had thrown him for a sixer, and he had begun to realise how short and tenuous life could be.

He'd been wasting time, and it was time to make some hard decisions. He needed to get away where he could think and not be distracted.

The clearing was well away from the side of the small river that wound in from the west. He checked around for snakes and then set to gathering firewood—with his left hand. It was surprising how he'd learned to do so many things left-handed over the past week.

By the time the sun had set, Matt was leaning against a log in front of a crackling fire. He stared into the flames and waited for his dinner to heat up in the camp oven hanging from the tripod above the flames. Maisie had insisted on cooking him a couple of meals to take away; she was the only one who'd understood why he wanted to get away and think.

One night, after Jenni's two kids had gone to sleep, Maisie had offered him a wine, and Matt had shaken his head.

'Thanks, Maisie. I don't drink.'

She'd nodded and sat back on the sofa. 'Unusual for a bloke up here.'

He pulled a face. 'I have my reasons. Or reason.'

'Overindulged once, did you?' she persisted.

'No. I've never drunk at all. Let's say I had my fill watching my father as I grew up. And I don't want to be like him.'

Maisie sat up straight. 'Matt McDougall! If you think you're anything like your father, you need to forget that quick smart. Bloody hell.' She shook her head. 'I'm going to have to go outside and have a ciggie.'

When she came back inside, she stood in front of Matt and wagged her finger. 'I knew your father. He played poker with my husband. Trust me, Matt, you don't have anything of him in you. Please believe me.'

'I don't want to find out the hard way. That's why I don't drink.'

'You think it was the drink that made him that way? I know he was your father, Matt, but believe me, he was a cold, mean man. Sober or drunk. It wasn't the drink; it was the way he was. Your mother deserved a medal living with him and putting up with his shit.'

'Thank you, Maisie. That means a lot to me.'

She flopped onto the sofa beside him and picked up her wine glass. 'Now you can have a social drink and enjoy it!'

##

Matt stood on the edge of the ridge and looked out over the valley. In the far distance, the Gulf glinted silver. The vegetation was a mix of beautiful purple and blues, and he took a deep breath.

He walked back to his campsite and reached into the small esky that he'd brought with him.

It was a test.

In it was a six-pack of beer on ice he'd picked up at the IGA on the way out of town. He lifted out the first bottle, still cold from the ice around it and popped the top,

He put it to his lips and drank a mouthful. Putting the bottle on the ground beside him, Matt tilted his head back and waited for the sun to set. An hour later, he was still looking at the sky and thinking, but now there were brilliant stars above.

Sara would be back in town, and he wanted to have his path of action very clear in his mind before he spoke to her.

He picked up the bottle, took a few mouthfuls and waited.

The stars twinkled above, the fire crackled, the aroma of Maisie's beef stew surrounded him, and Matt didn't feel any different. Maybe a little bit more relaxed. He waited for the anger and the frustration to kick in. And maybe a bit of mean.

But all he could think of was how happy he was that Jenni was on the road to recovery and Sara was staying in Second Chance Bay.

With a shrug, he picked up the bottle and finished the beer.

If he was honest, he didn't even like the taste very much. A grin spread on his face as he thought how ridiculous he was being.

What had he expected?

To have a transformation like the Hulk? To have his muscles bulge and pop out of his shirt?

Matt McDougall, you're a moron.

He opened the esky and picked up another beer before he lifted the lid of the camp oven and stirred the stew that was now bubbling away.

It was serene out here. No lights, just the stars above and the wind in the trees. One day he would bring Sara to his secret spot.

Matt swallowed; his decision had been made for him by his heart—and maybe his common sense and a bit of Maisie wisdom thrown into the mix.

He had a lot to be thankful for. It didn't matter that his father had been a violent man. Jenni was recovering; he was part of a warm and loving family, his mother was happy, and if he was right, a cute and quirky woman with red curls had some feelings for him.

Before he could think about it anymore, Matt popped the top off the second beer and held it up to the sky.

Here's to my future. A future with Sara in it.

Well, you idiot, why are you out here in the scrub by yourself while she's back in town?

As Matt pondered rolling up the swag and packing up camp, the sound of a car coming down the bush track caught his attention. He sat up straight and frowned.

A few minutes later, a truck with McDougall Fishing Charters written on the side pulled up at the side of his camp.

As though he was expecting them, his two younger brothers jumped down from the cabin and sauntered over. They looked at the beer in his hand, and then both looked at each other.

'Having a party out here by yourself, are you, big bro?' Dane reached into the esky and pulled out two beers, threw one to Donny and then popped the top of the other.

'What are you two doing out here? And how did you find my secret spot?' he spluttered.

'Secret? Jeez, we used to come out here when we were kids. We've come to talk some sense into you, mate,' Donny said.

'And we've got something for you,' Dane added. 'Mum told us to bring you a present.'

'I don't need any sense talked into me. I've come to them by myself.'

'Does it involve a certain young woman?' Donny wiped the back of his hand over his mouth.

'It might,' Matt replied with a grin.

'About bloody time you got some sense into you.' Dane sniffed the air. 'That smells pretty good. Do you think we should stay for dinner, Donny?'

'Nah, we've both got a lovely woman waiting at home.'

'Not like this idiot.' Dane gestured with his head to Matt.

'Hey, watch it. So, what did you come out here for? What's this present Mum sent out?'

Matt shook his head as his two younger brothers walked to the truck and high-fived each other before they climbed into the truck.

'Mad bastards,' he muttered. 'But I do love the pair of you.'

The truck engine flared into life, but before the large vehicle pulled away, a door slammed, and Matt looked up.

He squinted and then rubbed his eyes as the truck disappeared into the distance.

'Hello, Matt.' Sara's voice was soft as she held out a parcel wrapped in Alfoil. 'Your Mum sent me out with the bread to go with the stew that Maisie made for you.'

Matt's mouth opened and closed as he stared at her. For the first time ever, he was lost for words.

Sara walked over and put the bread on the ground beside the fire before she moved closer to him. She lifted her hand and put it on his heart.

'Matt? A few days ago, before Jenni got sick, you were about to be honest with me. It seems your whole family and half the town know something we don't. Is it a good time to tell me what you were going to say that night?'

Matt nodded and looped his arms around her slim waist. Her eyes were bright as she looked up and held his gaze.

'It is. I've known this for eight years or more, but I was a coward. I'm so very sorry that I took all those years away from us. I was about to pack up and come to town and find you to tell you.'

'Tell me what, Matt?' Sara's soft lips were a rosy pink in the firelight as she whispered the words. Her breath warmed his mouth, and Matt inched closer.

'I knew I loved you, and I knew even then I wanted you in my life, but I made a huge mistake. I was scared I was my father, and I didn't want to risk that with you.'

Sara's lips moved closer to his. 'You are Matt McDougall. No one else, and I love you just as you are. With your fears, and with your uncertainty, but you have to know I love you unconditionally.'

'I love you, Sara Sweeney, and I always have. And I always will.' He looked over at the swag. 'Maybe it's just as well I packed the double swag?'

'Maybe it is.' Sara's lips widened in a sweet smile as she lifted her face for his kiss. Matt closed his eyes and breathed in her scent before he slid his mouth gently over her soft cheek, slowly making his way to those lips.

The night was silent around them, and the stars smiled down as Matt kissed Sara properly for the first time in years. She lifted her head a fraction before he deepened the kiss.

'It was worth the wait, my darling Matt.'

Epilogue

The spring afternoon was filled with soft cloud, and the whisper of gentle rain was carried on the slight wind. Sara didn't care what the weather was like as Claire and Nicole fussed about her and straightened her dress.

'Mercy me, girl, aren't you ready yet?' Maisie burst into the room at the back of Mrs Plummer's—now Sara's—house. 'You don't want him to change his mind. He's standing under the tree in the backyard, pulling at his tie as if it's choking him.'

'Matt won't go anywhere,' Sara said with a smile. 'And I think we're ready, aren't we, girls?'

Nicole and Claire smiled and nodded. 'We are.'

'Well, what are you waiting for?' Maisie said.

They walked down the back stairs, and Sara's heartbeat quickened as she saw Matt, flanked by his brothers and his brother-in-law, standing at the end of the garden. Jenni was sitting in a chair at the bottom of the steps, and as Sara reached her, Jenni held up her hand and took Sara's. Sara leaned over and kissed her cheek.

'Are you ready, Jen?'

Jenni nodded and stood, walking between Nicole and Claire. 'I wouldn't miss this for the world. I've waited a long, long time to see my big brother happy.'

The strains of a slow love ballad floated in the air as the four girls walked towards their men. Jenni's two children waited at the front, each holding a basket of petals.

Helen, Rick, and Sara's Nan sat proudly in the front row beside Hector and Caro. Sara took another step towards her future and smiled when she saw the doctors' hands clasped together. Dan and Marcy sat in the row behind them; they'd become good friends over the past three months since Sara arrived in town.

The family members and the other guests and the awareness of her surroundings left Sara as she took the last steps towards the man waiting for her.

The man who loved her.

Matt held out his hands, and she lifted her eyes to his as a wave of love suffused her. His eyes held hers unwaveringly, and the connection between them was as strong as though it was bound by one of the ribbons floating on the children's petal baskets.

'I love you, Sara,' Matt mouthed over the music as it swelled to a crescendo.

He held out his hand and entwined his fingers through hers as the celebrant began to speak.

'And I love you, Matt,' she whispered.

THE END

Other Books and Series from Annie

Daughters of the Darling
From Across the Sea
Over the River (2024)
Porter Sisters Series
Kakadu Sunset
Daintree
Diamond Sky
Hidden Valley
Larapinta
Kakadu Dawn

Pentecost Island Series
Pippa
Eliza
Nell
Tamsin
Evie
Cherry
Odessa
Sienna
Tess
Isla

The Augathella Girls Series
Outback Roads

Outback Sky
Outback Escape
Outback Wind
Outback Dawn
Outback Moonlight
Outback Dust
Outback Hope

An Augathella Surprise
An Augathella Baby
An Augathella Spring
An Augathella Christmas
An Augathella Wedding

Sunshine Coast Series
Waiting for Ana
The Trouble with Jack
Healing His Heart
Sunshine Coast Boxed Set

The Richards Brothers Series
The Trouble with Paradise
Marry in Haste
Outback Sunrise
Richards Brothers Boxed Set

Bondi Beach Love Series
Beach House
Beach Music
Beach Walk
Beach Dreams
Second Chance Bay Series

Her Outback Playboy
Her Outback Protector
Her Outback Haven
Her Outback Paradise
The McDougalls of Second Chance Bay Boxed Set

Love Across Time Series
Come Back to Me
Follow Me
Finding Home
The Threads that Bind
Love Across Time 1-4 Boxed Set

Bindarra Creek
Worth the Wait
Full Circle
Secrets of River Cottage
A Clever Christmas
A Place to Belong

Others
Whitsunday Dawn
Undara
Osprey Reef
East of Alice
Four Seasons Short and Sweet
Follow the Sun
Ten Days in Paradise
Deadly Secrets
Adventures in Time
Silver Valley Witch
The Emerald Necklace
A Clever Christmas

Christmas with the Boss
Her Christmas Star

About the Author

Annie lives in Australia, on the beautiful north coast of New South Wales. She sits in her writing chair and looks out over the tranquil Pacific Ocean. She writes contemporary romance and loves telling stories that always have a happily ever after. She lives with her very own hero of many years and they share their home with Barney, the ragdoll puss, who hides when the four grandchildren come to visit.

Stay up to date with her latest releases at her website: http://www.annieseaton.net

Awards

2023: Winner of the long contemporary RUBY award for Larapinta

Finalist for the NZ KORU Award 2018 and 2020.

Winner ...Best Established Author of the Year 2017 AUSROM

Longlisted for the Sisters in Crime Davitt Awards 2016, 2017, 2018, 2019

Finalist in Book of the Year, Long Romance, RWA Ruby Awards 2016 Kakadu Sunset

Winner ...Best Established Author of the Year 2015 AUSROM

Winner ...Author of the Year 2014 AUSROM
Best Established Author, Ausrom Readers' Choice 2017